Also by Judith Krantz

PRINCESS DAISY

SCRUPLES

JUDITH

MISTRAL'S

KRANTZ

DAUGHTER

Crown Publishers, Inc. · New York · 1983

Published by Crown Publishers, Inc.,
One Park Avenue, New York, New York 10016 and simultaneously in Canada
by General Publishing Company Limited

Printed in the United States of America

Grateful acknowledgment is hereby made
to the New World Music Corporation for permission
to reprint lyrics from "Someone to Watch Over Me,"
copyright 1926 (© renewed) by New World Music Corporation.

Library of Congress Cataloging in Publication Data

Krantz, Judith.

I. Title.

PS3561.R264M5   1983   813'.54   82-17966

ISBN 0-517-54906-9

Design by Camilla Filancia

10   9   8   7   6   5   4   3   2   1

First Edition

For Ginette Spanier

Who opened the doors of Paris for me.

With much love and the memory of many years of friendship.

For Steve

Who has all my love.

This book could never have been written without him.

I feel deep gratitude to these friends for their answers to my questions.

Jean Garcin, *Le Président, Conseil Général de Vaucluse*

Jacques and Marie-France Mille of *Le Prieuré*,
     Villeneuve-les-Avignon

Bill Weinberg of the Wilhelmina Agency

Karen Hilton and Faith Kates of the Wilhelmina Agency

Joe Downing

Aaron Shikler

Micheline Swift

Betty Dorso

Grace Mirabella of *Vogue*

Ann Heilperin of Van Cleef and Arpels

MISTRAL'S
DAUGHTER

1

Fauve dashed through the lobby, her Stop-sign red slicker flapping around her, and managed to squeeze her way through the elevator doors a split second before they closed. Panting, she tried to furl her big striped umbrella so that it wouldn't drip on the other people who were jammed in with her, but, in the crowd, her arms were pinned to her sides.

Earlier in the morning Fauve would have had the elevator pretty much to herself, but there hadn't been a single empty taxi in Manhattan on this rainy September morning in 1975. She'd had to wait endlessly for a bus on Madison Avenue and run the rest of the way across Fifty-seventh Street. Soaking and uncomfortable, she cautiously swiveled her neck around to survey the mob that hemmed her in. Would any of them get off before the tenth floor? No hope of that, she realized. The creaky, ancient elevator that rose so slowly in the Carnegie Hall office building was charged with a palpable cloud of tension and terror. Except for the operator, the small space was packed with young women who were gripped in silent, fierce and frightened concentration. Each one of them had grown up knowing that she was, beyond any question, the most beautiful girl in her high school, in her hometown, in her state.

This elevator trip was the last step toward a goal they had been dreaming of feverishly for years. Before them lay an audition at the Lunel Agency, the most famous of all the modeling agencies in the world, the agency with the most prestige and the most power. Fauve felt the almost unbearable weight of the quivering anxiety and nervous anticipation that palpitated around her, and, closing her eyes, she prayed for the ride to be over.

"Casey asked if I'd seen you," the elevator operator said to Fauve, so loudly that everyone heard him. "She's waiting for you upstairs."

"Thanks, Harry." Fauve hunched deeper into her coat collar, trying to disappear as she felt twenty pairs of eyes immediately turn toward her in a wave of hostile awareness. On each side her profile was being evaluated in naked competitiveness, her neighbors sweeping their glances from her forehead to her chin and finding no flaw. Behind her they were estimating her height and noting, with a misery that vibrated clearly, that she was as tall or taller than any of them. Even in the rear of the elevator there was no girl whose view was so completely blocked that she couldn't see the conflagration of Fauve's tumult of hair, of a red so extravagant that it could only be natural.

There was absolute silence as Fauve was inspected.

"You're a model, aren't you?" the girl on Fauve's right asked her, accusation and desperate envy clear in her tone.

"No, I just work there." Fauve could feel the relief in the elevator as if it were a solid substance. She straightened up, invisible now and blessedly unimportant. As soon as the elevator doors opened on the tenth floor she sprinted out into the corridor and ran through the entrance to the Lunel Agency without a backward glance.

She knew precisely what the girls behind her would do. Each one of them would take her place on the line that had begun to form a half-hour ago for the open auditions that were held three mornings a week at the agency that had been founded more than forty years earlier by Maggy Lunel, Fauve Lunel's grandmother. Out of the many thousands who auditioned each year, only thirty were accepted.

As Fauve walked rapidly to her office she thought that perhaps one of those girls in the elevator might have the slightest breath of a faint percentage of a chance to succeed. Perhaps one of them had that quality everyone in the agency called "lightning." How could they know, she wondered, as she pushed open the door to her office on which the sign said, "Director, Women's Division," that it had never been enough just to be beautiful?

Casey d'Augustino, Fauve's assistant, looked up in surprise from the chair on which she was perched, leafing through an advance copy of Vogue. Tiny and curly haired, Casey, at twenty-five, was older than Fauve by several years.

"You look as if you're wanted by the Mounties," she chortled, amused by Fauve's expression.

"I've just escaped the furies . . . got caught in the elevator with a large batch of young hopefuls."

"Serves you right for being late."

"How often does that happen?" Fauve asked with mild belligerence, shucking off her raincoat and sinking, with a sigh of relief, into her chair. She pulled off her wet boots and put her feet, in their kelly green tights, on her desk. She always dressed to defy bad weather and today she wore an orange turtleneck sweater and purple tweed trousers.

"Rarely," Casey admitted, "but no need to apologize, you're still right on time for the emergency of the week."

"Emergency?" Fauve looked out through the glass door of her office, her red eyebrows raised in inquiry. Everywhere she looked she saw the normal activity of the agency, dozens of bookers talking into their batteries of phones. As long as the telephones functioned, there could be no real emergency at Lunel.

"Trouble with Jane," Casey said, looking unnervingly serious.

"Again!" Fauve, who had started to doodle on the pad on her desk, slammed down her pencil with as much force as if it were the gavel of a hanging judge. "After that warning I gave her last week. Trouble again?"

"She was booked for Bazaar yesterday—Arthur Brown was shooting. Bunny, his stylist, called first thing this morning, absolutely livid . . ."

"Did you know that livid means black and blue?" Fauve interrupted hastily, not anxious to have her already harried day utterly ruined by hearing the latest about Jane, Lunel's top model, a girl who worked only under her plain first name, needing none of the catchy, inventive appellations of others, for she was the best blue-eyed blonde in the world, possessing a cataclysmic beauty about

3

which there could be no ifs, ands or buts. It was all there with Jane, locked into the bone, irrefutable. She was the only model Fauve had ever known who was completely satisfied with how she looked, insufferable Jane, who knew she was perfect.

"Livid as in furious," Casey went on. "Jane showed up two hours late yesterday which Bunny had anticipated, since she's always late. So that wasn't the problem. Her hair was filthy. That wasn't the problem either because the stylist washed it. She proceeded to mortally insult the makeup man but he forgave her because he's heavily into being insulted. Then she felt too shaky to work because she hadn't had lunch so they fed her, sending out for three different kinds of yogurt before she was happy. After that she had to make a half-hour phone call to her personal astrological adviser. All par for the course, so far. The thing Bunny was livid about was that after fawning over Jane all day *Bazaar* still didn't get the picture. She wouldn't let them cut her hair."

Fauve leapt to her feet, her lovely, vivid face a study in disbelief, her great gray eyes wide with outrage. "Jane *knew* it was a beauty editorial. She knew they had to cut her hair two inches—that was the whole point. Damnation! The difference in hair next season is a *mere* two inches—I had it all out with her last month when she accepted the booking."

"Ah, but our Jane changed her mind, you see. Her astrologer told her not to make any changes until the sun moves into Neptune."

"That's it! Jane's got to go. I'm going to terminate her contract today."

"Oh, Fauve . . ." Casey moaned, thinking of the next three solid months' worth of bookings on Jane's schedule.

"Nope. Jane's made us look bad once too often. How can I expect the other girls to behave and work hard if I let her get away with this?"

"If you terminate her she'll be working for Ford or Wilhelmina tomorrow. People will put up with anything to get her—there's only one Jane," Casey warned solemnly.

"Wrong, Casey. There'll always be another Jane, sooner or later," Fauve said quietly. "But there's only one Lunel."

"Point well made. Point taken. Still, aren't you going to talk it over with Maggy first?" Casey asked.

"Maggy!" Fauve said, astonished. "She's not supposed to be in

4

today—it's Friday." When her grandmother was away on her habitual long weekends, Fauve was in full charge of the business.

"She told me it was raining too hard to go up to the country until tomorrow. The Boss is in her office," Casey informed her.

"Of course I'll tell her about Jane," Fauve said thoughtfully. "Any more emergencies?"

"Only one you can't do anything about. Pete's working on it now," Casey said, referring to the telephone repair man who spent half of every week unscrambling their hundred outside lines and dozens of intercoms. "One of the bookers' phones is screwed up—she's getting some shrink's calls and he's getting ours. She's telling everyone to have a good cry, then take a cold shower, two aspirins . . . and pray."

"Couldn't hurt," said Fauve as she pushed open the office door and headed in the direction of the big corner office where Maggy Lunel had long reigned over the world of fashion modeling.

Certain great beauties age gracefully; others hang on relentlessly to a particular period in their past and try to maintain themselves there, withering, nevertheless, just a little every year; and still others lose their beauty quite suddenly, so that it can only be fleetingly reconstructed in the imagination of those who meet them. Maggy Lunel had aged *agelessly*. From twenty feet away she was still that seventeen-year-old who had once been the loveliest artists' model in all Montparnasse. At a distance of ten feet she was clearly the most sophisticated woman in New York, a woman who held her slim body with an élan that generations of women had tried to copy. From a closer view it was impossible to realize that she was in her sixties, for her charm was too potent to leave room for such mean-spirited calculations.

"Magali! What a shame about the country . . . was Darcy very disappointed?" Fauve rushed forward to kiss her grandmother, calling her by her true first name as no one else had the right to.

"He was a bit grumpy but then he called Herb Mayes and they made a date for lunch at '21' which cheered him up immediately," Maggy answered, hugging her. "Last night the radio said the power lines were out so I refused to budge . . . I tend to lose my famously sweet disposition when I have to creep around by candlelight and grill a hot dog in the fireplace."

"And I thought you'd be more romantic—another illusion

5

gone. Anyway, I'm awfully glad you're here. I've decided to cut Jane loose . . ." Fauve looked at Maggy with a mixture of inquiry and determination.

"I rather wondered when it would happen. Loulou and I've had a bet on it for the last three months."

Fauve's mouth opened in surprise. Loulou, the head booker and Maggy's particular crony, had never indicated anything but resignation over Jane's unpredictable behavior.

"Who won?" she gasped.

"Loulou, of course. In five years of trying I have yet to win a bet from Loulou. Still . . . someday . . ." Maggy grinned and shrugged. Fauve, she thought, was looking particularly enchanting on this gloomy morning, in her wild combination of clothes, and her green feet. Any of *Les Fauves*, the school of painters after whom she'd been named, would have been overcome by her. Indeed, in Maggy's opinion, any man at all would be overcome by her, although it wouldn't quite do to tell Fauve that. Not that she was vain, but it might sound like some ordinary grandmother's normal prejudice. For decades Maggy had possessed the most expertly trained eye in the world for spotting beauty and she was deeply thankful that Fauve hadn't decided to be a model. She could have been the best of them all—in her own way outclassing Jane—but Maggy had never wanted that particular career for her.

"What time is it?" Fauve asked suddenly. "I left my watch at home—that's what comes from dressing in a hurry, and I don't want to miss Angel's new cottage cheese commercial."

"It's almost ten-thirty."

"Good. We're just in time. Shall I switch on your set?" Fauve gestured toward the television set that Maggy kept to monitor the various commercials in which her girls appeared. "Or are you busy? I can watch on my own set if you are."

"No, stay here, darling. I'd like to see it and I don't have all that much to do today. I hear that Angel's interviewing business managers . . . she's doing as well as you thought she would."

Fauve turned on the set and sat down in the chair in front of Maggy's desk. The two women both turned their eyes to the screen and watched as Angel managed to convince even them, for thirty astonishing seconds, that skim milk cottage cheese could be an object of gourmet devotion.

When the commercial was over they shook hands in congratulations, laughing together, each on the same rollicking thrilling note of freedom from all convention, a laugh that made everyone who heard it stop to listen and wish fervently to hear it again.

"You were right to move Angel to the Big Board," Maggy said. "That spot should run forever."

"I can just see her trying to decide whether to buy an apartment house or a herd of cattle with the residuals. She'll probably settle for a Jaguar."

As Fauve reached up to turn off the set, the words "News Center Flash" popped onto the screen and she kept it on to see what had happened. An anchorwoman appeared, speaking rapidly.

"Julien Mistral, considered to be France's greatest living painter, died today of pneumonia at his home in the South of France. The artist was seventy-five years old. His daughter, Madame Nadine Dalmas, was with him at the time of his death. Details at noon."

Neither Fauve nor Maggy moved. Shock held them in their chairs as another commercial ran its course. Suddenly Maggy jumped up and turned the set off but Fauve still sat immobilized, the light of her eyes extinguished. Maggy went to her, leaned down, put her arms around her shoulders and pulled the motionless red head to her breast.

"My God, my God, to hear it like that," she murmured, rocking Fauve in her arms.

"I don't feel anything. Absolutely nothing. I should feel something, shouldn't I?" Fauve said, almost too softly for Maggy to hear.

"It's the suddenness . . . I don't feel anything either, but I will." For a moment they were both silent, clinging together, listening to the wail of a siren in traffic on Fifty-seventh Street without hearing it. Julien Mistral was dead and time had come to a stop for the two women, both of whom had loved him.

On Maggy's desk there was one framed photograph. As if they were joining her in their shock, each of them found herself looking toward that picture of Teddy, the greatest fashion model of all time; the girl who had been Maggy's daughter, Julien Mistral's mistress and Fauve's mother.

Finally Maggy stood up and released Fauve as her French practicality swept over her arrested emotions and told her what had to happen next.

7

"Fauve, the funeral . . . you'll have to go. Come on—I'll go back to the apartment with you. I'll help you pack. Casey can get your plane ticket."

Fauve moved for the first time since the television announcement. She walked over to one of the windows and looked out at the rain. She spoke without turning her head to Maggy.

"No."

"What do you mean 'no'? I don't understand."

"No, Magali, I can't go."

"Fauve, you're in shock. Your father is dead. I know you haven't spoken to him in more than six years but of course you must go to his funeral."

"No, Magali, no, I won't. I'm not going. *I can't.*"

2

Paris was *en fête,* in love with itself. It was a Monday in May 1925 and everywhere neighbors agreed with each other that never, in their memories, had the chestnut trees carried so many creamy pyramids of flowers. But they only stopped to notice the parade of blue days and star-filled nights when they weren't busy gossiping, for never, even in the history of this capital city of all capital cities, had the ferment of the worlds of art and fashion and society yielded such a pungent, intoxicating wine.

In her workroom on that morning in May, Chanel was busy creating the very first little black suit; on that morning Colette was putting the finishing touches to the scandalous manuscript of *La Fin de Chéri.* Young Hemingway and the half-blind James Joyce had been out on that dawn, drinking together, while Mistinguette had opened the night before at the Casino de Paris, proving once again, as surely as a great bullfighter claims the applause of the crowd, that the art of descending a staircase belonged to her. The Cartier brothers had bought the most extraordinary necklace in the world, three perfect strands of pink pearls that had taken two centuries to gather—and many people wondered to whom they would sell it.

Maggy Lunel cared nothing about pearl necklaces as she stood on a street corner in Montparnasse, called the Carrefour Vavin. She was devouring her second breakfast, a handful of hot fried potatoes she had just bought for four centimes from a street vendor. She had been in Paris less than twenty-four hours and, at seventeen, she found that running away from home in Tours to seek her destiny was an infernally hungry business.

Passersby on the rue de la Grande Chaumière turned to cast a second and often third glance at her, planted there as if she owned the pavement, tall, long-limbed, unselfconscious and apparently totally unaware of the contradiction between her face and her clothing. She wore the boyish, athletic silhouette of the day following the latest mode in a trim skirt of pleated navy serge that covered her knees and a white crêpe overblouse, which was belted below her waist.

But, in a day when no lady, rich or poor, was seen on the street without a hat, she was bareheaded and her face had not been tweaked and painted into the cupid-bowed, heavily powdered, highly rouged version of a Kewpie doll that was so in favor that women everywhere had managed to make themselves all look alike. She had the strong, bold beauty of a day in the future, of an era that wouldn't dawn for another quarter-century. Her cheekbones were twin scimitars under the white stretch of her skin and she carried her head on her long neck as proudly as a war flag.

In a time when all women had cut their hair, hers was a long, straight fall of shiny stuff, the dark orange of apricot jam, and her thick, unfashionably unplucked eyebrows were only a few shades deeper over eyes that were set almost too far apart. They were frank and spangled and wide open, the whites fresh and bright, the irises the yellow-green of a glass of Pernod before it has been diluted by water. Maggy's lips were so full and well marked that they were the focus of her face, a signal as emphatic as a signpost.

As Maggy Lunel regretfully chewed the last of the potatoes she looked like a large golden cat who had walked into a breeze. Nothing about her self-confident stance would have revealed her age to an observer, but her skin was as tender and new as a baby's palms and where it lay over her well-formed, straight nose, it was dappled with faint freckles.

Maggy dusted her hands off with her handkerchief and looked about the Carrefour Vavin. She was standing a step away from the boulevard Raspail. Across that wide thoroughfare was the beginning of the rue Delambre. From her spot on the sidewalk every other street seemed to be going downhill. She had the feeling of being on top of a gentle hill in the center of a great open place, as if this crossroad were the main avenue of a great city, complete in itself. In every direction she had large views of the fresh, blowing sky of spring, pierced by the tops of the chestnut trees. But there was nothing peaceful in the prospect. The very air was charged with sparks of energy, and even the pigeons looked busy. It seemed to Maggy that the passersby were almost running to get to their mysterious destinations.

Oh, she thought, how madly she wanted to crunch Paris between her teeth, to chew and chew until she possessed this city, this unopened treasure chest crammed with objects of desire. She shifted from one foot to another with impatience to *begin*, tapping her neat, "Louis" heeled pump with the instep strap buttoned on one side, swinging her head to try to look into the windows of each passing taxi, so overwhelmed with curiosity and eagerness that she didn't notice that she herself had become the object of the attention of a growing group of people who had clustered around her. They were an oddly assorted band: young women in cheap, brightly colored clothes, old women in aprons and slippers; grandfathers smoking and small children tugging at their mothers' hands; boys and girls who should, surely, have been in school, all waiting with an air of resigned patience that made Maggy look like a nervous filly straining at a starting gate.

Gradually they formed a rough circle around her and their conversation trailed off as they looked at the stranger and nudged each other.

"Are you waiting for someone?" asked a buxom woman of thirty-five.

Maggy looked up in surprise, glanced around the circle and smiled.

"I certainly hope so, Madame. I'm in the right place, aren't I?"

"That depends."

"The models' fair? Isn't it here that I wait to get work as an artist's model?"

"It's the spot," said a twelve-year-old boy, peering at her with ardent interest. "Me, I'm of the *métier*. I wasn't even born when I was painted for the first time," he boasted. "But my ma, she was in her last month."

"Shut up, imbecile," said his mother, shoving him behind her. "You're no model," she said to Maggy, accusingly.

The *foire aux modeles* was an institution that had started in

Montmartre some seventy-five years earlier, when professional artists' models gathered to be hired around the fountain of the Place Pigalle. As the artists had moved to Montparnasse the models had followed them, still standing on the street waiting for work every Monday morning.

Entire families had lived by this trade for generations and Maggy's appearance among them was greeted with the deep resentment any group of professionals shows toward an obvious amateur.

"If someone will pay to paint me," Maggy retorted, "won't that make me a model?"

"So you think that's all there is to it, do you? It's a stinking hard job of work, my fine young lady."

"Good," Maggy said decisively, jamming her hands into the pockets of her skirt and standing straight and sure in her tight new shoes.

The models who had gathered closely around to hear this exchange, blocking the pavement, suddenly drew back as they all turned to watch a pretty girl wearing a close-fitting, jade green cloche over her shingled dark hair, who was swinging along the street with an admiring man on each arm. As she caught sight of Maggy she looked her up and down with a sharp eye. She raised her eyebrows in surprise and then shrugged her shoulders in dismissal. Loudly enough for all of them to hear she commented, "So that's the kind of savage coming from the provinces these days, is it? That beanpole's never seen a pair of scissors obviously. I wonder if she's even heard of soap and water . . . there's a strong air of the farmyard somewhere." She laughed in contempt, pretending not to hear the wave of sniggers her comments had caused and disappeared down the street.

"Who is that . . . individual?" Maggy asked indignantly.

"That's Kiki of Montparnasse, and you didn't even recognize her? Now *there's* a model—the queen of us all." The woman was glad to underscore Maggy's ignorance. "Everybody knows Kiki, and Kiki knows everybody. You *are* wet behind the ears and no mistake."

As Maggy was about to reply she felt a hand fall on her arm and turn her around abruptly. "What have we here?" Two men were looking at her. The one who had spoken was shorter than she, dressed in a dandy's piped jacket and perfectly pressed trousers, a stickpin in his tie and a straw hat tipped to one side of his head. He had small, clever eyes and a grin that showed tiny, yellow teeth.

The second man was as monumental as the massive tree trunk against which he leaned. His eyes, as blue as open water, were disconcerting in the steadiness and the fixity of their gaze. He was six feet four inches tall, and there was a wild, yet noble air about him that was doubly startling in this crowded city scene because it was untamed by urban custom or consideration. He might have been a mountain climber surveying the world below from the height of a conquered peak. He had a splendid head set arrogantly on a thick, strong neck, a broad open brow, a dominant, high-bridged, confident nose and a wide mouth. His hair was dark red, curly and unkempt. As he looked appraisingly at Maggy he had the air of a gallant, battle-bound cavalier riding out of the past, in spite of his workingman's brown corduroy trousers and open-necked blue shirt.

"Mistral," the smaller man said to him, "what do you think?" He put his hand under Maggy's chin and slowly turned her head from one side to another. "Very interesting, eh? The eyes—a most curious color. And decidedly there's something unusual—even odd—about this mouth, just a touch cannibalistic, wouldn't you say? Van Dongen couldn't make much of it." He fingered Maggy's hair as if it were fabric in a shop, rubbing it between his thumb and index finger. "Hmmm—at least it's clean and she hasn't cut it."

Maggy stood rigid in shock. No man had touched her like this in her lifetime. In automatic self-defense she focused on a neutral object, three bunches of leeks the taller man was carrying under his arm as if they were a book. As the shorter man's fingers lifted her hair away from her ears so that he could inspect her profile, she stepped forward, reached out and snatched a big white leek by its hairy, grayish roots. She held it up to her mouth and bit the vegetable cleanly in half, its long green leaves falling to the pavement. The man in the piped vest, Vadim Legrand, known to all as "Vava," let his hand fall as he watched her chewing. She took another bite.

"You could say 'please,' " said Julien Mistral.

"When you look at the animals in the zoo, you must also feed them," Maggy answered, her jaw moving vigorously. Mistral didn't smile.

"Mistral," Vava said with an air of decision, "I'm going to take her into the academy and see what she looks like. Come on." He motioned to Maggy to follow him into the painting academy of La Grande Chaumière, a few steps away.

"Why? You've been looking at me. What more do you want?" Maggy demanded.

"He wants to see your tits," the boy told her with an air of importance.

"In there? Now?" she asked, bewildered.

The boy's mother laughed with malice. "Get your ass moving, my girl. Go strip down in any empty classroom just like the rest of us. Do you think you're hiding something special that they've never seen before? Oh, these debutantes! She thinks it's made of mother-of-pearl."

"Are you coming or aren't you? Make up your mind," Vava insisted. "I don't really need a model today."

"Yes," Maggy heard herself saying. "Of course."

She turned and followed him rapidly, trying to get out of sight of the crowd of models before they could notice the wave of heat she felt rising on her face, the blush that tormented her life.

"Wait up, Vava." Mistral passed her in one stride and stopped the smaller artist. "I'll take this girl."

"I saw her first."

"What the hell difference does that make? Do you have me confused with someone who gives a shit, Vava?"

Vava gave his yellow grin. "That makes a dozen times you've done this to me."

"When I want something, not merely to annoy you."

"Ah, bravo! That's as close to an apology that anyone has ever had from you, Mistral. Take her. Take her! I have to work on the portrait of Madame Blanche anyway. Nobody buys your stuff so you have the time to indulge your curiosity; just tell me, can you afford to pay a model?"

"Who the hell can? But I can't afford to spend my time doing flattering portraits of rich women either," Mistral said with indifference, not caring if Vava was insulted or not.

"Come along," Mistral said to Maggy, giving Vava's hand a quick shake of farewell. He took out his pocketknife, sliced the roots off another leek, handed it to her, and began to walk down the boulevard du Montparnasse without turning to see if she was following. Maggy took the leek and tucked it like a handkerchief

14

into the pocket of the young boy who had talked to her, and rushed after him, whistling a phrase from the melody of the Java—an insistent catchy dance tune that she had heard the night before, floating up to her window from the open door of the *bal musette* next to her cheap hotel.

Julien Mistral was in a filthy mood as he took the shortcuts to his studio on the boulevard Arago. For years now he'd been pounding at his painting as if he were a convict in chains, given a mighty rock and a small hammer and ordered to reduce the rock to dust. He was engaged in the struggle that had become his only goal from the day he had walked out of a class in the École des Beaux-Arts of the Sorbonne and decided to paint his own way, to paint from his feelings and not from his brain. In the four years since that day, Mistral had found that it was almost impossible to turn off his head, to escape from the narrow prison of French education, to go freely beyond the classicism that has always dominated the core of French painting. He was consumed with the attempt to get the paint on the canvas *without* the rule of his trained French brain.

The tall man hurried under the ancient trees of the park of the Cochin hospital, ignoring the girl who had to run to keep up with him. He forgot her existence as he thought wrathfully of the exhibition he had visited with Vava earlier that morning.

Even that bugger Matisse, even *he* is stuck in chess playing, not painting. He uses the contrast of two colors to create a third color—one that just isn't *there*, damn his eyes—why doesn't he call himself a mathematician and be done with it? Or an interior decorator? And as for that damned acrobat Picasso and his friend Braque, gray, boring, imitative, *dreary* Braque, the two of them are no better—chasing Cézanne's bullshit about reducing all nature into a cone, a square and a circle, beating it right down into the ground until they drain out all the life, all the air—to the lowest circle of hell with all of them!

He was so angry that he walked right past number 65 and only realized that he had passed his destination after half a block. He turned abruptly, with a curse, and, with Maggy close on his heels, flung through the open doors that led to a covered passage.

The artists' *cité* of the boulevard Arago, built in 1878, was like a village in Normandy. A cobbled street led to rows of two-story, half-timbered houses with high gabled roofs and walls of glass. Long gravel walks bordered an overgrown garden filled with apple trees, hollyhocks and geraniums. Each of the small studios also had its own small private garden, enclosed by boxwood hedges and low gates.

Maggy followed Mistral as he climbed three steep steps and opened his front door. He went to his shambles of a kitchen and looked angrily about for a place to put the leeks while she stood just inside the doorway, intimidated by his silence and the way he seemed to project himself through the air as if it were an enemy. She was flushed from the long, fast walk, her chin tilted high to cover her sudden and inhabitual shyness.

Finally, Mistral threw the leeks on the floor and turned into the big studio, jerking his head at Maggy to follow him. She looked around in amazement. Everywhere there were canvases and everywhere there was color, such color as she had never seen before, such color as she had not known existed within any walls of any room, color on which she felt she could swim as on a great river. There were rainbows and clouds and stars and giant flowers; there were children and circuses and pinwheels; there were soldiers and naked women and flags and horses jumping and a fallen jockey and always there was the river of color torn from the sun itself.

"That's the bedroom," Mistral told her, pointing the way. "Go get ready. The robe's in there." Maggy found herself in a small room containing little more than a bed. On a hook behind the door hung the dusty red silk kimono Mistral kept for models.

Maggy took off her skirt and blouse, folded them neatly and put them on the bed. She stopped, dry-mouthed. "Painters paint *skin*," she told herself in a panic, turning to her high school art lessons for reassurance. "Rubens painted mountains of white skin with red patches. Rembrandt painted yellow-green skin. Boucher painted pink and white skin. Skin is the single most painted substance in the history of painting." With shaking fingers she unrolled her lovely new silk stockings. "Painters are like doctors—a body is only a body—an object, not a person," she told herself in a rising inner wail.

Many times in her life Maggy had propelled herself into a situation through which only her inborn self-confidence could carry her. She had realized, when she first determined to run away to Paris and become an artists' model, that of course she would have to pose naked. With her usual bravado she had decided that she could do it, and gone on with her plans.

Now, on a sunny morning in May, she found herself shivering and trembling and sweating all at once. She had reckoned without taking into account her life's experience. No man had ever seen her naked, not even a doctor, since she'd never been sick in her life.

She tried to whistle a phrase from the tune of last night's Java as, with frantic resolution, she let the straps of her chemise slip off her shoulders, but her mouth was too parched by fear to whistle as she shrugged out of the garment she had only possessed for a few days, her first grown-up underwear. Underneath the white batiste chemise, oh, the shame of it, she had on only a new pair of wide-legged, white knickers, as flimsy as the new style dictated. Nothing, no power on earth, could make her take them off she realized.

"What the hell is taking so long?" Mistral called roughly from the studio.

"Coming," she answered faintly. The impatience of his voice made her throw on the kimono over the knickers and wrap it tightly around her waist. The floor was so cold under her bare feet that she put her shoes back on. Flustered, she fumbled with the little buttons, gave up and walked out of the bedroom with the straps of her shoes flapping and making a little noise at each step she took. She stopped ten feet away from Mistral, who stood ready before an easel, and waited for instructions. All the light of the room was sucked toward the clash of her orange hair and the red Japanese silk.

"Go stand by the window, one hand on the back of that chair."

She obeyed and stood very still.

"For Christ's sake, the kimono," Mistral snapped.

Maggy bit the inside of her lip and felt her hands trembling as she undid the sash and let the robe fall to the floor.

Maggy had broad shoulders and the long vertical curve of her neck, as it met the sweeping horizontal of her collarbones, was strong and passionate. Her breasts were tenderly alive, so young that they were almost like cones, high and well separated, with tiny nipples that stood out in firm points. The line of her rib cage from armpit to waist had a fine tension and a perfect clarity. Her skin was so polished, so white, that it drew the lapping, splashing light into it and then reflected it back so that she glowed as if she were illuminated from within.

Instinctively Mistral reacted against her beauty. He was accustomed to the easily proffered nakedness of the professional model who wore her skin as casually as an old dress. Nakedness to him

17

had value only because painting the nude body was an intensely serious business. Maggy, who stood as resolute as Joan of Arc at the stake, seemed instantly, furiously erotic. As he realized that she had aroused him, he became angry in self-defense.

"What the hell do you think this is—the Folies Bergère? Since when does a model pose in her knickers and shoes? Eh?" He glared at Maggy. She kicked off her shoes and began to undo the buttons that held her knickers together at the waist. A tear of humiliation and rage slipped out of each eye.

"Now what? A striptease? Is this a whorehouse? Is that what you think I hired you for?" Mistral shouted. "Enough, don't bother!"

"It's all right," Maggy muttered, her head bowed. A button resisted her fingers and she struggled with it.

"Out!" ordered Mistral. "I said enough. I can't paint a model who is embarrassed. You're absurd, ridiculous! You should never have come. You've wasted my time, damn it. Out!" He gestured to her as angrily as he might have chased away a cat who had walked over a freshly painted canvas, sending her rushing back into the bedroom with the kimono bundled around her like a blanket.

"Fool, fool, *fool!*" Maggy lashed at herself as she scurried, fully dressed, out of Mistral's studio. She had not dared to look at him again before she left, but if she had she would have seen him staring at the chair by the window, the image of her naked body imprinted on his unwilling mind.

3

Shaking and furious with herself, Maggy fled in the direction of the Luxembourg Gardens and almost fell onto the first empty chair she could find, indifferent to the scampering world of children at play. In the space of the last half-hour the dream that had ruled her for four years had turned into such a stinging misery of failure that she wrapped her arms protectively around herself and bowed her head in shame.

A young mother sat down next to Maggy and busied herself with tending her baby. Her feelings of importance and pride communicated themselves to Maggy even through her own emotions. She raised her head and gazed about her at a dappled world in which the old sunned themselves as the young ran about intent on their games. Her heart began to lift when a small boy tottered over to her and laid a big rubber ball in her lap. She unlocked her arms and rolled it along the path for him. He brought it back, as hopefully as a dog with a stick, and soon she found herself the center of a group of children who were attracted by the novelty of a grown-up who would condescend to play with them, so unlike their own mothers whose words were a litany of French childhood: "Don't touch; shake hands nicely; don't get dirty; don't run too fast; take that out of your mouth."

Maggy played for an hour, escaping into a world of simple games that carried the flavor of her early schooldays when she had been a hoyden, a tomboy with a fan of wild hair that flew in the wind like the wings of a big bird, the only girl in school who could throw a stone better than any of the boys, catch any ball, climb any wall.

Soon after the last child had been dragged home for the midday meal, Maggy, too, left the park. Hunger drove her back to the Carrefour Vavin but every restaurant she passed was full. It was just after noon and on the terraces of Le Dôme and La Rotonde there wasn't an empty chair to be found. Waiters whisked about adding extra chairs and tables so that the terraces sprawled out almost to the edge of the pavement, but there was no place for the uninitiated to sit, since no one was fool enough to leave a front-row seat at the most exciting theater in the world.

Maggy stopped at a street vendor and bought one red carnation and pinned it to her blouse. Her spirits rose abruptly and she turned, head high, into the Select, hoping that the smaller café might have room for her inside. She zigzagged sharply left at the door to avoid the crowd of men standing in front of the long bar and discovered a tiny empty table in the far corner of the room, next to the big, lace-curtained window, sheltered and inconspicuous.

Thriftily, she ordered only a cheese sandwich and a lemonade, staring at the crowd of rowdy, roaring, bizarrely dressed, carefree people packed in together behind the little wooden bar tables as if they intended to spend the day. The sound of raucous, high-pitched conversation, swelling like a river in spring, mounted around her. As the room grew smokier she caught snatches of French spoken in a dozen different accents, for this was the era in which foreign artists dominated Montparnasse; the days of Picasso, Chagall, Soutine, Zadkine, and Kisling; the years of de Chirico and Brancusi and Mondrian, of Diego Rivera and Foujita. French artists, like Léger and Matisse, were in the minority as Americans, Germans, Scandinavians and Russians flocked to the *quartier*.

Happy in her anonymity, feeling invisible because she knew no one, Maggy didn't notice the interested glances that were directed at her. Here at last was the exotic spectacle she had expected to find. This was the life Constantine Moreau, her high school art teacher, had talked about. A failed artist, he had filled his pupils' minds with high-flown tales of the cultural life of Montparnasse, stuffing their heads with half-accurate stories of parties to which he had never been invited and feuds in which he had never been involved. What he lacked in teaching ability he had made up for in the pas-

20

sion he felt for the life of the artist, in the aching exile he conveyed as he made real the violently pigmented, tempestuous drama of a Paris to which he had so vainly yearned to belong. It was Moreau who had given Maggy's imagination the home it had been seeking, Moreau who made a bohemian life in Montparnasse her ever-present fantasy, he who had assured her that Renoir himself would have wanted to paint her even if she were taller than most of the other women in the world. She gazed, almost open-mouthed in wonder, at the display of deliberate eccentricity inside the Select. This is what heaven must be like, she thought. If only she were part of it.

"Well, my little one, so you're the new girl, no? Let me offer you a drink."

Maggy turned, startled. She hadn't even noticed a woman who sat at the next table, inspecting her closely from the outrageous orange of her hair to the remarkable and almost equally outrageous boldness of her features.

"Well, are you or aren't you?" the woman asked.

"Oh, I'm new, that's for sure," Maggy said, startled, looking around at the stranger. She must be over forty, Maggy thought, and yet still so rosily pretty, even though she was more than just plump, like one of the luscious girls Fragonard painted, who had grown middle-aged and fat.

"I am Paula Deslandes," the woman announced, with an air of importance. "And you?"

"Maggy Lunel."

"Maggy Lunel," she repeated slowly, as if she were tasting the name. Her shortsighted eyes, the warm brown of an expensive cigar, peered intently at Maggy. "Not bad. It has a certain charm, a certain dash, a brio—perhaps it will do. In any case it has the essential two syllables and since there isn't another Maggy working in the *quartier*, that I know of, and I know everything there is to know, I approve, in principle, for the moment anyway."

"What luck for me. And if I hadn't met with your approval?"

"*Tiens, tiens!* She sits up and barks." Paula's smile, which had the power to banish all despondence, broadened. "You're cheeky for a provincial."

"A provincial!" Maggy exploded. "That's the second time in one day. Oh, it's too much!" Although she had never known a Parisian other than Moreau, she understood that the provincial is a matter

21

of constant superior amusement to anyone who has the sovereign luck to be born in Paris.

"But it jumps right out, my poor little pigeon," Paula said without apology. "Never mind. Ninety-nine percent of the people in the *quartier* are provincial. But I—I am the exception." She was intensely proud of herself, this child of the streets of Montparnasse, a "flower of the pavement" as she liked to say with a romantic sigh, the daughter of a framemaker who had been brought up within a few hundred feet of the Carrefour Vavin. All Paula Deslandes knew or ever wanted to know of nature was contained within the walls of the Luxembourg Gardens, all she knew of mankind, and she was steeped in the subject like a cherry at the bottom of a bottle of old brandy, she had learned during the thousands of hours she had spent posing in the studios of painters or seated in a café. Paula represented, in her round, abundant and buxom form, the embodiment of the passion for gossip, endless gossip, that was embedded so deeply in the artistic life of Montparnasse.

Meeting Maggy put Paula into the highest category of the only three moods she permitted herself. She rated her emotional temperature every morning and never admitted to a mood that was not good, better or superb. Superb had long been reserved for an addition to her list of lovers—there were and would always be men who appreciated a woman who embodied that classic trio of pleasures: fair, fat and forty. Recently she had found that uncovering a fresh item of news before anyone else in the *quartier* had wind of it was able to make her feel a mood that deserved the designation of superb, and Maggy promised a great feast of novelty.

Every Monday, when her restaurant, La Pomme d'Or, was closed, Paula treated herself to a tour of her village of Montparnasse, knitting together the many threads of gossip to which she had been privy during the busy week. Each night she presided over the dinners of artists and art collectors from all over the world who had made her restaurant so profitable. Paula Deslandes was a natural, untutored historian, who could easily put stray bits and pieces of information together so that they formed a coherent social fabric.

"Well then, Maggy Lunel—so it didn't go well this morning with Mistral, eh?"

"Oh!" Maggy cried. "How could you possibly know anything about that? You've never even seen me before!"

"The word travels fast in this little corner of Paris," Paula answered smugly.

"But . . . who told you?"

"Vava. He dropped in on Mistral right after that big bastard threw you out, poor thing, and being Vava, naturally he couldn't wait to spread the story. He's an old woman, I always say."

"Oh, no!" Maggy hammered on her new skirt with both fists, punishing her bold pink knees. She felt drenched in a blush, once more intolerably shamed, shown up again as a childish little prude from the country.

"It's not important," Paula said urgently. "You mustn't take it seriously—everyone has to start somewhere."

But Maggy had stopped paying attention. Two women and three men had just taken complacent possession of a table in the center of the room. One of the women was Kiki de Montparnasse, who stared openly at her, elbowed her friends and pointed toward Maggy and Paula. Her male companions fixed Maggy with their eyes and raised their hats to her with satiric politeness while the women giggled.

"That one again! Just what I needed," Maggy muttered angrily.

"What has Kiki to do with you?" Paula asked.

"She insulted me this morning when she passed me in the street."

"Ah. Did she indeed?" Paula murmured.

"I don't find it amusing," Maggy said, not liking Paula's thoughtful tone.

"Nor do I, I assure you. I find it fascinating . . . that bitch is too condescending to bother to insult just anyone . . . so she's noticed you already . . . well, I have to grant her an eye."

"So you know her, too?"

"Yes. I know her. Let's get out of here. There is a bad odor suddenly in this café. I'm inviting you to a real lunch. Come on—last night I won three hundred francs at poker, took them off Zborowski and God knows that dealer can afford it. Stop looking at that slut and her riffraff. Pretend they don't exist. We're going to Dominique's for a *chachlik*. Sound good?"

"*Chachlik?* What is it? Something to eat I hope—I'm starving—I'm always starving." Maggy stood up quickly, desperate to leave, unfolding to her full five feet nine inches. Paula's eyes squinted as she looked up.

"My God, how much will it take to fill you up? Never mind, come along, it's crowded there but they'll find a place for us." Paula herded Maggy out of the Select as briskly as a terrier, never glancing at the table of Kiki's friends who watched them maliciously until they reached the door.

Around the corner, halfway down the rue Bréa, the two women turned in at an inconspicuous door that seemed to lead to a *charcuterie*. But beyond the display cases, filled with selections of cold Russian hors d'oeuvres, was a small, low-ceilinged, red-walled room with marble counters and high stools.

Once they were perched before a counter and Paula had ordered for both of them, she returned to her questioning of Maggy. "Tell me all about yourself. Mind you. I'll know if you leave something out."

Maggy hesitated, not knowing how to begin. No one in her seventeen years had ever asked her this question. In Tours, where she had lived all of her life, everyone knew everything there was to know about her. Should she gloss over the facts? Something about Paula's eyes disposed her to tell the truth. They were infinitely knowing, yet infinitely kind and Maggy needed someone to talk to even more than she needed food. She took a deep breath for courage and plunged in to get the worst of it said as quickly as possible.

"The most important thing about me has always been that my father died a week before he was supposed to marry my mother—he had smallpox. If he'd lived, I'd have been just another premature child—as it was—I'm illegitimate."

"Evidently—but these things happen, even in the best of families."

"But not in respectable Jewish families. They just *never* happen. I'm the only bastard in the whole Jewish community of Tours and I've always had my nose rubbed in it."

"Your mother then, why didn't she just leave Tours and go to live somewhere else, pretend that she was a widow like so many other women?"

"She died when I was born. Aunt Esther always blamed her for dying and escaping the scandal of her conduct."

"Charming! Such sympathy! Did this agreeable aunt bring you up?"

"No, I lived with my grandmother until she died four months ago." Maggy thought wistfully of the gentle old woman who had raised her so tenderly in her small house, who had been made happy by Maggy's smiles, whose uncritical love had made Maggy brave, who had always resisted Aunt Esther's irrational conviction that somehow Maggy had to pay for the shame of her birth.

"It was my grandmother Cecile, my mother's mother, who named me Magali. She always called me that, even though everyone else calls me Maggy, because it was one of her family's favorite names. The Lunels moved to Tours from Provence after the Revolution and in Provençal Magali means 'marguerite' . . ."

"So you're from the South, when it gets down to it?"

"Yes, on my father's side too. His name was David Astruc. Astruc means 'born under a lucky star' in Provençal . . . but not for him! My grandmother used to tell me stories about my family to cheer me up when the other kids called me a bastard. She said that even though my parents had made a mistake they came from the oldest Jewish families in France—from many hundreds of years before the Crusades—and that I should always remember it with pride."

Maggy gestured with her long arms in an ardent arabesque, fired by memories of the tales her grandmother had woven of a life in cities with musical names: Nîmes, Cavaillon, Avignon.

"But what happened after she died?" Paula asked, touched by Maggy's almost childish sense of vanished grandeur.

"Ah, that's why I'm here, that's why I had to leave Tours forever and why I'll never go back. My aunt couldn't wait to get rid of me. The funeral was hardly over before the hunt for a husband began. Not in Tours of course—there I'd always be the Lunel bastard—but in other cities. Finally she found a family in Lille whose son was so ugly that they couldn't find a girl who would even go out with him, much less marry him . . . and they arranged it!"

Furiously, Maggy pushed her hair away from her elegantly positioned ears. "An arranged marriage. In this day and age . . . yes, they still do it. As soon as I heard I started to make my plans."

As she paused to eat the marinated lamb she remembered the day on which her rebellion had changed from an insubstantial dream into a necessary act. The proposed marriage took the idea of running away to Paris out of the realm of fantasy. She had saved five hundred francs over the years out of her grandmother's little gifts and she spent three hundred of them in the department stores on the rue Bordeaux for a cheap suitcase and a few ready-made garments. Her only extravagance had been the silk stockings, three pairs of them, but how could she confront Paris in black cotton?

"So," Paula interrupted her thoughts, "you are, in short, a beautiful, orphaned Jewish virgin."

Maggy laughed at this interpretation, on a rising, blithe note,

showing the glint of her perfect teeth, her yellow-green eyes spar-
kling like the target of a treasure hunt in the dimness of the
restaurant.

"Nobody ever put it precisely like that before and I've been
called a lot of things. My grandmother used to send me to the rabbi
of our town, Rabbi Taradash, to be properly scolded because she
knew that she could never do it convincingly. And I'd go to him in
disgrace at least once a month—it gave him a change, he said, from
preparing bar mitzvah boys—and he'd get so involved in the logic of
my explanations that finally he'd just make me promise not to do it
again and I never did. I'd do something worse. But 'beautiful'—no,
nobody but my poor grandmother ever called me that. Or 'virgin'
either."

"Are you a virgin then?"

"Of course I am!" Maggy looked startled. She'd been in trouble
all of her life for running wild with a bunch of boys but they had
been companions only, partners in troublemaking.

"So much the better," Paula said, "at least for the moment. You
have everything still ahead of you and that's the best way to begin
in Paris."

Paula had seen generations of Montparnasse girls come and go.
She had seen them drive off in Bugattis with millionaires and never
return and she had seen them die in a week of a raging form of
syphilis; she had seen them marry artists and turn into proud
housewives, and more often, she had seen them marry artists and
turn into harpies. She didn't believe she'd ever seen a girl with the
promise of Maggy Lunel. This girl, she thought consideringly, was
someone inevitable.

"Well, that's it, that's all there is to me. Except that I've made
the worst possible start." Not even a full stomach, not even the
novelty of a listener as interested as Paula, had made Maggy forget
her experience with the painter she knew was called Mistral.

"Listen to me, my little one. You must put Mistral and his
abominable manners out of your mind. Vava tells me he's a genius
but if that's true, I ask, why doesn't he sell? How much of a genius
can he be if he can't afford to eat at my restaurant?" Clearly this was
Paula's yardstick of worldly achievement.

"That woman, Kiki de Montparnasse, does she eat at your
place?" Maggy asked curiously.

"She wouldn't dare to put her foot in the door, that dough-

26

faced bundle of bones and pretensions. And her name is Alice Prin. 'Kiki de Montparnasse' indeed!" Paula's face grew as grim as its round contours would allow. "To call herself that when she wasn't even born in Paris—it's too disgusting."

"But they told me she was queen of the models . . ."

"They told you a lie. They know nothing. Once, and not so long ago either, *I* was queen of the models but Alice Prin has never rivaled what I was, she hasn't come close." Paula's lips closed in an unforgiving line. She could hardly explain to the innocence of Maggy that the one who called herself Kiki had stolen not just one but many of Paula's lovers, and then, not content with those victories, she had boasted to all Montparnasse of them.

"I wonder why she insulted me? I've never done anything to her."

"Because she is so proud of herself that she has to make fun of every other woman she sees. But her little group of sycophants mean nothing. Listen to me, Maggy, you look like no one else in the world. You were *born* to be painted."

"Born?" Maggy stopped. Paula's words, stated with such authority, were so unexpected that they robbed her of speech.

"Yes, born, as a hummingbird is born to seek nectar, as a bee is born to sting, as a chicken is born to be roasted. But this business of offering yourself in the street in the *foire aux modeles*, that's out of the question for you, understand? I'll introduce you to the painters who can afford to pay more than fifteen francs for a three-hour pose—they're all my pals. Did Mistral pay you anything, by the way? No, of course he wouldn't—that doesn't astonish me. But from now on you work only for the maximum. Of course you have to learn a thing or two first, but nothing I can't teach you. It's all a matter of making up your mind to take off your knickers—how difficult can that be, after all? You see, it is a painter's business to learn how each woman is made. Whatever we may think, they need us far more than we need them."

"They do?" Maggy's voice was astonished.

"But yes. Just imagine it, Maggy. For fifteen hundred years, ever since the Dark Ages ended, artists have been running after this ordinary thing, the body of a naked woman. Nothing calls more upon an artist's strength, nothing shows up his weakness as quickly. Show me a man who cannot paint a naked woman and I'll show you a man who cannot truly paint."

27

"Constantine Moreau never told us that. He only said . . . that, well, that Renoir would have wanted to paint me."

"Perhaps Moreau merely wanted to keep his job. What, I wonder, would you schoolgirls have repeated at home? Well, what do you say? I propose to *launch* you! Not just out of the goodness of my heart, mind you. I want you to beat that bitch, that insufferable, intolerable Alice Prin who has the arrogance to think that because my youth is gone, because I've put on perhaps a kilo or two, that she has taken my place. Mine! She can't see into the future, but I can, and one day her youth will go too—as will yours, my seventeen-year-old pigeon—even yours. Well, Maggy?"

Before the girl could answer Paula held up a warning hand. "Are you sure you're up to it? I don't want to waste my time if you're not. It's boring work, you'll always feel too cold or too hot, and most of all it's far more difficult than anyone realizes to hold a pose. You'll want to cry with pain but you must never let your client know it. When the half-hour is up, then, and only then, may you move. And ten minutes later, back to work. So. Shall we make Alice Prin regret the day she insulted you? Shall we attack?"

"Oh, yes . . . yes, *please!*" Maggy sent her glass of tea crashing to the floor with her instantaneous gesture of impatient acceptance. Suddenly the old dream lay within her grasp again all the more precious for the fiasco of the morning, suddenly she felt that she had only to reach out to hold Paris between her arms. What did it matter, after all, if Renoir was dead?

4

Listen to me, Maggy Lunel,"
Paula said severely. "Does an egg wear a skirt?"

"Not the eggs I know," Maggy answered, rolling her eyes dis-
respectfully. In less than a week's acquaintance she had learned to
love Paula—and those she loved, she teased.

"Don't make the mistake of not taking me seriously, my girl!
You must imagine, with all the power you possess, that your body
is a *basket of eggs*, eggs of different colors and sizes, your breasts the
eggs of an ostrich, your pubic hair the spotted egg of a gull, your
nipples the eggs of an undernourished sparrow. A naked egg is the
most natural thing in the world. It is so basic, so complete that not
even Brillat-Savarin ever suggested that an eggshell should be
decorated."

"What about Russian Easter eggs?" Maggy protested, but
sooner than she would have believed possible, she learned how to
feel genuinely unconcerned as she exposed her body to the eyes of
the painters who first gave her work as Paula's *protégée*, only to
quickly find themselves in hot competition with each other for her
time. If she felt a blush about to betray her, Maggy learned to shield
her face with her hair for the few seconds it took to recover the egg
image, but within weeks she moved easily from pose to pose, her
body just an object.

Pascin painted her with roses in her lap, an icon of sensual
authority; Chagall painted her as a bride flying in wonder through a

purple sky; Picasso painted her over and over again in his monumental, neoclassic style and she became the preferred odalisque of Matisse. "You, *popotte*," she said to him, "are my favorite client. Not for your beautiful eyes, but for your oriental carpet. Here, at least, I can sit down—it's like a week's vacation."

The day after she met Paula, Maggy moved out of her hotel into one room with a fireplace and a sink and a bidet, high up in the building next to La Pomme d'Or, Paula's restaurant. It cost her eighty-five francs a month, furnished only with a big, gilt-trimmed bed. Maggy bought herself fresh new bedding. Paula gave her an overstuffed chair, she picked up a battered table and an old armoire in a junk shop and once they were installed she had no more space for anything but a mirror above the sink. When Maggy looked out of her window at the mansards and chimney pots of the gray-white roofs of Montparnasse, outlined against the ever-changing skies of Paris, she wished for no other view on earth.

The building in which she lived boasted that rarest of creatures, a good-natured, happy concierge. Madame Poulard sat in her dark *loge* working all day at her Singer sewing machine, toes up, heels down, toes up, heels down, *petite couturière* to the immediate neighborhood. Childless, she adopted all the girls for whom she sewed, pouring over *Le Journal des Modes* with Maggy as they looked for designs to copy, since the two ready-made skirts and two blouses Maggy had brought from Tours were totally inadequate for her new life.

By October of 1925 Maggy had established herself as Kiki's only rival and equal and even if Kiki was still "*de*" Montparnasse, Paula gloated over the fact that Maggy needed no such qualification after her own name.

It was just as Maggy, unique Maggy, the one and only Maggy, who always sported a fresh red carnation in her buttonhole, that she jumped in and out of taxis, too busy to walk from one job to another; it was as Maggy that she danced all night at Le Jockey and La Jungle to the music of a tango or a shimmy; as Maggy that she moved to the insinuating melody of the beguine at La Bal Nègre where she felt as foreign to that world of dancers who had been born in Martinique and Guadeloupe, as did Cocteau and Scott Fitzgerald, who danced there as well.

Maggy was invited to the twenty-round boxing matches at the

Cirque d'Hiver, which she attended with several masculine admirers to protect her from the rough crowd, and she went often to the steeplechases at Auteuil, cheering when her horse cleared all the jumps and lavishing all her winnings afterward on champagne for her pals. She never went to the races without a tip on a horse and she rarely lost because the tips were excellent, given in return for a smile and a sudden hug from her strong, slim arms.

When Maggy arrived at La Rotonde or La Coupole, there was always a chair for her as she joined first one table and then another of her *copains*. Now Montparnasse felt like her own village too and that fall she celebrated her eighteenth birthday with a party in her room. Maggy decorated the bidet by filling it with bunches of red carnations, piled the one table high with bottles of wine and invited a hundred people. Everyone came, bringing friends, and they sat drinking and singing on the staircase until the police finally arrived.

Occasionally she would spend an evening alone at home, on her quilt, watching the sky from her window and trying to arrange in her mind all the new things she had seen, all the new people she had met. Rabbi Taradash would have disapproved deeply, Maggy smiled to herself, if he knew how she earned her living, in fact he wouldn't have believed it possible, but she suspected that he would still call her, as he used to, "my little *mazik*," a Hebrew word used to describe a beloved child who is also a swift, clever prankster.

She wasn't homesick although she still grieved for her grandmother, particularly on Friday evenings when, on the eve of the Sabbath, peace and cheer had filled their small house with the illumination of the two candles on the dining room table and the blessing of the light and the wine. None of the Lunels had been particularly observant or pious Jews yet this weekly ceremony had been comforting to Maggy and every year she had looked forward eagerly to kindling an additional candle on her grandmother's fine Chanukah menorah day by day, until all the candles blazed sweetly in memory of those flames that had once burned in the Temple in Jerusalem for eight days with only one day's supply of oil. Now all that belonged to a life she had put behind her. Certainly, she thought, she didn't miss the family seder on the eve of Passover that had always taken place at Aunt Esther's house. Maggy's gathered relatives had somehow never failed to make her remember her shameful status; each year she would once again feel that her mere existence was a stain on their family's good name . . . no, she

31

thought defiantly, no, I couldn't have endured that existence a minute longer and now I can forget it forever.

Maggy needed these occasional quiet hours of reflection as a balance to the many nights of dancing when she escaped from the immobility of her hours of posing into the wholehearted dash toward pleasure, ever more pleasure, never *enough* pleasure, that made Montparnasse the center of all that was mad and joyous and abandoned in Paris.

As Paula never failed to point out to her, there was a dark side to Montparnasse life, a world in which drink and drugs were a constant. But even without her warnings, Maggy would have gamboled immune through the never-ending party of Montparnasse nights. She would have been untainted by that sky that burned so red, illuminated as it was by the dozens of nightclubs and bars that attracted all of Paris to its lights. She still was shielded by essential and untouchable innocence, the legacy of seventeen years in her grandmother's house.

Often Maggy danced barefoot, not just for comfort, but because she was taller than many of her partners. She still refused to cut her hair. Before she went out at night, in one of the simple sleeveless chemise dresses with low necklines that Madame Poulard made from the ends of bolts of material Maggy found on sale at Le Bon Marché, she parted her hair in the middle and coiled it over her ears, or she wrapped a sequined scarf around her head, knotting it on one side and letting it fall over a shoulder. But do what she would to simulate the hairstyle of the time, after half an hour on a dance floor, Maggy would find that the scarf had slipped off, or that the tight coils of hair had somehow come undone and the masses of her hair were swinging from side to side as if she were galloping about in open fields.

It was not just a whim that prevented her from adopting a more modish hairstyle; the painters she posed for preferred it long, and even paid a few francs extra because of it. An artist's joy in a woman is based on her flesh in all its manifestations, from her toenails to the crown of her head, and, to a man, they detested the style that decreed that a woman's hair should be cropped and flat. However, like most of the other women in the Western world, Maggy had adopted the line of dress imposed by fashion, the waist barely marked at the hips, the breasts flattened. That whimsical painter, Marie Laurençin, protested that a woman was not a stick, but Chanel and Patou and Molyneux had decreed that she must try to look as much like one as possible, and within her limited means, Maggy tried to follow fashion.

"You needn't give yourself airs and graces," she cheerfully assured Picasso, as she cocked an eye at the way he had distorted her body in his paintings. "It's not only your own idea, *chouchou,* for we women too can reinvent anatomy. Did you notice my new dress, eh? And don't forget it, they belong strictly to us, those breasts and thighs and all the other bits and pieces you play fast and loose with. *No touching!*"

For her work she had bought herself an apple-green silk robe and during her minutes of rest she would often wrap it around her body and walk around the artist's studio, stalking the unfinished canvas like a heron.

"So that's the way I look to you, is it? Well, I may not have a full-length mirror in my place but I have only to look down to see that both my nipples are the same color. D'y' see that you made the right one look like a raspberry and the other like a strawberry out of season? And my eyes—do they really have so many different shapes? I've heard that the Eskimos have twenty-five different words for snow—are you of the Eskimo school then? Still, you might have a lick of talent. Who knows? I'm no expert certainly."

On her clients, "*mes popottes,*" Maggy lavished her sarcasm, her generosity and her incurable impudence. On Paula she bestowed a solid love that was untouched by capriciousness and suited the older woman very well. She regarded all of Maggy's triumphs as if they were her own and from time to time, as the two women ate an early dinner together in the kitchen of La Pomme d'Or, Paula noted that the girl had still not found a man. Not with that monstrous appetite of hers, the appetite of someone who had never known a lovesick day. Time enough, she thought to herself approvingly.

While Maggy conquered Montparnasse, Julien Mistral found himself facing a financial crisis. For years he had carefully eked out the modest patrimony he had inherited at the death of his mother, almost three years earlier, but now, he realized with a shock, it was almost gone. Yet no strict economies were possible to an artist who used paint and canvas as lavishly as he did.

He had always bought in such quantities that he had persuaded Lucien Lefebvre, the owner of Lefebvre-Foinet, the art supply store on the rue Bréa, to give him a small discount. There were cheaper paints to be sure, but only Lefebvre ground his by hand and mixed them with poppy-seed oil instead of the usual linseed oil so that they smelled like honey, and possessed, Mistral was convinced, a richness of tone that other paints didn't have. But even with the discount he had run up an uncomfortably large bill. Yet to limit himself? Impossible!

Restraint, economy, husbanding of resources, living within his means; all of these virtues Mistral practiced in his daily life, drinking only a little cheap red wine in cafés, and paying almost nothing for rent or food. Women, he thought, as he got ready to leave home on the evening of the Surrealist costume ball, to which he'd been invited by a rich young American woman, Kate Browning, were no expense. As plentiful in his life as the burrs on a dog, not one of them had yet cost him a centime.

Mistral stretched and almost hit his head on the ceiling of his bedroom. He decided not to bother shaving or brushing his tangled red curls, since his only concession to the need for a costume was an old-fashioned, wide-brimmed, black hat he had picked up in some secondhand clothes store. He was not disposed to take any more trouble for the Surrealists whose definition of beauty—"the chance encounter of a sewing machine and an umbrella on a dissection table"—was, to him, an abomination.

All "isms" were equally loathsome to him, and in that group he included political parties of every type, all religious groups and anyone who believed in some clearly formulated system of morals. Art had nothing to do with words like morality or immorality; it was above morality, above definitions of beauty. Why, he often wondered, did people bugger themselves up by getting involved in ideas instead of paint?

Still, he was willing to take the time to go to the ball. Kate Browning might buy another painting soon, he thought, and God knows he could use the money. She was not unattractive in her severely groomed, almost ascetically pretty, blond, and obviously American way. In the last months he'd sold her two small canvases, which made her even more attractive to him than perhaps she deserved—he liked a less austere type.

In any case, he would not, could not skimp on his materials. Mistral hurried out, rolling the Lefebvre-Foinet bill into a ball and flipping it into the garden next door. There was no artist so serious or so busy that he didn't go to costume balls, not even Julien Mistral.

Were there more costume balls in 1926 than there had been in 1925? Or would there be more in 1927? No one could be sure during those fine festive years for no one could keep track. Every week there was another ball sponsored by a different group. In this second week of April 1926, the Russian artists had already given their *Bal Banal* and the homosexual international had held their *Bal des Lopes* at Magic City. When the Surrealists organized a *Bal Sans Raison d'Être* to celebrate nothing at all and everything at once, everyone agreed it was not to be missed.

Just a year before, the Surrealists had created a great scandal at a banquet given at the Closerie des Lilas that ended in an attempted lynching only broken up by the police. Freethinkers of the most doctrinaire kind, they made a violent stand against the government, the military, the church, and for full measure, against business as well, glorying in their nickname "The Terror of the Boulevard Montparnasse." When two of their number, Miró and Max Ernst, created the decor for Diaghilev's *Ballet Russe*, dozens of Surrealists broke up the performance by blowing trumpets, making speeches and attacking the spectators.

With their exciting reputation who, with any pretense to position in the world of art or letters or fashion, could possibly stay home that night?

"Surrealist or not," Paula had announced a week earlier, "I'm going in what suits me best, just as I always do."

"Not the Pompadour? Not again!" asked Maggy. "You're impossible—I'm tired of your costumes and you should be too."

"There is only one reason to go to a costume ball," Paula said serenely. "You go to show off whatever part of your body the accident of living in this banal era has prevented you from revealing in your everyday clothes. I'm not trying to be clever—I leave that for those with nothing special to reveal, who don't have my magnificent white shoulders, my delicious pair of breasts, my still small waist. But—just for a change—I'm going as Du Barry, to make a little change from the Pompadour, no?"

"So little that it's unimportant. Again your wide pink taffeta skirts, the tight blue satin bodice, a lace fichu, more lace at your wrists, your powdered wig and your beauty patch—you disgrace me!"

"Ah, I'm always underestimated," Paula sighed. "Instead of the lace fichu I will wear a stuffed python attached at my right shoulder, passing under my bare breasts and fastened securely along my left shoulder until the tongue of the beast licks my ear."

"Bare breasts?"

"But naturally—I thought I'd explained."

"*Félicitations!* I'm proud of you."

"It's a small effort. Only the python to be borrowed, and I'm set. What about you?"

"I'm going as a bowl of fruit."

"What a horror! Lemons in your hair and a dress like an apple? Maggy, that's unworthy of you."

"Wait and see." Maggy stirred her coffee and lowered her lids over her eyes. The thick, straight sweep of her lashes, darkened with mascara, looked like two long, spiky caterpillars on her cheeks.

"Who are you going with—Alain?"

"Alain and three of his friends—four men to be precise."

"As always, safety in numbers, isn't that so?"

Maggy puffed out her lips and blew at an imaginary hair as she did when she was embarrassed, a childish habit she had often been teased for in the past. Paula, as usual, was right.

Montparnasse was like an overstocked sexual zoo. Every possible kind and variety and assortment of sexual partnership was to be found there in examples by the dozens. From the domestic household of the heterosexual couple, to the most unrestrained cases of fetishism, no aspect of Eros was foreign or antipathetical to the *quartier*. Everything was possible and permitted.

In this atmosphere of unbounded, and therefore frightening, permissiveness, Maggy had found herself, from the beginning, more comfortable as a spectator than a participant. She scolded herself as the months slipped past, berating herself for virginity of which nobody but Paula suspected her, but in spite of all the arguments she found in favor of having a lover, the fact was that she remained a virgin although her eighteenth birthday was months past.

Maggy concealed her state of stubborn, unfashionable chastity from everyone. Only Paula was not misled by her free and easy airs, the saucy impertinence with which she treated her men, her laughing rejoinders to their importuning, her casual nakedness. Since everyone assumed that she must have a lover, the fact that Maggy rejected every man's attention whenever it became serious, simply gave her the reputation of being some fortunate man's faithful and secretive mistress.

It took Alain and his friends all afternoon and evening to create Maggy's *trompe l'oeil* costume. Her right breast was painted as a bunch of pale green grapes, her left as a small melon of Cavaillon, the kind that is served whole, with sweet wine in its cavity. Her arms and shoulders became bunches of bananas, some ripe, some still showing a hint of green, and a pineapple grew down under her breasts and over her navel, its sharp leaves losing themselves in her pubic hair. Each hip was a slice of pumpkin and her thighs were stalks of rhubarb. From her knees to her feet she was entwined in painted grapevines and her armpits held apples.

Her face was left unpainted except for two honey bees on her forehead, her hair was held back by a garland of flowers. She had refused to bow to the protests of the artists who insisted that the green chiffon scarf she intended to wear as an improvised G-string was incompatible with the spirit of the occasion.

The artists had constructed an oval, wooden fruit bowl, six feet long, covered with silver paint, on which they planned to carry Maggy at shoulder height. Each of the four men wore painted sandwich boards, over black tights and sweaters. André represented a Brie, Pierre an entire Camembert, Henri a slice of Roquefort and Alain half of a Chevre . . . each huge block of cheese painted so realistically that they looked edible. The four artists were part of a school of Realist painters and their ensemble of cheese and fruit was meant as a protest against the Surrealists and their distortions.

"Wait," Maggy protested as they made a trial attempt to hoist the fruit bowl, "I need something to do with my hands. Can't I carry a flower or something?"

"No, you'll ruin it. Just rest your head on one elbow and lie absolutely still and don't, for the love of God, sweat. Damn it, Maggy, why wouldn't you let us use oils instead of water colors?"

"Because I don't intend to spend tomorrow bathing in turpentine," Maggy answered. "As it is, Alain, the silver paint feels a bit sticky. I'm not sure it dried properly. Didn't some king paint slaves with gold paint once? I believe they died of it."

"Rumor, rumor. Anyway it's only going to come off on your

37

ass, if at all. Now let's go—the ball started an hour ago. Maggy, get off there and walk with us. When we get to Bullier we'll put this miracle together."

"Just let me put on my coat and shoes."

"Why bother—it's warm out," André protested.

"But it's three streets away."

"Don't you dare smudge anything," Pierre said anxiously.

"On second thought, I'm taking a taxi—in a coat. I'll meet you there."

"Oh, the little bourgeoise," André mocked.

Maggy advanced on the little artist menacingly. "Do you want to die, mosquito? Strangled by two bananas? Take that back."

"You wouldn't get mad if it weren't true," he cried, dancing out of her reach.

"Hey, there's no time for lovemaking," Alain shouted. "If we get there too late everybody'll be too far gone to notice us—onward! Everybody to the barricades!"

Five hundred people were jammed together at the Bullier by the time Maggy arrived. In the crowd were Darius Milhaud, Satie and Massine. The Comtesse de Noailles was there and so were Paul Poiret and Schiaparelli, joined by Picasso wearing his picador's costume. Gromaire had put on the habit of a Spanish Jesuit to which he had added balloonlike woman's underpants trimmed with rose red ribbons and Brancusi had gotten himself up as an Oriental prince with beads to his knees and a Persian carpet around his shoulders. Pascin, followed as always by his tame troop of gypsies, jazz musicians and pretty girls, wore his usual black.

Astonished "Bravos" sounded at the first sight of Maggy at the tip of the great staircase. She made her entrance borne aloft and perfectly balanced during the perilous descent. One by one the musicians caught sight of Maggy through the smoke, and with a toot and a blare and a blast of every instrument in the orchestra they heralded her slow passage around the huge ballroom, lying motionless on the silver platter. Everywhere she passed sections of the crowd stopped dancing to press around the group of Realists, applauding and screaming their approval. Maggy had been so skillfully painted that only little by little did everyone realize that, except for a wisp of chiffon, she was utterly naked, a realization that only added to the roar of approbation.

"What on earth is *that?*" Kate Browning asked Mistral, from her vantage point at one of the raised tables that circled the dance floor.

"A Realist manifesto," he shrugged. He had recognized Maggy as soon as she appeared. No one else in Montparnasse had ever flaunted hair of such a flamboyant shade of orange, a color he'd never forgotten. But he could scarcely reconcile the awkward, embarrassed girl who didn't know the first thing about posing with this shamelessly revealed creature, lounging naked before a thousand eyes, and laughing. *Laughing!*

He had heard about her from dozens of people as she became well known, he had often glimpsed her hurrying about the streets from a distance, but they had never exchanged a word in the eleven months that had passed since her first day as a model. If he had been honest he might have admitted to himself that he had avoided her, he might even have recognized that he was ashamed of the manner in which he had chased her away—but such thoughts were foreign to Mistral's attitude toward life. Second thoughts about a silly girl? No, life was too short, there was too much work to do.

"Julien! Do you know how to dance?" Kate Browning asked in the quietly imperious manner that she was unaware she possessed, although she was only twenty-three.

"Dance? Of course I dance. But not well. I warn you."

"Well, don't you *want* to dance?"

"In this mob?"

"Come on, I'm in the mood," she said, not to be frustrated.

"What's that they're playing now?" he asked.

" 'Mountain Greenery.' It's nice and bouncy and you can't just sit here."

Reluctantly he got to his feet, inches taller than anyone in the room, and followed the trim American onto the infernal dance floor on which the bodies were so pressed together that his lack of dancing skills wasn't important. For a few minutes they moved inexpertly almost at the edge of the crowd as the music changed to a pulsing ragtime beat. Suddenly Mistral and Kate were squeezed from both sides by scores of dancers crowding to get a better look at Maggy, whose four bearers were approaching.

Maggy, on her perch, was wrapped in a mounting delirium induced by the warm bath of cheering admiration whirling around her. There was an immense liberation in being naked yet covered by paint as if she were visible and invisible at the same moment. She

39

felt as if she were hovering over the ballroom floating free. From every side hands reached out to try to touch her but she was aware of no menace as the artists raised the silver oval higher and higher to keep her out of reach.

Suddenly, from the crowd, a voice shouted, "Down with the Realists!"

"Down with the Surrealists!" screamed a dozen other voices.

The crowd, which only a second before had been good-natured in spite of the suffocating pressure of the dance floor, joined battle vigorously—this is what they had been waiting for all evening. Kate Browning, aware of danger, adroitly slipped out of Mistral's arms and threaded her way to the edge of the crowd, leaving Mistral to follow her.

Jostling, shoving, elbowing each other, howling slogans, the dancers closed in on Maggy's four artists, almost knocking Alain and André off their feet. Pierre and Henri, the Camembert and Roquefort, still struggled manfully. However, without the careful balance the four artists had achieved, the big wooden platform tilted alarmingly and, with a start, Maggy realized that she was in danger of falling and being trampled underfoot. She looked around, suddenly alert, keeping her wits about her. Everywhere there was a mass of bodies, men punching each other, women ducking and screeching. The place had erupted into a riot.

Crouching, Maggy gathered herself together, coiled herself up into a tight ball and launched herself off the platter with a strong leap sideways, aimed right at the only point in the room that seemed stable—Mistral's black hat.

He caught her with an "Ouf!" of surprise but he stood rocklike, too strong to lose his feet in the mob. Maggy lay in his arms like a child on a swing, no fear, no alarm in her eyes, still under the spell of the moment in spite of her instinctive spring to safety.

She curled her arms around Mistral's neck and let her head fall on his shoulder. Automatically he tightened his arms and held her to him as she compressed herself into a compact oval, bending her knees sharply so that her legs and feet protected the backs of her thighs and her bare, silver-splotched bottom.

Finally, Mistral moved. There was a door to the street not more than a hundred feet away and he pushed strongly toward it through the swarm, clutching Maggy as if she were someone he had rescued from the sea.

As he reached the street, Maggy spoke.

"Where are we going?"

"Not far."

"I hope it's an unpretentious place."

"Oh, it is."

Mistral crossed the street, turned a corner and walked into a large building with an ornate, sham-Moroccan façade. Inside there was a counter behind which a woman stood waiting for customers.

"Good evening, Monsieur. For one or two?" She showed no surprise at the sight of a man carrying a multicolored, naked woman.

"One, please. Do we have to wait?"

"No, you're in luck tonight. I have something ready—just follow me, Monsieur, 'Dame."

The woman led the way down a hallway lined with doors at regular intervals. She opened one of the doors, ushered him in and shut the door behind them.

In the middle of the bare room stood a huge tub filled to the brim with hot water. On a chair by the tub lay a towel, a cake of soap and a washcloth. Still holding Maggy, with a rapid movement Mistral bent down and tested the temperature with one finger. Satisfied, without letting her feet touch the floor, he plunged her into the water, getting his arms wet above the elbows.

"*Assassin!*" Maggy sputtered.

"It's not that I don't admire your costume but it was coming off all over my shirt," he said, vigorously lathering the washcloth.

"Give me that."

"Certainly not. It's man's work." He took off his damp jacket, rolled up his wet sleeves and knelt on the floor by the tub. Maggy tried to stand up in the water but she couldn't get the right leverage in the deep tub. She floundered, heaving herself halfway out only to slip back again. Mistral ignored her struggles and briskly applied the washcloth to whatever part of her body presented itself. Within seconds the water turned a murky gray.

Maggy started to laugh helplessly. She let herself lie back in the water and watch uncomplainingly while he scrubbed her shoulders and her legs. Only when he approached her breasts did she pounce, with an overhand blow from her two hands, her fingers firmly interlaced, right to the back of his neck. His hat fell into the water and he let go of the washcloth just long enough for her to grab it. She slung a hatful of soapy water directly into his eyes and, while he swore vilely, half blinded, into the the towel, drying them as best he could, she finished scrubbing off the last of the watercolor from her body, laughing harder than ever at the sight of him kneeling on the floor, dripping onto his shirt, his eyes red and smarting.

At last Maggy dropped the washcloth on the wooden floor and sat in the opaque water that rose to her shoulders, her arms folded on the rim of the tub, her chin on her hands. Her damp hair clung to her shoulders, her eyes wet with tears of mirth, but her lips were curved in an old tomboy grin, and she'd clapped Mistral's sopping hat on the back of her head.

"Nice work," she congratulated him. "But what have you planned for the rest of the evening?"

Mistral sat back on his heels. What indeed?

"I'm getting cold and I'm getting hungry," Maggy menaced. "And when I'm cold and hungry I get mean. D'y' want to risk it?" There was challenge in her voice, in her eyes, in the cock of her head—even her red eyebrows were challenging. She might be naked and submerged but the very way she'd appropriated his hat defied him.

"Don't go away," Mistral said, jumped to his feet and walked out of the room, taking his jacket and the damp towel, closing the door behind him.

"Oh, that son of a bitch!" Maggy cried out loud. She looked disgustedly at the rim of the tub where a gray ring was forming. She tried to let in some more water but the faucet was locked. She shrugged and stood up in the tub, sloshing water over herself with the palms of her hands. She was reassured to see that she hadn't turned gray. She stepped carefully onto the floor and shook herself mightily, shuddering like a great dog, wringing water out of her hair. Fortunately the night was warm and the room was even warmer, filled, as it was, with the steam of the bath.

Suddenly, the door opened and Mistral walked back into the room. Maggy straightened up, shielding her lower belly with the big hat, one arm over her breasts.

"You forgot to knock."

"Sorry." He passed her two fresh towels. "Dry yourself off—go on—I won't look. And here's my jacket—put it on when you're finished. I have a taxi waiting."

"I hope we're going somewhere nice for dinner."

"Eventually."

"You *do* know how to treat a girl." Maggy struggled into his jacket. The sleeves dangled below her knees, hiding her hands. Clumsily, she wrapped her arms around herself to hold the jacket together. She was entirely covered up except for her bare legs and feet. "Well, I'm all set, and rather grand too, but you don't look like much. Your shirt's all wet," she grumbled.

"I think we both look . . . clean," Mistral said, leading the way to the front door of the public baths. "As long as you're clean, the rest isn't important."

Padding in her bare feet, Maggy followed him to the street door of the public bathhouse. They darted across the pavement into the taxi that waited outside.

"Sixty-five boulevard Arago," Mistral told the startled driver.

Still barefoot, but wearing the red kimono, which she had put on with a smile of surprise at finding it just where it had been a year before, surprised that it could still hang from the same hook like a remote memory, Maggy entered the studio, dimly lit at night when the work lights were off, and looked for a place to sit down.

The studio was as crowded as the bedroom was bare. Mistral had the habit of visiting the *brocantes* of the neighborhood, the dealers in objects that could not be called antiques, yet were certainly not new, and picking up odd bits and pieces that caught his questing eye; a huge casserole of Quimper pottery with a hole in it; a ship's figurehead, half eaten by worms; the last remaining piece of a once splendid set of painted tin soldiers; a Victorian chair of purple satin trimmed with moth-eaten braid.

However, although his discoveries filled a room they fell short of furnishing it. Maggy picked her way toward the Victorian chair, which at least seemed to have a recognizable function, and sat in it with a sigh of pleasure. She was brimming with a mixture of curiosity and adventure. She had never expected to find herself here again and the evening seemed filled with tentative wonder.

"Soup?" she called into the tiny kitchen in which she heard Mistral moving about.

"What do you think this is, a restaurant? If I want soup I go out for it. You'll get bread and cheese and sausage and wine and be glad for them."

"You're not much of a host."

"I don't entertain often," Mistral said, looking with irritation at the sausage he was slicing. It had an air of antiquity to it. On a tray, he hastily arranged a few mismated dishes, a bottle of wine and two glasses, one of them chipped, and carried it out to the studio. He stopped in mid-stride at the sight of Maggy in the purple chair, her orange hair spread out on the red Japanese silk. It was as if a fire had been lit in the corner of his studio.

"You can't sit there."

"Why not?"

"That chair is about to fall apart."

"What do you suggest then—the floor?"

"I have a little table outside in the garden—I thought we'd eat out there."

"But do you also have little chairs out there in the garden?" she asked with a flick of laughter in her voice.

"Yes, believe it or not."

"Ah, well in that case, who could resist such magnificence?" Maggy followed Mistral outside where overgrown lilacs, their white blooms just in full bloom, hung glimmering faintly over a table of white painted wood. Two bentwood chairs stood in the unmown grass, with heart-shaped backs and striped cotton cushions on their wooden seats. Mistral lit a tall candle in a short, twisted copper candlestick while Maggy bent over the plate and inspected the sausage.

"Go on, take a slice," he urged her.

"It lacks . . . how shall I put it . . . a certain youth."

"Better not eat it," he said, hastily putting the plate on the grass. "I think the cheese is probably safe. Are you really hungry? I can go and get something—there's a *charcuterie* that stays open late . . ."

"No, no, I'm teasing you. But did you have dinner?"

"Oh."

"What is it?"

"I just remembered where I had dinner."

"And?"

"It was with a woman . . . a rich American art collector of sorts who invited me to that Surrealist madhouse."

"In that case she has serious reason for complaint." Maggy raised her wineglass, gravely leaning forward and gesturing to Mistral to raise his glass to hers. "To the lady, let's drink to the lady

44

who began the evening with Monsieur Mistral. Who knows with whom she will end it? I wish her good fortune."

"Good fortune," said Mistral, touching her glass with his. And as he drank all memory of Kate Browning disappeared. Nothing existed outside of this still, dim corner of a fragrant little garden, this space that seemed to have been dreamed into an existence far from the real world, a space in which the music of Maggy's voice, impudent, low and as free as running water, insulated him from his former life; a space in which his familiar plot of garden seemed to be newly created, as fresh-minted, secret and hidden as if it were the floor of a rain forest.

He felt his will, his reliable, intractable will, slipping away from him like a heavy garment he had worn for too long. He felt ten years younger, he found himself aware of the warm touch of the April air and the lush whisper of the tall grass and the sweet scent of the lilacs and the harsh taste of the wine. Maggy was a lovely shock. He hadn't been prepared for her. He hadn't expected her. What was she doing here? He drank again and the question dissolved, not in wine, because he hadn't had much wine, but in the sight of her.

Without any light but that of the single candle, she decorated the night. Her skin reflected the moon when she moved. The flame of the candle kindled an answering spark in the green of her eyes, a spark so alive that it made the April moon, tucked among the trees, look insignificant and far away. The sound of her voice seemed to be arousing him to feelings of confused mutiny . . . against what he could not have said.

Almost reluctantly, as if obeying an order, he yielded to an unfamiliar yet irresistible command. He flung himself on the grass and took Maggy's bare feet in his hands, rubbing gently.

"Poor feet—they're cold," he murmured.

She didn't answer. The touch of his hands, big, flexible, powerful, the heat and the slight roughness of his skin, made her shudder with an emotion she didn't understand. She flung back her head and it seemed to her that the haze of stars was humming.

Now his lips were on the soles of her feet, tentative, questioning, barely brushing the skin. She caught her breath, afraid to move, spellbound by the sensations that shot from her feet to the very roots of her hair, piercingly urgent sensations that were like a foreign language, heard for the first time and, mysteriously, understood. She bit her lips as his tongue touched the arch of her foot, outlining, exploring, bolder each second. She moaned out loud as she felt his teeth graze her heel, and she tried feebly to pull her feet out of his grasp, but he only tightened his hold. She felt her knees falling apart under the Japanese silk as his tongue ran up the calf of one leg then up the other, finding that soft, private curve behind her knees.

"Stop it," she gasped. "Please."

Mistral stood up, a huge figure in the dark, and gathered her in his arms. He looked at her with a frown of concentration.

"Stop? Are you sure?" He kissed her lips fleetingly and drew back so that he could see her face. "Ah, not so sure, not completely sure," he sighed and kissed her mouth, its succulence both carnal and innocent, slowly kissed those lips that stood out from her pale face like an opulent flower.

Maggy's confusion and sudden alarm disappeared under his kisses. She laughed, not just with pleasure, but with a new note in her voice, the outlaw that had always lived within her rising to the surface. Her lips became an outlaw's lips, her hands an outlaw's hands as she caressed his powerful neck, and reached up for his curly head to pull it down to her again. She wriggled out of his arms, finding her feet, and boldly pressed all her long length against his body. They stood together for a long, long moment, growing together like two tall trees, swaying slightly as their lips parted, then almost immobile as they strained together, seeking a knowledge beyond knowledge. With a grunt of need, Mistral parted the heavy silk kimono, mad to touch the body he knew only through his eyes, mad to feel her skin, to hold her breasts in his hands, to learn the tight buds of her nipples with his fingertips. She spoke in a trance. "Not here—inside." Stumbling, unbuttoning his shirt as he walked, he followed her to his bedroom, to that wide bed under the window through which moonlight fell on the sheets. In seconds he stood naked, erect, magnificent.

"Let me look," she commanded in such a tone of urgent curiosity that he stood still while she approached, all her coltishness gone as she delicately ran her fingers over his shoulders and his chest and down to his waist, lingering over the unfamiliar shapes and textures, the sinewy muscles of his arms, the astonishingly hard points of nipples that hid in the springy hair in his chest. Only when she had satisfied herself, when his body was no longer completely strange to her, did she untie the sash of the kimono and let it fall to the floor. She lay down on the bed, waiting for him.

At last, Maggy thought, at last. She didn't submit to his hands, she encouraged them. Arching and stretching like a cat she played with him, holding her breasts in her hands and offering them to his mouth, letting him raven on them until, with a swift, lithe movement she withdrew and flung herself at his chest, her lips seeking his nipples. Imitating him, she sucked on them until he almost screamed and held her off, unable to endure the excitement. "Ah, so two can't play at that game?" she murmured and soon she had her answer, as with unsteady hands, he parted her legs and bent over her, kneeling on the bed, his hot open mouth questing between her thighs, his tongue flickering. A vast silence seemed to envelop them. Maggy found herself immobile, rigid, almost without breath, as she waited, all playfulness gone.

Still kneeling, sitting on his heels, holding her waist in both hands, Mistral launched himself into her body. She was so moist that he was able to advance several inches before he reached the barrier. He persisted, not understanding, and got no farther.

"What . . . ?" he murmured, heat consuming him as he looked down at the darkness of the triangle where they were joined. He tried again, without success. Now, the spell of inaction broken, Maggy gathered herself up with all her courage and pressed forward, willing herself to open to him. Every muscle in her long, strong legs was tensed, her toes were pointed, her hands clutched the mattress and her back arched as she raised her pelvis upward, his jutting, hot spur of flesh the only focus in the universe. There was a flash of pain but she ignored it, launching herself anew, met halfway by his mighty thrust. Suddenly he was inside of her, suddenly the spear, point and shaft and hilt, now a heavy fullness of mortal flesh, was encompassed by her body and they lay still, panting like two gladiators evenly matched who pause to salute each other before renewing the struggle.

"I didn't know," he whispered, his astonishment so great that it had only commonplace words.

"I didn't tell you. Would it have made a difference?"

"No, no." Now they lay on their sides, looking into each other's eyes. One of Mistral's arms supported her shoulders and, with his free hand, he gently probed the damp tangle of her pubic hair, finding the tender flesh he sought, and caressed it stealthily, steadily, without stopping, even when she begged, until she cried out in bewildered joy. Only then did he take his own serious pleasure, but still carefully, with an unaccustomed caution, that added to the swelling, rising fever that shocked him with its power when at last he burst into her as potent as a great bull.

5

The first time Julien Mistral painted Maggy, the first time he went after the shadow between her breasts, the first time he dipped his brush, unthinkingly, into vermilion and painted that shadow, he heard a cosmic "Ah ha!" rock his brain. Stunned, almost knocked off his feet, he *saw*, he saw as he had never seen before, he saw with his entrails as he ravished the canvas, his brush flying almost out of control, his fingers numb with discovery, the temperature of his body rising so that he had to tear off his shirt, his impatience to follow his vision so great that finally he dropped his brushes and squeezed paint onto the canvas directly from the tubes.

He was painting at last as he had always known he could paint, without inhibition, without calculation, with freedom so vast that it was as if the walls and the ceiling of the studio had been knocked away and he was standing under the blue, open sky.

Fascinated, Maggy watched him, as she lay motionless on a heap of green pillows, not daring to move until, long after an hour had passed, he finally stopped his attack on the canvas and dropped at her side, radiant, bathed in sweat.

In a gesture he had never dreamed of before he wiped his paint-smeared hands on her pubic hair, branding her with smears of green and Titian red as if she were another kind of canvas. He tore open his pants, without taking them off, and plunged into her violently, grinding her down on the pillows with his big, hot, wet body until he found a huge release that he met with a sound that was a roar of triumph.

Weeks passed while Mistral painted Maggy. He knew that something about the way light interacted with her flesh had been the inspiration for his breakthrough. It was not only a technical matter, a phenomenon that could be explained by the translucent whiteness of her skin or the way her hair broke into shafts of fire or the fact that his imagination was prepared, why he did not know and did not ask, to seize on her particular physical qualities and use them to make the leap forward. It was also his spiritual conviction that light poured out from the inside of her body, *emanating from it*, so that when he painted her the very canvas became a source of light. Maggy knew that something surpassingly important had happened to him but when she asked him about it the few words he found were not enough. Since the experience was not an intellectual one, it escaped words, and Mistral felt a superstitious awe that prevented him from wanting to talk about it.

After that first night in April it was the one perfect spring of Maggy's life. It was the spring by which all other springs would be judged and found wanting, and while Maggy lived it she also watched herself living it. She knew, in the part of her brain that felt no emotion, that only recorded and filed memory, that this was her age of gold. She knew, with the knowledge born in all women, that nothing as glorious ever lasted forever, and yet, as day followed day, she never looked ahead, never considered the future, never asked herself what would happen tomorrow. Each day was enough, round and full and as complete as an apple of the sun.

For Mistral, too, it was a time of surpassing joy, but before he was a man he was a painter, and his happiness sprang more from the work he was doing than from Maggy herself.

It never occurred to Julien Mistral, following the night of the Surrealist ball, that Maggy had a life that could prevent her from posing solely for him seven days a week. He took all her time as his right, expecting her to hold her pose for abnormally long periods since he was tireless and never stopped until she was in such muscle pain that she had to beg for a rest. He assumed, with a selfishness so total that it was regal, that she was entirely content to leave her own life behind, to abandon her room and share his studio, to forsake her circle of friends, to go without normal diversions, to give up any vestige of personal freedom. When he dropped his brushes it was only natural that she be there waiting to relieve the nervous tension of creation by opening her body to his hungry, violent lovemaking.

Maggy questioned none of his careless convictions. She offered herself to him on every level with simple generosity, as if she were a field filled with tall, blowing flowers, that grew only to be gathered at his pleasure.

Hour after hour, she gladly endured the concentration of his gaze, knowing that he wasn't thinking of her or even seeing her as Maggy. Her love asked nothing for itself but the satisfaction of watching him work. He was a man consumed, a man filled with so high a passion for creation that she thought of it as holy. The two months during which Mistral painted the seven pictures of Maggy, the series that later came to be called simply *La Rouquinne*, "The Redhead," were months that soon would become isolated from all that Maggy or Mistral knew of ordinary life. They would become as legendary, to each of them, as if they had once been joined together in some heroic adventure never before attempted by man. The series became a milestone in the history of art, but neither of them was ever to discuss it.

By the end of May of 1926, Mistral felt sure enough of his new powers to attack other subjects. When he had finished the seventh portrait of Maggy he abandoned his concentration on the nude as suddenly as he had begun. Now he turned to still life. His neglected garden, heavy with June flowers; each corner of his junk-filled studio, bright with tatters as a flea market; a vase of purple and white asters; a melon split in half—all these objects presented themselves to his freshly inspired vision as if he had never seen them before. They *lived*, as surely as Maggy lived. Light fell on them and they breathed it in. The world was new.

Mistral never painted except from life, and, as his mind danced he changed forever the way people would focus their eyes. With the rhythm of a bandit, with the bravura of a pirate, he let loose that sense of play he had not been in touch with since childhood. He plundered the secret clearings of his spirit, opening them to sun and air and wind, using his brushes as if they were a trumpet on which he could blow his way to the gates of heaven.

Maggy's disappearance with Mistral from the life of the *quartier* had provoked a storm of gossip and, when Mistral released her from posing for him, her reappearance was a cause for more questions.

"Of course," Paula said, "you did it all in the name of love?"

"Paula!" Maggy said, shocked. "You don't expect me to ask him for money!"

"No, unfortunately, I don't suppose I can. God, what fools women are."

"But you just don't understand," Maggy said mildly. She was too happy to get angry.

"On the contrary. I understand perfectly and I disapprove totally. It's *la folie furieuse*—only to be expected—but don't think I'm going to congratulate you. I thought you'd learned to be a professional."

"As for that—you old cynic—Julien has given me my favorite picture—the largest and the best of them all and the one I love more than any other—the first one he ever painted of me, on the green cushions."

"Wonderful! Months of work and you own a painting by an artist for whose work there is no demand! Oh, Maggy, I never thought you'd end up a painter's maid of all work. That's for other girls, not for you," Paula scolded, too upset to hide her feelings. "And now that he's finished painting you for the moment, now that you have time to go back to work where you get paid, I suppose you give him the money you make posing for others?"

"That's just not fair," Maggy protested. "Julien is working like a demon and he hasn't a sou—naturally I'm pitching in and paying for things—it's only natural, but just until he begins to sell, Paula."

"Tell me this, what does Julien Mistral do for you besides paint you and permit you to share his bed?"

"*Oh!*" Maggy could hardly believe that Paula could have misunderstood so utterly the nature of the ties that bound her to Mistral.

"'Oh,' says the goose," Paula echoed her severely. "And who cooks the meals and who cleans the studio and who takes the dirty laundry to be washed—or perhaps, heaven forbid, washes it herself—and who makes sure there's enough wine and goes out for the morning croissant and brews the coffee and makes that much-used bed? Does Monsieur Mistral do all this in return for the money you bring home?"

"Paula, how ridiculous you can be. Of course he doesn't have time to do those things. Why, I hardly have time myself—I just buy something at the *charcuterie* and we have a picnic—"

"Not another word!" Paula said. It was worse than she suspected. The women she had known, and there were many of them, who lived with painters, had, with almost no exceptions, finished badly. Painters, even bad painters, had the egos of giant babies. Monstrous infants, each was the center of his own universe and other people existed in orbit around him only to gratify his needs.

Sometimes, when Paula was in a charitable mood, she conceded that the struggle to be recognized as a painter in a world in which, in her private opinion, the greatest work had already been done, was so great that *only* a man with an enormous ego could possibly take himself seriously enough to persist. Perhaps *without* those egos they would have to give up and become bank clerks. Perhaps their ego was all that stood between them and utter panic. But she didn't give a damn what kept them painting when, to her wisely unexpressed way of thinking, one trip to the Louvre would compel them all to cut their wrists in despair. She didn't have a sou's worth of sympathy to spare for them when a woman's fate was concerned. Sometimes, for one had to be fair, sometimes a painter married his model and sometimes a painter and his wife even stayed married, like good old Monet, who painted gardens and lily pads because his wife threatened to leave him if he brought a model into the house, but that was long ago.

Paula had no illusions about Mistral. She didn't trust such careless, indisputable beauty in a man. It was disquieting and indecent. Beauty, she told herself, should be reserved for women who had need of it in dealing with the world. Why, even she, Paula Deslandes, who didn't like Mistral, had found herself staring at him in the street when he passed like a highwayman, wondering what it would be like to lie warm and sticky after love, in the fierce protection of that huge, well-muscled body; even she had caught herself thinking that if she were still young she would tame him, that arrogant swaggerer who had, to her sure knowledge, fallen into short seasons of passion with a dozen girls around Montparnasse. No, this man was not a potential husband for anyone. And as a lover—oh, why couldn't Maggy have found a less selfish man?

La vie bohème, thought Paula with a sinking heart, has never been more than a poet's pea-green fantasy and here was her Maggy, her own dear Maggy, still innocent, thinking that she was living it.

"Never mind," Paula said, pulling herself out of her reverie. "I lost fifty francs at liar's dice last night and I'm suspicious of human nature, particularly my own. Pay no attention."

"I hadn't," Maggy answered truthfully.

Had Paula known more about Julien Mistral she might have understood him better but she would have been no less concerned about Maggy's love for him.

The painter had been born and raised in Versailles, an only child. If both of his parents had been at home while he was growing up, he might have been drawn into a normal family atmosphere but his childhood had been oddly barren, empty of laughter.

His father, an engineer, a builder of bridges in the service of the French government, was away much, if not quite all, of every year, working in the Colonies, and his mother seemed quite content with this arrangement. She would probably have accepted any way of life that left her alone to pursue the needlework that was her only real interest. She embroidered magnificent ecclesiastical garments with a passion that had nothing to do with religion although she might well have been happier as a nun. Without a piece of embroidery in her hands she quickly grew restless, plaintive and eventually angry.

Madame Mistral had attended to her son's needs while he was a baby but as soon as Julien could be sent to the École Maternelle she left him to fend largely for himself with a clear conscience. The boy was healthy and well formed, there was a servant to keep him fed and clean and to take him to school.

From a point in the past that went as far back as he could remember, Julien had always known that most of what he could learn at school was not worth the trouble. He lived for other information, the lessons he taught himself. Like all children he was a natural artist, with a basic set of symbols at his command to represent people, houses, trees, the sun.

By the time he was six, before most children become enamored of realism in their drawings, Julien had started to use his eyes to put the elements he drew into a coherent whole, a composition. Soon he lived for the sheets of paper he carried about in his schoolbag, the precious pencils he kept so sharp, the colored crayons on which he spent all his pocket money. As drawing became the focus of his being he grew less verbal, less aware of the passage of time as he bent himself to the ultimate questions: *the shape of things*, the relation of one shape to another and the relation of all the shapes to the whole. Grammar, spelling, mathematics and even reading itself had nothing to do with the crucial problems of pattern and structure with which his mind was concerned.

When his teachers protested to his mother she agreed that Julien's inattention was deplorable. But even the formidable French educational system can't force a child to do well when he doesn't care about the opinion of others, when punishment is merely a minor annoyance and when his mother forgets his crimes as soon as she escapes from the principal's office.

Uncaring, soon given up as a dolt by his teachers, he held down the place at the bottom of every class until he was old enough to leave school. Years earlier his schoolmates had given up trying to communicate with the absent boy whose remoteness was so complete that it had long ago ceased to be a challenge for them. If he had been shy, he might have been victimized, but his undisguised lack of interest in his schoolmates protected him from them quite as well as his unusual height and strength.

At seventeen when his schoolmates were volunteering to fight the Kaiser, Mistral entered a private art school in Paris where he worked brilliantly within the academic tradition until he passed the exam for the École des Beaux-Arts. After a few years at the Sorbonne he began to find himself at odds with any traditional approach to art. First only to himself, then openly, he said that art cannot be taught. "Technique, yes; color, yes; anatomy, yes . . . as for the rest, no." He abandoned the Beaux-Arts when he was barely twenty-one and his father, from Algeria, unprotestingly sent him enough to live on until he died a year later. When Mistral was twenty-three his mother, too, died, and except for a legacy to her best friend, she had left the little she possessed to her son and only child.

Now Julien Mistral was almost twenty-six and still unknown in the art world except for the reputation he had earned among some of his contemporaries. To him all gallery owners and dealers came under the category of the enemy. When Mistral heard that Marcel Duchamp had called art dealers "lice on the backs of the artists" he roared that Duchamp hadn't gone far enough.

"What about Cheron, who paid Zadkine ten francs for sixty drawings? He's the same shit who threw Foujita seven francs fifty centimes for a watercolor! *Merely* a louse? He should be hung, taken down while still breathing and disemboweled. Twenty francs to Modigliani for a portrait—it's unspeakable."

Yet his inheritance was almost gone and Kate Browning, the prim, rich American who had invited him to the Surrealist ball, hadn't returned to buy another painting. Should he perhaps, Mistral wondered, have written her an apology for his disappearance? He considered the thought briefly and then dismissed it to return to his easel.

Katherine Maxwell Browning of New York City had a small talent. A very, very small talent, and what was infinitely worse, she *almost* knew it. Her intelligence was keen, her eye for the beautiful acute; she had been born with the painful capacity to appreciate the best, to aspire toward it, but without the ability to produce it. She referred to herself as a sculptress, her family of rich stockbrokers thought of her with admiration and puzzlement as a true artist since none of them had any intimate knowledge of art nor cared to have. Even her professors at Sarah Lawrence had been encouraging. She had always been able to trap and stamp upon the truth about her own talent before it rose to her consciousness.

Kate Browning had come to Paris in early 1925 to study with Brancusi, but he would have none of her. However, the professor in charge of the *atelier* at the Beaux-Arts, where Kate next presented herself, was lenient enough to allow her to join, even after she had shown him the required photos of her best college work. He expected that once she had bought the obligatory round of drinks for the other students, she would attend a few classes and then quietly drop out as so many Americans did in those days.

His attitude was dictated not by any un-French, untraditional desire to be nice to foreigners but by a very French appreciation of her immaculate prettiness—a look as quietly emphatic as the power of will which had driven this essentially ungifted woman to position herself in the heart of the artistic life of the world.

She was twenty-two, and she had the rare kind of perfect oval skull that permitted her to part her short ash-blond hair in the middle with impunity. Her high forehead loomed over eyebrows plucked into a thin line and the prominent bones of the clearly marked sockets around her gray eyes gave her face a distinction that might otherwise have escaped it because of the relentless regularity of her features. Kate's nose was slim, her lips were thin, her chin was sharp, yet it was these very hard edges that, in the ensemble of her wonderfully shaped skull, made her a striking woman.

In the early spring of 1926, Kate Browning, who spoke French with a tutored fluency that made up in vocabulary what she lacked in gesture, was taken to visit Mistral in his studio by one of her fellow students at the Beaux-Arts.

With the first savage pounce that his canvases made on her trained yet unrigid eye she was consumed by a rage to possess this man's work. She *knew.* She looked at his work, she let herself plunge into the great river of color and she knew for once and for all. There was never any doubt in her mind, then or ever, that Julien Mistral was the greatest painter of his day, nor that others would eventually agree with her.

Yet Kate was clever enough and disciplined enough to resist the voracious impulse she felt to buy as much of Mistral's work as possible. At their first meeting she had quietly listened to him fulminating against private collectors.

"I've known some who buy everything a poor wretch of an artist will give them, they take everything, at bargain prices, and wait until the market catches up with their tastes. Then, hup! Huge profits! They're even worse than dealers—at least with a dealer you know it when you're being robbed."

Julien Mistral would have shouted with outrage if anyone had suggested that even as he spoke Kate was seeing herself as his future patroness, the custodian of his talent, the protector of his career. Yet, from that day on, she found herself waking in the middle of the night thinking of him, planning how she could make him as famous as she knew he deserved to be.

Her acquisitive nature was covered only lightly by a smooth fabric of civilized rules. She was cunning, deeply cunning, and as tenacious as she was cunning. There were primitive forces alive under the spareness of the personality she presented to the world and she directed the flow of this power to biding her time. Carefully she chose one of Mistral's works and then, a month later, bought another. She held herself in check for she had understood from the beginning that in spite of his financial need—of which the perceptive antenna of the rich had immediately informed her—Mistral was intensely suspicious of anyone who seemed to want to own a piece of him. And what was his work but himself, flung raw onto canvas?

She had contrived to invite Mistral to the Surrealist ball in the most casual manner and when he decamped with Maggy she merely murmured "Patience" to herself, refusing to take his act as an insult.

Was Kate Browning's decision born of the fact that her devotion to Mistral's work enabled her to put aside her own utterly minor abilities without having to make any excuse, even to herself? Was it born of this perfect opportunity to lay down with honor her own, fruitless struggle to create? Or was it the prize of Mistral himself that she sought, rather than his work? Was not this rough, lawless, remote man the most essential part of her interest? This redheaded man whose tall body moved with such an outdoorsman's grace, whose face was so unforgettable in its beauty, its strength?

She never asked herself these questions in the middle of the night, nor would the answers have mattered. Everything had come together for her in one instant of awareness and in her spare, predatory and absolutely determined way, Kate Browning dedicated herself for life.

As Maggy stood in the kitchen of Mistral's studio, humming to herself and peeling potatoes on a Saturday afternoon in early July, she heard a knock on the front door. She glanced into the studio where Julien was working. When the knock was repeated he didn't hear it. Maggy opened the door with a feeling of mild curiosity. Outside stood a young, finely boned, obviously self-possessed woman who looked much too elegant for the neighborhood. She was dressed in an immaculate, white, crêpe-de-chine dress intricately fagoted and scalloped with a deep white cloche of the finest straw covering her head. The man with her, Maggy thought, had the look of a farmer dressed for a visit to the big city, as if he'd just had a good scrub and struggled into his only proper suit.

"Is Monsieur Mistral at home?" the woman asked.

"Yes, but he's working." Maggy wouldn't dare disturb him at the whim of a casual caller.

"But I am expected, Mademoiselle," Kate said with a polite smile.

"He didn't tell me . . ." Maggy broke off as Kate brushed quickly by her. Open-mouthed, she watched the pair advance into the studio. Mistral put down his brushes with ill grace, but he walked forward and shook Kate's hand, frowning as he loomed over her.

"So! You did forget, Julien. Never mind—I told Adrien that I didn't think you'd be expecting us. Adrien, this is Julien Mistral— Julien, this is the friend I told you about in my note, Adrien Avigdor." As the two men shook hands Kate laughed a social laugh, a drawing-room laugh, a laugh that could cover any situation with its characteristic note of total confidence and perfect assurance that anything the owner of that laugh did or said was correct.

Maggy hastily took off her apron and dried her hands on it. She was barefoot, as usual, and wearing a sleeveless, flowered, cotton smock she wore only in the kitchen. She pulled back her shoulders and marched into the studio with her limber, long tread. Thank God I'm tall, she thought as she shook hands with Kate Browning and Avigdor, both of whom were shorter than she. Why, she wondered, hadn't Julien warned her that he expected visitors? That was what must have been in the little blue telegraph message he'd received earlier that day and tossed away with a grunt of annoyance.

"A glass of red?" she heard Mistral offer. "Sit down somewhere," he said gesturing vaguely. "Maggy, bring the wine."

As she searched the kitchen for four intact glasses Maggy felt a wave of heat rise from her throat to her forehead. *Damn* him for not telling her. That woman looked as if she had just stepped off a yacht—so that was the American he'd ditched the night of the ball. He'd never said she was young and good-looking. And that marvelous dress! Oh, what a dress! Why were they slumming? Avigdor couldn't be her boyfriend—he looked too simple to even know her—yet his name was familiar somehow. She found an almost full bottle of red wine, settled on four glasses, unmatched, two chipped and two unchipped glasses—to hell with being a scullery maid—and brought them into the studio.

As Mistral poured the wine, Kate kept up a flow of chatter, her voice with its level American drawl charmingly at odds with the formal correctness of her French. Adrien Avigdor looked around the studio, Maggy noticed, with the inattentive eye of a man who was thinking about his vegetables and wondering if it would rain before evening. He seemed to scarcely listen to Kate yet, as soon as she left a pause in her observations, he spoke directly to Mistral.

"I've seen the two paintings Kate bought from you. They pleased me very much."

"That's what she wrote me," Mistral replied in brusque dismissal, as if the compliment were false.

And damn him again, Maggy thought. If this farmer is even possibly a customer Julien could at least be courteous. What does he expect us to use for money when I go to market? The shopkeepers won't let me put food on account the way he does his paints. It's my francs we spend.

"Would you mind if I looked around?" Avigdor asked, his open and guileless light blue eyes beaming with frank good nature in his round face. He had an air of trusting pleasantness, a kind of decency and kindness that Maggy responded to in spite of her annoyance at this surprise visit.

"Look, Avigdor, *dealers* like you don't just 'look around,'" Mistral said, suddenly vicious. "You don't go visiting artists to kill time on a Saturday afternoon, not unless it's to put something in your pocket, don't think I'm a fool. Why, it's dealers like you who . . . ."

"Monsieur Mistral, you're making a mistake," Avigdor interrupted mildly. "Don't lump all dealers together, that's really not at all fair of you, you know. What about Zborowski—why, he finally got Modigliani's price up to four hundred and fifty francs for a portrait, eh? And who else would have been able to get that American, Barnes, interested in Soutine? And consider a few of the other decent middlemen of art. What about Basler, and Couquiot and Francis Carco, the poet—you can't tell me that they're all dishonest, now can you?"

"All right, there are some, one or two maybe, exceptions—but as far as I'm concerned, dealers, as a group, are common thieves, whoremasters and first-class shits!"

Kate's calm, tinkling laugh greeted his words. "Well said, Julien! But as I wrote you, Adrien is another of the exceptions. I wouldn't have presumed to bring him otherwise. So may he have his look around? And for that matter, may I? I haven't seen your work in months."

"Go ahead, go ahead, since you're here," Mistral grumbled, ungraciously. "But don't expect me to stay around and watch you. I have a horror of people saying the kinds of things they think they have to say when they look at pictures. I'll be out in the garden until you've finished. Come along, Maggy. And bring the bottle."

Alone in the studio, Avigdor started to walk around the room, looking intently at the pictures on the wall.

"No, Adrien," Kate said impatiently, "let's see the new work . . . you can look at the rest later." She started to pull at a large canvas that was standing on the floor, tilted toward the wall, its front hidden. "Help me with this."

Quickly, expertly, Avigdor turned all the paintings Mistral had propped carelessly against the wall, so that they faced into the room. He didn't stop to look at them as he placed them side by side. He worked with the rapidity of a cat burglar, fearing that Mistral would change his mind and come back into the studio at any minute. Finally all the canvases were in place and he and Kate stood surrounded by them, each silently looking, Avigdor panting from exertion, Kate trembling from excitement, and an emotion she couldn't identify, an emotion that made her feel angry, furiously angry.

As his eyes went from one of Mistral's paintings of Maggy to another, Adrien Avigdor thought that it was like pressing himself naked on living flesh, like feasting, gorging, literally eating youth. He wanted to roll on the canvases, he realized with amazement, he who trusted only his calm judgment, he ached to throw himself down and roll all over them and kick up his heels with spurting excitement. The pictures of the girl—ah, he could mount her! They excited him far more than Maggy did in living flesh.

Finally, he tore himself away from the seven large canvases and turned toward the still lifes. Looking at them, he felt as if he were outdoors, lying in long, sweet grass, pagan, blissful, innocent of everything but the flood of his senses. As eager as a young dog after a bone, he rushed from one canvas to another, unable to contemplate each one for more than a few seconds because another beckoned out of the corner of his eye.

As Kate watched him, crystals of triumph hardened within her. Certain as she had been of Mistral's genius, she had waited tensely for Avigdor's reaction. He was, in the opinion of many people, the shrewdest of the avant-garde art dealers of the day. In only one year his new gallery on the rue de Seine had been the scene of a series of successful exhibitions of work by a group of new artists who had not been widely exhibited before and he had created a fast-moving market for his discoveries.

She turned her back on the nudes. There was something about them, she thought, that utterly disgusted her, something sickening. But the other work! She was astounded by it. Mistral's earlier work that still hung on the walls, and her own two paintings as well, all faded in comparison with the new energy, the explosion of vitality that charged his still lifes. Here a single huge zinnia, with its double circle of stiff pink petals, hovered against the sky, drawing into itself the essence of every flower that ever grew. Next to the zinnia, a big canvas showed a corner of the studio, in which every object radiated a life force so powerful that the canvas grew in mystery the longer she looked at it until, finally, it blotted out its surroundings and she felt dizzy, mystified, overwhelmed. Everywhere in the studio she felt as if there were holes that had been punched into wonderment.

"So?" Kate said at last to Avigdor in English, which he spoke well. To her it would always be the language of business and business was what she had brought him here for.

"I am indebted to you, my dear," he said vaguely, as if in a dream turning back to the pictures of Maggy on the green cushions.

"Adrien, pay attention." Kate walked up to him and snapped her fingers under his nose. "I know the way you feel but I didn't bring you here just to gape."

"My God, Kate, my knees are weak, my eyeballs are popping. I feel as if I've been struck by lightning—give me a chance to recover, I can almost smell thunder," Avigdor said with his countryman's open smile.

"So," Kate pounced, "you agree with me?"

"Without reservation."

"Then what about the one-man show? You said you were totally committed for the next year, that you had absolutely no way to fit in another artist—what do you say now?"

"I have suddenly discovered a new month in 1926—we will baptize it October."

"The opening show of the season?" Kate's thin eyebrows flew upward.

"But naturally," he said with the simplicity of a prosperous peasant discussing the price of beets.

"Naturally," Kate echoed, breathless with the magnitude of her victory. She had been buying from Avigdor since he opened and her respect for his astuteness had grown as she watched him moving from strength to strength in the risky waters of the art market. Now, as she saw him make a decision with the same swiftness and commitment with which she operated, she understood the man better than she ever had.

How right had been the calculation she had made to bring him here without even giving Julien a chance to say he didn't want to see him. Avigdor, like many dealers, bought outright the paintings he planned to exhibit. The difference between the price that he paid for them, and the price that he sold them for, represented not only the risk he took but his potential for profit.

62

He would, she knew, pay Mistral the least he could get away with, in all due fairness, but that suited her perfectly. Mistral's financial independence was the last thing she wanted. A painter who can control his dealer needs no patroness, Kate thought, and when the time came, as it soon would, for his prices to go up, she intended to be the agent of that particular piece of good news.

They stood in a sudden silence, conspiratorial yet with an edge of caution, each waiting for the other to speak. Finally Avigdor said, "I'd better go and talk to him."

"Oh, no, Adrien."

"But, my dear Kate, one thing must be understood. This Mistral of yours may be allergic to talk of money, as you told me, but unless I have signed him to an exclusive contract we have nothing to discuss."

"Adrien, trust me. Today isn't the right time to mention the contract to him. Today isn't the right time to tell him *anything* except that three months from now you're going to give him a one-man show. I haven't been wrong so far, have I?"

"Kate, I can't tell this man that I'm going to go ahead and do everything I can to establish him unless I have an absolute assurance that he's not going to leave me and go off to another gallery someday," Avigdor said, with a firmness of a breeder discussing the stud fee of a prize bull.

"You have *my* assurance."

"Do you expect me to go all-out on nothing but your promise? What makes you so sure that you speak for him?"

"You just take my word for it," Kate insisted, quietly.

Adrien considered her for a moment. He was not certain that he liked Kate Browning but he admired her. She had a sureness of taste that was remarkable for someone not in the business, and she had distinction. Could Mistral, that haughty, impatient, rude giant be under her influence? There had been nothing in the way he greeted her to indicate it, and yet . . . and yet . . . it was impossible to doubt Kate, as she spoke with such fine, clear determination. It was a risk worth taking. In fact he did not see how he could avoid it. The same instinct that had led Avigdor to decide to open his season with the paintings of a man whose recent work he had never seen until little more than an hour ago, told him that he could not get to Mistral except through Kate. He made a gesture of acceptance and turned toward the door to the garden.

"Shall I tell him, Kate, or will you?"

"Adrien! *You*, of course. It's your decision, your gallery." Kate's precise mouth curved in delicate mirth.

Oh, *yes*, Avigdor thought, she *was* clever. A tiny shiver touched his spine. No wonder she had never appealed to him physically. He didn't like women who were as clever as he. Or more clever.

6

Adrien Avigdor was only twenty-eight when he first met Julien Mistral, but he might, with truth, have said that he had spent his life preparing for the day when he would be able to change a painter's future in a single moment of decision.

He had been brought up in the antique business. "We," his father used to say, gesturing grandly toward his flourishing shop on the quai Voltaire, "were selling them antiques before they built Notre Dame." "We" were the Jewish Avigdors, "they" everyone else in France. Adrien, who loved his grandiose father, as much as he laughed at him, wondered why he had stopped short of saying the Avigdors had been selling the Pharaoh antiques while *they* built the Pyramids.

As a child, Adrien traveled about the countryside with his father on buying trips. So quickly that he seemed to be drinking rather than learning, young Adrien had grasped the profound difference between the way antique dealers think and the way antique *buyers* think. When he was only eight, he could judge merchandise by imagining himself looking through the window of his father's shop and *having to have* a certain pair of goblets. Better yet, by the time he was ten, he could just as easily distinguish the teapot or inlaid box that would never call out to be bought, that would be admired, even picked up and discussed for a quarter of an hour, but was destined somehow to never change hands. Presented with two dozen Limoges teacups, his hand, as if of its own volition, would pick up and turn over the only cup with a tiny crack on its base.

When his father died, rather than work in the family business with his two older brothers, Adrien opened his own shop, in the rue Jacob, only a few steps from the church of St. Germain-des-Près. He was convinced that people bought more freely from a shop that was built in the shadow of a church, preferably a cathedral. By the time he was twenty-five, his fortune was made and, unheard of for an Avigdor, the traffic in antiques had ceased to fascinate him. He realized he had reached a dangerous point in his life when he sold a chocolate service that might not have—perhaps—belonged to the Empress Josephine, but should and could have. He got five times what he paid for it, and had trouble keeping awake during the transaction.

"We," he said to himself, looking as if one of his pigs had died, "have been selling them the debris of centuries for too long." Within a matter of hours he had determined to make a change of *métier*. He would move from the world of antiques, in which everything that could be sold already existed, to the world of art in which profits beckoned on works as yet uncreated. His well-trained assistants could continue to run his business, with an occasional visit from him.

All threat of boredom vanished as Avigdor contemplated the challenge of making a place for himself in a trade that already included such giants as Paul Rosenberg, the Bernheim brothers, Réné Gimpel, Wildenstein and, richest of them all, Vollard, whose fortune was based on the two hundred and fifty Cézannes he had once managed to buy from the artist for an average of fifty francs apiece. It wouldn't be easy, starting from scratch, in a profession dominated by establishment dealers who handled the work of the most important modern painters, such as Matisse and Picasso, and who at the same time were able to attract the custom of the biggest customers, many of them American millionaires, by the ease with which they could conjure out from their storerooms a Velásquez, a Goya drawing, or a work by one of the great Impressionists.

In spite of the dignified solemnity of these great dealers, with their gray-velvet-covered walls, Avigdor knew that their tightly knit world was a snakepit of snarling envy and open, spiteful rivalry which mounted as news grew of the success of the New York branches of French dealers. What tearing of hair there had been at the news that the Bernheims had gotten twenty thousand dollars for a Matisse, that Wildenstein had sold a large Cézanne for sixty thousand dollars, both prices previously unheard of in France.

Clearly, Adrien Avigdor calculated, if there's that kind of money to be made in men who were absolutely unknown only twenty-five years ago, there's going to be a similar market for the work of men who don't yet interest the major dealers. Only a few princely collectors can afford to purchase old masters to ensure their own immortality. Nor are there many collectors who will risk thousands on artists with reputations that have been freshly made. Yet there must exist many would-be collectors who will risk lesser sums than those needed to own a Matisse.

Yes, he told himself, as he walked along the rue de Seine on which busier Left Bank galleries were already located, buyers come in three sizes: the Andrew Mellon size who only want artists who have stood the test of time, the Picasso size, in the medium range, and the Avigdor size, who want to get in on the coming thing, on the ground floor.

As he scanned the people sauntering along, he realized that the world had been organized so that men like him could prosper. After all, nobody needed to own works of art to survive. And yet, human nature is so constituted that once survival is ensured, once a level of comfort is established, proprietorship of nonessential objects becomes an immediate desire. The savage who adds a second necklace to the first, and John D. Rockefeller buying the Unicorn tapestries, weren't that different from each other, were they now? And the peasant's wife who waits for a good harvest and promptly buys a painted jug to adorn the top of a chest—how different is she from Henry Clay Frick, that cold-eyed Maecenas, who spent a million dollars for the eleven Fragonard panels that Madame Du Barry, thinking them too suggestive, had refused to accept from Louis XV? Yes, falling somewhere between the peasant's wife and the Rockefellers, there are a lot of potential customers out here, Adrien Avigdor told himself happily.

For two years he dedicated himself to learning his new trade. Outwardly he seemed as leisurely as that fixture of the eighteenth century, the gentleman amateur. He visited and revisited every one of the best galleries where he was welcomed as a wealthy, cultivated colleague from the world of antiques. He smiled his honorably intentioned, if countrified, smile and spoke of thinking about taking up collecting paintings . . . about which, alas, he had to confess himself a complete neophyte.

At Gimpel's he said shyly that he wasn't thinking of anything as rare as a Greuze drawing or even a tiny Marie Laurencin—too rich for his blood—but perhaps something by a younger man? At Rosenberg's he reflected sadly on Picasso. He admired Picasso but he didn't think he could afford him—not at a hundred thousand francs a picture. If only he could afford three hundred thousand francs for the Monet, the one of the red boat—but of course the day to buy Monet was long past, was it not? Perhaps a younger man? At Zborowski's he admitted that he was sorely tempted by the Soutines. Was it true that they couldn't give them away a year ago and now they were fifteen thousand francs each? Fascinating! That's what he heard. What an unpredictable affair the art market was, to be sure.

Avigdor sought out the advice of a number of carefully chosen art critics, those who worked for specialized publications with readers who bought art regularly. Flatteringly, he asked for their guidance in forming his projected collection. Some, as was common practice, undertook to advise him for a fee, others he was able to lead to exceptionally fine bargains in antiques. What man does not enjoy living with a bit of fine old silver, an Empire chair, a few Meissen plates? They became his friends and well-wishers.

Eventually he plunged into the sordid warrens of the artists' studios in Montparnasse, working his way through La Ruche and the cité of Denfert Rochereau and number 3 rue Joseph-Bara, neither rejecting nor accepting, but looking, always looking.

By 1925 Avigdor, now twenty-seven, was ready to open the gallery he had rented and handsomely renovated on the rue de Seine. He picked seven artists who interested him, a stable of men who still had a long way to go, and in choosing them he was lucky, he was brilliant, his eyes functioned sublimely—and again, he was lucky. In a year he was considered an avant-garde dealer of exceptional discernment. Soon the entire art world buzzed with news of his every move. His good friends among the critics applauded, for had they not taught him everything he knew? Was he not a good fellow? Those critics who were not his friends attacked him viciously and that brought even more sales, for in Paris if new art does not cause a scandal it is hardly worth bothering to look at it.

With well-concealed relief Mistral agreed to the one-man show. Somehow, once that had been settled, it seemed relatively unimportant, as Kate explained it to him, to sign the contract of exclusivity. It stood to reason that you couldn't have one without the other, she said in a matter-of-fact way that shortened the discussion, particularly as she had advised him that he had not set high enough prices on his work.

"Let me bargain with Avigdor for you," she said. "Everyone knows that nobody asks enough for his own work—you need somebody who isn't emotionally involved. And I like doing it—that's the sort of thing we're good at in my family—really, Julien, you'd be doing me a favor." Mistral, who hated even to think about money and didn't relish the idea of a haggle with Avigdor, put his financial affairs in her hands with gratitude. Now he was able to supervise the mounting of his exhibition with growing attention.

For years he'd been careless with his finished canvases, impatiently leaving them unstretched and unvarnished, propped against his walls or stuck up on a nail anywhere he could find a space, but now, his pride in the work he had done in the last few months was so great that no detail was too unimportant to demand his full attention. In the three months before the date of the exhibition, he was almost too busy to paint. Maggy continued to support him by modeling as he allowed himself to be interrupted at any time by Kate, who came by frequently and carried him off in her blue Talbot convertible to inspect the proofs for the catalog, to choose a type style for the cards of invitation to the opening, or to meet Avigdor for a drink.

Kate established an excellent working rapport with the framemakers who had to be handled carefully, for their craftsmen's testiness was notorious. Mistral found himself more and more dependent on her services as a go-between between himself and these artisans who took no badgering from impatient painters, but who seemed to enjoy cooperating with the charming American girl who spoke to them with such proper deference.

Maggy watched and waited, with an unadmitted premonition of fearful grief daily growing in her heart. She had no weapons except her body and her love, but Mistral's attention was focused on the exhibition and he turned to her less and less often. When he did make love to her there were shadows between them, the shadows of her unadmitted jealousy, the shadows of his scarcely surfaced feelings about the exhibition.

He lived in an unsorted jumble of exultation and worry in

which anxiety mixed with hope, excitement was tinged with panic. Underlying it all was a growing, swelling, terrifyingly strong intimation of victory. This man who had sneered at his fellow artists for so long, who had gone his own uncivil way, who had railed contemptuously at the commerciality of the art world, now found himself craving desperately with all the power of his barbaric, famished character to take his rightful place in that world, to be recognized at last.

As the date of the opening of the exhibition, the *vernissage,* grew closer, Mistral grew more and more agitated.

Somehow Kate, with her utter conviction of his genius, was able to find just the right words he needed to hear to feel a momentary reassurance, a solace for which he asked her more and more frequently although he affected to almost ignore her when she spoke.

Even if Maggy had known what to say he wouldn't have paid attention to her. She was too young, too ignorant for her opinion to carry any weight with Mistral. Naturally Maggy thought his work was wonderful. Why shouldn't she? What did she know of the painting that she didn't pick up as a pigeon picks up crumbs in the street? How could the judgment of an eighteen-year-old model give him the support he found in conversation with a cultivated woman of the world, a rich man's daughter who, at twenty-three, had quickly come to know everyone who counted in the artistic circles of Paris? Kate's delicate fingers seemed formed to take the pulse of that world and judge its condition.

That past June, Paul Rosenberg had exhibited Picasso's work of the last twenty years. On October 5th of 1926, when Avigdor first exhibited Mistral, it was clear that the second major artistic event of the year had taken place. The crowds who are invited to a *vernissage* are as without pity as they are without false pride. If they find work uninteresting they quickly turn their backs to the walls and chat with each other, take a quick glass of wine if it's available, and leave for something more interesting without even a word of apology to the dealer.

But when the work speaks to them, when they smell new talent, they are capable of shoving each other aside to get a better look with as little courtesy as if they were snatching the last taxi on a rainy night. And when they decide to buy, a wave of desire begins to mount in the gallery, rocketing from one spectator to another, as infectious as hysteria, as if these finely dressed collectors were badly behaved children at a birthday party, openly covetous, grabbing for the last slice of a delicious, but inadequately large, yet essential cake.

Avigdor, besieged, put a small red "sold" sticker on the last of the fifty canvases less than two hours after the collectors and the merely curious had begun to trickle into the gallery, many of them alerted by the critics who knew that Avigdor would provide them with the occasion for a rousing debate. He needed all his patience and good nature to deal with the complaints of former customers who were angered at the unavailability of the pictures they insisted on having.

"Come back tomorrow," he repeated, with a confiding appeal in his kind eyes, "and I'll see if there's something I can spare you—but I can't promise miracles—it will be small. Forgive me, my friend. No, I assure you, I didn't reserve any for myself—you know I never do that. Tomorrow—yes, I'll try to find something." He would, he thought, get rid of all of Mistral's earlier work at this rate.

Mistral brooded, a silent island in the middle of the long crowded room. He understood his success intellectually, but instead of the glory he expected to feel, there was blankness, emptiness, confusion. And there was something worse—there was fear. Success, disdained for so long, then sought at last with such an unleashed need, success was too great a change for him to accept. The territory was too unfamiliar, the position too exposed, the prize too rich.

Each time another stranger came up to him to congratulate him the words seemed to mean less and less. The people surging excitedly around him, chattering at him and at each other, didn't connect in his mind with the pictures on the walls. He couldn't forge a link between his work, the work he did alone, the work that poured from his belly, with any of the compliments that were being paid him. He muttered his thanks, keeping his eyes focused above the heads of the people who talked to him, absently pushing his dark red curls away from his forehead that was damp from the heat of the room.

Only with Kate who slipped effortlessly through the throng and returned to his side from time to time, was he able to look down and grin faintly. They exchanged a few words, unimportant comments on the size of the crowd and the success of the frames, but the less they said the more intimate was their communication. Mistral drew strength from Kate, who felt none of the unwelcome emotion that was poisoning the moment for him. For her the victory was at second hand, removed enough to be under control, yet close enough to fill her with the sweetness of being the instrument of it all.

Maggy stood in a corner, holding herself particularly tall and proud. A ferocious malaise had gripped her as she watched the crowd cluster excitedly around at the seven canvases that displayed her in all her nakedness. It was one thing to pose for an artist, but quite another to be displayed for laymen to see, she thought. If she had known how she was going to feel, she wouldn't have come to the *vernissage* at all. She mustered all the experience of the past year to calmly accept the congratulations that accompanied the perfunctory shakes of her hand, the rapacious, avidly inquisitive, scrutinizing glances.

It was almost, she thought, as if she were an animal, a horse who had just won a race or a dog that had been named "best in show." "Magnificent, Mademoiselle," or "splendid, quite splendid," they said to her, and passed quickly on, as if she were not a human being to whom one could talk reasonably. Soon, she speculated, some man would doubtless try to pop a lump of sugar in her mouth—that one would lose a finger.

If only Julien would come and stand by her, if only he would even catch her eye, but he was as immobile in his position in the center of the room as if he'd been planted there. Why did he ignore her so, today of all days? she asked herself, and a cramp of misery settled behind her eyes.

Even Paula, who had first stayed close to her side, had drifted off to inspect the crowd of collectors, artists and critics, the very people who came to her restaurant every night. It was as if this was a party in Paula's honor, for if it had not been for her, none of it would be happening. If Paula Deslandes had not launched Maggy Lunel, Mistral might well still be unknown, she meditated, not at all sure she was pleased with her largesse. She was looking about with that indefinable air of the insider, the person in the know at a public event, when a man she'd never seen before spoke to her.

"It's an extraordinary event, Madame, don't you agree?"

"I do indeed," said Paula with a subtle inclination of her head that Madame the Marquise du Pompadour would not have found unworthy. She could tell immediately from that one sentence that the man was the particular kind of American who speaks acceptable French but still has enough trouble with the language not to have the insupportable pretension to imagine himself fluent.

"Is Madame a collector?"

"In a minor way," Paula answered, looking at the man with interest. "And Monsieur?" As always, she responded first to his masculinity, his good looks. Then she noticed that he was exceptionally well turned out, yet he wore his expensive clothes with American forthrightness, a kind of brusque immaculateness that proclaimed his origins.

"In a minor way also—can one live in Paris and not collect something?"

"Some do . . . but I have no use for them," Paula said with a disdainful sniff of her pert nose.

"May I present myself? Perry Kilkullen."

"Paula Deslandes."

As they shook hands she took stock of her new acquaintance. He was probably close to forty, and his aura of prosperity contrasted pleasingly with his thick blond hair that was just beginning to go gray at the temples and his gray eyes that held a youthful enthusiasm. He was, Paula thought, the sort of splendid American that the English are regretfully forced to concede is a gentleman in spite of his birthplace.

"Have you bought anything in the show?" Paula asked.

"Unfortunately, no. The only pictures I really wanted were all sold."

"Which ones would you have chosen?" Paula asked with her most adorable pout.

"Any one of the nudes—I think they're the finest things here."

"Monsieur has a taste for the sublime," Paula teased.

"I noticed you talking to the young lady," Perry Kilkullen said, indicating Maggy across the room. "She's the model, isn't she?"

"Surely you don't imagine there are two like her in the world?"

"I suppose she's the artist's wife?"

"God forbid!"

"His friend then?" he asked delicately, giving the word "friend" the particular tiny nuance of pronunciation, a mere fragment of a tone that to the French indicates a sexual partner.

73

"Certainly not," Paula said protectively. "Maggy is a professional artists' model—the best one in Paris as anyone will tell you. She works for many painters."

"Maggy?"

"Maggy Lunel—my *protégée*," Paula said preeningly.

"She's so very beautiful. A girl apart," Perry Kilkullen said in such a voice that Paula glanced at him sharply. He was staring openly at Maggy with a look of such poleaxed yearning that Paula would have laughed if her self-esteem hadn't required a split second to regain its equilibrium. Ah, but what did she take herself for? Her forty-three years, luscious as they were, would seem nothing when compared to Maggy's resplendent eighteen, Paula thought, shaking herself mentally.

"How does she come to be your *protégée*?" the stranger continued, not trying to hide his curiosity.

"Ah, that's a long story," Paula said evasively. She had to grant eighteen its full glory, she reflected, but she didn't have to humble herself before it. This handsome Kilkullen would have to try much harder to find out anything he wished to know.

Maggy, still trapped in the corner, looked at Mistral who stood some twenty feet away. Oh, this was intolerable. She couldn't endure another minute without some contact with him. Perhaps he would put his arm around her, or at least take her hand in his. She needed some loving word, some gesture. Why was she so childish? Even a single smile would help her to get through these moments. Maggy began to struggle through the mob in Mistral's direction. She found her passage blocked by Avigdor, who had been collared by a stout man with dyed black hair.

"Adrien, who owns that nude lying on the green cushions? I want to find the lucky son of a bitch and get it from him. It's only a question of how much he wants—I'll pay anything—be a good chap and tell me."

"It's not for sale," Maggy said gently.

"Mademoiselle Lunel is right," Avigdor agreed. "It belongs to Miss Browning."

"The hell it does!" the stout man said. "Where is she—I'd like to talk to her."

"Monsieur Avigdor is mistaken," Maggy spoke up firmly. "I've owned that particular painting from the very day it was painted. Julien gave it to me and it has no price because I'll never sell it."

"What do *you* say, Avigdor?" the man insisted, unimpressed.

"There seems to be some confusion . . . ah, perhaps Miss Browning can . . . I don't . . ." Avigdor looked as if the heavens had opened and hail had ruined his hay.

"Look, just follow me," Maggy told the stout man. Avigdor obviously didn't know what he was doing or saying. With difficulty she cleared the way toward Mistral, and clutched his arm.

"Julien, that dealer of yours has just told this gentleman that my picture doesn't belong to me—explain to him, would you, please?"

Mistral turned his head and glared at both of them from under his frowning brows. His mouth, always set in a stern line, was tight with annoyance.

"What's this nonsense, Maggy? You sound as crazy as everyone else in this lousy menagerie."

"Julien, listen. It's about *my* picture, the first one you painted of me on the green cushions. Avigdor told this man that Mademoiselle Browning owns it."

"That's perfectly true." Kate spoke calmly. She had appeared at Mistral's side just as Maggy reached him.

Mistral shook his head angrily. "What the hell is going on!"

"It's quite simple, Julien," Kate proclaimed in her unimpassioned voice. "I reserved all the nudes for myself before the exhibition opened. Obviously they are far too important to be sold separately. I wanted to make sure they'd be preserved as a series—it was the only way to insure it. Otherwise, they'd be dispersed in the hands of seven different people by now."

Maggy let go of Mistral's arm. "You *couldn't* have bought it for yourself, Mademoiselle Browning. It was *never* for sale. It's mine. Ask Julien! Julien, *tell* her! You remember, you must remember—"

Mistral closed his eyes as if to blot out her words and Maggy saw, in a flash, that moment when he had fallen on her with that pounce of absolute possession, his great hands, still sticky with paint, rubbing with rough victory on her pubic hair.

"He'll paint you another," Kate said without raising her voice. "Won't you, Julien? Be reasonable, Mademoiselle, calm yourself. You simply can't expect him to keep any hasty promise he may have made about that first canvas—it's too significant to the body of his work. I'm sure we all agree."

"Julien! Why don't you say something? You know you gave me that picture." Maggy's voice rose furiously, suddenly out of control.

Mistral looked from one woman to the other. Maggy's face had flushed with anguish and disbelief, she was immobilized, ineffective in the tightly packed crowd and her prominent mouth was thrust forward in a grimace of emotion. Kate stood quietly, fastidious and graceful, the pure oval of her head poised on her neck in a way that indicated, as no word could have, that the rightness of her position was beyond dispute.

"Stop carrying on like a child, Maggy!" Mistral commanded roughly. "Kate's absolutely right, the seven pictures belong together. I'll make it up to you, damn it! It's not going to kill you to give up one picture, for Christ's sake!"

For the space of a long moment Maggy looked straight at his face. She had grown absolutely still and severe composure fell like a mask over her vivid outrage as she listened to his words. The clatter of voices dimmed around her as she absorbed the stance of Kate and the meaning of what Mistral had said. She knew more about them in that instant than they knew about themselves—perhaps more than they would ever know.

Maggy had always recognized that Kate was an antagonist—now she saw that the American had the eyes of a wolverine. She had not bought the paintings because she loved them but because she hated them, because she wanted to make them disappear. Mistral, whom she had willed herself to trust, because to do otherwise would have been against all her loving nature, had turned on her in a spurious irritation that amounted to a shameful lie.

Here, in what should have been his moment of triumph, it seemed to her that he reeked of the furtive and the diminished—a wild animal trapped, tamed and caged. In Kate, Maggy smelled a ruthlessness the size of which she could only begin to understand. She stood powerless, friendless, in an arena in which there could be no victory, from which there was no escape except an honorable retreat. She felt as if some essential plug in her body had been pulled. If she stayed facing them any longer she would begin to howl in outrageous, indecent pain . . . and to no purpose.

Slowly, quietly now, she spoke to Kate.

"Since you want my portrait so badly, Mademoiselle, that you are ready to steal it, I give it to you. There is no price. Keep it where you can always see it but remember—it will never really belong to you." She turned to Mistral. "You can't 'make up' anything to me, Julien. You gave me a gift, you've changed your mind, now you've taken it back . . . it's so simple that even I, child though I am, can understand such an action."

"Shit! Maggy, stop exaggerating . . ."

"Farewell, Julien." She nodded formally at Avigdor and Kate, turned and walked out of the gallery, as stiffly as if her legs had turned to ice, but with her head high on the long stem of her neck. As Maggy moved, in cold dignity, people found themselves moving aside to let her pass and looking after her. Surely, more than one of them thought, she isn't, after all, the same girl who modeled for those nude paintings. That model had been a laughing, erotic creature, and so young, so succulent. But this was a woman, austerely beautiful, untouchable, regal, above all, adult.

7

When Perry Mackay Kilkullen finally tore himself away from Mistral's *vernissage* he knew that he should find a taxi since he was running behind schedule. It is equally far to travel, either as the crow flies, or on foot, from Avigdor's gallery to the Hotel Ritz, where Kilkullen lived, or in the other direction, to the Carrefour Vavin. The heart of the art world and the center of the grandeur of the Right Bank are both a comfortable walk from the rue de Seine. They are an even shorter taxi ride but Perry Kilkullen found himself unable to make the physical leap out of the Paris evening into the enclosed interior of one of the square, dark red Renault taxis. The early October dusk had a dreaminess, a warmth still lulled by summer's scents, fruity with promise, that it would be criminal to miss.

As he walked back to the Ritz to change for a business dinner he stopped for a minute on the Pont du Carrousel and looked toward the great ship of the Ile de la Cité, that noble island in the Seine that bore aloft the crouching silhouette of the façade of Notre Dame. He turned his back on that immemorial reminder of his faith and looked west, into the lemon distance, along the winding river bordered by tall, narrow, gray buildings on the left and the alluring shadows of the blue Tuileries garden on the right, a sight that usually made him concentrate with all his senses in order to engrave once more on his memory the view he considered civilized man's crowning achievement.

Tonight he saw nothing except a girl, a tall girl like a young queen with red hair, with a mouth that looked as if it had been formed for him alone, and a body he felt he would die if he never touched. He was all longing and torment, and even in his flood of emotion he remembered Shelley's phrase, "the desire of the moth for the star," and laughed for happiness at feeling an emotion he had never known before, an emotion he had thought poets described with deliberate malice in order to make nonpoets envious.

Perry Kilkullen, at forty-two, was an example of the flower of American Irish Catholic aristocracy. Related to the Mackay family of the vast Comstock Lode riches, he had been married young to one of the vast and distinguished McDonnell clan, a graceful and intensely pious young lady who could prove that her particular branch of the big, important family was directly descended from the Lord of the Isles himself, and spoke of the thirteenth-century McDonnells as if they were first cousins.

As the years went by, Mary Jane Kilkullen's love of genealogy had to substitute for a love of progeny as she and Perry found themselves almost alone among their contemporaries in having no children. Like their many friends, they sailed at Southampton in the summer and skied at the Lake Placid Club and went to Pinehurst for golf in the spring, but the absence of those sons and daughters who would have united them as staunch Catholic parents did not make them turn to each other for solace, as so often happens in childless marriages.

At first their barrenness was a frustrating, inexplicable absence and then, as it was prolonged into an acid acceptance, they turned away from their personal relationship, which had been founded on a mere fleeting, youthful attraction, and plunged, separately, into matters that guaranteed them some fulfillment.

Mary Jane Kilkullen became indispensable to the Guild of the Infant Saviour, the Catholic Big Sisters, the Catholic Center for the Blind, and the Foundling Hospital. Perry Kilkullen immersed himself in his firm of international bankers, and by 1926 he spent more of the year in Paris than he did in their large apartment at 1008 Park Avenue.

Paris had become his true love, his consolation for the aridity of his personal life and Paris had kept him young, as she does all who truly love her. As love of London will give a man mellowness, as love of Rome will impart to a man a patina of history, love of Paris will guarantee an available heart.

Perry Kilkullen kept a three-room suite facing an inner garden of the Ritz and although his Parisian life was filled with cables and conferences and business lunches and formal dinners with other members of the international banking community, he often dismissed his chauffeur and set out on foot, at random, to walk the endlessly alluring streets of his city.

Now women, many women, glanced at him as he hurried, already late, toward the Place Vendôme. While Paula had scrutinized his voice and clothes and his manner, the women who noticed him, although deprived of such clues, all knew he was not French as they were caught by the sight of his tall outline, by an impression of casualness and litheness and vitality. There was something about his step, quick, martial, confident, that looked as if he were walking to the beat of drums.

Perry Kilkullen saw none of them as he approached the Ritz and dashed up the steps, already crowded by men in tailcoats and women in brocade evening capes, their many bracelets clinking and clashing together. He rushed through the buzzing, perfumed, gray and gold lobby, forgot to nod to the stately concierge, neglected his usual greeting to the white-gloved lift boy, brushed wordlessly past his valet, ignored the handful of letters waiting for him and flung himself into his dinner clothes with only two words beating in his head. Maggy Lunel. Maggy Lunel!

It took only a half-hour of inquiry the next morning to find out that Madame Paula Deslandes was the owner of La Pomme d'Or. She had said that Maggy Lunel was her *protégée*, Perry Kilkullen thought. Just what would that mean?

He had his secretary book a table for him for that night, and he dined alone, not noticing the excellence of the rare *gigot* or the ripeness of the Brie, waiting for the moment when Madame Deslandes would condescend to stop by his table. She had greeted him pleasantly as he arrived but as she made her way from one table to another in her crowded restaurant, each party seemed to demand an endless amount of her attention. She watched him sit impatiently, scarcely eating, out of the corner of her eye as she chatted with her regulars at greater length than usual. Let him wait, she thought, not without a small but undeniable residue of offended pride. As he drank his second cup of coffee Paula approached his table and nodded. Perry sprang to his feet.

"Will you take a brandy with me, Madame?"

"Willingly." Paula sat down opposite him, put her plump elbows on the table and thoughtfully rested her saucy chin on her folded hands. How, she wondered, was he going to get around to the matter that brought him here without being obvious?

"Madame, I must meet her."

Paula raised one eyebrow in admiration. The attack direct. Not bad for an American.

"Can you help me, Madame?"

She raised her other eyebrow, her cosily distributed features arranged midway between receptivity and hesitation.

"Madame, I'm in love."

She snapped her fingers dismissively. "Like that? It's not possible."

"Madame, I am a serious man, I'm not whimsical, you understand, not given to flights of fancy. Things like this have never happened to me . . . but now it has. I'm a banker . . ."

"A banker? *Tiens*—more and more impossible."

"I assure you—please don't laugh—look, I'm a partner with the Kilkullen International Trust—here's my card—all I ask is an opportunity to meet her."

Paula looked at the card as long and as seriously as if she were trying to read the future in it. Maggy had spent the night in Paula's apartment and they had talked long past midnight. Maggy was through with Mistral. It didn't matter if he had made love to Kate or not, she had said, and Paula had recognized unmistakable truth in her voice. It was a matter of Maggy's own pride. She had been treated as if she were of no worth. She had been rejected slowly for weeks and she had refused to acknowledge what was happening. Now that she knew that Mistral held her in less esteem than the American woman, now that she finally understood, she would never again seek the slightest gesture from him. Nothing. Ever. It was one thing to be made a fool of by love—that could happen to anybody—and there was no dishonor in it, but it was totally different to make a fool of oneself.

Paula had listened, careful not to encourage her at first, since she knew that a wise woman takes no sides in lovers' quarrels. If Maggy went back to Mistral after all these brave words, Paula's agreement would ultimately be held against her.

But as the hours passed she saw that Maggy had truly gone too far to turn back, that events had tutored her slowly, unconsciously, over the past weeks, in an unwilling comprehension of Mistral's character; that she had no reservoir of illusion to drain, no stored-up years of shared emotions to comfort her with false hope.

Paula didn't doubt that Maggy still loved Mistral. A passion, a first passion, like the one she had lived with him, marks a woman for life. No woman truly recovers from such a love. But the loss of the painting had, as no other event could ever have done, shown her his true nature. It was a conclusive proof that Julien Mistral had never had the commitment to her that Maggy had made to him. She could never love him blindly again. The generosity that she had bestowed so purely on Mistral depended on her belief—no matter if it had been hasty or foolish or even utterly false—that he had loved her as she loved him. With that belief destroyed there was nothing left for her to hold on to.

Maggy was beyond anger now. Mistral had, in all fairness, never said that he felt as she did. She had taken it for granted with a credulity that now seemed to belong to a childish innocent she hardly knew. She was dry-eyed, firm and decisive. It was the only way she could deal with the situation. To wail would have been to injure herself even further, and that would have been unendurable. She had sent a boy to pick up the belongings she had left at Mistral's studio, and, even now, she was resettling herself in her own little place.

"Madame . . ." Perry Kilkullen thought that if she looked at his card any longer it would turn yellow at the edges and wither with age.

Paula looked up. He was a good man. She could hardly be mistaken about something so basic. He was rich—that jumped out from every thread on his vest. He was sincere. Whether he could really be in love with Maggy without having spoken one word to her was a matter for debate, but he certainly thought he was. Lust—of course—but love was another matter. He was probably married but that was not an issue. The rawness of Maggy's wounds shouldn't be allowed to go without some salve, and the sooner the better. God knows this Kilkullen was marvelous to look at. What better tonic to help Maggy begin her recovery from a stupid misadventure with Julien Mistral than a good, rich, handsome American? Even if he was a little crazy? Every Frenchwoman should have at least one American—at least once.

"Tomorrow night, Monsieur Kilkullen, you may invite us to dine with you," she said gravely, feeling a bit like Juliet's nurse.

"Ah . . ." he sighed with huge relief. He had been prepared to go to Avigdor next if Madame Deslandes refused him but he felt less ridiculous talking to a woman.

"At Marius and Janette," Paula continued, "since oysters are in season." And, she thought, since Maggy doesn't have the clothes for Maxim's. Madame Poulard's creations could only carry her so far—certainly not into Maxim's.

"How can I thank you?" he implored.

"By not noticing when I order a second dozen Belons—by begging me to have a third dozen—but not permitting me dessert. I'm not a difficult woman. I prefer the simple pleasures."

"I *wish* I had a brother," he said, with admiration.

"Oh, so do I!"

During that first awkward dinner, as Paula devoted herself to her oysters—for one may bring people together but after that they must fend for themselves—Perry Kilkullen saw clearly that underneath Maggy's tense exterior there was a deep and terrible grief, a heavy burden of sadness she could hardly attempt to hide. This encouraged him more than if she had been gay because it meant that she must be suffering, and whatever it was, he meant to cure it. The operetta of sound that filled the bright, busy restaurant just off the place d'Alma was a background for the luxurious low charm of her sad voice in which there was a mourning note of which she was unaware. He was prepared for enchantment but, as the dinner went on, he was appalled by the recklessness of his emotions, appalled and unafraid.

In the weeks that followed he courted her as gentlemen had courted ladies when he had been unmarried, in the early years of the 1900s. For all the youthfulness of his forty-two years, Perry Kilkullen's manners were marked by Edwardian grace, by the restraint of a period in which there was ample time for all things.

Maggy's apartment was filled with baskets of flowers that arrived every day from Lachaume, but he did not permit himself to offer her anything else. He walked up the rue de la Paix every morning as he left the Ritz and looked wistfully at the entrance to Cartier. He would have liked to rush in and buy her—anything, everything!—but he knew it was utterly inappropriate. As often as she would agree, he took her out to dinner. In an era in which evening clothes were the rule at the grand restaurants, he bowed to her desire to go to simpler places where she was comfortable in her little chemises and her black cape. Gently, as if she were a rare, wild bird, he led her to talk to him of her childhood, of her grandmother, of Rabbi Taradash and the gang of young rascals she had been a member of less than two years before. In turn he told her of his legendary relative, "Honest Ned Kilkullen," who took on the power of Tammany Hall and won—for a while—and he explained to her the difference between the Irish and all other immigrants to the United States.

"They love a good fight, Maggy, and they love a good song. They're scrappy and devilishly proud and they'll do anything to win freedom and justice as they see it. They always think they're in the right, of course, even when they're wrong, but that's just Irish fire."

"I think I'd like the Irish," she said, amused at his fervor.

Suddenly Perry saw a vision of his wife in whom the Irish fire had been quenched years ago, if indeed, the Eastern seaboard stiffness that had been drilled into her by her governess had left any fire burning. Mary Jane Kilkullen had turned into a dry, duty-bound committee woman whose name evoked dim images of a big antique-filled apartment in which the valuable silver was always highly polished and the fine linen sheets freshly ironed; of a golf ball neatly hit; a cocktail perfectly mixed, but no memories came to him of the feeling of her hair under his hand, of her scent or her lips. As quickly as her image had drifted into his mind it faded. Reality was the roundness of Maggy's shoulder, the unquenchable spangled flash of her eyes, set so far apart on her face that they had that touch of peculiarity without which mere beauty is empty.

Two weeks of this gracious courtship passed and Perry Kilkullen, who had been able to be so direct with Paula, began to damn himself more as day followed day and he realized that he was paralyzed by the power of his feeling for Maggy. He felt that he'd been turned back into a timid adolescent who hesitates to even reach out a hand to the girl he loves for fear of rebuff. How, he asked himself, as he neglected his correspondence and forgot to return phone calls, how had he allowed a situation to develop between them in which he was behaving like some sort of benign, doting *uncle?*

Another week went by before Maggy, who couldn't avoid realizing how much he seemed to cherish her, started observing him for signs of what Paula, as inquisitive as an old concierge, called his "intentions." She had never known a man could be so gallant or so shy. One night, as they finished a massively gastronomic dinner at Le Grand Véfour, Maggy discovered that she suddenly felt like dancing. It was more than a feeling, she explained gravely to Perry, it was a physical necessity.

"Where?" he asked, delighted at an interruption in what seemed to be an endless series of meals.

"Le Jockey," she answered. Maggy hadn't returned to any of the Montparnasse nightclubs or bistros or cafés since the *vernissage.* On the Right Bank, she had been as unlikely to bump into Mistral or any of their scandal-loving friends as if she'd taken an ocean voyage, but tonight when she chose Le Jockey it was a sign that she didn't care whom she might encounter, for it was the artists' favorite nightclub, so casual that they often went there in their painting clothes.

Perry and Maggy soon found themselves jammed into the narrow, dark room that was perhaps the noisiest place in Paris. Owned by two men, one a painter, the other a former steamship steward, the walls and ceiling of the first and most famous Montparnasse nightclub were decorated like a Western saloon, covered with posters pasted up in every direction, punctuated here and there by blackboards on which saucy limericks were written in American slang. Lee Copeland, an ex-cowboy, played the piano, accompanied by two Hawaiian guitarists, and if they grew tired, a phonograph beat out the latest jazz and blues records from the United States.

A tribal and primitive excitement throbbed in the tiny Jockey for the four years of its brief, legendary existence, and every night limousines, like Perry's, swung to a stop before the black walls of the club, on which Indians and cowboys had been painted in bright colors, and couples who had fled formal balls quickly disappeared inside to drink endless glasses of whiskey and dance in a delirium all night long. A record was blaring out the "Black Bottom" from George White's *Scandals* as Maggy and Perry sat down. On the tiny

85

dance floor couples were flailing around madly.

"Hell—I don't know how to do that one!" Perry said in exasperation.

"I don't either—I haven't been here in months." Maggy sipped her whiskey. "You could break an arm out there."

Then Lee Copeland slid into the first phrase of "Someone to Watch Over Me" and Perry grinned in relief. "I can manage that—shall we?"

Maggy rose, and in a reflex, kicked off her shoes. It was the first time he had held her in his arms and the eloquence of the body was never more immediate as in that moment when they touched. Physical compatibility is a question of skin first and foremost. If the contact of one skin on another isn't *immediately* pleasing nothing else can possibly matter, but if it is, all other things may follow.

One of the great simplifications of life took place when ballroom dancing was invented. It was no accident that for years far-sighted matrons refused to let their daughters waltz. Once a man is permitted to put his arms around a woman and move to music with her, an infinitude of additional arrangements can be contemplated that no gavotte or minuet had ever led to.

Of all dances known to Western man in the twenties, the fox-trot, or the "Slow" as it is called in France, was the most dangerous, more fatal by far than the sexual explicitness of the athletic tango or the exuberant shimmy. A "Slow" is simply an embrace to a simple step, and the size of the dance floor at Le Jockey made even that simple step almost impossible to take.

As the Hawaiian guitars wailed out the Gershwin masterpiece, Maggy became magically accessible to Perry as the constraints he had been imprisoned by for the last three weeks simply vanished into the melody.

> "I'm a little lamb that's lost in the wood . . .
> Oh, how I would try to be good."

The lyric of the imperishably banal words would be, for Perry, the source of an unreasonable happiness as long as he lived. They held each other until the music ended and as the piano glided into the next song, they stood still, clasped together, and looked into each other's eyes. Without moving a muscle Maggy gave Perry the feeling that she was in motion, leaning against a spring wind.

"I could ask him to play that song again," Perry said longingly.

"Or you could take me home," Maggy whispered with a curving, poignant note in her voice. Without letting go of each other's hand, pausing just long enough to drop money at the table and for Maggy to retrieve her shoes, they walked out of Le Jockey and into the waiting limousine that took them the few streets to Maggy's tall, narrow building next to La Pomme d'Or.

Maggy still hummed the melody as wordlessly, hand in hand, they climbed the dilapidated badly lit staircase, toward her fifth-floor room. As they reached the third floor they had to pick their way carefully between baskets of flowers, still fresh, that had been carefully deposited on each tread of the stairs. The corridor to Maggy's rooms was lined with more baskets and when she opened the door Perry gasped—the huge, gilt-trimmed bed in her bedroom was born aloft, entirely adrift on a sea of flowers.

"I guess I overdid it," he muttered.

"A girl can never have too many flowers."

"There's no place to sit," he said, bemused.

"And there's no room for me to make you a cup of coffee."

"And you can't get to the fireplace to toast a marshmallow."

"And I can't open the door of the armoire to hang up your coat."

"I'm not wearing a coat."

"Ah, but that simplifies things. We have no choice, do we?"

"No. We have to lie down on the bed or stand here all night."

"My feet hurt," she said plaintively.

"Then the alternative—the alternative . . ."

In the pause before he kissed the lips she raised, in that humming second in which everything seemed possible, in which every happiness was offered, he thought he was approaching a destination toward which all unknowing he had been traveling all of his life. And when he bent his mouth to hers and felt her breath mingle with his, he knew he had arrived.

They stood, kissing in a field of flowers, for a long time, until their hearts beat so turbulently that they were both shaking.

"The alternative?" she murmured and at last they lay down together on top of the quilt and slowly, with trembling fingers and many kisses Perry got undressed as Maggy watched him by the dim, pale gold of the streetlamp that filtered up to her window. Naked, he stood startlingly young; without the fine suit, the vest, the starched linen, he was a man with rumpled thick blond hair and the long, flat muscles of a skier.

He slipped the thin straps of her chemise off her shoulders and pushed her dress down to her waist. With one arm he held her up so that she was half reclining on the bed, as he stroked her from her neck to her waist, his warm hand taking possession of her body inch by inch, gentling her down until she relaxed completely, her head thrown back on the pillow. Now he slid her dress off, threw it down over a basket of violets and soon she was as naked as he was, her body calm yet filled with riotous promise as she waited, deliberately and deliciously passive, for whatever he would do next. He looked long at the perfect and untroubled youth of her body. Then he molded himself closely to her as they lay facing each other, side by side, almost equal in height, lips to lips, nipples to nipples, heart to heart.

"Maggy, I love you so. Will you let me love you?"

"If you don't . . . if you don't," she threatened with a quiver of a shivering laugh. "Oh, yes, love me . . . darling Perry . . . love me . . . don't ask any more questions."

At first there was a dissonance in their rhythms. Maggy, accustomed only to Mistral's urgency and roughness, was several paces ahead of Perry, who brought a grave, slow rapture to his caresses, taking one step at a time and lingering over it, but, as she felt herself swelling with readiness, budding hotly and wantingly, and then swelling even more demandingly, Maggy realized that she had no need to hurry toward quick satisfaction. She matched herself to him, abandoned her haste for languorous waiting, almost holding her breath, proffering herself to his fingertips and his mouth with blissful curiosity. Each moment was enough in itself, one blending into another like notes of music. He smelled like honey, she thought, driftingly, as he finally took her, sure of himself, strongly. As they strained together, suddenly she felt as if a fluttering flight of bright butterflies had just been released from her body, borne in soft surprise between her thighs, launched into the quivering air.

Twice during that perfect night they woke from sleep and turned toward each other, deepening and confirming their need.

When Maggy finally woke it was bright daylight outside and Perry was sleeping as if nothing could possibly arouse him. She slid out of bed, put on her silver-kid evening shoes, and, stark naked under her black cape, she dashed down the stairs to the bakery at the corner where she bought six still-warm croissants. He was sleeping when she returned and picked her way carefully through the flower baskets toward her single gas ring to make coffee and heat milk. Maggy filled two enormous cups half-full of the strong brew, put them on a tray with a pitcher of the steaming milk, a bowl of sugar, and the croissants and cleared a place for the tray on the floor next to the bed.

Perry lay flat on his stomach and, at some point in the night, he had dragged the quilt so far up that everything was hidden but the top of his head and one outflung hand. Should she pull his hair or . . . Maggy bent her head and licked the knuckles of his little finger. He groaned and lapsed back into sleep. She slipped her tongue between the top of his little finger and his ring finger and slid it back and forth between his fingers. He moved his hand away but she imprisoned it and sucked the tip of his index finger. The quilted mass rose from the bed as if a bell had been rung in his ear.

"What the hell? . . . where? Maggy, you devil!" He lunged for her and threw her on the bed. "Why are you wearing your coat? Take it off! Kiss me! Kiss me!"

He captured her, and pushed her back on the pillow so that her hair spread like red banners against a white cloud. It seemed to him, as he felt her lips open against his, that he had awakened as a child again, with every hour full of possibility, every moment stretching before him, free and shining and ready to be filled with his dreams, with no day yet used up, none tarnished or forgotten.

"The coffee!" she managed to gasp finally. "It'll get cold."

"Why didn't you say *coffee?*" he demanded, releasing her. "I smell it but I don't see it."

Maggy squirmed to the edge of the bed and managed to raise the tray carefully so that nothing spilled.

"My God! Where did it come from?" he asked, as she poured the hot milk into the big cups. "Last night you said there wasn't room to make a cup of coffee . . . this morning there's a feast!"

"In the morning certain things become . . . more important, so I reconsidered. Have a croissant."

"It's so *good*. It's the best thing I've ever eaten in my life. How did you get them?"

"I went down to the bakery before you woke up," she said hungrily, taking another.

When everything on the tray had been consumed Perry lay back on the bed and stretched. He looked around him and really observed his surroundings for the first time. The only beauty of the room was in the flower baskets and now his clothes, cast aside so hastily, covered a number of them. The walls were covered with a faded and splotched wallpaper, the gilt of the bed was scratched and tarnished. Maggy's tenth-hand armoire sagged in the middle and the ceiling was low and confining in spite of the sun that poured in from the two open windows.

"Could I use your bathroom?" he asked.

"Down the hall, second door on the left."

"You don't have your own?"

"One to a floor, sir. I have a sink and a bidet—cold water only—but whenever I want a bath I have to go to Paula's. And when I want to go to the bathroom I go down the hall."

"You don't happen to remember what happened to my trousers?" he asked, casting his eyes around the room.

"They must be here somewhere."

"If they're not, I'll have to piss in the bidet," he threatened, surprising himself. He'd never spoken to Mary Jane so freely in twenty years of marriage.

"There they are on those pink roses—no, stay, I'll get them." Maggy prowled catlike among the flowers, at ease in her miraculous nakedness, with a total lack of modesty that made Perry waver an instant between awe and shock. Never in all of his married life had his convent-bred wife walked around like that.

By the time he had returned from the bathroom Maggy had hastily brushed her teeth, washed her face and made a collection of his clothes on the bed, where she was perched, covered now in her peignoir of lilac silk.

"Maggy." He sat on the bed with the air of someone about to make an announcement.

"Was the bathroom all you had hoped?"

"And more. Listen, my darling love, you can't stay here."

"But why not—I have the best view in Paris."

"Because we can't live on coffee and croissants. Because I can't stand to think that you don't have a bathroom. Because there are so many things I want to give you. Because I can't sleep here every night and get to work in the morning without going back to the Ritz to bathe and shave and change and I don't have time for that. Because there isn't enough room for your flowers."

"Sleep here every night?" she asked, seizing on the one phrase he'd used that had really caught her attention.

"Don't you want me?"

"Oh, yes, I want you!"

"Every night?" His gray eyes insisted on affirmation.

"I'm not sure about *every* night." She caught him around the waist and lay in his lap, looking up at the thatch of blond hair that covered his chest. "But certainly tonight, and tomorrow, and the day after . . ."

"Then, you see, my beautiful girl, you have to move. There isn't room here for my clothes."

"Or your valet."

"Especially my valet. Would you like to live at the Ritz? No, forget that—in five minutes the whole hotel staff would be talking about it and I don't see why anybody should know our business. Maggy—will you let me find an apartment for you? Will you let me make the arrangements so that we have a decent place?"

"But you're so proper," she protested. "Here you have a chance for an adventure in the real Paris, the part of Paris only the artists and the French really know—the place all those other visiting Americans are trying so hard to make their own—but immediately you want to change it into something else; a nice place to live, to sleep, with servants no doubt, and the best meat from the best butcher and all the bills paid on time . . . this 'decent place,' would it be for me or for us?"

"What's the difference?"

"I won't move into *any* man's apartment or house or suite—I'd rather keep my little room here. It suits me. But if it's a place of my own, a place to which I alone have the key, my own, private place, like this one, I might begin, *just begin*, mind you, to consider it . . ."

"I promise! Your own, absolutely. Only one key. I'll call for an appointment. Is Mademoiselle free this evening? Would Mademoiselle care to receive Monsieur Kilkullen? Is Mademoiselle in the mood to entertain a gentleman caller? Does Mademoiselle want to be kissed on the back of her neck or does Mademoiselle have more unorthodox desires? Does Mademoiselle want to be touched between . . ."

"Stop!" Maggy wriggled away. "Mademoiselle has no desires left this morning."

"But do *you* promise, Maggy? Will you move? You still haven't said yes." He looked at her anxiously. She was so unpredictable, he thought, so *unownable*, that he feared she might prefer a way of life that offered her complete freedom. There was not a domestic hair on her head. But he couldn't bear to think of her living here in this impossible room in which he'd spent the most beautiful night of his life. Daylight did not become it.

"Perry, what you want, put quite plainly and without chichi," Maggy said, with sudden seriousness, "is to *keep* me. My own key or no key, I'll be a kept woman if I agree, won't I?"

"That's such a sordid word!" he said, horrified. "Why put it like that?"

"But am I correct? Isn't that exactly what other people would say? What else would I be but a kept woman, *une femme entretenue?*" she kept on, relentlessly.

"Oh, Maggy, you're impossible," he said wretchedly.

"And I suppose you'd want me to dress in couture clothes—you wouldn't think my own things are good enough—and you'd want to buy me jewels and furs . . ."

"*Yes!* Goddamn it, I would! What's so terrible about that? Damn!"

Maggy jumped on the bed and a wide smile began to appear on her lips as she whirled around and around with her lilac peignoir swirling about her bare legs. "Diamond bracelets all the way to my elbows? Chinchilla to the floor? Trips to Deauville? My own car?"

Perry looked up at the mischief in her face. "Bracelets on both arms, to your shoulder if that's possible . . . ten fur coats . . . a coach and four . . . six tall footmen . . . one of each number in the new Chanel collection . . . and that's only the beginning!"

"Oh . . . oh!" She whirled faster and faster until she collapsed on top of him. "I've *always* wanted to be a kept woman! It was the dream of my depraved youth—oh, the thrill of it . . . *kept* . . . just like in *la Belle Époque.*" She shivered deliciously. "What would Aunt Esther say if she only knew?"

"Let's not tell her," Perry said hastily.

"I wouldn't dream of it. Listen, darling—how soon do you intend to start keeping me? To tell you the truth, I want to leave Montparnasse and never come back. I'm finished with my life here. It's over, this chapter, and done with . . . everything except Paula."

"Today, this morning. I'll get a suite for you at the Lotti—it's just a few steps from the Ritz and we'll start looking for a place."

"Oh, *yes!* I knew being kept would be heaven—but kept by a rich, tall, handsome, generous, crazy American!" Maggy covered his face with a torrent of kisses. "*Ça, alors, Ça c'est la vie, mon chéri—la bonne vie!*"

"The good life," Perry echoed, "yes, my beloved, I promise."

8

He isn't working," Kate said as she sat with Avigdor in a café. "He hasn't even been able to pick up a brush since the *vernissage*." The dealer stiffened. An artist who doesn't paint regularly, as if he were going to an office, may prove as bad an investment as a vein of gold that dwindles into rock.

"It's that damned girl. She never came back, did she?"

"It wasn't that at all," Kate snapped. "Naturally he was furious after she kicked up such a stupid fuss—that revolting little scene she made was disgraceful—but he's hardly the type to pine away over a woman. He doesn't need her as a model anymore and I gather they'd only been together a few months—not enough to make a man like him stop work. She's essentially unimportant."

"As you say." Avigdor, in agreeing, reserved his thoughts. Could an unimportant girl have been the inspiration for such impassioned work? But something forbidding about the smoothness of Kate's high forehead, an icy note in her voice, told him not to speculate further, at least not out loud.

"I have a theory that it's some sort of letdown—postpartum blues. The *vernissage* was such a high point that afterward there had to be a reaction. I've been feeling a bit . . . flat . . . myself so I can imagine how it must have affected him."

"Has he even tried to paint?" Avigdor asked.

"Yes. That's the thing that worries me most. It's been two weeks now and he stands in front of his easel and just looks at it, hour after hour, day after day, while the paint dries on his palette.

Every time I drop in I see him there with nothing on the canvas. Then, at night, he gets reeling drunk on red wine—he never did that before. And he won't talk about it. Adrien, he looks . . . *frightened*—that's the only word I can think of to describe his eyes. It's almost as if he's in some sort of private panic . . . I just don't understand it."

"He's got to get away for a while, see something besides his studio walls. He isn't the first artist to be unable to lift a brush after a big success."

"I've been suggesting that he should take a trip somewhere."

"And?"

"He says he's not in the mood. He says he's not the kind of man who takes vacations. He says he hasn't done a decent minute's work in months and he has to keep at it until it begins to come again."

"Shall I talk to him?"

"I wish you would, Adrien. He thinks you did a good job on the exhibition."

"Thanks," Adrien said dryly. He'd *made* the man into the sensation of the season. But if dealers expected normal gratitude from artists they'd go to bed every night severely disappointed. Any dealer who was in business for gratitude should abandon his gallery and become a breeder of dogs, nice big slobbery ones.

Two days later, early one morning in mid-October, Mistral left for Provence. The night before while they were having a farewell drink, as if it were an afterthought, Kate had offered to drive him down.

"I only know Paris and a little of Normandy. I'd like to see Aix and Avignon myself but I don't like traveling alone . . . and you wouldn't have to take the train . . ."

Mistral was affronted. "You take too much for granted, Kate. Do you think I want you driving me all over the place?"

"*You* drive . . . I don't care," Kate said, exasperated.

"I don't know how—how typically American to think that I would, as if I had a car."

"I'll teach you in half an hour as soon as we get into the country. There's nothing to it."

As soon as they had passed Fontainebleau, Kate turned off the main road and, after the briefest of demonstrations and instructions, turned the Talbot two-seater sports car over to Mistral. She knew that he possessed instantaneous reflexes, that his reactions were as fast as if he were in danger, and that his concentration on anything visual was prodigious. She was curious to see what he would make of this challenge. Without giving him a word of guidance she watched his big, exceptionally elongated hands with their finely articulated fingers deal deftly with the wheel and the shift.

He mastered the machine in ten minutes and they turned back to the main road and sped toward Saulieu, going southwest along an almost deserted route at ninety kilometers an hour.

Kate sat silently, relaxed and warm in her beautifully cut brown-and-rust tweeds, wearing soft leather gloves and a felt cloche. They drove through the countryside of the flat *département* of the Yonne, between endless rows of plane trees bordering fields from which the last wheat had almost all been gathered. It was the kind of fall day that contains no touch of melancholy, the kind of day on which some tantalizing promise lies almost visible in the depth of the sky and the snap of the air, particularly when the traveler's destination is south.

In Avallon they had a quick lunch and continued on their wordless, swift flight until the destination she had planned for that night lay behind them. Mistral seemed to have fallen into a trance of motion in which thought or memory played no part.

From time to time Kate looked at his profile and noted that his mouth, normally held in a commanding, peremptory line, had relaxed. She couldn't see his expression because his eyes were so deeply hooded, but nothing about the set of his imperious head invited conversation.

"How far are we going?" Kate finally asked as the afternoon drew on and she began to feel the chill of evening in the open car, in spite of her heavy suit and sweater.

"Until we get to Lyon, where the Saône joins the Rhône. Long ago it was a sacred place. For me it's the true beginning of Provence, although any Provençal would say it's too far north. No stopping until Lyon."

"That's almost two hundred kilometers," Kate protested.

"Yes, but it's all downhill," Mistral assured her. "South is always downhill."

In Lyon they found a small hotel, ate excellently for little money and went to their rooms windburned and exhausted. The next day they followed the majestic Rhône, that quickly moving and unpredictable river that has been venerated for millennia, driving through villages whose names followed each other like a great wine list, a prodigious pathway of vineyards, one more precious than the next, from Lyon to Valence to Orange and finally to Avignon. There they crossed the river to Villeneuve-les-Avignon, where they stopped at last almost at midnight, at a *pension* Mistral had visited once before, during a vacation trip while he was still at the Beaux-Arts.

Madame Blé had bought her *pension* from a gentleman farmer. The original building had been a cardinal's palace and then a priory from 1333 until the Revolution, when it had returned to secular use. Yet it still basked in an atmosphere of utter peace. It was built in a U-shape around a courtyard where the mossy marble columns of the former cloister stood sentinel in the dark garden. This ancient priory had nothing of the monastic about it, nothing ecclesiastical. Its warm tranquillity was that of a refuge from the world, but not from the fruits or the joys of the earth. The center of the courtyard was punctuated by a flight of steps that descended into a wine cellar as old as Cardinal Arnaud de Via's palace, and this was the true heart of the building.

"I've got to find some sort of guidebook to this area," Kate said the next morning after a late breakfast.

"Why?"

"We've been traveling so fast I feel utterly disoriented. I don't know what's to the east or to the west of this place but I do know it's terribly historic and I don't like feeling ignorant."

"Historic?" Mistral lifted his heavy eyebrows in feigned surprise.

"Oh, for heaven's sakes, Julien—full of ruins, churches, museums, all sorts of things we should see. Stop looking so amazed. What's wrong with my wanting to know? We've driven damn near the whole way from Paris to the Mediterranean in two days and I want to know why you picked this one particular place to stop in, out of all the rest of France."

"And will a book tell you that?"

"Well . . . why not? We can't just wander around without knowing."

"We can't?"

"Obviously it's possible, but that way we're sure to miss things," she said tartly.

"You could have ten guidebooks and ten years in which to follow them and you'd still miss something marvelous right under your very American nose. Why don't you relax and look around. That's what I came to do—just look around."

Kate abandoned the discussion. Although her fundamental sense of order was put out of joint by the idea of drifting about without some authority to refer to, she didn't want to argue with him about anything.

All the rest of the day and the following one they wandered around Villeneuve-les-Avignon on foot, exploring the city that had grown up during the fourteenth century when the pope moved from Rome to Avignon. Church dignitaries had settled in Villeneuve and created a bustling city with a great monastery and a magnificent fort, a city that had now retreated into a few sleepy, fragrant squares and several narrow, arcaded streets where the last stones of episcopal palaces could still be distinguished.

On the third day, they headed east past Avignon itself and took the road that led to the market town of Apt and bisected the Apt basin, a rich fruitful valley that lay cupped between two mountain ranges some six miles apart. Far away to the north lay the Monts de Vaucluse and, to the south, almost bordering the road, was the Montagne du Lubéron. It was this side of the Lubéron, *Le Versant Nord*, that had captivated Mistral on his previous visit. He had never forgotten those fantastically eroded limestone cliffs, on which sparse vegetation clung as fiercely as did the huddled villages that perched a thousand feet above the main route, apparently unreachable until Mistral found the thread of narrow dirt road that led to each one of them: Maubec, Oppède-le-Vieux, Félice, Ménerbes, Lacoste and Bonnieux.

In prehistory man had lived where these fortified hill villages now stood, each one of them nearly invisible from the road along which enemies had so often come marching in the past. For hundreds of years they had endured bloody battles against tyranny from the north, these tiny, sleepy villages with streets as steep as stepladders, whose houses tumbled close together, soft gray and softer ocher, mantled with vines, splashed with the fluttering, mythological silver of olive groves and the deep coral of the flowers of the vine called "Fairy's Fingers." From these villages, at night, rose a

98

mist, peopled, it was said, by the ghosts of the former inhabitants, Protestant dissenters who were mercilessly slaughtered by their countrymen in the Wars of Religion. These now peaceful villages were the homes of shopkeepers and craftsmen whose trade came from the many small, prosperous farms of the Apt basin.

Mistral was widely excited. He had no sooner climbed up to the white marble ruins of the château-fortress in Oppède-le-Vieux, where he would see, from that steep vantage point, some particularly enticing farm that lay down below and he'd hurry down the precipitous path he and Kate had just climbed, dragging her protestingly behind him, to throw himself back into the car and drive back to the rolling, richly cultivated valley searching for the farmhouse he had spied from above.

Each big farmhouse, or *mas*, as it was called in Provence, was a collection of stone buildings, built roughly in a square around a central courtyard, with so many connected outbuildings and small towers, so many different heights of roof and such a diverse, asymmetrical collection of shuttered windows and arched doorways that it resembled a small hamlet set in the middle of a wealth of fields and vines that grew till they touched the walls of the buildings on every side.

Mistral would ignore the signs that warned that the road to a *mas* was private property and drive right up to it, get out of the car and circle around lost in admiration, ignoring the warning barking of the farm dogs, until a peasant woman would come out to investigate. Then, while Kate watched from the car, he'd engage her in conversation. Invariably she'd invite them both in for a glass of wine. He was passionately intent on penetrating into the interiors of these rural strongholds, no two of which were alike, with their three-foot-thick walls and fireplaces so large that he could stand in them.

The Provençal peasant women, taciturn and wary of anyone unknown, would never normally have asked two strangers into their homes, but Mistral's robust appreciation and interest charmed them as much as did the sight of him, so much a fine cavalier in spite of his rough workingman's clothes. The farm women's suspicions were replaced by friendliness and curiosity for they could sense in this tall man of the north, with his red hair and ocean-blue eyes, an emotional rapport, an immediate sensitivity to their way of life that made him seem not quite a stranger even though they clannishly called their own neighbors from the next village "foreigners."

"There isn't a more beautiful place in the world," he told Kate after they had spent three days driving about the mountains and plains of the north Lubéron, returning the forty kilometers to Villeneuve each night before dinner. "At least in my opinion."

"Have you seen enough of the world that you can be a fair judge?" Kate couldn't prevent herself from wondering.

"I don't need to. Some things are self-evident. What more could you ask of nature, Kate, and what more of man, than these villages, this sky, these trees and stones and earth? I was right to come back here. In Paris I'd forgotten the horizon—I'd forgotten green. Nothing, Kate, *nothing* on earth is as green as the leaves of a vineyard with the late afternoon sun on them."

Kate had never seen him so expansive with visible pleasure. He looked as if every pore of his being was flooded with the particularly pure and vivid light of the Provençal countryside, that land the poet Frédéric Mistral had called "The Empire of the Sun."

She felt different herself. These days outside in air that smelled of heather, rosemary and thyme had made her shed the thick layer of sophistication within which she normally moved. The hard edges of her features, which she had always before covered with pale ivory powder, were all softened by a sunburn that rounded and warmed her face. Her thin lips, no longer touched carefully with bright red lipstick, looked fuller and softer against the flush of her cheeks and her high forehead was covered by the fine ash-blond hair that had been so blown about by the wind of the open car that she had abandoned any attempt to maintain her neat center part, forgot to wear her hat and just let it fly about as it wanted to. The perfection of the shape of her face was enhanced by this new abandon. Now, as she slid into a country mood, she seemed less formidable and as young as her twenty-three years.

"You were right about the guidebook," she admitted as they finished dinner in the garden of the *pension* of Madame Blé.

"But, Kate, think of what you've missed! There's the Popes' Palace in Avignon—we haven't even been inside and it's just across the river—and the Roman Arena in Arles and the fountains of Aix—oh, don't forget the Maison Carrée in Nîmes—here you are in the middle of a hundred famous antiquities that tourists have been visiting for centuries and all you've seen is a few sleepy villages and a dozen farms."

"Why do you keep teasing me, Julien? I said you were right; do you want a formal apology?"

"An apology? From you, the haughty New York lady, the rich and elegant American who darts about organizing people so neatly that they hardly know she's doing it?" He gave her a condescending grin.

"Now that's just not fair. I resent that." Kate spoke calmly but she felt anger grip her. Why did he turn on her the minute she made a concession? What made him so contrary?

"Fair? Of course it's fair—you just don't want to see yourself as you are. You're different here, I'll grant that, but in Paris when you're in your element, I've never known a woman who managed to have things more her own way. You're remarkable, Kate. What's wrong with being rich and perfectly dressed and looking down your nose and making life turn out the way you want it to? There are a lot of women who would like a chance to change places with you."

"Goddamn you, Julien! Who the hell are you to tell me what sort of person you think I am? Nothing, no one, matters to you, does it? Besides your work, is there anything you truly care about? If so, I haven't seen it. You're a *monster*." Kate could hardly believe the words she heard pour out of her lips. Her composure, her sense of proportion, the neat stitches of her normal speech had all disappeared in a storm of fury.

Mistral smiled like a small boy provoking a kitten.

"And you, dear Kate, will of course, permit anyone to walk all over you because you're too good-hearted to stop them. Flexible, soft-minded Kate, undemanding Kate Browning who only asks from life the small fruit that falls from the tree to her feet."

Too angry to reply, she fell silent, biting the inside of her lips, fighting back a bellyful of rage.

Lazily he spoke. "Two such thoroughly decent people, two such splendid characters as we, might make an interesting combination. What do you say, Kate? Shall we experiment?"

Kate jumped up from the table and walked into the dark garden, outside of the pool of light. Mistral followed her, and with his powerful hands, turned her toward him. She stiffened her body in resistance and averted her head, her jaw tense. With one hand he held her in place and with the other he forced her head around to face him but she didn't raise her eyes, whether still in resentment or not, he couldn't be sure, nor did he care. She had begun to appeal to him these last few days and surely she hadn't invited herself along on this trip just for the sake of the scenery. Women didn't work like that, in his experience. Not even rich Americans in expensive tweeds.

"Kate, let's go to my room. I want to see you naked, spread out on my bed."

"Julien!"

"Now don't tell me you're shocked. Was I too direct for Miss Browning? Do you want pretty words, Kate? I want to fuck you. If that doesn't suit you, you have only to say so. I won't ask again. So . . . yes or no?"

"How typical, how romantic," she muttered.

"I said 'yes' or 'no.' "

In the little light there was he saw her whole face take on such a complex, shivering expression of unwilling but irrepressible yearning that it made him put his arm around her, without another word. All the way up the curving flight of stairs they said nothing to each other, their only contact was the light pressure of his arm across her back and his hand at her waist. Through his fingers he could feel her rigidity, her refusal to lean against him, her insistence on walking as self-containedly as if he weren't touching her, yet Kate didn't hesitate or resist him in any way. It was almost as if she were mounting the steps to his bed without thinking about what she was doing, yet her silence was charged with something so tight, so secret, so much stronger than ordinary sexual tension, that Mistral found himself puzzled by it.

He released her to lock the door of his room. When he turned back to her he found that she had retreated to the window and seemed to be looking in complete fascination at something in the garden. He crossed the room and stood behind her and brushed the back of her neck with one finger. She didn't jump or turn around but her hands grasped the window frame with determination.

"Kate, how can we begin to experiment if you won't even turn around?" he whispered to her teasingly. She didn't move, or indicate that she had heard him. Mistral bent and brushed the back of her neck with his lips. Kate gripped the window frame convulsively. He smiled faintly, and with the tip of his tongue he touched the nape of her neck at the exact spot where her bobbed hair came to a neat point and then he drew his tongue slowly down the back of her neck along the delicate ridge of her spinal column to a place between her shoulder blades. There he fastened his mouth against her skin and breathed gently, patiently, without a single additional motion, until her hands dropped to her sides and she turned around and faced him, white and shaking.

"You've never kissed me, Julien. Never even kissed me."

"A mistake, Kate . . . one of the few I'll admit to," he said as he reached down and lifted her chin toward him. Her lips were cool and held together so tensely, so ungivingly, that he drew back in surprise. "Kate, you don't have to go ahead with this—I don't force myself on unwilling women."

"No, no, Julien, I *want* to," she insisted although her words were contradicted by the timidity of her voice. She flung herself toward him, throwing her arms around his neck and pressing her lips on his in quick, short kisses that were almost like pecks.

For a moment Mistral, amused, let this awkward assault continue, but soon he held her off at arm's length.

"Not so fast and furious, Kate."

"Christ! Don't you ever stop making fun of me?"

For an answer he picked her up and carried her over to the bed. Still holding her in his arms he lay down next to her. "I'll admit to another mistake . . . I forgot how impatient you are . . . I'm going to teach you patience, Kate, you need to learn it badly—so badly." As she lay there stiffly he ran his hands lightly down the length of her body. She flinched but didn't protest. "I have no intention of undressing you, Kate, not for a long time," Julien murmured as he bent over her lips. "Lie still," he commanded and he kissed her closed mouth, concentrating all his curiosity, all his need—for it had been weeks since he'd made love to any woman—on her finely shaped lips, until they grew warm and swollen and finally parted willingly to allow his tongue to enter her mouth. He held himself back, touching only lightly along the inside of her lips, languorously sweeping from one corner of her mouth to the other, resisting her when she began to try to trap his tongue and draw it further into her mouth, then letting her have it for one brief second before he withdrew it completely and covered her whole mouth with his, his mouth that always looked so stern until it turned hot and tender in love. As he played with her, his tongue flicking in and out of her lips, pressing forward for only a tiny fraction of a moment, he could feel all the muscles of her body beginning to relax until she lay passively, no longer clenched in anxious anticipation, her entire being centered on his mouth and what it was doing to her. Soon that stage of abandon passed away and he could sense the gradual tightening of her arm and leg and pelvic muscles as she began to want more than mere kisses, but still he confined himself to her lips, laughing inwardly at the lesson he was forcing her to endure. She groaned and ground her teeth as he tantalized her. You'll beg for it, he promised himself, you'll have to beg for it, you cool American bitch, even as he felt himself growing almost unbearably excited.

"Julien . . . " Kate gasped. "Undress me."

"No, Kate."

"Julien . . . *please.*"

"If you want me . . . undress me," he demanded, flinging himself back on the quilt and kicking off his shoes and lying quite still. Kate looked at the splendid man who offered himself to her in such a maddening way and in a sudden, resolute fury of determination, with trembling fingers, ignoring her self-consciousness, she threw herself at the buttons of his shirt, almost ripping them open. He helped her to ease his arms out of his sleeves and she scarcely paused to run her hands greedily down over his chest before she attacked his belt buckle. But then she reached the buttons of his fly and she became conscious of the great hard outline of his penis straining under the cloth. She was seized by a sudden inability to continue and her hands fell to her sides. "You . . . Julien . . . *you* do it," she implored.

"Lost your nerve, Kate?" he taunted her, watching her carefully even though every impulse in his body was urging him to throw her on the bed and take her just as she was, her hair wet at the roots with the sweat of lust, her lips bruised, her fists clenched.

"No! Damn you!" she responded violently and took a deep breath before setting herself the task of opening his fly, revealing him rearing and naked, for he wore nothing under his corduroy trousers. Mistral was breathing as rapidly as she while Kate forced herself to unbutton each button. When she had reached the last one he ripped off his trousers in one swift movement and threw her back on the bed. "Good, Kate, good . . . you were patient . . ." he grunted as, with experienced fingers, he began to take off her clothes, finding, as he had expected, that her breasts and hips were small, her waist slender and her blond pubic hair as fine as that of a young girl's.

Soon they were both entirely naked and Kate lay on the bed in such a posture of modesty restrained by sheer willpower that Mistral had difficulty in not laughing at her. "Lovely Kate," he murmured as he grasped her slim body and hugged it, covering as much of her flesh with his own as he could. He held her, quietly warming her with his nakedness until he felt her begin to relax against him. Had she been another female he would already have entered her, but Kate, this unsensual, inexperienced woman presented him with a challenge he had no wish to resist. She wanted *him*—oh, yes, but she wanted to get it over with as quickly as possible, without losing herself, and that was something he had no intention of permitting.

Eventually, when her body felt as warm as his own, he began to trace her backbone with his fingertips while he continued to hold her locked tightly against him. He caressed her almost boyishly trim buttocks with a rapid movement and when she immediately grew tense, he muttered, "Patience, patience, Kate," and withdrew his fingers to the small of her back. Each time his hand returned to her buttocks he lingered there for a second longer until finally he felt her pressing them against his hands, offering themselves. "Patience . . . patience," he repeated, taking an altogether new pleasure in this leisurely arousal, he who had never bothered to gauge so carefully the state of readiness of any woman, he who had never explored the delicious, self-inflicted pain of holding himself back when release was there for the taking. With one arm he held Kate immobile as he finally probed between her buttocks, finding her astonishingly ready, although, as his fingers parted her, she jerked away in a half-hearted protest. Now he grew merciless as his long fingers advanced further between her slim thighs and found the precise spot he was seeking. His middle finger became as agile, as delicate as the tip of a tongue as he returned again and again to the attack, now pressing softly and moving slowly, now darting quickly and purposefully, all his lust centered on that one fingertip and the flesh it was awakening with such cleverness.

"Julien . . . my God . . . stop!" Kate cried out, but he answered only "Patience," and soon he felt her gathering herself together in an unmistakable clenching and hardening of her pelvic muscles. More rapidly, ever more rapidly his finger flickered until finally, he felt her shuddering and leaping, out of control, her shriek of release smothered against his neck. His fingers didn't leave her until the last spasm had left her body. She lay back, drained but wide-eyed. "You see what patience will earn, Kate?" Mistral whispered to her but she didn't nod or smile but looked at him gravely.

"That's never happened to me before," she whispered.

"Then our experiment is half a success—now, it's my turn, Kate," Julien answered and gave himself up to his own fierce mastery of her willing, open, pliant body.

Later, Kate, like someone coming out of a trance, began to cover his hands with fluttering kisses of gratitude. It was a long while before she realized that Mistral was sleeping deeply.

9

Kate Browning was in torment. Every night for the next week, after Mistral fell away from her and went to sleep she lay awake, her sleekly fashioned body echoing with a passion she had never known existed, for she had always been too cautious before. The thoughts of the pleasures Mistral had taught her so quickly pierced through her entrails like honeyed arrows that she would never want to pluck from her body. She put her fingers between her legs, to that tender kernel of flesh that was so unfamiliar to her touch. It was still alive, still ready to quiver again. All day long she had felt it distended, burning, aching for his hands and his lips. At meals she watched those hands tear bread and cut meat and found, to her mortified surprise, that she was rubbing her thighs together under the table. She moaned aloud at the sight of his mouth, so firm now, soon to be so hot and soft on her skin. Her nipples were sore yet she rubbed them stealthily across Mistral's arm.

The foundation of her life shifted and she felt heavy with inevitability. Her mind could not rest, probing Mistral's inner inaccessibility. How could she dare to swim, to just float along, in this mindless rapture when the man himself did not *belong* to her? The only moments when Kate felt certain that Julien's full attention was on her was during the actual act of love. But even in those moments he had never once wholly *given* himself to her, never once betrayed a need of her, never once said that he loved her. Was he holding back, as she was, she wondered, or was she simply a female body in a bed?

"*Je t'aime bien*, Kate," he said—that careless phrase with that careful nuance, that "*bien*" that turned the word "love" into "like." She was desperate to hear him say the simple, *necessary* words, "*Je t'aime*," but until he did she would not say those words to him. Yet every day she realized that she was falling deeper and deeper in love. Mistral had become the only prize the whole wide world had to offer her. There was an insatiable, ruthless completeness about her feelings that included everything she knew about him; all the difficulties he presented; all the faults clearly observed in him; the women he had had before she met him. They didn't matter. Nothing mattered except an avid, addictive obsession that would accept nothing less than possession.

Kate was a woman of enormous strength, proud, devious and subtle, yet her nerves were pulled so tightly by the strain of concealing her emotions that she wept, lying there next to the superb body of the man who slept without thought of her. But after she wept she stayed awake and scrutinized the situation with the cold, farsighted intelligence that no fire could extinguish.

Frustration was alien to Kate's deepest nature. She did not and never had believed that there was anything she couldn't have if she really wanted it.

During the second week in Provence, Mistral decided to drive west to Nîmes, that mellow city that had been declining with delicious serenity since the reign of Hadrian. There he and Kate went walking in the park, climbing up the many steep stone steps that finally led to the base of the Tour Magne, the ruin of a Roman watchtower that looked out over a vast panorama. They lay on the grass, agreeably tired, observing the few citizens of Nîmes who had sought out this high, cool place, from which, almost two thousand years ago, Roman soldiers had been able to see for a hundred kilometers. After a long silence, Mistral spoke.

"I couldn't, I wouldn't begin, or even dream of beginning to paint this view. It's too complete, too vast, it answers every question I might ask of it, it has no need of man."

"You haven't found anything . . . anything you feel like painting, in Provence?" Kate asked carefully. This was the first time he had mentioned painting since they had left Paris. She had obeyed his unspoken rule of silence on the subject.

"No," he said. No, he thought, no, I haven't *wanted* to paint—that's what terrifies me the most. *Not to want, not to need to paint*—I've never known such emptiness! That young couple on the bench over there, their hands are almost touching—they're not seeing the view, they've probably grown up on it, probably their mothers brought them here for years and years to play—and today they've realized that the other is *another*, a mystery, that strangest of things, another human being. Once . . . once I could have painted their hands not quite touching, painted those hands a dozen times, ten dozen times and never come to the end of what they make me feel, those four hands that don't quite touch, that don't yet dare to touch, that *will* touch—and perhaps—who knows?—change the world. But I don't *want* to paint those hands . . . I don't *have* to paint them. And if I'm not a painter, *why am I alive?*

"I suppose," ventured Kate, "that this country has been painted too often? Everything's so—picturesque . . . that it doesn't interest you?"

"Something like that, yes," Mistral answered briefly. The last time I was here, he thought, I wouldn't walk around a corner without my sketchbook, I was wild with excitement, nothing looked as if anyone had ever laid eyes on it before—much less painted it—all Provence was calling me until I thought I'd go as mad as Van Gogh. "Picturesque" my ass. You can't understand, Kate, and I can't explain. "Picturesque" will do as well as any other explanation but the fact is that I've lost it, *lost it*, and even Provence hasn't brought it back.

"Come on, Kate," he said abruptly, getting up. "This grass is still wet."

More and more often during the next week Mistral turned the car in the direction of Félice, the village that lay on the north flank of the Lubéron, east of Ménerbes and west of Lacoste. Félice held an attraction with which he became more and more obsessed as the urge to paint refused to return: the game of boules.

In the single café of the town every man who could walk and belonged to the village gathered each evening and each noon to have a *pastis* or two. Now, in autumn, their ranks were swelled by many farmers, who were making the most of this short, leisurely time of the year after the crops were in and before the hunting season opened. After a few rounds the men all wandered off to the flat, shady ground behind the café and played endless games of boules, that bowling game which is the equivalent, throughout the South of France, of soccer, bicycle racing and billiards put together, a game so complicated that its rules cover three pages of tiny print.

One of the farmers, a young man named Josephe Bernard, had looked Mistral up and down the second time he and Kate had gone to the café.

"Do you play boules?" he asked finally.

"I'm just a tourist," Mistral said to excuse himself.

"No matter. Would you like to try?"

In spite of the rules, boules is basically so simple that Mistral was able to acquit himself honorably with a minimum of instruction. His coordination and eye were so well developed that although he had never held one of the steel balls before, within an hour he was making a respectable showing and on that first day he managed to knock away the boule of another man from its position close to the target, delighting his sponsor who invited him to be part of the game any time he was in the neighborhood.

Mistral had returned often, charmed by the high drama of the game, which involved endless arguments, filled with wit, insults, laughter and shrewdness, as well as the never-failing pleasure of throwing a ball, that one skill all men love to use.

Kate watched from the sidelines, amazed at Mistral's ability to lose himself in a game that she found infinitely boring. But while he played she was able to look at him without his realizing it. How easily he fell into the manners of the boules players, she thought. He threw his arm into the air as widely as they did, argued as earnestly, laughed as loudly, played without noticing the passage of time, and every day his command of his boule grew greater.

"You're sure you're not from this country?" Josephe Bernard asked his new friend. "Provence must be in your blood . . . and in your name. Mistral—that's 'master wind' in Provençal. I have some cousins named Mistral from over near Mérindol, on the south side of the mountain . . . perhaps we're related?"

"Maybe I am but I can't prove it. I don't know where my great-grandparents came from. I wish I did, but my family's all dead and while they were alive I never listened—never bothered to ask."

"Most strangers, if they try to throw a boule, they make fools of themselves. It only looks easy. If you practiced for a few more weeks you could be on my team. There's a tournament the last Saturday in November."

Mistral threw his arm around the young farmer's shoulders and ordered a round of drinks for everyone in the café. He knew how much such an offer meant from a man to whom each boules tournament was a matter that would be discussed with an intensity of interest for years to come.

"I wish I could, Josephe, but I have to work for a living." But how, Mistral wondered, am I going to go back to work? Boules had let him forget for a few hours, boules had let him stop trying to find someone whom he could blame for the fire that had gone out: Avigdor because he was a dealer and all he wanted was product to sell; Kate because she had caused the exhibition to happen and before the exhibition he had been painting as simply as he breathed; Maggy because she was a fool and a child and the only woman who had ever left him; the exhibition itself because it opened his eyes to the cupidity of collectors who buy in a minute what it takes a man months of labor to create, collectors who don't respect, don't understand, but just open their purses and purchase a piece of him—he realized that none of them was to blame but still he circled them in his mind, trying to find the culprit.

"We have to work too," Josephe replied, "but there's always time for boules—if not, why bother to work?"

Besides the café and the game, Félice held another lure. Below the village in the valley not too far from the main road, Mistral had discovered a deserted *mas*. One day, spurred only by idle interest, he had followed a deeply rutted path that wound up and around a low knoll covered by an orchard of precious live oaks, the only trees at whose roots truffles grow. The shade of the orchard opened into an avenue of excited, pointed, green-black cypress beyond which stood a high wall surrounding a *mas*.

Mistral parked the Talbot on the strip of meadow that lay between the cypress and the walls of the house, a sunny, dry stretch of tiny yellow thistles and wild grasses. Tall, broad, double doors barred them from seeing inside. There was a silence, laced, as always, by the sound of the cicadas, a dry but pleasant crackle that was so much a part of the countryside that it was a part of the silence itself. None of the familiar sounds of a farm rose from behind the walls that surrounded the buildings; no dogs yapped, there were no kitchen noises nor the calling of children. Honeysuckle, growing thickly and curling over the walls, released an intense sweetness that was almost as tangible as if it were visible; a swarm of red and orange butterflies hung above the meadow like a Chinese kite and a sleepy, swarming hum indicated that here was a paradise of bees.

Together Mistral and Kate walked around trying to peer inside, but the walls were surrounded at their base by wicked brambles and the tendrils of honeysuckle grew up into the air just above Mistral's head.

At one point the wall turned into the bottom of a big round tower with two unshuttered windows open high above them, but whoever had abandoned the *mas* had made sure that there would be no intruders for there was no gap anywhere. As they made the circuit they could see five tilted roofs of various heights, and the tops of some window frames. The walled *mas* was the hub of a wheel of wedge-shaped fields, each separated from the other by tall windbreaks of cypress or cane. One section of the wheel was an olive grove, the next an unworked expanse of red earth; then came a vineyard heavy with unpicked grapes; and next to this lay an apricot orchard, laden with rotting fruits; then another vineyard and more sections of unplanted fields, the earth clumped as if a plow had never passed over it.

"It's incredible!" Mistral exploded. "Here, in a land whose every millimeter of good soil is used—I can't believe the shame of it! Look at those grapes, look at the olives! And the apricots! They grew and ripened and no one picked them. It's a disgrace!"

"It must be for sale," Kate ventured.

"There's no sign posted. All I saw was the name on the mailbox. *La Tourrello*—a Provençal word—must mean tower—little tower, or something like that," he said angrily. "It's probably part of an estate and the heirs are fighting about it—that's what often happens. If they don't agree to work the land in shares they have to sell it at auction."

"Why don't we find out? They must know in Félice," Kate suggested. "If it's for sale, we could at least ask to visit it."

"No, I don't think so. I don't want to go in." Mistral sounded troubled.

"You? You've been inside every *mas* from Maubec to Bonnieux. Why not this one?"

"I can't explain it. It's just a feeling." He was protecting himself. An intuition told him that he would never forget the look of this securely locked, valuable, walled domain. Even though he had seen only the outline of the shallow slant of the tilted roofs inside, their simple geometry had such a rightness that they had touched his heart. The *mas* on the knoll was perfectly at one with nature and he preferred to see no more of it than the outside since it was empty and therefore available.

Mistral had never owned a house and the house-lust that most of the human race feels had never touched him before. He had been content to look at the farms of Provence with the simple understanding that they were the only possible structure that could be perfectly mated with this wondrous countryside. It was an esthetic joy, not tainted by the itch to own; but one step inside the doors of this *mas* would change him forever.

"All right," Kate said, respecting his wish. Both she and Mistral were profoundly alike in the limitation they placed on the things they did not want to know.

In the week that followed, they returned four times to the deserted *mas* and she never repeated her suggestion although she was irritated almost beyond bearing at his fascination with the place. He's courting that old farmhouse, she thought jealously, wooing it as if it were a woman, prowling around the walls like a lovesick adolescent. Between the café and the boules and mooning around this farm he manages to put in a full day without accomplishing one damn thing. When will he paint again?

In the café in Félice, several days later, Josephe Bernard questioned Mistral.

"You say you're a painter, eh, Julien? We've seen them come and go for years—there's always a painter hanging around in these parts. But I never saw one who did anything but paint the countryside. I say that a real painter should be able to make a picture of another human being that looked *exactly* like him. What do you say to that?"

"Not every painter does portraits, Josephe, and not every portrait looks like its subject, or the way he thinks he looks, which is never the same thing at all."

"I was afraid you'd come out with high-class crap like that," Josephe replied, disappointment evident in his open face. "So you couldn't paint me the way I look in the mirror, is that it?"

"Maybe yes, maybe no, but I can do something that will make you smile, my friend." Mistral took a pencil from the bar and drew rapidly on the back of a slip of paper used for the game of Lotto. "What do you think of this?" He shoved the paper over to Bernard. In a few spare lines, in less than a minute, using a knack he had had since he was a teenager, a knack he never thought twice about, he had distilled the essence of Josephe Bernard into a caricature.

"Damn if it's not me!—big nose and all!" Bernard bellowed with laughter. "Now do Henri—he's got another ugly mug!" He grabbed an old farmer and thrust him in front of Mistral and slid another piece of paper at him. Soon Mistral was surrounded by men, all clamoring for their caricatures, vying with each other like schoolboys for the next turn. He ripped them off with an ease that astonished the crowd.

Now that was something, they told each other, an image that looked so much like you that it could be no one else in the world, and done so quickly that it seemed like magic. Each one of them pored over his caricature—how had the painter managed it? Those of them who lived near the café hurried home to bring their wives and children back with them, all waiting in line for one of the amazing slips of paper. Better than a game of *belotte*, this was. Soon Mistral had to take another pencil and then another, as the points wore down, but nothing stopped the slashing strokes of his cunning hand. Finally there was no one left in Félice who hadn't been caricatured, who hadn't carefully carried away a slip of Lotto paper, to look at over dinner and compare with many a friendly insult.

It was late, almost seven o'clock, when Mistral and Kate finally left Félice to go back to Villeneuve. His heart was so swollen with thanksgiving that he didn't want to talk. Caricatures, a simple party trick he had forgotten he could do, *caricatures*, by all the saints in heaven, had given him back the demon of creation. His fingers itched for the feel of a brush, his nose craved the smell of oil paint and turpentine, his gut was alive again with images he *had* to throw on canvas—and all because he'd taken a pencil without thinking and spilled out foolishness to entertain those simple folk he liked so much. They had responded with such wholehearted appreciation, the caricatures had gone directly from his hand into their hands. Theirs was the only reward he could accept with ease, without feeling disconnected from his work.

For the first time Mistral enjoyed that feeling of triumph he had not been able to absorb into himself on the night of the *vernissage*. Every muscle, every nerve and sinew of his body was newborn, as full of power as it had ever been. Mistral could scarcely contain his excitement. How could he wait till morning?

After dinner that night Mistral set out by himself for a walk. He felt a wild energy that was too great to be contained under a roof and his jubilation was all the companion he wanted as he roamed along the banks of the Rhône, accepting with pleasure the feeling of the chill of the air against his skin, rejoicing in the free rustle of the trees, the tumble of water. As he walked he understood, with so clear a conviction that he marveled that it had not come to him sooner, that he must never leave Provence.

Never again, he thought, never again the loneliness of cities. Never again the anthill of Montparnasse, where too many people spoke too many languages in too many cafés, and talked too much rot about government and religion and schools of painting. Never again the cold Parisian winter with the dismal rain killing the light. Never again a day without a view of the horizon.

Even as he enumerated for himself the reasons for not going back, he knew that he didn't need them, they were only the outward expression of an inward feeling that held him in the tightest grip. *He must not leave Provence because here he could work.* It was as if he had had a revelation, as if he had seen a vision, it was stronger than any superstition and clearer than any logic.

At dawn he awakened Kate.

"The vacation's over, Kate. I'm going back to work."

Kate blinked with relief. "Give me half an hour—I'll dress and pack as quickly as I can."

"No, don't rush, no need. Stay on awhile if you like."

"But you just said you're going back to work. What are you talking about?"

"I'm staying here, Kate."

"What?"

"Right here. Madame Blé is open all year around, which solves one problem and there are plenty of empty houses in Villeneuve to rent as a studio. As soon as the store's open, I'll telephone old Lefebvre and have him ship down all the supplies I need on the next train and send the bill to Avigdor—nothing could be easier. I've got it all planned."

"I suppose you're doing all this to be on that damn boules team," Kate said viciously.

"That wouldn't be a bad reason, but no, I have a better one." Mistral paced restlessly around the room, not seeing Kate's face, white with shock. "It's this place, Kate, this place." He didn't know how to explain his conviction to her, and, he realized, he didn't need to. "It's the light here, don't you understand?"

"I see perfectly," she said evenly. Nothing could be gained by further discussion. One thing Kate was never wrong about was the strength of another's position and Mistral's was of unquarried marble. "I'll stay on a day or so then."

"You don't have to rush back—stay as long as you like, unless you'd be bored when I start working all day. I'd enjoy having you here Kate, very much."

"We'll see." Did he think she'd hang around like a house cat? she thought furiously. Kate realized that his announcement snapped her out of a coma. Love, concealed with so much difficulty, had made her inattentive. She'd been dreaming the days away, dangerously sidetracked by her body. "Since you're staying, I don't think I'll go sight-seeing today, Julien. I'll be in that car long enough on the way back. I've got a few things to put together—and I have to go into Avignon to buy some heavy sweaters for the trip, or a decent coat if they have such a thing. I'll get the taxi to take me into town."

"No, you can have the car. I'm going to walk around and see what's for rent." He didn't try to conceal his eagerness.

Kate was out all day, not returning for lunch. When she finally appeared late in the afternoon Mistral was impatient. It was a good forty-minute drive to Félice and he was anxious to announce his decision to his friends in the café.

A thousand meters along the small road that led to Félice Kate put her hand over Mistral's. "Turn left," she said.

"Why? We'll be late for the game. I can visit *La Tourrello* any time now."

"There's something I want to show you. It won't take long. Please."

He turned the car onto the path and parked, as usual, on the strip of meadow.

"A last look?" he asked. "I didn't know you cared that much about it."

Kate slipped out of her seat, walked to the big wooden double doors set in the wall and took a key out of her pocket. She put it into the lock and turned it with difficulty. As Mistral watched, astonished, she pushed one of the heavy doors open wide. She beckoned at him. "Come on!"

"What are you doing? Where'd you get that key?" he called, not moving from the driver's seat. He had no intention of going in.

Kate walked back to the car and held out the key to Mistral. "Take it. It's mine. Or rather it's yours. To be precise, it's my dowry."

He snorted with astonishment. She certainly had the capacity to surprise. And how grand was her scale! She did nothing by half and somehow, he realized as he looked at her grave and hopeful eyes, she was never preposterous, even now. Dignified, serious, intent, she made her extraordinary proposition a possibility just by her assumption that it could happen.

"Will you marry me, Julien?" Kate asked.

He was silent. He knew she had more to say and he found her profoundly interesting.

"I love you and you need a wife. You need a home, I saw the notary in Félice today and bought this farm. The former owner died leaving only a granddaughter who was anxious to sell. Next week a young farmer and his wife will move into the wing on the left and start hiring men to get the land back in shape, the groves, the orchards, the vineyards." She paused but still he said nothing so she continued, spreading out a delicious life before him as clearly, as distinctly as if she had flung a bright cloth on the grass and placed generous platters of fine food and bottles of wine upon it and invited him to a feast. "I'm looking for an architect to design your studio. I've already hired a master mason in Avignon. He's meeting me here tomorrow. A plumber and an electrician will come with him—there's a great deal of work to be done before the house is—"

"Could *you* live here—in the country—at *La Tourrello*?" he interrupted at last.

"It seems that I can't imagine living happily anywhere you are not. God help me. I find myself curiously unable to go back to Paris and leave you here for the winter and drive down to visit in February pretending that I want to see the almond trees in flower."

"But I've never thought of marriage," Mistral said.

"Think of it then," Kate said with a flash of humor. "It's time to get started on our lives. It's time to do the real work. You've begun well, so that part's over, but now the harder part comes . . . to keep going forward, to enlarge, to reinforce, to gain new territory and make it absolutely your own . . . years and years of work that will take all your strength. Didn't Flaubert tell artists to be regular and ordinary in their lives so they could be violent and original in their work?"

"I've never read Flaubert," Mistral said. The important thing, the only thing, he thought, is that I want to paint again and I must not leave this place.

"Julien, imagine having your studio built here, looking up toward Félice."

She didn't gesture. The immoderate bounty that lay before his eyes all spoke for her. Her love needed no other adornment to make itself evident. He looked about and saw a future of order and peace and plenty, saw that it was possible.

"Think," she added in a voice that danced with nerves, as he remained silent, "think of the boules tournaments, the many boules tournaments, year after year."

"You're trying to bribe me, Kate."

"Of course." She stood her ground resolutely, the key still in her outstretched hand, the wind blowing her hair, the grave gray eyes warmed by the emotion she no longer hid. In her expression, her blind faith in him mingled with vulnerability.

"I'm trying to think of a single reason . . . to say no," Mistral said slowly.

"And . . . ?"

He jumped out of the car and took the key from her. He grasped it tightly, feeling the heavy, smooth iron press into his palm. Recognition flooded him. This piece of land, this woman . . . they were his future. They laughed together, complicit laughter and not for the first time. It had been so from the first day they had met.

"But how strange life is!" he exclaimed in wonder.

" 'Pray love me little, so you love me long,' " she murmured in English.

"What does that mean, my clever bossy American girl?" he asked as he pulled her into his arms.

"A poet long ago . . . someday I'll tell you . . . someday you'll understand."

10

No, decidedly no! Impossible, totally impossible. It's out of the question," Paula proclaimed to Maggy, looking more scandalized than Maggy would have thought possible for a woman who, self-admittedly, had seen everything.

"But why?" Maggy wailed.

"Two catastrophic reasons. Your lingerie and your shoes. They simply will not do! Oh, Maggy, just look at this. It's enough to make me cry." Paula waved distractedly at the scant pile of undergarments she had taken out of Maggy's armoire and spread over the bed, and held up three petticoats as accusingly as if they were dustcloths.

"This one is patched, this one is frayed at the hem, this one is missing half its ribbon as far as I can tell. You don't have a single complete set of lingerie in suitable condition," she continued, warming to her grievances, "and where, may I ask, are your corselettes and *soutien-gorges?* All I see here are ill-assorted garters, mended stockings, knickers that you must have brought with you when you left home and these disgraceful petticoats. I will admit that they're clean but beyond that!" She threw up her hands.

Maggy blew hair out of her eyes. "Oh, why are you acting like a duchess? You don't seriously think I bothered with all that, do you? I don't need them in my work surely. Or to go dancing. On the contrary! And as for my petticoats, they're perfectly good with just a stitch here and there . . . Madame Poulard can fix them up in no time."

Paula sat down on the bed with finality.

"Maggy, you must be mad. How do you expect to be treated with respect, when you go to Patou or Molyneux, if they see you in these rags? What would Mademoiselle Chanel say to such a beggar woman? I don't care how much money you have to spend, no couturier, no *vendeuse* and no fitter is ever going to take you seriously unless you have proper lingerie, proper shoes and a proper hat as well."

"Well, so much for my glorious career as a kept woman. Over before it began. I don't have the right clothes to wear in order to go and buy the right clothes, so how can I possibly move into a suite at the Lotti? Maybe I could tell Monsieur Patou that I've been in a shipwreck and lost everything? Or convince Mademoiselle Chanel that I was stolen by the gypsies who kept all my clothes and returned me unharmed? How *do* people ever manage to buy made-to-order clothes if they have never bought them before? It's worse than a Chinese puzzle."

Maggy flopped down on the floor of her room, crossed her bare legs and leaned rebelliously forward, her chin on her hands.

"It all seemed so simple this morning and now you've made it so complicated that I don't even want to think about it. A year ago you were instructing me in how to hop out of my knickers, now you want to put me in corsets! I'll just tell Perry we have to stay here and to hell with his valet and his business. If he doesn't like me the way I am, it's just too bad. Corsets be damned."

"Now, now," said Paula, hastily, "it's not that insoluble. Calm yourself, little one. It merely demands thought and planning, like all important events in life. For the lingerie we start from the beginning. Everything must be new. There is a shop, just off the rue St. Honoré—it's run by three Russian emigrées, all titled ladies, of great discretion and understanding and—what is more important—promptitude. They specialize in cases like yours . . ."

"What! Now I'm a 'case,' am I?" Maggy said indignantly.

"In this particular matter, yes." Paula went on imperturbably.

"If they get the order this afternoon, and I explain to them the nature of the emergency, you should have exquisite lingerie made within a week. And as for the shoes, there is a splendid little Italian *bottier* I know who is not far from them. Rue St. Florentin, up two flights, a very reliable address. For him there is no need to worry about the lingerie so we can go there today."

"I could just pop off to Raoul . . ."

"Raoul? That dreadful little place in the arcade with the shoes for eighty francs that have ruined your feet?" Paula was mortified.

"That's what I've been wearing all along and you never objected before."

"Forget what you endured before—don't you want Perry to be proud of you?"

"He is already." Maggy brooded, pulling her tender orange plumage around her face, all but hiding it. Her romantic fantasy of the life of a kept woman was rapidly falling apart in the face of Paula's practicality. It sounded like work, and work of the most boring kind; endless fittings; days wasted running around from one special workroom to another; *corsets*, all so that she could impress a saleswoman who would probably see through her anyway. She hated that saleswoman already, she thought in dejection.

Suddenly the memory of Kate Browning as she had looked the first time she came to Mistral's studio came into her mind, Kate Browning so sure of herself in cool, white silk, every stitch of which had to have been made by hand, Kate Browning with her spotless white gloves who always looked so stylish, so self-confident and self-possessed that it was impossible to doubt that she had tiptoed daintily out of her mother's womb in a pair of tiny perfect shoes and a marvelous hat from Rose Descat.

Galvanized, Maggy jumped up with a suddenness that startled Paula: "What about gloves?" she demanded, taking Paula by the shoulders and shaking her. "Foolish female, have you been in that kitchen of yours for so long that you don't know that without gloves no lady is dressed for the street? While you drivel on about corsets you have forgotten gloves. How can I start my new life without at least six *dozen* pairs of gloves since I intend to never wear a pair more than once, *once*, do you hear?"

She released Paula and danced around her room, picking up a stocking here and another there, inspecting them for darns and finally taking two that were intact. All the others she swept into a wastebasket. "Twelve dozen pairs of silk stockings, before lunch! Then on to the Russian aristocrats—I *crave* lingerie: all silk chiffon and stupendous appliqués of lace; peach-colored crêpe de chine; garter belts, teddies, *soutien-gorges* to flatten my tits, flared tap pants in pale green and lavender and mocha, red chiffon nightgowns . . . what else? Chinese pajamas! But no corsets!" Maggy halted her capering progress around her tiny room in front of the mirror she had hung above the sink. She studied herself intently, shaking her hair around her head. She pulled it all back behind her ears, then she lifted it in both hands and piled it on top of her head. Slowly she shook her head from side to side in disapproval.

"I need a haircut."

"Of course you do. You can't wear hats properly with all that hair and without the right hats . . ."

"Don't tell me—I know. Without the right hats no self-respecting *vendeuse* will even let me in the salon. Now just tell me one thing, Paula. Do I have to go and get my hair cut off *before* I go for a haircut by Antoine, or will Antoine deign to cut my hair in its present lamentably unfashionable condition?"

Paula's eyes widened. Antoine was the most famous hairdresser in the world. Twenty years before he had invented bobbed hair when the great actress, Eve Lavallière, let him sacrifice her hair to his scissors, an experiment that so unnerved him that he didn't try it again for another six years. Now he ruled supreme in his salon on the rue Didier that he had inaugurated by a ball for fourteen hundred guests with each woman dressed in white. Every female creature in France dreamed of presenting her head before the master.

"Antoine," Paula breathed, respectfully.

"But of course," Maggy said. "He will know, just by looking at me, that I am worthy of his scissors, poor though I have been and temporarily between one pair of knickers and another."

"How will you get an appointment?"

"I'll just go and see him. Will he be able to resist the chance to cut off this hair?"

"I don't see how he could," Paula said truthfully. Antoine was so impulsive that he had recently bid five thousand francs at a charity auction for a single glove that had been donated by his client, the poetess Vicomtesse Marie-Laure de Noailles.

"Then on your feet, my *coco*. You don't think I'm going without you?"

"I wouldn't let you—what if you changed your mind halfway through?"

"My thought exactly." With a caressing hand Maggy touched her hair. It had to go, that much was clear, but she was not nearly as brave about the prospect as she sounded. In fact her heart was fluttering in a way that made her want to give little yelps of anguish, but she flung on her best daytime clothes and bundled Paula into a taxi before she had a chance to change her mind.

It was never more difficult for a woman to be beautiful than during the 1920s. Fashion flattered no one, femininity in all its manifestations was truncated, hidden, distorted. Hats hid the forehead and the eyes; eyebrows were unnaturally tweezed, bodies forced ruthlessly into unflattering boyish forms; cosmetics used badly. Only three colors of lipsticks existed and hairstyles were so ugly that only the most authentic beauty could overcome them.

In this period a haircut could make or break a woman. Women who only ten years before had been considered lovely in their Edwardian draperies and the floating clouds of their elaborately dressed hair, were denuded and exposed to the cruel light of day without any grace or charm left to them—all in the name of fashion. Women who would once have been reigning beauties were revealed as scarecrows, with scalped heads perched like knobs on top of unfashionably plump shoulders. A poorly shaped skull could ruin a young woman's future.

Maggy sat in the chair before Antoine's mirror while the hairdresser hovered behind her, surrounded by a small crown of apprentices and assistants. Paula sat grimly off to one side.

"My God . . . your hairline," he said in excitement in his Polish-accented French.

"What's wrong with it?" Maggy asked, ready to explode. Any excuse would do if she could only leave with dignity. Leave *now* before he started. She looked around in a dizzy panic. The walls of the salon were made of great sheets of plate glass, the staircases themselves were constructed of glass, the chairs and tables of the salon and the decorations and lights were all made of glass to please this tall, pale Pole who lived in a crystal abode above the salon and slept in a glass coffin which, he claimed, protected him from dangerous electric radiation in the night air.

"How *could* you have kept it hidden for so long?" he asked reproachfully. "Elegance starts with the hairline, Madame, and yours is—a *poem*. This," he said, tracing a long thin finger high across her forehead, "is the essential shape without which no other elegance matters, without which no true elegance can begin. It must be *exposed.*"

"Whatever you say," Maggy muttered, closing her eyes as she saw him pick up his scissors. They made a horrible, softly shrieking sound as they flashed through her wings of hair, each lock of which was carefully caught before it fell to the floor by an assistant whose job it was to preserve long hair and make it into switches and chignons and braids that the shorn client could pin on in the evening. Maggy opened one eye and saw her head hunched into her shoulders as she cringed in the chair.

She sat up bravely for it was entirely too late now to act the coward, and forced a smile onto her lips. Was that her neck, that endlessly long, white *thing?* Were those her ears, those poor little pink projections? Now Antoine wet her head and took up a razor that glittered relentlessly as he gradually shaped her hair into a shining cap, as short as that of an English public schoolboy, the extreme Eton cut which only the most beautiful women could wear. It was combed straight back, parted precisely on one side, and in front of each exposed ear the cap came to a sleek point on her cheek. At her nape her hair was shingled so that the fine shape of her whole skull was clearly seen. Maggy's large yellow-green eyes, set so far apart, looked twice as big as they ever had and her sharp, fiercely curved cheekbones now had competition in the totally revealed, long, pliant column of her neck.

She threw off the cloth that covered her and stood up, gazing into the mirror, turning this way and that so that she could see herself from each side and from the back. There was a hushed silence from the crowd of onlookers. Even Antoine himself said nothing as Maggy anxiously looked at the new personage who faced her in the mirrors.

She felt faint. Her head seemed quite separate from her shoulders, as if it had been detached and allowed to fly upward like a balloon. The woman in the mirror was bold; the woman in the mirror was older than Maggy and absolutely in command of herself; the woman in the mirror was supremely chic even though she was wearing Maggy's suit and Maggy's deplorable shoes. Her head, that sleek, superbly cropped head, so bright that it looked painted on, a magnificent red punctuation mark, dominated the room.

Maggy stood expressionless. Paula held her breath. Slowly Maggy moved closer and closer to the mirror, her eyes never leaving it. The images she saw grew huge and she looked at it questioningly until her eyes merged and her nose touched the mirror. She remained there a second, misting the mirror with her breath and then, with a decisive motion, she kissed the mirror with her big, delicious mouth.

"Ah!" all the watchers breathed in relief.

"Madame is content," Antoine stated with an air of proprietorship.

"Madame is enchanted!" Maggy seized the astonished Pole, squeezed him hard and pressed a kiss on his ear. "Madame is to be addressed as Monsieur from now on." She took the carnation that was pinned to her jacket and put it behind Antoine's ear. "From one Monsieur to another, I love you," she told him.

Perry Kilkullen did not know the first thing about keeping a woman. It all sounded so easy, the phrase fell so naturally off the tongue; men, after all, had been keeping women for thousands of years, Perry reassured himself. The ancient Greeks and Romans had kept women or young boys, depending on their tastes. Perhaps both? Who knew? The history of any country was filled with legendary kept women and the ranks of the aristocracy were eventually filled with their children. How did the various Louises do it—XIV, XV and XVI? How on earth did they make the *arrangements*?

Feeling more American than he had for years in Paris, slightly abashed but infinitely determined, he went to a real-estate agent. A place to live had to be the first step for a Kilkullen, as for a Louis. Or did they just slip the lady into a set of spare rooms at the palace?

"In what quarter does Monsieur desire to live? How many reception rooms does Monsieur require? How many bedrooms? And how many will there be in staff? Does Monsieur wish a house or a flat?"

"Look, I simply won't know until I see it. Just show me the very best of what you've got."

He inspected a dozen houses and apartments in the fashionable parts of the Right Bank and rejected them all for one reason or another. He didn't include Maggy on these expeditions because he wanted it to be a surprise. Finally, on the avenue Vélasquez he walked into a vast, second-floor flat that opened directly onto the noble, green, lopsided rectangle of the Parc Monceau. As if he were a person with perfect pitch hearing the right chord, Perry felt at home in the empty rooms.

126

He took her there that evening at twilight and led her through the apartment. She was struck dumb as he proudly displayed chamber after chamber.

"Oh, my God!" Maggy burst out at last.

"Don't you like it?" Perry asked anxiously.

"Have you counted the rooms?" she asked on a wild note.

"No, not exactly. It seemed okay to me."

"There are *eleven* rooms, and at least two dozen closets. Heaven knows how many baths and that's not counting the kitchen and the pantries and laundry room or the servants' rooms you said are up in the attic," she quavered.

"Is that too big?" he couldn't help sounding dejected.

"Anything more than two rooms is too big as far as I'm concerned. And one of them should have a bathtub in it."

"But . . . but, you said you dreamed of being kept in style."

"Oh, Perry," she cried, huddling close to him, "I'm so *scared!* I know what I said but that was a fantasy and this is reality. I just want to go back to the Left Bank and find a tiny room in a tiny hotel and get into bed and pull up the covers over my head and not come out! Ever!"

Perry pulled her close to him and stroked her as firmly and as gently as if she were a large, terrified animal. He realized, as he held her, that he had grown up among rich New York women who had always expected that one day they would rule large establishments; women who had been in training all of their lives to move effortlessly, with quiet authority, through rooms far larger and more numerous than these on the Parc Monceau. But what did Maggy, his wonderful girl, his first, his only love, know of such things? It only made her more precious to him that she was reduced to terror by an eleven-room apartment, this girl who had had the courage to run away from home at seventeen, who took risks by nature, who was still at heart almost a tomboy.

"Look," he whispered to her, as if he were talking to a child, "if you want to, we'll keep living in hotels, don't worry. But why not give this place a chance? It isn't as if you have to move in tomorrow, darling. It'll take time to furnish and then, when it's finished, if you have even the slightest doubt, if you still feel it's too big, I'll simply get rid of it. What do you say to that?" As he spoke he knew how desperately he wanted to make a real home for Maggy, not in a hotel, but here, in this lovely space, where they could be together permanently, just the two of them.

Maggy's voice was muffled because her head was pressed to his vest.

"How many months will it take?" she asked suspiciously.

"Oh, a long time," Perry assured her, "a very long time." He wondered how people actually did furnish apartments. His wife and his mother-in-law and his mother had all been in a feminine tizzy for a while before his wedding, so long ago, and he supposed that it was apartment stuff that they were rushing around about but he hadn't paid any attention. Apartments, to men of his generation, *came* furnished, new of course, but somehow to a chap's taste. All that just got taken care of—was that not one of the things women spent their time on?

During the next six months it seemed to Maggy that she learned an amazing number of new things every day. First there was English. She had determined to learn English because it wasn't fair, it seemed to her, for Perry always to be at the disadvantage when they talked together, and anyway, no matter where they went, whether it was to the Bal Tabarin to watch the cancan, or to dine at Maxim's or to Frederick's for pressed duck, all around her she heard English spoken and it was infuriating not to understand the jokes.

The buying power of the American dollar was so high that Paris was filled with expatriates living well on fifteen dollars a week. They intrigued Maggy with their carelessness, their rambunctious gaiety, their way of irreverently throwing themselves on Paris, as if it were the world's biggest playpen. Who but Americans would play tennis inside Josephine Baker's nightclub with paper rackets and balls? Who but Americans could sit in with the musicians at Bricktop's and make such wild jazz as she'd never heard before? Not speaking English in 1926 in Paris was to miss the best party given in history.

Every morning, right after breakfast, Maggy took an English lesson from the earnest Bostonian wife of an American writer who couldn't seem to finish his novel. One of the first expressions Maggy learned was "writer's block" and, for the rest of her life, whenever she heard those words they would bring back the expensively draped, pale blue satin sitting room of her suite at the Lotti.

Perry had engaged Jean Michel Frank, the most talked about of the decorator-designers of the day—the leader of the practitioners of *Les Arts Décoratifs*—to work on the apartment, and while he went about his business, Maggy went about hers.

"Do you have any idea, Paula," she asked querulously, "how hard a kept woman has to work? It's a job and a half. Why, you can't leave the house in the morning if you're not in a suit from O'Rosen or Chanel, you don't dare show yourself in the afternoon unless you're in Patou, you can't just drink a cocktail, you have to dress for it, in something from Molyneux with tiny shoulder straps and a handkerchief-pointed hemline . . ."

"I hope you're not complaining," Paula said severely. "Every *métier* has its price."

"Being kept seems to amount to spending one percent of your time naked in bed and changing your clothes the other ninety-nine percent," Maggy said thoughtfully. "Aren't there any *métiers* that allow you to wear the same thing from morning till night? And the hats, Paula—a different one for each outfit and three fittings on each hat, all that fuss over the tilt of a brim or the width of a ribbon—who would have guessed it?"

"I could have warned you," Paula said knowingly, "but I was afraid you'd back out of the whole thing while you still had time."

"It's too late now," Maggy said, restored to her high spirits.

"Interview a butler?" she said incredulously.

"The apartment will be furnished next month," Perry replied reasonably. "We have to have a staff, and a staff means a butler—he can help you with the rest of the interviews."

"How would I know what to ask him?" Maggy huffed in indignation. "What do I know of the care and feeding of cigars, of the intimate love life of cases of wine, the protocol of announcing dinner or of the right way to polish silver? Or of the wrong way either, for that matter? If you want a butler, you must find him yourself and that goes for all the other 'staff' as well. I'm not sure yet that I'll ever move in."

"You haven't even been to see what's going on—aren't you curious?"

"No," Maggy lied. She found herself wondering at odd moments of every day just what Monsieur Frank was up to, but she didn't want to be drawn into the process because as soon as she expressed a taste or a preference it would be as good as agreeing to live in that enormous, deeply alarming, oppressively grand apartment Perry had bought. Hotel life, even in the high style of the Lotti, had something enchantingly harum-scarum about it. The elevators were crammed with amorous couples who couldn't possibly be married, the lobby echoed with music and laughter, the maids were always ready to chat for a moment and as for the dignified concierges, they pored over the racing form with her every day.

"Well then, I'll do it," Perry said with resignation.

"I know—let Paula. It's the sort of thing she does best. She can read character, that one—you can't fool her. At least I never could. And don't forget the last *shiddach* she made."

"*Shiddach?*"

"An introduction—as in you and me—well, only used loosely. Actually it's an arranged marriage, like the one my Aunt Esther wanted me to make. It comes from a Hebrew word '*shidukh*,' " Maggy said learnedly.

"And that bit of lore came, I assume, from Rabbi Taradash?" Perry was charmed by Maggy's rare use of Jewish expressions. They seemed as piquant and chipper to him as the red carnation in her buttonhole.

"Don't remind me of my poor sweet rabbi. A kept woman living in sin with a Catholic? Oh, I can't even think what he'd say."

"Would he explode?"

"Explode with anger, split with aggravation, burst with suffering—you can take your pick. But he would not understand, any more than your priest if you had one, would. However, I refuse to feel guilty! The Talmud says 'When a man faces his Maker, he will have to account for those pleasures of life he failed to experience.' That's one part of the Talmud I know and the one part I agree with entirely. It's probably contradicted in another part—I'm basically ignorant about religion and where we're concerned, I don't see that it has any relevance."

"Is that the only reason you don't feel guilty about me?" he asked, with sudden gravity.

"Oh, my darling, no. I don't feel guilty because I love you so much." There was no way to truly tell him, she thought, how she felt about him.

It was a love without mystifications, free of surprises or harshness, a love that could never wound her. Perry's arms were a bulwark against ever being hurt again. With him she was utterly safe, and now she knew the value of safety.

There were moments, she admitted to herself, when she was flooded by memories of Julien Mistral, when she would feel again just how the stern line of his mouth became so surprisingly tender under her lips. But then she would turn away resolutely from the unwelcome memory and count her blessings. What if she had lived with Mistral for years? What if she had been saturated with him, her heart stained through and through by the paint-obsessed man who cared for no one. How astonishingly lucky she'd been. Her brief months with Mistral had left her badly bruised, but she believed that she possessed a core that he had never touched. She bent her head to the back of Perry's hand and rubbed her cheek over it so gently that she could feel the tiny blond hairs tickle her skin. "About that butler . . ." she murmured.

"I'll attend to it."

"I knew you would."

"Close your eyes tight and promise not to peek. I'll lead you into the salon—I want you to see that first," Perry said to Maggy. It was April of 1927 and they stood outside the front door of the Parc Monceau flat.

"But that's so silly. Still, after all, why not? This whole thing is ridiculous." Maggy squeezed her eyes shut and took Perry's arm. It seemed to her that they walked a long time before he said, in a voice tight with emotion, "You can look now."

She opened her eyes on one of the first of the truly modern rooms of the twentieth century. She felt as if a fresh breeze had blown her into a new world, a gold and beige and ivory and white world in which the utmost luxury was expressed in the purest of forms. Nothing looked like anything she had ever seen before. The gloomy walls, that she had remembered as paneled in dark wood, had been stripped from floor to ceiling and covered with hundreds of squares of parchment, each one slightly different from all of the others. Uninterrupted by a single picture, they formed, in their assembly, a deliberate and masterful work of art that glowed, pale gold, in the light of the boldly shaped white plaster lamps.

The room, which had seemed impossibly big when she first saw it, now embraced her in its unexpected festivity. As she walked around on the white rugs she realized that she was moving in a new *sort* of space, a space in which she had never imagined people living, a space suffused with freshness and openness, that immediately made all other interiors seem crowded and fussy and old-fashioned. Maggy trailed her fingers along the backs of the simple armchairs, covered in the plainest, heaviest ivory silk imaginable, she caressed the tops of the low, gold lacquered tables and then dizzily, she dropped down to one of the large sofas. She lay full length on the soft, natural beige leather and, eyes half-closed, contemplated the essential shapes of everything in the room.

"What do you think? Isn't it terrific?" Perry asked anxiously, his words rushing. "The lamps are designed by Giacometti, there are forty coats of gold lacquer on the tables, the rugs are hand knotted in Grasse . . ."

"Don't bother me with details, my darling," Maggy said. "Just come lie with me here, it's like floating."

They moved in three days later. Jean Michel Frank, delighted with his American client, since a rich, open-pocketed single man—particularly if he is in love—is always the most desirable client any artist can have, had bent his great talent to making the Parc Monceau apartment a total expression of his revolutionary vision, a vision that would still be fresh and meaningful a half-century later.

On the first night in the new apartment Maggy found herself unable to sleep. Quietly, she got out of bed and wrapped herself in her maribou negligee. As she wandered around the apartment she had the nagging feeling that something was missing, something was not quite right. Yet Monsieur Frank had neglected no detail.

Never, Maggy thought as she passed by the linen and silver closets, had she dreamed that anyone could own so many objects. It would be weeks before she felt familiar with their contents. Nothing that could make life supremely comfortable was missing and everywhere immense cleanness reigned, a cleanness that made the satin-draped luxury of her suite at the Lotti seem shabby and even grimy by contrast.

Maggy drifted into the salon and stood by the French doors that looked out into the park. From the vantage point of the second floor she could see much of that most frolicsome of Parisian parks, the classic colonnade and the oval pond and the pyramid that the Duke of Orléans had caused to be brought there in 1778. Empty now, the park, surrounded by elaborate wrought-iron railings tipped with gilded arrows, was like a stage set, she thought, ready for some masque or entertainment of an archaic kind. It looked as if it were waiting for a procession of goddesses in Grecian robes or a band of fantastical fairies from a poet's imagination. But she knew that nothing would go on in the locked park until the children, those well-behaved children of this elegant quarter, arrived in the morning with their nurses. Restlessly she walked from room to room but in spite of her growing sense of something lacking that *should* be there, she could find no human need unaccounted for. Finally Maggy went back to bed and drifted into a troubled sleep filled with fragments of dreams.

The following day, toward twilight, Maggy let herself into the apartment, using her new key for the first time. Rosy with the coolness of the April evening, she didn't even bother to take off her coat as she crossed the entrance hall and almost ran through the long corridor to the dining room. Under her arm was a large, lumpy package wrapped in newspaper.

She had spent the afternoon poking through certain shops on the rue des Rosiers and the package contained the object she had gone searching for, the one thing, she had realized as she had awakened late that morning, that was missing from the apartment. Maggy stood in front of the vellum-covered sideboard. On it stood two heavy silver and lapis lazuli candelabras that had been designed by the famous silversmith, Jean Puiforcat, especially for the room. They matched the great covered silver and lapis bowl that stood on the dining table. Maggy took each of the candelabras from the sideboard and placed them on the table, on either side of the bowl. Then, very carefully she unwrapped the newspaper and uncovered a large, rather battered brass candlestick with seven branches.

"There! That's more like it," she said out loud as she put the menorah in the place of honor in her home.

11

Perry Mackay Kilkullen did not give one good goddamn. Not a damn for the shocked letters from his mother and his sisters and brothers. Not a damn for what the church had already said, would continue to say, was presently saying. Not a damn for the unspoken disapproval of his partners and the thrilled gossip of their wives. Not a damn for the rising tide of whispers at the Turf and Field, the Piping Rock or the New York Yacht Club. Not a damn for the opinion of anyone he had ever known or liked or even loved before he met Maggy. He was utterly indifferent to these shadowy figures, who had once seemed important, and to what they thought about a matter that was so fundamentally his own. He was forty-two, he had lived more than half of the years any man could expect on earth, and only now did he understand what it meant to be alive. *Maggy.* Without her he would have been an approximation of a man, and never known it.

He still performed his banking functions with precision; no one could accuse him of neglecting the firm, but otherwise he cut himself off from his past life deliberately and effectively. He no longer accepted invitations to dinner from his circle of friends within the Parisian banking community; when his Yale classmates visited Paris with their wives he avoided them. Carefully he arranged his business matters so that he didn't have to spend time in New York, where his wife, clad in her dignity and her religious convictions, waited with seeming serenity for him to outgrow a stage in life through which, as her mother assured her, many other fine men had passed. Mary Jane McDonnell Kilkullen was too proud to give her friends any indication of how she felt about the open scandal of Perry's keeping a French mistress. She continued on her rounds of good works, a slim, jeweled, gracious woman who refused, by her brisk yet bland bearing, to let anyone feel sorry for her. Nothing would ever make her descend to the vulgarity of acting like an outraged and deceived wife.

In the fall of 1927 Maggy turned twenty. She looked more worldly than her age, as she always had, with the urbane eyelids and bold mouth that made her, in any crowd of women, the most fascinating to watch, even if she was unlike the ideal beauty of the time. She was not, had never been, a "young thing," prettily engaging, nor did she fit into the fashionably childish and brittle flapper mode. In the past few months during which she had been able to indulge her taste, she had achieved a timeless, enigmatic, never-to-be-dated elegance.

To celebrate her birthday Perry took her to Marius and Janette, where they had dined together for the first time, and then they went on to their favorite Montmartre nightclub, Chez Josephine, where the absurdity of the nanny goat and the pig, Josephine Baker's bizarre pets, who ran about being spoiled by royalty from a dozen European countries, never failed to amuse Maggy.

Tonight however she felt oddly thoughtful. Twenty was very different from nineteen. It was a woman's age, not a girl's age. Her girlhood was over, Maggy reflected, and didn't know whether to be cast down or delighted. She sighed and twisted the double rope of pearls that Perry had given her for her birthday.

"Is something wrong, my baby?" he asked.

"I'll never be young—*really* young—again. And don't you dare tell me I'm being silly."

"Was being 'really young' so very wonderful?"

She shook her head at his misunderstanding her meaning.

"It meant that everything lay ahead of me. It meant that I didn't have to think about the future because it was so far off. Somehow the choices I made didn't really *count*. Nothing was final because everything was going to change anyway. But now, now I feel so . . . so," she gestured ineffectively and shook her head because the words disappeared even as she tried to find them.

"As if you have to make decisions?" he asked tenderly.

"Something almost like that. As if I'm *in* my future—as if my life should be going somewhere." She smiled wistfully and shrugged her shoulders with an uncharacteristically helpless air.

"You are going somewhere. You're going to marry me."

Maggy's hands flew up incredulously. "Don't say that! You know it's impossible! How can you say that, even as a joke? I've never thought of it!"

"I know you haven't but I have. It's all I've been thinking about, almost from the day I met you—the theoretically unthinkable plan of getting a divorce and marrying you and living with you for the rest of my life. Nothing else is natural or right or true. We belong together."

"You're a Catholic and you're married!" Maggy objected in wild consternation. She had acquiesced in all his arrangements for her even as she understood that nothing more was ever going to be possible. Every barrier stood between them; he was as little likely to marry her as if he had been the Prince of Wales, and she had loved him enough to accept the situation.

"My wife and I have been as good as separated for years—you know that. We don't have children to keep us together . . ."

"Oh, why did you have to bring this up?" Maggy cried. "You know you can't get a divorce."

"That's what they said to Henry the Eighth." Perry grinned at her. True, Catholics should not get divorced. But that was not to say that they *did* not divorce on rare occasions, through the use of infinite willpower and patience and a great deal of money and influence. Of course such Catholics were not what his family or anyone he knew would consider *good* Catholics. He himself would not consider a divorced Catholic a good Catholic.

But to marry Maggy, Perry Kilkullen was willing to become a bad Catholic. He had discovered that his faith was not nearly as strong as his love. Once the wheels of his imagination had begun to turn, once he had seen his life as barren, his marriage as merely the arid continuation of something that was long dead, no more than a social and theological convenience, he had become impatient with the laws of the church. Could rules that demanded that he be false to his deepest needs be right? Did he have to surrender all the good years that were left of his life as a man to a web of "musts" and "must nots" that had been decreed by Rome? Every time he made love to Maggy it was, by all the dogma he had learned, an occasion of sin. Yet when he lay within her he felt consecrated. Her breasts, her belly, her thighs—all were a benediction. Nothing as beautiful could be unblessed.

"Oh, how can you smile like that? Don't you know what you're saying?" Maggy cried, deeply shocked. "You've gone crazy."

"Wouldn't you want to marry me if it were possible?" Finally, Perry was struck by her reaction. He had expected wonderment, confusion, but not this refusal to be happy about his plans.

"I don't want to be the cause of all sorts of trouble for you," Maggy said stubbornly.

"I was *parched* before I met you!" Perry said violently. "I was dying of thirst and you saved me. I could have gone on for years and ended up withered, dry, bleached, as empty of sap as a piece of driftwood."

"But won't it cause trouble? Bad trouble?" Maggy insisted.

"Big, bad, terrible trouble." He grinned in relief. That was all that had upset her. "Almost the worst trouble you can imagine. But worth every minute of it, if you'll be there to marry me, if you'll say you'll love me always no matter how long it takes."

"You know I will," she said slowly. His utter need dissolved her fears.

"Even though you're not really young anymore? Are you sure you're not too long in the tooth to make such a decision? After all, it may well take a few years and you don't want to risk being an old maid."

"I may be reaching maturity," Maggy said, "but I'm not yet too old to take a chance."

"Then it's settled?" he said eagerly.

"Between us, yes, *yes*, my darling. As for the rest . . ."

"I'll leave for New York on the next crossing . . ." Perry promised.

"But now—while I'm still young enough, let's dance."

Less than ten days after Maggy's twentieth birthday Perry Kilkullen and his wife confronted each other in the library of their Park Avenue apartment. For two hours Mary Jane had not once raised her voice in anger or let an unguarded word escape her lips. She had listened quietly and without interruption to everything he had to say, her trim legs crossed neatly at the ankle, her pretty face almost expressionless, her hands lying quietly in her lap. She didn't even fiddle with any of her many rings. She wasn't making it tough for him, Perry thought, as he poured out all his arguments, all his reasons, all his pain at what he had to do to them. She seemed to be listening, really listening, to what he was telling her. Perhaps she, too, was anxious to make a true life for herself. Perhaps, in all the time he'd been gone, she had found someone who could love her as every woman should be loved. Finally he stopped, hoarse from talking. There was nothing now that she didn't know, nothing he hadn't confessed, and tried to explain.

A silence fell and lasted for so long that he almost began to speak again, to repeat himself, when she said, gently and so softly that he could barely hear her. "A divorce? I couldn't do that to you, Perry."

"But you'd be doing *nothing*. I'm totally to blame."

"I couldn't possibly abandon you, Perry. How could you expect me to be so cruel?" she said with a look of compassion.

"Mary Jane, stop twisting things. You wouldn't be abandoning me, I've abandoned you."

"You haven't done anything that can't be put right, Perry," she said, as kindly as if she were reassuring a frightened child. "You—oh, I suppose people would say that you've 'strayed'—people love to say things like that, I find—but as I see it, you've just made a mistake. It's serious but far from irreparable. Fortunately the church understands, the church will take you back when this is over."

"I thought you were *listening*, damn it!"

"I was. I heard every word. But Perry, poor Perry, you seem to forget that you have an immortal soul."

"Mary Jane, I'm a grown-up man. I'm forty-two—let me worry about my own soul."

"You're asking the impossible, Perry. Is it for *me* to decide that you are to be denied the life to come? If I *were* to agree, if you were able to get a divorce, if you married this girl during my lifetime, you'd be excommunicated. And it would be through my fault as much as your own."

"I'm willing to take that chance, Mary Jane."

"But I'm not willing to condemn you. And you know that you have no right to ask me to do so."

He looked at her narrowly. Was there the merest hint that she was playing a game with him, hiding behind piety? But on Mary Jane's face he saw only conviction and resolution and tranquillity, a fatal calmness that told him that there was no hope. She existed in a parallel world from his and there was no bridge of words that could be spun between them. Her belief negated the existence of his passion. Maggy and his love for her were not real to Mary Jane. They were merely an abstraction, a "state of sin" from which he could be redeemed by confession and penance and a return to her. He knew he had lost even as he continued to reason, to argue, to plead.

At last Perry left, defeated. Mary Jane looked at her watch and frowned. She had missed a meeting of the Guild of the Infant Saviour at which she had been supposed to preside. Still, nothing could be more important than making Perry understand that there was no circumstance under which she would weaken and doom him to an eternity without salvation.

As she picked up the phone to call and excuse her absence, she told herself that she could almost weep for him, for his pitiful delusion that he could hope to spend a single day of happiness outside of the church. Poor deluded, corrupted, dishonored Perry, so far gone that he was actually capable of imagining that Mary Jane McDonnell would ever allow herself to become the first woman in the long history of her clan to be divorced. That, she mused, as the phone rang, showed, more than anything else, how far into error he had fallen.

Perry lingered in New York for a few weeks, attempting to persuade members of his family who had influence with his wife to plead his cause for him. He failed utterly. The ranks of the Kilkullens and the Mackays were closed as far as the question of divorce was concerned. When he attempted to speak of Maggy only one of his sisters was even willing to listen, and she had always been the biggest gossip of the lot who just couldn't restrain her curiosity. He turned away from her, easily able to imagine what she would repeat in a horrified, delighted whisper, to one and then to another of his relatives. "A twenty-year-old artists' model, my dear—you know what *that* means."

How could he possibly convey Maggy's pure essence to them? How could he ever hope to make them understand? A few of his male relatives showed themselves not unsympathetic to his problem so long as he limited it to being nuts about some girl who wasn't his wife. It had happened to them too. To most of them, for that matter. But it had never led to divorce, not even to any thought of divorce. Why, several of them asked, wasn't he willing to just let things go as they had before? Many a Catholic had a girl on the side, why the hell was he rocking the boat?

Almost eight weeks passed before Perry was able to extricate himself from the business demands made on him by his partners now that he was in New York. He was buying time, he wrote Maggy. It would be at least another year before he had to return to the United States—perhaps longer.

He arranged for his Paris lawyer, *Maître* Jacques Hulot, to take charge of the household, so that she need never give it a thought. Hulot paid the servants, checked and settled all the household accounts and took care of Maggy's personal bills as well. One of the lawyer's clerks delivered a supply of cash to Maggy every week since no Frenchwoman was allowed to have a bank account in her own name. He didn't know what she might want to spend cash on, Perry wrote, but he wanted her purse always to be so full that any folly, any caprice could be satisfied. The only matter he neglected to recount in his daily letters to his love was the result of his meeting with his wife, and Maggy, in her own letters, didn't press for details.

Her mood was high-hearted, she assured him, she saw Paula frequently, she'd ordered a sable coat as he'd insisted before he left, she'd gone back to her English lessons and was becoming genuinely fluent; yes, she missed him terribly but since there was no one she truly wanted to be with but him, it wasn't quite the same feeling as being *lonely*, it wasn't as if he weren't coming back as soon as he could.

As he reread Maggy's letters in his rooms at the Yale Club, Perry Kilkullen thanked God that he was rich. So very, very rich that he need never worry about the approval of the rest of the world. His family could close its doors to them socially, but they couldn't prevent him from creating his own world with Maggy, a sweet, wide, adventurous world in which every desire could be fulfilled with the exception of a legal marriage. It would be a permanent arrangement of the kind that the French had a knack for understanding; Maggy would never feel that he was less than a true husband to her, divorce or no divorce. Of course she'd be bitterly disappointed when he finally had to tell her, but she was French, so she'd accept reality.

And as for the life to come and his immortal soul, about which Mary Jane was so damnably concerned, when he thought of Maggy, Perry Kilkullen knew that he was indestructible. His immortal soul could shift for itself.

Maggy came to meet him at Cherbourg. While Perry waited for his baggage to be cleared he saw her on the other side of the barrier, her face tense, almost drawn, with excitement. This was the moment he had conjured up, over and over during the long days of the stormy ocean crossing. Now, all at once, just seconds away, was the end of the painful weeks of separation, but even as he longed impatiently to take her in his arms he found himself wishing that she had not driven out to Cherbourg but had let him take the boat train into Paris. That train trip, those four dull hours of gentle progression, would surely have inspired him to find the precise words in which to present the future to Maggy in its best light. Mary Jane's refusal still hadn't formed itself into just the right, optimistic yet final, sequence of explanation, try as he would to find it.

Suddenly Maggy slipped under the barrier and ran toward him, throwing herself into his arms, covering his face with kisses. To the protesting customs inspector Maggy said something in such rapid slang that Perry couldn't understand it, but it left the man chuckling, blushing and unexpectedly benign.

"Oh, my darling, I have such news! It can't wait, really it can't! I was up at four in the morning to make sure to be here on time . . . oh, Perry!" She stopped abruptly and fell suddenly silent.

He scarcely made sense out of her words as he felt himself enter the circle of enchantment that her charm had created for him from the moment he had first seen her. Automatically he fell back into their teasing mode, as if they were continuing a conversation that had just been interrupted, even while he pressed her head closely between his hands, tenderly caressing her cheeks. "If it can't wait why don't you tell me?"

"I'm too shy," she said, her face rising out of the high collar of her fluffy, silky dark fur like a bunch of white violets.

"Since when have you been shy?" he asked. He had forgotten exactly how young her skin felt under his fingertips, he thought abstractedly.

"I've always been terribly shy. I just don't act it. People don't understand that about me because I don't have a shy look, I'm too tall," Maggy said rapidly, nervously.

"Is that what you got up so early in the morning to tell me? It's a fascinating subject, your height, but to lose half a night's sleep over it . . ."

"Guess," she demanded, drawing back a little, and putting a finger over his lips.

"You fired the cook?"

"Be serious," she pleaded.

"Darling, I haven't seen you in almost two months and your letters haven't hinted at the smallest mystery. Wait—I have it! You found a pearl in your oyster at Prunier's yesterday and you're having it made into a tiepin for me?"

"That's close, very close," she murmured.

"You've discovered a brilliant new little milliner no woman in Paris knows about yet, you've been offered a part in a film with Valentino, and you're leaving me to go to Hollywood, you've found a little château in the country that we can buy for weekends, you've learned to ice skate, you won a tango contest . . . must I go on or can I just kiss you again?"

Maggy took a deep breath and switched from French to English. "I am going to have a baby. No, *we* are going to have a baby."

"*That's impossible!*"

"I already have sickness in the morning," she said with timid pride.

"Maggy, you *can't* be pregnant . . . I've never been able to father a child . . ."

"When you change your woman, you change that possibility." Her mouth smiled but her eyes were tremendously anxious.

"I just can't believe it," he said numbly.

"Then you aren't happy? Oh, I've been so afraid you wouldn't be happy about it, oh, Perry, I'm so sorry . . ."

"No! My God, no! Don't be sorry, don't ever say that . . . it's the most incredible, the most—oh, darling, Maggy, you can't possibly know how much I've always wanted a child. I gave up hope so long ago . . . this is the most glorious news . . . sweet Jesus, I can't even begin to tell you . . ." Tears of joy sprang into his eyes, and fell down his cheeks and when she saw them, a touch of color came into her white face.

142

For weeks, Maggy had been caught between terror and exultance, between wild excitement and a million fears. Yet was she not to be his wife? It hadn't been until Perry had left for the United States that she began to wonder if she might be pregnant. Somehow she didn't dare to write about it. What if she were? What if she weren't? She had waited until a few weeks ago to see a doctor, as if not knowing for sure would make the whole situation disappear. Yet now Maggy was almost three months into her pregnancy as far as she and the doctor had been able to determine.

"Just thank heaven that it didn't happen sooner," Paula had said to her when she heard the news. "If Mistral, God forbid, had given you a baby, my girl, I'd advise you to get rid of it and don't think I don't know a dozen fancy doctors who'd do the job. But Perry is a man you can trust, an honest man, a good man, if I've ever met one. Granted, this matter of a divorce is inconvenient, but everything will be arranged, sooner or later, I don't doubt—Americans get divorced right and left, day and night, as far as I can make out. And then think, Maggy, a fine husband and a baby too, ah . . . a baby's the only good thing I've ever missed in my life, the only regret I have. But you my little one, you are going to have everything—and in such style! I have to admit it, I envy you."

Maggy had held on tightly to Paula's words, willing them to be true. Now she lay her head on Perry's shoulder. "Hug me, hug me, you don't know how much I've needed you." It wasn't until the chauffeur was driving the big Voisin steadily toward Paris that she brought herself to ask with studied lightness, "What happened, then, with your wife?"

"It's going to be absolutely all right, darling," he responded instantly. "It's just a question of time, that's our only problem."

"The Vatican can't be persuaded to rush, I suppose? Just a little tiny nudge?"

"Are you asking if I'll be divorced by the time the baby is born?"

"I guess . . . I *was* hoping for it," she admitted.

He hesitated before he spoke. "I'm afraid that will be impossible. But, Maggy, there's nothing, absolutely nothing to worry about—I swear, I *promise*. By the time our baby is grown up enough to know the difference it'll be ancient history—we'll be just another old married couple. The important thing is to take care of yourself so that nothing goes wrong."

143

"Wrong?"

"I want this baby so much, Maggy."

In May of 1928 Théodora Lunel was born. The name means "Gift of God" in Greek and both Maggy and Perry thought it perfect. She was a wise baby from her first day on earth, a baby who rarely cried, nursed efficiently, slept in the most satisfactorily thorough way and woke without a moment's crankiness. And she was extraordinarily beautiful. People who think all babies are beautiful have only to walk through a hospital nursery to discover that while all babies may be endearing in their smallness and helplessness, almost none are beautiful. Teddy, whose features were already arranged in a classic pattern of excellence, whose light red hair curled entrancingly, whose limbs were straight and perfect in every way, was the wonder of the nursery.

Perry Kilkullen felt marvelously justified. That undeniable, atavistic need for a continuation of his own existence that he had repressed for so long, burst forth with more power than any emotion he had ever known, until he had met Maggy. The deep human magic of a baby, his baby, absorbed him so completely that Maggy, confined to bed for the two weeks that were deemed necessary for a new mother, felt almost jealous, and then felt ashamed of herself as she recognized the source of her irritation.

The moments she most enjoyed were in the middle of the night when she was left alone to nurse for twenty minutes at a time. "Little bastard," she told the child in a low, loving whisper, "little adorable bastard, how can you look so contemplative? Such dignity, such a look of meditation on your face, even as you empty my breast, anyone would think you were born an heiress to a throne. Aah, but you take yourself seriously, don't you? Not even a thought for your poor old mother. Bastard that you are, and daughter of a bastard—little double bastard—you should pay me more attention. Just look at all the trouble that has gone into putting you in the world. I demand some respect. But what do you care about it? I didn't have a mother to nurse me, yet I survived. You are a luckier baby in every way, but . . . nevertheless—a bastard."

When Maggy and Perry were together they never talked of the fact that the baby bore Maggy's name. All that, as Perry repeatedly assured her, would be changed as soon as they got married. However, it preyed on Maggie's mind to a degree that surprised her. She

144

had not thought often of her own illegitimacy once she had put Tours and all those who knew her history behind her forever, but giving birth had brought it back as if she was still in the cruel schoolyard, fighting anyone who taunted her with such ferocity that even the strongest of them had learned to leave her alone. It seemed to her that if she called Teddy a bastard, no one else would do so . . . she was drawing out the poison before it had a chance to circulate in the baby's veins.

The only person to whom she revealed her fears and anxieties was Paula. Shortly after they had brought the baby home, Paula, who had often visited at the hospital, came to call for tea and scolded her roundly.

"For a Frenchwoman you are a proper fool, my girl, worrying about something that you know will be regularized. *Regularized*, I tell you! We have a national genius for regularization, we French. Why, just look around you—what could be more solidly luxurious, more perfectly organized, more *comme il faut* in every way than this magnificent establishment of yours? I personally cannot find the slightest fault with it, from the little Théodora's English Nanny Butterfield to those superb pearls you wear so casually around your neck. Look about you, Maggy. You are surrounded by everything a woman could possibly want to make her feel secure, by every evidence that Perry intends you to become his wife. You should be ashamed to even *think* the word 'bastard' about that glorious baby. All these legal details will be put right in a twinkling when the time comes. It's your unfortunate childhood that makes you so nervous, that's all." She helped herself to another miniature chocolate éclair. "Why, you even possess a pastry chef who has no equal, right in your own kitchen, you ungrateful girl."

"How materialistic you are, Paula," Maggy protested, laughing.

"Of course I am. And what is wrong with that? Now, where are you hiding that delicious scrap of an *enfant*? I want to take just one tiny bite out of her. You owe me that much."

Teddy had been born in a vintage year, a year in which the Kellogg-Briand Anti-War Pact was signed in Paris by fifteen nations, the pact that outlawed war forever. The sensation of the salon of 1928 was a full-length nude of Josephine Baker. The French public flocked to the movies to see Mary Pickford, Charlie Chaplin and Gloria Swanson, the house of Hermès made the first useful handbag that any woman had ever carried and Coco Chanel had become the mistress of the Duke of Westminster, the richest man in England. Jean Patou, who had had the idea of importing pretty young American girls on whom to show his clothes, was enjoying a great success with the development of a strong bias cut, and a new neutral called "greige" became the color for the most stylish women.

It was such a gentle, fruitful year that Maggy forgot her apprehensions and relaxed into the absorbed and playful life of a pampered young mother. The great world seemed to have nothing to do with her. Perry would read out loud to her from the newspapers as she lay watching Teddy perform the incredible act of sitting up and she would reply with an abstracted noise to the fact that two American men had gone around the world in the record time of twenty-three days, fifteen hours, twenty-one minutes and three seconds by steamer and airplane. She seemed to have abdicated an interest in the immediacy of his divorce, Perry decided, listening to her sing as she fed the baby on Nanny's day off. Maggy could wait placidly for it to come about, certain that wheels were turning mysteriously but surely in the Vatican, but he was not self-deluded enough to share the optimism for which he had been responsible.

Divorce was the first thing he thought about when he woke each morning and every day he resolved to take some action, but then, as each day wore on, he remembered the adamantine rejection with which Mary Jane had responded to the proposal and he allowed himself to be seduced into immobility because he was living the happiest life any man could hope for.

Teddy's first birthday passed and still he did nothing, in a trance of peace. During the summer of 1929 Perry and Maggy took the baby, her nurse and Maggy's personal maid to spend six weeks in a great beachfront hotel in Concarneau, where the cool air of Brittany was known to be so good for growing children. Teddy had become mobile, not a toddler but a swift-running little creature who remained miraculously upright until she reached the object of her lovely flight.

As Perry rolled a ball to her one day at the beach he noticed a group of four people sitting on a blanket not far away, under a big umbrella. He glanced at them and, in the instant that he did so, they glanced away. As Teddy ran up to him with the ball and collapsed in his lap with a laughing cry of "Papa, Papa!" his heart drained of blood. On the blanket sat two of his business associates and their wives. He looked at them again and saw that they had rearranged themselves adroitly so that none of them was facing in his direction. In spite of their tactful backs Perry knew that all they could be thinking about was the sight of him and his child, that all they would talk about as soon as they left the beach was Perry Kilkullen and his bastard daughter.

He picked Teddy up and walked off the beach, holding her in such a tightly protective grasp that she squirmed. Bitterly, savagely he damned himself for a coward. Oh, he had bought happiness all right, bought it for almost two years at the cost of lying to Maggy every minute of every day although she didn't know it. Yes, she had been willing to live with him before there had been any question of marriage. But reminding himself of that didn't help him to feel less ignoble. Maggy had exercised her right to choose. But what rights did Teddy have? What future was there for her? What kind of father was he to his child, his only child, the child of his heart?

Perry went to consult the lawyer, *Maître* Jacques Hulot, before he returned to do battle with Mary Jane in New York. If there was the slightest chance of some legal wrinkle that he could take advantage of by becoming a French citizen, he was ready to change nationalities. Hulot ponderously announced that he was unable to help him, he could not use French law for his convenience. As Perry rose to go, the lawyer leaned forward over his immense desk. "One moment, Monsieur Kilkullen," he said, raising his hand commandingly.

For two years he had supervised the payments of enormous sums of money that this rich and headstrong American spent so easily to maintain what must be a juicy and accomplished mistress. He had resented being used to expedite the man's private life, so that no one of his American world would know how he lived and with whom. How dare Kilkullen, who could afford to dissipate such vast amounts without thinking twice, presume to discuss French citizenship? Why did he not avail himself of his own Reno, Nevada?

"We are both men of the world, are we not?" Hulot said with satisfaction. "This need not, after all, be considered a tragedy. It must seem to you now that everything is conspiring against you to deny you your wish to marry Mademoiselle Lunel. Yet, in ten years, in even five perhaps, will you not be grateful that the church and the state, which possess more wisdom than you realize, have prevented you from escaping into this impetuous liaison? When the day comes that you find a new, different . . . *friend* . . . will you not be glad for the restrictions. . . ?'' He stopped, as Perry came around the desk and grabbed him by the lapels until he was pulled out of his chair.

"Never, *never* speak of Mademoiselle Lunel again!" He released the lawyer. Until he could engage another one, he still needed this man's services, damn him. Hulot had all the financial reins of the household in his hands. Perry Kilkullen rushed out of the legal chambers and stalked, enraged, through the streets of Paris. Perfumed gusts of insinuating air drifted alluringly around every corner. When, Perry asked himself in angry despair, did the cynical French, the mean-minded, hardhearted French, *keep* all the promises that they made implicit by the fatal fairness of their skies and the wanton intoxication of their city? When a man and woman who should not fall in love, did fall in love, as everything French invited them to do, then God help them.

As soon as it was possible after his conversation with Hulot, Perry left once more for New York, determined to wrest a consent for a divorce from Mary Jane. It was the middle of October before she would agree to see him. He found her thinner than ever and looking far older than the passage of two years should warrant. She was a graying, middle-aged woman, only dimly pretty now, he thought with surprise, while she gazed at him with her pale blue eyes and noted, with a searing flash of bitterness, that he looked positively young. She could see in him too much of the man she had married. Time had treated him lightly. Unfair, oh, *unfair.*

"Mary Jane, I have a daughter."

"Surely you don't think that's news to me, Perry? I don't believe I have a friend in the world who hasn't managed to let slip that information. Do you expect me to congratulate you?"

"Doesn't her existence change the picture, for Christ's sake? It's no longer just a matter of your religious convictions or my excommunication, it's a matter of my only child's future. If I'm willing to risk hellfire and eternal damnation and any and all punishments the church promises me, why won't you let go?"

"I feel no responsibility for her future. She was conceived in sin and born in sin and she is nothing to me. But God's law is clear and I, at least, intend to obey it."

"Mary Jane, I can't believe you mean that. You're not a hard woman . . ."

"How would you know? How would you know what kind of woman I've become? How many years has it been since you turned away from me? Go away, Perry. You and your bastard disgust me!"

She left Perry alone in the library looking out at the unfriendly gray stones of Park Avenue, touching in his pocket the photographs of Teddy he had brought with him to soften the heart of this woman who, he now realized, would only have been further inflamed by them. He was glad Mary Jane had finally gotten angry. Now that she had vented some of her real feelings, now that she had given up her pose of the saint who was thinking only of his salvation, they could surely find a way to work it out. He would be back, in a week, in two weeks, every week for a year if that was what it took. The essential thing was not to give up. Eventually she must give in. He went back to the Yale Club and tried to exorcise his frustration on the squash court. It was that or howl out loud.

Two weeks later, on October 29, 1929, the stock market collapsed. "Coolidge prosperity" vanished as almost seventeen million shares of stock were sold at steadily declining prices. For the next frantic weeks Perry had all he could do to help cope with the panic of the investors whose money he and his partners handled. He saw no chance of leaving New York at any time in the near future, so he wrote Maggy to leave Paris and come to the United States with Teddy.

"Thank heaven I learned English," Maggy said to Paula as she supervised the packing of one of her six steamer trunks.

"Has this American financial trouble affected Perry's fortune?" Paula asked in concern. In just a few weeks the number of free-spending American customers at her restaurant had dwindled to almost nothing.

"I don't know, but I shouldn't think so, he's so clever, after all. I've never discussed money with him. It's been like a magic carpet— often I have even forgotten to ask a price when I buy something."

"No!" Paula was horrified. It was one thing to be kept in the manner of a duchess but not to ask a price was un-French.

"But yes." Maggy giggled. "Like one of those American tourists. I'm so glad to see I've finally shocked you. I knew there was something that could."

Paula sniffed dismissively. She didn't really believe Maggy . . . it was too exaggerated to be true, she thought, looking at Maggy, who was holding a drift, a river of gauzy, quicksilver luxuriance, the silks and velvets and metallic brightness of her dresses rustling and shimmering as they dripped softly from her arms.

Maggy dropped the clothes on the bed and darted over to Paula and gave her a hug. "Why don't you come with me? I invite you—you've never been anywhere outside of Paris, darling sewer rat."

"Thank you but no. I'm too old to displace myself. Why should I travel to see skyscrapers when I've successfully resisted the temptation to view Mont St. Michel? Paris will always be sufficient for me. But when will you be back?"

"I can't really be sure—as soon as all this quiets down."

"I hope it's soon," Paula grumbled. "It's bad for business, this stock market nonsense."

Nine days later Maggy disembarked in New York. She walked down the gangplank holding Teddy's hand firmly, trying to control her own excitement and leaping anticipation. Behind her followed Nanny Butterfield, the pleasant Englishwoman who was still Teddy's nurse. The passage had been quiet and uneventful, the ship crowded with subdued, worried passengers, many of them expatriates coming back to see what had happened to the investments that enabled them to live in Europe. Perry had arranged to meet them at the pier and take them directly to the furnished apartment he'd rented.

Maggy stood under an enormous letter L in the long, dark customs shed, looking about her with wide, smiling eyes. She had dressed so carefully for this reunion. The tiny veil of her green satin cloche just reached to the tip of her nose. Her slim, sable-collared, green wool coat had a short attached cape, trimmed in another wide band of dark sable—nothing, she thought, could be more romantic, yet she couldn't help but shiver in the New York wind, a chill, whirling dirty wind that smelled so unfamiliar. Her smile faded after a while as an officious inspector insisted that she open every last trunk and suitcase. Teddy was whimpering, and Nanny Butterfield was anxious to feed her lunch. Where was Perry? Why wasn't he here to take charge? All around her people were directing porters to put their luggage on trolleys. The gloomy shed was almost empty before Maggy was cleared to leave. Three porters loaded her belongings and one of them asked her, "Where to, lady? Is there a car waiting for you or do you need a taxi? All this stuff won't fit in less than two cabs."

"I must telephone," Maggy said distractedly, looking everywhere for Perry's tall figure.

"Right over there."

She was in the phone booth before she realized that she had no American money in her handbag. How could Perry be so late? So inconsiderate? It was inexcusable. Maggy went back to the porter. "Could you please lend me the necessary coin for the telephone? And please, could you also show me how it works?"

"Sure, lady. Your first visit, right? Come on, follow me." He put the nickel in the slot for her and gave the operator the number she told him, that of Perry's office in Wall Street. Then he shut the door of the phone booth and waited outside, wondering with what she expected to tip him.

"May I speak to Mr. Perry Kilkullen, please?"

"Oh. Oh, I'll let you speak to his secretary. Who may I say is calling?"

"Miss Lunel."

"Just a moment."

When a second woman's voice answered, Maggy said impatiently, "Please, this is Miss Lunel. Can you tell me where Mr. Kilkullen is? He was supposed to meet me hours ago."

"Is this one of Mr. Kilkullen's clients?" the woman asked, uncertainty and caution in her voice.

"Certainly not," Maggy said in mounting anger.

"Are you a friend of his, Miss Lunel?"

"Yes, of course," Maggie snapped. "Now may I speak to him? This is absurd!"

"You don't know," the voice said blankly. It was not a question, yet not a statement.

"Know . . . know what?"

"I'm sorry to be the one . . . it's most . . . everyone here is so upset . . . Mr. Kilkullen had a heart attack playing squash four days ago. I'm afraid . . . he didn't survive."

"Mr. Perry Kilkullen?" Maggy said mechanically. It must be one of his relatives, one of the other Kilkullens. The mouth of the telephone gaped at her, like a crucial organ that has been chopped in half. Blood would gush from it.

"Yes. I'm so sorry. The funeral took place yesterday, it was in all the newspapers. Is there nobody else here you'd like to speak to? Is there anything I can do to help you?"

"No, no, no."

12

If it had not been for Nanny Butterfield, Maggy asked herself when she was again able to think coherently, how could she have lived through the next minutes, the next hours, the next days? The sensible Englishwoman had taken over completely, coping with all the practical necessities while Maggy was made mute and blank with shock, and all but paralyzed by a disbelieving grief, a rending anguish that snapped through her flesh and bone like the metal jaws of a trap set for an unwary animal.

Nanny Butterfield hunted up the ship's purser and changed Maggy's sum of francs into dollars, she asked him for the name of a hotel and settled them in two adjoining rooms at the Dorset and she put Maggy to bed with the aid of the hotel doctor. For the next few days she treated the shattered woman as if she were the age of Teddy, coaxing her to eat a few mouthfuls and sitting with her until she fell into a drugged sleep.

When Maggy woke in the morning it was to raw pain, so brutal that she couldn't bear to remain under the covers because of the thoughts that attacked her there. Trembling with cold, no matter how warm her robe, she stood in front of the bathroom mirror, afraid to meet her image, tears draining from her eyes into the washbasin for long moments before she could bring herself to make the necessary movements to brush her teeth and wash her face. Every detail of grooming was like a pinnacle of ice over which she had to haul the burden of her bruised, aching body.

Getting dressed was impossible. Maggy spent the week in a nightgown and robe, pacing her overheated room gazing at the walls obsessively, as if their bland cream surfaces could blot out the unbearable. For hours on end, with the curtains tightly drawn and the lamps lit all day long, Maggy walked, shivering, shoulders hunched, toiling back and forth, as if she might die of the torment if she dared to stop her ceaseless movement. She was afraid to go to bed until she dropped on it from exhaustion.

Only when she was worn out did Nanny bring in Teddy to cuddle for a minute in her arms. Maggy held the child in weary blankness until Teddy, lively and easily bored, climbed out of her arms and ran off to play. Her baby was the only warm thing in the world, Maggy thought, her brain working slowly. Her hands were freezing even when she put them in her armpits to warm them. Her feet were icy, although they were snug in her fur-lined slippers. She was like someone who had been skating, fearless and agile, on a sunlit silver lake, until, in the space of an instant, she had fallen through the ice into the lethal chill of Arctic water. Drowned . . . drowned. But Teddy was warm. She could not drown, she must not drown because Teddy was still warm.

"Are we to return to Paris, Madame?" Nanny Butterfield asked, seeing that Maggy was ready to face the future.

"How much money do I have left?"

"About three hundred dollars, Madame."

"I must cable *Maître* Hulot for more—that won't be enough for the tickets," Maggy said dully.

His answering cable arrived the next day.

DEEPEST REGRETS FOR YOUR LOSS. MR. PERRY KILKULLEN LEFT NO INSTRUCTIONS TO DISBURSE MONIES BEYOND THAT OF PAYING HOUSEHOLD AND PERSONAL BILLS ON A MONTHLY BASIS. THESE HAVE BEEN ALL SETTLED. NO FURTHER SUMS CAN BE ADVANCED. HAVE TURNED ALL ESTATE MATTERS OVER TO HIS NEW YORK ATTORNEY MR. LOUIS FAIRCHILD OF 45 BROADWAY, ADVISE YOU CONTACT HIM FOR ANY FURTHER ASSISTANCE.   MAÎTRE JACQUES HULOT

"Look at this," Maggy said, handing the cable to Nanny Butterfield, too stunned for indignation.

"He's washing his hands of us," the Englishwoman said bluntly.

"I'd better go and see Mr. Fairchild," she said listlessly.

"Quite so, and soon . . ." She looked at Maggy, dead pale, standing helplessly, her eyes raw and rimmed with red, her face swollen from the endless, futile tears. "Why don't you write to him and make an appointment? And, Madame, today you really should get dressed and take a nice walk with Teddy and me. It's very pleasant in the park and it will make a change for you. Lovely, brisk weather they have here."

"Oh, no, Nanny, I couldn't."

"Indeed you *must*," she said with a mild authority that no child and few adults had ever questioned.

Three days later Maggy faced Louis Fairchild in his office. She had spent hours every day in the park with Teddy and that morning she had had her hair done in Richard Block's salon where they were able to set it almost as well as Antoine had in another life. Maggy had put on her bravest red lipstick for this interview.

"Thank you for making the time to see me," she said to the worried-looking, gray-haired man.

"Not at all. I must say I was astonished when I received your letter . . ."

"You *do* know who I am?" she asked anxiously.

"Of course, but poor Perry never told me you were coming to New York. May I say how terribly, terribly sorry I am. He was a very good friend, a dear friend. I still can't believe it . . . such a young man and with no history of . . ."

"Mr. Fairchild," Maggy begged, "please stop. I can't talk about it. I've come to you for advice. Would you read this cable and tell me what I am to do?"

He looked at it carefully for long, considering minutes and then shook his head. "I *told* Perry to make a will! I told him once if I told him a dozen times, but he just never got around to it. Like most men of his age he thought he had all the time in the world."

"I don't understand . . . just tell me please what is my *position?*"

"Position? I'm very much afraid that you have . . . none."

"But he was getting divorced! We were going to be married!" she cried.

"He died a married man, Miss Lunel. Legally you don't have any claims. Unfortunately there's nothing on paper."

"But Teddy, our daughter! What about her? Doesn't she have any rights?" Maggy's voice was incredulous.

"I'm sorry—but no." Louis Fairchild thought that if Mary Jane

155

Kilkullen wasn't so bitter he might have been able to persuade her into giving the child something, however little. But it was because of the bastard, she insisted, that her husband had died in a state of mortal sin, that Frenchwoman and her bastard.

"*But he promised . . .*" Maggy broke off. The only emotion she had felt since she had arrived in New York was loss, endless loss. Now rage closed her throat. She saw herself as she must look, sitting there keening "he promised," like millions of other women since the beginning of time. Foolish women, childlike women, victimized women, stupid, *inexcusably, criminally stupid* women who believed in their men, those careless men who took what they wanted, those loving men who failed to make the most basic provisions for the women they should have protected. Men who lied and lied and lied. Julien Mistral and Perry Kilkullen. She pulled herself up tall in her chair and looked at the unhappy lawyer.

"Please, Mr. Fairchild, what precisely do I own in the world?"

"Your personal property, such as jewelry and furs and any other specific gifts Mr. Kilkullen may have made to you, a car perhaps?"

"Our apartment in Paris?"

"It will be disposed of, with all its contents, before the estate is settled."

"Disposed of," Maggy said, fury making her voice calm and businesslike. "I hope somebody remembered to pay the servants."

"*Maître* Hulot is in correspondence with me about that."

"They, I trust, will get some compensation for being thrown out of work without warning? That's only proper, is it not? And, fortunately for them, they have lost only their jobs. *Tiens*, I should have taken lessons in something useful."

"What are you going to do?" Louis Fairchild said. He really didn't want to know, he didn't want to sit and contemplate the future of this dazzling, but utterly dispossessed woman. However, mere decency demanded that he try to be helpful.

"Ah, that is something I shall have to consider carefully." Maggy gathered her silver fox furs about her and began to put on her long, gray gloves.

"If there's any advice I can give you . . ."

"Perhaps you could give me the name of an honest jeweler. I think that it would be sensible to get rid of some of those small pieces I never seem to find time to wear," Maggy said as casually as she could. The hotel bill was due again at the end of the week.

Fairchild scribbled a name on his card. "This is the fellow I always go to for my wife's birthday. Tell him you're a friend of mine. Look . . ." he hesitated, embarrassed to propose a loan to the most desirable woman he'd ever seen in his life, "if you need some cash, I'd be glad to be of service . . ."

"Thank you, that's very kind, but it won't be necessary," Maggy said with a reflex of pride. There were some things she just could not do. Not yet at least.

Louis Fairchild saw her to the elevator and then returned to his desk miserably. What an unholy mess. He supposed she'd go back to Paris and find a husband. Girls like that could always find husbands. And if he were to be honest with himself, he didn't really blame Kilkullen. If he'd had a chance at a girl like that himself, he'd have grabbed it too. Only he'd have had the common sense to make a will. At least he hoped he would. A girl like that could make you forget a lot of things you were supposed to do.

That night Maggy opened her jewel case for the first time since she'd been in the United States. The pretty, flashing pieces looked like childhood toys, long forgotten. Thoughtfully she put the real jewels into one pile. In another heap, much larger than the first, she laid the costume jewelry she much preferred for its cleverness; the lapel pins and necklaces she had collected from Chanel, who dictated, "Wear anything you like so long as it looks like junk."

Nevertheless, there should be enough here to keep them in comfort for a long, long time, she mused. Perry had loved to take her into a jeweler's for no reason at all, when they were out walking in the neighborhood of Place Vendôme, and demand that she pick out something to celebrate the sheer joy of the moment. "To celebrate Teddy's fourth tooth," he'd declare, or "Because you have the pinkest nipples in Paris."

Resolutely she took all the real jewels, with the exception of her pearls—a woman had to have her pearls—and her favorite bracelet, out of their velvet cases and tucked them into her handbag. She couldn't afford to be sentimental and, besides, she was finished, utterly finished, with sentiment, finished with an emotion that led, sooner or later, to mortal weakness.

Maggy found it impossible to forgive herself. She had been a "poire," that classic French laughingstock, the foolish true believer, the butt of practical jokes, the person who almost asks people to take advantage of her. Since her interview with Louis Fairchild, Maggy felt as if she had grown centuries wiser and harder. She would never believe in a man again, Maggy knew in her soul, and as the knowledge flowed into her she felt warmed, strengthened and oddly alert. It was not a happy thing to find out, at twenty-two, that no man—whether he loved you truly or not—could ever be trusted. It was not a happy thing to finally realize that you could depend on no one but yourself. But it was a clean realization without the possibility of question marks or exceptions. The dirty, freezing, winter water in which she had been struggling receded, leaving her on dry land, barren and unwelcoming land perhaps, but so much less frightening now that she understood that she had only her own two feet to support her. She had been in that situation before and survived . . . it was familiar territory.

Maggy drew herself up to her full height and looked at herself sternly in the mirror. You have nowhere to go but straight ahead, she told herself, and firmly put her mind to planning the perfect costume in which to sell her jewelry. First the black, plainly cut, Vionnet dress. Then her black Schiaparelli coat, a complete transformation from last season, with its wide, padded epaulet shoulders and double-breasted, wooden-soldier silhouette. It looked as martial as she wanted to feel, severe, dashing and above all, absolutely new. With it she'd wear a strict black Caroline Reboux felt hat, its angular line strikingly defined. Did she look widowed? Surely that was the effect all that black gave—but not a pathetic widow who could be led into a mistake of judgment.

The next day, clad in her arrogant armor, Maggy walked calmly into Tiffany's in search of the salesman whose name Louis Fairchild had given her. He brightened as she introduced herself.

"I find myself with some jewels that no longer suit me," Maggy said casually. "Mr. Louis Fairchild told me that you might be able to help me dispose of them."

The salesman's face fell. "You mean buy them back from you?"

"They weren't bought here—they were made in Paris."

"But, Madame, we never buy back even our own jewelry, it's a policy of the company."

"Do other American jewelers have the same policy?" Maggy asked casually, allowing herself to sound mildly surprised.

"So far as I know. Particularly these days, Madame. There are so many ladies who are discovering that they have more jewelry than they need."

"Indeed. Ah well—how—inconvenient." She hesitated, sighed and then gave him a lightning, sideways look, overtly conspiratorial and mischievous.

He coughed discreetly. "Look, you'd have more luck in a smaller store. Those little jewelers are more flexible. They're in business for themselves so they're always on the lookout for a good buy."

"Do you recommend any of them?" Maggy asked with a wicked appealing note in her voice that made him yearn to kill dragons for her.

"Recommend? No, I wish I could go that far. But there's a fellow around the corner, on Madison, down a couple of blocks, who's got a nice little place—Harry C. Klein. But it is only a suggestion, not a recommendation, you understand."

"Of course, and I'm grateful to you. You've been most kind."

"Say, listen, it was a pleasure. You're the first person I've talked to all day. But this Wall Street panic can't last. So when you're in the market again come back and see me. Tiffany's will still be here." He looked after Maggy with wistful lust. He'd give almost anything to see her wearing that new ruby and diamond necklace with the matching earrings. And nothing else, no, not even a pair of high-heeled shoes.

Harry C. Klein had had a bad morning. An old customer had come in to have a sapphire ring he'd sold her a number of years ago put into a new setting. She had insisted on "sitting with" her stone while the work went on so that it couldn't be switched for one of less value. Paranoid! Everybody was going bananas. He'd almost told her to go away and find a jeweler she could trust but, business being what it was, he'd agreed. The men in the workroom would be furious. And now this young woman had just tipped out a bunch of pieces on his counter. Did she think he was Santa Claus? Nobody in his right mind was interested in adding to his inventory. He looked at the clips and earrings and bracelets with a quickly appraising eye.

"I can see you're definitely no gold digger," he sighed to Maggy. "Too bad. Melée—that's what you've got."

"*Melée*—but in French that means a fight, a struggle in a crowd," she said puzzled.

"For jewelers it just means a lot of little stones." Morosely he flipped over a pair of large clips thickly paved in tiny diamonds. "See, no big stones."

"But big stones are dull!" Maggy exclaimed. "I only wanted to wear amusing pieces, the witty ones—big stones are for old princesses at the Opera or for the Dolly Sisters—they are too serious for me."

"Big stones are for *resale*," he said, wagging a lecturing finger in her face.

"I never thought of jewelry as an investment," Maggy said in a low voice. She pushed out of her mind the gay lunches in the Ritz garden followed by the lighthearted search for a glittering folly in a jeweler's window. So even there she had been a *poire*—Perry would have given her anything she fancied; acres of those thick diamond bracelets she had scorned as "service stripes."

"Lady, lady, don't you know that jewelry is only an investment if you plan to hold onto it for fifty years? And even then it's a crapshoot. Sure you can always sew it into the lining of your skirt and flee the country. But where would you go? I'm talking *resale*, lady, not investment. I'm talking about getting something *close* to what you paid for it. Resale means big stones and even then only if they're good quality, good clarity. Better a two-carat ruby with the right strawberry gleam than a five-carat ruby that's a bit off."

"But look at these designs, this workmanship!" Maggy exclaimed angrily. Could all her treasures be worthless? This man must be trying to rob her.

"Means nothing. Only the weight of the stones and the value of the metal settings count when you go to sell *melée*. Look, I have a safe full of loose stones upstairs, little ones like these, maybe not as fine, but fine enough. I bought them at wholesale. I couldn't offer you anything except considerably less than wholesale, because with your fancy, funny piece there's a lot of labor involved just to break them up to get the stones out. Anyway, I can't buy them because my business is strictly a question of supply and demand and ever since the Crash, demand has disappeared." He looked at her pearls and nodded in regret. "Those cost a fortune, didn't they? Burmese, I'll bet? And then the Japanese learned how to cultivate them and now . . ." He sighed mournfully at the sight of the gleaming, once

160

coveted objects that even Maggy had known were impossible to sell.

"So," Maggy sighed, echoing his mood, touching her lovely, devalued fantasies, "*Bubkes* . . . nothing."

"*Bubkes?*" he said, startled. "You're a Jewish girl?"

"But of course. Does that turn my *melée* into one big valuable ruby?"

"No such luck. But what's a beautiful Jewish girl like you doing without her basic diamond solitaire?" Harry C. Klein demanded severely. "How come you didn't get, at least, your major sapphire, your important ruby? Smart you weren't."

"Smart I wasn't," Maggy agreed emphatically, grinning in spite of herself at his outrage. She unfastened the row of big brass curtain-ring clips that Schiaparelli had used in place of coat buttons and slipped out of her narrow sleeves. Mr. Klein's shop was overheated and it had occurred to her that in her black dress she looked even more definitely widowed than with her coat on. Perhaps this nice man had a soft spot for Jewish widows? It was worth trying to sell her *melée*, even for next to nothing.

"Wait a minute—what's this?" He grasped her arm and took a look at the bracelet she had decided to keep.

"More *melée*, I suppose, plus some emeralds."

"Those emeralds look interesting. Take it off, I'll take a better look—with your luck there's something wrong with them." He examined the bracelets with his jeweler's loupe, scrutinizing each emerald in turn. Finally, with a grunt of satisfaction he gave it back to Maggy. "Good, very good. For these emeralds I don't mind making an exception. So what if I don't sell them for a long time?"

"You mean you want to buy the bracelet?"

"Definitely, and I'll give you the fairest possible price. Have it appraised first if that'll make you happier, be my guest."

"But Mr. Klein," Maggy said sharply, "I don't want to sell just the bracelet, I want to sell everything. The person who buys the bracelet has to take the other pieces too."

Totally dumb she wasn't, Harry C. Klein thought with a mixture of pleasure and gloom. The chances of a small jeweler like himself ever being able to buy four perfectly matched emeralds of two carats each was remote. An important jeweler might have to wait a long while before laying his hands on such a set. You could make two pairs of magnificent earrings from them or even a necklace—no, *two* necklaces with two emeralds in each, surrounded by diamonds. If stones like that ever lost their value, nothing they've dug up since the days of King Solomon's Mines would be worth anything. Even if he had to sit on the emeralds for years, he couldn't pass them up.

Maggy put the bracelet back on and reached for her coat.

"Where are you going?"

"To find somebody who'll buy the lot."

"All right, all right. Don't start to shop around, it'll only confuse you. We'll make a deal . . . don't be in such a hurry."

She looked at him suspiciously and then relaxed. He hadn't had to tell her that the emeralds were good . . . but first she'd get that appraisal.

By the time Maggy concluded the sale of her jewelry to Harry C. Klein they had become good friends. He knew her sad history: the French husband, handsome David Lunel, who had invested so unwisely in the United States and, while investigating the extent of his losses in New York, had died in an automobile crash, leaving her stranded with their baby daughter. He knew of Rabbi Taradash and of her grandmother and even of her grandmother's secret recipe for *pot-au-feu,* but he knew nothing of the fevers of Montparnasse nights or of a painter named Mistral or of a comic carefree girl who had let her green silk kimono slip off her naked body unconcernedly in front of the eyes of anyone who would pay to paint her. When the time came for the delivery of the twelve thousand dollars that Maggy's jewels finally fetched, of which the lion's share was paid for the emeralds, Harry C. Klein took a proprietary interest in her future.

"I suppose you're going to take the little girl and go back home? Maybe start a little business? You can do a lot with that much cash these days."

"I haven't really decided."

Maggy walked up Madison Avenue slowly, deep in thought, her check safely tucked inside her brassiere. She had a nest egg, enough to provide for herself and Teddy for four or five years in moderate comfort if she found a small flat in an unfashionable part of Paris. But when her money ran out, what would she do? What sort of small business could she establish, untrained as she was? And what if the business failed and she lost all her money? Could she get a job as a *vendeuse* perhaps, in one of those shops in which she used to lavish Perry's money without asking the prices?

162

She looked around her and sniffed the air. It was a few weeks before Christmas: the bright blue day flapped around her like a flag. New York was stunningly alive with a crackle of promise, an irresistible rush of vitality that made Paris seem old-fashioned, tradition-laden, unbeckoning. Why not make a clean break? Why not stay here where she was Mrs. Lunel, a widow, rather than go back to a country where too many people knew too much about her? Excitedly she turned and almost ran the short blocks back to the jewelry store.

"It's too late to change your mind. We agreed, fair market value," Mr. Klein said, looking up as she burst in, cheeks flaming.

"I've got to get a job! Here in New York! I'm not going back to France, I've just decided . . ."

"Doing what?"

"I don't know. Do you have any ideas for me?"

"A girl who's never worked a day in her life—are you kidding?"

"Well, I have done a little modeling."

"What kind of model?"

"For . . . fashion designers."

"So." He looked her over carefully. He didn't know anything about fashion models but he knew a stunner when he saw one. "I have a friend who's in the fashion business, we play poker twice a month, Italian fellow. He's done very well—a boy from the old neighborhood but today you'd never know it. Alberto Bianchi—we used to play stickball, today he's pretty fancy. I'll give him a call, see if there's anything doing." He retreated to his back office to telephone and returned beaming. "Maybe they can use a girl—just maybe. One of their regular models took off with the husband of their best client. The fellow decided to give himself a Christmas present for a change. Go quick—these days jobs don't stay empty long. Here's the address and here's," he said, giving Maggy a quick kiss on her cheek, "a kiss for good luck."

Maggy was as nervous as a goldfish as she approached the entrance to Bianchi's. The glass doors on East Fifty-fifth Street were smoked, and there were no show windows flanking them, merely the discreet bricks of a modernized townhouse.

She entered through the doors and, for the first moment since she'd been in New York, she felt immediately at home. Shocked, she stood still and breathed deeply. All around her the pulse of the establishment beat with a rhythm so familiar that she recognized it in her blood, the rhythm of a *maison de couture*. The sounds were the ones she knew: the voices behind fitting-room doors, those of the saleswomen deferential and unruffled, those of the customers high-pitched, indecisive and spoiled. The smells were the same; the mingled perfumes of a hundred rich women lingered in the air mixed with the smoke from their cigarettes, underlaid by the pungent aromas of new fabric and fur.

Her heart lurched as she drank in the atmosphere, that special distillation, that intensity that goes to a woman's head like a bolt of electricity, compounded of the million fantasies that had been brought to this place; fantasies of how a woman might look if she found that right, that perfect dress; of how that perfect dress would transform her; fantasies that placed a greater belief on the power of clothes than clothes could ever fulfill.

It was the Lourdes of vanity, Maggy thought. Here they came, not to be cured but to be made into their dreams of themselves; younger, more beautiful, thinner, more desirable. The concentrated force of these fantasies seemed strong enough to blow the walls of the dressmaker's apart, yet a controlled calm reigned over the gray-velvet, mirrored reception room.

Patricia Falkland, a beautifully tailored, dark-haired middle-aged woman, sat behind a polished desk on which stood only a single bud vase containing one white rose. She had worked for Alberto Bianchi for years, supervising all the salespeople and fulfilling the absolutely necessary role of mediator between saleswomen and clients. She never acted as a saleswoman herself but she was responsible for giving advice to vacillating customers, and for dealing with all the personnel of the house. Sizing up new customers was her specialty.

Miss Falkland could spot, in a dowdy, middle-aged woman, the wife of a major meat packer from Chicago who would spend thousands of dollars, as easily as she could pick out the young society woman, dressed in the latest fashion, wearing every evidence of luxury, who would never settle her bills. She knew each one of the wealthy women of New York who preferred to come to Bianchi for his brilliantly edited copies of Chanel and Vionnet and Lanvin, rather than going to Paris for their clothes. Throughout the 1920s, although fashion was dictated absolutely by Paris, there were many American women who refused to devote several months of each crowded year to traveling back and forth to France and subjecting themselves to the exhausting round of collections and fittings.

As Maggy entered, Patricia Falkland pursed her lips in an inaudible imperceptible whistle, that whistle of unqualified approval that few women ever elicited from her. Maggy embodied an ideal that the richest women couldn't buy. As Patricia Falkland's eyes traveled their customary swift path upward, taking in all the details of Maggy's ensemble, from the exquisite, perfectly polished shoes to the cunningly wrought hat, she knew that she was looking at someone who was dressed in the original of the clothes that Alberto Bianchi would be reproducing for his customers, someone who was dressed in the *real thing,* that uncapturable essence of Paris that could never be duplicated, no matter how closely they copied fabric for fabric, seam for seam, button for button. *How the hell do those bastards do it?* She always asked herself that question when she saw Parisian dressmaking at its best, and it was still the only question for which she had no answer.

For a second, neither of the women spoke. Maggy stood, looking around the reception room, with that inimitable air of a prospective customer that the atmosphere of the room had brought out in her, that stance; appraising, judgmental, yet absolutely sure of her welcome, which she had grown into during the last two luxurious years. It was a stance that could never be achieved by deliberate practice, never assumed by anyone who wasn't accustomed to spending a great deal of money. It came from an inner, unconscious attitude toward clothes. It said, as if she had spoken aloud, "There isn't anything you have to sell me that I cannot buy if I choose. But will I? It is for you to tempt me. And even then I may be so sated that I will refuse to be lured. Spread your best out in front of me. If I want it I will have it. Or perhaps not—that is for me to decide."

The instant of silence passed as Patricia Falkland rose deferentially and advanced toward Maggy. "May I help you, Madame?" she asked in the voice she reserved for the best customers.

"I hope so," Maggy replied.

"If you'd like to sit down, I'll call a saleslady immediately." Miss Falkland smiled as if to apologize because a saleslady had not materialized out of the floor at Maggy's arrival.

"No, please do not trouble. I would like to speak to someone about the modeling job."

"A job?" she repeated as her smile vanished.

"I understand that you need a model. I would like to apply for the position."

"That's quite impossible," Miss Falkland said sharply, a clear note of anger in her voice. How dare this woman waltz in the salon giving herself the airs and graces of a customer when she wanted a job? It was quite outrageous. It was unforgivable. Absolutely unheard of. Her heart hardened toward Maggy who had caused her to make a mistake in the judgment of which she was so proud. It was infuriating to have been caught putting on her most welcoming manner for a mere job hunter.

"I was informed by my friend Mr. Harry Klein that the House of Bianchi needs a dress model. Mr. Klein talked to Mr. Bianchi himself, no more than a quarter of an hour ago, so I came immediately."

"Mr. Bianchi is looking for a professional model, a working girl, not a dilettante. We pay thirty-five dollars a week, which wouldn't buy one of your shoes, and our girls work like brutes for that money, or they don't last a week. We'd never even consider someone without experience."

"Please, give me a trial," Maggy insisted. This female, she thought, is not going to get rid of me. I'm no longer a sniveling child who is too modest to take off her knickers. "Mr. Bianchi told Mr. Klein he needed . . ."

Patricia Falkland heard and noted the determination and stubbornness in Maggy's tone. For years she had deplored the masculine aberration that led her employer to continue to keep up an association with his poker-playing friends from his past, but she knew perfectly well how sentimental he was about it. She bowed to the fact that she couldn't brush Maggy off without trouble from Bianchi.

"Follow me," she said brusquely. "But it's a waste of your time." She led the way up one flight of stairs into a room, empty at the moment, where the new French originals hung on long racks next to the tables the models used for their makeup. She picked out a white satin evening dress, intricately cut on the bias, so low in front and in back that it was difficult to tell which was which. With a gathered peplum flounce that projected between the hip and the knee, it was, quite possibly, the most unwearable gown that Madame Jeanne Lanvin had ever created. She handed it to Maggy without a word and went back to her desk.

Damn that creature, Patricia Falkland fumed. She knew enough to wave Klein's name around like a sword, but she didn't have the sense to realize that she was totally unsuited to showing clothes. The last thing a model must do is to seem like competition to the customer. No matter how good-looking she is, she must not stir up any response of *envy* in the customer, she must never appear to be on the customer's social or economic level. The customer must be encouraged to feel superior. It was something bone deep, understood by everyone who sold clothes.

She was still immersed in angry thought when Maggy appeared at the top of the stairs, wrapped in an ermine cape she had appropriated from another rack in the model room. Her bare head revealed hair like a carefully tended bonfire, still parted at the side as Antoine had first styled it, but longer now and waved tightly over her ears. A living statue, she advanced at a subtle, gliding pace that was neither slow nor rapid, a pace calculated to allow the spectator to absorb the details of what she was wearing with ease, yet her eyes, looking serenely into the middle distance, did not permit any personal contact. Vanished, as if it could never have existed, was the unconscious, privileged challenge with which Maggy had entered the reception room and in its place was a demeanor that indicated clearly that she was there only and uniquely for the pleasure and service of others.

Look, look not at me, she seemed to be saying, but at what I'm wearing, because if it tempts you then it can be yours. I am only the medium who indicates to you how you can realize your dreams. I am neutral, the clothes are everything, and are they not beautiful? I am proud to wear them, for a few minutes. But they do not belong to me. Think how marvelous *you* could look in this.

Maggy reached the last step and walked across the reception room. Miss Falkland, regarding her with an unfriendly, impassive eye, noted that she had found a pair of white satin evening shoes from some model's cache. But anyone, even a born frump, could wrap herself in ermine and create something of an effect. There hadn't been a model who worked for Bianchi who hadn't fought to show that wrap and they'd all looked well in it. The test, the trial had been sidetracked and she was unimpressed.

Maggy turned in front of the desk and walked back to the foot of the staircase. There, slowly, with a gesture to which she gave all that she had ever learned of allure, a gesture that told all that could ever be learned about handling fur, she threw back the cape, unfolding it as easily as if it had been made of organdy, and let it trail from one hand as she revealed herself in the white satin dress that had, by the act of her having put it on, become ultimately desirable.

One of two fake diamond clips Maggy had picked up at Chanel marked the lowest point of the décolletage in the front, and as she turned again, another was clasped at the V of the dress in the back in a manner that no one in New York had yet seen. She circled the room, the ermine whispering on the carpet, and now a small, dreamlike smile warmed her face, enough, just precisely enough, exactly enough of a smile to gather the spectator into the sensuous pleasure of wearing such a dress, a smile that guaranteed temptation. She didn't look at Patricia Falkland for approval or disapproval as she walked, but if she had, she would have seen the woman's lips set grimly.

"Who's this?" a man's voice demanded. Miss Falkland jumped but Maggy stood still imperturbably, and waited, offering herself absolutely yet not losing her distance.

"Someone applying for a model job, Mr. Bianchi," she said. "I don't think she's suitable."

"Maybe you should have your eyes checked, Patsy. What's your name, Miss?" Maggy's neutral, bland look disappeared as she unfurled her unauthorized charm.

"Magali Lunel, but I am called simply Maggy in the business."

"You're the girl Harry called about—I didn't expect . . . when can you start?"

"Whenever you like. Tomorrow if that suits you."

"How about now? Patsy, Mrs. Townsend just called. She's changed her mind about leaving for Palm Beach after all, so she's desperate for new clothes for the Christmas parties in Tuxedo Park, and we're shorthanded."

"Now is even better than tomorrow," Maggy said. She liked the look of Mr. Bianchi, who had once been a boy in Harry Klein's old neighborhood. He had a perfectly tended look, splendid linen, a glossiness of hair and sleekness that was more continental than American. He was plump, as bright-eyed as a boy, and obviously a master at his trade. She understood a man like this one. He would be a demon if she disappointed him but kind, even generous, if she could give him the perfection he expected.

Several hours later, after she had modeled dozens of dresses and suits and coats for Mrs. Townsend, Maggy left the House of Alberto Bianchi with a job that paid thirty-five dollars a week. Her heart jumped as she thought gleefully that she had, after all, been trained for something useful. Years of taking her clothes off as quickly as possible for her artists, followed by years of watching fashion shows—and the ability to imitate the best models in Paris—had added up to a salable commodity. She would be making enough money to pay Nanny Butterfield and still have fifteen dollars left over.

Maggy arrived at the corner of Fifth Avenue and Fifty-seventh Street and paused to look around her, to absorb the almost tangible pledge made by the long, brightly lit thoroughfare in the winter twilight. Another Maggy, the seventeen-year-old girl who had stood in the center of springtime Montparnasse, and waited impatiently for her life to begin, seemed to join her, to stand by her side and say, "Courage." How little you knew then, Maggy whispered to herself. How little I know now. How much, how very much I am going to learn. She wondered where she could find a florist's shop. She needed to buy a red carnation for her buttonhole.

13

What was the reason for the hold Lavinia Longbridge had over the younger members of New York society? Even bridge-playing dowagers at the Southampton Beach Club bestirred themselves to ask each other. Mrs. Condé Nast posed the question to Mrs. William de Rahm, and Cecil Beaton, on his frequent visits to New York, had become enough aware of her power to inquire of Mrs. Herbert Weston if she understood the reason for it.

One cynic had said that in all of nature there were only fourteen different patterns into which objects from crystals to pineapples could stack themselves, but that at the top of each stack one would be sure to find Lally Longbridge. Yet this was too simple an answer, although it had first been observed when, as Lavinia Pendennis, she became the most fêted debutante of her year, her spectacular entrance into society so far outpaced the next contender as to make all the other girls seem to fall into one undifferentiated group.

When she married Cornwallis Longbridge she might have been expected to fall into the traditional role of rich young wife, but this she refused to do, maintaining in an era of couples, a separate identity, so that Cornie Longbridge became another, although the most favored, of her subjects.

Lally was as beautiful as she was miniature, with black eyes and black hair that sprang away from her white delicate face like a wreath above the whitest arms and shoulders and back in New

York, and the reddest lips, the only touch of color she allowed herself; but there were many beautiful girls in society: Mary Taylor, Isabel Henry, Helen Kellogg, Justine Allen and Alice Doubleday all had their champions for the queen of beauty.

No, it was not just popularity and beauty that accounted for her enormous influence—it was the generous manner in which she had pledged her life to having a good time. For the only way Lally could have a good time was when she bestowed it on others.

In Lally Longbridge the reckless gaiety of that great party of the twenties had danced right on into the first frightening year of the thirties. Cornie Longbridge's fortune was secure and her life was devoted seriously to entertaining unseriously; her home was like a reassuring campfire that could be counted on to warm everyone who came near. Lally was considered the best bartender in the city and certainly she knew all the best bootleggers. She invented the buffet supper; meals at her house always had the charm of picnics; and her roving taste for people was the spice that made her parties go like rockets. Lally asked jazz musicians to her parties and newspaper reporters and professional boxers and tap dancers from Broadway shows and songwriters from Tin Pan Alley and, jealous hostesses whispered, even gangsters, which only made the parties more thrilling. She welded them all into one bright unit by her laughter and friendliness.

Often after a party had taken off, Lally would step back into the shadow of an alcove and watch for minutes at a time the new and unexpected groupings she had caused to happen, feeling like the most successful of stage directors. Her entertainments were as frequent as they were spontaneous, never planned more than a day or two in advance, with the knowledge that her household was organized around hospitality, her servants chosen for their capacity to cope with large groups as carefully as if she were an ambassador's wife.

Lally Longbridge had had dresses made at Bianchi's since her debut. She was one of those exceedingly rare short women who possess the gift of dressing in a way that made her look tall. The heart of it lay in the fact that Lally never perceived herself as tiny—everybody else she felt was simply too big. Until Maggy came to work at Bianchi's she had never found a model who understood this and who would willingly show her dresses that, in theory, only tall women could wear.

In the last year and a half she had become increasingly interested in Maggy. Mrs. Lunel was far from being the usual house model, obviously, but what *was* the mystery of this widowed Frenchwoman who couldn't be drawn into speaking of herself? Everybody she took an interest in was *supposed* to tell Lally all about herself—it really was most curious, almost vexing.

One day in the spring of 1931, she astonished Maggy by inviting her to a party the following evening.

"Say you'll come, Maggy, do! After dinner we're having a scavenger hunt and there'll be a fabulous prize for the winning team— it'll be great fun."

Maggy hesitated. The house models never mingled with the customers. A social gulf, which everyone acknowledged, separated them.

"Now don't be stuffy! I know what you're thinking and it's too silly for words. Lots of women work these days—it's getting rather smart. That doesn't mean that you're prohibited from having a good time."

"I'd love to," Maggy said decisively. She owed herself some kind of romp. For the past year and a half she'd led a life of discipline and hard work, at the beck and call of Bianchi and his customers for as long as ten hours a day, rarely off her feet for more than a few minutes at a time.

But it was healing work that kept her from thinking about the past, exhausting work that let her sleep soundly, waking only occasionally to dreams of Perry Kilkullen, which made her weep, waking too often to dream of Julien Mistral, which made her rage. How could she still dream about a man she hated? She'd ask herself that uncomfortable question furiously, trying to deny the profound, rolling orgasm that had awakened her. She was, on those mornings, particularly glad to run off to a job that left no time for uncomfortable introspection.

Maggy was now the leading model at Alberto Bianchi's and the other nine models all looked up to her. Even Patricia Falkland had been forced to admit, if only to herself, that no one could show and sell a dress like Maggy. In the scattered moments that the models had to congregate in their dressing room the other girls asked Maggy's advice and there was nothing about which she didn't express firm, immediate approval or disapproval, from the line of a new hairstyle to the shade of a pair of stockings. Somehow Maggy found herself calming the girls when they had jitters or complaints or quarreled among themselves. She listened to their accounts of their many romances and administered stiff but compassionate doses of tough-minded advice in which her own hard-learned wisdom was mixed with bits of Paula's well-remembered admonitions. She even found herself scolding the girls who put on a pound or two, and advising them about the placement of their rouge and eyeshadow.

Charity fashion shows had become a rage in New York and the House of Bianchi was constantly asked to participate in them. Soon Maggy found herself in demand by the organizers of these shows who were all amateurs. She was able to run herd on the models, most of them dithering, nervous, awkward society women who had never walked on a runway before.

Because of this extra work Maggy's salary was raised to fifty dollars a week. She had had to dip into her precious nest egg to furnish the small apartment just off Central Park West, on Sixty-third Street, that she'd taken for her little family.

Nevertheless, Maggy's salary was just enough to support Teddy and Nanny Butterfield. Her own expenses were minimal; her Paris clothes were still in style, chosen as they had been from advanced designs that embodied ideas that were still fresh to the American eye . . . not that it mattered really, Maggy thought, since she had no occasion to get really dressed up.

The other manikins at Bianchi's had, in her first days there, invited her to go out to speakeasies and nightclubs with them— there were always many young men who wanted to meet her. But she had refused time after time, and eventually they stopped asking. She never mentioned her choice of solitude in her letters to Paula, who would, she knew, have disapproved deeply. As soon as work was over Maggy hurried home every night to have an early dinner with Teddy and soak her feet.

Now, reacting to the flattering surprise of Lally Longbridge's invitation, she felt that she'd gone as long as she could endure without an evening's break, just one night of sheer *fun*. The Jazz Age was finished, killed by the Depression, but an unsubdued audaciousness in Maggy told her how badly she still thirsted for the sound of a saxophone, the thrum of a guitar. The melody of "Sweet Georgia Brown," forgotten for six years, came back to her lips. As she dressed for the party she realized that on a May evening, even

New York, that lonely, tense city of metal and concrete, could turn electric and rosy with expectation.

When the impulsive business of inviting guests was over, Lally Longbridge gave an hour's concentration to the composition of the teams for her scavenger hunt. There was no point in putting the same kind of people together, people who already knew each other—a scavenger hunt was only as much fun as the team members made it.

Maggy Lunel, she thought, was so smart that she should be on the team with Gay Barnes, who spun nothing but nonsense in her bubbly blond head. Gay had been the most famous of the showgirls in Earl Carroll's *Vanities* before she married Henry Oliver Barnes, who must be thirty-five years older than she. Lally, who was always interested in how others packaged their personalities, realized that Gay had managed to win over stuffy New York society by two simple means: she was amazingly decorative and she had a killingly funny way of seeming to never know when a man made a risqué remark—remarks she had most definitely provoked.

Which two men with those two women? She bit her thumb pensively. Why not Jerry Holt? The entertainment column he wrote for the *World* was read by everybody in town and he was as witty as his reputation was dubious. And . . . yes . . . it would serve him right for being so hard to pin down; the other man would be Darcy, Jason Darcy, whom everyone called by his last name.

How amusingly outraged that rather too self-satisfied twenty-nine-year-old *wunderkind* of the publishing business would be to find himself teamed up with an ex-showgirl, a dress house model and a, probably, pansy columnist. It was the kind of team that would give Lally a special kind of good time. At every party she gave she arranged for at least one such ill-assorted group, a secret game she played, for her own delectation.

Hours later, after dinner, the ten teams gathered in Lally's fashionably sterile chrome and glass drawing room, filled with white tulips. There was groaning and protesting over the lists she had handed them.

One debutante of this season, only beautiful ones count
One of Miss Ethel Barrymore's shoes
One dog, must be pure white

One program from *Smiles* signed by both Adele and Fred Astaire
One tablecloth from the Colony Restaurant
One English butler—no fakes
One brand-new copy of *A Farewell to Arms*
One single yellow glove
One New York City policeman's hat
One waiter's jacket from Jack and Charlie's

"This is simply fiendish," Gay Barnes wailed. "We'll never win, never."

"How long do we have?" Maggy asked.

"Two hours," Jerry Holt explained. "The team wins that brings in the most by the deadline."

"I've had an inspiration!" Gay Barnes announced. "It doesn't say anywhere that we can't split up, does it? What's the point in all four of us going after the same things? I think Jerry and I should take the first five and you two take the others. How about it?"

"All I know is that somewhere I must have a yellow glove, I'm a much-gloved woman," Maggy said, wondering, why on earth, if she were going to plot to be alone with a man, the blond girl had picked out a *pédé*.

"Whatever you all decide," Darcy agreed. "But let's get going— we've wasted five minutes already."

Downstairs, on Park Avenue, Darcy handed Maggy into a long limousine. "Twenty-one East Fifty-second Street," he said to the chauffeur sitting in an open box.

"I suspected Lally was going to spring another scavenger hunt so I told the car to wait," he told Maggy.

The enormous dark blue Packard, which would have seemed appropriate for J. P. Morgan himself, was only one of the ways in which Jason Darcy set himself apart from other young men of his age. The only son of a wealthy Hartford insurance company owner, he'd been considered one of the most brilliant men of his class at Harvard, graduating at eighteen. In the following years he had borrowed family money to launch three new magazines, each of which had become immediately successful in that booming era.

The money soon repaid, Darcy used his large income to live as well as a pasha entitled to display three horsetails. He had affairs with an astonishing percentage of all the prettiest women in New York, whom he bothered only to divide into two basic categories, treating the society ladies like chorus girls, and the chorus girls like society ladies, an arrangement that somehow ensured everyone's pleasure. No one woman had managed to catch him and the ever-growing band of his disappointed, temporary flames all drifted toward the face-saving conclusion that he was married to his work.

Jason Darcy was a genuinely influential man who risked becoming self-important. Unfortunately for his character, he'd never wanted anything he couldn't manage to obtain; not the admiration of his peers or his own self-esteem. For the moment Maggy was the bauble he had decided to acquire. Twice, during dinner, he had caught her eye although they had been seated at different tables. Gay Barnes, nitwit that she was, had shown a most convenient sense of timing in splitting up the team, although if there hadn't been the excuse of the scavenger hunt he would simply have taken more direct measures.

Maggy was jolted by the memory of Perry's dove-gray Voisin as she leaned back into the deep, soft cushion of the Packard. She'd forgotten how such a car made her feel, cossetted, a rare object made of precious materials, fitted into a velvet nest. Nothing, no perfume she knew, smelled as sensuous as the interior of a limousine.

She glanced at Darcy with mild interest. He had a long, thin face of infinite distinction, a scientist's face or a philosopher's face, she thought, in spite of his youth. It was a face that was sharp with cool curiosity, yet he looked as if he could never be surprised. He moved with economy and grace; he had a straight, gray gaze in which she suspected some humor must lurk, and a straight hard mouth that looked as if it could be capable of great scorn. His dark hair fit closely to his head, and he was easily a few inches taller than she was. A man like a blade, she thought, and dismissed him from her mind. The limousine was so much more potent an excitement than any mere man could be.

She was disappointed when the ride ended too quickly and they entered the permanent carnival of Jack and Charlie's, the most clublike and most expensive speakeasy in New York, a wood-paneled cave of jovial shouts and hearty defiance of the Volstead Act, which opened at lunch and didn't close until dawn. It was the daily hangout for a merry mix of Ivy League undergraduates, sports writers and stockbrokers and it roared with the complex, excited noise that can only be made by a lot of happy people drinking, eating, laughing and flirting in an overcrowded room.

They were quickly shown to a table and Darcy ordered champagne, conferring a moment with the waiter. Maggy, still longing to return to the limousine, sat restlessly, until the waiter poured the wine.

"Isn't that a waste?" she asked. "We can't drink the whole bottle—just look at this list—the English butler, the policeman's hat . . . what time is it?" Her competitive spirit had begun to rise. This was hardly an appropriate moment in which to sit around lazily and sip bootleg booze, no matter how authentically French it was.

Darcy gave her a complacent, rather too lofty look. "I've just arranged to rent our waiter's jacket. I'll phone home and tell my butler to meet us on Lally's sidewalk with my copy of Hemingway—Clarkson used to work for the Duke of Sutherland—and we can pick up that yellow glove you said you had on the way back."

"Is that your idea of sportsmanship?" Maggy frowned. This man was draining all the fun out of it, with his smugness and his showing off.

"I call it basic wisdom. We didn't take a blood oath to win—just to play. Anyway, aren't you bored stiff by scavenger hunts?"

"Most certainly not! I've never been on one before. What gives you the right to turn this evening into drinks for two?" she snapped. How she hated them, men who thought they could dominate women.

He didn't answer but drank his wine and looked intently into the world of her angry, challenging green eyes. He could feel himself respond to her quality, one which seemed to him to be untamed in the deepest sense but yet well under control. He didn't know anything about her, but she could never be anonymous.

"Where did Lally discover you?" he asked. "And why have we never met before?"

"I work at Alberto Bianchi's," she said curtly.

"What do you do there?" So she was another one of those women who never worked a day in their lives before, who had accepted a "funny little job" to show how undaunted they were by the Depression.

"I model dresses . . . other women buy them."

"I rather tend to doubt that."

"It's quite true."

"You mean you're a *genuine* victim of the Crash, you work for a *living?*"

"For fifty dollars a week. I do very well, as it happens."

"Tell me everything," he invited, confident that she'd like nothing more. What woman didn't?

"Everything? You're *damned* rude, do you know that? Why should I tell you anything at all? I don't even think I caught your name, whatever it may be. You've ruined my scavenger hunt and now you're being utterly presumptuous. What's more, you didn't even ask me if I like champagne before you ordered it."

"You're absolutely right," he said, taken aback. "I apologize profoundly. Would you like something else to drink?"

"This is quite enough, thank you," Maggy said. She looked around her, paying him no further attention.

"Mrs. Lunel, I'm Jason Darcy and I'm twenty-nine years old and I was born in Hartford, Connecticut, of a respectable family. I've never been to jail, I don't cheat at poker, I love animals, my mother speaks highly of me, and I usually have better manners than I've led you to believe."

"Is that quite 'everything'?" Maggy asked, permitting him a small smile.

"I'm a publisher, *Mode, Women's Journal* and *City and Country Life.*"

"*Tiens, tiens,* three magazines for just one man," she said. "Just what precisely does a publisher do? Besides being obnoxiously inquisitive with unknown ladies?"

"Precisely? I'm the boss."

"What an unilluminating explanation. Who do you boss and why do you boss? Be more exact, if you please."

He looked at her, catching her scarcely hidden mockery.

"Couldn't you be a little more impressed?"

"Should I be? I have no idea just what a publisher does."

"I invented the magazines, I decided how they should look, I targeted in on my public, I established the standards, the formats. The editors report to me, and so do the business departments and everybody who physically produces the magazines."

"Is that a publishing empire?" Maggy asked. "Like the publishing empire of Mr. Hearst, for example?"

"Mine's more like a kingdom than an empire," Darcy admitted.

"How modest of you, Mr. Darcy."

"You don't feel any particular delight at drinking champagne with a fairly important publisher?"

"I'm far too old and too wise for astonished delight, Mr. Darcy."

"Darcy."

"Darcy. What little I've seen of the world has left me blasé, jaded, spoiled and, worst of all, hungry."

"So soon after dinner?"

"Dinner is a meal that invariably leaves me hungry."

"How about some chicken hash? It's a specialty here."

"Leftovers, how childishly barbarian." Maggy hadn't felt so impulsive, so to-hell-with-it-all, so intoxicatingly, splendidly silly since she had arrived in the United States. Ah, but it was droll to make an utter fool of a man again, she thought. Men had been invented to become fools—that was *all* they were good for, that and no more. Paula had said so and Paula had been right.

Jason Darcy couldn't stop looking at Maggy. She shot off more flames than a black opal, with those golden-greeny eyes and her orange hair, shining smooth over the lovely shape of her skull, breaking into deep waves just under her chin—she had the flushed brilliance of a child running loose in the first snow of winter. Who the hell *was* Maggy Lunel? Not a chorus girl or a society woman. And yet he was sure he knew all of the most beautiful women of the city.

"I've got it! You're a new Powers girl."

"And what might that be?" Maggy asked curiously. Recently she'd heard the phrase flung about more and more but she'd never had the time or interest to ask about this odd Americanism.

"A photographic model, with the John Robert Powers agency—come on, stop looking as if you didn't know."

"Truly, I'm not involved in that world. I merely model copies of Paris originals and help to run society fashion shows. The House of Bianchi has never used a Powers girl."

"Well, it's just a question of time before you do because Powers is getting bigger all the time. He's been in business for a couple of years, ever since the ad agencies and magazines all started using photographs instead of drawings."

"And what do these Powers girls make when they work?"

"As I remember they started at five dollars an hour in the first days but now the top girls are getting fifteen."

"Fifteen an hour! That's a fortune!" Maggy was awed.

"Damn right, especially if a girl works a lot and they're all getting busier and busier in spite of the Depression. Today either a business has to advertise or it goes under, and nothing sells a product like a pretty girl."

"And Mr. John Robert Powers, what does he earn?"

"Ten percent of whatever his models make."

"And how many models does he have working for him?" she persisted.

"I'm not sure—I'd imagine about a hundred, including the men and the kids. If you're really only a fifty-dollar-a-week dress model, you should be working for him."

"Thank you," Maggy said absently.

Jason Darcy was still far from convinced that Maggy Lunel was what she said she was, not because anything she'd told him was impossible but because there was something about her that was so unique in his own experience that it made him suspicious.

Maggy Lunel was not behaving normally. There was nothing in her manner, in her eyes or her words that indicated that she was trying to attract him, and this, to Darcy, was incredible. He knew, as well—or better—than anyone else that he was one of the most eligible men in the United States. He had everything: first of all, at only twenty-nine, he had accumulated enough influence to make him eligible if he'd been a gnome. In addition he was unattached and rich, which would have made him eligible if he'd been a werewolf. But he was neither gnome nor werewolf, he was a man who admitted, each time he looked in the mirror, that he was handsome, an accident of genetics to be sure but not to be despised.

Why then, *how* then, could this woman sit here drinking his champagne while she interrogated him about the Powers Agency as if he were a conduit of information and nothing more?

Perhaps she was in love? That was the only reasonable explanation. And yet she had come to the party alone. A fury to know more about Maggy stirred in him, as she seemed to engrave a pattern on the air with a gesture of her eloquent hands. "And where is this famous chicken hash?" she suddenly asked him. "And why is my glass empty? Shall we go dancing?" She was matter-of-fact, not provocative, he noted with fresh wonderment, but her vividness was a triumph.

"What about Lally's scavenger hunt?"

"But it's a ridiculous and boring American custom—isn't that what you think?"

"Where would you like to go? The St. Regis Roof, the Embassy, the Cotton Club?"

"Le Jockey," Maggy murmured.

"The Jockey?" he said puzzled.

"Did I say that? Never mind, it's been closed for years. Let's go on up to Harlem."

Adrien Avigdor was sure of his ground. Since Julien Mistral had gone to live in Félice five years ago, since that improbable marriage to Kate Browning, the man had had three sell-out, one-man shows in Paris, each one a greater triumph than the one of the year before.

Now, in the spring of 1931, it was time for him to show in New York. His production of paintings was small, or, to be precise, he painted a great deal and showed very little. Mistral exercised to the full the legal position possessed by every French artist to obtain, by writing a simple phrase on the back of a painting—*ne pas à vendre*—the right to withhold from sale any canvas or even to prohibit the exhibition of the canvas, although he was under contract to Avigdor for all he agreed to actually sell.

Each year, four months before the planned exhibition, Avigdor drove down to Provence and spent a draining, difficult week living at *La Tourrello* and arguing with Mistral about his new work. Once in 1928, Mistral had not been satisfied with a single painting and there had been no show in the autumn of that year, Avigdor remembered gloomily. Mistral destroyed the work he didn't like in an annual bonfire, capering around and feeding canvas after canvas into the flames like a devil out of Hieronymus Bosch, a man who heartlessly, gleefully, invited Avigdor to watch as hundreds of thousands of francs of marvelous painting turned into oily smoke.

"That's in case I should fall down dead, Adrien, and you got your hands on stuff I never meant anybody to see—who would make sure that you wouldn't sell them, eh?" He was as suspicious as the peasants he lived among and trusted no one except Kate. And he trusted her only so far. Obviously not far enough to believe that she would obey the prohibitions he scrawled in large letters on the backs of hundreds of paintings.

It was agony for Avigdor to watch Mistral's mountainous bonfires but there was a miserable measure of satisfaction to be derived from the fact that while he never had any extra Mistrals left to sell when an exhibition was over, no other dealer in Paris ever had so much as a single one. As far as Avigdor knew, no collector who had ever bought a Mistral had resold it. Mistral himself always retained his favorites.

The man's prices had mounted far beyond anything Adrien had planned because of the scarcity of his available work. But, after all, Avigdor mused, there were only thirty-six Vermeers in existence, so perhaps Mistral knew what he was doing?

In any case, artists should not be allowed to marry rich women, it gave them too much freedom. No matter; Mistral had finally agreed to a New York show of new work and of selections from his output since 1926. Various American collectors were lending canvases so the show would be a large one. Many art critics from American newspapers and magazines were already in busy contact with Avigdor. *Vanity Fair* had commissioned a long article on him and Man Ray had gone to Félice to photograph Mistral in his studio. Mark Nathen, whose gallery was one of the best in New York, was planning a *vernissage* that would attract all of artistic and social New York. The show would be one of the major events of the spring of 1931 since everybody in the small, inbred world of art was extraordinarily curious to see the work of this man, who lived like a hermit stuck away in the Lubéron, indifferent to his gathering fame, his growing legend.

"Before dinner I thought we might drop into the opening of the new show at Nathen's," Darcy proposed to Maggy on the telephone.

"What show?" she asked idly. She had no time to keep up with the wide-ranging cultural life of the city.

"Mistral—the French painter—you must have heard of him."

She held the telephone in one hand, and with the other she steadied herself against the mantelpiece, feeling the cruel beat of her heart knock against her breasts. The shock of Mistral's name, spoken so unexpectedly, had made her mind a blank of ice. Her stomach contracted in fear. Why fear? she wondered. Automatically she said, "Yes, I know who he is, but I don't feel up to going out tonight."

"Maggy, what's the matter?"

"I'm just so tired I can't move, too tired to dress . . . I think I'm catching cold."

"I'm very, very disappointed," he said gravely.

"I am too."

In the three weeks since he had met Maggy, Darcy had asked her out far more frequently than she had been willing to go. Each time he saw her he grew increasingly baffled by her deep reserve, her gentle but obstinate refusal to speak of herself. She seemed to have told him all she was ever going to tell him on the night of the scavenger hunt. She always insisted on meeting him at a speakeasy or a restaurant. She never offered him any hospitality, and when he left her at the elevator of her apartment house—for she didn't ask him to come up—Maggy shook hands briskly, not even coming close enough for him to risk a brief kiss.

In his limousine, she sat far away from him, her hands folded tightly in her lap, she danced with a tension in her body that imposed a delicate but insistent formality that turned a song like "The Night Was Made for Love" into a satire. Was she frigid, was she frightened, was she suffering from some damn French neurosis he hadn't heard of? Did it have something to do with her being a widow?

Darcy thought about her in obsessive curiosity, for her widowhood and the existence of Teddy were two of the few details of her life that she had let escape. He examined the little he knew about her with as much fascination as if it were a piece of a map that would lead to buried treasure, but she remained tart, aloof, serenely and mysteriously unknowable. What was worse, damn it to hell, was that she was as untouchable as a princess in a tower. Every now and then, as he talked to her, he had the almost unendurable suspicion that something he had said was making her go through a polite agony of suppressed laughter, but he'd never actually caught her at it. What colossal nerve she had!

"Look, I'll call you tomorrow, but take care of yourself, don't get sick. Will you go to bed early?" he asked anxiously.

"Yes," she agreed tonelessly, "I will, I promise."

As Jason Darcy wandered disconsolately into the Nathen Gallery he found he was reassuring himself that, at the very minimum, Maggy Lunel must *like* him. Darcy, sought after, hard-to-get, powerful, proud Darcy, started to review his virtues to balance the fact that he had never even been allowed to come close to her lips. Then quickly, like a man touching his tie to make sure that it's properly centered, he told himself how preposterous he was, piling one worldly asset on top of another, listing his magazines, his well-staffed household, his Harvard summa cum laude, his youth, his health, his desk piled high with invitations and solicitations from every part of the worlds that were touched by his publications, as if to prove that he had enough value to be allowed into the hidden garden of Maggy Lunel's private, guarded world.

He surveyed the crowd in the Nathen Gallery, surprised at the broad cross section of New York he saw there. He knew a great many of the people and, as he listened to the moneyed hum of conversation he thought that it sounded more like the Metropolitan Opera at intermission than an artistic event. He supposed that the unusual number of society women he recognized and greeted were there because the show had been organized as a benefit for the Children's Hospital; it was rare to find the Whitneys, the Ochses, the Kilkullens, the Gimbels, the Jays, the Rutherfords and the Vanderbilts all mixed up with the most famous faces of Greenwich Village and Southampton.

Then as Darcy began to look at the pictures, his mild interest at the composition of the crowd vanished in an instant. He had the sudden sensation of being picked up by a pair of great strong hands and set down under a new horizon. Each painting was like a step along a pathway into another world, an alternate world, a better world. Reasoning, deliberation, logic, time, and space itself all dissolved into an unqualified radiance, a splendor of paint that had the texture of a living, breathing substance.

And yet, Darcy asked himself, stunned, what has the man chosen to paint after all? A café table and chairs under an orange awning, a stand of poplars quivering in the heat, a market basket filled with bread, radishes and a bunch of dahlias, a woman bending down in a garden in the morning—the simplest of subject matter, nothing that had not been painted by a thousand painters before Mistral.

Yet the emotion of the artist as he looked at his subjects had so merged with the images he put on canvas that a transparency was created, through which a bridge was flung from the world in which Mistral *felt* to the world in which the spectator *lived*, so that for an essential moment, Darcy existed with Mistral's eyes, Darcy entered into Mistral's vision.

Wondering, amazed, buoyant with the blooming of his senses, feeling as if he had left New York and walked into open, sunlit, cloud-dappled country, Darcy went through the big gallery not noticing, as he entered the far room, that it was unusually crowded and filled with buzzing conversation.

Maggy! He shivered violently, the hair rose on his neck as he confronted the big canvases of Maggy on every wall, naked and so utterly abandoned as she offered the glory of her flesh, exposed, shameless, happier than he had ever dreamed she could be, available to every eye, Maggy, more erotic, more violently and generously sensual than any woman he had ever seen in paint or in the flesh.

Lust, palpable as smoke, a pungent, hungry, raw lust quivered on the canvases of Maggy with her legs sprawled wide apart lying on an unmade bed, one arm dangling to the floor; Maggy with wet hair washing between her legs with a soapy cloth; Maggy thrown down on a pile of green cushions, laughing, her nipples tender and inflamed, her pubic hair caught in a shaft of light so that each red filament was alive and separate.

As Darcy stood immobile, frozen, unable to look away from the pictures, he caught words rising from the talk in the room. There was a delighted, high-pitched, scarcely repressed excitement in the babble that greets any out-and-out scandal.

"Bianchi's model, my dear, that French girl . . . mistress . . . Perry Kilkullen, of course . . . what *skin* . . . I saw them together in Maxim's . . . did you say Bianchi? . . . . widow, my foot . . . incredible breasts . . . didn't they have a child? . . . met her at Lally's, yes, I'm sure . . . a child surely . . . how the hospital committee let this pass I'll never . . . the Kilkullens will . . . shocking . . . don't be so provincial . . . shocking . . . painted when, you say? . . . Bianchi's model . . . poor Mary Jane . . . Perry's *what?*"

Why the hell didn't he paint them in sperm? Darcy thought to himself, why not just fuck the canvas? He shook with uncontrolled laughter. Life had never attacked him so unexpectedly. That lily maid, that contained and elusive princess—oh, how beautifully she had outfoxed him! What a formidable woman she was! His admiration for Maggy swelled within him like a great chuckle as he watched the faces of all the men in the room, their eyes greedily roving the canvases—he'd bet that half of them were trying to control stiffening cocks—he knew he was. Oh, Maggy, darling Maggy, so you "had heard of Mistral" had you—and how many times did he stop painting to fuck you? How, in fact, was he able to pay any attention to his paint and brushes? The man must have had the concentration of a diamond cutter to get any work done at all under the circumstances—oh, Maggy, no woman has ever surprised me like this—I feel a virgin fifteen again. *Bravo!*

By noon of the next day Maggy was without a job. She didn't blame Bianchi; her usefulness to him was clearly over. He'd received a dozen outraged phone calls before he'd asked to see her and if none of them had actually used the term "scarlet woman" it was only because they knew it was old-fashioned. Obviously Maggy couldn't possibly organize another society fashion show and as for normal modeling for the house, her notoriety would get in the way of the dresses. People would come to see the cause of the scandal but they wouldn't dream of ordering the garments she wore. Just by putting a dress on, she would invalidate it.

As he said goodbye to Maggy, with a check for two weeks' salary, Alberto Bianchi felt two emotions; sorrow at losing this valuable model and a burning impatience to run up to the Nathen Gallery to see for himself what Maggy looked like stark naked—God knows, he'd wasted enough time wondering.

Darcy tried to reach Maggy at Bianchi's as soon as he left the Nathen Gallery, without success. She'd gone to bed, Nanny Butterfield had told him. He phoned her at home repeatedly but Maggy refused to take any calls, not even from Lally, who also had called several times. She asked Nanny Butterfield to answer the phone and say that she was out of town and wouldn't be back for a while.

When he couldn't reach Maggy by phone Darcy went to her apartment but the doorman had firm orders to allow no one upstairs but deliveries. He sent flowers twice a day with notes begging her to call him at the office or at home, but she did neither. He stood impatiently on the street outside of her apartment house for hours, but she never emerged. He did everything but disguise himself as a delivery boy. He could hardly believe his own behavior, yet he couldn't stay put.

Four days after the opening of Mistral's exhibition Darcy telephoned once more in the late afternoon, hoping that by now she might be ready to come out of her isolation. Maggy was in her bathroom when the phone rang, Nanny Butterfield was making Teddy's supper, and Teddy herself dared to answer the phone, something she was forbidden to do.

She was three, a prime age for little girls, one of their peak years.

186

Teddy had already grown accustomed to the exclamations of strangers in the park who saw her beauty for the first time, she had already learned that there were certain laws that she could break without being reprimanded just because of how she looked. However, these laws still applied at home; Nanny and Maggy tried to be strict with her because they were joined in a conviction that it would be fatally easy to spoil her. A ringing phone was already an object of greedy veneration for Teddy. She picked it up with guilty delight and said a muffled hello.

"Who is this?" Darcy asked, thinking he had the wrong number.

"Teddy Lunel. Who are you?"

"A friend of your mother's. Hello, Teddy."

"Hello, hello, hello." She giggled and arched her neck. "I have new red shoes."

"Teddy, is your mother there?"

"Yes, but don't you want to talk to me? What's your name?"

"Darcy."

"Hello, Darcy, hello, Darcy. How old are you?"

"Hello, Teddy—I'm—oh, never mind—is your mother there?"

"In the bathroom . . . . no, here she is . . . Mommy, telephone for you."

Hastily Teddy held out the phone to Maggy, who looked around wildly for Nanny Butterfield, almost replaced the receiver, but finally snapped her fingers in anger and answered curtly, "Yes?"

"Maggy, thank goodness, I thought you'd never come out of hiding."

"I'm not hiding!" she said furiously.

"Hibernating then. Your daughter sounds charming, much nicer than you. How about dinner tonight?"

"Absolutely not. I'm not going out."

"But you're the toast of New York."

"Darcy, you were never malicious before."

"I'm telling you the truth. The gallery is mobbed with people who've heard how luscious you are. You're considered the beauty of the decade."

"A *succès de scandale*—do you think I want that?"

"This is New York, Maggy, any success is a success, nobody really cares what it's based on as long as they talk about you," he said, trying hard to make her feel better in the only way he knew how.

"If that were so, I'd still have a job," Maggy answered, bruised by his practicality. Didn't he understand how embarrassed, how humiliated she was?

"That's different, Bianchi has to mollify his clients, but they aren't everybody in town . . . oh, they think they are, but they really don't count except in their own world."

"Nevertheless, Darcy, I earned a living in that world, such as it was."

"Maggy, remember what I thought about your being a Powers girl . . . why don't you go see him?"

"No!" Maggy exclaimed sharply. "I'll *never* model again, not for any reason. I've been a painters' model and a fashion model—I was seventeen when I started and now I'm twenty-three and out of work—and I've never made more than fifty dollars a week—no, thank you, that's not for me, it hasn't done much for me, has it? On the other hand . . . well . . . I suppose it's silly of me . . ." She stopped, unwilling to continue.

"Tell me, Maggy, come on."

"It's a foolish idea. No, no—perhaps not absolutely, totally foolish . . . do you remember telling me that Powers had a hundred models working for him and that he took ten percent of what they made?"

"Sure I do. What about it?"

"I'm used to telling models what to do and how to do it. At Bianchi's, all the girls came to me for advice—it's something I seem to know in my nerve endings. I haven't any idea what photographers require of a girl but it can't be so different from what painters expect, so, well . . . I thought I might . . . try . . . to open an agency myself!" she finished on a burst of bravado.

"*Compete* with John Robert Powers?" he asked doubtfully.

"And why not? Just what does some man do that I could not do? And perhaps better? He's only another kind of dealer and I've known dozens—believe me, there's no magic to them." She rushed on, spurred on by his reaction of doubt. "As it happens, Darcy, I have a little capital to risk."

"Maggy, you're bloody marvelous! Do you want some business from *Mode* and *Women's Journal* and *City and Country Life?*"

"Of course I do! Oh, Darcy, it *could* happen, it could really happen, couldn't it?"

"*It's already happened!*" How he'd missed that laugh of hers! It

188

made the world dance. "Maggy, come out with me tonight and celebrate—champagne to baptize the new agency?"

"On one condition—you must allow me to pay."

"Why, for God's sake?"

"The Lunel Agency wishes to offer champagne to its first customer."

Oh, shit, he thought, *shit!* He realized too late, far, far too late, that he *adored* this impossible woman whom he'd as good as started in her own business. "You're right, Maggy," Darcy said glumly, "you don't have much to learn after all."

14

Maggy's Girls, as everyone called the Lunel Agency models, at first were only a choice handful, but soon their ranks grew to many dozens; exquisite girls, butterfly girls who were so much more glamorous, so clearly more sophisticated than their only rivals, Powers's often corn-fed "Long-Stemmed American Beauties."

Maggy's Girls pranced through the thirties as if there were no Great Depression. Wearing corsages of big lavender orchids pinned to their wide-skirted strapless ball gowns, they banished reality as they danced at the Stork Club and at El Morocco, escorted by at least two men on each arm. They embodied escape for millions of Americans who crowded the movie theaters to see films about rich people in whose lives all telephones were white. Like *Vogue*'s earnest report that the silly new hats have "killed discussion of the Stock Exchange and the rise of Mr. Hitler," Maggy's Girls filled the public's avid need to have fun, even if it was only vicariously. A *New York Daily News* poll asked women if they would rather be a movie star, a debutante or one of the Lunel models and 42 percent decided they would prefer to work for Maggy.

While Maggy prospered in New York, Julien Mistral painted in a fever of energy in Félice. He had entered into his "Middle Period" which was to last for the next twenty years. No longer, as he had in the twenties, did he paint at random the scenes or objects that caught his eye. Now he devoted himself, for two or three years at a time, to one subject, and out of this concentration, out of the thousands of studies and work sketches he made and eventually destroyed, would emerge a series of paintings, as few as a dozen, as many as thirty-five.

Défense d'Afficher, his series of paintings of walls covered with layer upon layer of peeling posters, was the first of these historic series. Next came *Vendredi Matin,* images of the bounty of the weekly outdoor market that took place in Apt. *Stella Artois,* the series that was named after Mistral's favorite brand of beer, illuminated as it had never been before, the intense inner life of the men of the village as they passed their evenings in the café of Félice, drinking, gambling, talking. *Jours de Fête,* the most important of the Middle Period series, was inspired by the celebrations that took place in each village of the Lubéron on the day of its patron saint, a day of mountains of cotton candy and dizzy children riding wooden horses, of processions and fireworks, of wild overexcitement and budding country passions.

Mistral spent every day in his studio from breakfast till dinner. Cold meat, bread and a bottle of wine were brought to him on a tray, and he devoured everything standing up in front of a canvas, unaware of what he was tasting. Kate took the opportunity given her by her husband's abdication of interest in anything but his work, to take more and more control of his business life. She handled all the contracts with Avigdor, she carried on the correspondence with the galleries in many foreign countries who wanted to show Mistral's work, and it was she who made the decisions about the management of the farm.

Once a year, at the time of the harvest, Mistral abandoned his studio and worked in his fields with his men, but otherwise he lived in a world entirely his own. He had no time for newspapers. The changing political tides in Europe were no more his concern than the train of cock feathers on the latest Paris evening gown. As for the boules tournament in Félice, yes, that still meant something to him, but the burning of the Reichstag was an event utterly without interest. If he found that he was down to his tenth tube of raw umber he raged, but the catastrophe of the Dust Bowl, when Mistral heard about it from the farmers in the café, didn't touch him enough to cause him to mutter a word of commiseration. He had as little interest in the Italian aggression in Ethiopia as he did in "Amos n' Andy."

Julien Mistral was at the height of his powers, at peace with himself at last, and his natural selfishness was only reinforced by the knowledge that never had he painted as well. How could anything that was happening in the world have the slightest importance, when he woke up each morning with an absolute need to stand in front of his easel burning strong inside every cell of his body? No human fate, no current of history had the power to affect him so long as he knew that nothing could stop him from spending the day in his studio.

Kate Mistral, on the other hand, never lost touch with life beyond Félice. She went to Paris several times a year to keep in touch with the art world and buy clothes, for live in the country as she might, she continued to be well dressed at all times. She worked closely with Avigdor on Mistral's shows, as she had on his first one, and she represented her husband at the *vernissages* he always refused to attend. Occasionally she left him alone for a month at a time and returned to New York to visit her family. He scarcely noticed these absences.

In the aftermath of the Crash, Kate was no longer rich. In hindsight, she had been lucky to use so much of her own capital on buying the domain of *La Tourrello*. Although she had fulfilled the pledge she had made to win Mistral and given him the title to the land as her dowry, it had been an excellent investment. Her husband had absolutely no idea of how rich they were growing. The many fertile hectares that surrounded the *mas* were crowded and orderly and sweet with fruits and vegetables destined for the wholesalers of Apt. They had fine pigs, flocks of chickens and ducks, a few horses, the latest in farm machinery and many hands to cultivate the crops. Whenever new, adjoining land came on the market, Kate snapped it up. The farm itself could support them in comfort, she thought with satisfaction, even as she counted and recounted the ever-growing sums from the sale of paintings that she deposited in the bank in Avignon.

Although the bank account was, of course, in Mistral's name,

Kate's financial expertise compensated in many ways for the lack of close communion that she was dimly aware of at the heart of her life with Mistral. He rarely spoke to her of his work, he never asked to paint her because of what he explained was a "matte" finish to her skin that prevented the light from entering into it, and he almost never invited her to visit the studio. However, Kate had become a famous hostess. The *mas* was superbly comfortable and everyone she or Mistral had ever known in Paris was eventually invited to spend long weekends. She was house-proud and gloried in showing off *La Tourrello*.

During those periods of the year when the boules players were gathered outside behind the café, Mistral almost always joined them after he finished painting, coming home for dinner only when the last game was over. In the winter, when it was too cold for boules, he worked all day and went to bed early, like an exhausted farmer. Yet she possessed his body, that ever-hungry massively passionate body and the rough direct greed with which he frequently turned to her and satisfied himself was always enough to bring her to a climax, for Kate existed in a state of ready arousal caused by living within the field of sensuality that enveloped her whenever she thought of her husband. All he had to do was murmur "Patience, Kate, patience," and she was ready for him.

She was as addicted to Julien Mistral as she had ever been, Kate realized, as she sat downstairs alone by the great fireplace after he had gone to bed. She regretted nothing she had given up of the worldly life she had led before she met him. What little there was of Julien Mistral that did not belong to his work was, she felt certain, entirely hers. She smiled into the embers, safe within the thick walls of *La Tourrello* as the leaves of autumn flew outside and a low, red moon rose above the frosty, bare fields, the stripped vines.

Kate made as little as she could of the Spanish Civil War in 1936—"Spaniards against Spaniards," she said, guarding her peace of mind, for she, unlike Julien, read the newspapers. On September 29, 1938, the Munich agreement was signed and millions of French, English, and Germans as well, told themselves, in relief, that there would be no war.

In the summer of 1939, Kate, who hadn't seen her family in two years, went to New York for a visit. The city of her birth was particularly gay because of the World's Fair with its theme of the "World of Tomorrow."

Hitler had occupied Czechoslovakia two months earlier but every day twenty-eight thousand people, to whom this distant event had no particular significance, waited on line to visit the "Futurama" where they were treated to General Motors's wonderfully convincing version of the year 1960. It was to be an era in which diesel automobiles costing two hundred dollars each and shaped like raindrops, would race on accident-free highways; there would be a cure for cancer; Federal laws would protect every forest, lake and valley; everybody would have two-month vacations each year and women would possess perfect skin at the age of seventy-five.

"Kate, you absolutely must come back home," said Maxwell Woodson Browning, Kate's favorite uncle, who had been a career diplomat before his retirement. "It's dangerous to stay in Europe."

"Uncle Max, why are you so pessimistic? What about the Munich Pact? Surely Hitler has what he wants? And he couldn't be so foolish as to try anything against France—we have the Maginot Line, and Hitler's soldiers are nothing but a poor, ill-equipped rabble—everyone knows that. The Germans haven't got arms, even their uniforms aren't made out of real wool."

"Propaganda! Don't believe what you hear."

"How silly! Why would French newspapers and radio be full of propaganda? Aren't they free to print whatever they believe?"

"Kate, the situation is dreadfully serious. I'm in contact with a number of men who believe as I do that it is only a question of time before Hitler will try to invade the rest of Europe. You could easily be trapped over there during a war."

"But, Uncle Max, nobody wants a war, *nobody* wants to fight again, aren't you being an alarmist?"

"Kate, you've turned into a fool!" At such words from a man whom she had always admired and respected, Kate Mistral began to pay attention to what he was trying to tell her. By the end of the evening she was so convinced that she immediately wrote Julien to come to the United States.

When Mistral received this first letter he put it aside without rereading it. Such aberration was not worth the postage she had put

194

on the letter. He was busy developing a concept for a new series of paintings of olive groves. At such a time he became ferociously protective of his mental processes. Nothing must intrude on that slow, steady fermentation. Her second and third letters, increasingly shrill, finally forced him to reply and he wrote angrily and briefly that no one in the village believed that there would be a war. Hitler didn't have the stomach to face the French Army. Weren't Kate's relatives aware that the English had fixed things up with surprisingly good sense for once in their history?

Now Kate took matters into her own hands and started to search north of Danbury for the kind of farm on which Mistral could be happy. She was sure that as events grew more ominous, he would see that she was right, as she had been throughout their life together. Knowing Julien she understood that it was crucial to find a comfortable studio before she could expect him to move. But then he would follow her, as he always had, reluctant to the last. She would return to Félice to drag him back with her as soon as a studio was organized.

On the first of September 1939, Germany invaded Poland, and, two days later, England and France, bound by treaty to defend the Poles, reluctantly declared war on Germany.

There was still time for Julien Mistral to get out of France if he had really wanted to, and thousands of Frenchmen did, but now he had begun painting in earnest the series that would be called *Les Oliviers.* The light had turned that limpid, deep golden color that meant that the summer was over, the wind, that rough, icy exhilarating mistral that he loved, had blown all the glare away from the groves of olive trees and he was plunged in ruthless, blind concentration. Mistral could no more pick up and move away from Félice than if he had been a woman in the last stages of childbirth.

All winter long in his studio, Mistral painted the olives of the summer, those strange mythic trees, hermaphrodites, with their ancient, masculine trunks, twisted, brutal, almost ugly, above which sprang feminine branches and leaves, silver and slender as they joined in a constant dialogue with the sun.

When Mistral visited Félice he found the mood in the café calm. After the defeat of Poland there had been no further aggression on either side and everyone agreed that there must certainly be a way short of actually fighting to get out of this *drôle de guerre* that the

Germans themselves called the *Sitzkrieg*. But while Mistral was thinking of nothing but his olive trees, the Germans, refreshed and rested, overran Europe. On the seventeenth of June 1940, Pétain, the old marshal of the French Army, now premier of France, asked for an armistice or a truce, or a surrender, or a cease-fire, depending on each man's political convictions. The trap was closed.

Why now, Mistral raged violently, cursing his evil luck. *Why now*, when I have so much to do! *Why now*, when I haven't a second to spare, *why now*, when I'm painting as never before, *why now*, this stinking, foul *interruption?* What if I can't get any more supplies from Paris? There still isn't a decent paint store in Avignon. And what the hell am I supposed to do about new canvases?

He rampaged about his studio, stacking up empty canvases and grimly taking count of how few remained. There had been no shipments from Paris for months. He, like all painters, hoarded paint, but who could tell when he'd start to need more? And if that wasn't bad enough, if that wasn't enough damnable, ill-begotten trouble for him to worry about, there was the matter of the *mas*. Ever since Kate had gone on her trip to New York the farm had deteriorated steadily.

Jean Pollison, the young farmer Kate had engaged before their marriage to work the land, had always hired many additional men to help him during the time of heavy work, in the spring and in the fall, but since last spring there had been no men to hire; either they had been drafted and were now in German prison camps, or they were needed on their own farms to replace other men who had left for the army. Pollison had done his best by himself, assisted by the farm machinery Kate had bought which the other farmers of the region so envied, but now he had come to Mistral—actually *broke into his work*, Mistral thought incredulously—and told him that he feared a shortage of petrol to run the cultivators. The new government in Vichy was beginning to ration everything.

"*Merde*, Pollison! Is that my affair?" he roared.

"I'm sorry, Monsieur Mistral, but I thought I must tell you, since Madame is not here."

"Pollison, do whatever you can, but *never* bother me in my studio again, you understand?"

"But Monsieur Mistral . . ."

"Pollison," he shouted, "enough! Figure it out yourself, that's what you're here for."

As Jean Pollison hastily retreated from the studio he thought to himself that no matter how Monsieur Mistral played at being a part of the life of the village, no matter that he was the boules champion of the region, no matter how many rounds of drinks he bought for everyone at the café, he was still a stranger from Paris, and nothing would ever change that.

Five days after the cease-fire of June 17, Marte Pollison knocked timidly at the door of Mistral's studio late one afternoon. Normally she just left his lunch tray outside the studio, but today her errand was so important that it overcame her terror of angering him.

"What is it?" he barked.

"Monsieur Mistral, I must speak to you."

"Come in, damn it! What the hell is it?"

"People have arrived in a car filled with baggage asking to spend the night. It's Monsieur and Madame Behrman with their three children. I told them to wait outside until I spoke to you. They're driving to the border, trying to get into Spain. He said it's no longer safe for Jews to stay in France."

Mistral punched one big fist into the palm of his other hand in rage. Charles Behrman, and his wife, Toupette, were old friends. He had known Behrman, a sculptor, since the days of Montparnasse. They had rented the studio next to his on the boulevard Arago and often fed Mistral when he was broke. But now they had three small children, and when Kate had invited them down for a weekend several years before, Mistral found the children annoyingly bois-terous. Mistral thought quickly. It was intolerable, Behrman's thinking that he could just drop in with his whole irritating family, expecting food and lodging. And who knew how long they might stay once they were comfortable? If he chose to chase off to Spain because he was a Jew, that was his own problem. The war, after all, was over, the cease-fire established all over France.

"Did you tell him I was here?" he asked Marte Pollison.

"Not exactly, just that I would have to ask you before I let them in."

"Go back and tell them you can't find me, that I've gone out and you don't know when I'll be back. Tell them that you have no authority to allow them to spend the night without my permission. *Get rid of them one way or another.* You didn't let them inside the gate?"

197

"No, it was closed."

"Good. Make sure that they drive off, keep a good eye on them until they've gone beyond the oak forest."

"Yes, Monsieur Mistral."

The day after the Behrmans had been turned away from *La Tourrello*, Mistral went up to the café in Félice and bought a round of *pastis* for his friends. He listened with unusual care to the words of the men at the bar. Genuine ill feeling and bitterness had begun to divide them for the first time since he had met them. Men who had enjoyed good-natured, long-running, political arguments for years now had formed into two angry camps, those who thought Pétain's cease-fire had saved France and those who thought he was a traitor.

There was only one subject on which everyone seemed to agree, the infuriating invasion of the countryside by the blasted northerners, people who had escaped from the Occupied Zone into the South before the line of demarcation had closed, and those others, amazing in their numbers, who were still managing to filter through the line illegally. The strangers were everywhere, ill prepared, often in panic, desperate for unobtainable food and petrol, swamping the local authorities with their presence, a pest and a plague on villages and farms. Resentment was high against these hordes who couldn't stay peacefully where they belonged.

Mistral returned home thoughtfully. He knew too many people in Paris. He knew many too many Jews. Because of Kate and her constant hospitality, her years of exhibiting their contentment at the *mas*, too many friends had learned the road to *La Tourrello*. They knew how many extra bedrooms it had, how rich its fields were, how self-sufficient the property had become. There were bound to be many more unexpected visitors like the Behrmans and there was no way to know when they would arrive, or in what condition of need.

He called Marte and Jean Pollison together in the kitchen.

"Pollison," he said to the man, "I want you to build a high fence where the road to the *mas* branches off from the road to Félice. I don't want anyone coming here and disturbing me at my work—the whole country is crawling with people who will try to take advantage, and I must *not* be bothered by them."

"Yes, Monsieur Mistral."

"And, Madame Pollison, I don't want any more interruptions of my work. If anyone should ignore the gate and come through the woods, don't come to let me know. Tell them that I haven't been here for a while and that you can't receive them. Don't open the gate for anyone, under any circumstances, use only the little postman's window. For no one. Do you understand?"

"Yes, Monsieur."

In the two years that followed, a number of old friends and acquaintances who had known Mistral for years were to make their dangerous, laborious, terrified way to *La Tourrello*, sometimes aided by Frenchmen and Frenchwomen who risked their lives to help them. All of them hoped for just a single night's shelter from those who hunted them so efficiently and mercilessly. Many of these despairing and hounded refugees disregarded the stout fence and managed to make their way to the *mas*, but the great wooden doors were always kept tightly locked and Marte Pollison responded grimly and negatively to the frantic ringing of the doorbell that sounded in the kitchen.

Most of those who came were Jews and only a few of them survived the war.

In June of 1942, as he followed his mother's small funeral procession, Adrien Avigdor realized that now he was free to leave Paris . . . if free was a word that could be used at all at such a time. He made sure that the yellow Star of David bordered in black, as big as the palm of his hand, with the word *Juif* inscribed on it in black letters, was clearly visible on his jacket. Women were being picked up all over Paris for carrying their handbags in a way that obscured the star; a man had been arrested only yesterday for wearing a star that wasn't sewn on tightly; last week an old lady who lived near him had been caught and taken away when she ventured outside to pick up her mail in her bathrobe, forgetting that it bore no star at all. Three stars for each Jew, the order of the twenty-ninth of May 1942 had decreed, and he had been made to give up tickets from his textile ration card for each of them.

He had not foreseen this, no one had foreseen this, when Avigdor had made his decision to stay in Paris. His mother was too crippled by arthritis to move, and together, during those hot weeks in June, two years earlier, they had watched the exodus from behind the closed shutters of Avigdor's apartment on the boulevard St.-Germain.

By night and by day they had watched the mute, terrified herd struggling southward. Most of Paris, entire villages to the north and the east, hundreds of miles of countryside, were abandoned to the oncoming enemy. The population had taken to the roads in whatever vehicles they possessed, only to leave them when they ran out of petrol and to continue on foot, carrying miserable children, umbrellas and Sunday hats, pushing baby carriages filled with pathetic, useless household treasures; farmers lugged chickens in cages and prodded cows bellowing with thirst.

"Go Adrien, go!" Madame Avigdor had begged him. "I'm an old woman. You mustn't stay to be with me . . . Madame Blanchet across the hall has offered to fetch me whatever I want. Leave now, Adrien, while you can!"

"Maman, don't be foolish. Just look at those people—bedraggled, hypnotized, a rabble—I assure you that I have no intention of joining them. How can I abandon my artists, how can I leave my gallery?"

He didn't tell her that he had no confidence in her neighbor's promises, that he could not possibly leave her alone to face the arrival of the Germans. And it was true enough that he was busily engaged in saving the hundreds of paintings that had been entrusted to him by many who had decided to flee. They represented the finest works of the artists for whom he was a dealer and it was up to him to make sure that they were securely secreted. Who knew what the Germans would do when they came? Hitler hated new art. Even old Picasso was a "degenerate" in Nazi eyes. Someone had to stay.

Now, two years later, he could only smile grimly at his bravado, yet he would make that same decision today. He had been able to make his mother's last years bearable and he was glad she had not lived long after the decree that made the wearing of the Star of David mandatory for every French Jew over the age of six.

She had lived long enough, however, to have had to be helped stand on her crippled legs to line up to register as a Jew at the Préfecture of Police; long enough to have seen the word *Juif* written in large letters on her identity card, long enough to have learned that all non-French Jews had been rounded up and sent away.

Thank God she had not lived to know, as he did, that now all French Jews, even those who had lived in France for many centuries, were forbidden to practice any profession, to work in any business, prohibited from using the telephone, from buying a stamp, from going to restaurants, cafés, libraries and films. Even from sitting in public squares. Nevertheless, we retain one right, Avigdor told himself in grim humor, we can buy food during one hour each day, from three to four o'clock—when most shops are closed.

The trains still ran from time to time and civilians traveled, but not without the *ausweis*, or German permit. As Avigdor thought over the possibilities open to him he realized that all over France millions of people were traveling to weddings, funerals and christenings, were visiting sick relatives or moving to another part of the country for their health or their business. Life, under the Germans, for most Frenchmen, continued under the meanest and most miserable of terms from the point of view of nourishment and heat and rationing and restrictions of every kind, but nevertheless they were allowed to *try* to survive.

Soutine, he knew, had sought refuge in Touraine, Max Jacob in St.-Benôit-sur-Loire, Braque was in l'Isle sur la Sorgue, his friend, the great art dealer Kahnweiller, lived in Limousin under the name of Kersaint, Picasso was still working busily in Paris and so were the collaborators, Vlaminck and Cocteau.

Avigdor's gallery had been confiscated and turned over, by order of the Germans, to a non-Jewish dealer who now did a lively trade with the enemy, selling the daubs of tenth-rate artists. During the last months Avigdor had sought information on the best way to escape from Paris, although that great source of all valuable gossip, Paula Deslandes, had died several months ago of a heart attack and La Pomme d'Or was closed for good.

From the earliest days of the Resistance Paula had been busy helping people who were in danger. "I've been in training for this all my life," she'd told Avigdor gaily. "I knew there were many reasons never to leave Paris and now I've found the best one of all— I stay put and find ways to get others out."

Most Parisians had soon returned to their city after the first fright; pretty women wore new hats, and those with money could eat openly in black-market restaurants without feeling guilty since 10 percent of their check went to the national charity. In the cafés the intellectuals still talked; people still fell in love and went to church; and women gave birth. Nevertheless, there was no one whose life had not been profoundly changed.

Each Frenchman and Frenchwoman reacted differently to the presence of the Germans, and Avigdor, whose understanding of other humans had once been directed toward selling them antiques and paintings, now used his sharp instincts to decide to whom it was safe to go for a false identity card and an *ausweis*. *Everything* was obtainable, every degree of false card, including the "real" false card that came from the police, right down to the most lamentable and obvious forgeries.

As he had cared for his ailing mother, Adrien Avigdor took note of the comings and goings of the neighborhood. Like almost every other Frenchman, Avigdor had been able to keep from starving by recourse to the *Marché Parallèle*, an institution which might have been called the black market except that almost everyone who could afford to make use of it, did so. The rations permitted by the Germans were simply not enough to maintain life and, in any case, were rarely available.

Oh, he had his sources, he had his friends, he had been reserving them for a long while for this eventuality. Thank God he had the money to pay to escape the prison of Paris.

More than two weeks later, armed with an identity card that did not bear the word *Juif*, the indispensable ration cards for food and textiles, and a valid *ausweis*, Adrien Avigdor, wearing the blue garb of a farmworker, and clutching a precious bicycle, was jammed into a train carriage traveling south. He had been en route for days, most of the time spent waiting for a train in various squalid, overflowing stations, packed with people whose unscheduled trains had not yet appeared and who waited patiently, exhausted, sitting on their bundles and packages all night. Once nine o'clock came, the curfew imprisoned them in the stations until the next morning.

Several times, Germans working their way through the trains had inspected his papers methodically, checking his face against his photograph. Open, amiable, frank, not too clever, his ordinary farmer's face had never aroused the slightest suspicion, his new cards, adroitly "aged," which had cost him as much as a country estate, were impeccable. Avigdor was on his way to make contact with the large Resistance operation in the mountains near Aix-en-Provence but he had resolved first to stop and see Mistral.

Who knew if he would ever see the painter again? He had to

satisfy himself that the man was safe. What if he had been sent to Germany for forced labor as so many had been? There had been no communication between them since the fall of France. What if Kate, who had always retained her American citizenship, had been rounded up and deported? Avigdor had kept in touch as much as possible with what had happened to most of his artists under the Occupation—somehow news filtered through—but he had been deeply troubled by the lack of the slightest scrap of information about Mistral.

It was a long and wearying bicycle ride from the station in Avignon to Félice, but Adrien Avigdor relished it. Being in the open country after years of confined city life was pure joy. He realized that he would be lucky to reach *La Tourrello* by curfew as he toiled up the road from the hamlet of Beaumettes. Everywhere he saw fields left untilled, vines neglected. In every corner of France, the Vichy regime, who had done the Germans' work for them in the Unoccupied Zone since the armistice, had taken away many able-bodied men to work in German factories, replacing German soldiers. However, the production of food was always a necessity and Avigdor saw many people still in the fields, women and children as well as men of his age, old men and boys.

Exhausted, he pushed his bike up the hill leading to the *mas*, through the forest of live oaks, crossed the meadow and pounded on the tall gates he knew so well. After a long wait Madame Pollison opened the small window of wood and looked out forbiddingly.

Avigdor smiled at the familiar face he had come to know so well during his visits of the past years. "So you think you've seen a ghost, do you? It's wonderful to lay eyes on you, Madame Pollison, absolutely wonderful! I hope you still have a bottle of wine left in the cellar for me? Well, come on, open up—where is Monsieur Mistral?"

"You can't come in, Monsieur Avigdor," the woman said.

"Is there something wrong?" he asked, instantly alarmed by her expression.

"No one is to come in, Monsieur."

"What are you talking about? I've cycled all the way from Avignon. Are you afraid of something, Madame Pollison?"

"Nothing, Monsieur, but I have my orders. We can receive no one."

"But I must see Monsieur Mistral!"

"He is away."

"But, Madame Pollison, you *know* me! How many times have I stayed here, for God's sake? I'm a friend—more than a friend. Come on, let me in—what's the matter with you?"

"That was before. Monsieur Mistral is not here and I can't admit you."

"*Where is he?* Was he taken away for labor? Where is Madame?"

"I told you, Monsieur is out. Madame stayed in her own country. *Au revoir*, Monsieur Avigdor." The housekeeper drew back from the door and closed the window of wood in his face.

Avigdor stood there incredulously. The *mas* was shut as tight as any walled village of the Middle Ages. That beastly woman! He'd never liked her but it was incredible that she had not welcomed him. She knew perfectly well how close he was to the family. Where could Mistral have gone? What would Mistral do to her when he found out that she had sent him away? He started to pound on the door again but looked up at the sky first. It was still light, but darkness and the curfew were coming soon. There was just enough time to get back to Beaumettes with its one country inn.

Furiously, cursing, Avigdor quickly headed the bicycle down the hill but before plunging into the oak forest, he stopped, turned and gave one last unbelieving look backward toward the *mas*.

There, in the high window of the *pigeonnier* was a massive, unmistakable head. Julien Mistral stood watching him depart. With his keen sight, Avigdor could even see the fierce, determined, set expression on the painter's face. He stopped as abruptly as if he'd been shot and gave a great shout of relief. Their eyes met for a long minute over the distance. Mistral withdrew from the window. Avigdor, his heart pounding, rushed back to the gate and waited for him to come and open the gate. It was all that moronic housekeeper's fault. She had acted on her own without ever asking Mistral.

Minutes passed in the twilight hush, long minutes during which the silence of the *mas* grew more solid, long minutes before Adrien Avigdor finally understood and remounted his bicycle. He had not wept when the Germans marched down the Champs Elysées, he had not wept when he sewed on his yellow star, he had not wept when his mother had died, but he wept now.

Five months after Avigdor started to work with the Resistance, the Allies landed in North Africa and the Germans took over all of France. The Unoccupied Zone no longer existed, a large German garrison with its inevitable branch of the Gestapo was established in Avignon, and troops were stationed five kilometers from Félice, at Nôtre Dame-des-Lumières.

For almost two years Julien Mistral had worked in the fields. Even he had been forced to accept the fact that unless he worked officially at food production, as did everyone in Provence, he risked forced labor. In any case if he expected to eat he had to till the soil. The shopkeepers of Félice had almost no food to sell at any price. The farmer was now the one who ate, if not his fill, at least better than people in the big towns who were dying of hunger every day while the crops, the butter, the milk and the meat of France went to the Germans.

Mistral gave his toil of the day for the promise of painting at night, the shutters of the studio tightly closed, so as not to show the mild illumination he managed to create with the candles that had been stockpiled before the war by Kate, who believed as firmly as any French *châtelaine* in a bulging larder, far-sighted Kate who had piled up bars of soap as if they were gold ingots; who, much to Mistral's scorn, had filled armoires with blankets and dozens of heavy, hand-woven linen sheets that had never been used.

Now these sheets, treated with a kind of sizing made by boiling rabbit bones into a glue, served him as canvases. They were priceless, his most precious possessions. Bitterly he regretted the bonfires of former years. What would he not have given to have those paintings back so that he could paint over them? With growing despair he saw his stock of paints dwindle, although he rationed himself as severely as possible. Still, while he was working, sometimes he would forget, and lost in the trance of creation he would use paint as he always had. Then, as the candles guttered, Mistral was overwhelmed with the blackest misery as he confronted the half-empty tubes that had been almost full mere hours before.

A few weeks after the Germans came to Avignon a black Citroën stopped before the gates to Mistral's *mas*. A German officer in his green uniform got out, followed by two soldiers with cocked machine guns. Rigid and pale, Marte Pollison made haste to open the gates so that they could drive in.

"Is this the home of Julien Mistral?" the officer asked in passable French.

"Yes, sir."

"Go and get him."

No Frenchman answered the summons of a German officer without fear, even Mistral, who had no hidden radio tuned to the BBC wavelength, who had taken no part in any Resistance effort, who was perfectly *en règle* with the Vichy authorities.

The captain introduced himself with a flourish. "Kapitän Schmitt." He extended his hand and Mistral shook it. The German waved his arm at the soldiers and they lowered their guns.

"It is a great honor to meet you, Monsieur Mistral," Schmitt said. "For years I have admired your work. In fact I am a bit of a painter myself—only an amateur, of course, but nevertheless I have a great love of all art."

"Thank you," Mistral replied. The man sounded like one of the dozens of daubers he had taken pains to avoid in the past. His uniform seemed totally at odds with his friendly words.

"I was stationed in Paris until recently and I had the pleasure of visiting Picasso in his studio. I had hoped that if it wasn't inconvenient you might allow me to see your own studio—I have read so much about it."

"Certainly," Mistral answered. He led the way to the studio wing of the *mas*. Schmitt looked carefully at the canvases Mistral had piled against the walls. His exclamations of pleasure were perceptive and intelligent and showed a thorough knowledge of the body of Mistral's work. Before the war, he explained, growing more talkative, he had visited Paris every year in the autumn to see the new exhibitions and tour the museums. At his home outside Frankfurt he had his own little studio, and even now, in Avignon, whenever he had the time, he worked at his portable easel. "I can't resist painting, it's my weakness. I painted in Paris every weekend for two years, you understand how it is."

"Perfectly."

The captain gave his soldiers an order and one of them ran out to the black car and returned a minute later with a bottle of cognac.

"I thought . . ." the officer said with a trace of shyness, present-ing the bottle to Mistral, "please allow me—I would be honored."

Mistral stared hard at this polite, enthusiastic, cultivated man who was the only person to have seen his new paintings in two and a half years. Paintings that were his body, his heartbeats, his breath, his every vital function. The soldiers had disappeared.

"Sit down," Mistral said, "I'll get some glasses. Let's have a drink."

Kapitän Schmitt became a regular visitor, dropping by every two or three weeks. On his first visit he offered to bring Mistral tubes of paint and Mistral accepted them eagerly.

Later in the year, when the Todt Organization, which was fast becoming the largest employer in France, swept through the Lubéron, drafting thousands of farmers to build submarine bases, blockhouses and airfields, Schmitt took Mistral's dossier and marked it in such a way that he was exempt from the work which would have finally forced him to leave his studio.

If his neighbors concerned themselves with his friendship—for that was what it had become—with a German officer, Mistral never knew about it, for he no longer went to the café in Félice. The atmosphere there was closed, suspicious and dismal, there was nothing left to drink, and only a few old men and young boys ever ventured out to play boules.

One day as he came back late from his cabbages, Mistral found Madame Pollison shrieking with anger.

"They came and took everything! *Everything.* The last chicken, the turnips, the jam, the ration books—they searched the house, the young bandits, they even searched me! Oh, Monsieur Mistral, if only you'd been here—"

"Who came?" Mistral demanded roughly.

"I don't know, I've never seen them before, not anyone from around here—young savages, gangsters, criminals—they went toward Lacoste through the woods . . ."

"Did they go into the studio?"

"They went everywhere, there wasn't a door they didn't open . . ."

Mistral ran to the studio and examined it quickly. He came out screaming, "*Where are my sheets?*"

"They took those too, and the ones in the house as well, and all the blankets . . ."

"*All the sheets?*"

"What could I do, Monsieur Mistral? I ask you?" she cried, indignation mingled with fury. "I tell you they were gangsters."

When Kapitän Schmitt came, the next day, on one of his regular visits, bringing as usual a painting he had completed for Mistral to look at and criticize, he found the painter haggard.

"What's wrong? Has anything happened?"

"I've been robbed," Mistral answered grimly.

"Was it Germans? If so, I'll look into it, rest assured."

"No, I don't know who they were—young bandits, my house-keeper says. A bunch of thugs."

"The *Maquis?*"

"All I know is that they were strangers, she'd never seen them before."

"What did they take?" Schmitt asked, concerned over the mask of despair that was Mistral's face.

"Many things, of no importance, damn them to bloody, eternal hell, but why did they take my *sheets?* How can I work? I haven't a single canvas left. I could kill them! Bastards! Scum!"

"Where did they go?"

"I don't know—Madame Pollison said toward Lacoste, on the forest road. By now they could be anywhere."

"I'll see what I can do to get you some canvases—it isn't easy, there is almost none anywhere, but I'll try."

Two days later Schmitt returned with his car filled with the wide linen bedsheets.

"No canvas—but I got you your sheets back," he said beaming.

"How . . . ?"

"We found the thieves in the woods, near where you said they'd gone—a regular nest of them . . . they were loaded with stuff—they'd been out 'requisitioning' all over, or so it looked. *Maquis.*"

"*They weren't Maquis!*"

"Oh, yes, Julien, they were. Twenty of them. Don't worry, the little swine won't bother anyone ever again."

15

Shortness, Teddy Lunel thought with wistful, hopeless longing as she looked about her in the class-room, shortness is the answer. It must be.

There had been so many times in the past seven years at the Elm School, a small, private school just off Central Park West, when she had finally decided that her lack of popularity must be due to one or another of the things about her that made her different.

She didn't, like all the other girls, have a father or a family. Her mother, unlike any of theirs, worked all day. She had skipped third grade and was a year younger than her classmates. Eventually Teddy had worked it out that it had to be her height that caused her to be relegated to the ranks of the outsiders, the few girls who were lumped together like untouchables by the formidable band of the acceptable girls, who decided, with as much gravity as if they were electing a pope, which of them was the most popular, which the next most popular, right on down to that fatal line that excluded Teddy forever.

She had never been invited to a birthday party unless some mother democratically insisted on inviting the entire class; during the lunch hour no group ever saved a seat for her in the cafeteria; when clumps of girls formed to giggle at secrets during recess, Teddy had never been beckoned to join their priceless intimacy.

This exclusion seemed to have reached back to the first day of first grade, there was no appeal that could be made to change it, no person from whom she could seek an explanation—it simply existed, with mysterious finality.

There was no one wise in the ways of little girls who could have told Teddy that her extraordinary beauty was, at her age, a calamity that set her apart; nobody to point out that her peers weren't able to deal with a beauty so uncompromising, so inescapable, that it made her seem to belong to a different species from their own. When adults complimented her, and few of them could resist, she completely discounted whatever they said for they didn't know that no matter how she looked no one liked her.

Just as Teddy couldn't see herself in the mirror and know that she was already a classic beauty, neither could she draw back from the situation and understand the ways of school. How could a thirteen-year-old girl be philosophical about the need that exists in children, as it does in all other social groups, to form up into layers of clubbiness and that in order for any of the layers to seem ultimately desirable, there must always be one group that does not belong to any of them?

This same phenomenon operates in leper colonies, among whores, in jails and on the sidewalks of Calcutta. None of this knowledge would have comforted Teddy Lunel, who, at thirteen, had reached her full growth of five feet ten and a half inches, standing three inches above Mr. Simon, her eighth-grade teacher.

Maggy had no understanding of Teddy's position as one of the pariahs of the class. Teddy had never been able to admit it to her mother, who loved her with such a proud love, a love that made an implicit demand that Teddy be happy, be exceptional, be all that Maggy had ever dreamed of in a child. Teddy was terrorized by the possibility of jeopardizing her position as the joy of her mother's life if she diluted that love with the reality of her sad, lonely chagrin and bewilderment. She hid her wounds from Maggy as if she had indeed done something so awful that she deserved them. Very early in her life she learned to deceive, quickly she discovered that she could create a fantasy of an untroubled day that Maggy would believe and find reassuring.

Maggy often thought that Teddy lacked normal vanity. But perhaps it was just as well, considering how young her daughter was, she concluded, feeling wise and careful, for to Maggy, whose business was based on women's beauty, it seemed that Teddy had been designed by witchcraft. She was a creature of the most romantic contrasts, her hair, a dark red, its curling strands held a bewilderment of colors from almost brown to almost gold, her skin was so pale that when she flushed she seemed to flash into a moment of passionate fever, her delicate mouth was so mobile, so firmly outlined, such a riotous natural pink that it looked as if she were wearing lipstick. Under wonderfully astonished eyebrows, she had her father's eyes, blue and green and gray by turn, but they were set as far apart as Maggy's own. Her nose was splendid, a real nose, Maggy thought proudly, a fine, shapely firm nose that gave Teddy a faintly haughty air. It was, admittedly, perhaps too important a nose for a face without makeup, a child's face, to carry, but time would take care of that. Maggy never really saw Teddy as another child among children, because her practiced eye, alert to detect beauty, saw the woman she would become, not the too tall, too proud, too different-looking girl she was.

Although Maggy had no idea that Teddy would have joyfully traded her beauty to be little and cute, she had always been concerned about the fact that Teddy had not one relative in the world, no family but herself.

In the earliest days of the Lunel Agency, when Maggy was still working from home, she had watched with gratitude as her first models treated Teddy as if she were their baby sister. Soon, when Maggy moved to a suite of offices in the Carnegie Hall building, adding more phone lines and more assistants and more office space every year, she had asked Nanny Butterfield, and later Mademoiselle Gallirand, who replaced her, to bring Teddy to the office after school to play for a few hours several times a week.

Later, when Teddy had homework, there was a special desk set up for her in a quiet corner and the Lunel girls, who now numbered a hundred and twenty, would pop into Teddy's "office" to give her a quick hug, show her a new picture of themselves, complain about their aching feet or ask for an apple from the pile that Maggy kept heaped in a basket on Teddy's desk. They were a wonderful band of honorary relatives, Maggy thought defiantly, as she shopped at Saks and De Pinna on Saturday, when the office was closed, for yet more pastel cashmere sweaters, yet another expensive imported tweed or flannel skirt for Teddy to wear to school.

The Elm School was only a short walk away from the big high apartment Maggy rented in the handsome San Remo, at Seventy-fourth and Central Park West, overlooking the park. The towers of Fifth Avenue rose facing them across the entire width of the park and it was precisely this separation that had made Maggy decide upon the apartment, although she could easily have afforded to live in the most elegant part of the East Sixties or Seventies and sent her daughter to one of the better known, more fashionable schools. But on the East Side, Teddy would have been in constant danger of bumping into a Kilkullen or a McDonnell or a Murray, or a Buckley: the East Side was the *quartier* of the Establishment Catholics, and after Maggy had lost her job at Bianchi's, after the scandal of the Mistral exhibition, she had tried to keep her child at a distance. It is ridiculously easy in any city to just drop out of the small circle of fashionable neighborhoods and schools. Particularly, Maggy thought, when you have never been a part of it.

Teddy roamed the Sam Remo as if it were her fief. There wasn't one of the black elevator operators whose life history she didn't know; she was a favorite with the doormen who were always ready to lend her a piece of chalk for sidewalk hopscotch, at which, with her long legs, she was a natural champion. When she wasn't in school she was a volatile, talkative girl, always in motion, on roller skates, on her bike, or belly-flopping down the hills of the park on her sled in winter. Like the Pied Piper, she often led a romping file of children much younger than she, and when they were tired of playing, Teddy told them complicated stories about tropical jungles and raft trips down the Amazon.

There were other days, usually in the spring when a soft rain fell and the first forsythia splashed its yellow promise over the gray park, on which Teddy would take solitary refuge in Anne Hathaway's Garden, at the foot of an old stone tower. There, her imagination flaming, her hopes dancing, her heart high, she would dream her vague, glorious silvery dreams of love, and wonder when, oh, when, would it happen to her?

When Teddy, at thirteen, graduated from eighth grade, she led the class into the auditorium, a decision reached in a half-hour of wrangling among the teachers about whether her height would be less noticeable if she were first in line or last, since putting her in the middle was obviously unthinkable.

As she walked across the stage in her white dress to get her diploma there was an outburst of applause from the audience.

Maggy had invited Darcy, the Longworths, Gay and Oliver Barnes, and a dozen of her favorite models to come and see her daughter finish elementary school. The twelve top cover girls of 1941, decked out in their best hats, whooped and hollered and whistled as they watched Teddy, her eyes downcast so that she wouldn't trip, walk with a grace that some of them would never be able to learn. "My God, Doe," said one of them who had just had her twenty-fourth birthday, "wouldn't it be wonderful to be young again?" "I still am, darling," Doe replied but a sudden finger of doubt touched her heart. She, too, was twenty-four.

In high school Teddy resolutely forged an alliance with a few of the unpopular girls. Sally was a bookworm who wore thick glasses and sweated too much; Harriet stuttered and wore orthopedic shoes, and Mary-Anne was the teacher's pet, always sitting in the front row of every class, ready to wave her hand triumphantly when others failed to know the answers, but the three of them became her best friends.

Teddy stopped going to the park or to the Lunel Agency after school in favor of doing her homework with her new allies. The four of them would gather at one another's houses and finish their assignments as quickly as possible so that they could get down to the real business of these afternoons, the discussion, in unfailingly fascinating detail, of their romantic dreams. They had no actual boy in mind, just a vague notion of someone male, somewhere in the distant future. The most burning question they dealt with was that of the wedding night. How could you wear a nightgown like those their mothers possessed? After all, it was possible to *see through* those nightgowns—they had all sneaked into their mothers' drawers and held the pretty, fancy things up and made sure of this incomprehensible, frighteningly strange fact. How could you get from the bathroom to the bed wearing a gown that was almost transparent? How could you, assuming that you wore a bathrobe over the nightgown, *ever* take the bathrobe off? Would you actually get *into* the bed? Or would you just lie on top of it? *And then what?* At that point they all stopped talking in a flurry of giggles and went into the kitchen for brownies and Cokes.

One day Teddy had tried to tell them what happened next. "The father takes his penis and puts it in the mother's vagina and seeds come out that swim . . ." She was interrupted by a chorus of

213

disgusted shrieks and squeals. Her friends didn't want to hear such revolting details and they could not believe that Teddy's mother— even if she did work—had ever really sat down with her and told her these horrible things. At barely fourteen they hadn't really recovered from the shock of their first periods and what Maggy called "the facts of life" were far too unromantic and entirely too clinical for them to bear.

What then, Teddy wondered, would they think if they knew the whole truth about *her*? If they couldn't even listen to how a baby was made, what would they say if they knew she was a bastard? Oh, Mom had used a different term, of course, but it didn't change the truth.

She couldn't remember how old she had been when Maggy, finding it easier to express herself in the French they spoke together than in the English they spoke with everyone else, had told her that she was "*une enfante naturelle*"—but it was so long ago that she had had to *grow up* to the knowledge, gradually working out what exactly it meant long after she had first heard the words. How had Maggy let her know that her background was something she must not investigate? How had she been taught to know how to say, in a way that stopped all further questions, that her father was dead? She couldn't explain it even to herself, but it was long ago and she accepted it absolutely.

Like some Melanesian native confronted with a dish of sacred food that is consecrated to the use of priests, Teddy stepped instantly, self-protectively away from the forbidden subject. It was an interdiction so strong, so total, that she dared not ask Maggy more about it. This taboo set squarely in the living center of her life kept Teddy apart from her friends. None of them had any real secrets. Indeed the prime objective of their friendship was to share secrets, to confide, to reassure each other, to be companions and comrades in the difficult business of puberty.

Maggy had offered Teddy few details about her father. When she thought Teddy was old enough to understand, she told her that he had been an Irish Catholic who, before he died of a heart attack, had been prevented from marrying her by the laws of his church. Her manner as she said these few, halting words was strained, tense and so forbiddingly sad that it would have warded off any demands to know more, even if Teddy had dared to make them.

Teddy worshipped her mother but she was a little afraid of her. Many people were.

The habit of command, of being in total charge of a growing, prosperous business had added a formidable dimension to Maggy's character that was lacking in almost every other woman of the 1940s. It was a dimension that if it made it hard to think of her as maternal, made it easy to think of her as "The Boss" as all her girls called her, except when she was angry. Then they whispered to each other that "Marie Antoinette" was at large. On those days any girl who had gained more than a single pound invented excuses to avoid coming into the agency, every model who had stayed out too late at the Stork Club or El Morocco the night before took special care with her makeup and no one, absolutely no one, was a minute late for any booking.

At thirty-four Maggy had the authentically proud, bravura air of the acknowledged great beauty. When she was seventeen she had looked years older than her age; now she looked younger than her peers. Time had only accentuated the daring line of the bones under her taut, still luminous skin. She had grown into her self-confidence of movement, the spangles of her Pernod-colored eyes were brightened by wit and experience.

At the office Maggy dressed in black and gray suits and, in the summer, white suits, tailored to an almost inhuman perfection of line by Hattie Carnegie. The Burmese pearls she had received for her twentieth birthday were always around her neck, a fresh red carnation always pinned to her lapel. Titania of Saks Fifth Avenue designed the enchanting hats which she wore even when she was seated at her desk, as did most of the top fashion editors of the day. Maggy was friendly with all of them; she often had lunch with one or another at the Pavillon where Henri Soulé reserved one of his best tables for her every day. If by chance she were not planning to go there, she would have her secretary telephone to free the table.

And at night, there was always Jason Darcy, her best friend, her lover of many years, her co-conspirator, the man whom she would never marry. It was something Maggy hadn't even been able to make her dearest woman friend, Lally Longworth, understand. She had tried, God knows, when Lally took her to task years ago. "Are you totally mad, Maggy Lunel?" she had demanded. "Darcy's dying to marry you. What on earth is stopping you from saying yes?"

"Oh, Lally, Lally, I must never depend on a man. If we got

married I know just what would happen. Slowly, inevitably, I'd have to spend less and less time at work until one day I'd just give up the business and be Darcy's hostess and travel with him and worry about our houses and our servants and our dinner parties—maybe even our children. I'd be *in his power*, Lally, and I don't want that ever to happen. I can *not* depend on any man to support me." Maggy put down her drink and almost shook Lally to make her understand.

"What if we found out that we couldn't be happy together and we got a divorce? Then, just tell me, where would I be? You can't build a business like mine and then drop it and expect it to be waiting for you when you get back . . . it isn't possible. It's much better to go on as we have—Darcy knows that he has me; there's no other man I care about. If that's not enough for him I'm sorry, but that's the only way it can be."

"And I was going to give you the wedding," Lally said in a tone of exaggerated disappointment, but she was privately appalled by Maggy's grim view of marriage. Lord have mercy, if every woman thought so clear-mindedly about divorce before she got married the human race would die out in a generation.

Maggy knew that Teddy must speculate on her relationship with Darcy, but if she couldn't explain it successfully to a woman as sophisticated as Lally Longworth, she wasn't going to try to make it comprehensible to a teenager. Oh, there was so much that she couldn't quite explain to Teddy, she thought with a familiar, guilty fear. She had never told Teddy that she, Maggy, was illegitimate herself. Instead she had invented a story of being orphaned early. Teddy, who was lost in *Wuthering Heights*, whose bible became *Gone With the Wind* and who saw *The Philadelphia Story* a dozen times, was too befuddled by high romance to question her mother closely.

And then there was the problem of Teddy's lack of a defined religion. Maggy's own Jewish identity had never depended on religious observance, although she had lived in a closely knit Jewish community during her early years, and Rabbi Taradash had been her example of the dignity and wisdom of Judaism. From the time she ran away from home she felt no personal need to carry on specific traditions that, to her, were somehow unnecessary. She felt that she *was* a Jew—but she had no obligation to be an observant

216

one. The menorah she had left behind in Paris had never been sent for and she hadn't had the heart to replace it.

Years too late for it to have been worthwhile, she sent Teddy to Sunday school at the Spanish and Portuguese Synagogue on Central Park West. Teddy spent one bewildered morning discovering that everyone else seemed to belong there, to know and care about what they were learning. She decided that nothing could make her return to a place that made even the pecking order at the Elm School seem comfortable in comparison. As soon as she was old enough to take a bus by herself she ventured into St. Patrick's Cathedral, sat down in an inconspicuous pew and looked about in frightened curiosity.

This immensity of stone, this softly buzzing cave of blue and red and golden lights, these ranks of candles, the many sober, self-contained people going about their business so confidently—what had they to do with her? No more than the Synagogue school, she decided. She was no more Catholic than Jewish—no more and no less. To Maggy she announced that she thought she was a pantheist, or perhaps a pagan, whichever it was that felt more strongly about apple trees in bloom, the Brontë sisters, weeping willows, Siamese cats, the hot dogs at Jones Beach, and the Staten Island ferry.

"Patsy Berg touched a boy's *thing!*" Sally said with an air of fascinated incredulity.

"I don't believe you!" Mary-Anne said, stunned.

"If she did, he must have *forced* her," Harriet said with the look of someone with superior knowledge.

Teddy said nothing. She would give almost anything just to *see* a boy's thing. Touching it was even too much to dream about. She roamed the corridors of the Metropolitan Museum looking in vain for a statue that would possess a penis that was more than a marble curlicue, as insignificant as if it were a decoration on a birthday cake. Mostly they were broken off like the noses on the Greek statues. She *knew* that there had to be more to the whole mystery than the museum revealed.

But she was almost sixteen and only one boy had ever asked her out on a date, Harriet's second cousin, Melvin Allenberg. Melvin was short, almost elfin, and he wore thick glasses, but he was a senior at Collegiate, and when he smiled she told herself there was something about his grin that reminded her, for a split second, of

Van Johnson, except that he wasn't blond or tall or handsome. But on the other hand, he didn't have pimples. The next time that little Melvin Allenberg asked Teddy to go to the movies with him she accepted.

From the moment Melvin had first seen Teddy, his rampaging imagination had grasped her in a hold in which reverence mingled with longing. Her height only seemed one more uniquely wonderful thing about her. His fantasy was to live on an island peopled only by tall, beautiful women, who would, at his command, do anything he asked.

Before her date Teddy shaved the fine golden hair on her legs, the first of her friends to do so. The others watched in gloomy depression. "The hairs will grow back in like the stubble of a man's beard—real tough and scratchy," Mary-Anne warned. "Now you'll have to do it every week," Sally said with malice, "for the rest of your whole life." "I can't believe you're going through this for my icky, second cousin, Melvin, even if he is eighteen—you're crazy, Teddy Lunel," said Harriet, the most disapproving of the lot. "Do you know what his mother told my mother about him? He's *weird*, that's what. He's supposed to have this terrific I.Q. but he says he doesn't want to go to college, he's not interested in any sports, he doesn't care about anything except his stupid camera and that dark-room he's fixed up in his closet—Aunt Ethel can't keep a decent maid because Melvin is always bothering them to pose for him—the maid, for goodness sake—that's *bizarre*, Teddy. My aunt found hundreds of dirty magazines in his room once. You'd better watch out with him. He may only come up to your shoulder but who knows what goes on in his mind?"

Teddy smiled at Harriet and started on her left leg. They're all envious, she thought. None of them has ever had a date.

She sat through *See Here, Private Hargrove* without daring to meet Melvin's eyes, but she was conscious from time to time he would stare at her profile with something considering and earnest in the attitude of his round, curly head.

As they had waffles after the movie Melvin said solemnly, "You *are* the most beautiful girl in the world, Teddy Lunel."

"*I am?*" she gasped.

"Without any doubt." His glasses glittered at her. "I'm an acknowledged connoisseur of feminine loveliness, ask anyone at Collegiate."

"I don't believe you!"

"It doesn't matter what you believe. That has nothing to do with it."

Teddy blushed, her ears buzzed and she was afraid that tears were about to come into her eyes. None of the compliments she had received in her life from grown-ups had ever meant anything, but this! It was impossible not to know that Melvin meant what he said. He spoke as if he were making a documented academic pronouncement, there was an evaluating quality in his voice and she saw that behind his glasses he had bright, clever and very big, very clear blue eyes. His whole funny little face was set in an expression of total conviction. He looked like some kind of fluffy bird concentrating on an exceptionally fat worm.

"I've decided to call you Red," he continued. "Every beautiful woman needs a nickname that keeps her from being too intimidating and Teddy makes me think of Theodore Roosevelt. When a guy looks at you, Red, he sees something he never really believed existed except maybe on the movie screen, so he gets terrified that he won't have anything interesting enough to say to you. That's going to be one of your problems, getting people to treat you normally . . . to make ordinary human contact . . . in fact it's going to be damn near impossible. All the most beautiful women suffer from the same thing. It takes a special kind of man to understand them."

"You're nuts, Melvin Allenberg." Teddy was overcome with the intimate, flattering things he was saying to her so calmly, with such authority.

"Think about it, Red, just think about it," he said quietly. "One day, when we're both rich and famous, you'll tell me I was right."

Teddy couldn't answer. His words, that casual "one day" had acted on her as if they had been a beam of light that shot all the way into the future, illuminating undreamed-of vistas, as though Teddy Lunel was someone else who moved lightly in a world where the impossible became possible. Teddy looked down and slowly drew lines in her maple syrup with her fork. With the first absolutely calculated provocativeness of her life she asked, "What's a dirty magazine, Melvin?"

"Oh, so Harriet told you. I can't even make a collection of art photos without my family thinking I'm a dirty old man. Red, do I look like a dirty old man to you?"

"Harriet never said you were a dirty old man," Teddy said hastily, to defend her friend. "She never talked about you at all until you asked me to the movies."

"Well, she certainly never mentioned you either so that's fair. Anyway I never see her—our mothers have a mutual avoidance pact."

"Did Harriet never tell you about my family . . . my father?"

"No—should she have?"

"Well . . . he was a member of the Abraham Lincoln Brigade . . . he died fighting the Fascists in Spain . . . he was a great hero."

Melvin blinked with emotion. "God, you must be proud of him!"

"I am. My mother . . . she hasn't really gotten over it. She buries herself in her work . . . carrying on. She's French, you know. Her family was noble—there was a marquis who lost his head in the French Revolution . . . then all their land and money was confiscated . . . but not their pride. Mom's the last of her line . . . or rather I am . . ." Teddy said in a dreamy voice.

Melvin swallowed three times in awe. No wonder Red was not like any girl he'd ever met before. "Do you go out much?" he ventured, after a silence that seemed a fitting tribute to the unfortunate marquis.

"Mom's terribly strict. She only lets me have two dates a week on Friday and Saturday. She makes me go to bed early on Sunday because of school."

Reminded of the time, Melvin looked at his watch. "Come on, Red. She said home by eleven-thirty. I don't want to get you in any trouble."

At the door to Teddy's apartment Melvin Allenberg looked up at Teddy, who had been strangely quiet during the walk home.

"Have you seen *Jane Eyre* yet?" he asked. He might be short and funny-looking but he believed in always asking for what he wanted, no matter what the odds.

"No," said Teddy, who had seen it three times.

"Would you like to go next Saturday? If you're not busy already?"

"Umm . . . could we make it Friday? Saturday's taken I'm afraid."

"It's a date," he beamed. Once again his simple approach, unknown to most boys of eighteen, had let him achieve his goal.

"Thank you for a lovely evening," said Teddy, who had been grudgingly coached in this ritualistic phrase by her three friends.

Melvin grinned his not-quite-Van Johnson grin, reassured by this conventionality. "I hope you had as good a time as I did. Listen, I can tell that you're not the kind of girl who lets a guy kiss her good night before the third date, but don't you think it would be good for your soul to make one exception?"

Teddy didn't hesitate. She took off his glasses, and wrapped her long arms around him tightly, crushing his face into her collarbone with passionate gratitude. He struggled free. "Not like that, Red! Come on, bend down, and hold still." He planted a chaste kiss on her lips. "There! Now don't let anybody else get away with that. Promise?"

"I promise," Teddy whispered. Male lips felt different from female lips, they were prickly at their edges. Who would have guessed it? With her first conscious smile as a flirt she swayed forward and kissed him fleetingly before she gave him his glasses back. "Just don't tell anybody," she murmured. "It'd ruin my reputation."

16

Y ou told him *what?*" Bunny Ab-
bott, Teddy's roommate at Wellesley was astonished. Just as she
thought she had gotten used to the glorious excesses that had made
Teddy an instant legend among the four hundred freshmen who
had entered college with her in the fall of 1945, another caprice
surfaced.

"I simply lied by an inch and a half and said I was six feet tall,"
Teddy repeated calmly, as she came back from the phone booth in
the corridor. "When they hear that they suddenly lose interest unless they're six two or three—it eliminates the shrimps."

"Why do you still bother with blind dates?" Bunny asked. "You
can't even fit them into your datebook anymore."

"Oh, they just amuse me . . . it's like opening a Christmas
present." Teddy sounded casual because she knew she could never
possibly explain the feelings of embarrassingly violent love she felt
for everything about her new life, for every detail of college, from
blind dates to each and every girl in her dormitory. From the very
first day she had arrived at Wellesley she had been reborn into an
intoxication so unexpected that at night she lay awake to try to pin
down and fully explore the dimensions of the unbounded joy that
possessed her.

Teddy's life had become a high drama of popularity; every afternoon the dormitory phone rang at least a dozen times for her and
the girl on "Bells" who answered it would come to the head of the

222

corridor and shout "Lunel" in ironic resignation, yet without any growing trace of resentment. At Wellesley, Teddy had found at last the miraculous arena where it was acceptable to be different.

Her class had its share of brilliant girls who studied half the night; other girls were dedicated to winning a place on the crew that rowed against Radcliffe; there were those girls who clearly arrived at college already running for president of the class, girls who cared for little except art or music or philosophy, and still others who played fierce bridge all afternoon while simultaneously knitting argyle socks. If Teddy Lunel was almost exclusively interested in boys, who cared, as long as she didn't flunk out? She was smart enough to have been admitted to Wellesley so she was automatically one of them, her identity was, before all else, a member of the class of 1949.

The Wellesley campus was the noble proscenium for the epidemic of dating that had unfolded ever since the distribution of the little red Freshman Handbook, which contained photographs of each member of the class above their names and hometowns. The book was printed to help the freshman get to know each other but before it had been out for twenty-four hours, copies found their way to every man's campus in New England, now swollen by the ranks of newly returning veterans of World War II as well as the usual freshmen.

At the second week of freshman year, Teddy had been invited to every major Ivy League football weekend until Christmas vacation; she had her choice of nine dates for the Dartmouth Winter Carnival and, if her studies had permitted it, she could have gone out to dinner with a different man from nearby Harvard every night of the week.

When she went home for Christmas vacation that year, Maggy realized that her tall child had become a young woman who beckoned and tempted even when she stood still. The refrigerator held a heap of orchid corsages, love letters arrived in the mail every morning, Teddy went out every night and slept till noon. Still, better to be a prom queen, Maggy decided, and from what she observed, an utterly heartless and merciless flirt, than to be a girl who could be taken advantage of by a man because she imagined that he loved her.

Teddy waltzed through the first years of college, amorous, fanciful, vainglorious, as memorable as a first kiss and as impossible to recapture. She whirled from romance to romance as changeably as the tides, developing an authentic affectation of personality as she felt her power grow. She began to acquire a kind of learned self-confidence that was translated into a bewitching air of happiness as if nothing on earth had ever caused her to feel ruffled, or flustered or perturbed. She started to enter every room with a buoyant certainty of welcome, she accepted any change as if it had been planned for her enjoyment, there seemed to be no disappointment in her world, no potential for diminished expectations.

I don't believe this is happening to me, she whispered to herself, over and over, but she never said it out loud, for under all her triumphs always lurked the fear that she might suddenly find herself again the outsider just as suddenly as she had attained her fantasies of popularity.

Reality was never enough for Teddy. Somehow reality didn't manage to penetrate her unconscious in a way that allowed it to become a rock of experience on which she could base her emotions. She had been just a child, only six, when she learned the habit of changing reality into something brighter in recounting her days at school to Maggy. Now reality was as highly colored as she could ever have imagined, and it still didn't satisfy her. Outer success did not, could never, translate fully into an inner self-image that allowed her peace. Little by little the fantasy that dwelled within Teddy, that had inspired her to invent a father who died in Spain and a noble French background for Melvin Allenberg, was allowed to grow, to blossom.

At a Harvard-Yale game Teddy told her date, "My father went to Harvard, you know. Before he died he used to take me to all the Harvard games that were played near New York. He was mountain climbing in Tibet when he was killed—but he managed to save all the others." At Princeton, in a group that was discussing summer plans she grew nostalgic. "While I was growing up I spent every summer at my family's château in the Dordogne—the Lunels have lived in the Dordogne for as long as anyone can remember—the château has a hundred rooms, half of them in ruins—I haven't been back since my grandfather died." At the Dartmouth Winter Carnival she confided in her date. "Would you mind if I didn't go to the ski jumping? You see my father was killed right before my mother's eyes—he was ski jumping in the Alps, training for the

Olympics . . . she's never been the same." When the talk turned to Christmas vacation Teddy remembered her own. "We used to go to my great-great-grandmother's in Quebec. She always had the tallest tree I've ever seen—a living pine, at least thirty feet tall—and I'd dance around it with all my little cousins—there must have been two dozen of them—no, I don't see them anymore—my mother quarreled with my father's family after he died. They blamed her for letting him join the Free French when France was invaded. He was killed when his plane was shot down—he was on a special secret mission for General de Gaulle . . . no one's ever known what it was about, to this day."

Her tales were never questioned; a girl so extraordinary to look at must surely have tragedy and romance in her life, and she talked this way only to men she didn't intend to see in New York where they might meet Maggy when they came to call for her.

Maggy made it a point to inspect Teddy's dates as often as she could. She was reassured by the ever-changing parade of polo-coated youths who looked so fresh-faced, so respectful and essentially innocent. They were only children, she thought, and harmless.

"There's no question that there's safety in numbers," she told Lally Longworth. "I'm happier that Teddy's going out with dozens of boys than just one or two. And she treats them all so badly . . . I don't understand her anymore . . . if I ever did. I know it's too late now that she's gone away to school but I feel uneasy, as if I've lost touch with her . . . as if there's a beat missing . . . I keep thinking that there must have been something that I should have done to be closer to Teddy, to know her better. She mystifies me, Lally, and yet I gave her everything I could . . . I love her so, she has a comfortable home, she's always been beautifully looked after, I bought her the best clothes . . . oh, I just don't know . . ."

"Half the mothers I know say the same thing about their girls," Lally said comfortably, speaking from within the untroubled fortress of her little-regretted childlessness which entitled her to tell her friends how to bring up their offspring. "Once they go to college they become strangers. Are you sure there isn't anybody serious in Teddy's life? She'll be twenty soon. What were you doing at that age, I wonder?"

"Having fittings all day—and living like a woman," Maggy said thoughtfully. "We grew up so much faster in France. Or maybe it was just the twenties—I don't know, but her boyfriends all seem barely hatched to me. They're still groping their way out of the shell. Teddy assures me that these boys don't even expect—much less try—to make love to her . . . do you suppose that's really true?"

"Of course it is! What *are* you talking about, Maggy Lunel? Nice boys *never* expect to make love to nice girls."

It all depends on your definition of nice, Maggy thought, remembering how the blue frenzy of the Hawaiian guitars used to sound in her blood, remembering the wildness of the red sky of Montparnasse, remembering the melody of a Java that had the power to make a girl of seventeen be embarrassed by her virginity, remembering a spring night on which five hundred people had howled their delight at the sight of her naked body.

But Lally Longworth was right, at least for the second half of the 1940s, that profoundly conservative period. An overwhelming majority of the class of 1949 at Wellesley remained virgins until their marriages, and in that era of the tease, Teddy Lunel was responsible for more aching groins than any other girl in greater Boston. She had been influenced more than she realized by Maggy's deep suspicion of men.

A few of her favorite dates were allowed to kiss her for hours, rubbing themselves frantically against her in the back seats of convertibles or on the sofas of darkened rooms in eating clubs or fraternities, striving to gain their orgasms through the thickness of the clothes that separated their two bodies, for Teddy would never permit any of them to unzip his fly, to insinuate his hand under her skirt. She triumphed over their desire by refusing it any release except whatever they could gain without her seeming to notice. None of them was calm enough to guess that Teddy always had an orgasm too, easily, without a sound or a movement that could be detected, produced magically just by the pressure of a rigid penis straining inside a pair of trousers, a secret orgasm that could happen even on a dance floor. She never granted any of them the closeness to her that knowledge of this would have produced and, for her cruelty to them, she received the tribute of their proposals of marriage.

Teddy was not indifferent to the men who loved her, but somewhere deep within her there was a profound lack of concern with their pain. She was so in love with the idea of her popularity that she never fell in love with any one individual man. This inaccessible, heedless, faraway sensuality was like a few drops of water to men longing to drink their fill; it drove them mad, far more than if she had refused them the kisses she spent so lavishly. To have felt the points of her breasts through her dress, to have held her tumbled fragrance so closely, to have made her lips swell with too many kisses, but to be stopped there as if by an iron will . . . "I just hope, Teddy Lunel," one of them had said in a rage, "that someday somebody makes you suffer the way you make me."

She looked suitably regretful but she knew it could never happen.

If premarital Ivy League sex was rare in the late 1940s, drinking was the rule. At the very first football game Teddy ever attended in the Harvard stadium, she had been initiated with a paper cup of the powerful rum punch that was smuggled up into the stands in one of the red fire buckets that usually stood along the corridors of Eliot House. The buckets were intended to be filled with sand to throw on flaming wastepaper baskets but they were most often used as cocktail shakers or punch bowls.

After the game everybody went from party to party, sampling the various lethal, fruity concoctions, based on the cheapest available gin, which were served in each suite of rooms. Drunkenness was a normal way to end a Saturday night throughout the Ivy League, but Wellesley was a resolutely dry campus. Once there had been rumors of a single beer party in Munger given by a group known as the Lousy Eleven, but nobody believed them because the risk was too great: immediate expulsion for anybody drinking on college property.

Teddy loved to drink. Really loved it. There were few better feelings than the shift in perception that only liquor could produce, that sudden sense that the world was finally comprehensible and that it lay within her hands. Teddy studied, because it was essential, and dated and drank her way through three years at college, each more memorable than the last.

On a Sunday afternoon in the early fall of her senior year five members of a Harvard singing group, the Dunster Funsters, drove out to Wellesley to visit Teddy. They went frolicking about the famously beautiful campus, and after they decided not to walk all

227

the way around the lake, Teddy showed them the Arboretum, an almost hidden, little-explored collection of rare trees behind the science building. Part of the Arboretum is a thicket of pine trees, wonderfully scented, its floor covered with inches of fallen needles, slippery and soft underfoot. Instinctively they lowered their voices and slowed their pace. They seemed to have arrived at a place that was no longer Wellesley, that wasn't connected to the Gothic towers and the high sense of purpose that always hung over that marvelously lovely campus no matter how lazy the day.

"Drink, Théodora?" asked one of the boys, pulling a flask out of his pocket and sitting down under a tree.

"Harry! Are you mad?"

"Nothing like a schnapps in the fresh air—come on, there's nobody here but us and you know we're harmless, alas."

"*Don't you dare!*" she shouted, but the boys were already passing the flask around. The first time they offered it to Teddy she refused, but soon, under the soothing influence of the aroma of the pine needles and the out-of-season softness of the early October air, she dared to accept one small sip. And then another, and then a third. Harry was absolutely right about drinking outdoors, it heightened senses that didn't get properly exercised unless you were a part of nature. And oh, how blissful, how truly blissful it is to be a part of nature, she thought as she had a generous swallow of Scotch from a second flask.

"Gin smells bad, bourbon is too strong, rye is utterly horrid, but whoever invented Scotch was a good man and true," she announced. She felt that she'd made an important discovery.

"Robert Graves survived the trenches in World War One by drinking a whole bottle of Scotch every day," Harry's roommate, Luther, told her. "I can get by on less than a half of that."

"And you can't even write," Harry said.

"But I can sing, can't I, Harry?"

"Luther, you can sing, we all can damn well sing, we all *should* damn well sing!"

And sing they did, softly at first, harmonizing sweetly on old ballads, their voices so low that the birds could still be heard. Teddy lay back and listened in a haze of pleasure. How fine it was! One by one they sang all the Funster specialties. Really, she mused, it would only be fair of Harvard to give me a diploma when these boys graduate—I'm as much a part of their classes as they are. When

228

they started singing football songs none of them noticed that their voices now rang loudly through the little pine forest. "With the Crimson in Triumph Flashing . . ." Teddy found herself joining in but her voice was drowned out by the boys' voices, so she rose from the pine needles and did a little wild and antic dance. The five Funsters applauded wildly.

"More, Teddy, more!"

"Sing the Yale song—then I'll dance more."

"Never."

"Traitor—you're a traitor to the Crimson, Théodora."

"Sing the Notre Dame song," Teddy insisted, capering wickedly.

"What the hell—we don't play the Irish—give the little lady Notre Dame—take it off, Teddy, take it off!" Their voices rose in the Notre Dame fight song and Teddy cavorted like a shooting star, a captivating demon in Bermuda shorts, hair-raisingly graceful and quite, quite drunk.

It was during her bacchic encore, performed to a roaring Navy finale, "Beat the Army, Beat the Army Grey!" that Teddy's philosophy professor and his wife, out for an afternoon's stroll, attracted by the noise, wandered into the pine grove.

Two days later Teddy left Wellesley for good. Her case had been investigated and settled with due formality but there had never been any real question of the outcome. The sin was too grave.

At Back Bay Station, Teddy waved a last goodbye to all the grieving and guilty Funsters who had come to the station to see her off. But, as the train gathered speed in the outskirts of Boston, she dropped her aching, hot head to her hands and thought, silly bitch, *silly bitch*, STUPID BITCH! My fault, totally and absolutely my fault, I knew better! Did I think I could get away with anything? Did I think I was invulnerable? Fool, fool, bloody, bloody *fool!* I've lost it all, all lost, all gone, kicked out of paradise for good and for ever . . . I'll never be happy again. She would have groaned out loud but she was in the club car and it was filled with passengers. She had never known such paralyzing hopelessness. All the fears that had ever plagued her, all the premonitions that life was too good to be true, that nothing so wonderful could endure, gathered together in one lump that bulged rawly in her chest and rose up into her throat.

Teddy sat quite still for three hours, lanced by misery, drowning in self-reproach as the train traveled along the route that she had taken so triumphantly to Brown and Yale and Princeton. All the way to Hartford she stared unseeingly out of the grimy window. Finally she roused herself enough to order a sandwich and coffee. As she ate she looked around the club car for the first time since she had entered it.

At first her gaze was indifferent, unthinking, her mind didn't process what her eyes took in, but after a few minutes she focused, narrowed her concentration. The club car was filled with business-men and wherever she looked there was approval. More than ap-proval, there was intense interest, there was frank invitation, there was fascination. Teddy felt the first faint relief from pain that she had known since that moment in the pine grove when Professor Tompkins stopped dead and said, incredulously, "Miss Lunel!" Some instinct made Teddy get up and walk the length of the club car to the little toilet. She pushed open the door impatiently and confronted her eyes in the cracked mirror over the washstand. No matter how she felt inside, she looked no different than she had only two days ago. She braced herself against the walls, swaying with the train, as each mile brought her nearer to New York and the confrontation with Maggy that she dreaded with a fear so great that she couldn't even begin to face it.

You have to do *something*, she told herself grimly, looking in the mirror. You can't just show up and say that three years have gone down the drain. You have to have some project for the future, some idea of how you plan to lead your life. Three years toward a degree in history is useless on the job market—but I can't come home without a scheme. I've got nothing left but my face, it's as simple as that. But am I right?

In her mind Teddy checked over every comment she had ever heard Maggy make as she pored over models' photographs at home in the evening. It had been seven years since Teddy had spent much time at her mother's agency, seven years of being absorbed in her-self, seven years in which an entire generation of models had re-tired, their places taken by new faces, seven years during which she had only given rare glances to fashion magazines except for the yearly back-to-school issues. Yet she had never forgotten the indis-pensable requisites for a model's face. How often had she heard Maggy repeat them as she discarded photograph after photograph?

Peering desperately into the grimy mirror, she went down the list, her heart beating faster and faster. Definite cheekbones; eyes set far apart; a nose with a distinct shape to it; but not too big or too small; hair that anything could be done with; clear skin; perfect teeth, a long, long neck; a small chin, clearly cut; wide jawbones; a high forehead; a well-shaped hairline; an *uncrowded* face . . . yes, oh, *yes,* she had them all. She knew she was more than tall enough, she had always been skinny enough . . . but was she photogenic?

Teddy knew that only the camera could decide this. The crucial question of whether the sum of all the parts, no matter how good, will add up to a face that *matters* in only two dimensions, without the third dimension of depth, and minus the help of color, can never be settled by the eye alone. Maggy never let herself get too optimistic about a new model's potential until she had seen the test shots because so many girls didn't photograph as well as they looked in person, just as some of the best models were oddly unexciting in the flesh.

No, I just can't be sure, Teddy thought, as she went back to her seat, but at least it's something to try for, something Mother might approve of . . . oh, you bloody, silly bitch, who are you kidding? If she wanted me to become a model, why would she have never mentioned it? Why would she have sent me to Wellesley? But better a straw than nothing.

After her disappointment, after her anger, Maggy asked herself a sudden question. Why was her daughter so punished, in such disgrace for drinking on campus when, at Teddy's age, she had been living in sin with a married man and bearing an illegitimate child? A little historical perspective, please, she said to herself grimly. It won't kill her not to graduate. From this, as Rabbi Taradash used to say, little children don't die. And it would be good discipline for Teddy to try her hand at modeling.

The Lunel girls were a regiment of foot soldiers, hardworking, motivated and unspoiled. No one, looking at the fashion pictures and advertisements they posed for would have guessed at the vast amounts of grit and energy and willingness to endure discomfort that the frivolous images represented.

With a few flighty exceptions, every successful model went to bed early to get eight hours' sleep to prepare herself for the difficult day ahead. Without nonsense, businesslike, and as cheerfully as possible, she got up early so as to be ready on the dot of her first appointment; punctuality was vitally important to editors and clients and photographers who expected to see every model arrive, made-up and ready to work, on the stroke of the hour. Dependability was the sister virtue to punctuality; a model wouldn't cancel a booking for anything less than hospitalization, and even if she shook with fatigue between shots, she never let herself show it when the camera was on her. Tiredness was something she accepted as part of the money she earned, now as much as forty dollars an hour for top models.

Forty dollars an hour. The sum still astonished Maggy even as she fought to push it still higher. In Montparnasse, when she'd arrived there, the average artist's model worked for the equivalent of sixty cents for three hours of posing. Of course, once Paula had taken her in hand, she'd made double that, forty cents an hour for standing naked in an unheated studio in the middle of a Paris winter. She'd managed to live on it, even to pay her rent, buy her clothes, wear a fresh carnation every day—even to support Julien Mistral for one unforgettable perfect spring. Maggy paused and tried hard to imagine herself back in the skin of that girl. What had she thought about, how had she felt? Flashes of memory were vivid, the rest was lost.

She shrugged. There must still be artists' models, poor souls, but those of her girls who posed for lingerie photographs made double the money of those who worked only in fashion although they paid dearly for it in a loss of status. Her top girls even refused to pose in nightgowns and peignoirs. At least no budding Julien Mistral of a photographer could ever order Teddy to drop *her* knickers. In that there was some comfort.

Maggy pondered the question of the photographer to whom Teddy should be sent for her test shots. Normally she no longer concerned herself with this sort of decision. She had twenty-two employees and among them there were six who could have settled the matter with one phone call. Maggy knew, of course, that she was being overprotective, but these pictures were crucial. If they were disappointing, Teddy's future as a model would vanish. If they were good they would be used for Teddy's first "composite," a glossy 8 × 10 collage of photographs that would be her calling card, passport and temporary identity papers until she had painstakingly, over months, built up a portfolio of a variety of pictures, her "book" that she would carry everywhere so that it could be shown to magazine editors, advertising agencies and photographers.

Suddenly Maggy, who was in the habit of hardening her heart toward the ambitions, hopes and dreams of a thousand girls a year, Maggy, who never took the model's point of view until she had the pictures to look at that would speak louder than any human voice, found herself as eager to get the pictures right as if she were trying to break into the business herself. She imagined herself flipping through Teddy's test shots, imagined herself weighing and considering Teddy's merits as against those of—oh, say, that great model, Sunny Harnett, whose chin and nose were far too prominent for beauty, whose mouth was entirely too wide, but who had a smile that swept you right into the page with her, a smile of such pure gaiety that it was transferable to the reader; Sunny Harnett, who projected a blond blast of Southampton chic, who looked as if she were out-of-doors and dashing after a tennis ball even when she was sitting down. Did Teddy have any of that energy? Maggy, for all her expertise, found that all she could really do to help Teddy in a practical way was to work on her rudimentary makeup which was fine for college but not remotely right for photography.

Coffin, Toni Frisell, Horst, Rawlings, Bill Helburn, Milton Greene, Jimmy Abbé, Roger Prigent—she could ask a favor like this of any of these top photographers, but even as Maggy ran their names over in her head she knew that she was not going to be able to resist asking one of the three photographers she considered the most gifted in the world: Avedon, Falk and Penn. But it was collection time in Paris and this particular season Avedon, whose star had risen so rapidly in the past few years, was there for *Bazaar*, and Penn was in Paris for *Vogue*. So Falk it would be because Maggy couldn't endure this suspense, even if Teddy could.

It was like being in a tumbrel on the way to the guillotine, Teddy thought, or standing on the edge of the high diving board looking down into the ring of fire in the water below. She stood, frozen with self-consciousness outside a converted coachhouse that housed Falk's studio between Lexington and Third Avenue. It was after five on a Friday evening and the street was crowded with people rushing away from their jobs, the weekend beckoning.

It was football weather, Teddy realized, as she shivered in the breeze, and she should be hundreds of miles away, dressing for a date—oh, Dunster, Leverett, Winthrop and Eliot! She mumbled an incantation of the names of the fabled Harvard residence houses on the Charles River—that's where she should be! Instead she was primped and polished, brushed and painted and dressed in new clothes, up from her shoes and out from her skin, as perfect as her mother had been able to make her. She had never looked better, and she knew it, but the knowledge didn't help.

Her eyelashes were covered in unfamiliar mascara, her skin in powder, base and rouge, artfully applied, and her hair had just been done at Elizabeth Arden. Maggy had turned Teddy out in the flawless, adult elegance of Dior's "New Look," choosing a tightly fitted, double-breasted, gray flannel suit with black velvet lapels. The jacket was nipped in savagely at the waist, the hips exaggeratedly rounded by a buckrum lining above a slim skirt that stopped a few inches above her ankles. Teddy wore high-heeled black antelope pumps, a small black velvet hat with a veil that reached below her nose, and pale gray kid gloves. Under her expensive new blouse, in spite of the antiperspirant that she had frantically applied three times since the morning, she was beginning to sweat from nerves. She jabbed at the doorbell. Maybe action would keep her dry.

Falk had agreed to take the test shots of the new girl from Lunel so long as she came after he was finished shooting for the week. If Dora Mazlin, Maggy's chief booker, hadn't called to beg this personal favor from Falk's secretary he would never have been bothered to make the time, but his secretary owed Dora that favor for help in past emergencies. Every photographer, even those in Falk's position, sometimes needed a top model in five minutes and Dora was *the* pipeline.

The door was opened, to Teddy's ring, by a small cheerful woman.

"You're the new girl from Lunel, right? Come on in."

Teddy looked around the reception room. There was a general air of casual comfort but nothing about the room was exceptional except the photographs on the walls. "May I look?" she asked the secretary, because she was too nervous to sit still.

"Sure, go ahead."

Teddy walked from one photo to another, growing more tense with each second. She had always paid a fraction more attention to fashion photographs than other girls her age, but these pictures were like certain dreams that reveal a world that is similar to the

234

real world, but mystically heightened, more significant, filled with a magic power. She recognized many of the faces; most of the models were from Lunel, but surely none of the girls she was familiar with had ever been quite so interesting. The camera's eye had caught a millisecond of a revelation of personality. Behind the patterns of beautiful features Teddy could sense the intimate *self* of each model. These were not merely fashion photographs, they were fully realized portraits of women thinking their most personal thoughts.

"Listen," the secretary said suddenly. "If I hang around any longer I'm going to be late for my date. The phone isn't going to ring again today so I'm leaving. Will you tell him I'll see him Monday morning bright and early?" She grabbed her coat, and rushed out the door with a brisk wave, slamming it behind her.

Teddy sat down on the edge of a chair in the empty reception room. Beyond an open door she could see a slice of studio, brilliantly lit. For twenty, quite nearly unendurable minutes, nothing at all happened. The coachhouse was quiet with that special late-Friday-afternoon hush that says so clearly that work is over for the week. Could there be a mistake? Could she be alone here? Teddy wondered at last.

Finally, hesitating at every step, Teddy got up stiffly and ventured slowly into the studio, stopping a few feet on the other side of the door. She tried to peel off the tight gloves that seemed to be stuck to her hands. There was no place to sit, nothing in the room but an intense, waiting blaze of lights, a camera on a tripod and a sheet of virgin white paper that stretched right across one wall and was spread out on the floor. Sweat, yes, definitely more sweat, she thought in horror, trickled down her sides under her new waist cincher. She realized that she wasn't breathing and drew in two deep breaths.

"Is anybody at home?" she quavered in a small voice. There was no answer. Suddenly the door to the darkroom was flung open and a man popped out, holding a sheet of paper in his hand and looking at it. He gave her a glance. "I'll be right with you," he said, frowning at the paper. Then he looked up again and dropped the wet photograph. He peered at her from the other side of the sea of white paper.

"Red?"

Teddy jumped and squinted but she couldn't see him clearly.

"*Red!*"

The expression on Teddy's face changed and grew as complicated as the moment before a spring storm. She stepped firmly on the unspotted paper and took a big stride forward, shielding her eyes.

"Only one person has ever called me Red and that's a son of a bitch rat-fink who took me to seven movies, taught me how to French kiss and then dropped me without a word of explanation."

"Red . . . I can explain."

"*Ah ha!*" Galvanized, her nervous anxiety forgotten, Teddy took five swift steps forward and grabbed his shirt. "I cried my eyes out for you, you louse! I thought I was a total failure for months, I pretended to my mother that I was fed up with you, I told your cousin that you'd tried to get fresh . . . why didn't you ever call, Melvin Allenberg?"

"Were you really sorry?" he asked.

"Oh, what a shit you turned out to be! Now you want to *revel* in how awful I felt. That stinks! Anyway, what are you doing here?"

"Working late."

"So, you talked your way into a photographer's studio after all . . . the black sheep of the Allenbergs . . . I'll bet your mother's still upset?"

"She's made an adjustment."

"Where's Falk? I've been here a half-hour," Teddy said imperiously.

"I'm Falk."

"Bullshit."

"Do you see anybody else here?"

"Prove it."

Melvin Allenberg began to laugh. "Oh, God, Red, you don't change." Teddy hadn't loosened her grip on his shirt and now she tried to shake him, but try as she would he was impossible to budge. Solid as a small bear, he roared with laughter at her efforts, making her so angry that tears came into her eyes. He reached up and forced her arms down at her sides and pinned them there.

"Come on upstairs . . . I live over the store. I'll show you all the evidence that you want."

He released Teddy and quickly walked out of the studio into the reception room. She followed, beginning to believe him because of the way he moved. There was, in the casual sureness of his tread, that unmistakable modulation that reveals proprietorship, and when she climbed the stairs behind him and saw the large room that seemed to have been made out of the entire second floor of the coachhouse, she knew instantly that he was in his own home. The room fit Melvin Allenberg. It was messy and warm and crowded everywhere with enormous blow-ups of photographs of beautiful women, some of them on the walls, some on the floor, others piled in corners. Dozens of books lay open, a desk was piled three feet high with magazines and the big low couches and armchairs were all covered in dark green tufted leather.

"Drink?" he asked, going over to a tray covered with bottles and glasses that stood on top of an old seachest.

"Scotch on the rocks, but it won't improve your case, Melvin Allenberg."

"Melvin Falk Allenberg."

Teddy narrowed her eyes without comment, in a way that let him know that he was on strict probation. He poured two drinks and sat down on a chair by the couch, leaning forward, his elbows on his knees and his hands folded under his chin. He looked at Teddy quietly for a while. "Take off your hat," he said finally.

"What?" She was outraged.

"Take off your hat . . . I don't like that veil, I can't really see you."

"I don't even know if I'm staying," she said with what she hoped was a completely colorless smile, a smile such as she had never given in her life, nor would ever be able to give in the future. She was restored to the fine bravado that three years of unopposed tampering with malleable masculine hearts had given her. "I don't even know yet if I'm going to let you take my test shots. It all depends on the reason why you never called me again. I don't give a damn that you're rich and famous, you bastard, just the way you said you'd be."

"I said that *we'd* be," he answered.

"You remember that? After five years?"

"I remember everything. When we met you were entering into your destructive phase. Even though I was just nineteen I could see it coming, as sure as sunrise, and I didn't want to be your first victim . . . it was rough enough being your first triumph. So I bailed out when I knew that one more date, one more of those wild kissing sessions standing up outside of your front door, would finish me off, probably for life." He fell silent, and then he added, "Needless to say I was wrong." It was already far too late for self-preservation.

"Hmmm." Teddy had heard this sort of declaration before, in every variety of version, but there was an enduring patience and a kind of accepting calm about his statement that was more convincing than the most passionate phrases. He continued to scrutinize her as she took off her hat with care and pushed her fingers artfully through her hair, redistributing the carefully set waves until the lamplight dodged through its bewilderment of reds.

Teddy sipped her Scotch, which would always taste like danger, and returned his steady gaze. Melvin Allenberg had grown up well. He still looked like a bird, with his beaky nose and his big glasses, but his big bright eyes dominated his face with an intelligence that was infused with the kind of energy that is the essence of charm itself. His was a completed face: years would only confirm its shape, the firm chin, the broad brow, the curly halo of dark hair. She'd never forgotten his mouth, the first she'd ever kissed. Cleverness and whimsy were stamped as clearly on his well-formed lips as if he'd been a warlock.

"I suppose . . ." she began, with something quivering on the corners of her own mouth that showed that she was inclined to forgive him. Then she stopped, stung by a sudden memory. "And I'd been planning to ask you to the junior prom the very next time I saw you. Oh! When I never heard from you again I was too proud to call."

"What about all those other guys you were dating?"

"I decided not to ask any of them . . . so I didn't go. I missed it," she replied sadly.

Abruptly he got up, crossed the space between them, sat down on the couch, took her firmly in his arms and kissed her mouth.

"Oh, my sweet Red, my poor baby, I'm so sorry . . . I should have called but what could I have said? There was no way then to explain . . . I was too dumb to know the right words." Tenderly he wiped her lipstick off with his handkerchief and kissed her again. In his arms she felt him as solid as a tree, his lips were familiar. Her lips had received thousands of kisses in the last years but sensory memory retrieved his particular touch and taste and warmth; yet he was so changed, different in a way she suddenly understood with a leap of gladness. He was a man and he kissed like a man, not a boy. Teddy kicked off her shoes and lay back on the couch, her eyes open, looking at the pink Tiepolo twilight on the ceiling. She sighed deliciously and let him lift her hair off her neck and kiss her behind the ears. They'd never kissed sitting down before, she thought, and childishly, willfully, she eluded him and rubbed noses vigorously.

"Friends?" he asked anxiously.

"I forgive you. Only for old times' sake," Teddy growled crooningly. He ran his hands over her smart jacket, a garment so stiffly interlined and boned that it could stand up by itself. "All those buttons," he complained, as he started to undo them carefully, "between me and my girl."

The attempted unbuttoning of any single button was like an instant alarm signal to Teddy but she permitted it because the blouse under her jacket protected her with yet another double row of tiny taffeta buttons. Soon she lay on the couch in her elaborate blouse and new skirt, floating and lifting and melting under the storm of his kisses. She gasped for breath. This suddenness, this lack of prelude, of courtship, this brevity; the realization that she was alone in the house with him, not in a fraternity surrounded by a dozen kissing couples, was abruptly dangerous until she looked at Melvin's face and relaxed again. He'd taken his glasses off, and he looked so dear and reassuring that she plunged back into the flood of his caresses, enjoying the heady sense of power she always felt as whatever man who was kissing her grew more and more excited, as the beat of his passion grew quicker and the rhythm of his heart quickened. But now Melvin did something that had never happened to her before in three years of dedicated necking. He lifted her right off the couch, without any preliminary warning, and he carried her with ease, across the big room and through a door she hadn't noticed before, into what was his small bedroom.

"Melvin!" she protested, kicking wildly. "Stop that! What do you think you're doing? I never lie down on boys' beds!"

"There's always a first time, and I'm not a boy," he said, his voice muffled with love but determined. Teddy struggled to heave herself up off the quilt but he was so strong that it was like fighting against an undertow, and all the while he kept kissing wherever he could: her fingertips, her chin, her hairline, her eyes, a skillful arsonist setting a hundred tiny fires. Many minutes later, when she was blazing from head to toe, he started on the buttons of her blouse. She protested feebly. Her trusted iron wall, beyond which

239

no male could penetrate, seemed to have crumbled and Teddy found herself without boundaries.

This just isn't happening, she thought, as he took off her blouse and opened the waistband of her skirt and slid it down over her feet. When his warm hands deftly unhooked her waist cincher and freed her breasts, when his warm mouth bent to her nipples, those inviolate virgin nipples that had never been touched in their nakedness, she thought, again, no, it isn't happening, but soon, as he drew them up into tiny points of brilliant sensation with his mouth, she thought, maybe it is happening after all. When she found Melvin Allenberg naked, pressing every sturdy inch of his body along her own nakedness, when she felt his penis, leaping like a fish, against her lower belly, she knew that it must at last and absolutely be happening, and that, although unbelievingly, she was ready. Lying down they fit together as if they were exactly the same height. Melvin was supremely slow, quivering with control, exquisitely patient but relentless. He took her inch by inch, took Teddy Lunel with a thoroughness that banished all her habits of withholding, took her with a completeness that left her without any secrets. And, at last, relieved of her baggage of rigid chastity, she lay next to him and was glad and grateful.

17

One hundred and fifty Molyneux spring dresses, each with its own pair of gloves painted to match. Odd, the details that popped into her mind whenever she was nervous, Marietta Norton thought, as the Lockheed Constellation broke through the clouds and the sun blazed in—that must have been back in 1933.

The senior fashion associate of *Mode* took a breath of relief as the plane steadied. She never admitted it to anyone but she was terrified of flying and it had been a rough takeoff from Idlewild on this windy September morning in 1952. She thought longingly of the days when editing a fashion magazine was still a fairly civilized procedure, those years during which everyone took the *Normandie* over to France for the collections: first class it had been, five days of pâté, caviar, champagne and a chance to refresh the spirit. But now she was expected to flop and lurch back and forth through the horrid skies as if it were nothing special.

This trip for instance: to France for next year's resort clothes that would be shown on twelve pages of the January issue—it could have been done perfectly well out in the Hamptons, in her opinion—after all, the clothes were all American designs—but no, Darcy had insisted on a full-scale production. "Marietta," he had said in that grand seigneur manner of his which never failed to annoy her, "we've consistently stayed ahead of *Vogue* and *Bazaar* because we're not afraid to go all-out. *Vogue* is shooting resort in Portugal, I hear, and you're going to France for *Mode*—let's not discuss it further." Marietta Norton shrugged. It was an old argument between them and she never won.

However, she knew that she was the most experienced fashion editor in the business and Darcy appreciated her in the only way she wanted to be acknowledged, by paying her generously in a field in which salaries were normally low. God knows, after thirty years in fashion she was working only for the money that had enabled her to send her four daughters to the best schools, not for the joy of it. The glamour was long gone as far as she was concerned, gone as totally as Lanvin's evening jacket with mufflike shoulders of silver fox and lunch for two for ten dollars at the Colony and Cobina Wright's circus party and floor-length dresses for the races in the afternoon and Mrs. Harrison Williams costumed in Winterhalter crinolines as the Duchess of Wellington for the Chicago Opera Ball.

There had simply been too many Paris collections, too many Christmas bathrobe pages shot in July, too many jolting taxi trips down to Seventh Avenue, too many fattening lunches with manufacturers who advertised in *Mode,* too many days on which she had had to find the words to announce that fashion had turned yet another new leaf and now women had to throw out the old and ring in the new, when Marietta Norton herself didn't give a hoot in hell what she wore and, what was worse, looked it, and knew she looked it.

Like many of the best fashion editors Marietta Norton was unabashedly dowdy. She had spent most of her life inspecting all the clothes of the Western world and deciding which were the best of them; she had an instinct for choice that, had it belonged to a young and slim and very rich woman, would have guaranteed that woman a place on the Best Dressed List, but Marietta Norton never had the time, interest or energy to waste on picking out things for herself. Worse, she reflected, she was short and plump, the kind of woman the English always said "looked like a cook" although even the English didn't seem to have many cooks anymore.

Still, she counted on this trip to produce resort pages that would make *Vogue*'s Portugal stuff look downright dull, if none of the bugs that plagued location trips came raging out of the woodwork.

Bill Hatfield, the rangy, flip photographer, was, for her money, one of the most tasteful boys in the business. Berry Banning, her assistant, seemed unusually efficient so far, although the jury was still out on Berry until they came back without incident to New York. Often girls from her moneyed Locust Valley, Bar Harbor, Spence-Chapin background didn't have what it took to succeed in the magazine world.

The only detail that hadn't been nailed down to Marietta's complete satisfaction was the model's haircut. She cast a baleful glance at the back of Teddy's head. The incomparable Miss Lunel, damn her glorious eyes, had adamantly refused to let her hair be cut in the new petaled chrysanthemum shape. It was the coiffure of the decade, Marietta was convinced of it, but when did Teddy Lunel ever do anything she didn't want to do?

She had never had to compromise from the very first day she started working, four years ago. Like Norman Norell and Mainbocher, the two star designers who had so much power that they allowed their clothes to be photographed only on the condition that four entire pages were devoted to each of them exclusively, Teddy Lunel was the only model alive who was never photographed with another model. Still, it was probably better that way, Marietta thought, forgiving Teddy her stubbornness about her hair, since even the greatest of the other models looked—well, perhaps "diminished" was the best way to put it, next to Teddy.

This was the sixth time Marietta had used Teddy for Europe. Only last spring they'd gone to Paris together for the Fall Collections and if anybody had ever been as supremely, heartbreakingly beautiful as Teddy in Balenciaga's hat of black tulle and roses, with the tulle spun out in the back like sugar candy, she'd like very much to know about it because it would be a bloody miracle. And just where, she wondered, was the stewardess with her martini? New York to Paris, an eighteen-hour flight, with refueling stops at Gander, in Iceland, God alone knew where, and again at Shannon, was at least an eight-martini trip . . . if only no one had told her that the most dangerous moments were landing and takeoff she might have been able to get by with only two or three.

Bill Hatfield didn't need a drink although he'd ordered one anyway. He'd been a Navy pilot in the war and he could get on any commercial plane and fall asleep before takeoff and wake in time for landing—just so long as he was carrying his three good-luck charms, the ones that kept the plane up. He was glad that Marietta, a smart old broad if ever there was, had booked him for this trip. Things were getting sticky back at the studio. Ann had finally moved out and if she did as she had promised, was arranging for her lawyer to meet with his lawyer about the divorce. All well and good. But Monique planned to move in and so did Elsa. Had he really suggested it to both of them? They certainly seemed to think so. The only thing wrong with being a fashion photographer was the models. Great girls they were, he'd never met one he didn't like—that was the trouble. He'd be out of danger for this trip at any rate—he'd already had his waltz with Teddy Lunel.

Out of the corner of his eye he watched her as she bent over a book. It had been the most marvelous six months of his life, way back when she'd stopped being Falk's steady girl, three years ago, but with Teddy, when it was over, it was fucking finished, stone cold dead, no embers, no remember whens. She didn't look back, that one. He wondered how many affairs she'd had since him. The mystique of sexual promiscuity was like a velvet cape that she drew about herself with a smile that could send a man straight to hell. Still, he'd lived through it . . . barely.

He thought of the other models who might have been making this trip with the *Mode* bunch. There was Jean Patchett, whose eyebrows were drawn by a master calligrapher, whose little round black beauty mark just above her right eye was the most famous beauty mark in the history of photography. Patchett's look was sophistication pushed to its outer limits—wrong for the kind of pictures he planned to take. Dovima, with her passionate face, her black hair and blue eyes, would have been a good choice for ball gowns, but he couldn't quite see her for resort clothes. Lisa Fonsegrieves, with her lunar loveliness, her porcelain princess face, that witty tilted nose and curly blond hair—yes, she would have been wonderful . . . but still a shade less perfect than Teddy. The only other possibility had been Suzy Parker. You just thought that no girl had ever been born more beautiful than Suzy . . . until you looked at Teddy.

Strange how beauty divided itself into levels. There were the hundred and fifty models in New York who were the pick of the loveliest girls in all of America and there were the half-dozen of those hundred and fifty who had broken away from the pack and stood alone, each a superb champion with her own special beauty, and *then* there was Teddy Lunel. He had never heard a better description of her than one he remembered reading in college, "O thou art fairer than the evening air, Clad in the beauty of a thousand stars," a line of Marlowe's that had somehow stayed with him, professional beauty watcher that he had always been, even before he became a photographer. You could add up all the parts but you still couldn't express the mysterious harmony of her beauty without resorting to poetry.

Bill Hatfield looked forward to working with her although there would be none of the undercurrent of sexual potential between them that there would certainly have been if he were working with a model he hadn't slept with yet.

Teddy had the knack of never looking the same that made his work an adventure in mutual creativity rather than a technical process. With each new change of clothes, Teddy drew on the life of another woman, a woman who would one day buy that particular dress and in it meet a man who would become the great love of her life, a woman who would remember until she died just what she had been wearing at that particular moment. How the hell she did it he had never understood. A sense of *authentic existence*, nothing less, was what Teddy produced for the camera. Still, that was, after all, what she got seventy bucks an hour for, more than any model in the world. And worth every nickel.

Where, he wondered, was the stewardess with his martini? The nice thing about flying commercial was that you could drink without worrying about your coordination. Landing on an aircraft carrier with alcohol in your bloodstream had never been recommended . . . although it *had* been done, and by him, now that he thought about it.

Berry Banning was too excited to notice the bumpy air as they took off. This was her most important assignment since she'd joined *Mode* three years ago. She'd never been on a European location trip before and her responsibilities were terrifying. Marietta had decided on the clothes, of course, and they'd all been fitted on Teddy before they left, but Berry had been in complete charge of every detail from that time on.

She had done all the complicated, cross-indexed packing of twelve large suitcases so that each outfit traveled with the wide range of choices of shoes, handbags, jewelry, scarves, hats, nylon

245

stockings and sunglasses that Marietta Norton demanded on a fashion sitting.

Like Diana Vreeland of *Bazaar* and Babs Rawlings of *Vogue*, Marietta Norton approached each photograph as if it were an art form. Even when she was planning to photograph only a single hat she would make sure that the model was wearing perfume that complimented the mood of the hat, had on perfectly fitting shoes, untouched white gloves and fresh stockings. She could tie a scarf to convey a hundred variations of style, with a flick of her wrist transforming any model from an Apache to a Gainsborough. She played games with accessories like a theatrical set decorator, but God help her assistant if Marietta didn't have enough choice. Should even a single suitcase be lost . . . one such slip, no matter if it was the porter's fault, and Berry would never be trusted again. Marietta Norton, whom she worshipped, could unquestionably improvise something because there had never been a Marietta Norton location trip that hadn't been successful, but her own career would die before it had been properly born and there was nothing in life that she wanted but a future in the world of fashion.

From the time that she had been a little girl Berry Banning had saved every copy of *Vogue* and *Mode* and *Bazaar* and, recently, *Charm* and *Glamour* and *Mademoiselle* as well, and studied their pages as if they were her one and only prayer book and she were a cloistered nun.

It had never occurred to her that how a woman dressed could be a legitimate expression of the woman's *own* personality that depended on her point of view toward life. Fashion to Berry was a *law* and the happiest of beings were those, like herself, who were rich enough to live under this law, who could dedicate themselves to carrying out every subtle shading of its marvelously inconstant dictates. She never stopped trying to be worthy of high fashion. She spent hours peering unhappily at herself in a full-length mirror, unsucessfully practicing the frozen and eternally quizzical expressions of remote self-love that appeared on the pages of the magazines, as if the models were asking "Will I do?" and then giving themselves the secret answer "Of course." Every dress she owned was exactly as *Mode* said it should be; a triumph of architecture, constructed as carefully as a bridge, insistently feminine, creating a tiny-waisted, low-cut, full-skirted line that looked natural unless you were trapped inside it.

246

But alas, Berry Banning had rich-girl hair, brown-brown and without direction, the kind of hair that only looked good drawn back and bundled under a tiara. Worse, she had rich-girl limbs, formed by the genes of generations of athletic Bannings, and she was too sturdy for the almost Victorian paper-doll elegance of the New Look. And worst of all, she had stubbornly rich-girl features, good but plain, pleasant enough but too straightforward to lend themselves to change through the use of cosmetics.

She always looked the *same*, Berry thought, with familiar despair, no matter what she did. She kept her eyes away from Teddy, who sat only one row in front of her. It was going to be bad enough having to look at her for ten whole working days. She had often worked with Teddy before, although only for a day at a time in various New York studios, and she was familiar with the hideous sick headache that she always developed after such a day when she came home and confronted her own face in the mirror.

It wasn't, she told herself scrupulously, that she envied Teddy exactly, nor that she was jealous of her—as a matter of fact she genuinely liked her—but simply that it just didn't seem *fair* that two girls of the same age could both have the same things on their faces, like eyes and noses and lips, and yet with such utterly different results. It was as if Teddy belonged to an absolutely different form of life. What must it be like for her to wake up in the morning and catch sight of herself in the mirror—*that face*—and know it was hers? Oh, where was the stewardess with her martini?

Sam Newman, Bill Hatfield's assistant, was watching Berry Banning without seeming to. Christ, but he *loved* her kind of woman! Nice full breasts, great legs, long and tan from the summer, the kind of laugh that rang with self-assurance that was bred in the bone, a laugh as rich as she was. There was, in his large experience, no fuck so satisfactory as a rich girl—they just seemed to enjoy it more, probably because it didn't really count when they were making it with the assistant instead of with the photographer himself, so they just let themselves go and had fun. He'd had rich girls from the staff of every fashion book in the business, and from the fashion departments of all the women's magazines too and he'd take them over models any day, and he'd had models aplenty, although, of course, never the likes of Teddy Lunel.

Rich girls were much less neurotic than models, for one thing;

247

less worried about getting to sleep on time; they enjoyed their food more; held their liquor better; often insisted on paying the check because they knew perfectly well how little he made, and they all felt guilty because none of them had to live on their salaries. Oh, but he liked their immaculate underwear, and their good shoes and their clean, unfussed hair and their strong passionate bodies, developed by years of swimming lessons and skiing lessons and riding lessons. One day he'd have his own studio and he'd marry a nice, plain, *grateful* rich girl and have a bunch of rich kids. Meanwhile, where the hell was the stewardess with his martini?

Teddy put down her book, sat back and closed her eyes. She let her mind fill with the loud noise of the aircraft, those familiar racketing vibrations that still gave her a great splurging sense of freedom although she'd made this flight to Europe more than a dozen times since she started modeling. On one level she felt as if she were still working in New York, her mind filled with drifting thoughts of the details that constituted the sum of her life.

There were the taxis, as many as ten or twelve in a day. Half the cabdrivers in Manhattan knew her for a big tipper and could recognize her silhouette as she dashed out of a building to the curb, always in a tearing hurry, weighed down by her huge Lederer bag, and they stopped in an instant when she gave her traffic-piercing whistle.

Inside the taxi, her magnifying mirror clutched firmly between her knees, she applied different makeup or put on a pair of false eyelashes on the way from one job to another. If she had an extra minute she tried to organize the handbag out of which she lived. Certainly it could do everything but give milk, full as it was with her bulging cosmetic case, her hairpieces, her three kinds of bras, her collection of slips to wear under any kind of dress, her own assortment of scarves, gloves and jewelry for those advertising sittings where there was no accessory editor, her three pairs of shoes of different style and heel height for the occasions when nobody had thought to get shoes in her size.

Of course for a job like this location trip she had only to travel with a lipstick and her own clothes because Marietta and Berry had provided everything else, but the ordinary working day always held at least one emergency. As the sun touched her face through the window of the plane Teddy remembered a trip to Nassau with

248

Micheline Swift, the superb Swiss model, and John Rawlings the photographer. He had bet the two of them that if they could list the contents of their bags without looking he would give them each a hundred dollars in cash and, as a handicap, he allowed them each to forget thirty items. They'd both lost by a mile.

She sighed and tried to forget the routine of her life but the sun through her eyelids only made her think of the lights of a studio. Whenever she looked in a mirror it was to make a routine inspection of the texture of a serviceable fabric. Her face was no more than a machine she owned, a machine that had only a certain, limited life span.

Had she danced too late at the St. Regis Roof last night? If so, tonight it must be bed at nine, no matter what she had planned. Nobody would keep paying seventy dollars an hour for Teddy Lunel if there was even the faintest hint of fatigue under her eyes.

Did anyone who envied a professional beauty ever think about the cost of maintaining the façade; the hours of upkeep, the ringing of the alarm at six-thirty every morning, the cold hamburgers that had to be eaten on the run for their power to keep her standing on her weary legs as long as ten hours a day? It was the exhaustion that finally got to you, the exhaustion that made you wait without too much fear for that first wrinkle. If a model's father had died, if she was going through a divorce, or if she had just discovered she was pregnant when she shouldn't be, she still had to be fully *there* for the camera. Only the camera mattered. Did anyone fully understand, besides another model, that there could be no narcissism in a business that demanded total concentration on what the photographer wanted from you, allied to a total lack of self-consciousness, so that you forgot yourself for hours as you gave it to him, moving constantly as you poured out pure energy? It was almost like dance when it went well but good God in heaven, *it was so endlessly boring.*

Still, it bought freedom. Her weekly paycheck had been almost three thousand dollars for several years now, she had moved from her little apartment where she had first been safe from Maggy's scrutiny, to an elegant set of rooms on East Sixty-third Street and, if she kept in training, there was no reason why she shouldn't work at this rate for another three or four years, or maybe more, depending on how well the face held up.

But was that what she wanted? When had she signed on for this? Teddy had celebrated her twenty-fourth birthday last spring and as far as she knew there wasn't a girl with whom she'd been at college who wasn't married by now and didn't have at least one child. She didn't want *that*, Teddy thought, or rather, not exactly that, not a bunch of kids in the suburbs. But she didn't want to end up like her mother either, still consumed by her business, beginning to feel just a trifle threatened by some of the new agencies that had opened in the late 1940s like the Fords and Frances Gill and Plaza 5.

As the sound of the motors changed and settled down Teddy wished that she were making this long trip alone. Lately there seemed never to be a time to just sit and look up at the sky and dream. Day tumbled after day, completely filled, crowded with obligations and appointments. Each evening after she came home from her last booking she'd phone the agency and find out what she would be doing during every hour tomorrow.

Then, if she wasn't so tired that she needed to go to bed early, she'd hurry to bathe and dress and go out to the Stork Club or "21" or L'Aiglon or Voisin for dinner with any of the twenty men she could summon at the last minute. There hadn't been anybody she wanted to make love to, for, oh, two months or more, she thought with dismay. Why were men all so alike?

This summer she had spent weekend after weekend in Connecticut or out on Long Island where all the house parties seemed, in the end, to be the same. Teddy didn't miss spending those hot summer weekends in the city, although they could have their special charm—ah, but only if you were in love and the city seemed to have been emptied just for you. Or rather, only if you *thought* you were in love, Teddy reflected sadly. She had almost believed she was in love a few times in her life but it had never come true, not even with Melvin, her darling Melvin whom she still loved but with whom she had never been in love no matter how hard she had tried to be.

It had lasted for an entire year and there was no friend more dear, no lover more tender, but Melvin had never fit her dream, although he had come achingly close, so close that when he realized that his kind of love and her kind of love were never going to lock together he had been so desperately unhappy that they had had to part.

Every time she had been seriously involved with a man, Teddy thought, there had come a moment when she realized that she was like a stranger in a foreign country who tries to pay in an unacceptable currency. The coins of her emotions, on which she planned to live, turned out to be worthless. She could search her pockets, empty her wallet, as if she were in a nightmare, but she could never seem to find the right amount of . . . oh, of whatever it took to be in love really and truly. Her deepest fear, so buried that she failed to articulate it, was that something in her, some incurable emptiness, had already doomed her to inspire love but never to feel it.

Teddy's most excessive fantasies had all been fulfilled many times over. She'd had everything the world of high fashion could offer, more adulation and attention in eight average working hours than any bride on her wedding day. But more and more often she felt the surfacing of a long neglected but unappeased child in her, a timid little girl who wanted to be taken care of, who craved some vaguely seen but all-powerful man on whom she could depend. Teddy snorted at her own absurdity. She made more money than almost any man she knew . . . but recently a lot of her days had felt like one long, dreary, late Sunday afternoon.

She stood up abruptly, smoothing down the white capeskin jacket cut exactly like a man's button-down shirt that she wore over gray flannel slacks. She surveyed the next rows of the first-class cabin of the Constellation and shook her head severely at her traveling companions. "I guess all you people just don't give a damn," she said, "but I'd like to know what the hell has happened to my martini? I'm going to find that stewardess. Does anybody want anything while I'm on my feet?"

Julien Mistral stood poised on the edge of the diving board. His powerful, tanned body was bisected only by the thin strap of narrow elastic bikini that men in Europe had been wearing for the past four years. He was fifty-two and his heroic proportions were those of a man of thirty. He had painter's muscles, the firm solid legs of a man who spends his life standing before a canvas or walking around a studio, and the well-developed arms and back of any man who wields a tool, whether it be a paintbrush or a shovel.

The look of a gentleman trained to knightly swaggering, that he had worn so haughtily in his youth, had not changed with years of ever-growing fame, greater mastery. But the arrogance with which he had held his head, that air of a conqueror, was no longer perceived as arrogance but as the outward sign of validated genius. His neck had grown somewhat thicker, there were deep lines around his eyes and others that led from his high-bridged nose to his mouth, yet the prodigious blaze of blue that had been imprisoned in his eyes had not changed in its fixity or intensity. His thick dark red hair was cut short, at the temples it was almost sandy, and his mouth was still hard, dominating, uncompromising. Mistral had the face of a chieftain.

He paused before diving into the pool that had been built two years before and looked about him, his hands on his hips. He frowned and seemed to forget the invitation of the water on this hot September day in 1952, as he listened to the sounds around him. The buzzing silence, that paradise of bees that had once surrounded *La Tourrello*, had vanished long before, almost from the first day that Kate had bought the farm and organized a battalion of builders and plumbers and electricians.

Now, new noises invaded the air of Provence; a half-mile away automobiles passed frequently on the road to Apt where once they had been rare; a tractor ground and rattled in a distant field where so recently men had worked with their hands; from time to time the plane from Paris to Nice passed directly overhead; in the kitchen of the *mas* the voices of three servants were raised in a sudden quarrel as they prepared for the dinner party that Kate had planned for that evening. The door of Kate's new Citroën could be heard on the other side of the house as she slammed it briskly and drove off with a squealing abruptness that indicated her habitual pre-party discovery that some detail had been neglected that made necessary a last-minute trip to set it right. While Mistral stood there, his senses concentrated on all the sounds that were eroding the peace of his countryside, he didn't hear the light footsteps that approached cautiously along the length of the diving board.

"Papa!" shrieked a child's voice right behind him.

"*Merde!*" Startled, Mistral jumped, slipped, lost his balance and fell into the pool.

Three months following Kate Mistral's return to France after the war she discovered she was pregnant again. She had had several miscarriages during their marriage but Mistral hadn't been particularly disappointed. He had never wanted a child the way other men did. Children, he would have said if he'd given it any thought, were disruptive, time-consuming, probably disappointing and certainly the source of unforgivable interruptions.

252

He had deeply begrudged the need to worry about Kate's new pregnancy at the ridiculously late age of forty-three. He wanted her full attention to be turned to putting the *mas* back in working order. He never intended to have to deal with practical matters again, and when Kate had arrived in the spring of 1945, her two suitcases crammed with Ivory soap, Kleenex, toilet paper, instant coffee, needles, thread, flashlights, and white sugar, luxuries unimaginable in France for five years, he drew a breath of relief. He wanted only to disappear into his studio at first light and forget the nagging problems of daily existence. A child would complicate his life—but certainly she would miscarry again. Ordinary men needed sons to prove to themselves that they had existed and left something behind on the face of the earth. Julien Mistral knew that he was immortal and that a son could add nothing to his place in the history of art.

However, when Kate gave birth, in February of 1946, to a skinny, solemn and somehow sour-faced baby girl, she was so proud of herself that even Mistral felt a certain sense of participation in her happiness. Kate named the baby Nadine and reassured Mistral by promptly putting her on a bottle and getting her own strength back in a few weeks.

In the next years Kate's organizational abilities were taxed to the fullest. Jean Pollison returned from Germany with teeth missing, skeletal from malnutrition, but he recovered rapidly and *La Tourrello* was the first farm in the Lubéron to bloom again, thanks to Mistral's money that Kate spent so liberally as soon as there was anything available for sale after the war. A Swiss nurse was imported to take care of Nadine while Kate dealt with the renewed explosion of interest in Mistral.

As early as 1946 France swarmed again with American dealers greedy to see what had been painted during the war, and Mistral's studio contained more canvases that he considered worthy to be sold than it had ever held before: all the paintings he had done in the five years since *Les Oliviers* had been completed.

"Have you heard from Avigdor yet?" Kate asked Mistral soon after her return.

"No, I've decided to change dealers," Mistral answered. "The man has always been more interested in discovering new talent than in getting the best prices for the artists to whom he owes his success—why did he never open an American branch, I ask you? That alone has cost me a great deal. My contract with him lapsed during the war—take advantage of it."

As Mistral had known she would, Kate obeyed him without further question. He had calculated from the beginning of their marriage that as long as he allowed her to feel powerful in certain areas she would be satisfied. Any dealer would have to reckon with Kate before he even got near Mistral. He wasn't giving up any authority he wanted to retain in letting Kate choose a new gallery, since it was the sort of necessary business that he loathed, on a level with coping with the neighboring farmers who were beginning to think of forming a cooperative to which they would all sell their grapes. An artist choosing a dealer, he told Kate, was like an elephant picking out a favorite louse. The dealer Kate finally settled on, Étienne Delage of New York, Paris and London, soon discovered that Julien Mistral was an exception to the rule that most painters only grow rich in the grave.

When the São Paulo Museum of Modern Art had its major Mistral exhibition in 1948 he didn't bother to make the trip although Kate was there for weeks in advance, overseeing the installation of the canvases. A year later she went to New York for the opening of the big Mistral retrospective at The Museum of Modern Art, but again Mistral preferred to stay at home. In 1950 and 1951 he had finally been persuaded to be present at the important exhibition at the Stedelijk Museum of Amsterdam, the Kunsthaus in Zurich, the Palazzo Reale in Milan, and the two-month-long celebration of the twenty-fifth anniversary of his first show which was celebrated by an exhibition that took over the entire Maison de la Pensée Française, in Paris.

Once that was over Mistral declared that he would never go to another museum show, no matter how significant. He detested the kind of elbow-rubbing and ceremonial duties of these occasions, he loathed the crowds of strangers who felt that because they loved his work they had the right to talk to him about their reactions to particular paintings. "Let Picasso, that mountebank, that marketplace of every kind of art—not excluding pots and pans—encourage the lionizers—I have better things to do than act like the ringmaster at a circus."

He kept to his resolve but each exhibition—and each major art auction—saw a dramatic rise in his prices. Étienne Delage discovered, as Adrien Avigdor had before him, that the very scarcity of

Mistral's paintings made them unusually valuable. After his wartime paintings were sold, he took to retaining most of his new work that survived his annual bonfire, but in 1951 alone he earned the equivalent of a quarter of a million dollars in American money without having to part with more than a half-dozen canvases.

In the late 1940s and early 1950s more and more journalists found their way to Félice and for the many dozens who were denied entry to *La Tourrello* there were invariably several so important that Kate eventually persuaded Mistral to grant a few grudging interviews. On the other hand, she protected him from art historians who were writing books on him, tourists who wanted to have their photographs taken with him, college girls who wanted his autograph, scholars who were doing monographs on his work, collectors who thought that he might be charmed into selling them a picture when Delage had nothing to offer. Yet nothing was so disruptive, so distracting to him as Kate's growing interest in playing the hostess.

Perhaps it was the swimming pool, put in by a special company from Cannes, Mistral thought, that had set her off, but during the last two years she had become the social queen of the region. Aristocrats from England had bought a château near Uzès, a great American expert on Cézanne had settled in Ménerbes, the Gimpels, art dealers for generations, had bought another château not far from Félice, and now all of them and others like them were entertaining each other and being entertained by Kate.

Mistral had lost any interest in her body soon after Nadine's birth. Otherwise he would have stopped her—what did he care to meet strangers, no matter how famous, what possible interest could he have in listening to their absurd, excited chatter about the new, so-called Abstract Expressionists, a scum-filled sewer of hopeless drooling idiots, every last one of them, who, lacking talent, vomited up their last meals and called it art, as if an apple could be abstract, or a full moon or a mountain or a naked woman . . . why waste time talking about them any more than telling malicious stories about that *pauvre con* of a Picasso and his ludicrous involvement with the Communists who used him to paint propaganda portraits of Stalin, but never understood what his work was trying to do . . . not that he had ever succeeded.

No, the only thing he agreed with Picasso about was Dubuffet. Picasso loathed him as much as Mistral did. And the only thing he agreed with Dubuffet about was Monet—they both liked him. Degas had had the right idea, Mistral thought. When he knew he was dying he'd said to his artist friend, Forain, that there was to be no funeral oration, but, "If there has to be one, you, Forain, get up and say, 'He greatly loved drawing. So do I.' And then go home." There was a man!

But Degas had not had an American wife to whom he made love less and less. There was just enough guilt in that, he admitted to himself, to make him feel that Kate had to be allowed the pleasure she got in dining with Charlie Chaplin and the Duchess of Windsor.

Yes, ambition came to a woman as the life of the body was denied to her, he mused. He had his women, of course, in Avignon now, for the sake of decency, one young and willing girl after another, no more important than a pair of shoelaces, yet indispensable as shoelaces are when you don't have them.

But Kate seemed content with her ever-expanding guest list and with Nadine, who was growing into more of a chatterbox every day. He had tried, once or twice, to let Nadine sit quietly in a corner of his studio because she had begged to be allowed to see him work, but the child had never learned to maintain a decent quiet. "Why are you using all that red, Papa? Is that big yellow thing a sun, Papa? Can you paint a bird, Papa? Paint me a dog!" And even, God help him, "Why are you standing so still, Papa . . . is it because you are thinking?" No! It was too much to be endured. He forbade her the studio although her tiny chin trembled and she pouted in the way the servants thought was adorable and pulled ever so wistfully on her pale blond hair.

Nadine, at six, already had all sorts of little tricks to get what she wanted. Frequently Mistral caught her out in lies, especially against the servants. When he insisted that she should be punished Kate grew angry. "She's just imaginative, oversensitive, at her age she can't be expected to know the difference—don't be so moralistic, Julien." Mistral thought otherwise. Like all adults he knew how easy it was to lie and he was deeply suspicious of a child who had learned so young to do it so well. But Marte Pollison, who had no children of her own, conspired with Kate to spoil Nadine in spite of the discipline that the nurse tried vainly to impose. When Mistral talked to Kate about it she just laughed and said that it was typically French to expect children to be like little adults. Didn't he realize that her daughter was not an ordinary child? She was special and she had a wonderfully inquisitive little mind.

As he swam underwater after he fell into the pool Mistral thought grimly that inquisitive mind or not, he would teach her not to creep up behind him on the diving board, but when he surfaced Nadine had prudently vanished. Sly. She had been born sly and manipulative he told himself and dismissed her from his mind.

As Julien Mistral floated in his pool he thought about his work. It had been six months now that he had been groping toward the beginnings of a series of paintings inspired by shapes of grapevines in winter. His studio floor was covered with sketches and studies but only he knew that when he woke up each morning he no longer felt the gut-filling urge to leap out of bed and paint until the light faded. Only he knew that he lay under the quilt of the bed with the taste of fear in his mouth, with a churning in his stomach, with a weak and contemptible desire to fall asleep again so that he wouldn't have to face the fact that his fire burned lower and lower. Nevertheless, Mistral sketched all day, every day, wandering through his vineyards and those of his neighbors, each stroke of his charcoal based on a fear of death. He worked to keep death away, every motion of his fingers a useless protest against even thinking about death.

Ever since his fiftieth birthday he had been obsessed by this thought. Which came first? he wondered. The idea of death or the loss of that urge to paint that was the same as death itself? Mistral had always cared nothing for the lives or opinions of other artists but he found himself wondering if any of them had ever lived through the arid stretch of sand and rock in which he found himself wandering. It was not that he could not paint . . . technically he had such mastery that he could continue to paint for as long as he lived, but something had disappeared from his work, and he could not deny it to himself even if the public could be fooled—who could not fool those credulous cretins?

He searched and searched for the reason. The nerves of his eyes were as alert as ever; he *saw* with the vision that had always possessed him . . . but he was not *driven* to record what he saw, except by that fear that he would die if he stopped. Where was the failure, he wondered, where was the lack of connection, no, no . . . not lack of connection but lack of *appetite*. Yes, that was it, that was what it was.

Julien Mistral shuddered even though the water he floated in was warm, for he knew that there were many things in life that could be learned and many that could be achieved with hard work but that *appetite* must spring from within a man, and well forth without his conscious effort. Just as no wise doctor has ever been able to explain why, at the end of nine months, the womb begins to work to expel the child, no one knows what causes the divine hunger of the artist, no one can tell you what temptation must be put before him to drive him to appease his appetite day after day. Should that appetite falter . . . should that appetite dry up . . . if he had believed in God, Julien Mistral would have prayed.

18

It's the oddest thing," said Marietta Norton to Bill Hatfield, "but I believe I'm actually feeling a bit apprehensive. I haven't felt apprehensive since I heard about Pearl Harbor."

"Apprehensive, hell, I'm terrified . . . The last three guys who tried to get Mistral's picture came home empty-handed—all they had on film was the back of his head. But they didn't have our secret weapon—La Belle Théodora."

The fashion editor and the photographer leaned back against the cushions of the suitcase-filled old Renault taxi they were taking to *La Tourrello* from Le Prieuré—the hotel that had once been the pension of Madame Blé—in Villeneuve-les-Avignon, where they had spent the previous night. Behind them in another taxi were Berry, Sam and Teddy. They had been in France for almost ten days and after this afternoon's work they would be ready to return to Paris, and a day later fly back to New York with their objectives accomplished. Marietta Norton's intention had been to photograph her resort fashions in the studios of the three greatest living French artists—Picasso, Matisse and Mistral—and through Darcy's connections in the art world she had been granted permission by all of them.

In one day, in Vallauris, Bill Hatfield had shot fifteen rolls of film of Picasso and Teddy. There, on the Chemin du Fournas, Picasso rented two large studios in a building and split them in half, one part devoted to sculpture and the other to painting and engraving.

In the sculpture studio Berry had hooked Teddy into a strapless, black silk organdy dress printed with enormous white bows. Balancing lightly on her thin, high-heeled, black sandals, she stood amidst the mountain of spare metal parts that Picasso collected for his sculpture: bicycle chains and handlebars, wheels and pulleys of every size, any piece of odd iron that he could find discarded on a junk heap, some of which would be transformed into his animal heads and female forms and the great She-Goat, while Picasso, an aging Pan in a boiler room, flirted delightedly as she tried to avoid snagging her thin stockings on nails and barbed wire. Teddy quickly changed into a cornflower printed silk and the entire entourage moved into his painting studio where Picasso, peeking out from behind a potbellied stove, proudly pointed out the thick spiderwebs he encouraged to swing everywhere in the forty-foot room. Bill Hatfield went mad with excitement, trying to capture the expressions on Picasso's face as he talked to Teddy. Whenever he dared, he shot picture after picture of the messy, crowded studio itself, filled with the pots of paint and tools and old cans and equipment of all sorts from which the wizardry was distilled.

From Vallauris they had driven to Nice to find Matisse, bedridden in his bright hotel room at the Regina, living in a magnificent muddle of plants, singing birds, cooing doves and the brilliant fantasia of the bright paper cutouts he made now that he could no longer paint.

Matisse had welcomed them with the sweetness for which he was famous, enchanted with Teddy in her harem-bright dress, a shocking pink shantung splashed with an orange print, with her lovely bare arms making an arabesque that, he told her, none of his odalisques could equal. Teddy's clothes had been changed often enough to fill eight pages of Mode with the new spring prints. Now, at Mistral's domain, Marietta Norton planned to wind up with shots of the packable clothes that would travel everywhere next winter, four more pages of pictures in all.

In the second taxi Teddy sat in the front seat next to the driver. She was happy to leave the back seat to Berry and Sam, who seemed to be achieving an interesting relationship based on the limp and dazed condition in which Berry had staggered back last night into the room she shared with Teddy. Happy Berry, thought Teddy, I envy you. This is a country for lovers.

As the taxi passed l'Isle sur la Sorgue, with its ancient water-wheels still turning in the canals that surrounded the city, Teddy consulted the map. At least another half-hour to Félice, she thought, and her stomach clutched into a ball of nerves. Did all the others know that her mother had posed for Mistral? she wondered once again. The seven paintings that formed the *Rouquinne* series had never been publicly exhibited since the show in New York in 1931, but anybody with any knowledge of the history of modern art must have seen them in countless reproductions. Yet how many people in 1952 would ever connect them to Maggy?

Teddy had been in college in a darkened auditorium in the art building when a color slide of one of the series had been flashed on the screen in Art 101. She had never really looked at the picture before with close attention, but then, as the lecturer talked on about Mistral, she had scrutinized the model's face and realized, with a hot black flash of sureness, that the abandoned redheaded girl who displayed herself with such ripe sensuality had the same features as her remote, businesslike, stiffly coiffed, perfectly dressed mother.

On her next vacation Teddy had screwed up her nerve and ventured to ask Maggy about the painting but she had been granted only a few careless words. "I modeled briefly for artists when I was very young—it was so long ago that I've forgotten the details. Naturally we all posed naked—I thought you knew that," Maggy had said in a way that clearly indicated that she had no intention of discussing her life in Paris in any further detail. Teddy had been too intimidated to try to find out any more. Somehow her mother's existence before she came to the United States was almost as much of a taboo as the mystery of her own birth, the never-to-be-asked questions about her father.

Did Maggy have any understanding of the baffled, tongue-tied bruised frustration that Teddy had felt for so long? Or, to be fair, Teddy told herself, was she not a coward herself? Why had she been unable to confront Maggy with her questions, to insist on getting answers, no matter how much it might have shamed her mother? Oh, the old dilemma, the two sides to the argument that she had held with herself all those years while she was growing up.

In the past four years, living on her own, financially free of Maggy, she had almost forgotten the tormented, twisted bewilderments of her childhood. They had come to seem less and less important as her life grew more crowded and self-centered. It was only because she would be in the presence of Mistral so soon, that now they were filling her mind again. Yet, had this entire trip not been a kind of search?

Maggy had struggled to prevent her from taking the *Mode* booking as soon as she had learned what it was to involve, but Teddy had insisted. She waited to see if Maggy would finally come right out and say *why* she didn't want Teddy to go to Provence, but Maggy had given a dozen reasons that had nothing to do with Mistral, and in revenge, Teddy had resisted all her arguments.

What could Maggy be afraid of? Teddy wondered, her heart beating faster as the taxi turned off the road to Apt. What secret could she have that would still shock anyone after all these years? Could she possibly be so naïve as to imagine that because she had once posed naked for a painter who must be an old man by now, that it would horrify her worldly daughter?

"Berry," she said softly, "we're almost there. Better put on some lipstick before Marietta gets a look at you."

"I'm sorry to keep you waiting," Kate Mistral explained to Marietta Norton, "but Julien is still working and I don't dare to tell him you're here."

"I hope the light doesn't go," Bill Hatfield said anxiously.

"Don't worry. I made him promise to stop at five tonight and I reminded him again at breakfast—he rarely agrees to do this sort of thing, you know, but when I can get him to say yes he's usually very good about it."

"We're awfully indebted to you," Marietta said, praying that one more expression of gratitude might hasten the emergence of Julien Mistral. Picasso had given them a whole day but Mistral had only agreed to the hours of the late afternoon.

"Not a bit—I've been a *Mode* reader all my life—I get it here by mail," Kate said, smiling, charming, very much the wife of the great painter. She had led them all through the *mas*, with its profusion of high, white-plastered, dark-beamed rooms, fashionably spare and shining with hexagonal terra-cotta tile floors. Baskets of dried lavender stood here and there amid the fine country antiques. At the rear of the house, two large wings, built of old stones, and connected by a high stone wall that protected them from the winds, faced each other across a central swimming pool surrounded by grass. One of the wings was Mistral's studio, its doors closed, and the other was the new pool pavilion where a room had been set aside in which Teddy could change. For almost an hour they all waited, drinking tall glasses of cassis-flavored lemonade in the shade of a vine-heaped trellis.

Kate Mistral took no interest in any of them but Marietta Norton. She had an unerring capacity to pick out the most important person in any group and as far as she was concerned the only one of this band worth talking to was the fashion editor. Not only could she catch up on news of some of her carefully tended friendships with people who shaped opinion in New York, but she could lay the foundations for a connection to Marietta that would someday, somehow be valuable.

Kate had watched with disgust as the attention of the art world turned toward the new painters, particularly those of the New York School, and although she had no fears that Mistral was not secure in the fame that had grown since 1926, she was too clear-eyed not to notice how Picasso, as firmly enthroned as Mistral, was no longer considered to have any relevance to what the new painters were doing, how he was attacked on every side by the younger generation of art critics.

It was not enough for Kate that the major museums of the world competed to give Mistral shows, that art historians took the most serious interest in him, that he sold every painting he allowed to be shown. She wanted continuing publicity, particularly in the most fashionable publications, that would prevent any public slackening of interest in Mistral.

She knew that Mistral had never given a damn whether his art was fashionable—she would never have dared to use the word in front of him when speaking of anything but a dress—but she, Madame Julien Mistral, did not intend ever to find herself the wife of a painter in whom the fashionable world had lost interest. The Impressionists had ignored the great Delacroix and the public had followed their lead. The new Abstractionists must never presume to discount Mistral. These pages in *Mode* would be helpful—all top-flight publicity was helpful, although "publicity" was a word she would have feared to use even more than "fashionable" in talking to Mistral.

263

While Kate chatted effusively on a wicker sofa with Marietta, the rest of the *Mode* group sat at a little distance. Only Teddy stood up the entire time in her sleeveless, white jersey Anne Fogarty dress. The top of the dress was tightly molded and finely pleated, crisscrossing over her breasts into a deeply wrapped *décolleté*, and spreading into a vast ballerina skirt that stopped less than ten inches from the floor.

To emphasize the illusion that Teddy belonged to some unseen *corps-de-ballet*, Marietta had added a belt like a tight gold ring, gold ballet slippers from Capezio and a gold band that held her mass of red hair back off her brow. Teddy looked as insubstantial as an iridescent soap bubble in the dress that, in theory, was uncrushable. However, Berry hadn't dared risk letting her sit down in it for there were eight stiffly starched crinolines underneath holding out the light fabric. Teddy leaned over carefully and sipped a mouthful of liquid from a glass that Berry held for her. All she needed was to spill the pink lemonade over the dress, she thought. Ridiculously her hands were shaking. Why the hell didn't he come out?

"Stage wait," Berry muttered sympathetically. It was odd to see Teddy visibly nervous. She'd treated Picasso and Matisse as if they'd been old beaux from dancing school days.

"How are my eyebrows?" Teddy asked. The style of 1952 demanded heavy, arched and strongly emphasized eyebrows placed halfway between anyone's normal brows and the forehead. No model, not even Teddy, could depart from this cosmetic convention, but unlike other models, Teddy had refused to shave or pluck her own light red eyebrows. She had covered them with makeup and penciled false brows above them, a delicate, painstaking process that took at least a half-hour to do perfectly.

"Still on," Berry reassured her.

"I have this awful feeling that they're slipping."

"Don't worry, I'd tell you if they were."

The tall doors of the studio opened and Julien Mistral walked slowly toward them along the side of the swimming pool wiping his hands on a paint-stained rag that he stuffed in the pocket of his corduroy pants. Kate introduced him to Marietta Norton and then she asked the fashion editor to introduce her colleagues. Marietta, flustered by Mistral's martial bearing, by his unmistakable look of a man who would prefer to be elsewhere, presented them as quickly as possible, using only their first names. When Mistral took Teddy's hand he looked at her a shade more closely than he looked at the others.

"Come into the studio," he said in French. "Let's get this over with."

They understood him. Berry had finishing school French; Marietta, Paris Collection French; Teddy, her mother's French and Bill Hatfield, photographer's French.

Inside the great space of the studio they all fell silent. Here reigned a kind of sublime disorder that made the mess of Picasso's studio seem almost banal.

Only Bill, cursing to himself at the need to choose between looking at the paintings and taking his pictures before the sun dimmed, was able to move. The others simply stood as speechlessly shy as schoolchildren, not daring to venture a word because anything they said would sound inadequate as they gazed from one big canvas to another. Each canvas was a meditation on a world in which the commonplace became a marvel, each a meditation on a human vision that could articulate the commonplace so that it was perceived for the first time.

Finally Bill picked his spot. "Come on, Teddy," he said, grabbing her arm. "Go stand over there next to him and make like you're having fun." Mistral was waiting impatiently in front of his easel, on which stood an empty canvas.

Gathering all her professionalism about her, Teddy walked over to him, the skirts of her Swan Queen dress swaying as she moved so lightly in her ballet slippers. He was so tall that she had to stretch her neck the full length of its supple ivory arch to look up at him. She had never felt so small next to any man, Teddy realized, as she tilted her finely cut chin, her head pulled backward by the heavy mass of her hair. Her changeable eyes were an unnameable color that held in it the bewitchment of a thousand twilights. Her smile was an adventure.

Mistral took her chin in his hand and turned it to one side and then to the other, expressionlessly. His blue eyes, blazing twin conflagrations, scanned her face. He pulled the rag on which he'd wiped his hands out of his pocket. It smelled of turpentine, Teddy had just time enough to think, before she realized that he was holding her head firmly in one big hand and wiping off her eyebrows with the other. In unison, Marietta squawked, Berry shrieked, Bill cursed and Sam hooted.

"That's better. You use too much paint," Mistral said so softly that only Teddy heard him. "Just like your mother." He smiled for the first time. "But you are a thousand times more beautiful."

After the furor had quieted down, everyone from *Mode* went back to the room in which Teddy had changed and Marietta Norton inspected the damage. She told them all to wait while she went off to straighten things out. She found Kate with the cook.

"Madame Mistral, we have a problem," she said grimly.

"Oh, no—is there anything I can do?"

"Monsieur Mistral has, unfortunately, removed my model's eyebrows."

"What!"

"They were penciled on and he wiped them off. He also seems to have messed up the makeup base on her forehead. It's going to take her at least an hour to match the top of her face to the bottom—by that time the light will be too low for color pictures."

"But why on earth . . . ?" Kate was furious with him. How could he be such a boor—and after all her careful arrangements?

"I haven't the slightest idea—an artistic decision no doubt—but the fact is that it puts us in a devil of a spot—we have four pages left to fill, and nothing to fill them with."

"I can't tell you how sorry—I can't imagine what he thought he was up to. Look, I wouldn't dream of disappointing you, not after you came all this way—I'll go and talk to him. If he could give you some time tomorrow morning, would that work out or do you have to be somewhere else?"

"We're not going anywhere," Marietta said grimly.

"Let me give you a gin and tonic and get this sorted out."

"Don't bother with the tonic," Marietta said with a sigh of relief. She understood Kate Mistral's kind of woman. They were both equally professional. She'd get her four pages and that was the only thing that mattered.

The next day, after breakfast, as they drove back to *La Tourrello* Teddy was more confused than she had ever been in her life. That moment, that brief moment when Julien Mistral had held her chin in his hand, was embedded in her mind as if she'd been shot between the eyes and the bullet had lodged there. He hadn't said another word to her—bedlam had taken over—but she thought about nothing else since it had happened. It was as if her life were a film and when Julien Mistral had touched her the director had yelled "Cut." Until she saw him again the screen must remain blank, waiting.

As soon as Teddy saw Mistral frowning impatiently at the invasion of their troop into his studio, she knew that he had been waiting for her as eagerly as she had been waiting for him. There could be no doubt about such passionate certainty. She walked over to the easel, holding her breath. He put out his hand and she took it and their hands clasped each other tightly without moving for a long second until they both remembered that they were supposed to be giving the conventional handshake greeting of France.

"Bonjour, Mademoiselle Lunel. Did you sleep well?"

"Bonjour, Monsieur Mistral. I didn't sleep."

"Nor did I."

"Teddy," Bill Hatfield said, "turn a bit—we can't see the dress."

I must touch his face, thought Teddy, as she moved a few inches to her right. I must put my hands on either side of his head and feel the place at his temples where his hair starts to grow and the skin looks so smooth.

"Chin down a little," Bill called, "as if you're looking at the canvas."

I want to kiss his eyes. I want to feel his eyelids with my lips, Teddy thought, as she stared blankly at the canvas.

"Teddy, could we have a little more animation?" Bill asked.

I want to put my lips on his chest where his shirt is unbuttoned at the neck. I want to unbutton his shirt and lay my head on his chest and then button the shirt up again so that I'm inside it. I want to breathe with his breathing, I want my heart to beat with his heart.

"Teddy, back to me, please—I'm getting a rear view of the dress again."

I want to make his mouth grow sweet. I want to feel him laugh under my mouth, I want to beg him for kisses, I want him to beg me for kisses.

"Damn it, Teddy." Bill was more surprised than impatient, Teddy never needed this kind of direction.

"He is not happy, your photographer," Mistral said quietly.

"His happiness does not concern me."

"But he won't stop until he has the photographs he wants."

"No, you're right."

"And the sooner he stops the sooner we can talk."

"What are we going to talk about?"

"Teddy! You know I can't get anything with your lips moving, for Christ's sake!"

"What are we going to talk about?" she repeated.

"The rest of our lives."

"I'm leaving for New York tomorrow."

"You will stay here with me."

"Can that be true?"

"You know it is true."

"Look, guys, Monsieur Mistral I mean, this isn't working. What if you both went over to the table in the middle of the room and you show Teddy your palette?" Bill said with exaggerated calm.

"Where can we talk?" she asked.

"At the Hiely Restaurant in Avignon, at eight-thirty tonight. Understood?"

"Understood." Teddy gave Bill a smile that he spent the rest of his life wishing he'd captured on film and began to go through her poses as automatically as a well-trained animal, her head tipped so that she could look at Julien Mistral without meeting his eyes, because if she met his eyes she would not be able to stand up.

All these years, she thought, all these long years of dreaming and dreaming and falling and falling through the dream to this place, this minute. No one has ever been real before. No one else will ever be real again.

As soon as Teddy put herself seriously to work Bill Hatfield was able to get his photographs quickly. Kate Mistral, who returned from Félice just as they finished, asked them all to stay for lunch but Marietta had to refuse because she was afraid of missing the afternoon train for Paris, and all their luggage still had to be collected back at Le Prieuré.

"Are you all packed?" Berry asked over her shoulder. Teddy was lying on the bed in the comfortable room they had shared, with its walls covered in pale yellow fabric printed in a tiny Provençal flower design.

"I'm staying."

268

"Please, Teddy, you know that I have no sense of humor about anything to do with *arrangements.*"

"I'm not going back with you."

"Did you see my list? I've got all the suitcases, but oh, God, I can't find the *list.* Why are you just lying there?"

"You weren't listening—I'm staying on in Provence . . . for a while. I've never seen any place I like as much as this."

"But you can't just do that!"

"Why not?" Teddy's voice was calm yet it was filled with a kind of feverish necessity, and there was a bright flare of pink under her cheekbones. Berry looked at her anxiously.

"Are you sick? Don't you feel well enough to make the trip?"

"Of course not. It's a whim . . . don't you ever have whims, Berry?"

"Certainly not. I won't be able to have them for a dozen years. Well, okay—so stay . . . I've found that list—God must have listened. Your return ticket's right here—I'll put it on the bureau. You could have mentioned it earlier, that's all."

"I didn't know earlier," Teddy said in a voice from a dream. "I'll send the agency a cable so they'll have the news before you get home."

"What about your mother? She's not going to like this, is she?"

"Oh, she'll understand," Teddy said slowly. "I have the feeling that she'll understand better than anyone."

In a French city of medium size the best restaurant in town is often characterized by a straightforward lack of decor that announces clearly that here everything is focused on great food.

The restaurant Hiely in Avignon was located in one large but unassuming rectangular room, plainly paneled in wood, its comfortably large tables spread with plain yellow cloths, its plain parquet floor highly polished. On a center table stood a whole smoked ham surrounded by bowls of fresh fruit, and platters of cooked lobsters and bottles of wine reclining in individual baskets. However, there was no other display, the windows were undraped, there were no flowers on the tables and the unupholstered wooden chairs stood around the table in a dignified and reasonable manner that indicated that this place was devoted to gastronomy with a philosophy of total concentration.

As Julien Mistral and Teddy Lunel sat facing each other at a quiet table in a window alcove Teddy wondered why nobody had ever warned her that love at first sight would strike her dumb. Veteran of thousands of first dinners she had never found herself so at a loss for speech. They had already said so much to each other, in front of other people and protected from its consequences by the fact that they were in public, even though unheard, that now that they were finally alone together she was tongue-tied, reduced to a few banal words about the food.

Julien Mistral, who had never hesitated to make his opinions known, a man to whom shyness was the most unfamiliar of states, found himself almost as silent as Teddy. A lamentable performance, he told himself. He was choking with things that had to be said but he too scarcely managed to push his food around on his plate. Where to start? Not at the beginning because this had started a long time ago; yesterday seemed another era of his life. He couldn't begin in the middle because this strangely solemn, awkward dinner *was* the middle. They didn't know each other after all, yet he could see no future for them that was not a continuation. The necessary presence of this woman must never be withdrawn from him.

To Teddy the rather ordinary lamplight in the room seemed to tremble as much as her hands as she tried to make a show of eating. She found herself singularly unwilling to use any of her easily summoned arsenal of allure. She wanted only to touch Mistral, to hold him. She had no impulse to flirt because they had gone beyond flirtation the instant that they had admitted to each other that neither of them had slept the night before.

Mistral's face, that famous face, so much more beautiful than she had ever imagined, was grave. He didn't try to joke, he seemed to be thinking, and the inconsequential comments she might have used to bridge this moment stuck to her lips before they were spoken. The questions that she wanted to ask him were either too unimportant or too important. There was no middle ground. Teddy had to know everything about Julien Mistral from the day he had been born—his life was dense, complicated, foreign—yet something informed her that only the thinnest of veils separated them from knowing each other better than either of them had ever known anyone.

When the meal was almost over Teddy looked up from her wineglass and confronted Mistral's gaze, dropping even the pretense of speech. One single tear, of some emotion she didn't dare to name, ran slowly down her cheek. He touched it with his finger, let it be absorbed by his skin, and around them there fell a web of confused, hesitant joy that was so fine and fierce that he was freed to talk to her at last.

"Last week," he said, "I was sure I'd never feel young again. I looked up at the sky that I used to love and the sunlight was glaring through a thin layer of clouds and the light had a flat skin of utter hopelessness. I told myself that it was the human condition and that all that was wrong with me was that I'd had the ego to think that the human condition could never apply to me."

"And now?" Teddy asked gravely.

"I feel as if I had never been young before, never known what it was, as if all the years of my youth were spent in a kind of emptiness. I thought it was being alive because I couldn't envision anything better. I wasn't unhappy—I worked and I lived like any other man and I didn't ask myself questions because I was painting and I've always believed that was the only thing I wanted. I can't tell you that I missed you then because I didn't know you existed. It's only now that I understand how incomplete I was."

"But during half of your life I didn't exist." She smiled gently as she spoke.

"Does that seem even remotely possible to you? I know it's true, but I can't make myself *feel* it."

"We should have been born on the same day," Teddy cried passionately. "We should have grown up together! You could always have been with me—oh, I've been waiting for you *forever*. Those hours in which I felt unhappy and only half a person—oh, so many hours—it was because you weren't there. I was afraid this could never happen to me," she said, liberated by a great wind of gladness. "I never expected to be a girl like this."

"And I," Julien Mistral said incredulously, "I never expected to be *a man like this* . . . it is so . . . *thorough* . . . it makes me understand other men, men who give up everything for a woman, men I used to be so scornful of—it makes me feel . . . *human*, just like everyone else."

"Is that a blow?" Teddy said, her laugh a promise.

"It would have been until yesterday. Now it is such an extraordinary . . . *relief* . . ." Even as he spoke he listened to himself and marveled. He had never talked to any woman like this, never dreamed it was possible, never known that these words could come to his lips, never imagined himself swept up by an emotion that clearly announced itself as the most important feeling he had ever experienced, a rapture.

"I can't survive you." His declaration was a mixture of wonder and certainty.

"You don't have to."

"You will not leave me." It was an elated command, not a question.

"How could I?" Teddy asked. Her entire face was illuminated by such an unconditional declaration of love that it was as if she had taken her heart and was holding it in her eyes for him to see.

"You could not."

Together they laughed like pagan gods. In the space of five phrases they had agreed to banish the outside world, they had swept away all the problems they would face, resolved, even as they saw the consequences, for neither of them was so simple as to imagine that they would be allowed to escape, that nothing could stop them. Chaos had been accepted, madness—that *folie à deux* that overcomes lovers—was to be their daily bread.

"Come with me now," Mistral said.

"Where?"

For an instant Mistral looked blank. He thought of the Hotel Europe, once the magnificent residence of a nobleman of the sixteenth century, built around a courtyard with splashing fountains. It had been turned into a hotel a century before. At this time of the year they would have empty rooms. Tomorrow he would make arrangements, permanent ones, but for tonight the Europe would harbor them as it had so often welcomed lovers in this profoundly sensuous city where the papal court had known many joyous sinners.

"Just come," he said to Teddy. "I'll take care of you, don't you know that?"

She flushed with a new kind of happiness. None of the men in her life had seemed to know that she wanted to be told what to do, yes, even to be ordered to do it. Melvin almost understood . . . a thought of him drifted into her memory and then was extinguished utterly.

She stood up and walked across the restaurant with him, not noticing that dozens of Frenchmen had paid her the ultimate honor of ceasing to eat or drink so that they could look ar her undistracted.

Irrevocable. The word beat in her mind as Julien Mistral entered her for the first time. *Irrevocable.* Once inside the door of the hotel room they had fallen on the bed together without a second's hesitation, their madness of desire too severe to leave time for any conventional, ritualistic approach to each other. Almost fully dressed they made love with a clumsiness, an urgency that was final and necessary. It had to be done quickly, their pact to be sealed by this act.

Only when it was over did he undress her and take off his own clothes and make her lie quietly on the pillows while he touched her softly with his long hands, felt her as slowly and delicately and deliberately as if he were blind and could know her only from his fingertips.

Now Teddy delighted in being docile, taking a rare pleasure in not moaning or moving, as if he had ordered her to be still and wait. Now that she belonged to him they had all the time in the world. She let him move his hands back and forth with infinite care, never quite reaching that tender flesh that lay between her legs, until she burned too hotly to endure it any longer. She rose up and covered his body with her own, discovering him as urgent as a boy.

Irrevocable. He moved powerfully within her as he filled her in a way in which she had never been filled before. She clasped him deep within her, every one of her senses expanding until she knew that she had floated free beyond her own boundaries, that she had dissolved and he had dissolved and that together they had formed one being. Forever, she thought. *Forever.*

19

Even in the middle of winter a particular gaiety always rules in Avignon. As Teddy hurried down the rue Joseph Vernet to the hairdresser she was bundled up warmly against the brisk, dry cold that covered the South of France. But a festive sun shone out of a clear sky on to all the ancient stones of the town, stones of silver, stones like brown sugar, stones the gold of champagne, stones of rose and soft faded purple. Rue Joseph Vernet, curving and narrow, was as chic as a small street of Paris, bordered by townhouses whose ground floors were converted into *salons de coiffures*, flower shops, antique stores, and elegant little clothing boutiques. Teddy had a Friday morning appointment to get her hair done, the only fixed appointment in any of her weeks, for Teddy Lunel and Julien Mistral had made a life together that existed outside of ordinary time.

From the first night they spent together they had not once been parted. He had never returned to *La Tourrello*, he had abandoned it as if his house, his studio, his wife and his child were but a single worn-out sock, and they had lived together in a condition of astonished happiness that, in the last four months, had isolated them from the realities of everyday existence. They were so untouched by ordinary considerations that together they were like one sailing ship, lifted by a keen and steady wind, endlessly headed toward a rosy island.

After their first days at the Hotel Europe they had discovered a big apartment for rent inside the medieval walls of this queenly city with its opulent Tuscan light, its hundred bell towers, its history of pageantry and jubilation stretching from the days when seven popes had held lavish court, taking under their protection—for a price—those who did not feel safe outside the borders of the town: Jews, smugglers, escaped prisoners and, Teddy imagined, many other lovers like themselves. Avignon, lively, prosperous, laughing within its golden ramparts, contained everything to make life delightful, she thought, as she lay back and felt the expert hands of the shampoo assistant brush out her hair.

The apartment they occupied formed the entire second floor of an eighteenth-century mansion that had formerly belonged to a rich merchant in the fashionable Préfecture quarter. Its tall windows opened onto the flower beds and lawns, dotted with strutting peacocks of the Calvet Museum. Mistral had turned the largest room into a studio and next to it, in the bedroom, they had installed an enormous canopied bed with royal blue velvet hangings embroidered on the inside with scenes from a stag hunt. On chilly nights the hangings could be closed to shelter the bed on all sides.

There was no central heating in the apartment and each of the rooms had a huge fireplace, where, from early November on, fires of spicy eucalyptus and pine burned all day and all night. The studio was kept warmer than any of the other rooms of the house by a baroque Viennese stove, made of white porcelain, like a mound of whipped cream, taller than Mistral himself, that he had bought from an antique dealer to keep Teddy warm as she posed for him, as she did almost every day in the afternoons.

Never before in his life, he told Teddy, had he stayed up as late as he did now, sitting with her captive in his arms in front of their bedroom fire, talking and laughing far into the night, cracking walnuts, roasting chestnuts and sipping from the contents of the tall, slender-necked bottles of the colorless brandies distilled from fruits, which she bought for their irresistible names: *prunelle de buissons, mûre sauvage, églantine* and *myrtille des bois*. Nor had he ever slept so late. Now, when he woke, he lay and watched Teddy sleep until she opened her eyes. Then, often, they made love in luxurious forgetfulness of time and even space. Afterward Teddy would discover that she had so lost herself that she didn't know where she was for an instant, as she looked up into the embroidered forest with its running huntsmen, leaping hounds and tiny-petaled wild flowers.

"Does Madame want another soaping?" the assistant asked. Teddy nodded in assent and relaxed even more deeply as she contemplated the details of her new life. They lived like sovereigns, secure in their whirlwind of love, content to kiss and look at each other and know that they were right.

Every day before lunch they went for an *apéritif* to the Café du Palais, where they never wearied of the spectacle of the Place de l'Horloge, a vast, open square bordered by rows of venerable plane trees with their motley, piebald bark, filled with swooping flocks of pigeons and animated by the citizens of Avignon who promenaded there every midday, crowding the many cafés. At twilight they often walked to the top of the Rocher des Doms, where they found a park planted in roses that flowered till Christmas. Sometimes, when there was a film starring Gérard Phillipe or Jean Gabin or Michele Morgan, they went to one of the local movie houses, and in the intermission, when the ice cream sellers sold their wares up and down the aisles, Teddy would eat two Esquimos and Mistral would eat four.

It seemed to Teddy that although she sometimes noticed people glancing at them on the street or in a restaurant, no one in Avignon concerned himself with them. Mistral was a figure they had been accustomed to seeing for many years, coming and going, and if he now appeared with a young woman, it would be indiscreet and impolite to stare.

They had made no friends except for the doctor and his wife who occupied the *rez-de-chaussée* just below them. Two friends were all they needed, for Julien Mistral knew painful primitive feelings. He wanted to stand guard over Teddy and never let her out of his sight. He hid his suffering every time she left the apartment on an errand, he woke in the night to listen to her breathing; when men looked at her he would have gnashed his teeth at them if he could have. She was all woman to him, his bride, his child, sometimes as tender as a mother or as playful as the sister he'd never had, always his treasure, unknowable by anyone but him.

Under her turban of soapsuds Teddy made a wry face as she remembered the letter she had received today from Maggy. It had been conciliatory, very different from the first cruel and angry letters Maggy had sent after Teddy had written about her new life with Julien. Now, Maggy wrote, her only concern was Teddy's future. She was terrified that in some way history might repeat itself, as if Julien's intention to get a divorce would be no more successful than Teddy's father's had been.

How could she compare the cases? Teddy wondered. Kate Mistral was a Protestant, not a Catholic, and she had married Julien in a civil ceremony, not a religious one. Teddy tried to reconcile the Kate Mistral her mother described, a woman Maggy said she had feared from the moment she met her, a woman she described as having a willpower greater than Mistral's own, with the woman she herself had met; colorless, rather fragile, middle-aged and all but fawning over Marietta Norton.

No, Teddy assured herself as her head was gently massaged, her mother was wrong, she was seeing ghosts. Times had changed. Surely no woman today would continue to hang on to a man she had utterly lost?

It took the hairdresser a long time to towel-dry and brush out the long hair that Teddy no longer bothered to have set. Nor did she wear any makeup now, except for mascara. She looked younger than she had since she had started modeling, and her face was rosy from all the time she spent with Julien in the open air. All the eating and drinking, all the lazy parade of her days in which the only work she did was to pose for three or four hours, basking in the heat of the Viennese stove, had made her gain weight. The Korrigan skirts she had bought once she had decided to stay in Provence were growing tight, the slacks she had worn over in the plane from New York were difficult to zip.

I could never work for *Mode* today, Teddy thought, as she strolled to the Café du Palais to meet Mistral. Marietta Norton would faint if she saw me now. She stopped in a market to buy a jar of Mont Ventoux lavender honey, a long loaf of warm bread, a chalk-white cylinder of goat cheese and a half-kilo of pale yellow farm butter. The only meal she made was breakfast, the others they took in restaurants or bought from the *charcuterie* and ate as a picnic in their dining room where the only furniture was two wide, deep *bergère* armchairs covered in faded yellow brocade and an old, elaborately inlaid card table on which stood four unmatched, heavy silver candlesticks. After Kate's immaculate, well-appointed house Mistral delighted in this approximation of bohemia.

Teddy looked at her watch and began to walk quickly toward the Place de l'Horloge. As she swung the shopping net that held her few purchases she saw Mistral hurrying down the street to meet her, the top of his curly red head, tilted as cavalierly as ever, clearly visible from a distance above the crowd. Scattering the pigeons on the street by the force of her eagerness, Teddy began to run.

Kate Mistral stood thoughtfully in the big, windowless, fire-proof room off Mistral's studio where sliding metal racks had been installed for storage of his paintings. There, in row after row, protected from the daylight and from dust, stretched, dated and varnished, but not signed or framed, stood the best of over a quarter-century of his work. Mistral had never sold the pictures he thought were the most successful of each year's work. Some years he had kept a half-dozen canvases, some years only one or two, some years as many as twenty. Kate knew each canvas by heart, knew on which rack it was held, knew almost to the penny how much each would bring if Étienne Delage were ever allowed to offer it for sale. She turned on all the lights and walked through the aisles that had been created to give easy access to the paintings and slid out a rack from the very back of the storage room. On it stood the painting of Maggy, naked on the pile of green cushions, the most famous of the *Rouquinne* series. Kate had not looked at that painting since 1931 when it had come back from exhibition in New York but she had never forgotten that it was there, along with the six others, like a growing lethal radioactive substance inside a metal container, unseen but alive.

Oh, yes, she thought, it's easy to understand. What man wouldn't, after all, what man could resist? Young flesh, they all want it at his age, and if they could all afford it they would line up at the market to buy it by the pound. Julien is no different—if anything he's more susceptible than others, I've always known that nothing matters to him more than the way things look, than what his eyes can see, surfaces, nothing but surfaces. But what a fool he is, what a vast, childlike, typically middle-aged fool. You don't *marry* this, you don't throw away your life for *flesh!*

How long did it take him to realize that about the mother? Only months. How I loathed her, that sulky Jewish girl with nothing but a pouting mouth and a ripe body, that girl who had never understood what a genius like Julien needed from a woman. Kate's mouth turned sour in disgust as she thought of Maggy. That greedy loose-living girl must have had many lovers after Julien, for obviously this American was a bastard, why else did she bear her mother's name?

Could it be the mother that Julien saw in the daughter? Did the man think he could travel back in time and become young again just by pressing himself into firm young flesh once more? Her hands were clenched with the effort not to rend the canvas, not to attack it with one of the sharp tools that lay about in the studio only a few feet away.

Abruptly, she pushed the rack back into place. In the seven years since the war, the seven *Rouquinne* canvases had tripled in price as the finest examples of Mistral's early work. It was the best investment she'd ever made, she thought grimly, and she'd sell them tomorrow if she wasn't certain that they'd triple or even quadruple in value again in the next ten years. She had nothing to gain by parting with them now at any price. But if she did sell, if she finally decided she couldn't endure their presence on her property any longer, even hidden in the storage room, she wished she could do it through Adrien Avigdor. If she had to do business with Jews—and in the art world it was impossible not to—better to deal with the smartest of them.

Kate remembered her trip to Paris after the war and her last interview with Avigdor. It had been necessary to see him because he still had a number of Mistral's paintings that he had sequestered before the Occupation. She had been afraid that he would insist that they were still his to sell although his contract with Mistral had expired, but the man had been more than willing to hand them over to Delage.

She hadn't understood until he had told her why he would never do business with Mistral again. Turned away from *La Tourrello*, had he been? Well, what of it? Any Frenchman sheltering Jews did it at the risk of his life, didn't Avigdor appreciate that? And what did she care that he had discovered that the same thing had happened to other Jews who had come to Julien for help? She didn't give a damn if there had been a dozen or a hundred or only one Jew.

What right had they had to jeopardize Julien, she demanded of Avigdor as he sat sternly behind his desk in his sumptuous Right Bank Gallery, wearing the ribbon of the Legion of Honor in his buttonhole, won, he didn't fail to tell her, for his activities in the

Resistance. She had asked him angrily if he thought that a genius like her husband had to live by the rules Avigdor had made for himself? Did he know so little of artists, after all these years, as to think that they concerned themselves with politics unless it suited their need for subject matter? Avigdor was a fool, too, she told herself, and she would forget him. He had served his purpose.

Kate wandered down the aisle at random, stopping to pull out a large canvas of an apple tree in flower, the hidden voice of the painting speaking of an atmosphere so dense with spring that she could have heard the sap rising in the branches if she had looked at it with any attention. But Kate saw it without seeing it, as she remembered a conversation she had had with a notary she had gone to see in Nice only a week ago. One of her few friends in Félice was the notary's wife and since she suspected that her friend might hear things from her husband, she had made the long trip out of Haute Provence to the large city where she could be certain to find a notary who had no idea of who she was.

The visit itself had not taken long, and answers to her questions were simple. The institution of civil marriage in France he assured her was respected as in few countries of the world. Since 1866 divorce had been possible only *pour faute*. He had leaned back in his chair expectantly, knowing that he had not yet earned his fee. "*Pour faute?*" she had asked, skillfully hiding her anxiety.

"After the presentation of facts that constitute serious and repeated violations, my dear Madame, of the duties and obligations of marriage which make continued conjugal life intolerable." He obviously enjoyed the sonorous rhythm of his words as he rolled them out.

"I don't quite understand," she had said. "Does that mean that if my husband has given me grounds for divorce, if he is at fault, I can divorce him?"

"Indeed, yes, Madame. It is only a question of time, and of the proof."

"But if I don't want to divorce him, in spite of the fault?"

"Then no divorce is possible," he answered.

"None? No matter if he should want a divorce?"

"Never, Madame, it is completely impossible." She had thanked the notary, paid him, and taken the long, winding road back to Félice, climbing slowly through the bare meadows of winter. She need not worry, she need not act, she need not respond. She was protected by the weight of almost a hundred years of French law.

Did that despicable imbecile, her husband, know? Had he learned the truth from another notary yet? She had no intention of telling him. Let him find out for himself, let him learn the facts and slowly grow to understand—for he would not believe them at first, he would rage and shout and declare that nothing could stop him from getting what he wanted—let him realize that he was utterly impotent, totally powerless for the first time in his life. She could almost feel sorry for him if she chose. But that she did not. He must have forgotten how patient she was, he must really not remember that she never gave up.

I didn't let you go when I was young, Kate thought, when I could have had any man I wanted, when I could have had any life I cared to lead, when I could have shaped my future in any direction, I chose you, Julien. Is it likely, when I've spent my life *making* your career, that I'll let you go now? Oh, no, you contemptible man, why did you even bother to write and ask? How can you dare to imagine that I'll ever give you to that sly, thieving girl who came and took you away? Do you truly understand me so little? You belong to me. I own you just as I own these paintings. I paid for them, I still have the receipted bill, they are my property. And like it or not, so are you.

Mistral put down his brushes suddenly and stood very still. Teddy still looked dreamily at the ceiling moldings of the studio, her half-focused eyes resting on the garlands of flowers, the bows and cupids that she had grown so familiar with during the hours of posing. Surely it wasn't time for the break yet? It seemed to her as if she had just lain down on the model stand—but perhaps she'd dozed off as she sometimes did after a particularly heavy lunch. He walked over and stood looking down at her in abstraction.

"What is it, my darling?" she asked. "Don't tell me that I was snoring."

He sat on his heels and put out his hand and traced a line on her naked body from between her breasts down over her belly.

"No, not snoring . . . you never snore, but you're putting on weight."

"I know. It's all this good living. I'm going to be a Rubens one day. But I can't seem to really care . . . do you?"

"No . . . no . . . of course not." He sounded just a bit unsure.

Perhaps he really did want her to be as skinny as she had been when she was modeling. Perhaps her nice new voluptuousness that she found so pleasant was making her less paintable in some way. The French were always so worried about *la ligne*—Frenchwomen anyway. Mistral took each of her breasts in his big hands and stroked them thoughtfully. Then he put his hands at her waistline, his thumbs touching, his long fingers spanning her waist. He looked as if he were listening to something.

"Hey, what's going on?" Teddy laughed. "Your hands are cold."

"You're pregnant," he said in a voice of incredulous joy.

"Oh, no, I'm not!" She sat up, her eyes wide in alarm.

"Oh, yes, you are. That's not fat, not the way it's distributed—believe me, I know the difference." He plunged his face into her stomach and kissed her skin in wild excitement. "My God, my God, you can't imagine how happy I am."

"You! You!" Teddy sputtered. "Oh, Julien, you're frightening me—how the hell can you know?"

"Isn't it possible? Think, Teddy."

"No! . . . yes . . . I suppose . . . oh, no! It *is* possible. Oh, shit, no, it can't be!"

"I'm right," he said triumphantly. "I knew it."

"*What am I going to do!*" Teddy grabbed a shawl and covered herself frantically.

"Do—why should you do anything?"

"Julien! You aren't even divorced, for God's sake . . ."

"Teddy, *I will be*. I promised you that on my life, on my love for you, on my work, on anything you hold sacred. I will be! Especially now that you're pregnant. When Kate learns about the baby she'll see that there is no use in clinging to me any longer. I know how she thinks, I know her well enough to tell you just what's going through her mind. But she doesn't yet understand about us. She still *will not* realize that you are the only woman—the only *person*—I have ever loved in my whole life."

He stood up and looked down at Teddy huddled in her shawl. "I'm still so amazed by it myself, I bless every day when I find you in bed with me! And when we form a *family*, when I recognize the child at the city hall and tell the world about it, when the news becomes public, Kate's pride won't permit her to be passive. Or even much sooner, as soon as she learns the baby's on the way, quietly, sensibly, she'll take action . . . for the sake of Nadine, for the sake of her own name, to stop people from talking. Yes, that's what *will* happen, I'm convinced of it."

"Do you know what you remind me of?" Teddy demanded ferociously. "Those stories I used to read in *National Geographic* about certain tribes where the men don't even consider a woman to be wife material until she gets pregnant and proves that she's not barren." Teddy's voice rose violently. "Julien, you're talking about *me*, Teddy Lunel, having an illegitimate baby! 'Recognizing a child'—at the city hall no less—that's barbaric! I'm a New Yorker, not some peasant girl. I make seventy dollars an hour! *I make three thousand dollars a week!* . . . Oh, Julien, you don't understand . . ." She faltered, stopped and burst into a passion of tears, clutching him like a child, feeling his arms enfold her and clasp her and mold her firmly, possessively to his body.

As she wept she realized that she wasn't Teddy Lunel who made seventy dollars an hour anymore—that Teddy Lunel who crossed Fifty-seventh Street and all but stopped traffic—she had turned into somebody else, a woman who loved a man, a woman who was pregnant with that man's baby, a woman who had become part of that man's history.

Her mind skittered about as she thought of how easy it would be to have an abortion. There were a dozen models in New York she could telephone for a certain well-known address in Sweden. It would be two hours by air from the Marseilles airport, a weekend in a spotless Stockholm clinic and back by next Tuesday or Wednesday. But even as she thought about it she knew that she wouldn't do it. Julien would understand if she did, his happiness with her didn't need a child to make it complete.

No, it was something else, an emotion she had felt only once before, a sense of inevitability that welled up within her. Already she felt changed, truly a woman now, no longer a girl. It was the same feeling she had had on that first night in the Hotel Europe . . . it was irrevocable, as irrevocable as her love for Mistral and therefore it must be as right.

Month by month Teddy traveled across the winter and spring of 1953, her destination growing closer and closer. The baby was due sometime in June, her obstetrician told her, and she lived, from the moment she had accepted the child, within a circle of enchanted harmony. She knew that Mistral was working hard on getting his divorce but she refused to worry herself with the details of the negotiations that she assumed were going on in an atmosphere of unpleasantness. Nothing disagreeable could touch her now. To ensure that Maggy didn't suddenly fly over and make a fuss she simply didn't write her about the baby in the monthly letters she mailed to New York. Time enough for that information when she could also announce her wedding day.

Now Julien insisted that they hire servants to live in several of the apartment's empty rooms and Teddy chose a young married couple, not because they were particularly well qualified for houseman and cook but because they were so visibly in love. Teddy was obedient, giving in to all Mistral's protectiveness, even letting him come to the doctor with her every month although she had never been in more robust health. She was one hell of a healthy animal, she congratulated her image, admiring herself as she never had when she sat before the mirrors in the dressing rooms of the world's best photographers. Her only complaint was that she couldn't keep from falling asleep over her *eau-de-vie* at night and Julien had to carry her tenderly to bed, lifting her, easily and tenderly, in spite of her bulk.

In the mornings they went for long walks and in the afternoons Teddy still posed. Mistral had never been captured by any subject as totally as he was by her budding body. His work had never been unreachable or enigmatic, drunk as he was on the mute rhapsody of form and color, but now, as he painted Teddy growing slowly big with child he began to interpret, to search, to think in paint, to penetrate the surface more deeply than he ever had. Maternity had not been a subject that had interested him before. When Kate had been pregnant he had been vaguely repelled by the way her womb seemed to stick out without reference to the rest of her spare frame, as if it were a growth rather than an organic part of her body. It had drained her face of energy and color and though she had endured it without complaint the child within her had been a stranger to him.

But Teddy flowered so rapturously: her breasts, once fashionably small, burgeoned in unabashed lushness; the blue veins showed clearly through the translucent whiteness of her skin; her nipples spread and grew pinker and softer; her arms and legs were less angular, more delicately rounded. Her body was a miracle of beauty, and in its swelling volume he felt the power of nature as he had never felt it in any landscape. No storm, no sky or star-filled night, no ripe orchards or grape-heavy vineyards had ever moved him so. It was an inexhaustible subject, a painter could paint nothing else but the mysterious volume of that glorious curve of her belly that was never the same from one day to another. Often he finished a painting in a single week and soon the studio was filled with the sight of canvases propped against the wall, more canvases in any one time than he had painted since he had first painted Maggy.

In the middle of June, Teddy went into labor. Mistral drove her to the nearby maternity hospital and, as was the age-old tradition in Provence, he was permitted to stay with Teddy while she gave birth. Teddy clung tightly to his hand but her labor was only six hours long and she bore it easily and bravely. When the baby emerged, the doctor had to give it several sharp smacks before it began to cry and when it finally did, it howled with outrage. A nurse wrapped it quickly in one of the pink blankets that were kept especially for the newborn and presented it to Mistral.

"A girl, Monsieur," she said as proudly as if she had had the baby herself. Mistral, stunned, overcome, stared at the amazing bundle. A purple face from which energetic yells of anger continued to emerge, bright orange hair, all wrapped in vivid pink wool. He studied his daughter intently and then he roared with delight.

"A *fauve,* by God. My darling, you've had a little wild beast. That's what we'll call her, eh? Fauve? Do you like that name?"

Teddy nodded her assent but the nurse protested. "Monsieur Mistral, that's not a saint's name . . . aren't you going to follow the custom?"

"A saint's name? The devil I will! Fauve's a painter's daughter!"

20

*M*aman," wailed Nadine, "Arlette said I had a new little sister. I told her she was a liar. I'll never play with her again, she's wicked and I hate her."

"Why did she say that? Come, Nadine, remember."

"She said that her mother heard about it from her sister who works in a hospital in Avignon."

"When did she tell you this?"

"Today in Félice when I went with Monsieur Pollison to pick up a package at the post office. Arlette told everybody."

"She lied, Nadine. You don't have a new sister, you'll never have a new sister. But your father has a bastard child. You tell Arlette that the next time she says something."

Nadine's eyes grew wide and she pulled her curls with both hands. She knew what the word meant, any seven-year-old of the neighborhood knew what it meant, for illegitimate birth was far from unknown in Félice and the children of the village were brought up listening to adult talk from the time they were old enough to be held on a lap at mealtime.

"I don't understand, *Maman*."

"Remember how long your father's been away? While he's been gone he's been with a bad woman and now that woman has had a child. That child is a bastard."

"When will Papa come back?"

"You know perfectly well that I'm not sure, but if you're patient, he'll come home sooner or later."

"Will he bring the bad woman with him?"

"Now you're just being silly, Nadine."

"Will he bring the bastard?" Nadine asked jealously, daring to use the word because her mother had. The household had cossetted her so much since Mistral had disappeared that she had almost stopped thinking about her father. He had always seen through her fabrications—she found him terrifying. While he was away no one corrected her table manners or told her to stop chattering at the table. But many of her friends in school had baby brothers and sisters and she knew that once a baby was born the older children were expected to make way for the youngest in their parents' affections.

"Of course not! Nadine, don't say stupid things!" Kate jumped up and left her daughter beginning to whimper without attempting to comfort her. She rushed to her room, locked the door, sat in her favorite chair and stared sightlessly in front of her. She had expected this news daily but she had never imagined that she'd learn it from her own child. How many other rumors had Nadine heard that she'd never spoken of?

Obviously the grapevine that fed news to the inhabitants of Félice, most of whom were related in one way or another to people in every hamlet and city for fifty miles around, functioned more effectively than her own lawyer in Avignon. She had heard from Mistral about the Lunel woman's pregnancy six months ago. She had even gone through the formality of meeting with his lawyer and laying out her position for once and for all. Her husband was the victim of an aberration, an illusion, a temporary madness that a million men of his age experienced, she told the man. Her own position was immovable.

But Mistral had never accepted this. He had continued to send her urgent, deluded, insane letters, attempting to convince her that she had nothing to lose by giving him a divorce since he would never again be a husband to her.

Nothing to lose? Her contempt for him was so absolute that she could have laughed. She, Madame Julien Mistral, who had received the deepest respect throughout the world of international art, whose power was legendary because she controlled Mistral; she to whom museum curators came begging; she who could make the name of any gallery by lending pictures for a Mistral exhibition; she who alone could refuse or grant permission to reproduce one of Mistral's paintings; she who had to be won over before any scholar or reporter could get near Mistral; she who was in complete charge of his complicated business affairs—*she* had nothing to lose?

What if she had never brought Avigdor to see his work? With Mistral's hatred of dealers he might never have had his first show. How many other painters had been buried long before their work was appreciated? Far too many to count. It was she who had given him that first indispensable chance and it was her money that paid for *La Tourrello* and later her clever watchfulness that had made it possible for him to work for the last quarter of a century in a total freedom from worry that no other artist could even dream of. Oh, no, she didn't intend to abdicate, to throw away all that, to let some little whore of a model move into her position. *He owed her his life.*

Kate made an inarticulate, grinding sound of rage and began to walk from one window to another. How could a man think that one drop of his sperm deposited in the body of that Lunel bitch could influence her to give up all she'd worked for? How little he had ever really known her. There was nothing that could make her more determined to hold on to her rights than the birth of that bastard child. Julien's letters had offered her everything; *La Tourrello*, which she had once given him as her dowry; all the paintings, the money in their bank accounts; as if it were only a question of finding the right price to pay her to give up her identity. She was Madame Julien Mistral. Nothing could ever be allowed to change that.

Kate smoothed her hair and unlocked the door. She had handled Nadine badly. It would only make things worse if the child repeated her words. The scandal had undoubtedly already given the people of the village the finest entertainment that they'd had for years. They lived to discuss their neighbors and none with more malicious interest than the ones who didn't really belong to the village.

Kate found Nadine, sitting dismally in a corner of the kitchen while Marte Pollison directed the cook and her helper in preparation for the big meal that the men who worked in the fields would expect to find waiting for them at the end of the day.

She led the child back to her room and took her on her knees.

"Nadine, darling, what I just said to you was wrong. Don't pay any attention. Mother was just being foolish . . . sometimes mothers are foolish, you know, just like other people. I don't want you to say a single word to Arlette if she asks you anything about your father or me—everything will be all right soon, Papa will be back with us, but it isn't a good idea to talk to people about it. They get it all mixed up and it isn't any of their business. It doesn't concern them. I don't want you to go into Félice for a while . . ."

"But, *Maman*, school isn't over till July."

"I know, baby, but I'll speak to your teacher and she'll understand. You're doing so well at your lessons that it won't matter. We'll just have a good time by ourselves, we'll go on little trips in Mommy's big car and you'll eat in restaurants with me and see new things and every day I'll buy a special surprise for you, something extra pretty. Won't that be fun?"

Nadine looked unconvinced. If only I could take her away to Paris or New York, Kate thought. If only I could get away from this damn valley where everybody knows everything. But I can't leave, not for more than a few hours at a time. If Julien heard that we'd gone away—and he would know the same day—he'd think I'd given up. No, I must act as if nothing has happened, as if I've heard nothing, as if there is nothing to hear. I must not react, I must go on as always. He must not provoke me into the slightest action. One day it will be over, an ancient, confused, unimportant story. But now no one, *no one* may be allowed to pity me.

"What are you thinking, *Maman?*" Nadine asked.

"I'm deciding what to wear tonight. There's a big party at the Gimpels—what do you think, darling, shall I wear my white suit, or that dress you like so much, the blue?"

Teddy and Mistral sat drinking *pastis* before dinner on the terrace of the Sennequier in St. Tropez. A year earlier *Vogue* had discovered the "happy life, the undemanding ease, the lotus calm" of this little fishing village, but it was still unspoiled. As soon as Fauve was two weeks old they had packed her up, with her nurse, driven down to the coast and taken a suite of rooms at the Hotel l'Aioli for the summer.

"I'm restless, Julien," Teddy said moodily.

"I know, my darling, I can feel it jumping out at me. Did I play boules too long this afternoon? I'm sorry—it's just that these old men here are fantastically good. I wonder why it never occurred to me to come here before? It's been a perfect vacation."

"And why not?" Teddy said in a sudden burst of irritation. "Even if Fauve doesn't hold still for long, she and I are the best models you could ask for. The artist's mistress and his illegitimate daughter—a classic subject, isn't it? You must have enough paintings of us now for at least three of your series."

"Teddy!"

"I know, I know, it's not your fault, I'm not accusing you of anything, for God's sake, but how long is this supposed to drag on? I loathe this situation, Julien!"

"Darling, be reasonable. Fauve's only two months old. You don't seriously imagine that Kate can hold out for years and years, do you? One day soon she'll understand how dog-in-the-manger she looks, how hopeless it is—we only have to endure."

"You make it sound like Napoleon's retreat from Moscow. What do I see ahead of me, Julien? Listen to me! Last year I was in a state of hormonally induced passivity—I was hibernating, holed up in the apartment like that, eating and sleeping and dreaming whole months away like some sort of mama bear. That's nature's little trick, but now I'm right back to normal again and I just can't stand not having any idea of what to expect."

"You've had another letter from your mother." He groaned.

"Damn right. And I'm beginning to wonder if she might have been on the button after all. What if history *is* repeating itself? She never managed to get herself married and most people would agree that she's one hell of a lot smarter than I am."

Mistral took both of her hands in his and pressed his lips into her palms. "Don't say things like that, my love, it's only making it worse than . . ."

"Teddy! Teddy Lunel! I absolutely do *not* believe it!" a girl's voice squealed. Startled, Teddy pulled her hands away and looked up. There on the sidewalk in front of the café stood two men and two women. Peggy Arnold, who had recognized her, had been a star model with the Lunel Agency for the past two years. Teddy jumped up and enfolded her in a big hug. She was amazed at how happy she was to see a familiar face. Suddenly Peggy Arnold seemed like her best friend.

"So this is where you've been hiding out! Everyone's been wondering for so long that they've almost given you up for lost. Your mother said you'd fallen in love with France, but good Lord! Teddy, this is Ginny Maxwell—she's with Lunel too—and Bill Clark and Chase Talbot—we're all here for the weekend."

Mistral rose and approached them. "This is Julien Mistral,"

Teddy said, possession plain in her voice. The sun-dappled shade of the Sennequier suddenly seemed to turn into the stage of a theater as she watched Julien shake hands with the four tanned, white-clad, startled Americans who had grown suddenly shy, stiff—definitely in awe of him. It reminded her of that day, so many months before, when she had first met Mistral and, looking at him now, she was moved again by his heroic head, his splendid height and the contained force of his eyes. She was proud and glad that someone from her old life had seen them together at last, and, by God, she wanted to show him off.

"Oh, Peggy, I have a billion questions to ask you!" Teddy cried. "Listen, can the four of you have dinner with Julien and me tonight?"

"We can't, honey, we've promised to go to a party, but listen, Chase has his sailboat or yacht or whatever you call it when it's seventy feet long, anchored right here in the harbor—why don't you both come on out and sail with us tomorrow and have lunch on board?"

"We'd absolutely adore it, wouldn't we, Julien?"

"We would enjoy nothing more," Mistral said to Peggy Arnold. He welcomed any distraction at this moment. He was convinced that Kate would give in eventually but he had begun to realize that it would take longer than he'd expected and he didn't dare to share his suspicions with Teddy. It was growing harder to reassure her with every passing day.

The next day Teddy and Mistral boarded *The Baron*, Chase Talbot's chartered yacht, at ten in the morning. A crew of four, including a cook, had been hired to sail the yacht on a leisurely cruise from one port to another, along the French and Italian coastlines.

As *The Baron* moved smoothly out of the St. Tropez harbor into the Mediterranean, all six passengers lounged on cushions in the sun, close to the bow of the ship. Teddy allowed her hand to fall casually on Mistral's arm as she chatted with Ginny and Peggy, dropping back with relish into news of the world she had abandoned without a backward glance.

She had been lonely for women friends of her own kind, she realized, as they talked. She and Julien had lived in such a purposeful solitude that it felt good, just for a little while, to get back into an atmosphere where the difference between Ben Zuckerman and

Norman Norell was, if not critical, at least acknowledged, a world full of assumptions and references that had once been so important to her, that was still important to them.

As they talked eagerly, catching up on the news of New York, with one finger she caressed the firm muscles on Julien's forearm. Just that light touch made her understand that nothing her old life had ever offered was more than a shallow facsimile of existence. She abandoned the conversation and half closed her eyes. Reality was Julien Mistral, the man who had made her life whole, the man who had turned her from a girl who feared she could never love, to a woman who knew that she could love forever. Reality was Fauve, the daughter she was bound to by a feeling that was so different in texture and power from anything she had ever thought of as love. When she took her baby, naked except for a diaper, in her arms and tucked Fauve into her neck and felt that silky, plump, soft and incredibly strong little body relax in complete trust against her, Teddy knew an emotion for which she had no words.

Reality was Julien and Fauve. Reality was the end of this vacation and the trip back to Avignon. Reality was settling in for the fall and winter in that champagne-colored city, hunting through antique shops for more furniture for the big apartment, taking Fauve for promenades in the park, getting in a huge supply of firewood, going to market—oh, reality was so full of lovely things to do and eat and drink and smell and touch! And if reality should include another child, Teddy grinned to herself, Kate would have to admit defeat. Why hadn't she thought of that sooner? It was a brilliant idea!

"Let's throw over the lunch hook," Bill suggested.

"What's that?" Teddy asked, roused from her reverie.

"It's a light anchor, a Danforth. We use it whenever we just want to stop for an hour or so and swim or eat. The other one—the Plough—is simply too much trouble to bother with unless we're staying for the night—it's a big heavy bastard and I keep it lashed under the bow as much as I can. I'm your average lazy sailor."

"Oh." Yachtsmen always told you more than you needed to know, Teddy remembered from her summers in the Hamptons.

"Do we want to swim or drink or both?" Chase Talbot inquired of the group.

"How's the water?" asked Ginny.

"Great. If you want your swim, now's the best time."

The yacht lay several miles off the coast, in quiet water. The sun was hot on the deck and everyone voted to swim first and drink later. For half an hour the six of them took turns diving from the pulpit, a U-shaped chrome structure above the bow from which two lifelines were rigged. The deck of *The Baron* was far enough above the Mediterranean so that the pulpit, which rose three and a half additional feet above the bow, made a good diving platform.

Teddy hadn't had a chance to dive into deep water for two years but after a few attempts all her muscle memory returned as she clambered up, using the lifelines, and curled her toes expertly around the top railing of the pulpit until it was time to let go of the jib stay and plunge into the ocean.

"Gin and tonic for all hands," Peggy called to her as Teddy took her place at the bow. She looked behind her. All four of her American friends had collapsed, laughing, on the cushions on deck, gathered around a tray of glasses brought by one of the crew. She looked out to the ocean. Some twenty-five feet away Julien waved to her from the water.

"Just one more quick one," she called. She'd swim out to Julien and put her arms on his shoulders and float there with him and kiss him and kiss him, and whisper her marvelous new idea to him.

A big fishing boat, unnoticed in all their noisy rollicking, had passed behind the stern of *The Baron* moments before. Just as Teddy let go of the jib stay, gracefully poised to dive, the heavy wake of the fishing boat smacked into the yacht. The whole boat rolled sharply. Teddy lost her balance, teetered in the air for a split second and somersaulted awkwardly. There were two sharp steel flukes, nine inches long, that protruded from the big Plough anchor lashed directly under the bow. As Teddy fell, her head smashed sideways into one of the wickedly pointed flukes. Mistral launched himself underwater as soon as he saw that she'd been hit. He found her almost immediately, caught her easily under one arm and brought her to the surface with a powerful stroke of his free arm. Chase and Bill helped him bring Teddy up to the deck. She had not drowned. There had not been time for that. Teddy had been dead before she entered the water.

Three days later, in the American Cemetery in Nice, Teddy was buried. Maggy and Julien Mistral had been the only mourners. Mistral had forbidden the four Americans from the yacht to come and they had been too much in dread of his monstrous anguish to insist.

Maggy had not yet, and would not now bring herself to look directly at Mistral. She felt such a surpassing hatred of him that it was almost impossible to utter even a few necessary words. She knew she had to stay calm enough to convince him that he must give her granddaughter to her. He had already killed her daughter.

"I want to take Fauve with me," she said at last.

"Of course," he muttered.

"Did you understand what I mean?" He couldn't have realized. He must not have listened.

"Naturally, you must take her. There is no one else. I have no home for her, I will never go back to Avignon, I never want to see *La Tourrello* again—I'm going away, I don't know where, I don't know for how long . . ."

"If I take her now, if you agree, you won't be able to change your mind," she said fiercely.

Mistral got up with a groping movement, hesitant, almost sightless, his monumental body shambling, his hands shaking and fumbling. His cheeks were covered in gray stubble, for he had not shaved or slept or eaten in the three days since the accident. His eyes weren't red for he had not been able to weep but the blue fire that they had always held was utterly gone. He was an old man with dead eyes.

"Go back to your home, Maggy. I can't talk anymore. Leave." He made his unsure way out of the hotel lobby and, a minute later, Maggy heard him drive off in his car.

She sat immobile for a moment, not daring to move lest she hear the car return. Then, galvanized, she went to the front desk and made a reservation on the next plane to Paris, ordered a taxi, and went to her room to pack.

"Madame?" It was the nurse, tiptoeing into the room.

"Pack one suitcase with the baby's things. Do you have a formula for her?"

"She drinks ordinary milk, Madame, for the last two weeks. But don't forget to warm the bottle."

"Thank you, Mademoiselle. I do remember that much."

A day later, trailed by a junior concierge from the Ritz who had been delegated to accompany her to the departure gate, Maggy

294

crossed Orly Airport in Paris on her way to board the plane for New York. Fauve was in her arms. As she passed a newsstand she stopped suddenly, clutching Fauve to her so tightly that the baby started to cry. A pile of copies of the new issue of *Paris Match* had just been deposited on the counter. The cover photo, in black and white, had been taken on board *The Baron*. There looking into each other's eyes, stood Teddy and Julien Mistral. They were laughing in the most careless happiness, utterly absorbed in each other. A lock of Teddy's wet hair lay on his muscular shoulder and he held her possessively close to his bare chest with both his arms.

How many minutes, at that moment, Maggy asked herself did Teddy have left to live? She felt as if a crucial membrane inside of her chest had been ripped away.

"What is it, Madame?" the junior concierge asked in alarm as he saw her face.

"Please get me a copy of *Match*," Maggy said tightly. She would have to face the story. She couldn't pretend it didn't exist, not when everybody in the world would read one version of it or another.

Maggy sat in the first-class waiting room, cradling Fauve in one arm, and fumbled with the magazine, her hands shaking so badly that the slick pages were almost impossible to turn. The cover head-line had announced "La Mort de la Compagne de Mistral"—at least they had called Teddy his companion, not his mistress, Maggy thought numbly.

Apparently there was no other major story in the world that week, or at least none that so appealed to the shrewd editors of the great French magazine, for they had devoted twelve pages of pic-tures and text to it.

Beyond surprise, or so she thought, but not beyond despair, Maggy turned the pages. There were three electrifying photographs that Bill Hatfield had taken of Teddy and Mistral in the studio, not the pictures *Mode* had published, but pictures of them talking to each other, ignoring the camera, already entranced, already lost. There were pages of photographs taken at *La Tourrello* of Mistral, Kate and Nadine, the artist and his devoted family, only two years earlier. Among the great pictures of Teddy that had been taken while she was modeling was a dignified portrait of Maggy, sur-rounded by her most famous models, which had been taken for *Life* three years earlier, and yes, there, just as she had assumed it would be, was a reproduction of that most notorious of the *Rouquinne* series, Maggy herself, on those damn cushions spread in full color across two pages. She didn't have to read the caption to know what it would say. *Match* rarely missed a trick.

She scanned the main body of the text, holding her breath in fearful apprehension. Until now there had been no news leaks anywhere about Fauve's existence. Maggy herself had only learned of Fauve's birth three weeks after it had happened . . . Teddy had waited until they had all arrived in St. Tropez to write to her. She had been too shocked, too outraged to bring herself to answer that letter. Now there was no need to, she realized in a grief so profound that it gave her the strength of utter loss that allowed her to search the *Match* story.

There, in the second paragraph, was the account of the investigation of the register of births at the town hall in Avignon. Fauve Lunel, *enfante adulterine*, was the civil status of her granddaughter. The baby was a child of adultery who, under French law, must remain forever unacknowledged, so different from the status of an *enfante naturelle*, a merely illegitimate child whose parents were free to marry each other if they wished, whose father could give her his name even without marrying her mother.

Teddy had long ago acquired American citizenship, at the time that Maggy herself had become a citizen, but Maggy knew that if the reporters had managed to search the right register in Paris they would have found still another fact: the record of the birth of Théodora Lunel: *enfante adulterine*. But the celebrated *Match* thoroughness had not operated at its full efficiency. This much at least they hadn't discovered.

Maggy let the magazine close without finishing the story. After all, what difference did it make? Why should anything so minor matter, now that Teddy no longer existed on this earth? Teddy was gone, her lovely, dreamy, heedless, sweet girl and nothing she had ever feared might happen to her had been even a shadow of the reality.

The baby in Maggy's arms woke up. Her eyes, a delicate, clear, smoke gray, were endless in their depth. She looked straight at Maggy with shocking clarity for such a young being. She blinked twice under her carrot fluff and when nothing happened she made a small but distinctly hungry noise. As Maggy searched her shoulder bag for the bottle that must be warmed, she remembered a saying that every French child repeats after two unplanned events of hazard of any kind: two bottles of spilled ink, two tumbles in the schoolyard, two splinters in the same finger. "*Jamais deux sans trois.*" Never two without a third. Magali Lunel. Théodora Lunel. And now—Fauve Lunel.

The baby howled so loudly that every passenger in the lounge turned to look at Maggy. She glared back at them. Had they nothing better to do? Did they expect her to give her granddaughter cold milk? "Listen to me, you little bastard," she whispered to Fauve, "shut up, it's coming, it's coming." The infant stopped screaming immediately. "So, you'd rather listen than eat? That, at least, is a sign of intelligence. Perhaps you'll be the lucky third." As she signaled the lounge attendant to heat the bottle, she held the baby close and, as softly as she could, sang her a lullaby with half the words missing. Where had it come from, this song? It was in French and she had no idea how she knew it. She didn't remember ever singing it to Teddy. It must come from her own grandmother, Maggy thought. Her gentle grandmother, Cecile Lunel.

21

H ow," Maggy asked Darcy, "do you expect a child who still hasn't learned how to walk, to play with a panda that is twice as big as she is?"

"It was irresistible—I was passing F.A.O. Schwarz and it was there in the window . . ."

"That trap—why, they probably sell a half-dozen every Saturday."

"No, this is the prototype, there isn't a bigger one in the whole store," he said proudly. "I checked it out."

"Well, I put it in her playpen and I haven't heard a sound from her room since, so obviously she liked it. That makes almost a half-hour of peace today. Let's enjoy it while it lasts."

A year had passed since Maggy had returned from France with Fauve. She and Darcy were sitting in the great drawing room of her resplendent new apartment on Fifth Avenue, a room purposefully decorated to give the impression that it must surely open out onto a vast private park belonging to a noble Georgian manor house in deepest Devon. However, it occupied a space even more expensive than rolling English acres, a full half-floor of one of the most indisputably impeccable buildings in all Manhattan, an East Side apartment house that had a pedigree that virtually guaranteed the background of everyone who was permitted to dwell in it.

Maggy had determined that in order to properly bring up a baby whose adulterous as well as illegitimate origins had been so thoroughly documented by the press of the world, she must do it in the highest of styles, in the most open and grand of manners. Every impulse that had made her tuck Teddy away on the comparatively unfashionable West Side, which had caused her to send her daughter to the little-known Elm School, was to be reversed in the case of Fauve. She would *establish* her granddaughter from the beginning. Everyone knew everything there was to know about her. Good! Since Mistral was her father, let that become an asset. Daughter of one of the world's greatest artists, granddaughter and only heiress of Maggy Lunel of the Lunel Agency—Fauve would become a *personage* even in the cradle!

She could have saved herself the trouble, she often reflected. Unless she was more of a doting grandmother than she believed, Fauve was a child who could have brought herself up. When she waved her arms and laughed her surprisingly deep gurgle, things happened, people came running, even strangers did her bidding. She didn't like to be cuddled for long, her firm body would squirm out of Maggy's arms as she continued her never-ending exploration of her universe; she liked nothing so much as a new face bending over her or a foreign object, any foreign object. Had she been in the vicinity of a thick snake or a large and dangerous dog she would have launched herself straight at it, shrieking with pleasure.

She was utterly without any sense of fear and she detested boundaries. At fourteen months Fauve was often furious because she fell down whenever she tried to walk and impeded locomotion was the worst boundary of all. In her playpen she rattled the bars like an angry little gorilla, shouting every word she knew, for she had an extensive vocabulary. When she was put down on the floor she would crawl about with amazing speed and a striking lack of judgment, bringing tables, lamps, vases and ashtrays crashing down about her and laughing heartily at the lovely noises she'd made. Even when she was hit by a falling object she only cried for a second. Life was too interesting for tears, unless they were tears of rage, and even those only lasted until she found some new and fascinating thing to look at.

Fauve had a nurse. Fauve had had a number of nurses, who, one by one, had left, unable to keep up with her energy. They loved the baby, they explained to Maggy, in fact they adored her, but they were just so *tired*. Maggy sympathized and hired another nurse.

Again she was trying not to make one of the many mistakes she

299

was convinced that she must have made with Teddy. She spent a great deal of time with Fauve, reorganizing the Lunel Agency in order to do so. She had hired three highly efficient people to do much of the work she had once been certain that she must oversee in person and the agency was prospering and growing as never before.

Saturday, today, was one of the nurse's regular days off and Maggy and Darcy had formed the habit of taking Fauve for a walk in the park in her stroller. Since "21" frowned on babies, even one connected to Darcy, their valued customer since Prohibition, they headed to the Russian Tea Room on Fifty-seventh Street. There they could have a drink in one of the little red leather booths opposite the long bar while Fauve gulped freshly squeezed orange juice. Every waiter in his red cossack tunic, every motherly old Russian waitress, competed to bring the glass of juice to that resplendent child who could call a half-dozen of them by name: "Katya!," "Rosa!," "Gregor!," she would cry imperiously. She demanded no one as often as Sidney Kaye, the owner of the Tea Room, who told her funny stories with Yiddish punch lines to which she listened intently, gazing up at him from her stroller, with her gray eyes opened wide in wonder and her red eyebrows lifted, chortling when he came to the end of the tale as if, in some mysterious way, she had understood him.

"Do I look like a grandmother?" Maggy asked Darcy suddenly, as they sat enjoying the rare quiet of the moment.

Maggy was forty-six now, and during some otherwise noticed week or month between the years of forty and forty-one, she had lost the look of being younger than she really was, that she had kept throughout her thirties. One day, she woke up and discovered a woman in her mirror who had arrived at that age from which it is never possible to retreat, that "certaine âge" as every Frenchman gallantly but depressingly puts it.

She was an astonishingly well-preserved woman, Maggy told herself. But once anything is described as "well-preserved" its original essence has obviously been lost. It was the difference, she thought, between a ball gown on the night that it is first worn by a waltzing Victorian maiden, and that same gown, in mint condition, displayed in a case in a costume museum.

In the following six years the changes had been gradual but unmistakable for anyone with Maggy's judgmental, unforgiving eye. She could never be one of those women who only looks at her best features when she confronts the mirror, avoiding, unconsciously and so cleverly, the areas that show age. Maggy knew exactly how often she had to have her red hair touched up so that a sprinkling of gray didn't show at her hairline. She looked at her mouth, that still lush and forward-thrusting flower, and saw clearly that there were a few faint vertical lines above her upper lip. Her jaw line had relaxed and blurred ever so slightly. Oh, she was middle-aged and no good night's sleep, no vacation, no plastic surgeon could ever give her back again that unconditional freshness, that film of newness that announces youth. It was, she decided, as inevitable, and as little worth railing against, as the sunrise, or the fact that every apricot that isn't eaten will one day lose its bloom.

She didn't see the other changes that had taken place in her in the year since Teddy's death. Maggy's beauty was still bone deep, her surface was brilliantly maintained yet she had, from time to time, acquired an air of vulnerability. She never knew that the grief she lived with could be seen in an expression of bitter regret that veiled her eyes when, fleetingly abstracted, she seemed to be peering into a far and fearsome distance.

Her business manner, which had never been easygoing, was more terse, more quick to impatience than it had ever been. Her new assistants knew that while The Boss would not be unfair or unreasonable they had better have a sound and defensible reason for every decision they made. Most of the Lunel models were frankly petrified by her. Maggy knew this and sometimes it annoyed her, sometimes it amused her and, more often than not, she considered it a healthy state for them to be in. Better that than slackness.

"Do I look like a grandmother?" she repeated.

"You can never look like a grandmother," Darcy replied. He cared nothing about any of the changes in her—he didn't see them. Maggy's golden-green eyes that had first captured him had never let him go. She was still the magnificent woman whom he'd never been able to make completely his own from the very first night he'd seen her at Lally Longbridge's scavenger hunt. In a way that he had gradually grown to value, rather than to fight against, she had retained an inner enigmatic core. There were things about Maggy that were unaccountable: riddles, puzzlements, areas of her life about which she had never confided in him, no matter how close they became, and every year they grew closer. Finally Darcy was content not to even try to guess at them. Although she would never be his wife, she was his lover and his best friend and that had come to be enough.

He knew that their long affair irked many people. If Maggy and Darcy are going to be together—and so damned faithful, so devoted—they grumbled to each other, why don't they just get married like everybody else? Because we're not like everybody else, Darcy would have told them if they had dared to ask him directly. He wasn't sure what he meant by that but he knew that he possessed as much of Maggy as any man could ever have had. Unless he'd known her *before* Julien Mistral. She had left something essential in that long past relationship, something that remained only on canvas—or perhaps in her memory—although he tried never to contemplate that possibility—and almost succeeded.

Maggy shot him a quick glance. No, he meant what he said. He had answered her question with that hard gray flash, that bladelike look that had first attracted her notice. His thin face was even more distinguished than it had been so long ago, his hair was beginning to go distinctly gray, but his questioning philosopher's look had only sharpened, not grown more mellow with maturity and the unmistakable authority of his expression had settled more firmly on his lips. She put out her hand to him, lovingly. How *right* she had been never to marry this man.

A cascade of books slid to the floor behind them with a loud, long series of thumps. They jumped and looked around. Fauve came tottering toward them on her little fat feet, as unsteadily as if she were dancing on bubbles, her arms open wide for balance, a look of ecstatic achievement on her face. "Panda," the new pedestrian yelled in self-congratulation, heading for Darcy, who had provided the means for her jailbreak. "Climb panda!"

Venice, London, Alexandria, Oslo, Budapest—cities were no damn good. The country was no better: the Swiss Alps, Tuscany, Guatemala. Nor were islands possible: Ischia, the Cyclades of Greece, Fiji—all of them were empty of whatever it was he sought and finally Julien Mistral understood that he might as well go home.

He had painted nothing in the last three years but he had drunk an enormous amount of whatever was the strongest alcohol available in each place he had settled in for a week or a month or a day. Sometimes he had checked into a hotel and left an hour later, without any reason. Sometimes, he'd stayed on in a city long past the time when it had any novelty for him, out of an immobility that was as deep as his restlessness. Now he was too tired to go anywhere but *back*. Félice was a better place than any he had found.

The gates of *La Tourrello* were closed as Mistral drove up. He pulled to one side of the meadow and parked without honking or ringing the bell that sounded in the kitchen. It was lunchtime: all the household would be gathered inside and he wanted to avoid the inevitable moment of greeting. He took the path, now almost overgrown, that led beside the tall, protecting walls of the *mas*, around to the side until it reached as far as the small back door of his studio. One key existed for that door and it was still in his pocket. It was the only thing he had taken with him, besides the clothes on his back and the car he drove in, when he had gone to meet Teddy Lunel for dinner at Hiely in Avignon on a September night four years before.

He opened the door and went inside. The studio was dark except for a few stray rays of sun that came through the cracks in the shutters. Mistral pulled on the ropes that controlled the heavy canvas that covered the glass and in a minute the studio was drenched in the full light of high noon. Nothing had been touched since he left. The empty canvas with which he had posed with Teddy still stood on the easel. On a cluttered table lay the palette he had held, crusted with dry paint.

Slowly Mistral looked around the walls. There were those paintings, so thickly hung that some of them all but obscured a corner of others, that had so silenced the visitors from *Mode*. He looked long from one painting to another, not moving an inch toward any of them. For as far back as he could remember having had rational thoughts about the act of painting he had considered that he was trying to put on canvas what he *saw* in the most direct way he could, without letting an intellectual process come between his eye and the canvas. Now, in a growing swell of realization, he understood he had painted what he had *felt* at the time that he was seeing. The paintings were a visual equivalent of his emotions. Not the activity of the brain but the tides of the heart had been recorded here.

This comprehension gave him the first comfort he had permitted himself since he had knelt on the deck of The Baron and realized that the body that he held so tightly in his arms was dead, that Teddy had abandoned him. The paintings were proof that Julien Mistral had lived, that he once cared, once felt. He swayed, overcome by fatigue and the shock of allowing a feeling to touch him. Mistral had fled feeling with such absolute concentration for the last three years that any emotion, even a kind one, made him dizzy with the fear that it might be followed by pain so annihilating that he would kill himself to escape it.

There was an old mahogany and leather chair in the corner of the studio. Made long ago for a tobacco planter in Martinique, it unfolded ingeniously so that a man could recline at full length in it. Mistral sat down in it and gave a great sigh of relief. Within minutes he was asleep.

Hours later Kate went to the pool for her afternoon swim and noticed that the sun was shining directly through the glass of the studio roof. Otherwise the studio was as completely shuttered and closed as it had been for four years. Either the canvas had fallen or a vandal or a thief had broken in through the door on the side of the house. Moving soundlessly she walked alongside the length of the pool and approached the studio. One of the thick wooden shutters sagged slightly at its hinge and she had a hairline view into the studio. She saw only a part of a man's hand, motionless, dangling. Immediately Kate turned, went quietly back to the house and entered the kitchen

"Marte, tell the cook to go out and kill another chicken for dinner," she commanded. "Send the gardener for more lettuce and tomatoes and grapes. You go yourself and open Monsieur's room, put fresh sheets on the bed. Make sure there's no dust, plenty of towels in the bathroom, a new cake of soap on the sink and tub . . . why are you standing there?"

"You didn't tell me you were expecting a guest, Madame," Marte Pollison answered with dignity. She disliked hurried, last-minute preparations.

"Monsieur has returned."

"Oh, Madame!"

"There is no reason for surprise," Kate said. She turned quickly so that Marte wouldn't see her small, calm, triumphant smile. "I've been expecting him."

On a late spring afternoon, four years later, in 1961, Maggy was dressing for dinner when Fauve burst into her room without knocking. She turned from her mirror but her intended remonstrances faded on her lips as she watched her splendiferous granddaughter skip across the pale carpet.

Fauve was almost eight, dressed, as always after a trip to the park, in tatters, her knees skinned, her shoes covered with dust, her ripped shirt pulled out of her cotton skirt, on which one of the pockets hung by a thread. At least she didn't have a black eye today, Maggy thought, or a bloody nose. Fauve, as all the boys in her class complained, "didn't fight like a girl." There wasn't one of them she hadn't punched out at one time or another, but still they wouldn't leave her alone. Irresistibly attracted to her, they manifested their fascination with eight-year-old pestering and sneaky tricks. If she'd had pigtails they would have found inkwells in which to dip them.

She had a disquieting, imprudent beauty, that sprang partly from an elation that soared so high that adults feared the tears that such a mood would have produced in an ordinary child. However, Fauve only wept, as she explained to Maggy one day, if there was a happy ending to a book she was reading or a movie she'd seen, but she didn't know why she cried and so she tried to hide those tears.

Her coloring bedazzled, the carrot fluff she had been born with had deepened into a red that had no name because it was so many reds, and it sprang out from her head in a thick tumble that mesmerized the eye with its electric energy, its meshed colors that in some lights made patterns that were more pink than bronze, in others more copper than gold. The light gray irises of her eyes were rimmed in a circle of the darkest gray. When she was serious, her glance was grave and level, and if Maggy searched her eyes she felt as if she were looking into heavy mist that parted only to reveal another curtain of mist behind which there was yet more mist. But today Fauve's eyes were so hectically bright that Maggy thought she seemed on the verge of something like hysteria.

"What have you been up to?" she asked anxiously. Unruly, more active than ten children, inquisitive, rebellious and strong-

willed as Fauve was—all normal characteristics Maggy often reminded herself to be expected from a gifted child—there was never
any way to predict what she would do next.

Fauve held one hand teasingly behind her back.

"I have a surprise, the most marvelous surprise, the best surprise in the world, Magali, Magali!" Fauve's voice cracked with the
effort of not telling it right away. Maggy had refused to be called any
variation on grandmother, yet Maggy seemed too informal, so
Fauve called her by the real first name that no one had used since
her own grandmother died. Maggy reached for her hidden hand but
Fauve stepped back.

"No animals?" Maggy asked. It was an old battle.

"I promised, didn't I?"

"Vegetables or minerals?"

"Not that either," she sang out, bursting with information.

"Then I give up."

"My *father!*" Fauve exploded and whipped out a sheet of sketch
paper and thrust it into Maggy's hand. On it was an unmistakable
sketch of Fauve sitting on a park bench, her chin leaning on her
hand.

As Maggy stared at it in mute shock, Fauve's words spilled out
so fast that she could scarcely follow them. "We were all playing in
the park and an old man with a beard came up and introduced
himself to Mrs. Bailey and Mrs. Summer—they got all surprised and
excited—and then he came over to me and said I must be Fauve
Lunel and I said yes and he asked . . . he asked did I *know* who my
father was? I said that I was Mistral's daughter of course, everybody
knows that, and then, Magali, he said he was my father, he was
Julien Mistral! For a second I didn't believe him because in the
picture I have he's so much younger and doesn't have a beard, but
then I *knew*, I felt it and I gave him a big hug, Magali, just the *biggest*
hug, as hard as I can hug, and he said I looked exactly the way he
thought I would look and he held my hands and kissed them and he
didn't seem to know what else to say . . . that's when Mrs. Bailey
and Mrs. Summer came over to talk to him, but he didn't want to
talk to them, so he asked me to sit still for a minute while he drew
my picture. He did it so quickly, even more quickly than I do,
Magali, and you know how quickly I draw, and then he wrote you a
letter and made me promise to give it to you. *My father!* Oh, Magali,
I'm so *happy!* I wanted him to come back home with me but he said

he couldn't, not yet . . . oh, here's the letter." She took a folded piece of sketch paper out of the one remaining pocket of her shirt.

"Fauve, go to your room now and wash your hands and face and put on something clean," Maggy said softly.

"But I want to watch you read the letter."

"Go on, darling, and come back in ten minutes. Remember, tonight's the Sabbath and I'm going to light the candles soon—you can't look a mess for that."

So it had happened, Maggy thought, not unfolding the paper. Had there been a single day during the past eight years when she had been free of the expectation of this minute? At first she had told herself it was only a question of time before he came, no matter what he had promised. Then as Fauve grew older, she almost persuaded herself that perhaps she had been wrong; perhaps this man who obeyed no laws but his own had decided to ignore an inconvenient child. But now she felt no surprise. She unfolded the paper.

Dear Maggy,

I thought I could see her just once and go away. I had to come to New York and once here I couldn't resist. Now I must see you and talk to you. I'll telephone you at your office tomorrow—or at home if the office is closed. Forgive me but I know you will understand. Julien

Forgive him? It would be as impossible to forgive him, Maggy told herself, as it would be not to understand. *As he well knew.*

Julien Mistral never comprehended that it wasn't any of his reasonable arguments that persuaded Maggy to let Fauve spend the summer at *La Tourrello*, he never knew that he could have spared himself the interview with her.

During the years after Teddy's death she had been attacked over and over again by a wretched, fruitless monologue that replayed history in her brain. Wouldn't Teddy's life have followed a different course if she'd had a father? Mistral was so much older than Teddy—wasn't it merely a search for a father that had attracted her to him? What if Maggy had been able to talk about Perry Kilkullen—wouldn't that have made Teddy *feel* that she had had a father who was more real than those few childhood memories, like wisps of happy dreams? Worst of all, if Teddy had known all about Maggy's relationship with Mistral, known how heartlessly he had taken everything she had to give; her virginity, her whole heart, even her money, and then just dropped her without a thought or a scruple for a rich American—wouldn't that have caused Teddy to hate him from the cradle? How many chances had she missed to change the course of events? How *guilty* was she?

Eventually Maggy would make herself turn away from this tormenting litany of mistakes and busy herself with practical ways in which to guarantee that, whatever else happened, on a practical level Fauve's life would be different from Teddy's. Fauve must have traditions she determined as she bought a menorah to replace the battered brass one that she had left behind long ago in Paris. From the time Fauve could remember anything, she carried an image of Maggy lighting the Sabbath candles—it was the first fire the baby saw and she clamored for it, fascinated by its magic. Every one of the eight days of Chanukah was commemorated by its gift, and the lighting of first one and then an additional candle for each night of the holiday. From the time she was old enough to memorize them, if not to read, Fauve always asked the four questions at the festive Passover seder Maggy now gave each year, making sure that there were never any younger children present to claim that privilege.

She spent hours with Fauve every day and long before the little girl could understand what it meant, Maggy told her that she was her most beloved illegitimate granddaughter, in the way parents of adopted children use the word "adopted" to create an acceptance from the earliest moments of the child's comprehension. As Fauve grew old enough to understand, Maggy told her of her own family's history, from the highly embroidered scraps her grandmother Cecile had told her of the ancient history of the Jews of Provence right down to the tragedy of Teddy and Julien Mistral. Before Fauve was four she had heard about Maggy and Perry Kilkullen, she knew the sad tale of the dashing David Astruc, Maggy's own father, and of Maggy's mother who had died in childbirth.

She had even been thoroughly introduced to the admonitions of Rabbi Taradash. Sometimes Maggy would wonder if she was right to fill the child's head with so much Jewish family lore—a child who had only one Jewish grandparent out of four—but what else did she have to give her? She knew nothing of the Kilkullens, nothing of the Mistrals, but on the Lunel women she was, alas, something of a specialist.

"Why doesn't my father ever come to see me?" Fauve would ask and it was the only question Maggy could never answer satisfactorily. "He's married . . . he lives far, far away, he's working very hard, he's a man who never travels . . ." What kind of answers were those? She had even considered writing to Mistral to remind him of his daughter's existence but she had never been quite ready to do it, reasoning that Fauve was such a happy child this single sadness would just have to be endured. But now that Julien had finally brought himself to see Fauve, Maggy set her teeth and gave her consent to Fauve's visiting for the summer in Provence. Only the thought of Kate Mistral made her uneasy.

"Maggy, I assure you, Kate wants whatever I want," Julien had said impatiently. "She accepts me as I am, she always has. A child of eight won't threaten her—think, Maggy, I'm sixty-one, she's almost sixty, we've been married thirty-four years . . . you don't imagine that she would be jealous of a little girl, do you?"

"I think she'd be jealous of a canary if you decided to make a pet of one."

"Maggy, you've never been rational on the subject of Kate."

"Kate is not a woman about whom it's possible for me to be rational. If she had agreed to a divorce so that you could marry Teddy . . ."

"We might have gone out on that boat anyway, Maggy. Who can look back and determine what combination of circumstances give fate its chance?"

"I never believed I'd hear you talk about fate."

"It's the only explanation I can endure."

"You don't wake up at night and ask yourself what you did that made things go wrong? You don't *blame* yourself?"

"I will *always* blame myself. I *live* with blame, but does it help? Any tiny change in events could have changed what happened. If the fishing boat had passed a minute later, if I hadn't waved at Teddy, if she hadn't let go of the line when she did, if the Americans hadn't come to St. Tropez, if we hadn't been sitting at the Sennequier, if . . . there is no end to the ifs. All I can do is to paint, Maggy. That, at least, is something, but blaming myself is worth nothing at all. Am I wrong?"

"No." Maggy fell silent. To entrust Fauve to Julien even for the short summer months was dangerous. To entrust anyone to him was dangerous. But did she really have a choice? "No," Maggy repeated out loud, but it was not to Mistral that she spoke. It was even more dangerous not to allow Fauve a father.

22

On a June day in 1969, at the Gare de Lyon, Julien Mistral and his sixteen-year-old daughter Fauve boarded the deluxe express train that runs from Paris to Marseilles. Each June for the past eight years Mistral had traveled up to Paris from Félice to meet Fauve at the airport, spend a night in Paris with her and then travel down to Provence for the entire summer. During all those years it had never failed to thrill Fauve that the train was called *Le Mistral.*

She had assumed, that first time she traveled on it, that the train was named in honor of her father and she still wasn't quite sure when she had finally had to acknowledge that the train was named for the dominating wind of Provence. The mistral, that infernal cold dry wind, blows only when the sky is bright, bright blue and the sun is blazing, or, depending on whom you discuss it with, turns the sky white and hides the sun, this wind—again depending on individual opinion—that blows for a period of three days or six days or nine days without stopping; a wind that forces every last tree in Provence to bend toward the south; that causes every house to be built without windows on its northern wall, a wind like a dragon that hides quietly until the countryside has almost forgotten about it and then springs, screaming down from the Alps to the Mediterranean at fifty miles an hour, entering the most tightly closed rooms and giving the inhabitants of Provence an excuse for every ailment from a headache to a murder.

Fauve loved the mistral, to her it was an intensely personal wind, and she was its intimate. She called it by its Provençal names *Le Mistrau* or *Le Vent Terrau*, and she grew madly exhilarated and elated when she heard the rushing, softly roaring noise it made in the branches of the trees around *La Tourrello*. To Fauve it was the spirit of the land.

Le Mistral's first-class carriages are divided into compartments holding two rows of three seats that face each other. Fauve quickly claimed two window seats, covered in a particularly nasty shade of moss green, while her father busied himself with the headwaiter of the dining car, buying the pink tickets that would reserve their seats at lunch. "Lyon, Dijon, Valence, *Avignon*," she murmured softly, wondering as she always wondered, how she would find the patience to wait the six hours it would take until they arrived. The period of time between Valence and Avignon was the most frustrating because she could see the countryside change dramatically as they drew near. Oh, the leap of her heart with the first welcoming stand of dark, jagged-branched cypress, the intoxication of the sight of the first groves of olive trees, the first long, low lines of grapevines!

"Fauve, don't you want an *apéritif* before lunch?" Mistral broke into her thoughts, standing before her as the train glided out of the station. She jumped up and followed him through the heavy doors that opened by an electric eye, into the dining car where waiters in their white coats were already pulling the corks of bottles of wine and serving whiskey and Perrier to the first-class passengers. This prelunch drink was another tradition that had started with her first trip down to Félice. She always had two bottles of sweet pineapple juice and then, after a little urging, a third, for they were very small bottles indeed.

"A sherry, please," Fauve said.

"Oh, so you drink now, do you?" Mistral put his hand over hers.

"Only on special occasions." She laughed at him, delighting in the passion of love she felt transmitted from his hand to hers. He was, she estimated, the most undomesticated man who had ever existed, yet she knew that anything that concerned her mattered to him more than anything else in his life.

"A sherry for my daughter," he said, "and bring me a *pastis*." Mistral searched her face, seeking as always with a painful mixture of hope and fear, traces of Teddy's classic, catastrophic beauty. But as Fauve grew older, it seemed to him that she possessed a loveliness that owed nothing to her mother but her height and the color of her hair. It was, he reflected, searching for the right word to adequately describe this child he so adored, an *intelligent* beauty. There was always something fascinatingly thoughtful in Fauve's expression, something that made him long to know exactly what was going through her mind at every minute, something that prevented him from ever being quite satisfied with a single one of the many portraits he had made of her. There was a brave and absorbing mystery about her almost unpaintable gray eyes—what would Leonardo have made of her?—there was a seriousness that lurked at the corners of her bewitching mouth up until the instant that it curved into a sorceress's smile.

Mistral had never found it possible to concentrate his gaze for long on Fauve's eyes or her mouth; he had to look at her face as a whole because to him it was like a landscape on a changeable day in the springtime. No one mood lasted for long, each moment brought a new enchantment, a new perception. No, he had never quite captured her on canvas.

As Fauve sipped her sherry she was aware of Mistral watching her carefully. It was always the same during the first week of each visit as he pored over the changes that a year had made in her. She submitted to his inspection with the cheerful resignation that came of growing up under Maggy's all-seeing eye. Did any other teenaged girl have to be scrutinized daily by the most knowledgeable woman in the world on the subject of the female face and then, on her summer vacation, be the object of the minute attention of a father who saw *everything?*

"Mascara," Mistral observed in a neutral tone.

"I thought you'd never notice."

"I suppose it goes with your drinking sherry?"

"Precisely. Magali says that it's perfectly proper at sixteen if I put it on right. She taught me how herself. Do you like it?"

"Not excessively, but, on the other hand, since you are otherwise fairly agreeable looking, why should I complain, particularly when I know it would avail me nothing? I've survived four years of miniskirts, which seem to be getting shorter each year, I lived through the era of the tiny white plastic boots, I scarcely blinked when you gave yourself a geometric haircut—Sassoon, was it not?—

half of one anyway, so why should I worry about a bit of black on your lashes that will undoubtedly come off before the day is over?"

"What a philosophical, patient, dear little papa I have."

"You always made fun of me, even when you were a little girl. You're the only person who ever makes fun of me, do you know that?"

"And lived to tell the tale?"

"Who even tried."

"What about my mother? Surely she saw how droll you are?"

"No, no . . . or perhaps yes, but she never mocked me—she wasn't like you, Fauve. No one has your nerve."

"*Chutzpa*, Papa, that's what Magali says it is. And it's not supposed to be a compliment. It means audacity in Hebrew."

"What's wrong with audacity? You'll get nowhere in the world without it."

"Well, it also means brazen effrontery and outrageous gall—I think Magali'd like my audacity to be a little more ladylike. Still, I'm getting better. This year I didn't have a single fistfight and I went to lots of awful dances in pretty dresses and made dumb conversation with terrible, dreadful boring boys . . ."

"Nobody who interested you, not even one?"

"I would have said in my letters, you know that. No, Papa, you have a daughter who finds the male sex much less interesting than she has been led to hope they would be."

"But you're only sixteen! Why should you find them interesting at your age? There's plenty of time for that when you're grown up."

"Sixteen is supposed to be grown up," Fauve said earnestly but Mistral only shook his head at her. Sixteen was a child. Sixteen was a baby. He was sixty-nine and sixteen was so young that he couldn't remember anything of what it felt like, and certainly he didn't choose to remember that Fauve's grandmother had only been a year older than Fauve when he'd first set eyes on her naked body.

He thought as rarely as possible of Maggy. He wanted Fauve to belong to him alone, to be just his, Mistral's daughter, and nothing else, yet there was Maggy, so beloved of Fauve, to whom he now found himself linked forever, linked by blood. His grandchildren would be Maggy's great-grandchildren and who among them would make any distinction between generations in that unimaginable future? He resented Fauve's use of an occasional Hebrew or Yiddish

313

word, he resented her observation of Jewish holidays about which she wrote him, he resented the way Maggy had indoctrinated her with Jewish family history—what had Fauve to do with all that? She wasn't Jewish!

Yet he dared not criticize Maggy, for it was the one way in which to make Fauve turn on him in anger. Last year she had discovered a poem in Provençal by the poet Frédéric Mistral—a song really—meant to be sung to a Neapolitan melody and he never told her how maddening it was when she sang it:

> Mai, o Magali,
> Douco Magali,
> Gaio Magali,
> Es tu que m'as fa trefouli.

"Wait till she hears it—'But oh, Magali, sweet Magali, lively Magali, it's you who made me shudder with joy'—how about that for sexy, Papa?"

"It should please her," he'd said carefully.

"Don't overwhelm me with compliments—oh, okay, so I can't carry a tune but at least I'm learning Provençal."

"And how useful is that?"

"In Provence at least, it's a lot more useful than any other language I could learn. I'm planning to use it to keep on working on old Monsieur Hugonne and Monsieur Piano to let me organize a girls' boules team . . ."

"What!"

"That's what they all say, as if I'd asked to belly-up to the bar and take a swig out of the bottle of Pernod! Félice is not exactly a beachhead for female team sports but I'm not giving up. The biggest problem is the girls—they still look so shocked when I even mention it. What's so sacred about a ball of metal anyway?"

"Fauve, don't try to change customs that are hundreds of years old. Do girls play football in the United States?"

"Pops, girls do everything in the United States."

"Don't call me Pops," was the only response he'd been able to make to her shocking suggestion, he reflected, bending toward the prix-fixe menu the waiter had just placed in front of them.

The first-class dining car of Le Mistral has a kitchen at one end in which two white-capped chefs turn out surprisingly good food

314

on the superior-bistro level. Fauve and Mistral both ordered the *lotte*, that fish that can only be found in France, and the rabbit stew with new potatoes and salad, followed by the assorted cheeses and the *bombe glacée*, an ice cream dessert Fauve looked forward to from one year to the next.

"What are you painting now?" Fauve asked. As the years went by Mistral painted more and more slowly, becoming more self-critical, finishing fewer canvases and destroying a larger percentage of those he completed.

"Never mind me—what are you working on? Still taking that life class?"

"Of course. Oh, Papa, there's so much to learn. Doesn't the day ever come when you feel that you *absolutely* learned something, just one single thing for good and all?"

"It's never come for me—not for 'good and all,' so why should it come for you? Each canvas must lead into a new problem, you must wake up every day wondering what you are going to discover, what you are going to teach yourself, what new things you didn't know this morning you will know by this evening . . . but how often have I said this to you, my Fauve? Will you ever start to believe me?"

"I keep thinking I should be better," Fauve muttered. Her painting was the only area in which she found herself increasingly baffled, unable to make progress because of a growing insecurity and frustration.

When she was little—and now, looking back it seemed like an innocent's paradise—she had had such daring, she had known no limitations to what she would try to draw or paint, but every year the burden of being Mistral's daughter had become heavier. She sometimes wished she had no artistic talent at all—it would make life so much simpler, not to want to work in the same field as her father.

As Fauve demolished her fish she remembered that first summer at *La Tourrello* when, after a day or two of consideration, Mistral had allowed her into his studio on the condition that she stay perfectly quiet while he worked. He'd given her sticks of charcoal, paper and then, as an afterthought, some old, almost used-up tubes of paint, and a few worn-out brushes and a canvas, and installed her in a corner.

At first she had just watched him, but he walked about the studio for so long between each lightning attack of his brush that she soon lost interest in his odd movements and turned to the materials he'd given her.

At home in New York she'd had only pencils, sticky crayons and pastels, which promptly broke, and sets of watercolors, with which she had tried, over the years, to copy the illustrations in some of her favorite story books, but no one had ever thought of letting her near oil paints.

The smell of the tubes was immediately inebriating, she could clearly remember that instant when she had rubbed the paint on her fingers and sniffed with rapture. Then, imitating what she had watched Mistral do before he started work, she squeezed a dollop of paint out of each tube and arranged them in a semicircle on the wooden board he'd handed her. What next? she had wondered, confronting the first blank canvas of her life. She wanted to ask her father but didn't dare to interrupt him. There were no books around for her to search for pictures to copy, no flowers in a vase or fruit in a bowl. The immense paintings on the walls all around her were too confusing, too complex for her to dream of trying to copy them, so eventually Fauve dipped her brush into the darkest of the paints, a deep, rich blue, and started to outline the most central object in the studio, her father's easel.

She pulled her red eyebrows together in a straight line as she concentrated on it, freely and boldly, undaunted by the problem in perspective since she didn't know what perspective was, and saw only what was literally before her eyes. She worked steadily and so quietly that it was an hour before Mistral remembered her. She was so engrossed that she didn't notice when he came up behind her and took a look at what she was up to. His hair rose on his arms and the back of his neck in a shock of recognition. *She sees the way an artist sees,* he thought, not needing to explain to himself what he meant. He made no comment that day but the next day he gave her a sprig of grass in a vase to work from, and the following day he gave her an apple.

"*Regard! Regard,* Fauve . . . use your eyes, my little one, you must learn to *see* . . . see that apple . . . it looks round, doesn't it? But if you look—if you truly look—you'll see that the top is higher on the left . . . it isn't round at all, is it? And why doesn't it roll like a ball, this apple? Because it's almost flat on the bottom—do you *see* that with your own eyes, little one? And that little scar on the skin of the apple . . . can you tell me where it starts and where it finishes? What color is the scar, Fauve? Is it almost white? *Regard!* Do you see how the red of the apple is touched by yellow? And do you see where the yellow becomes brighter, just at the side? Now— tell me, can you *see* where, on your board, you have placed these colors, this red, this yellow? It's all there, Fauve, if you only use your eyes."

Then, as he had been aching to do from the first day, in a moment that would never be forgotten by either of them, he had finally reached out and put his huge hand right on top of Fauve's hand and guided it with his powerful fingers so that her brush moved under his direction, his force passing into her own fingers. She relaxed her small hand but kept a firm grip on her brush and allowed her wrist and bones and tendons to *lean* into his, the way a good dancer follows a strong partner, neither too yieldingly nor too stiffly, and as she saw and felt her brush make stroke after stroke, she drank in knowledge with her muscles as well as with her mind.

This was what it should feel like, his hand was informing her hand, *this is the way it goes.* No matter how original an artist must become, Mistral believed that in art, as in language, there was a basic grammar that has to be learned before true speech is possible and it was in this grammar that he trained Fauve.

That summer of Fauve's eighth year, the summer when her art lessons began, was also the year that Mistral started to frequent the café in Félice again. After an absence of twenty years he began taking Fauve there with him before dinner every day merely to be able to order a drink "for my daughter, Fauve." Little by little the men of the town, who had almost never set eyes on him since the war had interrupted all of their lives, began to gather around and admire the little girl while he offered them round after round with a joviality he couldn't contain, a friendliness they began to accept, slowly at first and suspiciously, but won over by the lively, curious, friendly child.

Mistral had never taken his daughter Nadine into Félice with him. Even if he'd wanted to, Kate would have discouraged it. When he returned from his wanderings in 1956 he discovered, without any regret, that from the time she was eight Nadine had been sent to boarding school in England.

In spite of Nadine's first four years at the village school, Kate had always considered it unthinkable that her daughter should be brought up for long in the countryside, for she was to be a citizen of the great world in which Kate had lived before she met Mistral.

Nadine was very young when she had learned to consider Félice as a rather inconsequential and old-fashioned oddity in her own important life. It existed, like a backdrop, painted in a whimsically naïve style, a living Brueghel, that set off the qualities of Mademoiselle Nadine Mistral in a valuable way. Kate allowed her daughter to consider *La Tourrello* itself merely a charmingly unconventional choice of residence, dictated by the whim of a famous, therefore permissibly eccentric father.

As she grew older, Nadine discovered for herself that *La Tourrello* had great usefulness in her scheme of things, for it was famous all over the world, and when she spoke of it to her friends, its name was received with the same reverence as if it had been a castle. The *mas* became a showplace that she displayed from time to time to especially favored friends before she rushed off to stay with them at the more civilized and desirable spots where they spent their summers.

Nadine, exquisite Nadine, with her cool, aquatic green eyes, her straight, shoulder-length blond hair and that eternal little smile that was not a smile at all but the shape of the upper lip of her delicate pink mouth, was exceedingly unpopular in Félice.

When Mistral first brought Fauve to the café in the summer of 1961, no one worried overmuch about what Mademoiselle Nadine's reactions might be to the arrival of a little half-sister who had appeared out of nowhere, or rather out of the superb scandal they knew very well, for had it not been in every newspaper and magazine, and was it not the sort of story one could scarcely forget?

Nor were Kate's emotions treated tenderly in the torrent of gossip that inundated Félice at Fauve's arrival, another chapter in the endlessly chewy, delectably juicy explorations of Mistral's home life that occupied the villagers for many a pleasant hour over the years. Kate Mistral did all her shopping in Apt or in Avignon, ignoring the village stores, a detestable and unforgivable trait in anyone who lived in the vicinity, and one which guaranteed her an ever-mounting degree of enmity. Kate barely deigned to stop at the village gas station to fill up her car. But what could you expect of a woman who thought she was better than her neighbors?

None of the other rich families who had bought homes in the Lubéron were the object of anything like the speculation directed at

Mistral. The others' homes were used for summer vacations, they were visitors only, clearly not *of* the countryside. But Mistral's position was ambiguous from the day he had settled in Félice in 1926. He had become almost, but not truly, a part of the village in those years when he was the chief stalwart of the boules team, those years before the war when Kate had been content to live in relative tranquillity, entertaining too often, it was true, but then she was American, after all.

After the war the climate of the village itself changed; eight men from Félice had been killed and a dozen had spent years in Germany doing forced labor, while many of the younger men had been in the *Maquis*.

At the café, where once the most animated discussions had concerned the relative merits of the boules grounds of other villages, politics were now argued seriously and the talk had a way of turning ugly; the supporters of de Gaulle refused to drink with the men who voted Communist. Mistral, with his loathing of politics, avoided the café, and his absence was perceived as a feeling of superiority, a belief clearly substantiated when Kate ordered the construction of the swimming pool. No one single thing she might have done would have more alienated her from her neighbors whose incomes depended, in the most basic way, on the amount of rainfall every year.

The distance that both Mistral and Kate put between themselves and the life of the village after the war did nothing to stem the gossip about them; quite the contrary, for were they not still *there*, as if defying their neighbors?

Nor did it help when Marte Pollison couldn't resist dropping certain details about life at *La Tourrello* into the ears of her cousins who owned the hardware store in Félice. Soon every housewife in the town knew precisely how much Madame Mistral spent on champagne for those parties she gave, how many kilos of pâté de foie gras and smoked salmon were delivered from the finest grocery store in Avignon before a grand reception, how many extra servants Marte supervised during the busy summer season.

Nothing could surprise them, they said to each other, about this woman who had actually installed five bathrooms with hot water and tubs in *La Tourrello* when she had first come to live there, at a time when many of the richest farmers of the valley had not yet installed running water in their homes. What folly! Did the Mistrals not realize that the tax inspector could not fail to notice them?

It would not have made any difference if the people of Félice had known that, in 1960 at Parke-Bernet in New York, an early Mistral had sold for half a million dollars. They had enough trouble crediting the details of the decoration of the room that was installed for Fauve during the six weeks that passed from the time Maggy agreed to let her visit for the summer in 1961, and the day she arrived.

A stonemason who was employed on the project of restoring the circular upper tower room in the *pigionnier* was able to reduce them to silence by his account of its decoration.

"But yes I assure you, the walls are covered in fabric, from the floor to the ceiling, in deep folds like a curtain but running around from one window to another, hundreds and hundreds of meters of it, printed in lavender and white flowers. The housekeeper told me that it came from the factory of Monsieur Demary in Tarascon." He paused to make sure everyone was paying close attention. "And the bed," he continued, satisfied with his audience, "has a canopy of the same material and a headboard carved like one of the old chests in the Hotel de Ville, fit for a princess. Tiles on the floor, of course, but also a white rug that Marte Pollison said came from Spain, and a white birdcage with lovebirds in it. Yes, I saw them myself. You know that bathroom Mistral made the plumber put in so quickly? Well, the bathroom walls are also covered in fabric!"

It was this final detail that made most of the housewives of Félice disbelieve his account for not even Madame Mistral could be foolish enough to do such a thing.

They were quite right. It had not been Kate, but Mistral himself who had feverishly harried the workmen; he who had decided to convert the dovecote, because he knew that a romantic tower room would delight a little girl; he who had thought of how to employ the traditionally patterned fabric to make sure that the occasional cold mistral of summer wouldn't come whistling through the old stones, replastered though they were; he who had accomplished the impossible by getting Provençal craftsmen to finish the work they had promised to do by the time they had agreed to do it, with an efficiency unheard of throughout the Midi.

When Fauve arrived in *La Tourrello* that first summer she had fallen in love with her room from the moment she entered it, yet, as the summer started, she spent many a sad hour there pondering the reasons for the hatred she felt emanating from Nadine and from Kate.

Was it, she wondered, the fact that her father was teaching her how to paint that made Nadine treat her with an enmity so remote, so totally rejecting, that she couldn't seize and wrestle with it? Would her half-sister have detested her under any circumstances?

Was it the fact that she was a bastard that made Kate regard her with an animosity that was sensed by no one but Fauve, for Kate was much too clever not to know that anything unpleasant she could say or do to the little girl would cost her far more grief from her husband than it would be worth. She was careful to seem ungrudging and generous, yet her loathing existed in the very way she pressed Fauve to have more homemade apricot jam, in the gesture she made to fill Fauve's glass of milk, in the smile that went with her suggestion that Fauve might enjoy having a bicycle so that she could go to the village.

Finally Fauve's pride asserted itself. If Kate and Nadine hated her she would ignore them and go her own way. She would seek out the children of her own age in Félice and set about making friends of them.

She never suspected how united the tightly knit community of eight-year-olds had been in their suspicions of her, a tall, oddly dressed American girl with flying red hair who bicycled up from *le château*, as they called *La Tourrello*, a girl whose fancy room they had heard too much about. Fauve spoke to them in citified Northern French but yet she made so many babyish mistakes in grammar, she didn't understand that she must shake hands all around or that she must not play the "Babyfoot" pinball machine with the boys, this girl with a most uncivilized name who did not even have her own saint's day to celebrate.

They envied the way Fauve's father promenaded her around the café as if she were a baby just able to take her first steps instead of a gawky girl as old as they were; they envied the shiny new bicycle and her pretty clothes. Who was she to descend on their little group and try to get in?

But none of them could resist Fauve for long, none of them could turn away from her brimming, open and ardent *intention* to love them. She offered to help them cut grass to feed the rabbits they raised for market and she volunteered to take care of their little brothers and sisters while they played tag. Fauve taught them how to throw a baseball, and she invited them all home for many a sumptuous *goûter*, the afternoon snack of bread and brioche and chocolate and three kinds of jam that is the French child's favorite meal. Afterward she took them up to her room, to lie sprawled all over her astonishing canopied bed while she told them about her school in New York where, evidently, nobody really did any work at all, in comparison to what was expected of them in the village school. Then, during the winters, she wrote letters to each of them, so that when she came back each summer it was as if an old friend had returned.

Two of the girls in particular, dark, pretty Sophie Borel, whom Fauve nicknamed Pomme because of her apple-red cheeks, and Louise Gordin, called Épinette, or thorn, because of her hot temper that contrasted so strangely with her angelic little face, had become Fauve's two best friends. Pomme, a humorist and born trouble-maker, was a tremendous source of information since her father was the local postman. Fiery Épinette was one of Fauve's first champions. Almost from the beginning, she defended Fauve to other girls who had not yet been won over to the stranger's presence in their insulated and chauvinistic community.

She could hardly wait to see Pomme and Épinette again, Fauve thought, as lunch proceeded, and the waiters, as agile as acrobats, balanced the platters of spicy rabbit *ragoût*, serving everyone in the dining car with swiftly graceful motions, as the train, traveling at a high speed, swayed constantly from side to side of the sinuous roadbed.

Neither Pomme nor Épinette was a good correspondent and while Fauve was away from Félice she always worried that something might happen to change the village she loved so much. What if someone had built a supermarket or a Monoprix or a movie house?

Félice was utterly beautiful to her just as it was. It was as quaint, Fauve thought, as any town on this planet could be, but quaint was not the right word for anything so modestly, so naturally and utterly itself, a human dwelling place that put on no show to attract the casual visitor, a private world in which the way of life hadn't changed in basic ways for hundreds of years.

Often Fauve reflected on the difference between attitudes in New York and Félice toward her illegitimate birth. In Manhattan, as she grew older and more noticeable, she often was aware of an undercurrent of unwelcome and malicious attention whenever she went out in public with Maggy and Darcy or with Melvin Allenberg, who had become her guide to the art world. There was a certain type of alert, overly curious glance that moved too quickly away from her face; an unmistakable nuance in voices discreetly lowered at a nearby restaurant table, an unnaturally blank kind of impersonal look that managed to scrape over her entire surface and take in every detail of her appearance; all signs of recognition that told her unmistakably that someone had just whispered to someone else, "Look, there's that girl, Mistral's illegitimate daughter."

At such moments, without knowing that she did it, Fauve straightened up to her full five feet ten inches, threw her slim shoulders back and opened her eyes wide, without blinking, and faced the people who had noticed her with a look of such stern and frank pride that it would not have been inappropriate on her father's face, a look that could startle people into silence.

"Illegitimate," Fauve had once said to Maggy. "Why don't people bother to be original? I looked it up in Webster's *Thesaurus* and I could be called so many other things—by-blow, catch colt, *nullius filius*, whoreson and woods colt—I'd prefer woods colt, wouldn't you?"

"Yes indeed . . . pity more people don't have better vocabularies," Maggy had responded dryly.

But in Félice, when there were consequences of premarital sex, popular opinion held that the only fault lay in the parents not having been careful enough. No finger was pointed at a child who grew up illegitimate. In Félice, Fauve felt that she was fully Mistral's daughter, in a perfectly down-to-earth and natural way, accepted as the guiltless result of guilty passion, but *accepted*.

She looked impatiently out of the train window. They still hadn't reached Lyon and lunch was almost over. "Is there any news from the village?" she asked her father. "Nothing new since your last letter?"

"New? Not unless you count that accursed, tasteless rabble, that unspeakably foul pack of decorators from Paris who are buying up

323

old houses all over the valley—painting them green and lemon yellow and even mauve, by Christ, against all tradition, doing them over inside and selling them to foreigners or filthy, decadent Parisians for ten times what they cost—it's a plague!" Mistral growled.

"In Félice?" Fauve asked, alarmed.

"Not more than before, only a few outsiders have discovered us, but in Gordes and in Roussillon it gets worse and worse. The villages have lost all their atmosphere, they look the way your Disneyland must look, sickeningly picturesque, with old houses tarted up like whores at a wedding, and swarms of hundreds of foreigners, God knows what kind of barbarians, arriving in tour buses, drinking Coca-Cola in the cafés, buying postcards by the dozen, ignoring the village itself, getting back on the bus and going on to the next place—one day to see the whole Lubéron!"

He looks more like a gallant, heroic conquistador than ever, Fauve thought, as Mistral fulminated. As she grew older he seemed to grow younger to her, perhaps because she had learned to really look at him, perhaps because he had shaved off the beard that had kept her from first recognizing him. His big nose was more prominent than ever, and his mouth more tightly set, unless he was looking at her, but the bold, arrogant adventurous set of his handsome head hadn't changed; he seemed, as always, stronger, more upright, so much bigger than any man she'd ever seen. He's prodigious, she thought, using her newest favorite word. I have a prodigious father.

23

Pervert!" shrieked Pomme, "depraved . . . debauched . . . corrupted—you're *sick*, Fauve Lunel, that's what you are!"

"Backwoods . . . medieval . . ." Fauve gasped through tears of laughter as Pomme shook her as hard as she could. "You're living in another century, poor girl." When she'd put on her record of Three Dog Night singing "Easy to Be Hard" she'd known that her friends were far from ready for it. In the past she'd won them over to Johnny Cash and Engelbert Humperdinck although their hearts were really still with the Bee Gees. But she hadn't been able to resist bedeviling them. They enjoyed it as much as she did.

The teenagers of Provence were dance mad in spite of the fact that their taste in music lagged behind that of New York. Each village held two public dances every year so that in the Lubéron there was almost never a Saturday night on which it wasn't possible to go to a dance within an area that could be reached by car or by bus.

At fourteen and fifteen Fauve had been allowed to go to the dances with a group of girls chaperoned by one of their fathers, but now, at sixteen, they had all reached the age at which they were permitted—in fact, expected—to go to a dance with a date.

After Pomme and Épinette left reluctantly to go home for dinner, Fauve thoughtfully put away her records. It hadn't escaped her that there had been a basic change in her friends since last summer.

Today they had talked of little else but the dance that was planned in Uzès for next Saturday to which they had each been invited by a boy from the district. They assured Fauve that she was invited to go to the dance with the four of them in a car belonging to the father of one of the boys, but once there, Fauve asked herself, what then?

Last year it had been perfectly honorable to stand in the "girls' corner" with a bunch of giggling friends and, if no boy presented himself, to dance with one of them. Indeed, because of her unusual height she was much in demand as a partner. But this year she was aware it would be something of a disgrace to dance with another girl. Most of the young females of Félice were going with dates, according to Pomme's information which was as official as any engraved announcement.

Morosely, Fauve considered Provençal dances. At the *Salle des Fêtes* girls and boys migrated to their separate corners as soon as they entered, eying each other as slyly and secretly as possible but otherwise not communicating, even if they had arrived together. The first dancers were always couples who didn't care what anyone thought: the cheerful grocer with his five-year-old daughter; a nine-year-old girl who had trapped her six-year-old brother in a grip he couldn't wriggle out of; two cousins who had formed a jocular alliance; perhaps a newly married couple or two, showing off for the neighbors.

Eventually each boy claimed his date, if he had one, but without any air of grace or pleasure. Why were they all so crazy about dancing, she groaned to herself, when they seemed so miserable when they were doing it? In Provence people danced like marionettes whose legs moved in independence from their stiff upper bodies. The proper expression during a dance was of frozen despair. Conversation, or even a smile between partners, was out of the question. When the dance was over the couple darted apart, as brusquely as if they had been locked together in a prizefight and returned to their respective corners, where, at last, they could communicate happily with members of their own sex. And they called that a dance!

Why did she have to subject herself to it? She could stay home Saturday night without any comment from anyone. Some English friends of Kate's were expected for the weekend, and no one at *La Tourrello* would know about the dance at Uzès and wonder why she wasn't there. Yet, she reminded herself, she had chosen to make herself a part of the village of Félice and if she missed a dance it would be interpreted, and rightly so, as turning away from her friends. Lack of a date was not the slightest excuse. Every girl from every village kilometers around who could get transportation to the dance would be there, because this network of dances provided the only means through which they would eventually find mates.

Oh, if it were only *last* summer Fauve thought with a rush of nostalgia, if only the whole business of pairing off hadn't already started! Pomme and Épinette, who once had thought of nothing but eluding their mothers and getting into mischief with her, were so excited about their dates for Saturday night.

Within two years they'd probably be engaged or married and then, before she knew it, they'd be young mothers, proudly displaying their babies to her, their freedom utterly surrendered, freedom that would be almost forgotten and probably not even regretted except for a moment or two of memory.

In the most basic way Pomme and Épinette were already gone forever, she thought, with a premonitory shudder. Her summer friendships, which had seemed eternal last year, now revealed themselves as ephemeral—they had been replaced, in the passage of a single winter, by the shadow, as unmistakable as it was unwelcome, of the end of adolescence. *Why did it have to end?*

Fauve flung herself on her bed with an impulse of passionate purity. *Who needed boys?* Why did Pomme and Épinette have to give a damn about them? Couldn't they have waited just one more year? But she knew it was too late. They had both set sail on the sea of romance judging by the certain note of inhabitual tenderness that Pomme, normally a fountain of mockery, had used when she mentioned Raymond Binard, the young electrician from Apt. And where was Épinette's predictable, delightful crustiness when she proudly announced that Paul Alouette, her "friend," who was on leave from his military service, had borrowed his father's new Citroën for the occasion? What sort of accomplishment was borrowing a car?

In New York Fauve was part of a group of classmates at the Dalton School, boys and girls, who had gone to the same dancing school and now got together for rock concerts and parties. They were, she knew, considered the late bloomers in a class where others smoked pot and experimented with sex, but none of her friends were in any rush to launch themselves into the complicated game of man-woman that they saw beginning to be played out all around them.

If only the time could stand still! If only nothing ever had to change!

Startled to find herself close to tears, she sighed deeply with a sigh that she didn't understand was her first sigh of adulthood, a sigh of recognition of the passage of time and the bitter, useless knowledge that there is nothing that can be done about it.

Slowly, Fauve began to feel comforted by her room. It, at least, was something she could always count on not to change. The tower room waited for her to come home to it each year, it possessed an interior life of its own that she knew yielded only to her. Before it had been used as a dovecote it had been a windmill, and she could all but see the great sails that had made their slow circles outside the windows a century ago; she could practically hear the whirring of the wings of generations of doves that had nested where her bed now stood.

In the last eight years Fauve had added to her room until it was a museum of her growing-up. Generations of dolls sat primly against the walls, photographs of Fauve and Mistral together, which had been taken each summer, hung on the walls along with old-fashioned postcards she had found in local antique shops, and flowers she had pressed and framed, as well as posters announcing past village fêtes, the volunteer firemen's balls and other occasions dear to her heart. She never subtracted anything from these collections of memories, nor did she ever bring anything home to New York from Félice. Instinctively she kept her two worlds apart from each other, just as they were in reality.

As Fauve lay, half dreaming, she suddenly heard Kate's voice in the courtyard. How much like Nadine she sounded, Nadine who, thank God, only visited *La Tourrello* once or twice every summer now that she was married to Phillipe Dalmas and living in Paris.

Had Nadine ever experienced regret, even a second of it, when she slipped from being a cool, composed, superior fifteen to a poised and worldly sixteen? Fauve doubted it. If Nadine and any of her crowd had ever dropped in at a village dance it would have been to stand on the sidelines and stare with open amusement as if it were a particularly droll folklorique spectacle. Had they condescended to join in the dancing it would only have been to turn it into a clever story that showed how quaint the locals were.

At the thought of her half-sister Fauve clenched her fists and bounded up from her bed, her gloom vanished in a rush of combat, which translated itself into the one eternal question which can make any female creature forget even such profound questions as the brevity of youth, the fleetingness of time.

What was she going to wear?

Five days later Fauve stood in the girls' corner of the *Salle des Fêtes* in Uzès, a bustling market town of many medieval towers which is the seat of the Duke d'Uzès, the Premier Duke of France. The year 1969 was a particularly confusing year for personal adornment, but even in the Lubéron the miniskirt had made its presence felt. Fauve had spent hours all week trying on and discarding one dress after another. They all looked, to her suddenly self-conscious eyes, either too dressed up, as if she were expecting some occasion more grand than a village dance, or too casual, as if she hadn't bothered to put on her best, as she knew the other girls would. She had still been standing indecisively, clad only in a pair of bright tangerine tights, when Marte Pollison tapped on her door to say that her friends were waiting outside in the car.

In a sudden rush of defiance Fauve jumped into a shocking pink minidress trimmed with a long, wide, geometric slash of purple ribbon. She gave one more lick of the brush to her red hair. Each long and lively strand flirted with the air. She thrust her feet into a pair of bright green Capezio ballet slippers and ran down the staircase of her private tower without going into the salon to say goodbye. If Kate disapproved of her sense of color she really didn't care to know about it. Not ever—and particularly not right now.

The girls' corner of the room was buzzing, but Fauve was not listening to the conversation. She could see two young men approaching her from the boys' corner; each seemed to have clear-cut intentions of asking her to dance. One of them was Lucien Gromet, whose bad breath she still remembered from last year and the other, Henri Savati, was the kind of dancer who could only trudge to the music. Wildly she wondered if she should ask one of the younger girls to dance and avoid them both?

The two boys were approaching at the same rate of speed, neither one of them willing to seem to be in a contest with the other.
They were no more than a few feet away when suddenly they were
pushed brusquely aside by a third male figure who skidded to a stop
before Fauve. He turned to the two others with a flourish. "A
thousand apologies, my dear friends, but Mademoiselle has promised me all the dances on her card this evening." Lucien's and
Henri's jaws dropped at these words. The accepted way in which to
invite a girl to dance was to mumble to her, hook a thumb in the
direction of the dance floor and amble off without even looking to
see if she was following. Dance card!

Fauve blinked twice. "Ah, Roland, I was beginning to wonder
what had happened to you," she said, and put her arm through his.
"I thought perhaps you had had to stop to feed the nightingales."

"No, tonight it was the peacocks—the peahen is in heat and they
engaged in an unseemly tussle. Shall we waltz?"

"I would like nothing better—but alas, the orchestra is not in
agreement."

"Then shall we sit this one out?"

"Perhaps it would be wise, Roland."

"My name is Eric," he said, "but you can call me Roland if for
any reason you'd prefer it."

"My name is Fauve." Usually the young men of the neighborhood, who heard her name for the first time, made some silly remark. She waited but he said nothing, inspecting her openly with a
look of frankest fascination. She thought that she couldn't remember if she had ever seen a man—for he *was* a man, not a boy—who
looked so comfortably at home in his skin. Eric was well over six
feet tall and there was some one outstanding quality to him that
Fauve was intensely conscious of, yet she couldn't manage to put a
name to it as she looked at him. It wasn't just good looks although
he was exceptionally handsome, with strong, blunt, well-formed
features, deeply tanned skin and thick brown hair that sprang up in
an unruly way from a cowlick over his right eye and fell down over
his forehead on both sides. His lower lip was full and indented in
the center, the focus of his face, giving him a humorous and generous expression. But just what was it, Fauve wondered, that struck
her as an unusual and important aspect of this stranger?

"You're staring at me," he said, and grinned.

"You're staring at *me*," she said indignantly.

"Would you rather dance?"

"Perhaps we should."

The orchestra had just begun to play "La Vie en Rose" when Eric took her in his arms. Fauve, who had stood braced in the normal dancing posture of the region, found herself being held close to his chest and masterfully led into what was, to her instantly responding feet, most decidedly a waltz. Perhaps the orchestra wasn't playing the requisite *one*, two, three, *one*, two, three of a Viennese waltz but, nevertheless, they were waltzing magically, and so gracefully that the orchestra leader, watching them, signaled his men to play "The Blue Danube" next. When that waltz was over they stopped suddenly, both of them amazed to find themselves in the center of a circle of other dancers who were watching them with as much curiosity as if Ginger Rogers and Fred Astaire had materialized on the dance floor.

"That was wonderful!" they each said at the same moment, their words colliding in midsentence.

"Come on, let's get something cold to drink. I've discovered three important things about you and I intend to impress you with my intelligence," Eric said, leading her out of the circle. There was a café next door to the *Salle des Fêtes* where the chaperones gathered to play cards. Fauve and Eric found a table and ordered Cokes.

"First," he said, "you are a foreigner, second you're an artist and third, you smell better than any girl in the world."

"But I don't use perfume," Fauve protested.

"That's just what I said."

"Oh." She thought about it for an instant and discovered that she was blushing, that disastrous blush that had been passed down in a direct line from one Lunel woman to another. "How do you know I'm a foreigner?" Fauve said hastily, slipping easily into the accent of the Midi.

"Too late to try that trick, and anyway I can do it too. You waltz like a foreigner—divinely, to be blunt—the only girl in Provence who could have taken Archduke Rudolf away from Marie Vetsera. You didn't learn that here."

"Oh!" Fauve had seen a revival of *Mayerling* on television and her blush deepened. "How do you know I'm an artist?" she demanded nervously.

"Because only an artist would deliberately wear those colors—the dress with your hair could be just to be noticed but then to add orange tights and those shoes . . ."

"I'm interested in art," Fauve said evasively. She never told people that she painted herself. Only her family and Melvin Allenberg and a few close friends knew that she painted and, of them, no one had any true idea of how deeply she felt about her work.

" 'Interested in art'?" he said. "Is that all—just interest?"

"I go to a lot of galleries and museums—New York is the art capital of the world, after all."

"So the New Yorkers would like to think," Eric said defensively. No Frenchman would admit that after the war the center of the art world had indeed shifted to the United States.

"Oh, come on, you know it is. Every Saturday afternoon you can see more new art just walking in and out of the galleries of Madison Avenue than you possibly could in Paris—not to speak of the museums. My friend Melvin and I go out looking two or three times a month," Fauve answered.

"Your friend Melvin? Is he some sort of expert?" Eric bristled.

"Melvin is absolutely brilliant! It's amazing how much he knows . . . and he's such a darling."

"This paragon—no doubt he's handsome too?"

"Well, perhaps not in the obvious way, but it's extraordinary how many girls fall in love with him. They get hooked by his brains and his talent first and then they realize how very attractive he is and how sweet. Sometimes I think that there's nobody in the world I can talk to the way I can talk to Melvin—it's as if I can tell him everything and count on his understanding me."

"That sounds to me as if you're in love with him yourself," Eric said grimly.

" 'In love'? Oh, Eric, what a marvelous idea!" Fauve chortled.

"What the hell's so marvelous about it? I think it's in terrible taste for you to sit here with me droning on and on about brilliant, handsome, sweet Melvin with whom you share so many artistic afternoons."

"And evenings too, Eric—there are all the gallery openings, you know, and my grandmother lets me go to the really important ones with him," Fauve said, with a wicked grin.

"Oh, that's too much!" Eric drained his Coke and slammed the glass down on the table. "I'm going back inside."

"Eric!"

"What?" he snapped, glaring at her.

"Melvin is an *old* man—ancient—he must be at least forty-three or four—he's like my uncle or something—he used to go out with my mother, for heaven's sake."

"How old are you, anyway?" he asked, sitting back in his chair, barely hiding his relief.

"Sixteen," Fauve answered. Sixteen suddenly sounded absurdly young. Her nostalgia for her fifteenth year had vanished, not to reappear for decades.

"I'm twenty."

They smiled at each other for no reason and for every reason. Fauve realized what it was in Eric's face that had struck her from the moment she'd seen him. She trusted him. She had trusted him overwhelmingly and instantly. It seemed like a strange thing to have picked out as the dominant quality in that face. How could she trust a complete stranger at first sight? And such a handsome one? Pomme and Épinette said men like that were spoiled and full of themselves, and to be avoided at all costs. Well, Pomme and Épinette didn't understand as much as they thought they did.

"Besides knowing all about art, thanks to doddering, kindly, antique Melvin, I suppose you know everything about architecture too?" Eric asked.

"Nothing, except the things you pick up just walking around. I'm genuinely uninformed."

"Well, thank God for that," Eric said delightedly. "I'm an architect, or rather I soon will be . . . I'm at the Beaux-Arts."

"Why are you so pleased that I'm ignorant?"

"I want to have something to teach you," he answered.

"Okay. Start."

"I don't mean now, I mean tomorrow, the day after tomorrow, next week, all summer long . . . don't you have any romance in you?"

"I'm not sure . . . I mean, how do you tell?" Fauve asked seriously, drawing her eyebrows together in concentration.

"So you're a romantic illiterate too? That's even better. Come on, Fauve, let's go and waltz some more and then will you let me drive you home? Or did you come with somebody? It's impossible to figure out at these dances." He sounded suddenly unsure.

"I came with some friends but they won't mind if you take me home."

"Where do you live?"

"Near Félice."

"That's not exactly around the corner." He sounded jubilant.

"It's about sixty kilometers," she said apologetically.

"That's what I like about it. Now Fauve, you've got to stop blushing when I compliment you. I'm going to train you, just like a dog. A compliment every ten minutes for a couple of hours and you'll forget how to blush . . . no, perhaps that's not a good idea after all. I think I like your blush . . . it adds such an interesting shade of pink to all the others."

Dances in Provence never start before nine and rarely end before two o'clock, but Fauve insisted on leaving soon after midnight since the drive was so long and her father always waited up for her safe return.

Near Remoulins, where they picked up the National Route 100 that led almost due east to Félice, Eric tried to persuade her to make a quick detour to see the Pont du Gard by moonlight. "It's one of the supreme wonders of antiquity, almost intact after two thousand years—you'll never understand the Romans until you see that aqueduct, it's . . . no, you're sure? You can really live another day without an aqueduct? Well . . . we'll have to come back."

At Villeneuve-les-Avignon, he had another suggestion. "Let's just go up to my parents' place and say hello—they're never asleep this early and the view from their terrace of the Fort St. André is the best you'll ever see—it may well be the best example of a fortification with twin towers . . . not that either? Don't you *like* a good fortress? All right, all right . . . I'll go straight across the river, looking neither to the left nor to the right although you're making a mistake not just taking a peep at the Popes' Palace tonight—it's never as good by daylight."

"Home, Eric," Fauve insisted, and once past Avignon they sped across the flat, rich plain, Eric proposing and rejecting a dozen projects for the next day. He felt a heavy responsibility for choosing Fauve's first experience with architecture. Since the nearby countryside possessed the ruins of a Phoenician city founded six centuries before Jesus Christ and a hundred other wonders from every era since, what should he pick as a starting point? How much of a ruin should a ruin be? What was her tolerance level for stones?

Fauve found herself scarcely listening to him as they got closer to Félice. Her father had never seen her with any special boy before tonight, she reflected with apprehension. What would he think of her leaving for the evening with a group of old friends and coming back home with an unknown young man she'd picked up at the dance? Surely it must happen to other girls all the time? He *should* be delighted that she hadn't been a wallflower, she thought as she indicated the road to *La Tourrello* to Eric. He *should* be pleased that she'd met somebody who was studying something as interesting as architecture, shouldn't he?

The great gates of the *La Tourrello* stood wide open and the lights of the salon were blazing on the far side of the courtyard. "Just drive right in," Fauve said absently. Eric parked the car in the courtyard.

"Well, you'd better come meet my father . . ." Fauve mumbled and nervously led the way to the salon where she knew he always sat, listening for her.

As they entered the room Mistral rose from his chair near the fireplace and walked toward them, looking from Fauve to Eric in surprise. Only surprise, thought Fauve, immensely relieved, not irritation.

"This is my father," she said, not daring to look at Eric. She should have told him she was Mistral's daughter, she knew she should, but there just hadn't been an appropriate time, or rather the time at which it would have been natural had come and gone so quickly that she hadn't had the wit to seize it, and anyway he hadn't asked and in any case, what of it? He didn't like her because she was Mistral's daughter and he wouldn't not like her for it either, but now, when it was too late, she desperately wished it hadn't come as a surprise. Eric might think she'd planned it to impress him.

"Papa, this is Eric," she said faintly.

"I can see that," said Mistral, shaking hands with a smile. "But, what is this strange tribal custom of the young never to know each other's last names? Eric what, may I ask?"

"Good evening, Monsieur Mistral." Why, Fauve wondered, did Eric sound so strange? Was he angry at her after all?

"The name of my family," Eric continued, "is Avigdor. And the name of my father, Monsieur Mistral, is Adrien Avigdor."

"But you can't possibly forbid Fauve to go out with this young man," Kate said evenly. "That's really out of the question, Julien, in this day and age. Think about it. You have absolutely no reason that she could understand or accept. All that would happen is that you'd encourage her to ask questions you don't particularly care to answer, isn't that so? If I were you, I'd just let the whole mess alone—it'll disappear of its own accord unless you meddle."

"You didn't see his face, Kate. You didn't hear his voice."

"Did he say anything unusual?"

"No, he was perfectly correct as far as that went, but there was *something*—I know I'm not wrong about that."

"Julien, all he could know is that his father was once your dealer. Naturally Avigdor must resent having lost you, what dealer wouldn't? It's unquestionably a famous family horror story—how Julien Mistral got his start from Papa Avigdor and then was so thoroughly ungrateful that he changed dealers—you know how those people talk business all the time. Losing you was probably the biggest event in Avigdor's life—next to getting you."

"I don't want Fauve mixed up with him."

"She's just a child—she's not old enough to 'get mixed up' with a boy at sixteen, not seriously anyway. What harm could come of it? An artist has the right to change dealers, after all. Fauve said that this boy is only twenty years old, didn't she? Well, you haven't seen Avigdor since before the war—it was sometime in 1938 I think that he came here the last time . . . or perhaps even as long ago as 1937— I don't remember. That's more than thirty years ago! Be reasonable! I think you're taking this all much too seriously, just because it's Fauve. You never made this kind of fuss about anyone Nadine went out with and God knows she brought home a lot of young men in her day."

There was no reason, Kate had realized long ago, for Julien to realize that Marte Pollison had told her exactly what had taken place between him and Avigdor during the war, and that her visit to Avigdor had confirmed that, and other facts as well. There were many pieces of information about her husband that she had stored away in her memory. One never knew when they would become useful . . . they were a form of capital, perhaps in their own way as valuable as any of the canvases in the storeroom.

Meanwhile she relished the look of anxiety on Julien's face. She had so few weapons and he had so many. Strange. Once Fauve had seemed to be another of his weapons, a danger to her, a threat to Nadine. Now, as Fauve grew older and more precious to Mistral every year, more dear to him than anything—for Kate was too clear-eyed to ignore that—Fauve became a weapon she herself might find a way to use.

Some day, at some time in the future, repayment had to be made for the suffering Julien had caused her. Kate believed in the inevitability of revenge. Life could not, *must not* be allowed to treat her unfairly . . . not in the long run, not if she were patient. How deeply interesting it was that Fauve had met this young Avigdor. "What did he look like?" she asked lightly. "Was there much of his father in him?"

"Something . . . perhaps . . . but I didn't pay much attention. He's far better looking, taller, I would never have guessed they were related."

"You mean he didn't look Jewish?"

"That wasn't what I meant! Neither did Avigdor, as you know very well."

"Good heavens, Julien, there's no reason to lash out at me—do try to be less touchy. In two weeks Fauve'll be tired of visiting old buildings with this student and there will be ten other boys for you to worry about. So he was better looking, was he? How much better? Avigdor wasn't a beauty, after all."

"Very, very much better. Too much better."

"Try to get some sleep, Julien," Kate said sweetly. "You're seeing ghosts."

24

What were you thinking of, Eric, to begin this cultural project by going to the Popes' Palace?" Beth Avigdor said with mild, amused indignation. "Such a great barracks of a place, without even any furniture to make it look less inhospitable—and full of tourists as well? No wonder you're exhausted, Mademoiselle Lunel. I've avoided setting a foot in there for years."

"I enjoyed it . . . for almost the first hour . . . and by that time we'd passed the point of no return," Fauve answered, wriggling her sore toes, grateful for the umbrella that cast a cool shadow over the lunch table in the garden of Le Prieuré.

Eric's mother was a woman to reckon with, she realized, forthright and statuesque, with fine dark eyes and hair only beginning to show a thread of gray here and there. She looked as if she must be at least twenty years younger than Eric's father who sat, looking as much at ease as any man has ever looked, judiciously considering the fourteen-page wine list, which was wittily decorated by seven, full-page, ink drawings by Ronald Searle. Adrien Avigdor had never seemed particularly young even as a young man, and now he was pleasantly bald, pleasantly stocky, and pleasantly wrinkled, mellow, sturdy and as unremarkable as ever. His mien had always been so simple, so independent of any outstanding feature, so dominated by his expression of rustic goodness, that age had only enhanced it.

338

In 1945 he had married beautiful Beth Levi, who had fought beside him for three years in the Resistance. Their only son, Eric, who had inherited his mother's looks, and his father's mien, had been born in 1949. The Avigdors had a fine and harmonious marriage, and his gallery on the rue du Faubourg St. Honoré was one of the most successful and respected in France.

Many years ago, when he had bought a vacation house in Provence, he had chosen to live in the urbane, elegant little city of Villeneuve-les-Avignon, which was so different in topography and atmosphere from those savage hill villages of the Lubéron that still held memories he didn't care to resurrect. And now, by God, here was Eric turning up with Mistral's daughter, Avigdor mused, as he weighed the possibility of a potentially interesting Nuits-St.-Georges, Clos de la Maréchale against a highly promising Romanée-St.-Vivant.

It had been impossible to prevent Beth, her maternal curiosity immediately aroused by Eric's enthusiasm, from arranging this lunch. His wife had never known anything more about Mistral than the simple fact that her husband had once been the artist's dealer. "We didn't get along but it's too unimportant to discuss," he had told her years ago. Eric had grown curious, in the last year, to know the reason for his quarrel with the painter, but he'd resisted being drawn into an explanation with his son. "Just call it a mutual disagreement," he'd said, with such an uncharacteristic frown that it had only served to convince Eric that there had been a serious rupture between them.

There could not be anyone Avigdor was less anxious to see his son interested in than Mistral's daughter, but he resolved that he would be as pleasant to her as he would be to any other girl. Indeed, what man could not be, once he'd laid eyes on her?

The years had taught Adrien Avigdor certain things, and one of them was how lucky he had been to survive when so many had perished. It was important to him to be grateful for life, important not to dwell on old wounds. He asked only to live with dignity, and with decency toward others, but the hard-earned lessons of self-preservation he had learned during the Occupation made him turn his back whenever he heard people speak of religion or politics. If only, he thought often, those two forces that so violently and persistently divided humanity had been left out of the scheme of things, how sweet life could be for everyone. He wanted nothing to do with certain memories that, in spite of his philosophy, had never faded, and Fauve Mistral brought them back to life.

"So, Mademoiselle," he said, turning deliberately to Fauve with his benign air, "you go to school in the United States, do you?"

"Oh, please call me Fauve—yes, I live in New York but I come to visit my father every summer."

"Of course, of course, how pleasant. Ah, Jacques," Adrien Avigdor turned to Jacques Mille, director of the hotel, son of the proprietor of Le Prieuré, who had bought it from Madame Blé, "what do you think of the Nuits-St. Georges as compared to the Romanée-St.-Vivant? Your personal opinion mind you, among friends."

"If it were my palate, Monsieur Avigdor, I'd pick the Beaune Vignes Franches, 1955." Young Jacques Mille, dressed in a casual, distinctly English manner, possessing an open, upright charm, and brought up to preside over a masterpiece of a hotel and restaurant, was a man whose advice could be relied on in all things.

"Then that's decided," Avigdor said comfortably. The rest of the meal could now revolve around the wine rather than have the wine chosen to accommodate the food—he preferred it that way.

The garden of Le Prieuré was filled, as always, with festive groups: celebrating families and tables of serious gourmets, seated at round tables on bright blue cushions under red sun umbrellas. Waiters and busboys bustled about under the vigilant eye of vivacious Marie-France Mille, Jacques's soft-voiced wife who embodied that idealized brunette Provençal beauty that the Italian poet, Petrarch, had immortalized in his Laura.

What would the ghost of pious Cardinal Arnaud de Via, nephew of Pope John XXII, who had given his palace to twelve canons in 1333 to turn into a priory, have made of the merry lunchtime scene? What would the ghost of Madame Blé, who had run such a quiet *pension*, have thought of the Olympic-sized swimming pool and the two tennis courts that lay on the other side of the old rose garden, out of sight of the diners? What exclamations would she have made if she could have seen the splendid addition that had recently been built and perfectly integrated into the old buildings, with its air-conditioned suites and luxurious baths? And what would the ghost of Teddy Lunel have thought if she could have looked down from the room in which she had decided her fate and seen her tall, lovely young daughter sitting there about to have lunch with Adrien Avigdor, a man Julien Mistral never mentioned to her during their short life together?

"I'm so happy to meet you, Monsieur Avigdor," Fauve said. "My grandmother has told me of you."

"So Maggy hasn't forgotten me?" asked Avigdor, pleased.

"Of course not. Magali has always told me absolutely everything about her past. She believes that it's important for children to know as much as possible about their parents and grandparents—particularly when they're illegitimate."

Fauve chose her words deliberately. She wanted Eric's parents to know from the beginning that no matter what was in their minds about her birth they didn't have to treat her with cautious tact.

"I wish you'd tell me about my father, when he was a young man," she went on. "I've only really known him for the last eight years. Perfect as my father is, he refuses to reminisce. But you gave him his first show so you must have known him for—oh, more than forty years! What was he like then?" The most lively curiosity was fervent on her face.

Mistral as a young man? Quickly Avigdor searched for a pleasant memory. He could hardly tell this devoted daughter that her father had always been an accursed, bad-tempered, arrogant, selfish man. A man who had sent more than one Jew to his death. But he must find something to say.

"Well, now let me see . . . it's hard to describe him exactly. He was always impressive, always the most noticeable person in any room." He paused, searched a second and then found inspiration. "What I'll never forget, no never, is that very first time I met him. Kate Browning, that is to say your stepmother of course, brought me to your father's little studio in Montparnasse where he was living with your grandmother—why, I can still see Maggy walking out of the kitchen in her bare feet with the wine and the glasses—it's amazing how vividly I remember her, but, of course, she was so magnificently beautiful, such a superb girl and not much older than you are now, Fauve . . . just eighteen I think, and so much in love, so loyal . . ."

"Loyal," Fauve echoed in a small voice.

"But, of course loyal, that above all. I admired her a great deal, you know, supporting your father by her modeling before he began to sell—but, naturally when a woman is truly in love she will make any sacrifice, is that not so? Ah, they were a striking couple, both so tall, both with red hair, his so dark, hers so bright, they were the legend of the *quartier* . . . ah, yes, Julien Mistral and Maggy, *La Rouquinne*—they must have been together for quite a while before he met Kate. By the way, how is Kate now? I've totally lost track of her."

"She's . . . fine," Fauve said out of a confusion so deep that she spoke vaguely.

"Her health is good?" Avigdor asked.

"Perfect, as far as I know," Fauve said, forcing herself to smile politely. Adrien Avigdor spoke a moment longer before the arrival of the Dover sole turned the conversation to food but Fauve heard nothing more.

Her father and *her grandmother? They* had loved? *They* had lived together? But it had been her *mother* and her father who had loved, who had lived together! A wave of troubled confusion so strong and complicated that it prevented her from moving swept over her and only the anxious pressure of Eric's hand on hers under the tablecloth brought her back and enabled her to pick up her fork.

With a few nostalgic, well-meant words Adrien Avigdor had taken the design she had made to explain her own life and changed it forever, as irrevocably as someone giving a twist to a pattern in a kaleidoscope. The familiar shapes were lost, destroyed. Why did you never tell me *this*, Magali? I knew only that you posed for my father, nothing more. *What kind of man is he?* What really happened between you? What can I trust now of anything you've ever told me?

"Is your sole not good, Fauve?" Beth Avigdor asked gently. She would have kicked her husband soundly if she had had any warning that he was going to ramble on in that fatuous way, but to be fair, Fauve had brought it on herself, when she proclaimed that her grandmother had told her "absolutely everything"—did any parent or grandparent ever tell the young "everything"? This would have had to be the first instance in recorded history. For whatever reason, the girl was clearly lost in her own thoughts. "Fauve," she repeated, "is the fish not good?"

"Oh! No, it's excellent, thank you, Madame Avigdor."

"Fauve, I promise, no more architecture for twenty-four hours,"

Eric said contritely. "Two days? . . . a week? Whatever you say. We'll do whatever you like this afternoon."

"Let's go to the Pont du Gard," said Fauve, giving him a resolute smile.

"You're crazy—you look knocked out."

"I'm perfectly fine, and I'm panting to truly understand the Romans."

"Eric has this notion that you can't comprehend a civilization until you understand how they feel about water," Adrien Avigdor grumbled. "Why about water and not about wine? I ask you that. Ah ha! No one can give me an answer. They never can."

"You could probably get one from a Talmudic scholar," Fauve suggested, "if you really want to know."

"That's not the sort of thing they discuss in the Bible," Eric protested.

"The Bible?" Fauve laughed. "What has the Bible to do with dozens and dozens of books of debates and commentaries on the Torah, the Five Books of Moses?"

"Dozens and dozens of what?" Eric said, bewildered.

"Oh, stop kidding me. Monsieur Avigdor, there are bound to be at least two opinions in the Talmud, or maybe even a dozen, so you wouldn't ever really get an answer, but at least they'd give you a good argument. At least that's what Rabbi Taradash would have said, according to my grandmother."

Avigdor's jaw dropped in astonishment.

"Drink some wine, darling," Beth Avigdor said hastily to her husband. In her opinion it was a perfectly reasonable suggestion; old-fashioned, unexpected and quaint coming from such a young girl, but certainly not a reason for such gaping amazement. Mistral's daughter or not, wasn't Lunel a Jewish name, and a fine old one at that? What had come over the man?

By the time she went to bed that night, Fauve had drawn a self-protective shell of rationalization around the revelations of Adrien Avigdor. She no longer felt betrayed by her grandmother. Now that she could think over what he'd said without the element of surprise, it made perfect sense that Magali had not told her the whole story, had kept some part secret. When she was younger she simply wouldn't have been able to understand it. God knows, the family

343

history of the Lunel women and all those star-crossed lovers of theirs was complicated enough. It was really rather romantic—love across two generations—she thought sleepily, but somehow she thought that she wouldn't ask her father anything about Monsieur Avigdor's memories . . . she'd wait to question Magali about it when she got home. No one had hidden things from her . . . no one had betrayed her . . . she could trust them . . . everything was as it had always been . . . there was just one layer of mystery . . . unimportant . . . so far in the past . . . so long ago . . .

"Fauve, hurry up and finish your breakfast," Mistral said. "It's time for your painting lesson."

"I promised to spend the day with Eric," Fauve said. "He's taking me to the Roman Arena in Arles."

"I assume you're teasing. I've put aside that time for you every morning."

"No, I'm serious."

"But, Fauve, you have your whole life to spend in looking at Roman arenas—what are your priorities? With your talent you can't waste time sightseeing! It's simply not possible! How many days are there in the summer? Don't you know how much you still have to learn?"

"I know, Father. But I promised."

"Julien," said Kate, "aren't you being unreasonable? Why should Fauve want to spend the morning shut up in a studio with you when she can be out with such an irresistible young man? I know that at her age I certainly would have preferred to flirt than paint . . . don't be insensitive."

"Kate, this has nothing to do with you. Fauve, come along. When that boy shows up, Kate, tell him to wait until Fauve's through for the day. If he's interested, he'll still be here at noon."

"No, Father."

"No? What does that mean?"

"I'm not going to paint with you this summer—not at all. I can't anymore."

"What are you talking about?" Now Mistral was too astonished to be angry. "Can't? Can't what? You're not trying to say that you are *unable* to paint? How many times have I told you that you have a serious natural talent? What's this all about?"

"I've thought about it all winter." Fauve faltered at first but her voice steadied quickly. "Last summer, you remember, when I wanted to do some experimental work, you said that I'd been contaminated by all the vulgarity and chichi of the shows I'd seen in New York and we went back to painting figures and landscapes and still lifes—well, I wanted to tell you then that I couldn't keep on trying to paint like Mistral, that I wasn't Mistral and never would be Mistral and there was no reason for you to keep hoping that I could ever be anything like you—but I didn't dare. I promised myself that I'd have the courage to do it this summer . . . well, that's it, that's why I'm not coming to the studio with you."

"Fauve," Mistral said, struggling to keep calm, "you live in the center of a whirlpool of all the filth of the entire world of art, if you can dignify that money machine, that total anarchy that reigns in New York by calling it art at all. I can understand why you aren't completely able to avoid some infection. It's a kind of Broadway-Hollywood interior decorator's insanity, a bunch of talentless exhibitionists—but surely you don't take people seriously who make 'art' from fluorescent light tubes and modular shelving and Styrofoam and comic strips and things they find in garbage cans—Jesus Christ, Fauve, if you want to be amused by art go study Marcel Duchamp—at least he did it with style and he did everything first!"

"You simply don't understand what I'm trying to say. I don't want to do Pop or Op or Minimal—or any of the others—I don't want to do what anybody else is doing—and I *can't* do what you do—I don't want to paint at all!"

"You can't possibly not want to paint, Fauve. You *are* a painter, you have no choice." Mistral's voice was gentle, patient, as if he were speaking to an unexpectedly stubborn thoroughbred horse. "I've never asked you to imitate me, not that I'm aware of. I've simply tried to keep you from being swept away into a cesspool of so-called new ideas—they'll only distort and corrupt your natural gifts. You know what I've always said: that you can't fly until you've developed wings strong enough to lift you off the ground and into the heavens. You *must* have all the essential equipment— afterward you can do *anything*—why, even Picasso, worn out and obsessed by erotica as he is, can still draw like a thousand angels when he chooses to. He had to have the classic training *in order to leave it behind him*. I'm telling you only that you don't yet—don't quite yet—have all that necessary background, all those skills. Fauve, let's go on up to the studio. You do anything you like this

345

morning—no lessons—we'll just paint together quietly, no criticism, no suggestions, just paint."

"No, Father."

Mistral's lips tightened. He looked at Fauve and he saw something in her face that made him reflect for a second, and decide to meet her on her ground. "All right, then, if it's a Roman arena you feel you must visit this morning, go and have a good time. We'll talk more about this later, eh? It's not something we have to settle right now, after all."

The kitchen bell sounded. "That's Eric," Fauve said, jumping up from the table. "I'll be back for dinner . . . or if I'm not, I'll call." She kissed Mistral on his cheek. "See you later." She picked her shoulder bag off a chair and walked quickly out of the room.

"Well, Julien," Kate said, in her flat, uninflected way, "I must say I'm stunned. I had no idea that she resented your lessons so much—hasn't she any idea of the privilege it is to be taught by you?"

"Oh, don't talk rubbish, Kate. She's my daughter, and privilege has nothing to do with it. It's that New York world she lives in, all sense of values disappeared there long ago. It's the people she's permitted, God knows why, to associate with, that photographer, Falk, who's allowed to drag her to those disgusting new galleries, it's a contagion, it's a sickness . . ."

"Hasn't it occurred to you, Julien, that she may simply not be interested anymore? Why do you expect Fauve to be different from most other sixteen-year-old girls? They live and breathe horses or ice skating or ballet and then one day they discover a boy—like Avigdor's son—and they lose interest overnight in that one thing to which they've devoted years of their lives—it's a well-known phenomenon."

Kate stood up, shopping list in hand. Then, as if having a second thought, she continued. "After all, how many great women painters are there? How many times have you said that their energies go into childbearing? And how many children of famous parents manage to achieve anything important in the same field as their parents did, eh? Has there *ever* been a great—even a well-known—woman painter who was the daughter of an artist of your stature?" She put her hand on Mistral's shoulder. "Don't take it so hard . . . it was bound to happen sooner or later . . . young Avigdor just

346

provided the spark that made the mixture explode . . . and I must say I can certainly see why now that I've met him. What an extraordinarily good-looking young man! And how hospitable his parents were to Fauve yesterday . . . they seem to have been in quite a hurry to take her to the bosom of their family."

"What an absurd thing to say about one lunch," Mistral said, his face red with rage.

Kate made a philosophic face. "That's what happens with children," she said, watching Mistral carefully. "You spend your life worrying about them and doing everything you can for them and then, just when they get to their most interesting age, they dash off with the first person who comes along and leave you waving goodbye. Do I complain that Nadine practically never comes here? Since she married Phillipe they spend all their vacations in Sardinia or Marrakesh or wherever their friends are—it's all quite normal. You accepted it with Nadine—the same thing is happening with Fauve, my dear, that's all." She gave a shrug of resignation.

"It seems hard to believe that you used to be an intelligent woman, Kate." Mistral was so enraged that his voice lost all of its color. "Fauve and Nadine have nothing in common. Fauve is gifted, enormously gifted . . . she was born to paint. She's simply going through a moment of rebellion. Tomorrow or the next day she'll be back at work." He stood up and left the room without another word.

Kate sat down at the breakfast table alone, listening to the sounds of the countryside. A brief smile crossed her finely molded lips as she thought of the stricken look on Julien's face, at the fury she had watched him conceal from Fauve. Ah, Julien, she said to herself. Don't you know that this is only the beginning? You've just started to lose her. You . . . you who used to be an intelligent man?

"Why Cavaillon?" asked Eric as he drove the car. "I know that's where they grow the best melons in France, but I thought that we were set for Arles? Cavaillon is basically without architectural interest."

"Because a Roman arena will wait one more day but in Cavaillon there's something I want to see. Anyway, didn't you say I could do anything I wanted to yesterday? And didn't I go to that old aqueduct and listen to all your explanations?"

"And I thought you were really interested."

"I was, I was incredibly fascinated. Roman water systems have a mysterious allure all their own," Fauve drawled provokingly.

"I think you need to be kissed," Eric said sternly.

"Oh, no, I don't!" Fauve cried, alarmed.

"Oh, yes, you do." Eric turned the car into a little side road and stopped the motor. He reached across the seat and pulled Fauve toward him easily in spite of her attempts at resistance, but once she was securely pinned in his arms he didn't try to raise the chin that she held firmly tucked into her neck but instead he kissed the warm, silky top of her head. Slowly she relaxed and they sat pressed together listening to the sound of their breathing and communicating a wordless secret of which they each possessed a half. Long, sweet dreaming minutes went by and finally Fauve said, in a small, shy voice with her chin still lowered, "You may kiss me if that's what you want."

"Isn't it what you want?" Eric asked, smiling at her youth.

"If you have to ask . . ." Fauve raised her head and drew a finger across the indented twin pillows of his lower lip. With a groan he pressed his lips on hers, feeling a jolt in his soul as he received the innocence of her full-hearted kiss. "Oh!" she whispered in incandescent surprise. "Oh, *how nice!*" She opened her arms wide and laced them tightly around his neck. They clung together kissing each other over and over, each kiss complete in itself, not leading to anything except another kiss, each kiss a miniature cosmos in which they lost all sense of the existence of any other world. Utterly captured by the moment as she was, Fauve was aware that deep in her chest a new pulse had announced itself, beating for the first time, as if it were a drum heralding the birth of something that had been waiting within her, waiting for this particular man to kiss her.

Suddenly the little car began to rock from side to side. Fauve and Eric stiffened in alarm and looked around them. The windows of the car were blocked halfway up by fat, dusty gray shapes, a noisy, indifferent succession of strong, mindless bodies that buffeted the Renault as if it were an inconvenient bush.

"I didn't even hear the sheep coming," Fauve said in amazement.

"Neither did I . . . oh, Fauve . . . my darling Fauve . . . oh, damn, here come the shepherds—look in the rear-view mirror." Eric moved away from her to a respectable distance.

"Shepherds?" Fauve scoffed breathlessly, taking refuge from her new emotion in teasing. "They're used to nature in all its manifestations. Come back here at once!"

Cavaillon, some fifteen kilometers southwest of Félice, in the direction of Avignon, is a calm prosperous market town of eighteen thousand inhabitants. Fauve and Eric sat outside the café in which they'd had lunch, holding hands silently, looking on to a drowsy, unimportant square. Finally Eric said, "I truly don't care that there's nothing to see in Cavaillon, though I do still wonder what we're doing here."

"We're waiting for the guide to show up."

"The guide? There's nothing here to merit a guided tour—just us and the waiter—even the shops are closed till four."

"Wait," Fauve said in a superior voice.

"Whatever you say, shepherd's delight."

"We did rather make their day, don't you agree?"

"I didn't think to ask, but possibly they've seen people kissing before."

"Oh, come on, Eric, I see him!" Fauve jumped up and started to cross the square toward a flight of steps in front of an unremarkable three-story building where a young man in his shirt sleeves had just stationed himself. Eric followed her, shaking his head in bewilderment.

As they approached the young man, people seemed to spring out around the corner of every street leading to the square, popping from parked automobiles and pouring from doorways, almost out of the very ground itself. By the time they had reached the base of the staircase they were part of a group of some twenty-five people, all of whom, to Eric's amazed eyes, seemed to know perfectly well where they were heading. He tried to keep as close to Fauve as possible but it was difficult since everyone was eagerly trying to climb the narrow staircase at the same time. At the top there was a balcony and a tall pair of handsomely carved, closed wooden doors set into a massive stone archway.

"What . . . ?" Eric began, but Fauve motioned him to be silent. The crowd finally arranged itself in place around the guide and waited in an expectant silence. The young man flung open the doors with a certain grave ceremony.

"Welcome to the Synagogue of Cavaillon," he said.

"I don't believe it!" Eric muttered to her.

349

"I figured you wouldn't—yesterday when you got the Talmud mixed up with the Bible," Fauve said, delighted with her surprise. "I discovered this when I was reading the green Michelin guide to Provence last winter, they've got it listed under 'Other Curiosities' in Cavaillon along with the old cathedral and the archeological museum. I'd planned to come here when I got back."

"Well, what are we supposed to do now?" Eric asked.

"Visit it, of course. Don't you want to?"

"Well, sure . . . I guess . . . why not?"

"You amaze me, you really do. I mean, you *are* Jewish, aren't you?"

"Naturally—my parents are, so I am—but what does that have to do with it? They aren't religious at all, neither of them, and I've never even been to a service—oh, wait, once a cousin got married, when I was a little kid, and they took me to the wedding in Paris, but I hardly remember it. To me being Jewish doesn't have a connection with going to a synagogue unless you feel like it, and I've never had the urge. Anyway, why are you so interested? Is it some kind of hobby?"

"Yesterday, your father was talking about my grandmother, Magali, remember? She's Jewish, born in France, and *her* daughter, my mother, was half-Jewish and half-Irish Catholic. My father is French Catholic so that makes me one-quarter Jewish—more than enough to fascinate me because it's part of my history, my *personal* history, and it's the *only* part I have any information about. My father doesn't know a thing about his grandparents—he frankly doesn't care and he's not even sure if they're originally from Provence in spite of his name. All I know about the other side of the family is that my mother's father was an American named Kilkullen—that and two dollars will buy you a shot of Irish whiskey on St. Patrick's Day. I'm curious enough to want to visit the synagogue, got it?"

"Anything you say, little nut. I just can't believe all these tourists—they've got to be speaking fifteen foreign languages—where did they all come from?"

"Fifteen foreign countries. This is a place of pilgrimage, Eric. What's more, it's even got a water system inside somewhere according to the Michelin, even if it's not a Roman aqueduct."

"What is it?"

350

"A ritual bath," Fauve pronounced, her eyes dancing with mischief.

"Oh, no! That's where I draw the line."

"It's only for women, you ignorant idiot, and anyway this synagogue is a monument, it isn't used for anything anymore. Look, the guide has a book for sale. Let's buy one so we can look around by ourselves without following this crowd. I hate being trapped in a herd."

Eric bought the entrance tickets and paid for a thin book by André Dumoulin, conservator of the museums and monuments of Cavaillon. It contained a short history of the Jewish community of Cavaillon, as well as photographs and descriptions of the synagogue.

Fauve and Eric left the group of tourists all listening intently to the guide, and wandered alone into the central part of the temple. Neither of them had any idea of what to expect and they stopped abruptly after they crossed the threshold, taken utterly by surprise. They found themselves in an almost empty room that nevertheless gave an immediate impression of the most gracious harmony of spirit. It could have been a perfect small salon from some abandoned palace built in the style and at the time of Versailles. The synagogue had been constructed in 1774, on the site of an older temple that dated back to 1499, and the architect and craftsmen of Cavaillon who had worked on its interior had been trained in the unsurpassably delicate formality of Louis XV.

The walls of the tall, balconied room were painted a soft white and entirely paneled. Each panel was adorned with wood that had been carved and gilded in motifs of roses, garlands of palm leaves, baskets of flowers, seashells and musical instruments—all the fantasies and fancies so dear to the taste of the Marquise de Pompadour. A number of chandeliers hung from the high ceiling, some of them dripping fragile pendants of old rock crystal, while others, more solid, were made of well-polished copper, all carrying gay clusters of tall yellow candles. A pale golden, muted light drifted in from high windows.

Both Fauve and Eric found themselves irresistibly drawn forward to stand before a railing, some four feet tall, made of intricately detailed wrought iron. It stood protectively around a pair of superbly carved and decorated doors that were the unquestioned focus of the entire temple. The doors, which looked as if they must open into a noble space, were flanked by tall Corinthian columns supporting an elaborate series of pediments crowned by a basket from which burst a profusion of sprays of roses.

Fauve, searching in the guidebook, realized that they were the doors behind which the scrolls of the Torah, the Hebrew Bible, had been kept when the temple had still functioned as a house of worship. She stood in awe, trying to imagine what she would see if she were to be allowed to penetrate the enclosure, to open the closed doors of the tabernacle, but she failed. It was beyond her.

Eric heard her sigh wistfully and pulled her gently away, leading her to the opposite side of the gemlike temple where they climbed one of the two semicircular staircases to the paneled, garlanded balcony that stretched the entire width of the room.

Fauve leaned carefully on the balustrade, as delicately fashioned as lace, and thought that from this vantage point the temple looked like a ballroom in which she could imagine ladies in powdered hair and men in brocaded vests dancing. But the guidebook, again consulted, informed her that she was standing on what had been the rostrum of whoever conducted the service. Her vision of dancers faded as she looked down and tried to imagine the sumptuous little temple filled with benches, and the benches crowded by people dressed as they used to be dressed throughout Provence, in costumes that were now only worn by folksingers performing for festivals.

The past seemed close, as if it were lying just behind a curtain of light; so powerful, so palpable was the atmosphere of the lovely deserted place that it was as impossible to realize that it was empty as it was to know what it had truly been like when it had been in use. Like all abandoned holy places, in which once the human soul has poured out its deepest emotions, it hummed with a complex energy and silenced the visitor.

As the horde of other visitors started to enter the main part of the synagogue, Fauve and Eric hastily descended the staircase and penetrated to the basement of the building, where, in the former bakery of the Jewish community, the city of Cavaillon and the Beaux-Arts had installed a small museum.

There, again alone, they found themselves in a long, low-ceilinged room with a stone floor. Two glass cases, full of photographs and documents, filled the center of the room and on both walls stood illuminated cabinets that contained all manner of ceremonial objects used in the performance of the service. It even contained the tabernacle doors of the temple of 1499, Renaissance in style, adorned with a bas-relief of vases, holding branches of fruit and flowers and painted with the Hebrew letters of the tablets Moses brought down from Sinai. Fauve was contemplating these doors that had been new almost five hundred years before, trying to pierce the veil of time, when Eric pulled her away to another of the cabinets.

"Look!" he said excitedly. "Here's a Roman oil lamp from the first century before Christ. See the two menorahs on its base? It says here in the book that it's one of the oldest representations of the menorah ever found on French soil—it's a hundred years *older* than the Pont du Gard."

Fauve found herself abruptly appalled at the sight of the humble little object. "Oh, Eric, think of the earth under which it must have been found—so *many* feet of earth—too much history—too many years ago—how many generations are there in two thousand years, how many births and deaths? I can't bear to think about it—I'm having trouble going back two hundred years, much less two thousand." She turned away to the cases with relief. Photographs, no matter how old, were somehow of today.

She walked slowly up and down, almost weary, gazing with diminishing interest at old letters and proclamations. Suddenly she stood transfixed before a photograph, taken in 1913, of a dignified, handsome old gentleman with a trim white mustache, a double-breasted black suit and a black hat with an upturned brim of a typically Provençal style. He stood to one side of the railing that encircled the doors of the tabernacle in the synagogue above them and, standing on the other side, was a dark-eyed, stately woman in a long, tiny-waisted black dress with a wisp of veiling on her gray hair. "Eric," she cried, "come and look at this. Look, just look! It says that they were two of the last representatives of the Jewish community in Cavaillon."

"They're certainly very impressive," Eric said, puzzled by her emotion.

"Their names! Monsieur and Madame Achille *Astruc*—Astruc, my great-grandfather's name! Oh Eric, I haven't told you about him—David Astruc was Magali's father—these people might have been relatives of mine! They were old when Magali was a little girl—they could have been cousins, or great-aunt and uncle or—oh, I don't know . . . something—" Fauve had tears in her eyes as she pored over the photograph of the fine, serene old people. Eric stood quietly, rocking her gently with his arms clasped around her waist as she studied the picture, lost in speculation and wonder.

It was minutes before the other tourists started to trickle into the museum.

"I think we've had the best of it," Eric whispered to her and Fauve quickly agreed, casting one last glance at the photograph before she followed him up the stairs and outside.

"I need a Coke . . . don't you?" Eric asked.

"Something cold with a lot of sugar in it," Fauve agreed, and they returned to the café and almost collapsed at a table, with that peculiar, drained, but high-hearted exhaustion known only to sightseers who have somehow been allowed to travel in time and not been forced to merely observe.

Eric picked up the guidebook and riffled through its pages with curiosity. "I wonder how many Jews lived in Cavaillon—let's see . . . it says here that it was always a small number, never more than three hundred people at the most. This is interesting, Fauve, the municipal archives mention that there was a rabbi in Cavaillon as early as the eleventh century but when the Revolution came in 1790 the Jews began to leave Provence and spread out all over France and after 1793 there isn't even a *trace* of community activity. Look, here's a list of the names of the last members of the community—it's from the archives of Cavaillon and they've broken the names into groups to show their origins."

Fauve took the book. "There are more French names than any other," she said, "all taking their names from the various localities they came from . . . Carcassonne, Cavaillon, of course, and Digne, and Monteux . . . all place-names . . . and . . . and Lunel."

"Lunel?" he echoed.

"Lunel! Then there must be a *place* called Lunel! I never knew that! It never even occurred to me that it might be a place-name. Oh, Eric, we *have* to be able to find it on the map if it still exists!

Eric, when can we go looking for Lunel?" Her fatigue forgotten, Fauve looked as if she were ready to set out on the search at once. Eric smiled at the sight of her eager, open-hearted impatient beauty.

"It's got to be somewhere, Fauve, and I'll dig it up for you . . . places just don't disappear. But not today." He took the guidebook away from her and looked at the page from which she'd been reading.

"There are some other names with a Hebrew origin like Cohen and Jehuda and a few from the Latin—that's where your Astruc comes from, darling, from *astrum* meaning star. The last group are foreign, people from Cavaillon who came here from other countries . . . Lisbonne and Lubin . . . a Pole . . . and . . ."

"And . . ." Fauve asked, puzzled at his stopping.

"Damn *time!* It takes everything with it," he muttered. People named Astruc and Lunel had *belonged* to that temple he had just visited as if it were only a larger than ordinary curiosity from another civilization. The past, tantalizing, elusive, always just beyond reach, had rapped him smartly on his shoulder, and he shivered in wonder. If he knew enough, if there were documents—which there weren't—why couldn't he trace Fauve's family back before the Romans had built the Pont du Gard? Why had so much knowledge been lost? How had it come to be forgotten?

"Ah, don't be upset," Fauve said, understanding his emotion. "It just isn't fair, not being able to know, it's so frustrating . . . Eric, we're both so miserably uninformed and ignorant, aren't we? We're a disgrace."

"We certainly are."

"But imagine . . ." Fauve continued, her eyes bigger than ever with speculation, "just imagine . . . Lunels and Astrucs and Lubins and Carcassonnes all going to temple together . . . knowing each other . . . their families living right here for hundreds and hundreds of years . . . maybe one of them was that rabbi in the eleventh century—I can almost see them, can't you?"

Eric was silent, looking at her lovely, thoughtful face, so animated by the visions she saw. He found himself swooping back from the past and totally, marvelously alive in the present.

"It's impossible to see anyone but you."

"Eric," Fauve said chidingly. "What a lack of imagination."

"Because I'm in love with you."

"What?"

"I'm in love with you. Do you love me? Do you, my darling?"

"I don't know . . . I've never been in love before," she murmured.

"Look at me," he commanded. Slowly she raised her lids and what he saw in her eyes was so unmistakable that he almost cried out in joy.

"But I didn't *intend* to fall in love!" Fauve protested.

"It's too late now," he said triumphantly.

25

The writer who complains of the loneliness of his work, the artist who speaks ruefully of the solitude of his studio, the composer who announces that he is condemned to shut himself away to write music in a secluded room all share one trait: they lie. Were they to admit the unfashionable truth they would have to say that there are few places less lonely than that privileged space in which the mind is free to concentrate on its work, no privacy more jealously guarded from intrusion.

The vast studio in which Julien Mistral worked at *La Tourrello* had been his only true home for forty years. As he opened the doors he breathed in deeply, relishing the complex aroma composed by the smell of the poppy-seed oil-based paints, the prepared canvases, the seasoned pine used as stretchers, the agreeably rancid paint-smeared rags that lay about, all mixed into a pungent necromantic brew. Mistral found himself greeted by a population of images that represented everything he had ever cared about. In this studio he had expended his heroic resources. Brush stroke by brush stroke he had distilled his life itself and the release of this essence of each hour's work had left an imprint on the very air. The paintings that he had sold over the years seemed to him to be as constant in their presence as those he had kept for himself, as if they had refused to leave. He had never experienced a minute's loneliness in his densely peopled studio.

What then, Mistral asked himself savagely, was the feeling that plucked so insistently at his consciousness that he found himself looking blankly at a half-finished canvas for an hour at a time? What was this restlessness, this irritation, this sense of something not accomplished, something incomplete?

It was a month before he was willing to admit to himself that it was Fauve's absence, a month before he reached a point at which he could no longer tell himself that tomorrow she would be back, a month before he was able to isolate and define the realization that in the course of the past eight years the painting lessons he gave her every morning during her summer stay with him had become essential to him.

He needed her.

After Teddy's death Julien Mistral had resolved never to need another human being. He had given Fauve up without a moment's hesitation, he had stayed away from her for eight years because he was afraid that she would remind him of Teddy. When he saw no resemblance to her mother in her face, he had been relieved; no man could love twice as he had loved Teddy, and survive. He could not afford to give another such hostage to fortune. The nine months of the year that Fauve spent in New York passed without too much pain, although much too slowly, in the certain knowledge that every June she would come home to him, and they would be together all summer long.

Never would he have believed that she could desert him. There had been no sign, on the last trip down from Paris, only five weeks before, of any basic change in her. A new maturity, yes certainly, and a hint of dissatisfaction with her own work, now that he thought about it, but what true artist was ever satisfied? No, it had nothing to do with his disapproval of her ventures into Abstraction . . . surely Fauve must know that if she had really insisted on it she was free to paint with a broom instead of a brush, free to paint archery targets or jigsaw puzzles, free to make mudpies and plaster casts. All that was just a convenient excuse. The reason she'd left him was Eric Avigdor. Fauve had been his daughter until the night she met that boy.

It was so simple an explanation, and so obvious that Mistral didn't understand how he had failed to see it sooner. Kate had been right, entirely right—perhaps if she had said nothing he would have understood immediately, but whenever Fauve was concerned, he discounted any opinion Kate had.

Where, after all, had Fauve been all these past days? Arles, she said, and Cavaillon and Nîmes and Orange, Carpentras and Tarascon and St. Rémy and Aix-en-Provence. Oh, how banally touristic! What was her conversation about on those few evenings that she favored them with her company at dinner? An infuriating mixture of architectural wonders—not one of which Mistral thought was worth looking at as much as the sight of a single cherry tree in bloom—and the discoveries she was making, little by little, of that most confusing of all subjects, the history of the Jews of Provence.

Did she think that he gave a damn for one word of it? He had nothing against Jews, they simply didn't interest him, any more than Mohammedans or Hindus. Why was she fascinated by a past that had nothing to do with her, so little relevance to the modern world? Did she have any idea how farfetched the topic was?

Maggy, who had, after all, been Jewish, had never given it a thought as far as he could remember, and Teddy cared only for the present they had lived in together, and yet here was his own daughter, poking about in synagogues, in Avignon, in Aix, in Carpentras. Synagogues!

Only last night, irritated beyond endurance, he had asked her why, since she was going through a religious phase, and since three out of four of her grandparents had been Catholics, why didn't she visit cathedrals? "Cathedrals are just too accessible," she'd said, maddeningly pleased with herself. "They're everywhere, there isn't a town without one or two—they're old, but without mystery."

Mistral put down his palette and gave up any attempt to continue work. He paced the floor of his studio in a rising panic. It was almost mid-July. In six more weeks, Fauve's summer visit would be over and she was on the verge of drifting away from him. When she came back next year she'd be seventeen—no longer a child—and he would be seventy. Seventy—bah! It was just a number. He had more energy, more curiosity than he'd had when he was fifty.

It was the behavior of his teenaged daughter that bothered him, not the weight of his years. Exposed to the attention of the first young man who'd noticed her, she had turned flighty, giddy and filled with overblown, momentary enthusiasms. She needed to be brought down to earth, that was all.

During each of the past summers Fauve had posed for a portrait, but this year she'd been out gadding so much that he hadn't had a chance to claim her time. Everything they had been accustomed to do together—the painting lessons and the posing, the visits to the café in Félice, had been changed by the entrance of that abominable boy into Fauve's life.

Mistral took down the canvas on his easel and propped it carelessly against the wall. Moving as eagerly as a young man going to a rendezvous with a woman he loved, he went to the corner where his blank canvases were stacked and picked out the largest one he could find. Yes! A full-length picture, an ode, a hymn to Fauve Lunel and her miniskirt—she'd like that.

"I've found out why Avigdor means 'the judge,' " Eric said to Fauve. "It seems that in the Book of Chronicles the name is used twice and later interpretation says that it's one of the names of Moses. I told my father and he said not to get too exalted about it— there weren't any lawgivers in the family, he informed me, but only antique dealers until he came along, and now a budding architect."

"It's marvelous!" Fauve said proudly. The two of them were in a secondhand bookshop in Avignon, looking for volumes that might lead them somewhere in their quest for historical knowledge. So far they had had little real luck, finding only some minor references in books, but Eric was undiscouraged. "How did you find out?"

"I made a phone call. It was a wild guess but I knew that there had to be a rabbi in a big city like Marseilles so I just looked him up in the phone book, called him and asked. He said to call back in two days—give him time to look it up—and when I did, he told me. He didn't even sound surprised at the request. Maybe he gets a lot of phone calls like that."

"Hmmm . . . probably," she said, losing interest.

"Fauve, what's wrong?"

"It's my father."

"What about him? Look, I know he doesn't like me. Nobody could accuse Julien Mistral of being much of an actor. He hovers just at the very outer limits of tolerance when I come to pick you up, but I feel that as long as he allows me in the door, that's enough."

"No, it's not about you." Fauve sat down on the staircase that led to the upper floor of the bookshop, and folded her arms around her long legs. She was wearing a sleeveless, frilled, batiste camisole with a tiny peplum. It laced up in front like the underwear of an actress in an old Western movie and it was the latest rage in all the boutiques in Midi. Her sheaves of hair, bronze now in the watery light of the staircase, fell in heavy waves over her breasts. If she'd worn a petticoat instead of blue jeans she would have seemed like a Victorian maiden getting ready for bed. There was a richness of suggestion in her beauty, Eric thought as he looked at her, that would bring out the poet in the most mundane of men.

"He's always painted a picture of me every summer," Fauve went on. "He wants me to pose for him, starting tomorrow. I can't refuse, Eric, it's impossible, he'd be too hurt. It's a tradition with us. I feel guilty enough about not letting him give me painting lessons. He hasn't said another word about them, but when I see him at breakfast I know it's on his mind and he's just controlling himself. Oh, Lord . . ."

"I think it's remarkable that you've had the strength of mind to keep on resisting," Eric said.

"I have to," Fauve said simply. "It's a question of self-preservation. Father doesn't consciously understand that he *does* want me to imitate him. It's implicit in everything he shows me, everything he tells me, although he'd deny it and believe he was speaking the truth. You see, my father thinks that his way is the *only* way . . . he hasn't a good word to say for another living painter . . . the only ones he admires are dead. But his work comes from him, it comes out of whatever is inside of him, and that's not *teachable*."

"Then all these years of lessons . . ." Eric asked.

"Oh, they haven't been wasted—I do have technical ability—I'm not going to be modest about that—but so do a lot of other painters. If I have anything more I'll only know it when I start to work in my own style and I'll never find that style if I keep learning from him."

"Why did you wait so long to decide?"

"Until last year I was happy to paint 'little' Mistrals. I go to an art school in New York and the teachers are afraid to really criticize me because of who I am and because I've been doing work in his manner—they're so knocked out by who *he* is that I can't get an honest word out of them. It took me a long time to figure it out—I was dumb, I guess."

"Not dumb, darling, just young," Eric said.

"Father's always praised me too much," Fauve added thoughtfully. "I don't know if I'm ever going to be really good but I know damn well I can't be as good as he says I am. He's probably only

361

doing it to encourage me, but it works in the opposite way—since I know my work isn't worth such extravagant praise, I wonder—is it worth any praise at all? If I truly couldn't paint he'd say so, but I'm in an in-between position. I *can* paint, like a very much lesser Mistral, and I don't want that! If I'm ever to do anything of my own it would be fatal to study with him anymore."

"Couldn't you tell him all this and make him understand?"

"I don't think I could get more than halfway through the first sentence. You've never heard him argue, or rather pontificate. And even if he heard me out and managed to understand what I was saying, working there in that studio isn't possible. It casts such a spell that you can't imagine seeing things in any other way than his. It overwhelms my own imagination, such as it is. But I do have to pose for him, there's no way out."

Eric sat down at her feet. "What does that mean as far as time is concerned?"

"He wanted to work for a few hours in the morning and a few after lunch but I said that I could only sit for him in the mornings. He said that we had only six weeks left, that mornings wouldn't be enough, but I insisted. I feel torn in two, Eric. I've never felt disloyal before, and now I feel disloyal to both of you."

"Not so. You're being loyal to both of us. Darling, darling Fauve, don't torment yourself. I know how much of your time I've been taking and I can't blame your father. We still have the afternoons and evenings. Look, I was saving this for later but you need to be cheered up." Eric took out an old, leather-bound book from his knapsack and gave it to Fauve.

"Believe it or not my mother gave it to me just yesterday. She finally remembered that she had it put away somewhere—it was published in 1934 and when my grandmother died, it was in her house. Apparently no one in the family ever bothered to read it."

"*Histoire des Juifs d'Avignon et du Comtat Venaissin* by Armand Mossé." Fauve read the title of the book in a voice that rose in excitement. "That's it! That's got to have it all! The Comtat includes all the countryside around here. Oh, how terrific! Have you started it yet?"

"No, I thought we'd read it together, but now that we don't have as much time, you take it and read it whenever you get a chance. Maybe you can read while you're posing."

"Not with my father, I don't—no distractions, no eye movements, I hardly dare swallow." Fauve leaned down and took the book in her arms and cradled it against her breasts. "I'll take good care of it, I promise. I wonder how far back it goes?"

"I took a look at the first page and apparently Jews were being exiled from Rome and moving to France when Tiberius was Emperor—somewhere about twenty years after Christ—so if it's antiquity you're looking for, it's there."

"Oh—I had expected something a little more contemporary."

"A Jewish *Gone With the Wind?*"

"Well—why not, after all?"

Fauve stood by the model stand in the shocking pink minidress she had worn the night she met Eric at Uzès. Since she couldn't be with him while she was posing, at least she could wear what she'd had on the first time she'd seen him. She felt a need to be in some sort of contact with him at every moment of the day.

Now that she had resigned herself to the morning hours of posing, she found that they were welcome in a way she hadn't expected. They gave her time to really think about Eric that she hadn't had before. They'd spent almost every day of the summer together and when she came home she was too muddled with the slow, sweet momentum of his kisses to have any rational thoughts except an almost vertiginous astonishment that such happiness could exist. What a world of wonders in which an Eric could be alive, wandering around loose just as if he were like other people, a world in which he would *love* her. The amazement of it was so great that it was undecipherable, it changed everything, it turned all her past years into a far-off country that she had sailed away from without a backward glance.

She thought of the firm symmetry of his skull under her fingers when she ran her hands through that brown hair that was so clean and so thick that it resisted her fingers. She could actually feel the solid roundness of the bone in the tips of her fingers. She stood in her ballet slippers, her feet at right angles to each other, her weight resting on one leg, the other one slightly bent, her hands turned outward and her arms hanging loosely behind her back. It was a pose that Mistral had chosen as a tribute to Degas, saying that her pink skirt was shorter than any tutu and might even have brought a smile to the mouth of that vile-tempered, great old man.

To Fauve, posing patiently, the image of a small triangular scar on Eric's face, just below his right eye, the souvenir of a fall when he was five, was more real to her than the sound of Mistral's footsteps as he stepped backward from the easel.

On her lips she could feel how smooth the warm skin was when she kissed Eric at the edge of his ear and then, lowering her lips a quarter-inch at a time, kissed him lightly and softly down the side of his closely shaven cheek and along his jaw and finally, slowly, reached her lips up to his longing mouth.

He'd said that she had the softest lips in the world but Fauve told him that she couldn't make any similar comparisons because none of the other men she'd kissed in her life had had memorable lips. She smiled, remembering how he'd drawn back when she said that and demanded to know just how many men she *had* kissed before. A few, she'd answered, only a few, just a few, a miserable, pathetic few, knowing that nothing could be more calculated to infuriate him. She was unable to keep from making him jealous, because he was four years older than she was and, of course, she understood, although he never referred to it, that he must be experienced and she was not.

He was so infernally protective of her sixteen years, Fauve thought, frowning, unaware that Mistral was noticing every change of expression on her face. She wished fiercely now that she had lied to Eric when he'd asked her age. If only she'd said she was eighteen! With her height she could have made him believe it, especially since he had no way to compare her to an American eighteen and guess the truth. But he knew she was just barely out of her fifteenth year and he had a gallant, idealistic determination not to take advantage of her.

Last night they'd had an early dinner at a good, inexpensive little Italian restaurant called La Mamma in Villeneuve-les-Avignon, and afterward they had gone exploring in the garden of Le Prieuré, not the formal rose garden bordered by santolina and ancient urns trailing geraniums, but the hidden cutting garden, in which grew the fresh flowers that were placed in the guest rooms every day.

Because all the personnel of the hotel were concentrated on the busy arrival of the evening's guests for the restaurant, they'd been able to duck unseen through the garage and the boiler room of the hotel and emerge into the walled cutting garden, a paradise of blooms all bordered by those little hollow, elfin, red objects called Chinese lanterns.

They had wandered there—arms laced tightly around each other's waist, and finally come to rest leaning up against an old, overgrown, unpruned pear tree that stood in the far reaches of the garden.

Fauve and Eric were entirely alone and protected from sight by the branches of the tree and Fauve had flung herself on Eric, thrusting herself against him and rubbing up and down. She didn't care if she was awkward or clumsy or aggressive, whatever she didn't know about making love she could learn, she *would* learn, but he pushed her away, first gently and then with determination, holding her at arm's length.

No, he'd said, it was clearly impossible and she had to realize it herself. If he let her go on like that it must lead further and then even further and then they wouldn't be able to stop, wouldn't want to stop, didn't she understand? She was too young, it wouldn't be right, wouldn't be fair . . . Fauve sighed deeply, wondering if he was right, suspecting that perhaps he was, but oh, how she wanted him.

"Fauve! I can't work if you're going to make one grimace after another! Now will you try to keep your face quiet for a minute or shall we stop?"

Fauve blew her hair off her forehead with an exaggerated moue. "I'm not making a grimace, I'm thinking. Do you want to paint a picture of a mindless doll or a thinking woman?"

"Ha! You make a point, even if it's a bit premature. All right, let's take a break."

Fauve stepped out of her pose and uncoiled her body like a long piece of rope and stretched every joint. Then she walked over to the planter's chair in the corner of the studio and sat down, picking up the old book Eric had given her, and, within a few seconds, she was engrossed.

Mistral knew far too much about the book. When they had started on the painting she had brought it with her and, during every break, she had returned to it, often pausing to read bits and pieces of it out loud to him. Finally, exasperated, he had told her that it broke his concentration to listen to her, that it was bad enough for a painter to have to give the model a rest every so often without being forced to absorb a history lesson in addition.

"Well," she'd said mildly, "all right, but this is incredible stuff. I'll tell you about it later," and she'd gone back to her reading. Only last year, whenever it was time for her break, they'd talked about their painting, or she'd amused him with stories about those two friends of hers, Pomme and Épinette, who were, impossible though it seemed, the granddaughters of two of the members of his original boules team from the café in the village.

Sometimes, he remembered bitterly, they'd go to sit in the sun just outside the studio and discuss the status of the Union Sportif of Félice, the feisty soccer team that was engaged in a protracted and perpetual struggle with the other soccer teams of the neighboring villages. Often, in those precious minutes, he'd explained to her why art was the only thing worth doing in a world of chaos, the only thing that had any possibility of enduring. History, he had told her, was merely stories of what people think happened or want you to believe happened. History can't be trusted.

And now, there she was, obliviously plunged into history as if it were a revelation of an immutable truth. What would he give to have his daughter back again, to have the Fauve of last year in the place of this self-described "thinking woman"? Almost anything, Mistral thought, almost anything, but what was there that he had to give that a girl of sixteen could want?

"Ready to continue?" he asked.

"Oh . . . sure. But, Father, would you mind terribly if we stopped a half-hour early today? Eric's parents are spending a few days in Aix for the music festival and they've invited us down to lunch at the Vendôme—it's an hour-and-a-half trip and I don't want to be late. Is that all right, just for today?"

What could he say? Could he insist that she stay? That she make the time up tomorrow? This wasn't the first time the sitting had been cut short for one reason or another. To be fair, he told himself frowningly, it wasn't the first time he'd realized that in order to pose for him she was giving up some excursion that required an early start and a late return. When he painted her during all those other summers, their time together had been filled with a deep communion, the melody of which he only fully appreciated now that it had disappeared, to be replaced by duty and an abstracted fondness.

"Of course, Fauve, go ahead. We can stop now if you like."

"Oh, Father! You're a darling! Thank you!" Released, she gave him a quick hug and bounded out of the studio not even thinking to conceal her sense of relief.

Yet, he noticed, his jaw set in a grim, tight anger, a line of pain, and hurt pride, she hadn't forgotten to take that miserable book with her.

If style is achieved when your outer surface corresponds perfectly with your real personality, when you look like what you are, then Nadine was ultimately stylish, Fauve reflected as she joined her father, her stepmother and her half-sister for a rare family dinner. Nadine had just arrived from Paris for a few days at *La Tourrello*, leaving her husband engaged on the details of a business deal. Mistral detested the man she had married and a tacit arrangement existed between Nadine and Kate not to remind Mistral of Phillipe Dalmas's existence any more than was necessary.

When Fauve had come to Provence for the first summer, Nadine had been fifteen and a half, actually a half-year younger than Fauve now was herself, yet even then she had seemed more sophisticated than anyone Fauve had ever known before.

That early impression had only been confirmed by the passage of time. Today, at twenty-three, Nadine was all brilliant cutting edges. Her blond hair swung in two bright polished arcs under her chin as if it were a truncated wimple, her straight, long bangs looked as if they could slice into her forehead, her eyes were edged in sharply drawn lines of dark green, with an Egyptian precision.

The planes of her nose were whittled to a degree that just escaped being pointed, her teeth were so white and regular that they reminded Fauve that their primary purpose was to bite. There was a knifelike line to her jaw but her upper lip still curved in its eternal smile. She was compelling, Fauve admitted. It was all but impossible not to stare at Nadine. Wherever she sat or stood was, always, center stage.

Nadine Mistral presented herself as she was, with no attempt to mask her own high self-esteem. Superiority was manifest in the absolute perfection of her immaculately well-cut white linen slacks, in the starkly elegant lines of her black silk blouse that wrapped and knotted at her slim waist, in the splendid pair of onyx earrings rimmed in flashing diamonds that hung from the lobes of her ears.

She permitted herself no flaws, not so much as a single fingernail was shorter than the others. How many hours each week it took to maintain this ruthlessly gleaming exterior no one knew, but Fauve was sure that there were women who could spend their lives trying to emulate Nadine's glacial and insolent elegance without achieving it, because, at the last minute, they would be tempted to add a rope of pearls or brush a little softness into their hair or tuck a flower into a sash. Nadine was, in her own way, a Minimalist, who made her statement with the fewest possible elements.

Kate Browning's determination to devote herself to Julien Mistral, which had seized her on the day she first saw him and his work, had been largely transferred to her daughter Nadine. The four years during which Mistral had left her for Teddy Lunel and then, after her death, roamed the earth, had locked Kate into the most passionate of maternal connections. No matter how all-important being Madame Julien Mistral was and always would be to her, her second concern now was her daughter's happiness and her position in life.

Since Nadine's marriage, Kate had lived in a state of impotent fury against Mistral, who stood between Nadine and her rightful status as one of the great heiresses of France. In time, Nadine would inherit everything Julien owned, the treasure of paintings in the storage room, the rich, income-producing property of *La Tourrello*, their bank accounts, their investments; all this vast fortune would be hers by French law, but meanwhile, Nadine actually had been forced to take a job to maintain her style of life.

Two years ago she had married a man, Phillipe Dalmas, who, for want of a more specific description, was always referred to in the press as "an investor." He had been celebrated in the social and gossip pages of the media for many years before he met Nadine because of the liaisons he had enjoyed with a number of the most sought-after women of the day. Phillipe was often dubbed "the most elusive man in Paris" for, at thirty-nine, he had never been married.

By profession he was a deal maker, bringing together people who needed money and those who had it to invest. Somehow only a few of his deals ever came to pass, and his commissions on those that did amounted to just enough to support himself in great style as a bachelor.

Phillipe could afford to employ a houseman-valet, he had

enough money to order suits made to measure at Larsen, where he could choose from the seven hundred bolts of wool that lined the walls like rare books, and his collection of cashmere scarves—for he never wore an overcoat—came from the great house of Hilditch and Key. His small apartment was in an irreproachable building near the Arc de Triomphe, and it was handsomely furnished with some good Empire pieces, but his only real capital was his charm.

Phillipe Dalmas was the World's Best Guest. Amusing, handsome and splendidly heterosexual, he was the subject of every hostess's reverie.

When Nadine met this sensual man, devoted to pleasure, given and received, a man enveloped in an immense glamour of unavailability, she was immediately determined to catch him. For his part, as Phillipe saw his fortieth birthday approach, he decided that it was a sensible moment to terminate his triumphant bachelorhood. He had no intention of spending a middle age visiting in other people's houses, no matter how agreeably.

Nadine succeeded in marrying him, where so many others had failed, by the simple, banal means of appearing at the right moment in his life. Her twenty-one radiant years, her flashing flawlessness and, of course, her incontestable prospects as the daughter of Julien Mistral, made her an almost inevitable choice, for while Phillipe Dalmas would never have married only for money, he certainly could not afford to marry someone without it.

Nadine Mistral and Phillipe Dalmas shared the kind of profound, bred-in-the-bone superficiality that can become, when superbly mounted, a certain kind of meaningfulness. Their deep attention to façades gave each of them a high gloss and together they made an unforgettably decorative couple, like a pair of rare art objects, burnished to an enviable degree. Once all the hostesses in Paris had resigned themselves to the loss of Phillipe as a single man, they began to compete with each other for the presence of the Dalmases, who had one of those marriages in which the husband and the wife together become the single star of an evening.

Kate would have put away certain loftier ambitions she had long nourished for her daughter, for she couldn't deny that Nadine adored her husband, had it not been for Julien Mistral, who spent a half-hour with Phillipe Dalmas and decided that the man was essentially worthless. There would be no dowry, he declared, and his wedding gift to the couple was only a medium-sized apartment on the avenue Montaigne, the very least, Kate had managed to persuade him, they could decently offer.

Since then, the allowance he could so easily have made them, had not been paid—and never would be, as long as he was alive, he assured Kate. Nor was it possible now for her to give them lavish gifts. Mistral, who had allowed his wife to make all the financial decisions for him during their long marriage, suddenly insisted on carrying on his own correspondence with his dealers and his bankers.

Kate was effectively prevented from secretly handling any substantial sum and the only money she could still spend freely was that needed to maintain *La Tourrello*. She was reduced to little more than a housekeeper and estate manager, she thought venomously. But Nadine took the disappointment with the philosophy of one whose father is almost seventy years old. It was only temporary, after all, and in the meanwhile it was chic and amusing to say that she had to work for a living, more droll than if she had just been another rich girl, particularly since no one could doubt how immensely rich she would be.

Nadine had created a job for herself that displayed her to perfection. She worked with Jean François Albin, the only other French couturier who enjoyed the level of international importance of Yves Saint Laurent.

Her work was without specific title, its boundaries hard to define. She wasn't head of public relations, because that job, with its technical details of dealing with the world press, was handled by Lily de Mar, who had been trained at Dior; nor was she involved in the actual design of the clothes or the selling of them, or any of the business of the House of Albin. Yet, in a way that was as clear as if it had been official, Nadine was employed to be Jean François Albin's Best Friend.

She was the one human being in the world without whom he simply could not function. She acted as a buffer between him and the entire world that he saw as full of enemies, or, at the very best, brutes, people lacking in sensitivity. He believed that Nadine alone would never lie to him. He was convinced that she was the only person who did not seek some sort of advancement through her association with him, for what could the daughter of Julien

Mistral gain from closeness to any couturier, no matter how famous?

To Albin, Nadine Dalmas was the idealized incarnation of the woman he designed for. He invested her with almost mystical powers to comfort and inspire and refresh him. He now needed her by his side at all times of crisis. Henri Gros, the solid businessman who was Albin's partner in a couture house that was swollen with profits from three perfumes and a number of worldwide licensing agreements, was delighted to pay Nadine a pleasantly handsome salary for her devotion, no matter how vague her role seemed to be. The fragile, creative machine that was Jean François Albin must be, at all costs, nourished, comforted and comprehended so that he could continue to turn out two collections a year.

As Nadine talked about her job at dinner with her parents and Fauve, her proud, cool, jaunty manner that was not an affectation but her natural form of expression, didn't change. Yet clearly, she was engrossed in her life. She spoke, as always, in even and assured tones that were pitched just a bit lower than anyone else's, so that people found themselves stopping their own conversations in order to listen to her.

"You see, Father, Jean François was at the breaking point. The new collection is all finished down to the last button, but last Wednesday he telephoned in despair in the middle of the night and I rushed over to the *atelier* to find him about to take a pair of scissors to every single garment. I led him away as gently as if he were a sleepwalker, and told him that we were going to the very best clinic in St. Cloud, where he would give himself over to a sleep cure until Monday and I stayed with him holding his hand, until he was actually sleeping peacefully. On Monday, when I return, he'll be a new man."

"Does that happen often?" asked Kate.

"He's had nothing but trouble these past months," Nadine explained. "All five of our new black manikins deserted to go to work for Givenchy, and that vacation house in Sardinia I told you about is driving him mad with worry. Quite naturally, Jean François insists that the interior decorator take the most precious old brocades and drape them like muslin and use inlaid woods with the same ease as if it were raw lumber but the man just can't seem to follow orders."

Gee whiz! Fauve whispered—to herself.

"Fortunately," Nadine continued, "I've been able to take a lot of this off his hands and leave him free to concentrate on his art, but no matter what I accomplish, in the end it's his decision that is vital, and this is just the worst of years. After all, he can hardly be unaware that he has become a cult object—nothing makes a person more vulnerable than to be elevated to that sort of worship—yet what can he do? He *must* expose himself time and time again—he must risk, he must change."

"Change what?" Mistral asked, pushing away his plate.

"The length, Father, Jean François feels that it's time to impose the maximum length—the mini is dead—but how can those cows of the public possibly be subtle and daring enough to follow? Can they rise to his level? He had such a horror of the buyers and the press—I don't know if he'll be able to face them after the collection is over—"

"Then why does he?" Mistral growled.

"If he doesn't come out and take a bow, Father, the rumors will start again—they'll say he's dead or drugged or shut up in a madhouse—I can't imagine how he endures it. The temptation, of course, is to compromise, to create a length that is not revolutionary but merely evolutionary—but Jean François is too great an artist not to be faithful to himself."

"Tell me," Mistral asked, "just how old is Jean François?"

"No one is sure, not even I, but I think he must be close to forty."

"He sounds like a child. And if you live in a child's world, you descend to his level," Mistral said scornfully.

"Enough of Jean François," Kate said abruptly, rushing protectively into the conversation. She was all too familiar with Mistral's opinions about the value of the haute couture and she knew how icy Nadine would turn if Jean François were criticized. "Nadine, you must ask Fauve to tell you about her summer—it's been an absolute revelation."

Nadine looked at her mother and caught a purposeful spark in her eye. They had never needed words to communicate. She shrugged lightly and turned to Fauve.

372

"You've been uncharacteristically silent tonight, now that I think about it. And yet it seems to me that I've heard something about you and a rather attractive young architect. So, little Fauve has finally deigned to recognize the masculine sex? And how do you find first love, eh?"

Nadine spoke with a cold curiosity so penetrating that Fauve almost flinched. Instinctively she sought a way to deflect that curiosity, for Nadine, like a tomcat, with a small animal in its jaws, wouldn't release the object of her attention until she was satisfied.

"I find the masculine sex marvelously useful, thank you. How have I spent all my summers here without any other transportation than my bicycle? This fellow has his own car so I've been able to convince him to drive me around—I've seen more of the countryside in six weeks than I saw in the last eight years."

"Your interest is only touristic? Fauve, do you expect me to believe that?"

"Believe what you want—I'm investigating the history of the Jews of Provence."

"Good Lord, how utterly bizarre . . . I thought they were all in Paris!"

"So do most people," Fauve said, almost laughing at the success of her gambit. Nadine hadn't even asked Eric's name. "There have been Jews living right here for two thousand years."

"Two thousand years . . . are you sure, Fauve?" Nadine drawled. Her hard glance, the green of malachite, was distinctly dubious.

"Absolutely! And until the Crusades they were treated more or less like everyone else. Even the Vandals and the Visigoths and the Barbarians left them alone when they invaded the countryside—it wasn't until the twelfth century, when the kings of France went chasing off to recapture the Holy Land, that they really began to persecute the Jews."

Fauve had put down her fork, excited by a chance to talk about the revelations she had come across every day in Armand Mossé's book, to which both her father and Kate seemed callously indifferent. She grasped this opportunity eagerly although she was perfectly aware that it had only come about because Kate wanted to head off an argument.

Fauve was literally on fire with names and dates and statistics; she felt as if Pope Alexandre VI and Jules II, who had both employed Jews as their physicians, were her personal friends. Just as heartily she loathed Jules III who had ordered the burning of the Talmud.

She was too involved in her subject to notice the veiled disdain that passed from Nadine to Kate as Fauve grew increasingly indignant over the more than five hundred years, ending only with the Revolution, during which all the Jews of Provence had had to submit, from childhood on, to the wearing of a distinctive yellow patch on their clothes. Mistral listened without expression while she described the horrors of the old ghettoes, locked and barred every night, in which countless generations dwelled in miserable, jampacked airless hovels while all other men were free to live at liberty in the vast and rich valley of the Vaucluse. The rules, cruel and restrictive and arbitrary, that the authorities imposed on all aspects of Jewish life, came spilling out of her in one long, fervent monologue. Mistral stopped eating and his lips tightened angrily yet Fauve didn't notice. She had no idea how long and how passionately she had talked until Nadine finished her cheese, and said lightly, "Aren't you being a bit of a bleeding heart, Fauve? Those people have all been dead for a long time—it's so morbid to talk as if this still matters today—I find it distinctly odd of you."

"Not that odd, Nadine. Everywhere in Mossé's book I find the names of Lunel and Astruc—names of my family . . . my name in fact."

"Isn't that pushing what's probably a very distant connection?"

"Distant! No, damn it, I don't think there's anything distant about it . . ." Fauve responded furiously, when Mistral finally broke his brooding silence.

"*Enough!* When you came back from that place in Cavaillon you described it in a way that convinced me that the local Jews must have been well off and well treated and now you submit us to this endless catalog of misery. This is becoming a mania with you!"

"I was being an uninformed romantic, Father, living in an illusion." Fauve spoke up boldly, unintimidated by his disapproval. "That building isn't even two hundred years old and I was fool enough to think that it indicated an idyllic past. Now I know that it's a deceptive remnant of one of the brief periods in which the Jews were permitted to live in relative tranquillity—and even so, it used to be surrounded by a dreadful ghetto that's been torn down. There are still people, well-meaning people, who boast that Provence was 'The Paradise of the Jews'—well, it was, if you compare it to the dozens of other places in France where the Jews were all burned alive! Provence was a paradise in the most limited and ironic sense of the word, like saying it was the best of all possible prisons for people who had committed no crime."

"Prison?" Kate said, carefully watching Mistral's expression as Fauve defied him. She was the only person at the table who was aware of how deeply he resented Fauve's interest in anything Jewish, the only person who had enjoyed his reaction to every word Fauve had said. "Why 'prison,' Fauve? We weren't the people who were responsible for what happened to those people, we never were cruel to Jews, we never treated Jews as if they'd committed a crime. Really, Fauve, I'm surprised you haven't accused us all of sending them to concentration camps."

26

Kate Mistral had acted a role with Julien Mistral from the moment she met him. The closest he had come to awareness of her real self was in that moment she had asked him to marry her. Now, after forty-two years of marriage she was locked into a part that had evolved with the years, a part in which she had never revealed all her emotions to this most necessary of opponents. When she admired an actress on the stage or in a film it never occurred to her that in her own domestic life she had long been a habitual and consummate performer. All of her human relationships took place in an intimate theater in which she assumed that everyone was acting much of the time. The moments in which her dramatic mask could be partially dropped were rare. Sometimes she approached the truth—and a genuine inner moment of contact—with Nadine. Never with her husband.

Kate sat placidly in front of her dressing table, taking off her pearls while Mistral stood angrily in the door of her bedroom, unwilling to come in and sit down, yet unable to go off to his own room and try to sleep.

"What on earth are you so disturbed about, Julien?" she inquired mildly. "I'll agree that it's irritating that Fauve insists on boring us at the dinner table but why treat it like a major problem? All girls go through difficult phases in their teens."

"You deliberately encouraged her."

"Nonsense. You can't say a single polite word to Fauve these days without unleashing her obsession. You know yourself that if you just say good morning you risk a lecture about a thousand years at the Wailing Wall. There's no stopping her—whenever she eats with us I'm afraid we're in for it, unless you want to forbid it entirely."

"You can't forbid Fauve to talk about the things that interest her, she's not that kind of girl," he said grimly. "Goddamn that Avigdor brat! He's behind all this."

"You're being very unfair. Of course the boy adds fuel to the fire, but in my opinion it goes way beyond him. If you want to blame anybody, Maggy Lunel is the guilty one."

"What the hell does that mean?"

"The Jesuits say that if you give them a child for the first seven years they can form him for life. You gave Fauve to her grandmother and she lost no time in imposing her own identity on your daughter. After all, Fauve does have that Jewish streak no matter how little you like it. Don't underestimate its power, Julien. Every child needs a feeling of identity . . . or so they say."

"She's my daughter—she's a painter. Isn't that enough identity for her, by Christ? What more does a sixteen-year-old expect, for the love of God! But no—instead of taking advantage of this summer she's wasting her time chasing around imagining she's found a so-called tradition that has nothing to do with her. She's mad to imagine that the Lunels and the Astrucs in that cursed book are her family. She can't possibly find out anything—even if there were some sort of vague relationship, it's too unimportant to matter!"

"Perhaps just knowing that she's your illegitimate daughter isn't enough for Fauve." Kate put her bracelets away, closed her jewelry box and began to brush the fine hair that fell so neatly around her face. "Do go to sleep, Julien. You make me nervous standing there."

A minute later Mistral was on the way to his studio in a darkness that was illuminated by that light night sky of Provence in which the stars have moved in from space until they seemed as if they must sing to man as they do in the other great open lands of the earth, in the desert or in the great polar reaches. He didn't flick on the work lights but walked directly to the easel on which the half-finished picture of Fauve stood. He looked at the rectangle of canvas, an almost solid gray under the skylight, lost in thought. Kate's words repeated themselves in his mind. "Every child needs a feeling of identity." How could he deny that she was right? From the day Fauve was born he had been powerless to give her his own name. Under French law, he could not recognize her as his daughter, she could not call herself Fauve Mistral, so naturally she thought of herself as a Lunel—as one of them. All summer long she had been slipping away from him, eluding him more each day, and although he had captured her image on the canvas he knew that he had not, as in other years, come close to catching her spirit, for even as he painted her she was somewhere else.

Scornfully, Mistral turned his back on the painting—why even bother to finish that daub?—and prowled around the shadowy studio. How do you catch a sixteen-year-old girl and pin her down and make her see reason? It would be easier to talk sense to a hummingbird. If only she were French, brought up right here in Félice, under his eye. If only she didn't escape him every year, if only she could be frozen in time!

Restlessly he sought the only comfort he had ever found effective—the presence of his own work. He unlocked the door of the storage room, switched on the overhead lights and roamed the brightly illuminated aisles, pulling out a rack here and there, and contemplating the painting on it as if it were a strange object, as if he had never spent many weeks, often many months, of the most intense effort of which he was capable on each one of them. After a long while he began to reach out and run his hand over an occasional painted surface, feeling the rough textures of the canvas as if it were a sentient being. Little by little he allowed himself to be eased, slowly he accepted solace. *These lived.* He was as sure of that as he was of the fact that he was Julien Mistral. They lived now and they would live as long as they existed. This room was not full of finished paintings but of speaking, breathing creatures. Here was *his* identity, here in this windowless room was all that would ever need to be said about Julien Mistral.

There was a section of the room that he never visited. The paintings he had made of Teddy when she was pregnant and of Teddy and Fauve during the first two months of Fauve's life, during which he had worked more rapidly than he ever had before or since, were all kept on several dozen racks in the back of the large room. He had abandoned them in his apartment in Avignon after Teddy's death where they had been carefully guarded by the married couple who had worked for them. After his return to *La Tourrello*, Mistral had arranged for the paintings to be picked up and brought to the storage room, but he had never looked at them again.

Now he walked slowly to one of the racks and pulled it into the wide aisle. The rack held only one large unfinished canvas, the last picture he had painted of Teddy in St. Tropez. She sat in a garden on a blue-and-white-striped swing, holding Fauve close to her breast, her head bent as she studied the baby.

Even in his most tormented, longing dreams she had never been as beautiful. He had painted his love so clearly that the canvas seemed to cry out on one high, clear, wordless note of joy. Quickly, he shoved the rack away, out of sight, and rushed out of the storage room, locking it behind him. He took the back door out of the studio and hurried down the path that led around the walls of *La Tourrello*, stopping only when he found himself deep in the forest of live oaks. He sat down on the ground, his back to a tree, breathing deeply, as if he'd been running for his life. Why had he done that? Why had he risked such certain pain?

As instinctively as if he were jumping away from a stream of boiling water he preserved himself from feeling the wound by shutting out the image of Teddy and bringing into the focus of his mind the patch of canvas on which he had painted that scrap of a being, the baby Fauve. Even then she had possessed a burning vitality. He remembered her at the moment of her birth, wrapped in the pink blanket, only just out of the womb, but already so distinct that he had known her rightful name at once. The anger toward her, that had been building up in him all summer as she wandered out of his grip, evaporated as he thought of her as she had been at dinner tonight. Fauve's face had reflected every emotion she felt; she could no more restrain her idealistic, volatile nature than she was able to be hypocritical or diplomatic.

Julien Mistral was not a man capable of abstract compassion. Not only did he not empathize with people, alone or in groups, he lacked the slightest desire to do so. His art was totally personal; it embraced only those things that came within the dominion he claimed for himself; certain aspects of nature, certain elements of the human life of Provence, and the few—very few—people he loved. Without the motivation of love he was a stone—a stone who painted.

As he sat against the tree, his love for Fauve allowed him to enter into her mind, permitted him access to her spirit, and he became slowly aware of the questions she must be asking herself. Who am I? What is life all about? Where am I going? Who went before me? Is there a connection?

Of course she was searching for something that would answer those questions, for was she not a romantic, as romantic as Teddy had been? No wonder Fauve was confused, no wonder she was thrashing about with silly concern. For the space of a few seconds Julien Mistral allowed himself to imagine the glory of a life in which Fauve could have grown up, watched over and cared for under Teddy's eyes, a child who had both a mother and a father, safe, secure, beloved. He grunted under the blow of a useless despair and pushed the picture away, but, for the first time in his life he fully realized that he was not the only person in the world who had been bitterly deprived of the love of Teddy Lunel. And he had never even shown that painting of Fauve and Teddy to anyone. *Not even to Fauve.*

He sat perfectly still, so stunned with the idea that now came to him that he kept turning it over and over in his mind, searching for flaws, unable to believe that it had never occurred to him before. His stern chieftain's face expanded into an irresistible grimace of fierce joy before it hardened into a look of resolution so intense that he seemed to be enduring, even embracing, some deep hurt. He *knew* how to give Fauve the sense of identity that would bind her to him forever, that would imprint him on her life in a way that would make it impossible for her ever to seek out a heritage that had nothing to do with him. She was so desperate that she was reduced to skimming some sense of belonging from the shell of a Louis XV synagogue. Yet he alone on the face of the great wide earth had the power to give her an identity, a heritage, a feeling of belonging that would make her realize that her most basic, most important tie in the world was, and always would be, to him.

Julien Mistral had never made a will, but, when his parents had died, he had been involved with the details of inheritance. His mother had astonished and displeased him by leaving one-third of her tiny estate to a friend with whom she often worked on her needlework, a woman to whom she wasn't related in any way. When Mistral had questioned the lawyer about the legality of this, he had been told that everyone is permitted to leave one-third of his estate to a stranger. The remaining two-thirds must be distributed among his legitimate descendants whether he wishes it or not.

Fauve was legally a stranger to him. Nothing in French law allowed them any official connection. She had no legal status. As an *enfante adulterine* she could inherit nothing—but as a stranger, one-third! Oh, how carefully, how intimately, how intensely they would go over all the paintings in the storage room, how many hours they would spend in the joyously complicated, thoughtful process of putting aside the one-third that would become Fauve's very own property, separating them from those that must, of necessity, belong to Nadine, and to Kate, of course, if she outlived him.

Fauve would be locked into his life forever. What dusty history book could bind her more closely to him than the possession of the very best of the work of his lifetime? What architectural bagatelle, what book, what list of names of people long dead, could make her feel a greater sense of identity than to know that, while he was alive, her father had given her as much as he could of the treasure for which he had lived? The work that was *him*.

He stood up and brushed the debris of the forest floor off his trousers. As he walked back to *La Tourrello*, Julien Mistral's silhouette in the starlight looked as eager and young as it had on the day he had first approached the gates of the vast farmhouse that was to determine the course of his future.

"Kate, please make arrangements for two of the guest rooms to be prepared," Mistral said to his wife the next morning as she sat alone by the pool.

"Have you invited visitors?" she asked, surprised. He left their social life entirely to her.

"Two men are coming, who'll have to take their meals with us since there's nowhere around here for them to eat. They'll probably stay for a week or ten days."

"Julien, what are you talking about—that's absurd."

"I've decided to make a will. The paintings must be appraised. This morning I telephoned to Étienne Delage for advice. As a dealer he knows all the tricks. He told me that I shouldn't make a will until I've established the value of each of my works. Otherwise the government will do it for me after I'm dead and, naturally, they'll put the highest value on them so that my estate will have to pay the

381

biggest possible tax. But if it's done while I'm alive, I have the right to appoint one of the appraisers, and the government sends another—those are the two gentlemen who are coming—and between them they reach a fair compromise. Étienne has found me a man who will put the lowest realistic value on the paintings that he can—it's his specialty."

"How very thoughtful of Étienne. May I ask why you've decided to make a will?"

"I'm leaving Fauve one-third of my estate, the part that may go to a stranger." He looked at Kate for signs of distress but her dark glasses covered her eyes and her expression didn't change. "Last night I remembered that it was possible and I kept hearing your words—'every child needs a feeling of identity'—and I knew that it was what I must do. Of course you and Nadine will get the other two-thirds—I'm going to leave Fauve her share entirely in the form of paintings, since it would be useless to leave her one-third of a farm, or of investments in a country in which she doesn't live. That means that I must establish the total value of *La Tourrello* and of our bank accounts and other investments as well as that of the paintings in order to make sure that she gets her fair third."

"I see," Kate said tonelessly.

"All that will take time to establish—probably the details won't all be down in black and white until long after Fauve goes home, but Étienne says that paintings—like furniture or silver or jewels—can be left individually. In other words, a painting that's worth a particular amount will be left to Fauve, one worth the same amount to Nadine, and one to you, and so on."

"And so you're going to leave them all by name and description?"

"Yes. Oh, I haven't forgotten that you own all of the *Rouquinne* series, never fear. That was an intelligent investment you made, Kate."

"So it was."

"I intend to buy them back from you."

"Do you?"

"Yes—they should go to Fauve—after all, they're family portraits, so to speak." He grinned in a way she hadn't seen in years.

"Indeed—they are indeed. Have you any idea what they're worth?"

"Whatever it is, I'll pay."

"Good."

"Well." Mistral stood up, relieved. "It's settled then. You'll tell the servants whatever's necessary? The appraisers arrive in two days."

"Of course," said Kate. "Have you informed Fauve yet?"

"No, not yet. I'll speak to her tonight, when she gets back to dress—there's some sort of a party she's going to this evening." He disappeared into his studio, thinking that Fauve might as well run around all day today, for tomorrow she wouldn't be able to tear herself away from the discoveries of the storage room.

Kate sat perfectly still, wondering if she was going to be able to endure the slicing, writhing rage that cut into her flesh like engine-driven iron drills grinding into a piece of wood. So it wasn't enough to beggar Nadine, to force her to work for a living until he died, was it? Now he was stripping her, despoiling her, robbing her, lowering his own daughter to the level of his bastard.

Did he think that she was such a fool as to believe his explanation of the "fairness" of the process of choosing the paintings he would leave Fauve? Didn't he realize that she knew as well as he that between two paintings that are appraised for the same amount there will be an enormous difference in *importance* that the artist alone can assign? Didn't he even suspect that she knew perfectly well that he would give Fauve only the paintings that he was sure were his greatest? The masterpieces of his masterpieces? If Fauve received all of her one-third share in paintings, leaving out his land, his money, his investments, it might well be possible to give her at least *half* of the contents of the storage room—the image of that room made her suck in her breath and bend over, grasping her stomach in both hands.

How dare he do this to her? She, Kate Browning, had taken up an unknown artist and made him into Julien Mistral and goddamn him to hell everlasting, he *belonged* to her. He had no rights on the face of the earth unless she granted them. How could he prattle like an old fool about "sharing" his work, when everything, every last bit of canvas he had ever smeared paint on, was rightfully hers?

He was her creature. What would he be if she hadn't become his wife? *Nothing!* He would be nothing, an embittered old man, living in some shabby Paris studio, wondering why the world had not come to his door. He would have missed his moment and some other painter would have had the glory. And yet he dared, he actually *dared* to speak of giving his work to Fauve?

What was his work but what she had enabled him to create? If he gave his work he would be giving away the one thing in the world—the only thing—that belonged absolutely to her. That he could not do. That he must not do. Paralyzed by an onslaught of fury greater than she had ever known in her life, greater than the emotion she had felt when Julien left her for Teddy Lunel, Kate sat sightlessly in the sun while bubbling, bursting coils of violence grew in her belly until finally she had to jerk herself out of her immobility and dash into the pool pavilion in order to throw up the loathsomeness into the bathroom toilet.

When she was finished she felt steady, calm and very sure of what she had to do.

"Will you come into my room and shut the door for a minute, Fauve?" Kate asked as soon as she heard her come upstairs that afternoon.

"Sure—but I'm a mess and Eric's coming back to pick me up by six—do you want me for long?"

"No, not long. Fauve, I don't think you realize how much you're upsetting your father with the sort of discussion we were all treated to last night."

"Oh, I know I went on talking too long, Kate. I thought about it today and I realized that I'd sort of taken over the conversation. It won't happen again. I'm truly sorry."

"It's not how long you talked, Fauve, it's the subject matter. You never got off the topic of Jewish suffering."

"What?"

"I hoped I'd never have to tell you this but I see that you're really deeply involved in your maternal heritage—it's completely understandable and I find it quite touching and fascinating—but you see, your father . . . when you speak of Jews like that it opens old wounds."

"I suppose you mean that it reminds him of my grandmother? I know about that, Kate, and I can't believe that whatever I said would necessarily make him think of her. Maggy's not the only Jew in the world."

"I don't mean that at all. It had never even occurred to me. No, Fauve, it's something that's much more difficult for me to explain."

"What are you driving at, Kate?" Fauve asked, puzzled by the intent, concerned expression on Kate's normally controlled face.

"Fauve, you're only sixteen. You've always lived in a safe world, yet only ten years before you were born World War Two was going on, and catastrophes that you can't even begin to imagine were everyday events."

"Oh, my God," Fauve said slowly, "last night, when you said what you did about concentration camps, you were thinking of what happened to the Jews in the war, weren't you? You were trying to warn me off—oh, Lord, Kate, I'm so sorry! I didn't realize that it would upset him . . . I never thought . . ."

"Fauve, I haven't made myself clear. I'm talking about the Occupation of France and what happened to life here during that time. When I got back to Félice after the war Marte Pollison, who was here at *La Tourrello* the whole time, told me things that I thought I'd never have to speak of to anybody." Avidly, Kate watched Fauve's bewildered face, which had already been drained of the carefree, excited radiance with which she had walked into the bedroom. "Fauve, for weeks you've been fascinated by the Jews who lived in Provence and I've been a wet blanket about it. There was a reason for that—I thought you might finally lose your interest. But you haven't and now, before I tell you why you must stop bringing this subject up, I want to be sure that you truly understand your father. He lives only to paint. You realize what his work means to him, don't you? You know that his art is everything, his reason for being?"

"He's also a person, a man," Fauve said slowly.

"But not like the others. No genius ever is. I've had to learn it over the years, it's certainly not something I expect you to grasp fully, but there's a certain dimension that genius lacks, a dimension of ordinary humanity that is denied genius precisely because it *is* genius."

"I guess I don't 'fully' understand, Kate."

"No, I was afraid you wouldn't. An example can show you what I mean better than words alone. In those last years of the war there were Germans everywhere, no place was so remote that they didn't know what was going on, not even here in Félice. They took almost all of the able-bodied men away for forced labor in Germany . . ." Kate paused and shook her head sadly.

"And . . . ?"

"Your father would have been sent away too except for the protection of a high-ranking German officer with whom he became—very friendly, very close."

"I don't believe that."

"No, Fauve, of course you don't. That's exactly what I meant about the difficulty of making you understand, even such a little thing as that."

"A little thing?" Fauve's face had turned white, Kate noted with a thrill of satisfaction. And what had she told her yet? Nothing important, nothing at all. How wise she had been to stay in Marte Pollison's good graces over these many years. The woman was a tyrant but eventually she couldn't resist gossip.

"That officer was an art lover. He supplied your father with precious paints so that he could continue to work in spite of all the shortages and he took him off the list of those who were destined to be sent to factories in Germany. Some of his best work was done in those years, and yet if people knew about it they'd be quick to call him a collaborator."

"Why are you telling me this?"

"To make you grasp fully what your father's genius demands of him. When he told the German about the bunch of young good-for-nothings who stole his precious sheets—for years he had nothing else to use as canvas—how could he know that they were members of the *Maquis?* It was a terrible misunderstanding and he's never forgiven himself for it—twenty of them, all caught and executed on the spot. Why, he'd never even have known what had happened to them if the German hadn't returned the sheets."

"I don't believe a single word you're saying," Fauve said furiously. "It's a contemptible lie, and what the hell does it have to do with last night? I was talking about the way Jews lived in Provence before the Revolution, not about the war!"

Kate sighed and put her hands over her face for a brief moment. Now! She thought, *now!* "Oh, Fauve," she said wearily, her voice gentle, in supplication, as if willing the girl to make a leap of intelligence. "It was only an example of the sort of thing, the sort of horrible, tragic thing that can happen in time of war. It was to give you an insight into the situation with those Jews who came to him for help during the Occupation."

"*Jews*—what Jews?"

"Jews from Paris, trying to get out of Occupied France. They came and kept coming—people who had just presumed on the fact that they were old friends of his from the days he had lived in Paris, or from the fact that they'd been invited here before the war. Why, sometimes they were only friends of friends. Marte told me about it . . . oh, Fauve . . . this is just too hard to explain to anyone of your generation . . . what do you know about the war?" Kate slumped in her chair, her expression closed and guarded.

"What is too hard to explain?" Fauve said faintly, her heart beating so hard that she felt as if she must run away, as if the house were on fire and she was in mortal danger. Kate took a breath of resolution and spoke quietly, looking at the carpet.

"Your father ordered Marte and Jean to build a barrier to hide the entrance to *La Tourrello* down at the main road so that no refugees, Jews, any others, Jewish or not, would come up here to disturb him, to interrupt his work. Of course he had to close the big gates too because some of them actually infiltrated right through the woods—naturally they knew the house was here, if they'd been here before. But your father knew that if he weakened and let some Jew spend even one single night under his roof he could be in serious danger. Any Frenchman who helped a Jew was putting his own life in jeopardy."

"But what about all the French who did help Jews, who fought in the Resistance, who bombed German trains, who fought back?" Fauve asked tightly.

"Little people, Fauve, little people with less to lose than your father. He had to choose between painting and risking his life and I believe absolutely that he made the right choice and I pray you'll think so too—he decided that his only loyalty had to be to his work, not to sheltering people for whom he'd never had any responsibility. You must be grown up enough to understand that."

"Grown up," Fauve repeated, "grown up?"

"But Fauve, they simply had to be *made* to go away! Nobody invited them but they just kept coming. They would have destroyed his *peace of mind*. Why do you think it took him *eight years* to go to see you? He was afraid for his peace of mind, for his powers of concentration. Those Jews would have prevented him from painting, even if they'd never been caught, even if no one had known. *La Tourrello* is remote, I admit, but in the village everything gets talked about sooner or later and someone might have denounced him to the authorities. And that, Fauve, is why your keeping on about the

Jews is upsetting him . . . it makes him remember all the people who got past the fence at the road and kept on ringing and ringing the bell in the kitchen."

"How do you know any of this! You weren't here! Is it Marte again, because I wouldn't believe one single goddamned lie she told you!"

"You still truly don't understand. Ah, Fauve, why would I bother to lie to you? Your father's *work* was at stake, don't you know what that means? Nothing could be more important."

"*Liar!*"

"Ask Adrien Avigdor since you don't believe me."

"What?"

"You heard me. He was your father's best friend before the war. But your father had to turn him away too, had to refuse him entrance. Avigdor told me so himself in 1946 in Paris and all the time that you've been seeing Eric I've been terrified that the old man might have said something to you. He was horribly bitter about it when I saw him last. It seems that he actually kept track of the people who came here . . . artists mostly of course. His personal animosity was frightening. He acted as if it were all your father's fault that there was a war going on in Europe and many of those unfortunate people were caught and deported—they probably would have died no matter what your father had done."

"Deported . . . died . . . caught . . ."

"Fauve, I simply had to tell you. We must *not* have any more of your history lessons during meals. Will you give me your word . . ."

Kate's words trailed off as she watched Fauve run out of the bedroom. No, she thought, no, she didn't think she'd left out anything important.

As Fauve pushed open the door into the studio Mistral was working on Fauve's picture, alive in every pore with energy and insight. His ability to participate in Fauve's quest for a sense of herself had provided the element that had been missing from his work these past few weeks and in one day he'd conquered the picture.

"Thank God you're back! I have so much to tell you." He threw down his brush and started forward to kiss her. She stopped, just inside the doorway, and held up one hand, warding him off.

"Father, did you refuse to give shelter to Jewish refugees during the war—did you listen to the bell ringing and not come to the gate to let them in?"

Mistral fought back. The shock of Fauve's challenge left him with only a single thought. "*Avigdor*," he roared. "What the hell has he been telling you?"

"So it's true!" Fauve cried. All her desperate hope had died as soon as he'd said Avigdor's name. "Do you ever *think* about them— the Jews who died because of you?"

She turned, but not quickly enough to avoid seeing the truth that was branded so clearly on his face. He reached toward her but she was gone. *And he did not dare to go after her.* He stood, trembling, in the center of the empty studio, irresolutely, and then he began, with the haste of a man in danger of his life, to lock every door and window of his studio from the inside so that he would be safe from the hatred he'd seen in his daughter's eyes.

Eric Avigdor, arriving there three-quarters of an hour later, found Fauve waiting outside the walls of *La Tourrello*. Her suitcases were on the gravel driveway beside her and she carried her raincoat.

"Are we going somewhere, darling?" he said gaily. He was ready for all of Fauve's caprices.

"Please, Eric, take me to the train station in Avignon."

"I certainly won't. If you've had a fight with that so-called sister of yours I'll go right on inside and break one of her fingernails."

"Eric, don't, don't joke . . ." Fauve bowed her head and, with a pang of fear he turned to part the curtain of hair that almost hid her face. At his touch she gasped with a single rending sob and he saw that she must have been weeping long before he came, for her face was raw with tears that had run into her mouth and down her chin.

"My God, what's happened to you?" he cried, but she shook her head blindly and climbed into the car and huddled in the seat. He threw the suitcases in the back and tried to hold her in his arms and comfort her but she shook him off. "Get me away from here," she said in a way that made him start the car without another word. They drove off in the direction of Avignon. They had been speeding along the main road for five minutes before he tried again. "Fauve, tell me what's wrong. Please, darling, let me help. I know I can."

"No, Eric." Her voice seemed to have no home in her body.

"Fauve, don't you trust me? Nothing can be that bad."

"I can't talk about it." She had stopped weeping but there was a blotched, hopeless, creased look to her young face that terrified him when he glanced at her. He stopped the car and pulled off the road.

"Fauve, I won't drive you any farther until you tell me what this is about. I've never seen anyone in the state you're in."

She opened the door of the car and jumped out. Then she reached for one of her suitcases. He clenched his hand around her arm and dragged her back into the car. "What do you think you're doing? Are you crazy? Fauve!"

"If you keep asking me questions I'll hitch a ride to Avignon. Someone will come along and give me a ride."

"All right, all right. You win. But *why* won't you talk to me? Don't you know how much I love you?"

At that promise of tenderness, at that sweet watchfulness, she lost control of herself and abandoned herself to a tempest of wild grief, spasms of gulping, childish sobs mixed with a keening sound of such violent loss that Eric could scarcely prevent himself from stopping the car again. He felt as if the countryside around him had disintegrated. By the time they approached the outskirts of Avignon she had calmed down into a blurred, scattered emptiness.

"Please, let me off at the station. I'll wait there for the evening train."

"I'll stay with you."

"I wish you wouldn't."

"You can't stop me."

They sat on a bench outside the station, Fauve staring straight ahead of her as mute and barred-off from any contact as if she were in a concrete box. Eric tried to hold her hand but she drew quickly away from his touch and folded her arms tightly around her body, tucking her hands under her arms. Only her hair, burning with its inextinguishable flame, reassured him that this was Fauve, his teasing, blithe girl with her festival heart and mirthful impulses. Even when she'd been serious or sorrowful, she'd always been ready to explore difficult feelings without holding back, but now she was locked in a kind of a glacial trance that all his immense love could not penetrate. If only he were really grown up, if only he knew what to do, he thought in anguish, hating himself for being only twenty. He was not able to understand that she could no more tell him what she had learned than if she had been responsible herself for what Mistral had done. She felt extinguished by a weight of shame so great that it was no different from guilt itself. She felt contaminated by being her father's daughter, his monstrous love made her feel as if she must be tainted with his evil, and Kate's revealing words, one filthy secret after another, filled her head like grinding rocks that would rub against each other for a vile eternity.

"Where are you going?" Eric asked.

"New York."

"Do you have your plane ticket?" She nodded. "Your train ticket?"

"I'll buy it on the train."

"I'm going to get it for you now."

"No."

"Fauve, you must let me do something for you or I'll go mad!"

She shrugged her acceptance and he went off to buy the ticket and a supply of sandwiches and mineral water for the trip, and in an impulse of helpless grief, every magazine he could find, although he knew already that she would sit without moving all the way to Paris. Something frightful had been done to her and his passionate intuition told him that nothing on earth would ever give him back the same girl he had left at the gates of *La Tourrello* only a few hours ago.

"Thank you," Fauve said in a white voice when he came back with his purchases. "I'm sorry, Eric."

"Will you answer my letters?"

"Yes."

"Fauve, will you stop once in a while and remember that I love you, that I'll love you *forever* and I'll never stop? If you were only a few years older I'd never let you go, no matter what, you know that, don't you?"

"Yes, Eric," she answered but his heart shriveled as he heard the passive, faraway tone of her voice. She was just saying yes to everything to get rid of him, or make him let her get on the train that he could hear hooting in the distance. All around them people were standing and picking up their luggage and moving purposefully toward the platform.

The train came to a stop and Eric went ahead of Fauve, putting her suitcases on the rack over her head in a first-class carriage, finding her a seat and stowing away her provisions.

She slumped in her seat as limp as a dead animal and he stood over her irresolutely for a few seconds until he heard the guard's whistle blowing to announce the departure of the train. He took her by her elbows and made her stand up and face him.

"We never did get to Lunel," he said.

"No."

The train began to move slowly as he kissed her. It picked up speed and Eric released her. "I promised we'd go and we will. You're my one and only love, Fauve. Never forget me." He ran down the corridor and jumped off at the very edge of the platform, and stood there with tears running down his cheeks as he watched the train disappear to the north, taking his heart away.

On another late summer day, a year later, Kate Mistral sat alone after breakfast, waiting until Mistral left the house. For months he had been gone from morning to evening. He didn't tell her where his roaming took him, but she knew enough to guess that he was searching the countryside for a fresh idea. He had been in a long nonproductive period and for months he had spent no time in his studio. Kate was too realistic not to know that it was no coincidence that this dry spell had started when Fauve left *La Tourrello*. Since then, Mistral had written to Fauve six times. Marte Pollison, who collected the mail from the postman at the gate, reported to Kate when each of the letters was returned unopened. What lies, what attempts at explanations could Julien have concocted? Kate wondered. When Fauve had decamped he had told her only that it had been over a teenaged misunderstanding, a stupid fight about her spending so much time with that Avigdor boy and getting too involved with the Avigdor family.

Several weeks ago he had finally brought himself to write to Maggy and since then, Kate had waited with dread for a response that would reveal her part in Fauve's departure. Yesterday Maggy's answer had finally come, just before Kate left for an appointment in Apt, and Mistral had thrust it unopened into his pocket.

Last night, all through dinner, which was silent and gloomy as it had been for the past year, Mistral's expression had been angry and weary and bitter. It seemed to encompass everything; the fine meal he had been offered, the perfectly laid table, the deft service, even the deliciously scented night air. What could Maggy have written? She had to know.

As soon as Kate heard Mistral drive off she went upstairs to his bedroom and locked herself in. The room was, as always, tidy, impersonal, for his real life was not lived here. There was no letter on the night table where he kept that book on the Jews of Avignon which Fauve had left behind. Kate had seen it there before when, as she occasionally did, she checked his room in his absence and she could still not understand why he kept it around. It wasn't like Julien to torture himself. The top of his desk was bare as well. Deftly she went through its drawers and finally, tucked under a pile of unanswered mail from admirers from all over the world, she found the envelope she had seen him put in his pocket yesterday. It had been torn open. Quickly she read the short note it contained.

Julien,

No, I don't have any idea of why Fauve won't answer your letters, or even read them. I've tried to talk to her about last summer but she absolutely refuses to tell me anything except that she doesn't want to talk about it. She's been very sad and disturbed, more than I can say, and each time you write her it only makes her feel worse. When she saw that you had written to me, she said that I should answer your letter in any way I pleased but that in the future, if you wrote to her again, she didn't want to even know about it. From now on she has asked me to return any letters that you send without telling her that they have come.

I know nothing about this situation between the two of you and I do not intend to enter into it in any way. Whatever you did to make Fauve turn against you, is done and too late to be undone. My own experience with you is such that I have no inclination to grant you the benefit of any doubt.

Maggy

Twice Kate read the letter, replaced it and slipped out of the room, hurrying down to sit in the sun beside the pool.

She was safe now, quite safe, she thought. There would be no more letters to worry about, no possibility of Fauve writing to her father to tell him who had told her all that she had learned on that afternoon a year ago. Safe—all of his paintings, the land, the investments, the bank accounts, all safe from division, saved intact for Nadine to inherit. Her daughter's future would not be compromised, and she herself had nothing left to fear from Fauve.

Kate had never been without a sense of irony and it was that, and that alone, that now kept her sitting so quietly in the sun.

She had been on time for her appointment in Apt with Dr. Elbert yesterday. Elbert was the doctor who delivered Nadine and she preferred him to other specialists in Avignon. When she had begun bleeding again last week, fifteen years after she had gone through menopause, she had reluctantly visited the doctor whom she hadn't bothered to see for years. Cancer of the uterus, he had told her, and so far advanced that it had spread to her liver. How long did she have? A year, perhaps, a little more or a little less, but Madame Mistral, there is nothing that can be done at this stage of the disease. If anything could have been done I would have had to see you long before this . . . and even then, who knows?

Who knew indeed? Who ever knew? Kate asked herself. She looked around her. All was in order, a rich empire, magnificent, secure and absolutely intact. For the first time since Teddy Lunel had walked through the doors of *La Tourrello*, Kate finally could feel certain that she was in full possession again . . . for a year—or a little more or a little less.

27

It was Fauve Lunel's twenty-first birthday, in the middle of June 1974, and the second floor of the Russian Tea Room was crowded with two hundred people, each of them glowing with the unspoken satisfaction of knowing that their importance was validated by their having been bidden to this particular coming-of-age, a pleasure that is such a basic component of human nature that it must have been experienced by cave dwellers gathered around a particularly prestigious fire.

From behind his big glasses, Falk, whose closest friends still called him Melvin, scanned the horde that palpitated with noise at the decible level only achieved in New York; his eyes dilated with the intensity of an observation that was as profound as it was swift. Here, right here, he thought, were gathered together all the people who had the power to decide how the American woman would hope to look each morning when she woke up.

He kissed Diana Vreeland and Cheryl Tiegs, reaching up to do so with no more self-consciousness than that with which a short woman kisses a tall man, and, as he hugged Lauren Hutton, pleased by her particular conformation of features, he reflected that women believed that they made their own choices about their physical aspirations, yet it was photographers like himself who were responsible for the wind of change that sent women to hairdressers and cosmetic counters and department stores. Yet he realized that even he was not as influential as Maggy Lunel, who, by picking out new models and sending them to see the right people, could determine the way everybody in the world would eventually come to think about ideal female beauty.

But did the *ultimate* power really rest in the hands of the fashion or beauty editor who made the decision to use one girl rather than another, or, he wondered as he gave Christina Ferrare a kiss on each glowing cheek, did the power ultimately rest in the hands of these splendorous girls who offered themselves to the camera? Where would the entire establishment of fashion magazines, advertising agencies, cosmetic companies, photographers and model agencies find itself without a never-ending supply of beauties willing to devote their young lives to becoming icons for all other women? In any case, Falk didn't have to come to any hard and fast philosophical conclusions tonight since everyone involved in creating the standards to which women all over the country would find themselves responding was right there in this room. Everyone, that is, but Fauve. Where *was* Fauve?

In the last five years Falk had seen less of her than he would have liked. While she was growing up they had spent most Saturday afternoons making the rounds of the galleries, but in the early fall of 1969 she had, and there was no other way he could find to describe the change in her, quite simply turned her back on art. She had blamed this abrupt, and to Falk, shocking loss of interest on the experience of going to the landmark exhibition called "New York Painting and Sculpture: 1940–1970," which Henry Geldzahler had mounted at the Metropolitan Museum.

God knows, it *had* been enough to give anyone visual indigestion, that overrich slumgullion in which thirty-five different galleries had been used to give thirty-five retrospective exhibitions to thirty-five of the greatest contemporary artists, but Falk would have thought a sixteen-year-old appetite equal to such esthetic burn-out. Even he, veteran of the art spectacular, had found himself battered by the unheard-of gaudiness of the evening, bewildered by its excesses, deafened by the barbaric rock band and footworn from the sheer size of the show, but Fauve had responded with something close to hysteria, saying that she never wanted to look at another piece of art or sculpture again. He'd been sure that she meant only until the next interesting show. How could anyone with Fauve's passion for art become indifferent to the complex set of experiences that looking at new work must give her?

Yet as time went on, he found that her disgust not only endured but deepened into a kind of sadness, as if she were mourning the death of art. She had insisted that all the great men had already painted, all the innovations had been made, all the great themes used up, all graphic possibilities discovered, so that new artists were only using the sweepings of the studio floors of past masters.

Falk had laughed at Fauve's notions until he realized that she had stopped working on her own painting. When he questioned her about it she was direct. She didn't intend ever to paint again. How could she keep on going when she had nothing new to add? Although Falk had always recognized the unmistakable influence of Mistral on her work he had also seen a true and original talent struggling to emerge. He knew that it was merely a question of time before she came into her own, before all that was personal and fresh in her work grew strong enough to make her break away from her father and strike out on her own. But instead of making progress, she had quit, quit flat and by now, he was sure, quit for good and all.

Falk bit into a *pirojok*, savoring the hot, flaky puff pastry made from sour-cream dough, and, munching, reflected that what was, to his certain knowledge a real loss for the world of art had been a gain for the model agency business.

Who would have imagined that Fauve, graduating from high school at seventeen, would have decided to go to work for Maggy rather than go to college? And who would have expected her to be so astonishingly good at it? In the last four years she had not just learned the business through and through, but she had made innovations that had kept the Lunel Agency ahead of its competition, so that she had become Maggy's second-in-command. She had worked so hard, with so much ambition and energy and determination that her youth and inexperience had been overcome by the time she was nineteen and since then "Lunel" had come more and more to refer equally to Fauve as it did to Maggy.

Falk found himself standing with Dick Avedon and Irving Penn, the only other photographers who had remained at the very top for as long as he had, the only others to whom every new talent was inevitably compared. As he talked to them he reflected on the rareness of longevity, staying power and endless excellence in this world where change was the rule. Yet Maggy Lunel still moved in an aura of supremacy.

Now she was at that age that could best be described as "age-less," enigmatically, flamboyantly, triumphantly ageless. And age-less she would remain, he decided, saluting her in his mind, for at least another two decades, until she moved on, gracefully, into a period in which she would be known, no doubt to her vast annoyance, as a "living legend."

When he had greeted her tonight there had been an exchange of sad recognition beneath their smiles. Each had known the other's thoughts and shared an unspoken word of never-fading grief. *If only Teddy were here.*

Falk pushed away the thought, as he had done so many thousands of times, through three marriages to fashion models, through the birth of four children, all inheriting the genes of their mothers and now all taller than he was—thank heaven for great big girls—and looked around for the one person he sought in this crowded room. He was fond, very fond indeed of his own children, but Fauve had come into his heart before he had married for the first time, and by some process of wishful thinking that he never chose to examine, she had always seemed like the daughter he should have had with Teddy Lunel. But where *was* Fauve?

Maggy Lunel took a final look of self-appraisal in her floor-to-ceiling three-way mirror before she left her apartment to go to Fauve's birthday party. So she was a woman with a twenty-one-year-old granddaughter, was she? Well, so much the better! She pivoted, checking the back of her jacket, made of several layers of thin, drifting, black silk crêpe de chine printed with oversized flowers in melting Oriental shades of plum, lavender and deeper violet shading into purple. Did all women, she wondered, as she passed her hand over the back of her hair where it curved inward gracefully in a smooth pageboy at the nape of her neck, feel the same way she did? As if she had stopped growing older at some undefined age that never changed except on certain bad days? An age that hovered at some agreeably mellow yet fresh moment of time between twenty-six and thirty-two?

She picked up the edge of the jacket and inspected its leaf-printed lining. Now there was a refinement indeed, since the lining would never be noticed, but one that Karl Lagerfeld of Chloé, who had designed the vaguely kimono-shaped garment, and the small-scaled printed tunic dress that went underneath it, must have loved working out, for was he not the man who had quite seriously asked his mother to give him his own valet as a present for his fourth birthday? Yes, the costume was successful because the long, firm lines of the body under it had withstood the test of time, but when Maggy clasped the Van Cleef and Arpels diamond necklace around her throat she had to concede that her interior age level did not quite match the evidence presented by her neck. Why was it that most women who owned the kind of necklace that a jeweler, with an air that categorized the words as having an exact technical significance, could refer to as "important," were not likely to have unlined necks? Damn necks! If only all heads rested directly on shoulders how much more delightful the world would be. Her shoulders still could compete in any company.

As Maggy caught the fleeting, boastful thought she asked herself in a combination of amusement and irritation if she were growing vain? She could have sworn that any vanity she must once have had, had been absolutely knocked out of her by daily dealing with the youngest and loveliest of all the millions of girls in the world. Her neck must only be a stand-in for the milestone that was marked by Fauve's birthday.

Yet, in Fauve's case, twenty-one certainly didn't mean the beginning of maturity or adulthood. No, that change had taken place five years before and Maggy knew no more of what had caused it today than she did then, when Fauve had come home unexpectedly early from her summer in France. At first Maggy had bombarded her with questions, but Fauve had refused to discuss what had happened with a stubbornness, a leaden and inflexible tenacity that Maggy had been sure she couldn't maintain. But, as the weeks passed and she saw the differences in Fauve, the loss of her young girl's illusions, the disappearance of her innocent playfulness, she began to understand that once again she had sent a beloved child to Europe and once again that child had been changed, terribly changed, by Julien Mistral. But at least this child had returned.

After a year had passed, Maggy simply accepted the fact that she would probably never know what had taken place. Fauve, so spontaneous, so open, so alive that every enthusiasm that crossed her heart showed in her face, had somehow learned to keep a secret. It had been a deeply distressing year, that year between sixteen and seventeen, Fauve's last year in high school, Maggy reflected, secure now in the knowledge that it was long past. The mysterious hurt had never been resolved. Fauve never returned to France. After Maggy had answered the letter Mistral sent her, all communication between him and his daughter had ceased as completely as if those eight summers in Félice had never happened.

Fauve, so flexible, so loving and quick to forgive, had been utterly implacable on the subject of her father. She had cast him out of her life. At first Maggy had had to admit to an intense curiosity to know what had caused the rupture but, where Julien Mistral was concerned, it was unwise to think too long or too deeply.

For the first few years Fauve had received and answered frequent letters from that boy she'd met over there, old Avigdor's son of all people, but now the letters had almost stopped coming—Maggy couldn't even be sure if they still wrote each other now or not. But eventually, Fauve had pulled herself out of the depression in which she had been enveloped.

Time . . . it was partly the passage of time, Maggy decided, partly the blessed elasticity of youth and most of all it had been the remedy of work. When Fauve first announced that she didn't intend to apply to college but wanted to work, Maggy had thought for one despairing moment that Fauve intended to become a model. She wouldn't have been able to prevent it. Fauve had had the unassailable, mesmerizing quality that would have made her into the face that personified her era as clearly as Suzy Parker and Teddy had personified the fifties and as Jean Shrimpton had dominated the mid-sixties. But, thank God, Fauve had wanted to follow her into the business. She had turned her back on using the privileges of beauty as a source of identity just as resolutely as she had turned her back on her talent for painting. Fauve had no interest in becoming the vigilant caretaker of her façade, no wish to be obliged to deal in merchandising her own surface, and she had taken to the agency business as if she had absorbed it all of her life.

Fauve had immersed herself in work with an efficiency and a diligence that had amazed Maggy, and during those first two years she was given an opportunity to learn every job in the agency. By the time Fauve was nineteen, in the spring of 1972, Maggy grew accustomed to being able to count on Fauve to make decisions she had never allowed anyone else to make but herself. In action Fauve was crisp, forceful and effective in a way that demonstrated a solidity greater than her years.

It was then that Maggy dared to take a vacation, her first in a long time, and when she and Darcy returned from two weeks in London she found her agency flourishing and Fauve secure and serene. Maggy was invaded by elation, a giddy feeling, an intoxication of relief, glorious relief, that lightened her limbs and made her thirst for activities she hadn't allowed herself much time for in all those years since she'd started her own business, those years in which she'd supported herself and her daughter, vowing never again to be weak and foolish enough to depend on a man for anything but affection, and even to do without that if necessary.

She gave herself permission to sleep deliciously late in the morning, arriving at the office only two hours before it was time to go out to lunch with a friend, where she sat talking until the middle of the afternoon as heedlessly as if she had been doing it all of her life. She threw away all her hats and gloves—what were they doing in her wardrobe? She had her hair restyled and even changed its color, from the determined auburn that was appropriate for her office persona, to a softer color, artfully blended with titian and light brown into which a few stray strands of silver were allowed to wander as if by mistake. Maggy spent many hours shopping for new, less tailored clothes and she hired Susie Frankfort to give her grand, almost too dignified, apartment a whimsical and original charm. Oh, but it was bliss to begin to lay down the burden she had carried alone for so long, Maggy thought, but why had no one noticed? Everyone treated her just as they always had, she realized with increasing pique. She had been The Boss, that old reliable, a workhorse with business on her mind for so long that people saw her only in that light. She didn't expect them to act as if she had just been elected Queen of the May but surely someone might have noticed!

One night, late in that spring season that was like a rebirth, Maggy and Darcy went out to dinner. At "21," the headwaiter, Walter Weiss, led them to their table, the same table at which they had sat that first time they had been there together in 1931 when it had been the best speakeasy in New York.

Darcy, as was his unalterable, almost sacred habit of forty-two years, sat at table 7 in the first section of the bar, to the left of the entrance and in the center of the side wall. It was a prime, strategic, highly visible and much coveted banquette to which many other powerful men had aspired in vain.

401

Any table in the first two sections of the bar was utterly desirable, for "21" was the only dining place in New York that had retained the glory and the glamour of its legend, the only restaurant whose imperial status remained undiminished as it rode out the decades with the steadiness of a great ocean liner on which nothing could possibly go wrong; a world unto itself as no other restaurant in the United States has ever succeeded in being or ever will be again. The assurance of always being led to a certain specific and distinguished table in the bar at "21" was something mere money had never been able to buy, a symbol more valued than a membership in the most exclusive club or a seat on the most important board of directors since it signified a high and continued place in the power structure of the country. Darcy's lien on table 7 was part of the innermost organization of his life, and he sighed in visible contentment as they settled down on the banquette.

"Why," complained Maggy, "do we *always* have to sit in this bar? Do you realize that we've never eaten in the main dining room upstairs?" Darcy looked as astonished as if he'd found table 7 occupied by a rock star. "I understand," Maggy continued with a wistful air that verged on petulance, "that it's very agreeable upstairs. I hear it's less noisy and more spacious. Onassis always eats there and Dr. Armand Hammer and Mrs. Douglas MacArthur and Nelson Rockefeller . . . and we're always *stuck* down here. It does seem too bad."

"But you've never wanted to eat upstairs, you've never even seen it as far as I know." Darcy was outraged. The upstairs was all right, he supposed, solid and corporate and formal, but a man with any juice left in his bones would always prefer to eat in the bar, in which he fancied he could still feel and hear and smell those great days of Prohibition, when Jack and Charlie's served the best booze in town.

"That's no reason for you to make such assumptions," Maggy said plaintively. She plucked disdainfully at the distinctively checked red-and-white tablecloth. "On the tables upstairs there's lovely plain white linen, the heavy old-fashioned kind, all slippery and starched, at least that's what Lally said. And there are flowers on the tables instead of these ugly red match holders." She sighed with the resigned sadness of a penniless little girl pressing her nose against a candy store window and pensively adjusted the bow of the navy blouse that went with her new, dashingly nautical, white Adolfo suit.

"Damn it, if you're so unhappy here, why the hell didn't you tell me sooner!" Darcy said furiously. "Let's go upstairs . . . come on."

"Oh, no, it's too much trouble. It was just a thought, something that wandered through my mind," Maggy murmured. "Anyway I'm not exactly unhappy here, I'm just restless." She sipped the glass of champagne from the bottle of Bollinger Brut 1947 the waiter had opened as soon as he saw Maggy and Darcy sit down at the table at which they dined two or three times a week. "I wonder what tequila tastes like," she said in a forlorn, diminished voice.

"I'll order you some," Darcy snorted, raising his eyebrows.

"Oh, no, never mind, don't bother, I don't really care, it was just a passing fancy." She looked pitifully sorry for herself as she rejected the mere idea of tequila. "Champagne is quite good enough for me . . . or so you've always assumed . . . just pay no attention."

"What the devil is this all about actually?" Darcy asked, twisting around so that he faced her as she sat, as upright and slender as she had ever been and in so many infuriating ways as unexaminable a siren as she'd been on the first night he'd taken her here and looked into her great eyes of that color that was still just as much green as it was gold, and wondered who the hell *was* Maggy Lunel?

"I'm tired . . ." she almost whispered.

"We'll go home," he said, alarmed. Maggy was never tired unless she was sick.

"I'm tired of your thinking that I'm not open to new experiences, I'm tired of being treated as if any change in routine would be unwelcome," she murmured. "I'm tired of . . . of . . . your lack of attention, Darcy. You take me for granted," she said, broodingly.

"What absolute rot!"

"So you deny it, do you?" Suddenly she quivered with energy. Her words came pouring out. "I thought you would, an insensitive, thoughtless, unromantic man like you . . . a woman might as well go out for dinner with her old uncle . . . her grandfather . . . her *great-grandfather*."

"What!" he roared.

"Don't shout at me! Just how long has it been since the last time you asked me to marry you?" Her face was flushed with accusation and indignation.

"*How long?* As long as it's been since I decided to stop making a goddamned fool out of myself! That's how long . . ." he sputtered, with the injustice of her words.

"You haven't answered my question." She was implacable.

"Fifteen years—no, I think I asked you on Valentine's Day once, about a dozen years ago, like an utter ass. Yes—I remember it now . . . you seemed particularly loving that night and I just gave it another shot, just like poor, bloody, old faithful that I am, even though I knew perfectly well that there wasn't a chance. You'd think I'd have learned."

"Ah ha!" Maggy's anger was triumphant. "So now I know why you kept asking. Because you were *safe* and it cost you absolutely nothing to make the gesture. I've always thought so, I always knew you were just like the others, I've always seen through your act. I've had quite enough of this neglect, thank you! I despise your low tactics and I don't intend to put up with them for another minute. It's shameful, a disgrace!"

"You . . . you . . . ungrateful bitch!"

"Is that a proposal?" she demanded, eyes flashing fury.

"Absolutely not!"

"So! When it comes down to it you're unwilling to make a commitment, aren't you? Too big a decision, isn't it?" she sneered. "Okay, Darcy, you have exactly one minute to get your priorities straight."

"Is *that* a proposal?"

"Only a man who lacked gallantry to his very *soul* would ask a woman to answer such a question. How dare you?"

"Captain!" Darcy beckoned him over. "We're moving upstairs for dinner. Send up two double tequilas on the rocks. Madame and I have some arrangements to make and there's just too damn much noise in this saloon."

And so, Maggy remembered, they had been married two years ago, and high time too as Lally Longbridge had said, taking all the credit as usual. She was still standing in front of the mirror, almost in a trance, when Darcy came in, dressed to go to Fauve's birthday party. As she looked at their double reflection she felt a little, irrepressible jump of blithesome joy. How *right* she had been to marry this man.

Darcy ate another tiny potato stuffed with fresh caviar and dotted with sour cream and decided that Henry McIheeny, that bon vivant who had once said, "Caviar should never be served with cocktails. You have to be seated to enjoy it," had been entirely too

404

pompous. He took another and popped it into his mouth, making the most of a momentary lull at the top of the staircase where he and Maggy stood greeting their guests while behind them the party was approaching that moment at which it could be said to be in orbit. Yet *where* was Fauve?

Polly Mellen, of *Vogue,* who knew more about putting the absolutely right model in the absolutely right dress—and most important of all—in absolutely the right *way,* was there, with most of her staff members, and so was Tony Mazzola, who had been editor-in-chief of *Harper's Bazaar* forever, accompanied by his upper echelon, and so was Tom Hogan of Clairol and Estée Lauder with her entire family and Gilbert Shawn, president of Warshaw, the catalog producers and perhaps the most prolific employer of models in the world, and to Darcy's utter astonishment, so were Eileen and Jerry Ford, whose model agency had been Maggy's chief—and formidable—competition since the late 1940s.

The fact that Maggy had invited her only major rival was the most significant indication that the woman he had loved for so long had truly changed, Darcy mused. Three years ago, if he had been asked whether it was more likely that Maggy would marry him or that she'd ask the Fords to a party, he would have picked marriage, as impossible as it had then seemed. The competition between the two agencies had escalated with the years and with the steady raise in the hourly rates paid to the models.

Maggy's income, before expenses, on the fees earned by her girls, came to close to two million dollars a year and the Fords were not far behind. Each agency had, among its several hundred models, a group of a half-dozen or so top models, who would, while earning more than almost any man in America, always be called "girls" and never "women." These girls were property, as real as if each of them were a fully rented office building whose tenants always paid their rent on time.

For over twenty years Maggy Lunel and Eileen Ford had vied for these same precious pieces of property, and since neither woman took kindly to losing, and since one of them lost each time the other won, a truce, however momentary, amazed Darcy.

"We're like the oil-producing countries," Maggy had explained to him. "Eileen and I, and now Wilhelmina in the last seven years and even Zoli, since 1970, run the only games in town worth mentioning. We can't fix prices or form a monopoly because it's against those ridiculous antitrust laws. But we're responsible to our girls to maintain standards so that they don't get unfairly treated by the advertising agencies and the photographers—after all, they only have a few good earning years before they're over the hill—so, as their representatives I've always thought we should be on reasonably good terms with each other." Now Darcy understood her motivation; she was thinking about Fauve's future.

One day Fauve would be alone running the agency and Maggy wanted her to be as secure as possible, free of long-standing feuds. Darcy didn't believe it was an idea whose time would *ever* come but he enjoyed watching Maggy struggling with her attempt to be pragmatic. Basically, he thought, as he studied her now, she was the most splendid woman in the room, even though it also contained Karen Graham and Renee Russo, but sweet reasonableness wasn't her style. He enjoyed her most when she was her feisty, fiery, everyday self, but organizing this party had brought out Maggy's mother-hen side, and she had, for the event, managed to gloss over the viciously competitive spirit that existed, had always existed and would always exist in the model agency business. Her very inconsistency delighted him.

Jason Darcy knew he was a lucky man. He'd dragged Maggy before a judge before she had a chance to change her mind but even as the ceremony progressed he'd wondered what differences a legal tie could make to a union that had lasted for so long. While he was repeating his vows he'd been remembering case histories without end of people who had had long and loving relationships until they made the mistake of indulging in marriage. What then about the example set by novelist Fanny Hurst, who had lived in great happiness with her husband for many years during which they occupied two different apartments and made appointments whenever they wanted to be together? Might that not be the ideal way to conduct such an unnatural, inhuman, artificial arrangement as marriage? But Maggy, this ardent, wistful, girlish, springtime Maggy who had popped out one night at "21," apparently intended to become his wife and he hadn't dared to entertain too many second thoughts.

And it *was* different. It was, quite simply, *better*. Better to know that she finally trusted him, better to know that after all she was willing to depend on him a little, better not to wake up in the morning in another room on another street and not know what his beloved was doing or feeling until he reached her by telephone. He decided that marriage was such a lovely treat that it should be reserved only for the middle-aged. Young people should be forbidden by law to regularize any of their romances until they had passed fifty because they couldn't possibly appreciate the charms of matrimony as long as they thought of it as a right rather than a privilege. It should be a *reward* for being faithful and loving, reserved for those who had been true to each other. He did, however, have the good sense to keep these opinions to himself. His reputation for crusty toughness would be destroyed if they ever became public and, since Darcy still published one of the most successful groups of magazines in the country, he didn't want to sound uxorious.

"Where the hell is Fauve?" said a man's voice behind him.

"I thought she might be with you," Darcy said, turning to Ben Litchfield, his one-time *protégé* whom he had watched rise from a space-salesman's job in the advertising department of *Woman's Journal,* the biggest and most successful women's magazine in the country, to editor-in-chief, bewildering the world of women's magazines by reaching the top just before he turned thirty.

"I wish she were," he said, "but I haven't seen her since Monday."

Benjamin Franklin Litchfield was the most fervent, and seemingly the most successful of Fauve's many suitors, although she kept her own council and Maggy and Darcy could only speculate. Darcy felt a proprietary interest in the man's case for he had introduced them himself a year ago.

Fauve and Ben should know each other he decided one day when he had tried to telephone each of them on a Sunday morning and discovered them both in their respective offices, hard at work on matters they had put aside for the weekend when they wouldn't be interrupted. He had insisted that they both finish up in an hour and join him and Maggy for lunch. It had taken all his authority to persuade the industrious pair to agree to such a reckless waste of time but, since that first meeting, Darcy had reason to suggest that they were moving toward spending Sunday mornings in bed together, an arrangement he favored as much more humane, and better for the circulation, the complexion and the psyche.

Maggy, too, approved of young Litchfield. In some ways he reminded her of Darcy when she'd first met him: he had that intensity that masked a capacity to be amused by the major absurdities of life, he had Darcy's curiosity and much, she sensed, of Darcy's generosity, but physically he had none of the lean and philosophic, almost ascetic distinction that had first attracted her to her love.

Handsome Ben Litchfield was a habitually rumpled man. He started out each day with the best of intentions, tall, muscular, conventionally clad in a well-pressed suit, a clean shirt, and freshly shined shoes, but by lunch he was a disgrace to the world of *Gentleman's Quarterly*. He had pulled at his thick sandy hair in despair so many times that it stood up on end where it wasn't falling into his eyes, he had tugged impatiently at the knot of his tie until it reached the third, by-now-unbuttoned button of the shirt that was peeping out between his vest and his trousers, his pockets were stuffed with papers and stubs of other people's pencils and he'd usually lost all of the three pairs of horn-rimmed glasses he needed in order to see layouts or read manuscripts.

But when Ben Litchfield took off his glasses his enormous, myopic blue eyes were as startled and happy as those of a baby waking up to the sight of his first elephant. He greeted everything in life with that same look of surprise and acceptance, although his associates had been heard to mutter that he was about as innocent as a vice squad cop in Detroit. He had the sudden, sweet, half-astonished smile of a man who's doing what he likes best and doing it better than anyone else. He'd been so busy getting to the top that he'd never paused and looked around for a serious girl until he'd met Fauve.

"Not since Monday?" Darcy asked. "I thought you two were seeing a lot of each other . . . that's three days."

"I know," Litchfield groaned. "Listen, Darcy. You've taught me everything I know as you've reminded me on innumerable occasions, usually in public. How do you get a girl to marry you?"

"Exercise patience, my boy, patience."

"Thanks a heap. That's a big help."

"Lunel women do not take to marriage easily, if ever." In fact, Darcy thought with complacency, he was the only man to have managed to marry one of them, the only man to have actually lured one of the line of three, lovely, redheaded Lunel women into matrimony. One of the three illegitimate Lunel women, he mused, for Maggy had told him the whole story on their honeymoon and he was, he believed, the only person on earth besides Fauve who knew that Maggy and Teddy had been as illegitimate as Fauve herself. "I won't have a minute's peace of mind until I see Fauve safely married," Maggy had told him. "Three bastards in a row are more than enough."

"Come on, Ben, let me buy you a *blini*, and we'll talk this over seriously. I may be able to give you some good advice—I don't think, after all, that too much patience is such a good idea," Darcy said. Perhaps it wasn't altogether fair to corner the market on Lunels. He owed it to Maggy to be more helpful. But where *was* Fauve?

He looked down the staircase again. At last! There she came, as flagrantly gorgeous as he'd ever seen her, long red hair flying, dressed in a streak of silver sequins, cut like a short slip, her cheeks bright with a flush of excitement, bounding up the staircase two steps at a time calling, "Magali, Magali, I'm sorry I'm so late!" A succulent girl like a salamander whose natural element is fire, Fauve Lunel arrived at her birthday party, but not alone. She had her hand firmly locked around the wrist of another girl—at least Darcy supposed it was a girl—a six-foot-tall scarecrow of a creature, in overalls and sneakers, with her flaxen hair cropped almost to a crew cut and a bewildered look on her face as she loped after Fauve.

"Magali—look what I brought you! She's just off the bus from Arkansas—do you think what I think?"

Maggy inspected the girl. The look of top models of the day was elegant, sophisticated, sculptured, with flowing hair. The girl was all bold bones and ever-so-slightly buck teeth, freckles and winged eyebrows. She had stupefying promise. So the look was about to change. Trust Fauve.

"Is she why you're late?"

"Yep. I was upstairs at the office, just checking out a few things before the party started and she wandered in off the street. Her friends, the ones she came on the bus with, had dared her to come up. So, naturally, that meant talking to them and then phoning her parents and telling them why she wasn't coming home and convincing them that I wasn't a white slaver and finding a place for her to stay . . . you know."

"What's your name?" Maggy asked the girl.

"Ida Clegg."

"Hmm . . . well, welcome to the Lunel Agency. Do you drink vodka?"

"Darned if this isn't a day for firsts," the girl said in a soft southern voice. "Yes, Ma'am, I believe I will."

Maggy turned to Fauve and kissed her, whispering, "But why didn't you leave all those details till tomorrow?"

"Magali, she *also* had Eileen's address on a piece of paper—her friends had dared her to go there too," Fauve whispered back.

"Why didn't you say so right away, for heaven's sake? I was worried."

"Because look behind you."

Maggy turned and found Eileen Ford standing there, looking, as always, like the girl who will inevitably be elected president of any class she's in.

"Happy birthday, Fauve," Eileen said with a warm smile.

"Thank you, Eileen."

"You must be very proud, Maggy."

"Oh, I am!"

"And who is this?"

"A new girl we've just discovered—Arkansas."

Eileen gave Ida Clegg a quick, piercing look that saw everything, knew everything, understood everything. "Arkansas?" she asked. "Arkansas what?"

"Just Arkansas," Fauve replied.

"I see. How patriotic. Well, Arkansas, welcome to New York." Eileen walked away thoughtfully. She did not look happy.

"Who was that nice lady?" Arkansas asked.

"Ahh . . . that was . . ." Maggy began.

"Nobody you'll ever need to know," Fauve assured her hastily.

28

Fauve Lunel almost sprinted through the doors of the old elevator that opened so slowly on the tenth floor of the Carnegie Hall office building where the Lunel Agency was located. She was late for her regular Friday meeting with Casey d'Augustino, but Benjamin Franklin Litchfield had been exceedingly persistent last night and she'd overslept this morning. Fauve whisked through the reception room where the walls were hung with six framed magazine covers of former Lunel models.

"Only six," Maggy had once said, "out of all our hundreds and hundreds because when anyone waits to be interviewed in that room and looks at those covers she'll leave if she doesn't have enough self-confidence to make it. Then, when I have to turn her down, on her way out she'll find comfort in the same pictures because after all how could anybody be expected to be as beautiful as those girls were?"

The agency, as it had grown over the years, occupied more and more space in the fine old building and still it was crowded. All model agencies are crowded the way restaurant kitchens and army camps and backstages are crowded. There is never enough room for all the items needed to properly perform the functions for which the space is intended, and if by some miracle of design, enough room were provided, the work would suffer because of lack of communication between the necessary personnel.

Maggy's own office was large and comfortable but Fauve and

411

Casey shared two small offices next to one of the three booking rooms which were the heart of the agency. The bookers all seemed to be busy on the phones, Fauve noted automatically as she sat down at her desk and buzzed Casey to come in. The Men's Division, supervised by Joe O'Donnel, who had once been a male model himself, was across the hall, and occupied even more cramped and less elegant space.

Casey d'Augustino had been working at the agency for only a year but she and Fauve functioned as a team. She was a graduate of Hunter, the public high school that accepts only the best and the brightest of New York's students, and smart, *smart* Casey, born with what she considered the unimaginatively ethnic name of Anna-Maria to a large Brooklyn family two generations removed from Palermo, was Fauve's closest friend. She sat down in one of the two chairs opposite the desk and groaned, cautiously patting her curly, short hair down over her forehead as if searching for bumps or bruises.

"What's wrong?" Fauve inquired cheerfully.

"Champagne hangover. The worst kind. Everybody has one. The whole staff. It was drinking all those toasts."

"I feel fine," Fauve said, surprised.

"You can't drink a toast to yourself, so don't look so virtuous, it was only because it was your birthday and not mine. On mine I promise you a lethal hangover."

"I brought you a present."

"Nothing will make it better."

"It's a counterirritant."

"I don't like it already."

"It's the new issue of *Cosmo*. Article on Lauren Hutton by Guy Flatley. Listen to this. She's talking about a 'go-see' with Diana Vreeland, her first venture into high fashion.

"A dozen models were parading all about her. And there I sat like a toad, taking in the whole scene. Suddenly—in the middle of a sentence—D.V. stopped and pointed a long, white-gloved finger at me. 'You!' she said.

'Me.'

'Yes, you . . . you have a great presence,' she said, her great eagle eyes piercing me.

'Thank you,' I said. 'So do *you*.'

She gave me a tiny smile and went back to finishing her

412

sentence. And that afternoon I got a call to report to Richard Avedon's studio and have some pictures taken."

"Oh, *shit!*" Casey jumped up. "No, tell me it isn't true! Tell me you're making it up! Tell me that this is just a vicious practical joke and you did it to show how much you love me, to take my mind off my physical paralysis, to force my blood to try and irrigate my liver once again."

"Feel better already, don't you?" Fauve said, pleased.

"God, yes. I feel like I could tear out a lioness's throat with my bare hands. Oh, how can they do that to us? Do you realize that *millions* of women read every issue of *Cosmo* religiously and when they see that little story they're all going to think that it could happen to them? 'Sitting there like a toad,' my ass! Lauren never looked like a toad on the worst day she ever had. Anyway *Eileen*, for the love of God, sent her to see Vreeland, she didn't just drop by! And where are all those *Cosmo* readers going to end up? Right here in our hallway waiting on line for the open auditions Tuesday morning. We'd better put on an extra girl to process them."

"Yep. But, Casey, you know it can happen and you know it must have happened just like that because Lauren's so straight she wouldn't make it up."

"Sure. 'Lightning' has to strike once in a while—but that doesn't mean that if you go out in Central Park and wait for ten years it's gonna strike you. Anyway, what's this I hear about you and Miss Texarkana? Faith's out with her buying her some clothes—what's up?"

"More 'lightning.' "

The two girls exchanged a smile of anticipation and cautious excitement, like two miners panning for gold who just may have hit pay dirt. Modeling was a business built on an occasional flash of lightning and many long hours of sheer hard work, but without the lightning, the sudden arrival on the scene of a new and singular type of beauty, it wouldn't be the business that had grown more and more fascinating over the last few decades, until it rivaled moviemaking in its appeal to the public.

Like everyone else who works in a field that trafficks in the flimflam business of glamour, they knew the truths behind that elusive illusion; the vital importance of being equal to the daily grind; the incredible persistence and the unending discipline, to say nothing of the absolutely crucial need to be in the right place at the right time. And yet they knew that glamour *did* exist and that certain faces had it, a quality no more to be explained than charm could be explained. They understood that some faces inspired *emotion*, and they were trained to recognize those faces amid a sea of girls who were just plain beautiful. The difference was so small that in most cases it had to be a subjective decision.

Every year thousands and thousands of girls were seen by the Lunel Agency; those who wrote and enclosed photographs; those who won the dozens of regional modeling competitions that were held all over the world; and those who came in person to the agency. And out of all of them they selected no more than thirty to represent. Why did they take on those particular thirty? Neither Maggy nor Fauve nor Casey could have written it out in words or made a diagram. All the basic rules were well known, all other physical requirements for a model could be met by a large number of the hopeful girls they turned down. They saw so many applicants that only someone who was blatantly special caused them to take a second look. Casey called it "something *behind* the eyes" and Fauve called it a sense of "heightened reality" but they both meant the same thing—lightning.

"First on my agenda," said Casey, "there's the case of Miss Day O'Daniel who called me again this morning. She's ready to jump ship and come over here but she wants her own booker."

"How negotiable is that?" Fauve asked briskly.

"It's her own booker or no go."

Day O'Daniel was one of the top half-dozen girls at another agency. Recently she'd become restless in the fretful ways models occasionally did for reasons no one could truly fathom, and had let it be known that she'd consider changing to Lunel. Her contract, like all contracts in 1974, required only thirty days' notice by either party for termination, and Fauve and Casey were eager to represent the exquisitely fine-boned brunette whose range was one of the greatest in the business. Range, the ability to inhabit a Galanos dress with careless authority and yet to look unthreateningly lovely in a mass-market magazine ad, was one of the qualities necessary before any girl who was already a top model could aspire to superstar status—and Day had it. However, Lunel had a policy, laid down by Maggy, of not permitting any model her own booker.

"Day said that she wouldn't feel she'd really come into her own until she had her own booker, she said that she wanted someone with whom she could feel totally secure and comfortable, someone who would know all her needs, someone who would give her the feeling that she was being taken care of. I quote."

"Maybe she should go home to mother," Fauve said broodingly. "It's such a mistaken and naïve idea that having your own booker is the only way to prove that you've made it. Doesn't she realize that if I give her her own booker every other booker in the agency will mentally click her off and forget about her? What if her booker is out to lunch? What if her booker's sick for the week or gets another job—Day would never be properly protected. It's a crazy way to run a career. I hope you told her."

"Gee, no, Fauve. I thought I'd let you do that yourself because you do it so well."

"Droll. I see you're feeling better. It's frightening how nice you can be when you're really sick. I'm always reassured when you revert to your truly rotten self. So our Big Board isn't enough for Day O'Daniel?"

Fauve's eyes wandered to the activity she could oversee through the half-glassed wall of her office. She had a view into all three booking areas: the smallish Test Board room, where all new girls, whose careers were just starting, were handled by four bookers; the huge Center Board room, where fourteen bookers arranged the schedules for the majority of the Lunel models, and the legendary Big Board room, in which three top bookers handled calls for a mere twenty girls, the stars of the agency. "Did she actually come right out and insist that it wouldn't be enough to be on the Big Board?" Fauve persisted.

"I thought I'd let you find that out."

"I think I'll let Magali ask her," Fauve said.

"She's gone to the country for the weekend, remember, and Ms. O'Daniel wants to get an answer today. Day left her home number—you can call her tonight."

"Okay, next." Once again Fauve was reminded that from Thursday evening till sometime late on Monday, Maggy now spent her time in the country place she and Darcy had bought outside of Bedford Village. It was still difficult to realize that Maggy had actually brought herself to leave her agency entirely in Fauve's hands for two out of five days a week. But Darcy had trained his various editors to claim only three days of his time each week, finding in the

415

process that they became more efficient and self-reliant. He had always maintained that work contracted to fit comfortably into the least amount of time you were willing to devote to it, and when he and Maggy married he decided to fulfill his dream of spending long weekends in the country.

"Next," said Casey, "Miss Nebula, Miss Cosmos, Miss Super Nova, Miss Milky Way or whatever it was she won, declines to go through the Program. She says she doesn't need it—she's been through enough training for a lifetime. No, do not *dare* to ask me. I've already told her that everybody goes through the Program, without exception, unless she's a top model who comes over to us from another agency, and even then we make the decision on an individual basis, but she's Swedish, highly outer-galactic, and very stubborn."

The Lunel Agency conducted an evaluation, called the Program, of all new models they accepted, in which Maggy, Fauve, Casey and three of the most experienced bookers participated. The agency paid to send the girls to a photographer for an exhaustive series of pictures expressly designed to show how she worked in front of the camera in her own clothes and makeup. Every detail about her was then analyzed and the six of them decided how best to polish their new model. They asked each other if she needed help with her posture; whether her hair was the perfect length, style and color; what more must she learn to do with makeup to widen her range; whether she needed to have extra coaching on her expressions to gain flexibility and camera presence; or dance classes for ease of movement and poise. If she had come to them from a modeling school they asked, what did she have to unlearn?

"There's never been a Swede as stubborn as I am," Fauve remarked. "Unless she has her own flying saucer, Miss Sweden will go through the Program even if Revlon calls today and wants to sign her to an exclusive contract for the rest of her life. We made one mistake with Jane, when we decided she didn't need the Program—and that taught me a lesson I'll never forget."

"These top beauty contest winners do put in a lot of time before they make it," Casey said, in an attempt to be fair.

"None of which has anything to do with modeling."

"As I well know."

"I'll see Miss Truly Magnificent—I think it *was* the Universe,

Casey, when I have a minute. Meanwhile, let's get Loulou in here."
Fauve picked up the phone intercom and dialed the Big Board room
and asked Loulou, the booker with the most seniority in the
agency, to come into her office.

A half-minute later Loulou strolled in, flopping gratefully down
into a chair. She was thirty, a plump, fair, pleasant-looking woman
whose expression invariably combined deep worry and absolute optimism, so that she looked as if she were going down in the *Titanic*
with firm faith in the existence of Paradise. Loulou, like a great
racehorse trainer or a wise ballet mistress, had developed to an art
that special equilibrium that enabled her to deal with a different
race from herself. The model, highly strung, highly priced, highly
vulnerable, a natural aristocracy, separated by the class system of
beauty from ever being quite like other women.

"Hi, guys," she said. "Well, let's see. Betty won't pierce her ears
for the diamond studs for the De Beers ad. She says she's not a
coward, but she can't stand needles; Hillary booked out for the
entire month of October. She's going to the Himalayas to meditate
whatever with that guru of hers, whoever. *Glamour* gave me their
budget for the Tangiers trip and it will only cover two and a half
girls and they need three so I said I'd ask the girls if they'd take less
to see the Casbah. That new Canadian girl keeps telling me she only
wants to do catalog when I know she's ready for editorial . . .
somebody has to talk to her about her image problem. Nine phones
are out as usual but Pete, our semipermanent phone repair man, is
on vacation and since nobody else really understands our setup,
we're just lucky it's Friday. One of you is going to have to resign
Cindy because I haven't had a request for her for two weeks and
you know that means it's over for her here but, what the hell, she's
twenty-six and she knows this has been coming for a year or more
so maybe it'll be a relief. There's a sale in the Anne Klein showroom; Halston is giving a party and Linda didn't get an invitation—I
can't be responsible for what she might do—keep her away from
razor blades. I hocked and hocked Fabergé to use Jessica and now
they're in love with her, they don't want anybody else, they need
her tomorrow, but she's in Mexico; Dawn's father is in from Syr-
acuse and she picked this weekend to skip town with her guy,
what'll I tell old Dads? Doyle Dane suddenly called to remind me
that Patsy has to drive a stick shift in that Alfa Romeo ad—she's

halfway to the location and as far as I know she doesn't drive period; one of the booker trainees forgot to give Lani her wake-up call this morning so she overslept and kept ten people waiting for an hour and they want to charge her for it; Patsy just called and asked us to make dentist, doctor, facial and waxing appointments for her but we don't even know *what* she wants waxed . . . anyway, if you guys have nothing else to do but sit around and yak and complain that's grand, but I've a lot of work to do so if you'll just excuse me—oh, did you want to see me? What's up?"

"It's gracious of you to ask," Fauve said.

"Kind of you to make time for us," Casey muttered.

"Day O'Daniel will be joining our happy group," Fauve announced.

"Why not?" Loulou never showed surprise. Just as her expression never changed, her composure couldn't be shaken. If Fauve had decided to get rid of every single one of the twenty models on the Big Board, Loulou would have shrugged. Her philosophy was that every three months a new generation of models arrived from the vast reaches of that mysterious, unimportant world outside of Manhattan and her job was simply to put them to work as profitably as possible. The models on Lunel's Big Board earned seven hundred and fifty dollars a day, although a few among them had the notion that they were worth more, as much as a thousand dollars daily. No one, not Maggy, not Eileen Ford, not Fauve, and certainly not Loulou, had any idea that within a half-dozen years all the top girls at all the agencies would be getting three thousand dollars for a day's work.

Loulou had trained both Fauve and Casey and they knew that while Loulou had her favorite models, as did every booker, the agency was always more important to her than any individual girl.

"I'll set up a chart for her," Loulou sighed, stretching and yawning. "My *head*," she groaned.

"Loulou, don't you wonder why she's coming here?" Casey demanded.

"I *know* why. I've just won five bucks on it. Wish I'd bet more. Oh, God, why do I drink? Nothing's enough fun to feel like this for. Listen, guys, I have to get back to the board. It may only be a lousy job for you but it's life and death out there for me." She shut the door behind her as she left.

"One day," said Casey morosely, "I'm gonna surprise her."

418

"No, you're not."

"No, I'm not," Casey agreed. "*Bookers.*"

Surely, thought Nadine Mistral Dalmas, the bills from Arene must be wrong. How could she possibly have spent twelve thousand francs on flowers in the last few months? Arene was the most expensive florist in Paris and it was the most prestigious. It showed a lack of intelligence, in Nadine's opinion, to send a hostess flowers from any other shop, for no matter how much you spent elsewhere, they didn't make quite the same impression. Sending flowers, the right flowers, in the right way, from the right place, was one of the carefully calculated nuances Nadine had perfected in the course of seven years of being Madame Phillipe Dalmas.

They had been called the most envied couple in Paris, Nadine reminded herself as she sat at the desk in her modern salon and confronted the pile of bills with which she had finally brought herself to deal. Most of them were three or four months old, and many of them were from people who didn't care whether she was the daughter of the Comte de Paris, the legitimate Pretender to the throne of France, or the daughter of Julien Mistral, whose estate would make her so immensely rich when he died. *When* he died. Her father, damn him to hell, showed every sign of living to a hundred, and Parisian tradesmen had nothing in common with British tradesmen of a century before who would keep an heir supplied with money on the basis of his expectations.

Nadine inspected the Arene bill carefully. Two miniature cymbidium orchid plants planted in porcelain cachepots for the Princess Édouard de Lobkowicz. How could they have charged so much when she had provided the cachepots herself? She had been rather proud of that particular offering for she had invented the notion of buying the most charming of cachepots at Le Grenier de la Marquise, a fascinating old gift shop, on the rue de Sévigné, and taking them to Arene to be planted. Of course it did make the flowers far more expensive but how could anyone with the slightest claim to taste just send a banal bouquet to thank a lady who had been born Princess Françoise de Bourbon-Parme? A lady who had included Nadine and Phillipe with the Duke and Duchess d'Uzès and the Duke and Duchess of Torlonia at a dinner for twelve, served by four butlers on Meissen plates, a dinner at which the menu card before each plate had borne the crown of the Holy Roman Empire?

She didn't send flowers each time they accepted the Lobkowiczes' hospitality, but when she did, they had to be extraordinary.

Lilies of the valley to the Vicomtesse de Ribes, sent only after invitations to two intimate dinners followed by film screenings and one seated, black-tie dinner party for forty. Nadine had hesitated as long as she could before settling on the flowers to send to the most elegant woman in Paris. Finally she had realized that only the simplest blooms would do. Of course, in that case it had been self-evident that there must be four dozen bunches . . . any less a gesture would have been skimpy, attracting no attention. Flowers to Helene Rochas, flowers to São Schlumberger, flowers to the Princess Ghislaine de Polignac . . . she put the Arene bill aside. She had no doubt that it was as exact as it was necessary, one of the obligations she accepted in order to keep her place in the inner circle of Paris society.

While it might seem to outsiders that the society of Paris was loosely organized, for it included certain dressmakers and a few writers and one or two decorators and even the Borys, who owned the huge grocery chain Fauchon, Nadine was keenly aware, with the delicate attunement to every vibration of a tightrope walker working without a net, that in fact it was a world in which, were it not for her ceaseless vigilance, even "the most envied couple in Paris" could quickly disappear from sight.

Discrimination had always been an art in French society where standing is so finely calibrated that even among dukes, three—Brissac, Uzès and Luynes—are more ducal than others. It is a society still based on titles. It is a tiny section of Parisians, but they were the only people on earth who mattered at all to Nadine. A few outrageously rich foreigners were always permitted entry since they didn't count—how could they when they weren't French? They were permitted to spend money on entertainment to buy their way into a purely temporary place in society, a place that depended entirely on the extravagant and tasteful quality of their largesse. A well-mannered, attractive extra man with highly placed mistresses, as Phillipe had been, before his marriage, was often admitted, as were certain foreign diplomats for the length of the time they kept their posts, as well as a tiny handful of powerful politicians.

But the great hostesses never invited people simply because they had asked them before. Each invitation, no matter how big the party, was considered, scrutinized, weighed, measured and then carefully reconsidered. Why, Nadine could imagine a hostess asking herself, do I ask the Dalmases to my table? Are they still good value? He adds nothing by way of status, for he's been around forever, and has no historic name, no accomplishment, and now, not even the virtue of being unattached. But she is closer to Jean François Albin than anyone else . . . his last collection was a marvel . . . and they're both still terribly decorative . . . yes, I'll ask them again this time. She is, after all, Mistral's daughter.

Three years ago Nadine had asked herself how long would the period of tolerance continue to be extended for the Dalmases, that amusingly poor married couple? Another year perhaps . . . or less? It was then that she had realized that they could no longer permit themselves to seem impoverished, however temporarily, without slipping socially. If she had not made the decision that they *must* entertain, they would soon be tainted with the deadly stamp of people who only accepted hospitality, and never extended it.

This would have been followed by gradual social oblivion, until they would have found themselves as far outside of authentic society as those members of Café Society who buy tickets to every big charity ball and overtip the headwaiter at the Relais Plaza to get a table near the bar, all to bask in the delusion that they have established themselves in Paris, when actually they have simply been permitted to fill up a little unused space.

What do they *do?* those people who aren't invited to the right parties, Nadine wondered, her entire body stiffened with scorn and contempt. How could they endure their lives when they had to live outside the only world that mattered? Didn't they know how low they were, how little they counted, how abject their position? Didn't they realize that they inhabited a wasteland as empty and as void of meaning as outer space? As she watched them, the outsiders, ordering splendid gowns at Albin's, she was repeatedly struck by the incomprehensible fact that these clothes were being bought to be worn *nowhere.* The dinners they were asked to were beneath contempt, their gala restaurant evenings were despicable. They existed only to make Albin rich. She might even find them pathetic if they weren't so abhorrent to her, if their inferiority did not make them, as far as she was concerned, less than human.

Nadine bent over the bill from Lenotre, the outstanding caterer of Paris. Since she and Phillipe had no staff except for a cleaning woman, Lenotre's bill was the largest she had to pay. Every three months they gave a "cocktail," astutely planned to occur just before an important first night or a big ball, so that people were content to serve themselves from a superb buffet of hors d'oeuvres, knowing that they would eat again later in the evening. As Nadine wrote the enormous check she thought that nothing would be more stupid than to employ a second-rate caterer. Better a Lenotre cocktail than a seated dinner of less quality, she assured herself, yet remembering with a pang of envy so pure that it felt like a cold wind, the recent wedding anniversary celebration they had been invited to by the Duchess de La Rochefoucauld. Jeanne-Marie had asked a hundred and forty people for a seated dinner and another two hundred were invited to come and dance afterward. The only way you could tell that the hostess was half-American was in her witty choice of food: Virginia ham and potato salad among all the other delicacies—ah, to be so enormously, unimaginably secure that you could serve such food to King Umberto of Italy and Prince Charles of Luxembourg, Nadine thought, still rigid with envy. Jeanne-Marie was the luckiest woman—did she know how lucky she was? Did she appreciate it?

Nadine pulled herself away from her reverie, reminding herself that she was far more exacting, more careful, more selective in her choice of guests than the busy Duchess who gave so many parties that she received people Nadine would never ask to her home. No, Nadine Dalmas's little cocktails had become famous for their relentless exclusion of anyone not absolutely of the first quality.

Frequently she and Phillipe accepted invitations from people whose social rank was ever so slightly dubious, simply so that she could fail to invite them. They were always so ridiculously hurt, expecting no doubt that a cocktail had to become a catch-all for all sorts of people, believing that reciprocity was due them. There was no question that her formula was right. Four cocktails a year for only the best people gave a hostess an infinitely greater allure than if she gave dozens of sumptuous but less discriminating dinners. And it was so very much cheaper.

Who would dream that they were not rich? The best florist, the best caterer, the best clubs short of the Jockey—Phillipe's family, though good, did not entitle him to belong to the Jockey. Here were the bills from the Polo Club and the Golf de St. Cloud. Phillipe had belonged to them as a bachelor, one of his few expenses in that period of his life, and to have dropped them was unthinkable. His bill for rented polo ponies in the last two months, during which he played on the Aga Khan's team, was over four thousand francs, she noted, but it was acceptable to rent your ponies if you played well and at least it wasn't as expensive as his heavy gambling losses during the winter when the Polo was filled with gin-rummy players.

Nadine wrote out the checks as quickly as she could to finish the chore, and as she wrote, she meditated on the things for which they didn't have to pay. These bills, no matter how high, represented only a tiny percentage of the scale on which they lived. Nadine's enormous wardrobe constantly renewed, was made entirely by the House of Jean François Albin; the apartment cost them nothing, they traveled in their friends' private jets, skied from their chalets in Haute Savoie or St. Moritz, sailed on their yachts in the Aegean, spent weeks in the private palaces of St.-Jean-Cap-Ferrat, Porto-Cervo and Bavaria. She had charge accounts at the Relais Plaza and Maxim's for lunches, again paid by the House of Albin; and, of course, they dined out every night during the season in Paris.

Nadine spent little cash and only where it would be noticed. At Édouard and Frédéric, the most in-vogue of the hairdressers of Paris, where she went on an almost daily basis, she tipped lavishly. The man who kept her blond, the boy who shampooed her hair, the man who blew it dry, the woman who did her nails and toenails—they would always be the first to gossip. If a princess or a Greek shipowner's wife could afford to be stingy, plain Madame Dalmas could not.

Plain Madame Dalmas. Nadine left her desk and prowled around her salon. Why, she thought, and wondered why she even bothered to ask herself the bitter question once again, *why* had she ever married a poor man? Why hadn't her mother prevented her? Why had she been allowed to commit the folly of a lifetime? Dazzled as she had been, surely someone could have, *should* have stopped her. And not just a poor man but an ineffectual ass as well who had put together only a few of his nebulous deals in the seven years of their marriage?

She must have loved him once, incredible as that now seemed to her. But what else could explain how she had spent the money her mother had left her when she died? Kate had died of cancer four years earlier, leaving far more money than she had told Nadine to expect. Apparently she had owned some paintings that she'd been able to sell at a vast profit. In any case, the money was gone now.

Nadine had become a partner in Phillipe's dream, his stupid determination to have a home in the country. Half of her inheritance had been spent on buying a château in Normandy. Since then he had refused to give it up although they had never had the means to restore it properly, and make it livable. He'd yearned for a home of his own far too long, he insisted, and anyway, soon they'd have all the money in the world.

Love for Phillipe. It must have existed or why had she allowed him to invest the rest of her mother's legacy? There had been enough to buy a partnership in a new nightclub that was intended to rival Castel's, with its membership of three thousand. Jean Castel turned away hundreds of customers each night, so obviously another *boîte* was necessary.

Together, as Phillipe and his other partner believed, they knew everybody who mattered in that rarefied circle of the children of the night, those famous bored people, so bored that even their fame bored them, permanently displaced people who began at eleven each evening to look for a substitute for sleep. What they had failed to realize was that those people neither wanted, needed nor welcomed any place to go other than their own, dear, familiar Castel's on the rue Princesse. After a year Phillipe had had to abandon the horribly expensive undertaking at a total loss.

Yes, she must have loved him or else she was as criminally lacking in judgment as he had been. After the failure of the nightclub, Phillipe acted as if it had been her fault. He grew petulant and sulky with disappointment, punishing Nadine for not being able to provide him with fresh funds. He became too lazy to charm her any longer.

Was there any sourness to compare to that of living with a man who had nothing but charm when he let his charm drop away as if he were a fat woman releasing herself from a tight corset? Yet, should the phone ring, he sprang into charm even as he answered it. She could watch him at a party as dispassionately as if he were behind glass, observe how he was responded to by men and women both, this man who asked irresistible questions, who bestowed the most imaginative flattery, who listened with art and when he spoke of himself, did so modestly and only with humor. A coat of charm encased him like a matador's suit of lights. Every one of his tricks was nauseatingly familiar to her. Even his good looks were repellent. She cared so little about him that she was indifferent to his affairs. Fortunately he had the good taste to confine them to women of riches and power who were unfailingly hospitable. It was the only thing he did with any cleverness.

Nadine stacked the envelopes in which she had put the checks and carried them into her bedroom. She would take them to Albin's to be sent off on Monday. Why buy stamps when her secretary would put them in the mail? She opened the three sets of doors on one wall of her bedroom and appraised her wardrobe. A million francs' worth of clothes, shoes, hats, furs, lingerie; every single item but the lingerie made to measure, all at a cost to her of only dry cleaning and her pride.

It had been years since she realized she hated Jean François Albin. She didn't know when it had started, the recognition that she was no more than a glorified, dressed-up nursemaid to a whining, weak, utterly self-centered, frequently cruel little boy who had one single talent that the world accepted as enormously valuable. His best friend, his muse!

What a farce it was, a farce they both still played out; Nadine, because she could not afford to lose the free clothes and the prestige the association gave her; Albin, because once his brief enchantment with her had run its usual hectic and always disillusioning course, found that chic, superior Nadine Mistral had become useful to him. He now required her to take his neurasthenic Afghans to the vet, fire and hire his domestics, write his thank-you notes, lunch with the most tedious and wealthy of his customers, get rid of any overnight lovers who gave themselves pretensions, buy his hashish, and be at his service twenty-four hours a day.

Tonight Nadine would have to push and wheedle him through his own birthday party to which he insisted he wouldn't go after she had spent weeks planning it. Too many lobsters, he had complained, too many duchesses. Why had she not arranged something amusing, a picnic, for example, with sauerkraut and pickled pig's feet and lots of cheap red wine? Why had she been so conventional, so bourgeois? Nadine had laughed and told him to remember that red wine made him sick, but she was jagged with outrage. He was intolerable, she loathed the very sound of his voice, yet her job with Albin represented the only regular source of income that the enviable Dalmases possessed. It was only enough to meet a few of their needs, not quite enough to cover the florist's bill she had just paid.

Since the time the nightclub venture had failed they had lived almost entirely on money Nadine borrowed from Étienne Delage, Mistral's dealer. She hated going to him because each time she did she felt more in his power, but who else would lend her money against the day her father died?

Nadine flung herself down on her bed and lost herself in her eternally comforting daydream. He would die. She would inherit. The estate must be worth . . . so much . . . so much! She couldn't imagine how much. Of course she couldn't sell so quickly that she depressed the market but she would realize at least many millions of francs at once, enough to pay all her bills, enough to provide her with every franc she could spend. She would leave Albin at the worst possible moment, crippling him emotionally right before a collection when he was most vulnerable. She would throw Phillipe out in a manner so humiliating that he could never discuss it with any of his friends. She would buy a vast private house on the Left Bank—on the rue de Lille perhaps—and have it decorated by Didier Aaron with classical refinement that owed nothing, absolutely nothing to mere fashion. And she would begin her life. Nadine Mistral the great heiress would take her *own* rightful place in the heart of the inner circle of Parisian society.

But until that day she would do absolutely nothing to disturb the status quo. She could not possibly get divorced as long as her social position depended on the charm and friendships of her husband and the magic of her employer's name. She still needed to be Madame Phillipe Dalmas, the best friend of Jean François Albin— no amount of orchids in cachepots could keep her on the invitation lists if she were without those protections. She could triumph as a single woman only as a rich single woman. She would wait. *Christ, how much longer could that old man live?*

29

Fauve stretched. Oh, it felt so good. Stretching, she thought sleepily, was right up there with eating and listening to music and kissing. Thank God nobody was too poor to stretch. She yawned. A great yawn was almost as good as a great stretch. She yawned and stretched at the same time. No, they lost something in combination. With so many agreeable sensations going she couldn't concentrate properly.

She rolled over in bed and reached for Ben to tell him about it but he wasn't there. She opened her eyes and looked around the dark bedroom, an unfamiliar place since this was the first time she had awakened in his apartment. Was it still night? Where could he have gone to? She waited awhile, almost falling asleep again, but when he didn't appear she slid out of bed, groped her way toward the windows and opened the curtains.

The thin, grudging sunlight of a March morning in New York made her flinch. Small clouds, high above the city, looked crunchy and little fingers of cold air seeped in from the edges of the windowpanes. She dove back into bed and considered her alternatives. She could call out and he'd come running from wherever he was. She could go back to sleep or she could try to find something to wear, since she was naked, and go brush her teeth. Teeth first, she decided, picking the bedspread off the floor and draping herself in it, since there didn't seem to be any of her clothes in the room.

In the bathroom she found a note impaled on a tube of tooth-paste.

Darling,
    I've just gone out to buy some stuff for breakfast. I'll be back as soon as I can. I love you.   *Ben*

Now that is thoughtful, she told herself, as she looked around for a toothbrush. A really magnificent breakfast—a regal, volup-tuous, erotic breakfast—was the only way to start Sunday morning in New York. More important, it proved that he hadn't expected her to be here this morning or he would have stocked his fridge the day before. As she failed to discover any toothbrush other than Ben Litchfield's, she noted that he obviously didn't take the presence of a lady for granted or he would have had a spare. Well, a soggy and secondhand toothbrush was better than nothing. She took a quick shower, dried herself on one of his slightly damp towels and put on the clean but rather threadbare terry robe he'd left hanging on the hook of the bathroom door. Definitely a bachelor establishment.

Fauve padded out into the living room and knew immediately that there was no one in the kitchen making something marvelous. The room was not just empty, it had such a glacial impersonality that she was sure the decorator who had decorated Ben's office had done the apartment too. It had the same Barcelona chairs—did any-one ever have more than that predictable pair or was there a law against it?—and identical glass and chrome coffee tables. The rug, like the chairs, was obviously expensive and carefully coordinated with the tweedy draperies, but the unlovable plants looked as if they'd been chosen for their ability to survive under neglect, and the lithographs on the walls betrayed no indication of personal taste.

The only sign of humanity in Ben's living room were the copies of the Sunday *New York Times* and *Sunday News* that he had stopped to pick up at the stand at Fifty-eighth and Madison last night before they came back. She looked at the eviscerated papers lying all over the coffee table and rejected the idea of picking them up. Somehow they didn't fit into her cheerful mood. Her body felt tender all over and well used, as indeed it had been. How much *good* news could she reasonably expect to find in the *Times* anyway? Certainly nothing that was fit to print, she reflected, and tried to curl up on the unsensuous couch.

Why did bachelors invariably own furniture that was stuffed with foam rubber? Should she go into the kitchen, wherever it was, and hunt around for a teabag? No, she'd wait for Ben to come back. After last night, a lonely cup of tea seemed an unworthy way to begin this lovely, lazy Sunday . . . this necessarily brief Sunday as he knew, since she had to leave for Rome later in the afternoon with the five girls Valentino had chosen to show his clothes on the runway at the opening of his spring collection. They'd all be gone for two weeks, on to Milan and Paris after Rome.

Without success, Fauve attempted to snuggle into a bouncy pile of foam rubber cushions. Benjamin Franklin Litchfield, where are you? Last night had been the first time she'd spent the entire night with him, or with anybody for that matter, Fauve thought, considering the brief list of her lovers. She knew it was unfashionable but there had only been two besides Ben.

Fauve supposed, when she had time to think about it, which was seldom, that the way she had lived was odd for the liberated 1970s. Although she worked long and hard and late at her job and had established her financial independence in a way that many other girls of her age had not, she'd been content to live at home until two years ago. She'd been pursued by many men, but, for at least three years after her last visit to Provence, Fauve had been too haunted by the memory of Eric Avigdor to respond to anyone else.

Finally there had come a time when mere letters hadn't been able to sustain that love. Eric had had to do two obligatory years of military service after he graduated from the Beaux-Arts, and that had stood in the way of any opportunity for him to visit her in the United States. She had taken brief vacations but they'd never come at a period when he was free.

After a while Fauve began to sense that both of them were being unrealistic about their intention to meet again. As the years went by those brief weeks together, when she was sixteen, became more fragmented as they receded further and further into memory. Certain moments were fixed, so vivid and clear in memory that she could scarcely bear to examine them, but the connective tissue between those moments faded. She couldn't call back the whole fabric of an entire day with Eric, only bits and pieces.

Had they not been equal to their feelings, she had asked herself sadly, or had they simply misunderstood the strength of those feelings? Surely he too must have gone through the same dimming of the past?

Fauve immersed herself in the world of modeling, and eventually it became increasingly difficult to write to Eric. She would re-read her letters and ask herself how he could possibly be interested in the tradition-breaking action of high-fashion Lauren Hutton agreeing to pose for Avedon in nothing more than a black lace bra, a pair of black bikini underpants and a prankish hat? How could it matter to him that the major decision of her week had been to promote one girl from the Central Board to the Big Board? There was no way to adequately explain to him that it was important, because once a model made this crucial career move she couldn't go backward and if the move proved to be unsuccessful or premature, her career would be largely destroyed.

The details that filled her days, the preoccupations that seemed so crucial, because they concerned people she liked and because they had true business and personal repercussions, dwindled down to such triviality when she put them down on paper that she tore up five letters for each one that she finally sent.

If it hadn't been for the surprise of Magali's marriage, Fauve guessed, she'd probably still be living at home, happily joining Magali and Darcy for dinner several times a week. She'd been so comfortable and happy there that nothing could have pushed her out of the apartment except her determination to give them a chance to be alone together. Magali had protested that it was ridiculous to treat them like honeymooners, but Fauve had known her instinct and timing were right.

She'd found a cozy little duplex for herself in a narrow, old-fashioned brownstone in the East Seventies, near Third Avenue, and there, just before she turned twenty, she'd had her first love affair. And her second. Neither of them had been a particularly fulfilling experience, Fauve admitted to herself. Something, some essential element, had been missing, and if she had to put a name on it, damn it, there was only one word she could think of—romance.

Was she being absurdly nostalgic, was she looking for something that could only happen once in a lifetime? The physical experiences had been satisfactory, the men had both been intelligent and

430

amusing, but that other dimension, that blithe thread of melody, that sense of poetry underlining the most ordinary undertaking, that transformation of the world, that she had once known sitting in a little car on a road near Félice surrounded by sheep, no, it hadn't happened.

Fauve had never let either of her two lovers spend the whole night with her although there was no question that her bed was big enough for two, that four-poster with billowing draperies of rose-bud-sprigged gauze, so long that they trailed on the flowered, Victorian rug. It was just that she couldn't imagine *waking up* with either of them—waking up with someone seemed more intimate than making love in some ways.

Last night she had thought, as she fell asleep, that waking up with Ben Litchfield might be a revelation. Romance had seemed to be in the air, not quite close enough to capture, but definitely lurking, waiting to happen. He had tried to speak of marriage but she hadn't let him—it was the wrong time. She had felt as if she were listening to an orchestra tune up, an uncoordinated assortment of sounds that promised the arrival of music.

Right now, Fauve thought, conscious that her feet were freezing, she'd settle for food and let romance go wherever it went when it wasn't operating. Country farm sausage—the small, spicy kind, all brown and crisp—with pancakes, dripping with maple syrup, for instance. Perhaps that was what Ben was bringing back? Or waffles with melted butter and strawberry jam? Maybe he'd gone out for a brioche and croissants and thin slices of sugar-cured Virginia ham or even a Pepperidge Farm coffee cake, ready to heat, the kind with the *lovely*, sticky white icing and raisins? Or had he simply gotten stuck waiting on line to buy bagels? Pumpernickel bagels with sweet butter and slices of sturgeon, juicy white sturgeon from the Great Lakes? Oh, Lord, she wasn't asking for much—she didn't expect eggs Benedict with extra Hollandaise sauce; she wasn't insisting on a tall, frosty glass of freshly squeezed orange juice without the pulp; she only needed breakfast, not brunch, for God's sake, brunch with tender crêpes stuffed with chicken and covered with mushroom sauce or even . . . even oyster stew.

Fauve tucked her legs under her in the lotus position for warmth and in the hope that it might lead to meditation and that meditation would stop her from thinking about food. No matter what, she didn't intend to go poking about in the kitchen and spoil his surprise.

She had heard a great deal about Ben Litchfield before she started to go out with him, for his staff was full of wistful editors who yearned for him without success. She had observed him closely for signs that he took women for granted but found no sign of it in his courtship. He had a prickly mind, quirky and questioning and he understood her shop talk and her late hours. She liked his edges. He had an insistent energy and she felt at ease with his preoccupations, accustomed as she had become to the world of publishing through Darcy. Ben Litchfield had pursued her steadily and single-mindedly for a long time before she finally allowed him to make love to her several months ago. He was a most . . . comforting . . . lover, Fauve thought, searching for precisely the right word. She felt secure with him, safe and quiet and warm and . . . comfortable.

Fauve's stomach growled and she considered reading the news-papers after all . . . anything to pass the time without thinking about doughnuts, jelly doughnuts with powdered sugar on them, gingerbread doughnuts, whole-wheat doughnuts, chocolate-covered doughnuts—she didn't even *like* doughnuts, for the love of God. When on earth had Ben had time to go through the *Times* and the *News?* she wondered. Dimly she remembered half waking up in the middle of the night and seeing the light on in the bathroom and hearing the crackle of newsprint. Had he had an attack of insomnia and tried to read himself to sleep?

Ben Litchfield's key scraped in the door and he came in with his arms so laden that Fauve jumped up to relieve him of some of his burden.

"Two Kellogg's Snack-Paks, milk, eggs . . . *that's it?*" She wanted to whimper but pride prevented her.

"I didn't know if you preferred Corn Flakes or Rice Krispies," he said, "so I got plenty of both. There's butter in the kitchen, and some Wonder Bread." He kissed her on her nose, over a three-foot-high pile of newspapers.

"You've been gone for hours!"

"I thought you'd still be asleep . . . I had to go down to Hotal-ing's in Times Square and, wouldn't you just know it, the *Philadel-phia Inquirer* was late this morning so naturally I had to wait," he said as he carefully put down the Sunday editions of the *Boston*

Globe, the *Pittsburgh Press*, the *Washington Post*, the *Cleveland Plain Dealer*, the *Los Angeles Times*, *Newsday*, the *Houston Chronicle*, the *Atlanta Journal-Constitution*, and the *San Francisco Examiner & Chronicle*. "But on the other hand, I got lucky—look, a *Miami Herald*! You usually can't get one on Sunday . . . it almost makes up for not being able to get the *Chicago Trib*—that's never available till tomorrow. Give me another kiss."

"Isn't there any bacon?" Fauve asked carefully. "To go with the eggs?"

"Bacon crossed my mind, but I only have one frying pan so there's no way to cook bacon *and* eggs."

"Did you ever think of cooking the bacon first and then frying eggs in the bacon fat?" she asked in a hunger-inspired leap of her imagination.

"My clever darling—women know so many things. Let's try that some other time," he said absently as he started quickly going through the papers and putting certain sections to one side and flinging the rest on the floor.

"What are you looking for?" Fauve sputtered. "Has something terribly important happened?"

"Hmmm . . . no . . . nothing special . . . I have to read the Sunday magazine sections and the women's sections—Style, or View or Home or Leisure or whatever they call it . . ."

"You *have* to read them?"

"You'd be amazed at what fresh new ideas the out-of-town papers come up with on Sunday—they're very useful . . ." he muttered, searching feverishly through the *Cleveland Plain Dealer*. "Damn, *damn*, that bastard, he sold me a bummer! The magazine section isn't here! You can't trust those guys . . . it's a crime . . . well, what the hell, it's not the newsstand's fault . . . it's the people who bundle them up to get them on the plane on Saturday . . . oh, shit!"

"*Ben!*"

"Yes, darling?" He looked up.

"Let's go back to bed."

"*Now?*"

"Right now," she said, putting her arms around him and taking off his glasses.

"Before breakfast?"

"It's better on an empty stomach. Dangerous on a full one."

433

"Well . . ." he said, looking with an infinitude of regret and reluctance at his newspapers. "Well . . ."

"Or," Fauve suggested softly, "would you rather read your papers while I make breakfast—and then go back to bed?"

"What a marvelous idea! Oh, darling, I do love you."

"Ben, what's happened to my clothes?"

"Aren't you comfortable?"

"The bathrobe's too big and I don't have anything for my feet."

"I hung up everything in my closet while you were asleep . . . I hate to wake up in a messy room."

"Thank you," she said to him as he pounced on the View section of the *Los Angeles Times* with a junkie's avidity.

Five minutes later she let herself out of the apartment so quietly that Ben Litchfield didn't notice she was gone until it was too late. "Out to Lunch" read the message she had scribbled in lipstick on his bathroom mirror.

Maggy was sprawled on the floor of the big living room of the converted farmhouse, wearing brown tweed slacks and a toast-colored cashmere sweater. On the plaid rug was a long roll of graph paper, an array of colored crayons and the White Flower Farm catalog. Darcy, a book in his lap, sat looking into the flames of the fine fire he had built from the stack of wood next to the fireplace.

He sipped his martini and considered his happiness. Was there anything better than knowing that it was Sunday night and you didn't have to drive back into the city until late tomorrow? He and Maggy had gone for a long walk in the barely budding woods this afternoon, proving once again his theory that a martini never tasted better than after prolonged exposure to a large dose of oxygen and the brisk development of all the muscles. There was really no point in exercise if you didn't follow it with a drink.

"What are you doing, sweetheart?" he asked Maggy.

"I'm ordering some new plants for the day lily garden."

"But why the graph paper?"

"I don't just shove plants into the ground any old way, baby face. I measure my garden space and I work it out on paper, six squares to a foot, and I color in the outlines of the shapes of the patches of lilies so that they'll drift into each other naturally. Then I look in the catalog and pick out colors that harmonize with what I planted last year—and then I order them by mail. Actually I should have done this last month but I was too busy thinking out the new herbaceous English border."

"Oh, God, why did I *ever* say it?" he asked the white-washed ceiling beams. "Why didn't I know better, why didn't anyone *warn* me?"

"What are you talking about?"

"The day I said you didn't know anything about gardening. I could curse myself. That was the day you fired the gardener, remember?"

"It was a turning point in my life, darling. You made me so angry that I decided to prove to you that anyone, even a city girl like me, could learn how to garden from books. It's no harder than cooking."

"But, Maggy, you're *obsessed!* I understand that theory about the wisdom of planting a three-dollar rosebush in a six-dollar hole but, my God, you made sixty-dollar holes all last summer! You ate up half the lawn with those holes. Each one took you a full day to dig and prepare."

"I only wanted to be sure that my bushes had all the room they needed in which to spread their roots, and all the nutriments at the bottom of the holes to help them grow for the next hundred years."

"But what about those nights you used to go out weeding and I had to hold the flashlight so you could see what you were doing? Do you call that normal?"

"When you only have weekends you have to take advantage of every minute," Maggy said serenely.

"And last fall when you spent six days mulching everything three inches deep with dried cow manure? You were in it up to your elbows!"

"When you put your garden to bed in the fall, cutie pie," Maggy said with a learned look, "you don't just wave goodbye . . . you *mulch!* I'll get my reward next month when things start to bloom. Gardening has taught me patience. You should be pleased."

"I'm enchanted. It's a whole new Maggy, the queen of the potting bench. I think you could carry double your own weight as long as it's wet dirt in a clay pot. But what I don't understand is why you're determined to go into the office tomorrow. So what if Fauve won't be there? It breaks up our weekend," he grumbled, suddenly remembering the flaw in the next day that he had forgotten.

"Darling, you don't have to drive back till evening and I'll be waiting for you then, but I don't like to leave the agency without anyone in charge."

"Casey can be in charge for one day, can't she? You're always telling me how reliable she is, and what good judgment she has."

"It's not the same thing. Fauve has the business in her blood. When she's not there, I should be," Maggy said.

"Always a Lunel at the helm? 'O Captain my Captain'? That sort of thing?"

"Lunel stands for something and I just can't let them all run around without some sort of final authority who's instantly available." Maggy was firm.

"You know best. Actually I never believed you'd be able to stick to your plan to spend these long weekends here . . . I shouldn't complain."

"No, you certainly shouldn't," Maggy said, thinking, as she turned back to her graph paper, of how quickly she had grown to hate these four-day weekends, one after another, all year long.

When Darcy had bought this house his plan for their life had seemed to promise the ideal combination of work and leisure. But after a few months she had realized that she wasn't built for four days of relaxed country living every week. Maggy took golf and tennis lessons and loathed every minute of them. She prepared far too elaborate meals for lunch and dinner, and she had begun to look hopefully under the beds for nonexistent dust when the challenge of gardening had come along and given her something that absorbed her energy.

If it hadn't been for gardening . . . she could almost understand how the Duke of Windsor, without his role of monarch to play, had been able to fill his years in creating a marvelous garden. But it was only a substitute for real work as far as she was concerned. It wasn't *enough*, even during growing weather and from late October till late March, while the garden slept, she was reduced to planning for the following spring. Maggy would have had to tell Darcy that the plan wasn't working, that it made her too unhappy to be idle, that she simply wasn't ready for this form of semiretirement, if it hadn't been for Fauve, and the need to prepare her to take complete charge whenever the business became hers.

The Lunel Agency had never stopped growing since its inconspicuous beginning in 1931. John Robert Powers had closed up shop in 1948 and even with the emergence of Eileen and Jerry Ford, now, in 1975, Lunel remained the biggest and most established agency in the world. But model agencies depend on the people who run them for their success, so Maggy forced herself to stay in the country on Fridays and Mondays as firmly as she forced herself to accept the decisions Fauve made on those days. She made herself give Fauve the freedom to run the business on her own, to make mistakes, to learn the hard way.

And the plan had worked. All too well, Maggy admitted to herself ruefully. You can't *half* abdicate, Maggy thought, realizing that this knowledge came too late. Fauve had earned the right to exercise power and if Maggy tried to nibble away at that power, tried to gather it back to herself, she would undermine the capable, self-reliant businesswoman Fauve had become.

At least tomorrow, with Fauve off to Europe, she had a reason to be at her desk on Monday—lovely Monday on which there might just be some sort of emergency resulting from the weekend ac-tivities of two hundred high-spirited girls, to say nothing of eighty healthy boys, Maggy thought with glee. Trouble. She was in the mood for trouble. Maybe, she told herself hopefully, there would be the sort of really nasty mess that everyone thought went on all the time in the model business but, in reality, rarely occurred. Or, if nothing happened on this particular Monday, during the next two weeks that Fauve would be away, something must surely go wrong. She'd take Loulou to lunch. They hadn't had a good juicy talk in weeks. But as usual, the first order of business was to smuggle the mail back without anyone noticing, Maggy thought, remembering the suitcase she had stashed away upstairs in her little sitting room, a suitcase jammed as full as possible with a random selection of the hundreds of pieces of mail that arrived every week, from hopeful would-be models.

At Lunel, as at the other agencies, this mail was routinely opened and examined by a booker-trainee or even by the recep-tionist, both of whom were perfectly well qualified to pick out any picture that should be referred to someone with more experience. Maggy managed to get her hands on some of these lowly communi-cations, from which, in the history of the agency, only a few models had ever been found, and she brought them up to the country every Thursday night. Over the weekend, at odd times, when Darcy was busy elsewhere, she'd dart off to this treasure trove and, with a busy letter opener, she'd go through every last piece of mail. There was always that chance . . . always the possibility of . . . lightning . . . she thought as she cut open each and every envelope as eagerly as if it had been the most tempting of surprise packages. She hadn't discovered her last model yet. You never knew!

Fauve shepherded her five tall charges, as different from the hurrying Romans all around them as if they were a wandering band of wild gazelles, toward an empty table that she had miraculously spotted on the sidewalk terrace of the Pasticceria Rosati.

"Sit!" she commanded briskly, knowing from past experience that the successful capture of a table at Rosati's was like winning at musical chairs. Except for Fauve, who had visited Rome once, none of the group had ever been to Rome before. They all had the day free to get over jet lag before the models were due to start work and Fauve had chosen Rosati's for their prelunch drink because of its location on the Piazza del Popolo, that swooningly baroque ensemble of twin domed churches, the Bernini Fountain, the Rameses obelisk and the ceremonial gate of the Via Flaminia.

The piazza had been designed three hundred years earlier to impress the traveler as he first entered the Eternal City and it had succeeded so brilliantly that it almost seemed sacrilegious to sit and order a campari in a setting of such imperial pomp and ceremony. Yet that *was* Rome, the distillation of Rome, the unequaled theatricality of daily life in which laundry was hung out to dry on palaces designed by Michelangelo, a simple restaurant occupied the house in which Lucrezia Borgia was born, and children played tag in the gardens of the Villa Medici.

Nothing can surprise the citizens of Rome, nothing can impress them. They are a race that keeps itself aloof, reserved and private, notably taciturn toward tourists. They have had to share their city with pilgrims since the days of the Caesars. To Romans everyone else on the face of the earth is a mere provincial and they turn a deaf ear and a blind eye to the never lessening flood of visitors who surround them. There is only one exception, only one kind of stranger for whom the Roman will turn his head.

"Lordy," said Arkansas, "don't all these folks just look so friendly?"

Without surprise Fauve scanned the fascinated faces all around them, not even bothering to hide their interest. Never, in the history of modeling, had there been such a worldwide passion for

438

American girls, tall, skinny, dashing girls with acres of hair in which the wind always seemed to be moving, with a strong yet innocent sensuality, brandishing excessive beauty and new-coined youth. The Old World couldn't seem to produce anything like these superb creatures with their laughing ease and their raging glamour who stormed Europe.

American photographic models now presented the new collection of fashion designers who, only a few years ago, would not have considered showing their clothes on anyone but the house models on whom they had been fitted, European girls who knew how to walk on a runway ten times more professionally than any American who normally worked in front of a camera. But now the business of haute couture was like a tiny, luxuriously kept pet poodle that drew behind it a great freight train of mass-produced products that were sold under the name of each designer. Dresses were still made by hand in Paris, in London and in Rome, but the few rich customers who bought them, no matter how young, were referred to as "dinosaurs" because they were members of a breed that had all but vanished from the earth.

Yet, fashion shows had never been so theatrical, nor so spectacular. Models were hired at great expense from every major model agency in New York and flown to Europe for the collections because the vast amount of publicity they generated was immediately reflected in sales of licensed goods in stores from Indiana to Oslo, from Tokyo to Hamburg.

The hectic fever, the mounting craze for American models, had spread to European fashion magazines and it had become routine for Maggy and Wilhelmina and Eileen Ford to send their most promising new models to live in Paris or Rome for three months at a time. Once there, the unknown girl would immediately be booked by the best photographers, all of whom were avid for the gloriously fresh American faces. She'd learn how to wear clothes that were more expensive and intricate than anything made in the United States; top-flight hairdressers and makeup artists would experiment with her looks until she knew the furthest limits of her potential; and she'd be able to build up her book with dozens of pictures from Italian *Bazaar* and French *Vogue* as well as from the many other fashion magazines published abroad. When this relatively raw, high school beauty queen came home, burnished, exotic, glossy and no longer wide-eyed, from the finishing school of Paris or Rome, she was more firmly launched in the business than if she'd spent two or three years of steady growth in New York.

If she came home.

Maggy and Fauve were well aware of the hazards of sending their models to Europe. Although most of them lived in private homes and all of them were booked by local agencies who kept in close contact with Lunel, there was a list without limit of things that could go wrong with young girls far from home. Someone from the Lunel Agency went to Europe every few months to make sure that all was well with them and, on this trip, Fauve was charged with looking in on all the Lunel models working in Europe as well as to make sure that Arkansas and the four other models who had been hired to do the shows for Valentino in Rome, for Armani and Versace in Milan, and Saint Laurent and Dior in Paris, kept to their demanding schedules.

"What did I tell you about Roman men?" she asked Arkansas, who was smiling shyly at the next table.

"Not to trust them worth a damn," Arkansas said, her smile widening.

"And who do you suppose are those men you are grinning at?"

"Well, Lord knows, they *might* be foreigners like us. They aren't wearing name tags, Fauve. You know why you're so suspicious? It's because you're a city person. Why, you're positively unfriendly. They look just perfectly fine to me."

"And you look just fine to them. Oh, dear God, is it going to be like this for two whole weeks? No, don't answer. It's going to get worse. This is only the beginning."

"But, Fauve," protested Angel, one of the latest crop from South Carolina, the state that mysteriously provided more high-fashion models than any other, "my mama told me that if a girl doesn't get her fanny pinched in Rome it's positively an insult. She said it's the custom of the country and I'll look like a hick if I get all uptight about it."

"The latest on Italian pickpockets is while that one pinches you the other grabs your wallet—so much for Roman admiration. Tell your mama that times have changed," Fauve said ominously.

"Are we supposed to spend the entire next two weeks working? What about dinner? We all need nourishment," remonstrated Ivy Columbo in her Boston accent. Intelligent Ivy had been accepted by

440

Radcliffe and Lunel in the same week. Higher education never stood a chance.

"Look," said Fauve, "in Milan the men are different, more businesslike, slightly less dangerous. When we get to Milan you can go out to dinner if you still have the strength to leave the hotel after the day's work, which I doubt. But in Rome, stick with me. I promised to take you all to the best restaurants, didn't I?"

Fauve looked around at the circle of rebellious faces. A waiter approached bringing a bottle of wine.

"The gentlemen at the next table wish to offer the ladies a glass of wine," he said.

Fauve waved him away. "Thank the gentlemen but tell them the ladies' religion requires them to pay for their own drinks."

"Aw, shucks," Arkansas said.

"Meanie!" muttered Angel. "Spoilsport. Killjoy."

"It wouldn't hurt to be just a trifle more gracious," Ivy chimed in, shaking out her curly black hair in a manner calculated to attract every eye on the terrace. Even Bambi One and Bambi Two, who had said nothing until now, looked sadly at Fauve from their marvelous eyes.

"Listen, girls," Fauve said sternly, "this is the first morning of the first day of this trip and you're giving me trouble already. That's simply not fair, and I won't permit it. If I let anyone at all buy us a drink, it's going to be interpreted as an invitation to join us and then we'll have the trouble of getting rid of them, whoever they are. There's just no such thing as a *merely* friendly gesture from any man in Rome . . . not only can't you accept a drink but you can't return a smile, you can't even show that you've noticed them noticing you. Their whole lives are wrapped up in seducing women—Roman men are the most outrageous, untrustworthy Casanovas in the world—you wouldn't want to get involved with one under any circumstance. Do you all understand? Have I made myself plain? Not a word, not a look, not a smile . . ." she said, staring at them all earnestly as she spoke, for this was the first time that Maggy had felt she was mature enough to be entrusted alone with the taxing job of model-wrangler. She was in sole charge of this group and she didn't want them to have any doubts about her authority. Fauve was so absorbed in what she was saying that she didn't notice the man who was threading his way to a table on the other side of the terrace, a

441

man who stopped, glanced at her, looked again and turned and began to move as swiftly as possible toward her.

"... not even a gesture of a little finger," she finished, glaring at her charges. As she spoke the last words the man reached her, unnoticed. He stood behind her for a moment, gazing down at her incredulously and then as all five models raised wondering eyes at him, bent down and kissed the top of her head. Fauve's mouth opened in outrage. She swatted at her hair and stood up furiously, prepared for battle.

"How . . . dare . . . *you!*" she squeaked as Eric Avigdor took her in his arms.

The girls burst into applause but Fauve didn't hear them.

30

I've been timing her," said Ivy quietly, "and it's been a good five minutes since she's given us a single suspicious look." She sat, with the four other models, Arkansas, Angel, and Bambi One and Bambi Two, at a table in Dal Bolognese, a boisterous restaurant next to Rosati's. They were eating lunch at one table while Eric and Fauve sat together at another from which Fauve could see everything they did, although she was too far away to hear what they were saying.

"I'm so sick of pretending to maintain eye contact with you, Arkansas," Angel whined. "It's a good thing I can't see but halfway across this table without my glasses. Will somebody with good eyesight please tell me if that friend of Fauve's is as heavily into irresistible as I think he is?"

"My old high school teacher would say you're damning him with faint praise," Arkansas grumbled. "And why pick on me? Do your eye contact stuff with Bambi One or Bambi Two. It makes me downright nervous."

"It's easiest with you. You're the tallest shape I can make out," Angel explained. "I think Fauve is the meanest! It's all right for her to have lunch with a male person because he's an old friend, or so she says, and to prove that he's not one of those sinister Roman types he's got a French accent. So what? I say she's a big, fat fraud."

"If you weren't practically blind you'd know he's got to be an

443

old friend," Bambi Two objected. "You should have seen the way he looked at her. He's a bit more than just an acquaintance if you ask me." She sighed longingly.

"Spare me!" Angel said, annoyed.

"Don't start to bicker, lovers," Ivy warned the four other girls. "We're doing brilliantly. She's forgotten about us. Don't slouch, don't turn around, don't get silly. Who's got the guidebook?"

"I have," said Bambi One, arching her long neck in a manner that had caused havoc since she was twelve.

"Well, open it and read out loud to us," Ivy said.

"But I'm eating," Bambi One protested. "And don't call me Bambi One anymore. I've just decided to change my name. My poor mom tried so hard to be original but there are five Bambis in the business, four Dawns, seven Kellys, a dozen Kims, seventeen Lisas, nine Heidis—from now on, call me . . . Harold."

"Harold, lover, open the guidebook. You can eat later. We'll all take turns reading," Ivy promised. "Even Angel will put her glasses on when her turn comes, won't you, Angel?"

The table of models fell to forking up their pasta in sweet seriousness listening intently as Harold read out of a copy of Fielding's *Europe*.

" 'Dal Bolognese,' " she intoned plaintively, " 'is a favorite meeting place of lovely budding movie stars, gal painters and gals in the Creative Arts'—hot spit! Wouldn't you just know? If I'm not budding, who the hell is? And I haven't met anybody but the waiter and the busboy—not even another creative arty gal, not that I'd be interested."

"Shut up and keep reading, Harold," Ivy commanded. "Fauve just glanced in our direction."

Harold bent her lovely ash-blond head even closer to the fat red book and continued to read rapidly as the girls ate with single-minded concentration, eyes held straight, not noticing that their table was the focus of the entire restaurant. Had such a sight ever been seen in the history of Rome? Five divinities, undoubtedly American, with eyes only for each other and some sort of book? Could they be a new kind of religious order? Could they be a cult of lesbians? And that unimaginably tall one with the shortest flaxen hair ever seen . . . was *that* the coming style, the Roman women asked themselves in anguish? If so, they were in for evil days for only the greatest beauty could get away with a cropped head. Yankees go home!

"They're spying on us, I can feel it," Fauve said, sitting up self-consciously.

"Not at all. They're fascinated by the guidebook like all good tourists. They seem like a charming, serious-minded group of girls," Eric said.

After the first minutes of wild excitement in which he and Fauve had been too surprised and flustered to say anything coherent, he had felt a totally unexpected shyness paralyze him. She had become a woman, a disciplined, experienced, polished woman, so much in charge of her life. What had happened to his Fauve? She looked so . . . so businesslike in her man-tailored black cashmere blazer, her gray flannel skirt, her low-heeled, expensive shoes and her impeccable white silk shirt. Only a plaid scarf reminded him of the deliciously crazy way she used to dress and even the plaid was subdued in shades of gray and rust. Her beauty, in this severe garb, was only emphasized. Her head was like one amazing great flower poised on a perfect stem. She seemed so much more grown up than that tangle of pretty girls who had surrounded her. No wonder she had never answered his last letter . . . she wasn't the same person to whom he'd written it.

"What are you doing in Rome?" Fauve asked with composure.

"I've joined an architectural firm in Avignon and I'm here for a conference on housing. It doesn't start for a few days but I came early. An architect should visit Rome at least once a year, no matter what his esthetic theories are . . . don't you agree?"

"Oh, of course. So many . . . ruins."

"Not just that, so many buildings from so many eras that are still in good condition," Eric agreed, unsmilingly.

He's forgotten about the ruins, thought Fauve miserably. No wonder he never answered her last letter. But what could she have expected? She had been writing to a twenty-year-old enthusiastic, impulsive young man, in love with ruined aqueducts and Fauve Lunel, but now he was so grown up, so totally a man. His hair still jumped up in that intractable cowlick she had smoothed down so many times, his lower lip was as full and she still couldn't take her eyes away from the indentation in the middle, but he spoke with a kind of self-containedness and ease that distanced him from her. His handsomeness was fully finished and formed, almost intimidating.

"What a coincidence that we should both be here today," she said.

"It's the sort of thing that happens in Rome," Eric answered casually.

"To which all roads lead?" Fauve asked, thinking that they were making, actually making conversation. And what did he mean by "the sort of thing"? Wasn't it *more* than a *sort* of thing?

"Fauve . . ." Eric began when a voice interrupted him. Ivy had materialized next to their table.

"Sorry, Fauve, hate to break in on you and your friend like this, but we all thought that since we have only one free afternoon to see the city the best thing to do was to take one of those glass-topped bus tours with an English-speaking guide and cram it all in." Ivy had the copy of Fielding tucked under her arm.

"This is Ivy Columbo, Eric," Fauve said, glaring at Ivy. "Eric Avigdor."

"You're absolutely right, Miss Columbo," Eric assured her quickly. "There's also a Rome by Night Tour—unless you're too tired from the trip over."

"Oh, no, we're all too excited to sleep. So whenever you're ready to leave, Fauve, we'd like to get going. Nobody is awfully hungry."

"Well . . ." Fauve hesitated. She couldn't just get up and walk away from Eric, even if he wasn't *her* Eric. Blast those girls, why couldn't they just eat their lunch peacefully? What the hell was their hurry?

"Whatever you say." Ivy stood by the table, clearly expecting a decision. "We could all go to the Via Condotti if you think the bus thing is a bore, and see the Gucci store—maybe they'll have something on sale? Just let me know what you've decided and I'll tell the others so we can look it up and read about it while you finish up here."

"But surely, Miss Columbo, you don't want to miss the Vatican?" Eric said. He and Ivy exchanged a quick look of instant understanding.

"Neat! Terrific idea! Fauve, you want to go to the Vatican, don't you?"

"Well . . ."

"Aw, gee, Fauve, make up your mind. We're wasting precious time. We're all dying to send postcards home from the Vatican."

"Oh, damn it, Ivy, go on! I'll meet you back at the hotel. I've *seen* the Vatican."

Ivy moved off to the other table, quivering with self-satisfaction. She'd always known that it wasn't enough just to be beautiful. When she'd insisted on reciting a poem she'd written about the heritage of Thomas Jefferson instead of tap dancing, and won the Miss Teen America Contest, it hadn't been because she couldn't tap dance up a storm. Bossy old Fauve Lunel wasn't going to stop Ivy Columbo from doing whatever it was that Romans do while in Rome, with tall, dark, dangerous, curly-haired Roman men with their shirts unbuttoned to the navel.

"Let's go, lovers," she murmured as she returned to the four other girls, "before she changes her mind. That guy is hip. But no stampede. I want to see a dignified, ladylike exit. Arkansas, stop snickering. Bambi Two, don't you dare look back at Fauve's table, Harold, stop winking at that man . . ."

"Lordy," complained Arkansas, "some folks just can't seem to get into *La Dolce Vita*."

"Don't bet on it," snapped Ivy.

"Shall we walk?" asked Eric as they emerged from the restaurant into the fluid pageantry of the Piazza del Popolo where the marble cascades of the balustrades leading up to the Pincio Hill seemed no less in movement than the swaying pines in the high garden of the Villa Borghese.

"Which way?" Fauve wondered, bewildered by the need to choose.

"No fixed destination," Eric said, taking her arm.

"That's my favorite place. Oh, I feel as if I'm playing hooky. I should be guilty, allowing them to go alone, but I just couldn't endure the thought of the Vatican. I've only been in Rome once before and of course I thought I had to see it—by the time I finally reached the Sistine Chapel I was almost crawling. But how can you go to the Vatican and miss the chapel? It's a must. Obviously it would mean a lot to Ivy, but I just couldn't face it."

"Remember the Popes' Palace in Avignon?" Eric asked. "Ever

since then I've known you weren't the Vatican type. It was a totally safe suggestion."

"Oh."

"You didn't think I was going to let you go off with those girls, did you?"

"I . . . wasn't sure."

"I have a lot of things to ask you. First, did you ever go back to Félice?"

"No."

"And you still won't tell me why?"

"No," Fauve said abruptly. "How are your parents?"

"Both of them are very well. Flourishing. My father has retired to Villeneuve so he's delighted that I've decided to live in Avignon. What about your grandmother? Is her marriage a success?"

"She and Darcy bought a place in the country and she's absolutely blissfully busy doing all the things she never had time for before. Magali loves her life—she only comes in to the agency three days a week now—she feels enough confidence in me so that finally she can live for herself a little . . . heaven knows she deserves it," Fauve said thoughtfully.

They were walking down the crowded, narrow Via Margutta in the direction of the Spanish Steps, blindly passing by dozens of art galleries, when suddenly Eric steered Fauve through a pair of double doors in an old and badly kept building. Inside there was a spacious courtyard and, at the rear of the courtyard, there was the verdant plunge of the Pincio Hill that descended steeply, covered in thick, plumy foliage, all the way down into the heart of Rome.

"This is it . . . no fixed destination," he said and looked at her for her reaction to his surprise. On his face she saw that special rare quality of trustworthiness that had first struck her in the *Salle des Fêtes* at Uzès and suddenly the years that had separated them dissolved, faded, disappeared as if they had never existed. She faced him and looked him in the eye.

"Why didn't you answer my last letter?" Fauve demanded, finally able to ask the question she hadn't been able to put out of her mind.

"But I did! You were the one who stopped writing."

"That's just not possible."

"I *know* I wrote you last," Eric insisted.

"I *know* I did."

"We can't both be right," Eric said.

"We can't both be wrong either!"

"Perhaps we're both—both right, both wrong?" he suggested.

"I thought—I thought that my letters were too petty, that you'd grown in such a different direction from me that you'd just lost interest in what I had to say."

"I thought my letters were too dull compared to your life. All I could tell you about was the Beaux-Arts and the army. I cherished your letters . . . I kept every one. I have them at home in my desk."

"I decided that you must have fallen in love . . . and you just didn't want to write me about it," Fauve said in a muffled voice.

"I imagined that every man in New York was after you."

"Oh, they were. In fact they still are. Half of them anyway. I beat them off with sticks."

"And that you were probably involved with somebody . . . in love with somebody."

"I wasn't."

"Not even a little bit?"

"What I call love doesn't come in little bits. But you . . . in almost six years?"

"Oh, I tried. I tried all the traditional specifics against a broken heart, hard work, drink and other women. But they didn't help."

"What broken heart?" she demanded, her eyes the color of a rising river mist at the end of a perfect spring day.

"Mine. I never fell out of love with you and you never came back to me. So it broke."

"Oh, my darling." Fauve rocked against him, the world wheeling around her in a vast, giddy, glorious circle. "How far is your hotel?"

"Five minutes if . . ."

"But the traffic—nothing's moving."

". . . if we walk. Three minutes if we run."

It was a big bed with a mattress that sloped into a cozy valley in the center, and rose around them in soft, billowing puffs. It was like being lost in a warm snowbank, Fauve thought, as they lay so intertwined that she didn't know where her body stopped and his began. Her mind drifted through layers of feeling and emotion. So much had happened to her in the last hours that she was drunk, dazed and ripe and plump with discovery. Details were all mixed together;

the astonishing silkiness of the hair under Eric's arms, the pang of acute modesty she'd felt when he'd faced her for the first time in his nakedness, the breathless quiet minutes when he'd suckled at her nipples and she'd looked down at the top of his dark head and knew that she had never experienced true tenderness before, and then the moment at which tenderness had shifted to a specific wanting so transcendent that it abolished tenderness; the burst of pure passion in which the two halves of the secret they had first shared in a little car on a road in Félice had finally been joined into a many-petaled flowering of surpassing joy—past and present mingled; they were waltzing together to the sound of a village orchestra, they were sheltered by the branches of an old pear tree in a walled garden, they were lying in that pellucid, honeyed, red-gold warmth that only the time-gilded bricks and stucco of Rome can distill from the sun. His eyelids moved, fluttering under her lips.

"I'm not asleep," he said, "just closed my eyes for a minute."

"Never, ever in my whole life have I been so exactly where I want to be," Fauve thought and then realized that she had said it out loud.

"Rome?" he muttered into her neck.

"This bed. The world is this bed. I never want to leave it."

"Ah, love, you don't have to. I'll keep you here forever. I'll bring you lovely food and wonderful things to drink and once in a while I'll change the sheets even though they smell so good from the two of us loving each other that I won't want to . . . I'll never let you go. I should have made you marry me when you were sixteen."

"You are a dreamer—to think that," she sighed.

"No, it didn't have to be a dream. I *could* have made it happen if I'd had any sense, any foresight." Eric slid out from under her arm and propped his head up on his hand and looked down at her seriously. "You don't know how many times I replayed the scene at the station in my head. Instead of taking you to the station I should have driven you straight home to my parents' house and taken care of you until you were getting over that strange, terrible state you were in, and afterward we could have been married and all these years wouldn't have been wasted. But I was too young to know what to do and like a childish, helpless idiot I let you leave. I've never forgiven myself."

"But, Eric!" Fauve sat up laughing, teasing—her small, tender nipples half covered by the veil of her hair. "That's just like babes in the woods covering each other up in autumn leaves. We were just kids—kids don't get married and go to live in a small cottage by a waterfall—you didn't really imagine all that, did you?"

He looked down and didn't respond.

"Why, I could no more have gotten married then!" Fauve continued. "I didn't know anything, I didn't have any experience, I hadn't learned what it's like to make a living, to run a business—I would never have been satisfied to be a child bride . . . you're, you're just joking, aren't you?" She scoffed at him, but there was a question in her voice.

With his finger Eric traced the high, rounded little apples that jumped into being high in her cheeks when she smiled—the *pommettes*, that curved sweet shape that he had remembered so often. A silence fell between them, a waiting silence like that in an audience between the end of one movement of a piano sonata and the beginning of the next movement, a silence tense with awareness that somebody who doesn't know the music might think that the piece had ended and applaud at the wrong time.

"Of course I was joking," he answered her finally. "Soldiers have some very wild fantasies in the middle of the night and that was the least lurid of mine. I had too much common sense and so did you—even then."

"Ah, darling, sometimes I wish I didn't have so much common sense. I get so tired of being grounded in reality. Have you ever read books by all those people who keep on and on about how you should live your life as if each day was going to be your last? I think they're just a bunch of sadists, promoting universal dissatisfaction."

"I wonder what the world would be like if everyone really did live as if there would be no tomorrow?" Eric asked.

"I can't speak for other people, but if there wasn't going to be a tomorrow for me, I know what I'd do."

"What?" Eric asked.

"I'll show you," she said and slid back down into the valley of the mattress and imprisoned his strong shoulders in her slim arms, and bent her head so that her lips fell directly on the warm skin between his collarbones where a pulse beat strongly. "I'll show you exactly . . . I won't leave anything out . . ."

Outside the sun withdrew slowly but neither Fauve nor Eric paid attention. It wasn't until a light was turned on in a window in a room across the courtyard of Eric's hotel that Fauve sat up with a violent start. "Oh, my God, what time is it?"

Eric reached to the bed table and looked at his watch. "About ten to six."

"Oh, no. Oh, no." She jumped out of the bed and ran to the bathroom, turned on the light and faced herself in the mirror. She was bedazzled, rosy, disheveled. "Oh, no! They'd only have to take one look at me to know where and how I've spent the afternoon," she cried, panic in her voice. "I have to take a shower and put on fresh makeup and do something about my hair and even then they'll be able to guess. Eric, when does the Vatican close? Do you have any idea? Oh, I don't know where to start! What a mess!"

"Wait a minute, darling. Don't go crazy, let's just think."

"Think? Who has time to think? I just have to get back to the Grand as fast as possible and pray that they're there waiting for me. What if they're not?" Fauve raced around the bathroom stark naked, trying to adjust the strange shower, looking frantically and unsuccessfully through her handbag for a small hairbrush, splashing cold water on her burning face, turning around in circles, her wits scattered, appalled by the way she'd let the time get away from her.

"Darling, you're hyperventilating. And you're freezing, you're covered with gooseflesh." Eric trapped her inside of a quilt, wrapped it around her, picked her up and carried her, kicking, and protesting, back to the bed. "Now shut up and let me telephone. Did you say the Grand?" He spoke to the hotel's phone operator in rapid Italian.

"But, what on earth am I going to say? Hang up, for God's sake. I have to figure this out." She tried to wrestle the phone out of his hand but he held her down with one arm.

"*La Signorina* Ivy Columbo, *per favore*," he said.

"No! Not Ivy. She's the smartest one. Call . . . call Bambi Two."

Eric paid no attention. "Hello, Miss Columbo? This is Eric Avigdor, yes . . . how was the Vatican? Inspirational? I suspected that it might be. Fauve? She's resting on a bench and she asked me to call and check in with you. No, she's all right but she's feeling faint—it's a combination of jet lag and claustrophobia—we just got out of the Catacombs—yes, the Catacombs of St. Callisto . . . all the way outside of Rome on the Via Appia Antica. Miles and miles . . . it's all my fault, I'm afraid. It was my idea—I'd forgotten how dark and narrow they are and once you get down inside you have to stay

with the guide or you could get lost and never find your way out—
the visit goes on and on—but the Catacombs can't be missed if
you're interested in early Christian martyrs . . . you didn't know
Fauve cared? She doesn't—it's one of my hobbies—I'm afraid I was
very selfish. The thing is, my car seems to have broken down and
this is the rush hour and the gas station attendant wants to close
up—that's where I'm calling from—so I just don't know when we'll
be back. Very late I'm afraid—impossible to say when. She's upset
about abandoning you . . . no problem? Oh, you're all going to have
room service and an early bedtime? You're absolutely right—it's the
smartest thing to do. Everybody's exhausted? Well, why don't you
put the 'Do Not Disturb' sign on all your doors when you finish
dinner and I'll tell Fauve not to worry."

"Wake-up calls!" Fauve hissed at him.

"Don't forget to tell the operator when to wake you tomorrow
. . . no, don't rely on travel alarm clocks, they never work. Right, I'll
tell her. Good night, Miss Columbo—what? Ivy? . . . good night,
Ivy. Thank you for being so sensible. Fauve will be relieved." He
hung up the phone.

"Catacombs!" Fauve said. "There's no way she believed you."

"I thought I was very convincing."

"You were—I didn't know you could lie so well—but who on
earth would be so absurd as to go visit Catacombs on a marvelous
early spring afternoon in Rome?"

"The same sort of people who'd go to the Vatican."

"Oh."

"I believe it's what's called a Mexican standoff," Eric said tenderly, relaxing the arm that had pinioned her to the bed.

"And what's that?"

"It just means that nobody has the advantage, a stalemate."

"You mean I've lost my moral authority?"

"You're merely holding it in abeyance. Tomorrow you can put
on that impressively severe jacket and your sensible shoes and
round up your little flock . . ."

"But what do you suppose they're really up to? Did you believe
her?"

"Why not? She did sound tired."

"Ivy? No way . . . she's probably tap dancing around the room,"
Fauve said grimly.

"I'm positive about the room service," Eric said, kissing her

453

neck, and ending the discussion. How else could he have heard the distinctive sound of a champagne cork popping in Ivy's room?

The next morning Fauve was sitting in the lobby of the Grand reading the *Daily American* with the angelic and faintly put-upon air of someone who has been waiting patiently when the models drifted out of the elevator on time, and, as she was deeply relieved to see, obviously refreshed. She accompanied them to Valentino's, where they were to stay until evening being fitted into the clothes for Thursday's collection.

The day was, she thought, inevitably perfect, although March in Rome can be wet and cold. Already the outdoor cafés were filling up, the smell of espresso spiked the soft air, trees thrust their blooming branches from behind every wall, there seemed to be a flower stall, banked high with blossoms, on every street corner. Fauve bought hundreds of tiny, pungent, dark-red carnations, filling both her arms and her shoulder bag with as many as she could carry. Her heart was full of an unruly, intoxicating tenderness. She felt like a pink balloon, filled with helium, that had been released into the turquoise sky, its string dancing gaily in the breeze. Why did she have so many flowers, she wondered for a minute, coming back to earth, and remembered that she was on her way to visit the three Lunel models who had been working in Rome for the past six weeks. She found them in high spirits and she gave them each a heap of carnations and a hasty kiss before she was finally free to dash away to meet Eric.

Until it was time to pick up Ivy and company at Valentino's the day was hers, to spend with Eric—time outside of time, time that had no connection to real life, time to be grasped and lived minute by minute, not touched by any thought of tomorrow. It was only Wednesday morning and she didn't have to fly to Florence until Thursday night—it was an eternity if she just thought of it as a string of miraculous moments, each complete in itself.

As they ate lunch in a little restaurant near the Forum, Eric couldn't stop gazing at Fauve. She looked fifteen, her face bare of makeup except for mascara and her hair brushed out so that its brightness had become a vermilion cloud. She wore a soft turtleneck sweater the color of pistachio ice cream and off-white corduroy trousers that she had stuffed into low, honey-colored boots. With the bright blue cotton poncho she carried, and her shoulder bag, she looked ready for the first day of school, he thought, his heart so nearly unmanageable with love that he felt witless. After lunch they walked to the Forum and paid their entrance fees at that little ticket booth that is so extraordinarily ordinary, as if a mere ticket is all that is needed to travel backward into history.

"I came here the last time too," Fauve said, "the day after the Vatican, and I promised myself I'd always return if ever I was in Rome again. You don't mind, do you? There's not much here for an architect, I'm afraid."

"Broken columns, a couple of arches, some headless statues?" Eric said, looking about. "A wilderness of fragments—everything tumbling over everything else, the debris of centuries fallen in on top of each other, and the whole lot covered with ivy and vines and holly—plenty here for an archeologist anyway." He laughed. "What draws you to it?"

"It's the only place I found in Rome that seemed to give me a real feeling of how old the city is. Everywhere else the monuments are so kept up and restored that I lose that sense of the past—but here . . . well, there's so little left that I can dream, I can just surrender to its mood and let my imagination loose."

Fauve and Eric picked their way upward under the cypresses toward the crest of the Palatine Hill, where once the monarchs of all the known world had their palaces. No other tourists and certainly no Romans were anywhere in sight.

"This must be the most peaceful place in Rome," Fauve said in a low voice. The poetic hush of the Forum delighted her. There was something almost supernatural that came from being in possession of this mysteriously abandoned space where once crowds from all over the Roman Empire had jostled each other for room to see the fortunate citizens as they walked by in their splendor. She felt a thrilling sense of vainglory, as if she were stepping over millennia in seven-league boots. She picked a spray of dark green acanthus leaves and studied its classic form. She wished she knew how to make it into a wreath, she thought, looking up at Eric. She imagined that some young Roman consul, returning to report on conditions on the edge of the Empire, might have had the same look of adventure and strength that was stamped on Eric's blunt, bronzed features. His head demanded a garland.

They reached the top of the hill and climbed up the steep steps into the greenness of the small, overgrown boxwood garden that was all that remained of the once-great hanging gardens of the Farnese.

"How I love it here!" Fauve exclaimed. "Doesn't it smell marvelous? What *is* that smell?"

"The boxwood—or is it the centuries?" Eric asked, looking down over the entire littered Forum spread beneath them.

"I feel more alive here than anywhere in Rome," Fauve said in a wondering voice. "Even the ghosts are friendly."

"Yes . . . I feel it too . . . how did you know?"

"It was like that the last time . . . I was sure you'd feel the same way." They sat down on a stone bench and fell silent, enriched and comforted by the tangible vibrations of a past that had disappeared, yet would never die.

Eric was the first to break the silence. "Tell me about your painting . . . you haven't said a word about it yet."

"I don't paint anymore—I haven't since the summer I met you."

"You let it go?" he said in astonishment. "How could that happen . . . how was it *possible* when it meant so much to you?"

"Eric, darling," Fauve said in a voice that struck him by its deep note of puzzled regret, "don't ask me about it . . . I can't really explain, not even to myself. Tell me more about you. This conference thing, what's it all about?"

"It's thrilling, Fauve. Really truly important." He got up from the bench and walked back and forth on the gravel path, gesturing vigorously with his large, beautifully shaped hands as he spoke, his eyes full of fervor. "Do you remember all those hideous apartment buildings they put up outside the industrialized zone of Cortine on the outskirts of Avignon?"

"How could I forget them? They were the only ugly thing in the landscape."

" And they didn't *have* to be! The conference is about humanizing low-cost housing, making it good instead of bad for the same price—or less—than it costs now . . . it's a question of design, of *caring*. I'll never accept the idea that public housing can't be beautiful . . . and neither do a lot of other architects from all over the world. We're meeting to exchange ideas and techniques."

"Is that the only sort of buildings you're interested in?"

"Not a bit—just the most necessary, I think, but not necessarily the most fun. My specialty is restoring old farmhouses all over Provence. You wouldn't believe how many people manage to buy

456

an old *mas* and then want to turn it into a Tyrolean cottage or a Grecian villa. I give them a comfortable house that works for modern life and still doesn't ruin the beauty of the original. But my biggest excitement is when I get a chance to build a new house. There I don't just copy an old *mas*—that would be easy, but where's the challenge? To design a new house for the Provençal landscape, a modern house that gives the pleasure to the eye and shelter to the body and respects the demands of the horizon and the hills—and the neighbors—ah, now *there's* an architect's dream! I want to show them to you—will you come and see some of my houses? Don't go back to New York after Paris—look, it's easy to plan . . ."

Fauve drew back immediately from his impetuousness. She held up her hand, warding him off. "No plans! The most I can go into the future now is to figure out what we're going to do about those girls of mine tonight. I have the strong impression that they have a hidden agenda. I can't leave them unattended, but I can't bear to be away from you for a minute."

"Why don't I dig up some other architects? We can all go out to dinner together," Eric proposed.

"Architects? *Roman* architects?"

"This conference is like the Olympics, all nationalities are represented. Lots of them like me are in Rome already."

"Hmmm . . ." Fauve considered deeply. "Latins of all kinds are absolutely out. Swedes are dubious—there's got to be some sort of reason why so many porno movies have the word 'Swedish' in their titles—Englishmen—Englishmen . . . no, there's that ancient French theory that no woman is as highly sexed as a supposedly frigid Englishwoman. What if it holds true for Englishmen too? I can't take that risk."

"Finns," Eric suggested. "Why don't we take a chance on Finns? They don't seem to reproduce much."

That night, after a dinner that would live in the annals of Lunel history, Fauve made sure that all her charges were safely deposited in their rooms before she slipped back to Eric's hotel. The big meadow of a bed, in which they had only spent one night, welcomed them. It had already begun to take on a mythic quality, Eric thought, as he counted the hours left to them. So aware was he of the passage of time that the texture of the sheets, the rolling terrain of the mattress, the amber glow of the little bedside lamp seemed to have become as much a part of the past as they were of the moment.

"There's only tonight," he said, cradling her head between his hands. "Tomorrow you can't be with me except while the collection is going on and then you get on that infernal plane for Florence. Why, oh why, do you have to leave Thursday night?"

"Don't count hours. Don't count minutes—you'll spoil *now*. Don't make me sad—don't make me sadder than I am," Fauve pleaded. "The girls have to be up bright and early Friday morning, you know it as well as I do. The fittings will be going on all week-end long—Versace, Armani—I thought you understood."

"Unfortunately it's as plain and logical as a blueprint. The thing I don't understand is why you've eluded me every time I've tried to talk at all seriously to you since we met. I haven't pressed it because I figured that maybe the time wasn't right, but now . . ."

"Oh—let me elude you some more. I elude so delightfully," Fauve whispered, covering his chest with kisses.

"I will if you'll answer one single very simple question—do you love me, Fauve?"

"Oh, *yes*."

"Then we *must* make plans, we have to talk about the future . . ."

"You said that if I answered, you'd let me elude you," Fauve protested, breaking into his immoderate rush of words. " 'Plans . . . the future'—that's not the stuff that elusions are made of."

"If you'd said that you didn't love me I would just shut up and make love to you. But, you *do*—don't you see how that changes everything?" Relief transfigured his voice.

Fauve pulled away from his arms, left the bed and stood by the window, naked and white in the darkness that fell outside of the lamplight. She clasped her hands behind her bowed head and shook it from side to side in a barely perceptible gesture of confusion and negation. "Please, oh, please, Eric, not tonight."

"But *when*? You can't be planning to leave without . . . that can't *be*! Fauve, how many more second chances do you think we're going to have?"

"Eric, I just haven't wanted to think," she said slowly with her face turned away from him. "I've been living without reckoning or wondering about possibilities . . . I've been living—just drifting in the wind. I've been so happy just bobbing along like a soap bubble, but if we keep talking my lovely bubble will burst. *Please?*"

Eric came to stand behind her at the window and put his arms around her, holding the soft weight of her breasts cupped in his hands. He rested his chin on the top of her head and protected her with his big warm body.

"You're shivering. Don't stay here, it's too cold. Come to bed, my little love. And bring your bubble with you—it's such a bright bubble and you wear it so beautifully."

"Tomorrow, Eric, I promise."

"Tomorrow."

On Thursday, after lunch, Eric sat waiting for Fauve at Rosati's. He looked at his watch impatiently. The Valentino collection must have started by now. He and Fauve would have almost two hours in which to make their plans before she had to leave to pick up the girls and the luggage and drive out to Fumicito in time for the plane.

He saw her approaching and jumped up. She came toward him, wearing a sweeping travel coat. The spring wind was brisk in the piazza.

"Let's go and sit inside," he said, tipping her head up for his kiss. "Thank God you didn't get held up."

"Once that show started nothing but a bomb in the dressing room could stop my girls from performing—and probably they'd just walk around the rubble. I sneaked out. I have to be back in time to congratulate Valentino, but it's a long collection."

"Espresso?" he offered.

"What I'd really like is a big pot of tea. Do you have that in Italy?"

"There's a long tradition of eccentric Englishmen and women who came to Rome and never left it . . . I'm sure they make tea. Fauve . . . when will you marry me?"

"I was afraid you were going to say that," she said in a strange muted voice. Eric looked at her and it didn't seem possible that this pale girl, dressed again in black and white, with only her hair to give color to her face, could be the spirit of fire and abandon with whom he'd spent the night until she had left him just before dawn.

"Why afraid?"

"Because I can't."

"Why not, my darling? What reason is there why two people who love each other the way we do can't get married?" He spoke

459

calmly and quietly. He'd been sure that she'd put up some sort of resistance, it had been evident in her evasiveness, in her insistence on never looking beyond the present. "You're not sixteen anymore . . . I know that was just a crazy idea—but now everything's different—there's nothing to stop us."

"I'm not ready to get married. How can you expect me to spend two days with you—only two days—and make a decision like that? It's been *perfect* and nothing *is* that perfect in real life, nothing! It couldn't keep on being like this—this was an *interlude*, Eric. But that's not the only reason." Fauve's voice was strong, sure of what she had to say. "I have a responsibility to Magali that I can't ignore. If I left the agency she'd have to come back and work five days a week or else give it up—sell it probably. She spent her whole life building that business and I've spent five years learning it and she counts on me—she has every right to. Oh, she'd never stand in my way, but I know that if I had to leave New York it would change the whole pattern of her life—just wouldn't be fair! She'd be miserable giving up the agency, and she'd be just as miserable working full-time again at her age. And anyway what would I do with myself living in Avignon?"

"Wait a minute! That's three reasons—could you just stop for a second and catch your breath? Drink your tea. Milk? Lemon? Okay, marriage wouldn't be like two days in Rome. *Nothing* is like two days in Rome. Nothing is like a week in Florence. Nothing is like a month in the country. Marriage is marriage and each one is different—and ours would be wonderful; from time to time it probably wouldn't be perfect, but only children expect marriage to be perfect—and you're not a child. That's one. Two. From everything you've told me about Magali, she can take care of herself. She'd be outraged if she thought you were sacrificing yourself for her . . . I can't imagine that she couldn't work it out one way or another . . . she's managed to do just splendidly on her own for most of her life, hasn't she? Three—now there's a real problem, but not one that we can't find an answer to. I could move to Paris, for instance, join a firm there and you could find a job, or you could open a model agency if that's what you want . . . living in Avignon isn't essential to me . . ."

"Stop it, Eric! You're being so goddamned rational about this, you sound like a train schedule."

"But you're giving me reasons and I'm giving you the reasons why your reasons are wrong. If you want to give me irrational, I'll be quiet and listen."

"Oh—oh . . ." Fauve flung up her hands, speechless.

"Come on—give me irrational," he insisted.

"I'm frightened, I'm terrified, I'm scared shitless," she blurted. "I'm *paralyzed* at the idea of making such a big decision. It's too much for me—it makes my blood run cold just thinking about it— oh, Eric, I'm a natural-born late bloomer. I give up each stage of my life as slowly as I can, looking backward the whole time—I need old habits, security, familiarity—I'm petrified at the notion of spending the rest of my life with you—or with anybody, for that matter. I don't really know you, not the grown-up you. I don't even know *me*. I haven't had enough time to myself, I'm not ready to be a wife, I don't *want* to plan my future . . . it's easy for you, you're twenty-six, you've had time to discover yourself, to experiment. I feel rushed, pressured . . . how can you expect me to be ready?"

"That's not irrational, that's natural." He took her hands in both of his. "I understand that it's too soon to make a decision. Just come and live with me—just see how it is for us together. That's not too big a step to take, is it? No strings—only an interlude if that's all you want. Don't go back to New York after Paris . . . come and spend the spring in Avignon with me."

Fauve looked into her teacup, as addled as she'd been in her life. I can't make him understand . . . how can I say, after all, that I don't trust him, no, not in spite of thinking I did? I trusted my father, and look what he did . . . how can I trust any man, ever, ever? An "interlude" . . . only an interlude he says . . . it's always an interlude when it starts—before it does something terrible to you. It was just an interlude for Magali in Paris so long ago, just an interlude for my mother . . . interludes turn into preludes and then? What then, oh, God? *Springtime in Avignon?* No! It's dangerous, too dangerous. I'm right to feel the danger. There's always danger when you trust, when you depend on somebody else, when you put your life into his hands. Oh, I want the life I *know*, I want the life where I have a place, where I have an office, where people need me, a life where I grew up, where I'm safe. *Safe.*

"No," she said, looking into her teacup. "No, I can't. I have to go back to New York. Maybe when I have my vacation," she faltered, "the next vacation I have . . . maybe then . . ."

"Don't bother." Eric stood up. "I didn't realize that you really hated the idea," he said tightly. "I wouldn't have kept bothering you about it for so long if I'd known. You said you loved me but you don't—not enough. Not nearly enough. Sorry—my mistake."

He put some money on the table and walked away.

"I knew he wouldn't understand," Fauve whispered to herself.

"Is something wrong, *Signorina?*" asked the waiter.

"No," said Fauve, "nothing's wrong. It's just the end . . ."

"The end . . ."

"Of an interlude."

31

Falk was accustomed to the flattery of beautiful women and discounted it. He was so steeped in flattery that he believed he no longer knew what it was like to have the feeling of being flattered, but when Fauve Lunel invited him to have dinner with her alone in her apartment, the first dinner she'd actually ever cooked by herself, he felt . . . flattered.

"I'm probably not a good cook," she had warned him.

"Who said so?"

"Nobody, I've never cooked for anybody else before, so how could I be a good cook?"

"I'll take that chance."

As Falk waited for Fauve to come out of the kitchen where she was mixing drinks, he glanced around her living room. It was like looking into the attic of a family homestead, he thought, or through a pile of old scrapbooks. Hadn't Fauve ever thrown *anything* out? He could see only two examples of restraint; she had painted the floor emerald green and left it bare and the fabric she had used on her keenly overstuffed, exuberantly Victorian furniture actually matched; a pattern of giant cabbage roses on glazed chintz that, now that he looked at it closely, had surely been used as curtains in Maggy's Fifth Avenue apartment before she redecorated.

He could remember the genesis of so many of the objects he saw; there was the huge wire birdcage he had bought Fauve on Third Avenue one Saturday afternoon. It seemed to have spawned seven other birdcages that were artfully piled around it, making a complex structure through which no bird sang. And there was the giant straw hat he'd bought her back from a location trip to Yucatán now joined by dozens of others in every shape and size, all hung on hooks on the walls. The graceful old lyre he'd given her for Christmas when she was twelve was suspended from another wall, surrounded by a number of antique musical instruments; flutes, violins, oboes and even a battered clarinet that had been restored to a high polish. Fauve had baskets everywhere, baskets on top of baskets, some of them filled with growing plants, some of them with pencils, others crammed with notebooks and bolts of fabric and balls of yarn.

Pillows! Fauve seemed to have cornered the pillow market, he thought with the connoisseur's salute of a man who considers himself an expert on the cluttered look. This went beyond clutter—this was historical. The books in her jammed bookcases included a complete set of the Oz books, the many adventures of Mary Poppins, and the works of E. Nesbitt, as well as all the books she had read since she was a child, none of which she ever seemed to have considered allowing to escape her possession. A pair of draped stone sphinxes, life-sized, it seemed to him, although he'd never seen a sphinx while it was still in good health, guarded the fireplace, inside of which stood a polished brass grate.

There was no fire—it was a mild September day in 1975—but Fauve had lit a galaxy of white votive candles in little clear tumblers and distributed them on the grate so that the fireplace didn't look empty and dark. There was a round table that was set next to tall windows that looked out on a flourishing acanthus tree. It was covered with three different tablecloths. The first one, flounced widely to the ground, was crisp, bright red taffeta, the second was a small silky old flowered carpet in every shade of pink, and the top cloth was made of delicate white linen with a wide border of embroidered organdy.

On Fauve's desk, in ornate old frames, stood the only three photographs in the room; a snapshot of Maggy and Darcy sitting on the lawn in front of their house, a picture from a 1951 issue of Life showing Maggy surrounded by her ten most famous models, and an enlargement of one of the test shots Falk had made of Teddy in 1947. Teddy Lunel when she was twenty.

He turned away, unable to look at it for more than a moment, and his eye was caught by an extraordinary object, a gigantic stuffed panda that had seen better days, sitting in a place of honor on a rocking chair in a corner. Startled, he looked around for other animals. A fleet of ship's figureheads, an army of small statues, a collection of music boxes, a forest of unmatched candlesticks, and, on each table, clusters of bud vases of every height, each holding a single flower or a spray of tiny leaves or a few wild grasses—yes, all of that, but, he was relieved to see, no other stuffed animals.

"Very cozy," he said to Fauve as she handed him a glass.

"I haven't really done much to it," she said, "but little by little it's taking shape."

"What shape did you have in mind?"

"I don't know exactly. I'll know when I get there—probably when I can't walk across the room without tripping over something. That's why I don't have a rug. It cuts down on the confusion. If I had a rug I'd want to put another little carpet on top of it, and I'd need a hearth rug of course—something in pattern—I seem to keep finding things."

"I love things," Falk said. "There is *nothing* like a thing."

"I knew you'd understand." They smiled at each other in the most mutual possible pleasure. "You'd never ask me if it doesn't collect a lot of dust or what sort of neurosis it all represents, or comment meaningfully on my nest-building instinct."

"Never. But I do wonder . . . ?"

"What about?"

"No pictures?"

"Nope, I don't have any room for pictures. There's too much stuff on the walls and anyway, to do pictures justice you have to subordinate the room to them."

"This room is definitely insubordinate."

"Exactly. Oh, the chicken! Excuse me for a minute."

She came back, a plain white chef's apron wrapped over her bare-armed, barebacked dress of bright saffron cotton. "It's cooking, that's all I can say in its favor at the moment."

"What sort of chicken is it?" he asked hungrily.

"Hungarian. Chicken Paprika. I'm counting on the fact that there isn't anything in the world that can't be improved by a great deal of sour cream. I know it's cheating but I need all the help I can get."

"When did you start cooking? Did it just come over you all of a sudden?"

"I think it must be a maturation thing or maybe an unnatural craving like in *Rosemary's Baby*. Ever since I moved here if I'm not invited out to dinner I've picked up something at the Dover Deli. A few weeks ago, I was passing the butcher shop and I found myself just marching in and buying two lamb chops. I thought that I'd put them in a pan and cook them. Well, I'm still not sure what I did wrong but the kitchen filled with smoke, and lots of hot fat started to pop out at me. I got so frightened that I grabbed the pan off the fire and threw the whole thing out the back window. But that started me thinking that if Maggy could learn to garden from books, I could probably learn to cook. So I bought *The Joy of Cooking*. History will be made tonight." She began to set the table.

"Maggy thinks you're working too hard," Falk said. "She told me that you're letting the business dominate your life."

"She's got her nerve! Do you know what she did last weekend? She ordered five thousand daffodil bulbs. Five thousand! She's going to plant them herself on those low hills behind the house and next spring they'll come up as if they had been growing wild for years, in drifts. *Drifts*—she's constantly raving on about drifts. And once she's got the daffodils established she intends to make a shade garden in the woods, the way it would be in nature if nature had her sense of style. Can you imagine anyone who plans to dig five thousand holes telling me *I* work too hard?"

"You don't dig individual holes, you dig up a whole lot of dirt and sort of dribble the bulbs around, or so she said. Like sowing grain or something."

"Well, however you do it, it's work. You know, I feel that maybe Maggy's more interested in her garden than in the agency now," Fauve said, putting plates down on the linen cloth.

"What makes you say that?"

"It's something really weird about Thursdays. Every Thursday as the afternoon goes by, she gets more and more irritable, as if she just can't *wait* to get away, but refuses to admit it. She finds nonexistent mistakes everywhere, she walks around the booking rooms and double checks everybody's cards to make sure that nobody screwed up Friday and Monday, she starts worrying about models who are doing just fine, she goes into the bookkeeping department to talk about whether they're prepared for payday as if, after all these years, they didn't know that every model will be in for her check on Friday, rain or shine. She's driving everybody a little crazy. The new bookers are terrified of her. Then she keeps finding little things 'she has' to do as the afternoon goes on, so that we can't close on time . . . unnecessary things that Casey or Loulou or I could take care of on Friday perfectly well. It's as if she's forcing herself to work late because she feels guilty about taking so much time off, which is *totally* insane."

"Have you talked to her about it?" Falk asked.

"No, I guess I just don't want to say anything that might sound critical. I figure that the day will come when she'll figure out for herself that she just doesn't want to work three days a week and then she'll let me know," Fauve said, appraising her table and judging it complete.

"How would you feel about running the agency if she weren't around?"

"It's what I'm trained for, it's what I know. We have really reliable people working for us in every department. Casey can do anything I can do, Loulou has the booking side of things as much in control as booking can ever be—I know it's a big business for anybody my age to run, but I've been in it for five years and I think I could manage. Still . . . Maggy *is* Lunel. Every aspiring model in the world wants to get in to see Maggy Lunel, not Fauve Lunel. The magazine editors trust her judgment as they won't trust mine for years and years, the agency would *never* be the same again . . . but . . . if she really is fed up, I understand. I'd have to . . . oh, my chicken!"

When Fauve came back from the kitchen she looked relieved. "I tasted it and I do believe it's going to be vaguely Hungarian."

"Haven't you ever cooked anything for Ben Litchfield?" Falk asked.

"Ben Litchfield doesn't have any damn taste buds."

"I thought . . ."

"I know what you thought. That's all anybody thinks. Honestly, Melvin, all of Manhattan could be two blocks square the way everybody is involved in everybody else's private business." Fauve sat down next to Falk and drank half of her glass of wine. "I don't mean you, obviously."

"I know you didn't. So tell me all your private business."

"He wants to get married."

"What else is new?"

"No, I mean he *really* wants to get married. He used to mention it every fifth or sixth time I saw him, now it's every time. Pressure, pressure," Fauve brooded.

"Most girls," Falk said.

467

"Exactly. Most girls. All girls probably. He's a wonderful guy, he's brilliant, he's good, he's successful, he's serious, he's very, very attractive, he's somebody I can talk to, we have a lot in common, he's sweet, he's everything you could ask for."

"Oh, I don't think I like the sound of *that*."

"I think Ben and I are what people call good for each other," Fauve said with a wicked smile.

"If you'd said he was impossible, crazy, unpredictable, and you couldn't understand why you were so wildly in love with him . . . maybe."

"Maybe . . . maybe not. Even that wouldn't guarantee anything."

"Nothing guarantees anything, Fauve," Falk said gently. "It's all a crapshoot."

"Isn't there any way to be sure, any way to nail things down so that they happen under your control? If you're very, *very* careful?" Fauve asked wistfully.

"Not if you're going to risk making a change. Change just can't be shaped and organized and molded *before* it happens. The nature of change is that it takes you somewhere else than where you are now. You grow, that's the only thing you can really be sure of, growth. But any change has its share of surprises."

"I've never been all that fond of surprises," Fauve said with a shadowy look of such sadness on her face that Falk's heart contracted.

"Do you think the chicken is ready?" he asked. "It smells ready."

"I'll investigate. How will I know if it's ready?"

"When the leg moves easily in the socket. Also, take a long cooking fork, stick it in and see if the juice that comes out is clear—stick it into the thigh, not the breast."

"How do you know?"

"How many wives have I had?"

"Only three."

"One of them must have taught me, but I can't remember which. It's good to know that sort of thing even if it's wrong. It's called folk wisdom."

Carrying a platter, Fauve emerged from the kitchen, beaming.

"It looks quite good, if looks mean anything."

The chicken was good, the rice was good, the string beans,

French-cut and flash-frozen, were good, and the paprika-laced sour cream lifted everything into a realm in which sheer greed became a virtue, for not to eat it ravenously would have been a sin of omission.

When dinner was over, Fauve and Falk sat drinking brandy in front of the fireplace where the votive lights still winked. Fauve fell silent, pensive. After a long, comfortable silence she looked up and said, "All the most important people in my life, Magali, Darcy—and even Lally Longbridge, who's like an aunt really, and you, especially you, Melvin, with whom I can speak with more freedom than with anyone else—none of you will talk to me about my mother. I wonder why?"

"I've always thought . . . that Maggy had told you all about her . . . nothing's been hidden," Melvin answered, uneasily.

"Oh, the outline of her life, yes. The basic details, the things I have to be told. I've looked at so many photos for so many hours—there's a complete library of old magazines at the office and between 1947 and 1952 there are literally thousands of pictures of Teddy Lunel, but they can't tell me the things I want to know, no matter how long I stare into her eyes."

"What sort of things?" Falk asked, his heart beating heavily.

"I'm only a few years younger than she was when she died. Would I have loved her? What would she have told me to do about Ben? What did she care about most in the world? Why didn't she marry you?"

"You know about that? Who told you?" He put his brandy snifter down with a sudden, startled movement.

"Oh, I guessed a long time ago. There's something about your face when you look at me. I know you were in love with her. Were you lovers, the two of you?" Fauve asked softly, seriously.

"I was . . . I was the first boy who ever told her she was beautiful, I asked her out on her first date, I gave her her first kiss, I was the first man who ever made love to her—the only thing I wasn't, was the first man whose heart she broke."

"I'm sorry . . . I'm so sorry, Melvin, I wish she hadn't broken your heart."

"She didn't want to, she couldn't help it, she just couldn't *quite* fall in love with me . . . she was looking for something else, something . . . some *other* thing."

469

"Did she have many lovers?"

Falk hesitated. Did he have a right to answer? Did Fauve have a right to ask?

"You see?" Fauve said. "That's exactly what I mean. If she were alive I'd say, 'Mother, did you have a lot of lovers when you were my age?' and she'd have to tell me something, even if it was just to mind my own business. But I can't ask Magali, obviously, and now you get all closed off. What *would* she have told me?"

"I think she'd have told you anything you wanted to know. I'm not sure that she would have given you sensible advice, being sensible wasn't a priority with Teddy—but I think she would have been frank with you."

"Well?"

"I told you she was looking for some *other* thing. She looked for a long time and whenever she realized that she hadn't found what she wanted . . . whatever it was . . . she looked somewhere else . . . so, she had a number of lovers. I don't know what 'many' means exactly, but perhaps she had one lover for every hundred men who wanted her—every two hundred—"

"But she cared about them?"

"Each one, until she stopped caring and started looking again. And then, she found your father and he was what she wanted, God help her."

"Am I being unfair to you?" Fauve asked suddenly. "Luring you up here with my divine chicken and then asking you about things you don't want to discuss?"

"No! God, no. I think we've all been terribly unfair to you, not telling you more, not talking about Teddy because it was too painful. Her death changed all the people who were left behind. None of us has ever been the same since."

"Isn't that true whenever somebody young dies?"

"Perhaps. But your mother was . . . she was . . ."

"Different? Special?" Fauve's voice trembled in its yearning need to know.

"I wish I could even begin to explain her charm—I used to read e. e. cummings—everyone my age read e. e. cummings—and I'd always think of her—'the musical white spring'—no, I'd have to be a poet to convey even a tenth of Teddy. And yes, you would have loved her so very, very much and she would have loved you more than anything in the world . . . that's the saddest part of it all." He stood up and went to where Fauve sat curled up in her chair and hugged her.

"Just remember one thing, your mother finally did find what she'd wanted for so long and she was marvelously happy until the very last second of her life."

"Can I give you a little more brandy, Melvin?" Fauve asked, standing up so abruptly that she knocked over a big folder that lay on a table next to her chair. It fell on the floor and papers scattered all over. Fauve darted to pick them up and Falk bent to help her. The papers slid around on the varnished surface and after he'd accumulated a small pile of them he stopped to see what they were. He looked casually, peered again through his glasses, and then took the papers away from the dimness in which they had been sitting, and thrust them under the light of a lamp.

"They're nothing," said Fauve. "Just give them to me."

"Like hell I will. Like *hell* I will."

"They're just doodles, Melvin. Come on, don't make me mad. That's private." She stuffed the papers she had picked up back into the folder and tried to pull the rest of the papers out of his grasp.

"Don't tear them!" he threatened, backing away.

"So? What if I do?"

"Fauve, you've been drawing, you've been working . . . how long has this been going on? Do you have any idea of how good you are, you dumb, *dumb* girl?"

"I just . . . I get a kind of nervous need to draw things . . . it's like a tic—*please* don't make a big number out of it, Melvin. You know how I feel about art—this is just a minor little, unimportant thing, not even a hobby. Everybody doodles, show me one person who doesn't doodle."

"Jesus, Fauve, who do you think you're talking to? Somebody who doesn't know the difference? These are fucking superb! Are you painting too? Fauve, tell me!"

"There's absolutely nothing to tell. Okay—so I draw a little—I admit it—I don't paint at all . . . I'm telling the truth . . . no paints, you'd smell them if they were in the apartment." Fauve flung her arms out in a gesture of innocence. "There's no law against drawing, it's never been considered a vice. Come on, Melvin, stop looking at me like that. It's embarrassing. And give me back my drawings."

He handed them back to her and shrugged. "If that's the way you want to go, baby, there's nothing I can say. If you should ever decide that you'd like to give me a birthday present or a Valentine's Day present or just a present . . . give me one of your doodles. Don't even bother to frame it. You've found your *line*—your own distinctive style, and it has nothing to do with your father or any other artist! Do you understand what that means? No? Never mind, stupid. I think I'll take that brandy you offered. I never needed it more."

Marte Pollison, in her seventies now, had never wavered in her long devotion to Nadine. In her eyes Nadine was still the miraculously beautiful little daughter she could never have had. Nadine, who knew that Marte adored her blindly, had always shamelessly and instinctively appealed to the sentimental side of the crusty peasant woman, running to her for sympathy when she had a bump or scratch that was so minor that Kate would have laughed it away; sitting with her in the kitchen listening to her chatter about the village life for hours at a time, waiting for the delicious sweets that Marte made especially for her. After Nadine left home for boarding school, she forgot about Marte entirely until she came home for vacations and then the old, satisfying relationship was immediately resumed, Marte growing more worshipful every year. After Kate's death, Marte became Nadine's only contact with the world of *La Tourrello* for Mistral had been blunt about not welcoming her.

"Your life is a farce, your husband is worthless and I'm too busy to be interrupted. You're not welcome here, Madame Dalmas," he had said unpleasantly the last time she had suggested coming to Félice for a weekend and from that time on, a period of almost four years, Nadine had prudently decided to remain in touch with Mistral through an occasional phone call to Marte.

Oh, how many times had she heard that dreary, unvarying, infuriating report, given in Marte's cracked old voice. "He's just the same, *ma petite chérie*. He gets up, he has breakfast, he shuts himself up in his studio all day, he has dinner and goes to bed. No, he's in good health, he never says anything to me except to warn me to keep strangers away, as if I didn't know. What does he do all day? He keeps the studio locked and I've never been one to pry. It's been a quiet, lonely time since your mother died. He's let the land go, he fired the men, the machinery has all rusted, the vineyards and the olive groves are the shame of the neighborhood, but he doesn't care, not he. If it weren't for me, he'd probably starve to death, and not even notice. I only stay on because of you and in memory of your poor mother."

In the middle of September 1975, Marte Pollison called Nadine to tell her that her father had been coughing for days. He had worked steadily, refusing to change his routine, but that evening he had been unable to get out of bed. "He won't let me call the doctor, ma petite, but I believe he may have bronchitis—what must I do?"

"Nothing, Marte, I'll be there in the morning. You know how he is about doctors—don't upset him."

Phillipe Dalmas made a perfunctory offer to fly to Marseilles with Nadine and drive up with her to Félice, a matter of little more than an hour and a half, but Nadine spurned it. As she drove up to the gates, she was shocked. La Tourrello looked abandoned, a stone pile from which the life had drained. In the kitchen she submitted gracefully to Marte's hugs. "You are more beautiful than ever—how gay it must be in Paris," Marte exclaimed, as she fussed happily over Nadine.

"Why is the house shut up, Marte? Why are the shutters closed, the furniture all covered?"

"Oh, don't blame me, it's not my fault. The pool is empty too and the garden's overgrown, but there's no one here but me to do all the work. I've kept the house dusted and swept and the tiles on the roof are repaired when they need it, but you know Monsieur fired all the domestics after Madame died, and my arthritis gets worse every time the mistral blows."

"Poor Marte—of course I understand," Nadine said.

"For a long while I offered to make up a fire for him in the salon so he could sit there at night but he never wanted one. I gave your room a good cleaning and airing this morning, and I'll serve you dinner in the dining room if you like, or in the kitchen with me. How long can you stay?"

"Until I'm sure he's better," Nadine had answered, and mounted the stairs to Mistral's room.

"I don't know why the devil you're here," Mistral barked at her as she entered. "It was too late to stop you when Marte, damn her, told me you were coming."

"Marte is concerned about you."

"She's an old busybody. Senile! I have a bad cold. All I need is a few days in bed."

"Don't you think you should call the doctor?"

"Don't be ridiculous. I've never seen a doctor in my life. I don't need a doctor, I need a little peace and quiet."

"Marte thinks it's bronchitis."

"She doesn't know what she's talking about. Is she qualified to make a diagnosis? Just leave me alone."

"Have you been working too hard?" Nadine asked.

"Working too hard? Do you have any idea of what that means? I work, that's all. Work is work." He coughed, an explosive, unexpected, uncontrollable cough.

"Get out of here," he said when he regained his breath. "You'll catch my cold." He sipped water from a glass by his bed.

"No, Father, I'll keep you company a little longer. Don't pay any attention to me. I'll just sit here."

Mistral closed his eyes in indifference and after a minute he fell into a light sleep, snoring at intervals. Nadine couldn't stop staring at him. Was this the man Marte described as in good health? Perhaps it was simply that Marte hadn't noticed, living with him every day, but Mistral was so thin that his body made only a long lumpy ridge under the bedclothes. From the chair by his bed in which she sat, his body smelled musty and rank with sweat. She shook with disgust.

He was a tough old man and only seventy-five. He had been able to work as usual until yesterday. Who knew what reserves of strength were left in that body? When she was a little girl he had been the strongest man in the world. Great painters, like great orchestra conductors, lived forever if they didn't manage to kill themselves in one way or another in their youth. Certainly his manner was not that of a man who believed himself to be in any danger.

Nadine bit her lips in a passion of impotent temper. It was probably a false alarm, a fever, a cough, a sweat, nothing she hadn't had herself a dozen times. Still there was no question that he had lost a great deal of weight. But thin people live longer than fat ones, she thought angrily, and tiptoed closer to the bed to gaze into his face. His nose seemed twice as large as it ever had for now it stood out from a face from which the flesh had fallen away, a harsh mask, somber and archaic.

"Damn it, Nadine, leave me alone! I want to sleep!" Mistral rasped, without opening his eyes.

Her heart jumped and she fled down to the kitchen.

474

"Marte, I don't think there's any reason to worry about him. He's too bad tempered to be really sick."

"I couldn't take the responsibility, I had to telephone you," Marte muttered.

"Of course you did. Anyway, I'm glad I came if only to see you. Father's kept me away for so long. You know I would have come as often as possible but he refused to see me. I've never understood it, but what could I do? It's his house, after all."

"If only your mother were still alive. Do you remember the parties? And how beautiful the house was, filled with flowers, servants everywhere, the kitchen full of food? And all the famous people? Oh, Madame was the queen of the countryside," she said sadly.

"You look tired, my poor Marte," Nadine consoled her.

"I kept looking in on him last night, climbing up and down those stairs. I didn't get much sleep, but you mustn't worry about me."

"I think we should both go to bed early tonight. I'm just down the hall from his room so I'll keep his door and my door open and if Father needs anything I'll hear him . . . I sleep lightly. You *mustn't* climb stairs like that with your arthritis. And tomorrow, if I think it's necessary, I'll call the doctor no matter what he says."

"I'm glad you came, *petite chérie*. I feel much better with you in charge. It's all too much for an old woman like me."

As Nadine lay in bed that night she was too alert to sleep. She imagined herself taking a candle and creeping down to the kitchen and finding the key to the studio on the big key ring that hung there. She imagined walking through the silent rooms of the shuttered house and going out the back, past the empty pool, to the great wooden doors of the studio. She saw herself unlocking the doors and snapping on the work lights and walking through the studio to the storage room where the supreme works of France's greatest living artist lay on their racks, hundreds of canvases, more valuable than any jewels. In her mind she counted them, she estimated their value—yes, in the hundreds of millions of francs, if Mistral's dealer was correct, and there was no reason to believe he was not. A fortune too great, too vast to understand. In that studio was her brilliant, triumphant future, Nadine told herself, hugging her body with impatience. Not mere paintings—no, so much more.

The houses she would own all over the world, the marvelous objects she would buy and buy and buy, the receptions she would give; the inherited glory that would finally, conclusively descend on her, the allure that would allow her to know everyone. The world would be at the feet of Mistral's daughter. Soon. Very soon. *How soon?*

She got out of bed and walked softly into Mistral's room. His breathing was ugly to hear, so much more labored than it had been earlier. He struggled horribly to produce each strangulated snore. She observed him carefully for a long time, far enough from the bed so that he couldn't see her if he opened his eyes. Finally Nadine went back to her room and slept soundly until morning. She dressed hastily and returned to Mistral's bedside. He was half awake and the water glass next to his bed was empty. The chamber pot that Marte had put on the bedside table was half full. Nadine emptied it, sickened and rigid. She poured some water for him and held it to his lips.

"How do you feel?" she asked.

"Like yesterday," he said but his voice was a whisper and, even without touching his skin, Nadine could feel the hectic fever that was baking him reach its hot fingers out to her. She busied herself with a washcloth and warm water, dabbing away, concealing her revulsion. "I don't think I should try to shave you. I've never done it before," she said lightly. "Shall I ask Marte to make you breakfast?"

"Not hungry . . . more water," he muttered, coughing again in that savage, gasping way that seemed so deep that it might have come from his bowels, a cough that jerked him up in bed and bent him in half.

Nadine went down to the kitchen to find Marte just coming in, a worried look on her face.

"He spent a very good night," Nadine said cheerfully. "I've given him a sponge bath and made him nice and comfortable. He's gone back to sleep. That's the very best thing for him. I tried to get him to eat but he refused. I know exactly how he feels—when I have that kind of cold I don't want to even smell food, only sip liquids. My Paris doctor says that they still haven't invented anything to equal bedrest and liquids."

"Oh, I feel guilty about letting you do all this," Marte said unhappily.

476

"Marte, my old Marte, if I can't take care of my own father . . . ? Look, you make some good strong soup, a beef broth, and perhaps later I'll be able to get him to drink some."

"Don't you think we should telephone the doctor in Apt who took care of Madame?"

"That would put Father into such a rage that he'd get worse. You know how he prides himself on never being sick. I wouldn't want to be responsible for bringing a doctor to the house unless I thought he truly wasn't well. It would make him as mad as seeing a priest walk in! All he needs is good, plain nursing. Marte, I know what you can do to make yourself useful! Make me a beautiful roast chicken the way only you can make it. I'm starving! And one of your apricot tarts and a big platter of cheeses, just for me. I dream of the cheeses from Félice. And country butter."

"I'll have to go into the village, there isn't much in the house."

"Then go, go. I'll be here, don't worry."

During all that long, hot September day Nadine guarded the sickroom. She stood in the corridor outside of the half-opened door and listened avidly. Mistral coughed constantly and violently. Sometimes he moaned and called her name in a pleading, desperate voice that was so weak that it could barely be heard. He whispered harshly for Marte, over and over, and coughed again, more rendingly every hour and yet, it seemed to her, without as much force as before. Occasionally, he seemed to fall asleep but never for long. Downstairs, Marte, relieved and comforted, busied herself in cooking and making the house look welcoming.

"Open all the shutters, Marte, take those awful covers off the furniture, pick some flowers, build a fire in the grate—at night it's too depressing like this," Nadine had commanded, and Marte, delighted at the new life in the house, had been glad to obey. When Monsieur was well enough to come down to complain, it would be time enough to close the shutters again.

In the middle of the night Nadine woke up with a start, as if someone had called her name, but the house was quiet. Marte, she knew, was sleeping in her room behind the kitchen downstairs. Yet . . . something . . . there *was* something. She threw on a robe and went into Mistral's room. The second she entered the room she knew that he was dying. Death filled the space, a primeval presence, a thickness of the air, a withering that nothing could reverse. At last. *At last.*

He was drowning in the liquid in his lungs. She could hear it. She had never heard that hideous noise before but she recognized it. What else could it be, that choking, desperate gurgle? If only the stench in the room wasn't so revolting—but she didn't intend to leave, not until she was sure.

Nadine went to the window and opened it so that a breeze could enter and push away some of the loathsome vileness that emanated from the bed. She pulled a chair as close to the window as possible and turned on a standing lamp just above her head. Intently she inspected her fingernails. The polish on one of them was chipped. Oh, on two. She would have to find a manicurist in Félice before the funeral.

There was a faint new sound from the bed, a begging sound, a pleading sound. Water? Could he want water when he was drowning? Impossible. He was struggling to speak. Gibberish. Meaningless syllables. She didn't listen.

Soon there were no more sounds from the bed. None at all. Still Nadine sat quietly in the fragile pool of light. She waited until she was absolutely certain that she had won before she walked quickly back to her own room.

She needed sleep. The morning light would wake her. These things were so sudden.

32

It was still raining. It hadn't stopped all day, Fauve thought as she peered out of the window of Maggy's apartment, to which they had both retreated after hearing the news of the death of Julien Mistral.

"How long," Darcy asked Fauve gently, "do you think I'm going to be able to say that you can't talk to all those reporters? Aside from the *New York Times,* and the *Daily News* and the *Post,* there are wire service guys and half a dozen stringers from out of town, a bunch of photographers, and two TV news crews right outside the house. They haven't been allowed in the lobby but they're not going away, rain or no rain."

"Why can't they leave me out of it?" Fauve asked miserably.

"Unfortunately you're the juiciest part of the story, sweetheart. When all the media people went to their morgues to put Mistral's bio together, the most newsworthy angle, from their point of view, is Mistral's daughter, Fauve Lunel—unfortunately it's the part of the story with the most human interest and you're right here where they can get at you. His death would get enormous attention just by itself, but add your mother's story . . . well, you can see why they want you."

"Do I really have to talk to them and answer questions?"

"I don't see why Fauve has to do that, do you, Darcy?" Maggy asked. "Is it necessary?"

"It would be the simplest way to get it over with," Darcy answered. "Just bite the bullet."

"What sort of things will they want to know?" Fauve asked, utterly at a loss.

"First of all, they've all been asking me if you're going to the funeral. After that, I just don't know. When did you last see him, what's your reaction to the tragic event . . . you know the sort of stuff they ask family members."

"I never expected this," Fauve said slowly.

"I did," Maggy said bitterly. "I remember the way it was when your mother died . . . there's nothing they won't ask and nothing they won't print. Darcy, can't you write down a statement and read it to them—tell them Fauve is too upset to talk."

"It's worth a try," he said, dubiously.

"Just don't say I'm going to the funeral," Fauve warned, "because I'm not."

There was a silence in the sitting room, unbroken until Maggy and Darcy exchanged a quick look and, in response, he got up to leave. "I'll be in the library, writing the statement," he explained.

Maggy moved over to the sofa on which Fauve was sitting and took her hand. "Look, Fauve, assuming that you really don't go to the funeral, don't you see that it will just arouse ten times the amount of curiosity there is already? Whatever the personal problems you had with him, your father was a major figure to the whole world—not just to art collectors—and besides Nadine Dalmas you're the only other child he ever had. You *must* go." Maggy's tone was reasonable but confident. Since that morning they had avoided discussing Fauve's refusal to go to the funeral and Maggy had had time in which to consider the situation.

"It has nothing to do with personal problems, Magali," Fauve murmured.

"Darling, I don't understand you. There's going to be a big funeral in Félice in three days . . . we know that from the news conference that Nadine gave. You can't *not* be there. I'll go with you if you like. It will attract even more attention, but that's not important."

"No, Magali. That's not necessary. Thank you—but I'm still not going."

"Look, Fauve, every day thousands of people go to funerals and nobody asks them how they felt in their heart of hearts about the person who died—it's enough that they make an appearance. It may only be a formality but it's a deeply significant one, a gesture of respect if nothing else. Particularly in the case of a father."

"I can't make that gesture," Fauve said in a voice so low that Maggy could barely hear her. She moved closer and put her arm around her granddaughter.

"Surely you can find enough in his work to respect him—no matter what went wrong between you. The work remains, Fauve. Don't forget that. You really *must* do this . . . it's a responsibility that you have as his daughter."

"No. Let's not talk about it anymore," Fauve said, standing up.

"I simply don't understand," Maggy cried in distress and bewilderment. Fauve was never unreachable by reason.

"I swore I'd never tell you—about what he did, about why I never could bear to see him again . . . but I guess I must now—or you'll just never understand." Fauve knelt by the sofa on which Maggy sat and looked up into her face with a look compounded of a mixture of regret and misery and reluctance and some other emotion that Maggy couldn't identify, some emotion that made her draw back in fear.

"The work you talk about, the work I should respect, Magali, he sacrificed many people to that work."

"*Sacrificed?*"

"During the war he chose to paint while the rest of the world was fighting. Others did that . . . he wasn't alone. He collaborated with the Germans . . . he wasn't alone in that either. When a group of Resistance fighters—*Maquis*—stole the sheets he painted on, he denounced them to a friend, a German officer. They were all murdered—all those boys—but he got his sheets back so his work wasn't *interrupted*. But that wasn't the worst, Magali, not even that. Throughout the war whenever refugees tried to spend the night at *La Tourrello* he refused to admit them—people on the run for their lives—mostly Jews. They were friends from Paris, Magali, probably many of them were friends of yours. He even turned away Adrien Avigdor. He could have saved some of those people but they might have *disturbed* his work. Jews—no one can say how many—went to concentration camps because of his work. *And they died there.* Nothing, no human decency was allowed to come in the way of his work."

"How . . . who . . . ?" Maggy gasped.

481

"Kate told me, but he admitted it."

"*He admitted it?*"

"Yes. To me. That was the day I left. I never wanted you to know, Magali."

"My God . . . my God . . . why were you so afraid to say anything? . . . you were only a child . . . you should have told me," Maggy said, brokenly.

"I was too ashamed. Later, there was no reason to say anything, it was all over. He knew that he'd never see me again."

"*Ashamed?*"

"Ashamed that he was my father, a man who could do such things. Ashamed *for* him, most of all, ashamed to know what he was worth as a man. That's why I can't make a gesture of respect, Magali, not to him, not to his work. What work can be more important than human lives?"

Nadine Mistral Dalmas did not feel quite the degree of gratification she believed should be hers. As always, she told herself, trying to put things into perspective, no human event was without some flaw. The funeral had been almost all that she had intended it should be. The minister of the Beaux-Arts had arrived from Paris with an entourage, and the windswept old cemetery, at the very top of Félice, had made a most photogenic background for the long procession of people who had followed the coffin after the high requiem mass.

All the adult villagers of Félice had been there of course, as they would be in the case of any death in the community, but the crowd had been swelled by a crowd of art lovers from all over Provence who wanted to be able to say that they had seen Mistral buried. A fine turn-out, she thought, in spite of the fact that aside from Phillipe and a few rather unimportant friends of his, no one from Paris had been able to come down. Of course everybody she would have cared to see was still away on vacation. Quite naturally it had been impossible for them to fly from wherever they were to such an inconvenient place. If only the old man had died in October, in Paris, it would have been quite different, Nadine thought. Still it *had* been a perfect ceremony. Even in this provincial village the Catholic church could be trusted for its sense of style. Quite unerring. There was nothing she would have changed about the taste in which everything had been executed.

She felt a bit bereft now that the press had departed so unceremoniously, withdrawing their attention as soon as the coffin had been lowered into the grave. Still, it gave her a chance to relax for the first time since the death.

It was this business of the tax man that really irked her, Nadine thought. It was unquestionably the major flaw. How *dared* that little functionary forbid her to open the studio? Did he expect her to *steal* her own property, she had asked him as he sealed the front and back doors? He had grunted in a way that was too noncommittal to be actually impertinent—just routine in a case like this, he'd said, only until the gentlemen from Paris arrived, merely a formality. But when she had complained to Étienne Delage, Mistral's dealer—her dealer now, she reminded herself—he had told her that there was nothing she could do. The state must establish its share of the estate before anything could be moved, much less sold. It was infuriating to have to wait one more minute after she had waited for so long, maddening to have to admit the claims of the government, but she had no choice.

"And now," Nadine asked Marte, who had appeared at the door of the salon, "what is it?"

"*Maître* Banette, a notary from Apt, has just arrived. He asked to see you."

"I've never heard of the man. Tell him I'm sleeping, get rid of him."

"I tried to, *ma petite*, but he insisted. He says that it's important."

"Oh, all right." Nadine sighed. Everyone knew there was no way to avoid a notary. She had already dealt with death and taxes, how could a notary not follow?

The man who entered, plump and red-faced, dressed in a formal dark blue, had the pretension to give himself an air of importance, Nadine noticed in a surge of temper.

"You pick a bad moment to intrude, Monsieur."

"May I offer my deepest sympathies, Madame Dalmas? But of course you will appreciate that I had to come as soon as I could."

"I don't know why—*Maître* Banette, is it? Why are you here?"

"Madame," he said with reproach, "only my professional obligations could bring me to disturb you in your grief. But this matter of Monsieur Mistral's will must, of course, be brought to your attention. It is on file at the Fichier Centrale des Dernières Volontés in

Aix, as is proper, but I brought you my copy. I realized you would wish it."

"His will?" Nadine sat up with a jerk. "He made a will! I never knew." In alarm she asked herself if the old man could have possibly left some money to charity. No, that would not be like him. Most certainly not.

"He came to consult me three years ago, Madame," *Maître* Banette continued. "There was the question of the Law of the Third of January 1972 . . ."

"What law? 1972? I don't remember anything about a law then that affected property. My own lawyer in Paris would have informed me."

"Ah, no, Madame. It has nothing to do with property as such." *Maître* Banette bristled. "In 1972 the Parliament of France made it possible for the first time to legally recognize the children of adulterous unions. Monsieur Mistral made out an act of recognition of Mademoiselle Fauve Lunel."

Nadine sat speechless. *Maître* Banette continued. "Then there is his will, a very strange document. I found him a most difficult person to advise, Madame. At first he wanted to leave his entire estate to Mademoiselle Fauve Lunel. I explained to him that it was impossible under the laws of France. The most that he could do was to divide the estate between his two children . . ."

"Divide!"

"Madame, rest assured, it was not possible to divide in half, no, Article 760 of the law of *Les Successions* makes that plain. Mademoiselle Fauve Lunel is only entitled to one-half of what she would inherit if she had been legitimate, that is to say twenty-five percent of the estate, rather than fifty percent. You, Madame, retain seventy-five percent of what remains after taxes." He paused and waited for Nadine to say something but when she did not, he continued, warming to his task. "The will, Madame, is written in a way of which I do not approve. I informed Monsieur Mistral of my opinion but I regret to say that he did not choose to take my advice."

"Fauve," Nadine said in a venomous voice. "Always Fauve."

"Precisely, Madame. There seems to have been a . . . a leaning toward this particular child."

"What did he say?" Nadine demanded. "Here, give me those papers."

"Madame!" He held the papers protectively close to his portly chest. "It is only because Mademoiselle Fauve Lunel is not in Fé-lice—I made inquiries—that I came to you without waiting for her presence. She will have to be notified, sent for, but meanwhile I thought it proper to inform you of the contents of the will since I have no way to know where to find her."

"Read the thing, damn it," Nadine spat out.

"Madame, that is precisely what I intend to do," he said reprovingly, clearing his throat.

" 'I, Julien Mistral, wish to leave all my work to my most dearly loved and cherished daughter, Fauve Lunel. However, since the law prevents me from doing this, I wish her to have the series, *La Rouquinne*, that I bought back from my wife, Katherine Browning Mistral, the deed of sale to which is attached to this document. I wish my daughter Fauve to have all the paintings I made of her and of her mother, Théodora Lunel, who was the only woman I ever loved. In particular, I leave to Fauve the *Cavaillon* series, which she inspired me to paint. Because of Fauve, I learned at last, but to my eternal regret, too late, the most important lessons of my life. I hope that one day she will understand that I listened to her and changed. If my beloved daughter Fauve wishes, I would like her to have the domain of *La Tourrello* and all the land that belongs to it. If she does not want to accept the domain, I direct that it be sold and the proceeds added to my estate.'

" 'Under no circumstances do I wish *La Tourrello* and the studio in which I have worked to become the property of Madame Nadine Dalmas. To my certain knowledge she has never appreciated or understood either the beauty of any land or the nature of any art. The rest of my estate, up to an appraised value of twenty-five percent, I also leave to my daughter Fauve. I would be honored if she would call herself Fauve Mistral but I will understand if she does not choose to do so.'

" 'Whatever is left must, according to law, go to Madame Nadine Dalmas who will, I feel assured, sell it as quickly as she can to buy herself a continuation of the shallow, unworthy, valueless, and utterly vain life she has always chosen to lead.'

"That's all there is, Madame."

"That bastard! That slut, filth, rotten bitch! No! Never! She'll not have a thing, not one franc's worth, not while I live! He must have been totally insane! I'll contest the will, it won't go through!" Nadine's face, a Japanese mask of evil, spewed forth a voice that made the notary rise abruptly and back away, disgust frank on his face. He made an effort to pull his dignity around him.

"I must tell you, Madame," he managed to quaver, "there can be no question of insanity. If I had doubted Monsieur Mistral's sanity I would never have drawn this will. It is perfectly valid."

"Get out! What the hell do you know? I'll call my lawyer in Paris. You pompous little ass, you provincial, stupid fool—of course this crazy will can be contested. *Out!*" Nadine advanced on the notary so viciously that the man picked up his hat and fled the room without another word, taking the will with him.

No question but it was the best story they'd had in a long time, newspapermen agreed as they learned the details. "*Inconduite notoire de la mère*," Code Civile, Act 339—they hadn't heard of that one in a long time. "Notorious misconduct" on the part of Teddy Lunel, still the greatest cover girl who'd ever lived—not easy grounds to prove, the experts among them said, but without doubt the only way to attack that extraordinary will Julien Mistral had made, the text of which had been sought out in the files in Aix as soon as the news of the suit broke, a text that had given them one hell of a grand story too. All in all quite a windfall for an item that they had thought had ended in a graveyard high on the north side of the Lubéron. It should run for weeks, said one junior reporter in excitement. Months, you young ignoramus, months, corrected his senior, rubbing his hands together in pleasure.

"It doesn't matter if Nadine Dalmas can't prove anything," Darcy said. "She'll still have her revenge, she'll still drag Teddy's name through the mud."

"She's free to dig up anything about my mother that she can find, even if it doesn't apply, isn't she?" Fauve asked violently.

"I'm afraid so. That's got to be just what she intends to do. Why else would she have taken a step that made the words of the will public? If she hadn't sued to break the will no one would ever have known what contempt Mistral had for her."

Fauve was prowling about Maggy's sitting room, her hands balled into fists. Every muscle in her body was so tightly clenched that she was bent, stoop-shouldered, as she shuttled back and forth, unable to stop and sit still for even a minute. She was caught up in the grip of a rage such as she had never known could exist. It was like a rogue wave that had suddenly appeared out of the calm sea, towering over a small boat, lifting it fifty feet into the air. Nothing she had experienced in all of her life now seemed to matter compared to Nadine's attack on her mother's memory. She would kill Nadine right here, right now, if it were possible, Fauve realized, and felt no shock.

"I'm going to Avignon tomorrow. I'm going to prevent this from happening. My mother's not going to be called a whore! I don't give a damn about the pictures but Nadine *cannot do this*—I will not allow it."

"Fauve . . ." said Maggy, and stopped. She began again. "All of this happened before you were born . . ."

"I'm going to pack," Fauve said, ignoring her.

"Isn't there anybody you can call?" Maggy pleaded. "Somebody who could help from all those summers you spent in France? Can't you think of a single person?"

"Yes," said Fauve slowly, stopping on her way to the door, "yes, there is somebody. How could I have forgotten?"

Eric Avigdor was waiting at the airport in Marseilles. He was constrained as he expressed his sympathy to Fauve, remembering the manner in which they had parted six months before.

"Papa was delighted that you called him," he said as they sped up toward Avignon on the Autoroute du Sud.

"He must have been astonished—I just asked overseas information for his number and we were connected within minutes. I'm afraid it was almost midnight. I hadn't thought about the time difference."

"He never goes to bed early."

"That's what he said but I thought he was only being polite."

"Papa? He gave up being polite when he retired."

"Has he found a lawyer for me?" Fauve asked anxiously.

"The best man in Avignon. He's waiting for you at my parents' house. His name is *Maître* Jean Perrin. He fought with Papa in the Resistance."

"It's so kind of your father."

"He's very fond of you." Eric smiled at her for the first time, and Fauve smiled a little. Just thinking of Adrien Avigdor made her feel better.

They lapsed into silence again but it was less formal than the stiff words they had exchanged during the wait for Fauve's suitcase. She had flown down to Marseilles directly after getting off the plane in Paris and she was exhausted and crumpled, but the afternoon light of Provence in early October, the sight of the eternally renewed olive trees and the sentinel, pointed cypresses worked their familiar miracle on her and a sheer animal pleasure in being back quickened in her blood.

For the first time since she was sixteen Fauve permitted herself to remember how much she loved this countryside. They turned off the Autoroute where it crossed over the main east-west road, and instead of going east, which would have brought them to Félice, they turned west and within a half-hour they arrived at the Avigdors' house on the rue de la Montée St. André in Villeneuve-les-Avignon.

Fauve was immediately disappointed and concerned at the sight of the lawyer. She had expected Jean Perrin to be the age of Adrien Avigdor but how could this man be more than thirty-eight or nine? He was slender, short, almost boyish in his looks. However, at second glance, he had gray eyes that made her stand up very straight, for Jean Perrin was one of the breed of men who take in everything with one rapid, comprehensive, commanding glance.

Adrien Avigdor, unchanged, was wearing a sweater and an open-necked shirt but Maître Perrin was dressed in a double-breasted suit with the rosette of the Legion of Honor in his buttonhole. His elegant, citified attire gave him, Fauve thought uneasily, something of the look of an urchin dressed in his best.

Beth Avigdor hugged Fauve as warmly as if she were a favorite niece.

"You must be so tired, my poor Fauve. The guest room is waiting for you. Would you like to lie down for an hour before we dine?"

"No, thank you, Madame Avigdor. I'd prefer to talk to Maître Perrin right away."

Fauve and the lawyer went to sit on the wide balcony of the house, high above the city, with the Rhône in the near distance and the silhouettes of the palaces of Avignon beyond, steeples and towers like an immense sailing ship riding the turbulent river.

"Eric told me that you were in the Resistance with Monsieur Avigdor?" Fauve probed, still troubled by his youth.

"Well, you see I hated school. It was more fun to run away to the mountains of Aix and play at games of good-guys-bad-guys. I was thirteen when the war ended. Alas, there was still time to make me go back in school, and so as you can tell, I became, relatively speaking, a respectable citizen."

"How old were you when you ran away from school?"

"Ten." He shrugged with a grin. "But as tall as I am now." As he smiled, Fauve caught a glimpse of the reckless, preteenaged patriot he had been and she felt all lack of confidence drop away from her.

"*Maître* Perrin, can you help me?"

"It is all I have been thinking about since Adrien called me yesterday night. In fact, Mademoiselle, I have spent the day working on it, a more interesting day than those I usually spend in my chambers, I must tell you."

"You've been at work already? But we haven't even talked."

"The question evidently reduces itself to the question of character witnesses, does it not? Therefore I looked for them. And I have found one, I am pleased to tell you."

"One? *One character witness?*" Fauve cried protestingly. "What good can that do against a charge of 'notorious misconduct'? My mother was twenty-four when she met my father . . . obviously she had lived, she wasn't a nun—and now she's in the hands of my half-sister who's out to ruin her . . . oh, my mother is so *vulnerable*."

Fauve's confidence in Jean Perrin vanished as quickly as it had come. How could this man, who now again seemed naïve and inexperienced, begin to guess what could be discovered and distorted about Teddy Lunel who had captured the hearts of so many men who were alive today? "A number of lovers," Melvin had told her, and she'd known that he was being tactful.

How many of them would boast? How many of them would be able to resist talking about their affairs with the most beautiful girl in the world?

"Mademoiselle, what does your mother's age have to do with this charge?"

"Everything, I should imagine," she said in distraction. He just didn't understand.

"You have not talked to a French lawyer, not even to a notary?"

"My grandmother spoke to the French counsel in New York and I got on the plane the next morning."

"Ah, a diplomat. A pity. Yet how could he have been expected to know, after all? You see, Mademoiselle, the law of France is most explicit and firm on this question, it does not permit of any doubt, it does not allow malicious charges to be brought idly. The charge of misconduct would only apply to the period during which your parents actually knew each other, during which your paternity might be questioned. From what I have learned, they were never apart from the day they met until the day she died. This fact I intend to see established beyond a doubt."

He looked away from Fauve's face. It was indecent to watch such relief. When Jean Perrin heard her begin to sob he got up quietly and went back into the house.

"What's wrong?" asked Beth Avigdor. "Shall I go out to her?"

"No, I'd leave her alone for a while," Jean Perrin advised.

Eric ignored him and rushed out to the balcony. Fauve was huddled in a deck chair weeping uncontrollably, shaking in a way that frightened him. He scooped her up and held her tightly in his arms, letting her cry until his chest was running with her tears. He comforted her with soft noises, rocking her like a baby until, finally, she lifted her wet, swollen, flushed face and gasped, "Handkerchief." He fished in his pocket and found nothing. "Wipe your nose on my sleeve," he said.

"Oh, I can't," Fauve wailed. "Not on your sleeve."

"Then I'll do it for you." He laughed, as he unbuttoned a cuff with one hand. "Now, *blow!*"

Half an hour later, Fauve, with her face washed and her hair brushed, sat in the salon with the three Avigdors as *Maître* Perrin recounted the details of his day with such well-contained pride that only Adrien Avigdor knew how he felt. Jean's eyes had shone like that, Avigdor thought, when he had come back from one of his forays during the Resistance. He looked as shyly pleased as on the night on which he'd blown up that freight train that was carrying arms to the Battle of the Bulge.

"I started by asking myself what it is that two people, who have, so to speak, vanished from their customary worlds, would still do that ordinary people do. That is to say, people who are not living for love alone," Jean Perrin began. "And to that there is only one answer, is there not?" He paused but none of them ventured a guess. "They eat."

"They drink wine," Adrien Avigdor corrected him.

"Both, *mon vieux*, both. And where do they eat? In restaurants, at least from time to time, for two people, no matter how much in love, will never be content with home cooking for an entire year. And where in Avignon would the greatest painter in France eat?" Again he paused, and this time Fauve answered, shouting.

"Hiely!"

"How did you know, Mademoiselle?"

"My father used to take me there as a special treat," she exclaimed, and then stopped, astonished. She flushed deeply. She hadn't said the words "my father" in so many years that she couldn't believe how naturally they had jumped out of her mouth.

"Of course, at Hiely, the only two-star restaurant in Avignon. It was not difficult to guess. So I went there this morning and spoke to Monsieur Hiely. He was learning his *métier* in his father's kitchen in 1953 but he had often crept to the door and peeked out to admire your mother. He remembered her well. I asked to see their *Livre d'Or* because I knew that they would have asked Julien Mistral to sign it. And there, on one of the pages, I found his signature. More than a signature, a charming sketch of Papa Hiely. And, at the bottom, your mother had signed it as well."

"But . . . but . . . that doesn't prove anything," Fauve faltered.

"Indeed no. However, the family Hiely sends Christmas cards to their good clients, and they have a record of their addresses. With a little searching through their files, I was able to find out where your parents lived while they were in Avignon, and there I went, without, as Adrien would be amazed to note, stopping first for lunch. The house is still standing and the same concierge who was there then is there now. I imagine that Madame Bette will still be there in the year 2000. In any case, she was most helpful . . ."

"The concierge?" Fauve interrupted.

"No, Mademoiselle, do not look so dubious, it is not the concierge who is your character witness, although she could well serve if we needed more than one. Madame Bette told me that your parents had become friendly with a doctor who still lives on the ground floor of the house. Not more than two hours ago I managed to find this doctor at home. He told me that he and his wife knew your parents from the day they moved in—indeed they helped move some of the furniture your father had bought. The two couples used to have drinks together from time to time and go out to dinner as well, to Hiely, to the Prieuré, to places in the country.

They loved your mother very much, very much indeed. They never saw your father again, after your mother's death, but they have always understood why he disappeared from their lives. They spoke of your parents' total devotion to each other. The doctor, Professor Daniel . . ."

"Dr. Daniel!" exclaimed Beth Avigdor. "But I know him!"

"Naturally, Beth. He is one of the most distinguished men in all Avignon, a professor at the University of Aix, Mademoiselle Lunel," Jean Perrin explained, hurrying on. "Professor Daniel felt the most lively indignation at this odious and disgusting charge that has been made . . . he became quite outraged—indeed, one would have to say that he took it personally. Of course both he and his wife are ready to testify that your mother never had anything to do with any man other than your father during all the time she lived in Avignon. The attack on the will will be stopped before it starts. There can be no question of any further trouble from the quarter of Madame Dalmas." Jean Perrin gave his shy, rapscallion's grin of triumph.

"*Personally?*" Fauve asked. "Why did the doctor take it so personally? Was it just because of being so friendly with my parents?"

"It was he, Mademoiselle, who delivered you into the world."

33

Madame Dalmas, what a pleasure to see you." Madame Violette, the senior *vendeuse* at the salon of Yves Saint Laurent was too highly trained to betray her astonishment as Nadine strolled in, but there was a perceptible rustle of startled interest from the group of lesser *vendeuses* who stood waiting to lead clients to their seats before the collection. As Madame Violette escorted Nadine to the most advantageously placed chair in the room she asked, "Is there anything in particular that might interest you, Madame?"

"A new wardrobe, entirely new," Nadine said with an indifferent air. "I've lived in Albin for so long that it has become utterly boring, too predictable."

"Ah, but Madame is superbly turned out. However, I must agree that a change is always amusing. Monsieur Saint Laurent will be sorry to learn that you came while he was out of town."

Nadine picked up the traditional stub of a gold pencil and the little white pad on which she would write the numbers of the clothes that interested her enough to try on. It was disorienting to sit, like any ordinary client waiting to see a new collection. And wildly exciting as well. There would be none of the overfamiliarity that existed when she had watched Jean François's designs evolve over a period of months, so that each time she put on a new garment she felt that she had worn it for years.

Saint Laurent was the best designer in the world, but it would have been unthinkable for her to admit it to herself before yesterday. Today she was free, finally free of the tyranny of that overrated, whimpering infant, Jean François Albin, with his sulks and his tantrums. Today she was in a position in which she could not imagine any other woman in the world being in: she had all the money she could conceivably spend, and a great deal more, and in her rows of closets there was not one dress, not one blouse, not even one handbag, that she intended to keep a day longer than necessary. Even a new bride of the richest man in the world, she mused, must have something in her old wardrobe that she didn't want to part with, something she intended to wear again. But since her interview—if that was what you could call it—with Jean François yesterday, Nadine intended to jettison the lot. It had not been anything that he had said, indeed, very few words had passed between them. Nadine had simply walked into his office and told him that from now on he would have to do without her.

"Ah, I see," he had replied, so expressionless that he must have been too stunned to begin his habitual complaining.

"You do understand, Jean François, that now . . ." She had lifted her shoulders in a gesture that said to perfection what words could not: now I have no more time to waste with your tiny, petulant needs, now you are going to have to struggle along without me, now you will find your silly little life falling apart because I cannot be bothered with you any longer.

"I do understand, Nadine. I shall have to make the best of it. Forgive me, Nadine, but Princess Grace is in the fitting room and I promised to go to her. Will I see you at her dinner tonight? No? Of course, you must still be in mourning. Well then, *à bientôt?*" He had kissed her on the cheek in the dry way he kissed everyone, and had rushed off busily, humming, shouting for his favorite fitter to attend him, instructing a secretary to send coffee down to the Princess's fitting room, pausing only once, to pet the Afghans that lay at the entrance to his workroom. "Yes, my beauties, yes, you are the most beautiful creatures God ever made, yes, my babies, yes," he had crooned to the dogs, and disappeared down the corridor.

A good act, thought Nadine, and one that might have fooled anybody. She knew, of course, that she had dealt him a severe blow, one which might well send him into one of his nervous depressions.

Nevertheless there had been something—something she hadn't missed—that had made her decide to come to Saint Laurent today.

494

If she hadn't known Albin so well, she would have had to say that it was a look of . . . amusement? Was it possible? Certainly not, she thought, as she stared with only half-hidden contempt at the women surrounding her. This was not the right time of year to order new clothes; these were women from the provinces or foreigners who were thrilled to find themselves here. She didn't like finding herself watching the collection with them, but she chose not to wear Albin's clothes any longer. What could Jean François possibly have been amused *about*?

The first manikins passed in a quick-stepping flurry of suits for early day, designed for fall and winter, clothes which had first been shown earlier in the summer. By now, Nadine thought, all her friends who dressed at Saint Laurent had already received their new autumn suits, and were wearing them.

If she asked Madame Violette, she was certain that the time required to make her clothes could be reduced to a minimum. She would have to be treated as if she were a tourist with only two weeks to spend on fittings, she thought grimly. Never mind, she would see next spring's collection at the press opening, decorating the front row of chairs with Saint Laurent's other favored customers, as much a part of the ritual as the clothes themselves and, in certain ways, more significant.

She scribbled numbers on her pad while she tried not to reflect on the conversation she had had this morning with her lawyer. She had gone back to him in one last effort to persuade him to make a further investigation of the life of that whore, Fauve's mother. When he had learned of the testimony of Dr. Daniel in Avignon, the lawyer had told Nadine that her case against her father's will was over, finished. She'd gone to other lawyers and they had all told her the same thing: one and only one "*action en reduction*" of a will may be brought. She must accept the will as final: nothing could now prevent Fauve from receiving 25 percent of the estate in precisely the way in which the will had been written. She would have to satisfy herself with 75 percent, they had told her, as if that would prevent her from knowing that she had been irrevocably cheated, *stolen from!*

How typical it was of her lawyer to insist on having the last word, even in failure, Nadine thought. He was criminally unprofessional, she'd told him, to which he had merely retorted that he had advised her against attacking the will in the first place. As she remembered his smugness Nadine's pencil broke in half with the pressure she put on it. Madame Violette, who had been standing at the back of the room, observing her clients, immediately brought her another.

Now a group of pant suits appeared on the runway, man-tailored with that special Saint Laurent exaggeration that Albin had never been able to achieve. Very much her style. Precisely what she liked best, thought Nadine, as she turned over her paper and began a fresh sheet.

The women on both sides of her were watching her write numbers with such obvious envy that she could have laughed in their faces. What must it be like to come here and know that you could only afford to buy a single ensemble? Unimaginable, a life in which you would look in your closet and find only one custom-made garment? It would be like having one meal a year and living on bread and water the rest of the time. Why did they even bother? Nadine wrote more numbers, quickly, greedily, knowledgeably. She could hardly wait to get into the dressing room and see herself in these clothes.

She blamed her lawyer for more than the ruinous testimony of that doctor in Avignon. Why had he not properly warned her that the text of her father's will would be made public? Why had he not told her that reporters would swarm to Aix, to read the copy that was filed there? Could that sickening, self-satisfied excuse for a man not have foreseen that the will would be translated into every foreign language, would become news in every foreign city? At least, that was what Phillipe had said. Perhaps Phillipe was wrong, perhaps it was only in Paris that it had appeared? She didn't intend to investigate.

Phillipe's opinions were nothing to her now, not even minor annoyances. She had kicked him out the same day that the will had been printed in Le Monde and Le Figaro. Told him to get out within the hour. It had been amazing, even admirable in its own way, the speed with which he packed, and with what little protest.

He must have seen it coming, Nadine concluded, must have braced himself for it. A man with his experience could not help but know that once she had her money she would get rid of him. He had probably been planning how to put a good face on it from the day Mistral died. Phillipe wasn't stupid about things like that, she had to admit. About everything else, yes, but not about other people's money. A man who could sponge for an entire lifetime had to have some shrewdness.

In any case, she told herself with relief, she need never be burdened with his bills again, neither his debts nor his opinions. The only opinions she valued were those of her friends. They would realize that Mistral had been senile—mad, sick, senile. The others, those nobodies who made up the rest of the world, would have forgotten within the hour even if they had bothered to read those headlines, that story. So Monsieur Phillipe Dalmas thought that she had poured a bucket of ordure over her own head, did he? Typical words of a bitter man on his way down and out. How could he explain that no one, not one single person, had even mentioned the will to her?

What an absurd idea to have . . . that no one had mentioned it because they had not wanted to embarrass her. Yesterday, when she had run into Hélène and Peggy outside of Hermès, neither one of them had said anything about the will. But they had not expressed the conventional condolences. They had acted as if nothing whatsoever had happened to her, since they had last seen her, before her father had died. They had seemed—well, a touch offhand perhaps.

Sometimes it was difficult for even the most well brought up people to speak of death. Wasn't that why they usually wrote notes of sympathy instead of phoning? Hélène and Peggy. Had there been something . . . amused . . . about their glances? If one of their fathers had written a will so self-evidently insane, she might well have had the chic, the tact, to make a joke of it, but she would have made the joke out loud, so that they knew that she understood how ridiculous, how meaningless it was, how little it reflected reality. Nadine took out a tiny handkerchief and touched her forehead, under her bangs. It was much too hot in Saint Laurent.

Ah, the short dinner dresses. She had always particularly admired the way he did them, his flamenco bravura. She had always resented having to wear Albin's dinner dresses with their classically muted sex appeal. He overdid subtlety, Albin, as he overdid everything else.

As Nadine inspected the dresses, her trained eyes gloating over each detail, she wondered idly what the *Cavaillon* series could be. It was a joke, disinheriting her from ownership of a house in which she wouldn't dream of living, and a group of portraits of three generations of sluts, as if they could possibly be more important than the vast body of his work that would come to her. Cavaillon? A market town, a place of no interest whatsoever.

Her curiosity didn't extend to the point that she was willing to be there when the tax authorities opened the studio tomorrow. Étienne Delage, her dealer, would represent her. He would make enough in commissions on her, God knows, to go and stay put for as long as was necessary, keeping a close eye on the tax men while they made their infernal inventory.

As the first manikin came out in an evening dress she simply had to have, Nadine ran out of paper on which to write its number. She had completely filled her tiny pad, jotting down all the wonderful clothes she was itching to order. She raised her head to signal Madame Violette for another pad and caught her, whispering behind her hand to two other *vendeuses*. All three of them were staring straight at Nadine. They averted their eyes the instant she spied them, but, on each of their faces she caught the same look of amusement that she had glimpsed on Jean François's face, on Peggy's face, on Hélène's face. They were laughing at her. Sneering? No, *laughing*.

Nadine got up, walking down the row without regard for the legs of the women she passed. She walked faster and yet faster as she approached the exit to the showroom.

"Madame Dalmas? Is there something wrong? May I assist you?" whispered Madame Violette, catching up with her just as she reached the door.

"It's stifling here. You can't expect anyone to sit for hours without air conditioning on such a day."

"Ah, Madame Dalmas, you are absolutely right. I am desolate. Monsieur Saint Laurent will be desolate. If you will permit me, Madame, let me take your pad. When you return I promise you the air conditioning will be on and all the numbers you've picked out will be assembled in our largest fitting room."

"I saw nothing I wanted."

"Nothing?" Madame Violette echoed, disbelieving.

"Not even a blouse. A disappointing collection. Albin has spoiled me for anyone else."

Fauve Lunel could be, if such a thing were possible, almost as stubborn as her father had been, Adrien Avigdor told himself, as he sat in discussion with her in the library of his house.

"I still intend to go straight back to New York," Fauve repeated, gently because she had deep fondness for Adrien Avigdor, but with a resolution whose wisdom she refused to question.

"Of course you do, but not now, not until the studio has been opened, not until you have seen the pictures that your father left you."

"Can't you just accept the fact that I don't want to have anything to do with them?" she pleaded again. "That I *refuse?* I've asked *Maître* Perrin to handle everything for me and he accepted."

"I have complete faith in Jean but there are some things you can't ask—can't expect—somebody else to do for you."

"I'm needed back in New York," Fauve said, trying another argument. "You don't fully understand, dearest Monsieur Avigdor. Imagine hundreds of beautiful girls and three thousand prospective clients, all craving their services. How can I abandon them?"

"These beautiful girls, you're selling them?"

"I think you know what I do." She laughed at his grave attempt to tease.

"I also know that there are people who can manage the agency while you're here. My old friend Maggy, I presume, has not grown idle with the passage of time? I have every faith that she will not let even one of those girls wither on the vine."

Fauve hesitated while she studied his face. He certainly didn't look immovable, impossible and intractable. He looked as placid and relaxed as a man milking a cow, almost asleep in the sun, but she still hadn't been able to convince him that she was right. Now that the question of Nadine's suit had been settled, now that her mother's memory was safe, *why* was Adrien Avigdor so intent on using the full force of his authority to make her stay longer? She felt too much gratitude for his help to simply ignore his determination, but on the other hand he had not been swayed by anything she said.

"There's nothing left to decide," Fauve replied, summoning her resolve. "What would I want with *La Tourrello?* I only have a few weeks' vacation every year and I wouldn't always want to spend them there, would I? Well, what happens when a house is left unoccupied? What about fire, what about pipes that burst, what about the mistral that blows a hole in the tiles and lets in the rain? I'd have to rent it or hire a caretaker who'd live there full-time. It's just too complicated. I'm going to sell it, of course."

"Your father's will said clearly that you should do as you wished."

"Well then?" Fauve asked.

"Nevertheless, I believe that you must, at least, *see* your legacy, the *Cavaillon* series. It's your duty."

"Monsieur Avigdor," Fauve said with finality, "we could go on like this for days. But that's not the point. I know . . . I know how my father behaved during the war."

"Ah." He managed not to show the alarming leap of surprise and shock that he felt.

"I also know that you know, that you are aware of what he did, not just to you, but to many others—no, don't say anything! Now, just tell me if you still think I have a 'duty,' as you put it, to see my legacy."

"I do," he answered firmly.

"But why—how can you?"

"Because whatever else he was or did, you cannot deny that Julien Mistral loved your mother and that she loved him. And he loved you most dearly. That was made very plain in his will. The *Cavaillon* series, whatever it may be, was painted for you, Fauve, painted *because* of you. You cannot turn your back on it."

"Have *you* forgiven him then?"

"Yes, I hope I have."

"Why?" she asked again, leaning forward to try to understand.

"Why? In part, of course, because he was a genius. I know, genius is no excuse, but surely it is an explanation, a partial explanation. In the Book of Job, if I remember correctly, my father used to tell me that somewhere it says that 'Great men are not always wise.' Nor are they always kind or always brave, Fauve. But there is something more than that. I forgave him because he was a man and I too am a man—*merely a man*—not his judge." As he spoke this last word, Eric walked into the library and stood, listening to them. Fauve looked at Eric as she answered his father.

"Perhaps you are right, but still I want no part of the past."

"One visit, Fauve, that's all I ask," Avigdor insisted. "After that, do whatever you wish."

"I think," Eric said, "that the two of you could be said to have reached a Mexican standoff."

Adrien Avigdor looked with interest at the dark blush that mounted from Fauve's shoulders to her hairline as she nodded her reluctant assent. What made that rascal of a son of his think that he, Adrien Avigdor, needed to be told that he had reached a Mexican standoff, whatever bizarre thing that might be? He had merely won the negotiation, as he had always fully intended to, as he had always been certain he would. He was not in the habit of losing such matters.

Several days later, in the second week of October, the three appraisers who had been appointed by the Bureau of Estate Taxes were finally able to gather at *La Tourrello*. The government had waited until the top art experts in France were all available since the contents of Mistral's studio were too important a source of revenue to be evaluated by any but the most knowledgeable.

Fauve's anxiety mounted steadily as she drove toward Félice with Eric and his parents. She found it difficult to accept the fact that she had let herself be persuaded to come back even one last time to the house that contained the two rooms she had once loved most in the world: her father's studio and her *pigionnier* bedroom, the house she had been trying to forget since she was sixteen.

The horror she had felt, the scalding bitterness, the hopeless pity for those unknowns who had been denied shelter, the abiding shame, all the emotions she had been battered by as she left *La Tourrello* so many years ago came flooding back as the car continued past Mènerbes and drew closer to Félice. She felt chilled to the bone, apprehension and tension made her conscious of her spine as if each individual vertebra were a tooth that had been attacked by a sense of intense discomfort. Not pain but an almost unbearable *uneasiness*.

Fauve's senses were too vivid. The colors of the countryside seemed so bright that even her sunglasses gave her little relief, she was aware of the voices of Eric and his parents as if they had been exaggerated, distorted slightly, tuned up to a higher pitch than normal. And their gestures seemed to be fragmented, jerky, flickering. She struggled to touch reality but everything had the quality of a hallucination that grew steadily more unendurable as they mounted the narrow road through the forest of live oaks and she saw the ancient walls of *La Tourrello* rise beyond the avenue of whirling cypresses.

They parked outside on the meadow, covered with tangles of thistles and spiky grasses, that had been drying all summer long. Fauve slid reluctantly, slowly, out of the car. The odor of honeysuckle hit her like a blow. She had managed to forget so many details. She had managed to forget that the *mas* was covered in honeysuckle. She had managed to forget how she could never breathe in its sweetness deeply enough, how it never cloyed, never grew less tantalizingly fragrant, with a scent that contained a mystery she had never captured, a scent that was the very memory of happiness distilled.

"Look, cars are here already. The appraisers must be inside waiting," said Adrien Avigdor, to try to get Fauve to move forward. She stood rigidly, unwillingness plain in every tense line of her body, and something more. Something that he could only call fear. He felt deep and painful emotion himself. He had not stood on this spot since the summer of 1942 when he had been refused entrance by Marte Pollison and had looked back to see Julien Mistral letting him leave.

"Let's go," said Eric, taking Fauve's hand unceremoniously. He pulled her along, through the open doors, into the courtyard.

A group of five men stood smoking and chatting in the courtyard. One of them was Étienne Delage, Mistral's dealer who now represented Nadine Dalmas, three of them were the appraisers and one a supervisor from the Department of Taxes in Avignon. They all introduced themselves solemnly shaking hands with Fauve, Eric and his parents.

"There doesn't seem to be anyone to open the door," said one of the experts, a bearded Parisian, tall and elegant.

"I have the key," said the dealer. "I've been informed that the old servant has retired. The house is empty. All the keys were left with the notary of Apt, *Maître* Banette. He asked me to give them to Mademoiselle Lunel since he was unable to be here today. He also asked me to say that he is at her service should she need him on estate matters." He took a ring of keys and handed them to Fauve.

"If you please, Monsieur," she said, drawing back abruptly, "would you unlock the door?"

Étienne Delage nodded and led the way. Although he was less familiar with the house than Fauve, she hung behind the others, every step she took an unwilling one, as he directed the group through the dimly lit *mas*, across rooms where an occasional shutter still stood open and finally out the back toward the studio wing. Finally they all stood in front of the doors to the studio of Julien Mistral.

The tax inspector from Avignon removed the seals that had been placed on the doors only hours after Mistral's death had been announced.

"Mademoiselle?" he asked Fauve, indicating the door. She shook her head in negation and again it was Delage who unlocked the studio doors.

Now, with one gesture, everyone stood back and Fauve was impelled, by their politeness and sense of occasion, to go first. She squared her shoulders and took half a dozen rapid, determined steps into the shadowy studio before she came to a sudden halt. The shock she had received from the scent of the honeysuckle was nothing compared to the assault made on her senses by the well-beloved, deeply familiar aroma of this dominion, in which her father had painted for almost fifty years. She almost cried out as she collided with the most important hours of her past.

The studio was not dark although all the shutters had been closed. Part of the skylight was open and the work lights were still on, as Mistral had left them. Shafts of morning sun, swirling with a billion universes of dust motes, seemed like columns from which the pungency of oil paint was released into the air.

Fauve closed her eyes for an instant, assailed by memories and then, recovering herself, stood stiffly, looking at the floor. Finally she raised her eyes and faced the studio.

What was this? What was this leaping symphony of flying paint? What were these huge canvases breathing life, this feeling of creation so glad, so generous that it had wings stronger than an eagle's? From what place came the rhythm that charged through the studio with majestic thunder?

There was nothing in all that vast space but some enormous paintings, larger than Mistral had ever painted, each hung with an exactitude of placement that spoke of much thought. The only sign of his presence was a sturdy, movable stepladder in one corner, his worktable and the old easel on which was placed an empty, fresh canvas.

As Fauve looked at the walls she gasped, bewildered, dazzled, stunned by the complex imagery that swept dancing out at her. Her eyes darted to one canvas and found crowned lions rearing into the air, lambs cavorting, gazelles prancing and doves swooping about, all against a tangled brilliance of jewel-bright wild flowers and apple trees, the green of peridot and celadon. She looked further, at the

next canvas, her eyes captured by the majestic weight of piled
sheaves of wheat and barley, heaping plenitudes of pomegranate
and date, grape, olive and fig. Here, Mistral's lambent colors were
the deep, opulent greens and golds of full summer, grains waving as
splendidly as banners. The next canvas exploded with surging ripeness, the deepness, the intensity of the hues of the autumnal equi-
nox: amethyst, wine, pumpkin and ruby, vibrating with the
fulfillment of the harvest. Palm branches wreathed in willow and
myrtle were flung aloft as in a glorious procession that took place
beneath a full red moon and many stars.

Singing birds . . . the rose of Sharon . . . the cedars of Lebanon
. . . what did it mean?

Then, on the far wall she saw the largest painting of all and was
immediately claimed by its magnetism. All the brilliant profusion
of other images faded around her and she narrowed her vision,
approaching the gigantic canvas on which a seven-branched candelabra blazed with a crescendo of essential light, a monumental
menorah that radiated glory of thousands of years of faith against a
background of triumphant crimson. Fauve stood there speechless,
looking upward, her heart leaping, her mind empty of everything
but awe.

Out loud, from behind her, Eric said the words that Julien Mistral had painted in tall, bold letters underneath the base of the
menorah.

"La Lumière Qui Vit Toujours. La Synagogue de Cavaillon, 1974—
the light that lives forever . . ."

"He . . . he went to Cavaillon!" Fauve cried out in wonder and
joy.

"The Cavaillon series—that's what it means," Eric said slowly,
with reverence.

"But the other paintings? What . . . ?"

"There's an inscription on each one of them," Eric answered.
Throughout the studio the group of other visitors were spreading
out, forgetting themselves in the adventure of discovery, exclaiming
out loud, speaking as much to themselves as to each other, experi-
encing the uncharted seas of Mistral's genius.

Fauve didn't turn but continued to look searchingly at the great
candelabra that commemorated the sacred vessel that had stood in
the desert sanctuary and in the two Temples in Jerusalem. Finally
she turned and took Eric's hand. Together they walked back the

length of the studio and stopped in front of the first huge painting.

There two tall candles were set in polished candlesticks, a twisted loaf of bread and a silver goblet brimming with wine stood on a white tablecloth. Each of the simple, elemental forms passionately spoke of gratitude for the gifts of the Creator to man. A peace, a gaiety, a joyful solemnity poured forth from the painting and Fauve nodded her head in the beginnings of comprehension.

"*Shabbat*," said the bearded art expert from Paris, translating the inscription that was written not in French now but in the letters of the Hebrew alphabet. "The Sabbath." Fauve searched the strong, unfamiliar, evocative shapes of the letters and saw in them the brushwork that was distinctively Mistral's, vivid and fierce, yet contained within a discipline to which he had never bowed before.

She moved eagerly toward the next paintings and she realized that the three canvases, those on which gazelles were leaping and branches were growing, the first canvases to catch her eyes, had been hung so that they were clearly set apart from the others. She stepped back so that she could see them as a group.

Puzzled, yet raised to another peak of visual delight, she looked in excited confusion from one to another. What was the key to these passionate rhythms, the wealth of images?

At her right shoulder she heard Adrien Avigdor's voice, pausing between each word as he translated the meaning of the words of the Hebrew inscriptions, composed of letters that he had studied for a few years, a lifetime ago, letters that he discovered had never disappeared from his recollection.

"*Pesach*," he said in his resonant voice as he gazed at the first canvas.

"The Feast of Exodus," added the art expert from Paris. "The anniversary of the revelation at Sinai—he used the symbols of the Song of Songs."

"*Shavous*," Avigdor said, turning to the next canvas, and again the expert's explanation came. "The Summer Festival—the bringing of fruits and grains to the Temple."

"*Sukos*," Avigdor read from the third painting and paused. "The Autumn Feast," said the Parisian's voice. "The tabernacles made of boughs and reeds in which everyone slept for a week, seeing the sky above."

Fauve swayed and around her the immense shapes of the pictures seemed to reach higher and higher until they touched the roof of the studio, until they reached beyond it into a firmament filled with moonlight. The walls receded, the colors burned brighter and brighter, she heard the stars singing and the palm fronds laugh, she felt the wings of the wind as the images appeared to move, to lift off the canvases and to whirl around her in a towering, glowing, incandescent hymn of praise, a victorious hosanna of color.

Something deep in Fauve opened and finally understood; Julien Mistral had crossed the green fields of time and lived in old Jerusalem; his pagan brush had been transported and he had expanded his last and greatest forces on painting these celebrations of a people who had—who still—worshipped an invisible God.

He had respected the invisibility of their God. He had not tried the impossible; he had not attempted to paint the voice from the Burning Bush, but he had reached into the heart of their festivals and painted the spirit in which they commemorated their God, and painted it in a way that all the other peoples of the earth could understand, for all men lived by the ever-turned wheel of nature.

She closed her eyes and leaned on Eric's arm.

"Are you all right?" he asked anxiously.

"Let's go outside for a minute . . . I'll look at the other pictures later."

As they started toward the door Adrien Avigdor approached Fauve and put out his hand, a question on his face which was answered by one look at Fauve's transfigured eyes. He dropped his hand, satisfied, and let them continue. Fauve had passed Mistral's easel when she turned back, caught by the sight of a scrap of paper that was tacked into the wood. On it, in her father's familiar handwriting, was just one line. She paused. The bit of paper was worn, yellowed and smudged by a rainbow of fading colors, as if it had been much handled, yet it flew from the easel like a flag bearing a motto.

"Hear O Israel, the Lord our God, the Lord is One," she said, reading out loud. "That's all it says."

"Isn't that enough?"

34

It's so maddeningly inadequate trying to describe them on the phone like this—can't you fly over and see them for yourself, Magali?" Fauve pleaded.

"I will, but right now it's impossible. Things have never been crazier and I don't dare leave the agency to run itself with both of us away. The most important thing is that we know that your father was moved to make those paintings, we know that he wanted to create something that could be balanced against the past. I guess the only thing to call it is redemption . . . not a word I normally find myself using, my darling. I thank God that he had the time to do it."

"It's more than his having the time, Magali. You'll understand when you see them. He painted with the last drop of his blood. Monsieur Avigdor says that sometimes this type of overwhelming vision visits an artist in his old age, but only the greatest of them—Donatello, Rembrandt—something totally fresh that soars above anything they've ever achieved. Like everyone else Monsieur Avigdor had thought, because father hadn't produced any new work in eight years, that he'd lost it, that he was hiding out because he didn't want to admit that he couldn't paint anymore."

"Were they all as stunned as you?"

"Yes, although, except for the Avigdors, they didn't have the extra shock of knowing how father had felt before about anything to do with Jews. The experts were stunned—just knocked out—even though they deal with great art all the time. The person who touched me most was the man from the Department of Taxes. He doesn't have any background in painting but he wandered around in a kind of speechless rapture, purely enjoying himself—so carried away by the *Cavaillon* series that he completely forgot about all the other paintings in the storage room. I wanted to call you right away but luckily I remembered that it was still the middle of the night in New York, so I waited till I knew you'd be at the office."

"Oh, I'm here all right," said Magali. "After all, it's almost nine o'clock."

"The thing is, I just can't leave Provence right away, Magali. There's going to be incredible interest in the series and since it belongs to me I have to stick around. I'm not at all sure exactly how soon I'll be able to get away. I hate to leave you up in the air like this . . ."

"Don't worry about me for a second. Everything's under control."

"But your weekends," Fauve protested.

"Never mind about them. The garden has almost finished blooming for the year and until you come back we'll go up to the country only for Saturday and Sunday. Darcy will understand . . . when did Darcy ever not understand?"

"Oh, Magali, thank you, and thank Darcy. I'll call every few days or so. Give everyone a kiss for me, especially to Casey and Loulou and . . . I love you, Magali. I'm so very *glad*."

"I can hear it in your voice, darling. Take your time, make wise decisions, just don't rush into anything. I love you, Fauve."

Maggy hung up and sat back in her desk chair. Like Fauve she was in a shock of euphoria. The description of the *Cavaillon* series, although Fauve had considered it inadequate, had lasted for more than twenty minutes of excited, rapturous details. So that man had finally used his God-given talent to make a greater contribution to the world than beauty alone. Maggy discovered that as overwhelmingly happy as she felt for her granddaughter, she was also happy for Julien Mistral, the Julien Mistral she had loved and hated for so many years. They had accounts between them that could never be settled, no, not if he'd illustrated every last line of the Old Testament, but now, at least, she could think, "Rest in peace," and mean it. She sat thoughtfully for a long while. Then, startled out of her meditations by a glance at her desk clock, she buzzed Casey and Loulou to come into her office.

"I've just talked to Fauve, ladies. She sends you both very special kisses and says that she's going to have to stay over in France for a while. There are things she has to take care of."

"How is everything with her?" asked Casey, anxiously.

"Absolutely wonderful! Never better. Now! There are a few matters I've been planning to talk to Fauve about that can't wait till she gets back. Casey, I've been looking over the test shots of that girl you found at the Southwest Regional Modeling Competition. No way, Casey, no way." Maggy shook her elegant head in firm negation.

"Maggy, she was clearly the most gorgeous girl in the competition," Casey protested.

"You fell into a trap. You went and saw hundreds of girls and you picked out the best one. But did you remember to take some pictures of our own girls to compare her to?"

"Well, no, I forgot. But I spent three whole, long, long days judging those girls."

"That's the problem. After three days of seeing one girl after another you jumped at the best of the lot. It's incredibly easy to fool your eye, to compromise, to forget how supremely good a girl has to be. I've done it plenty of times myself. She *is* a very pretty girl, Casey, but not pretty enough for Lunel." Maggy shoved the series of test shots over to Casey who looked at them carefully and sighed in agreement.

"Point made," Casey said. "Ah well, she's engaged to a boy back home anyway. Maybe she'll be relieved. Certainly he will be."

"Loulou," Maggy said, "I've been listening in on the open interviews. I notice that our reception room never seems to empty out. Are you aware that Bobbie-Ann has developed a Pygmalion complex?"

"Oh, Lord, she's been in charge of the auditions for a couple of months and I've been too busy to pay much attention. What's up?"

"Loulou, there are a million ways to turn people down nicely. But Bobbie-Ann doesn't say 'sorry' and keep it short and sweet. This morning she spent seven minutes showing one girl how to use blusher before she turned her down and another eight minutes with a different applicant talking about changing her hairstyle—then she turned her down too. It's not fair to give anyone false hope, not even for a few minutes," Maggy snapped. "Talk to her, Loulou. If Bobbie-Ann doesn't shape up she can always run a beauty school. If an applicant has to experience rejection, it should come with a minimum of personal contact, *before* she starts to feel that she's made a new friend. It doesn't hurt as much that way, I promise."

"Yes, Ma'am! I'll pass the word. Listen, Maggy, Bambi Two is worrying me. She says she's homesick and she's eating like mad. I caught her at it yesterday."

"I'll talk to her. Maybe if you all just stopped calling her Bambi *Two* it might help for a start. Try it. Let's see, she's had three *Glamour* covers and *Vogue* is considering her. I suppose she knows that?"

"Yup."

"Well, of course she's homesick, naturally she's eating all the junk she can get her hands on . . . maybe she can gain enough weight to stay *off* the cover of *Vogue* if she gobbles fast enough. It's just your everyday, ordinary, reasonable and understandable insecurity surfacing. Who wouldn't be having a little identity crisis—she was overdue for it." Maggy beamed at the girls. She'd helped half a hundred Bambis over this particular hurdle.

"Anything else?" asked Casey warily.

"No, not right now anyway. Have I remembered to tell you that as far as I'm concerned both of you are absolutely indispensable? No? Well, consider yourselves officially notified. Oh, and will you send someone out to buy me a red carnation—just one, for my buttonhole?" She picked up the phone to call Darcy as they left her office.

"Hmmm," hummed Casey when they reached the corridor.

"What does that sound signify?" asked Loulou, still delightfully rosy from Maggy's unprecedented compliment.

"It feels kind of good to have Marie Antoinette on the rampage again."

"Didn't we just get our asses kicked?"

"Just enough," Casey grinned. "Just *comme il faut*, Loulou, if you follow my meaning."

Nadine Dalmas had decided to change hairdressers, to try Alexandre. As always, when one is nice to people, they tend to creep toward familiarity, forgetting that the line between those who are waited on and those who wait on them may be invisible but it is real, and must never be bridged.

When she had gone to have her roots touched up last week, Monsieur Christophe, whose job it was to do her color, had actually presumed to regale her with an account of how his grandfather had died without a will. He had had three sons, one of whom, it seemed to be her destiny to learn, had been Monsieur Christophe's father. The heirs had fought so stubbornly over the division of the family farm that the property had eventually been sold at auction. Nadine hadn't been able to simply get up and walk away from this sordid account since the man was actually in the act of applying the bleach, nor had she dared to indicate that she was outraged at being treated as a captive audience. When a colorist has his hands in your hair you take good care not to antagonize him, no matter who you are.

"So, you see, Madame Dalmas, he was wrong, my grandfather, to expect his sons to come to an amiable agreement. He should have made a will, but since he failed to, the property passed out of the family forever. A great pity, don't you think?" Her face perfectly calm and remote, Nadine had had to incline her head to show that she was listening. Why on earth was she being subjected to this family history? What gave Monsieur Christophe the right to inflict his personal experience on her? "Yes, Madame, even a bad will is better than no will at all," he had said before turning her over to be shampooed.

The astonishing impudence of the man, to speak to her in a *consoling* tone of voice. Was he her equal that he dared to permit himself this intimacy? To offer her *his* understanding, *his* allegiance? On what grounds did he believe that she needed comfort, fidelity? His effrontery took her breath away. Yet if she returned next week Monsieur Christophe might have more to say on this odious subject, which he had obviously seized upon to give himself airs of being on a level with her.

No, here at Alexandre's, which she had never patronized before, she would be treated in the way that was due her and, now that she was rich, she wouldn't have to be as generous with her tips as she had been, Nadine reflected as she sat on the circular, haremlike, oversized piece of furniture, covered with leopard skin, on which everyone but queens had to wait their turn.

It was horribly crowded, even granted that it was a Friday. One

511

of the advantages of her former salon was that everyone there was on her schedule, Tuesdays and Fridays for a wash and blow-dry, Mondays, Thursdays and Saturday mornings for a comb-out. It would take awhile to break in the staff of any new salon, Nadine reminded herself, determined to stick with Alexandre until she had worked out her maintenance routine to her satisfaction. She had no more worries about being late to the office, thank heaven. It was really astonishing how quickly Albin had been able to find one of the little Montesquiou girls to take over her job, thankless task that it was. She wouldn't stay with him long, that silly young creature. She'd be temporarily taken in by the chichi until she found out what a cesspool Albin's was.

Nadine waved away a pile of magazines that a young assistant in a smock presented to her. No, she did not want *Match* or *Jours de France* or *Marie Claire* or *Elle*. Thank you but no.

Indeed, she had already seen them. She had bought a pile of brightly colored weekly magazines at a kiosk yesterday and taken them quickly home to read in private, for each of them treated the *Cavaillon* series as its main story. What incomprehensible fit of madness had caused the old man to paint those monstrous things with Hebrew lettering on them? Nadine had asked herself in aversion and disgust. She couldn't endure looking at them—the inscriptions alone made her shut her eyes. How typical of the press it was to make such a fuss over them, such an inordinate fuss, as if Julien Mistral had been a new discovery, an overnight sensation, a revelation. She couldn't understand the amount of space, the covers and full-page photographs, that had been devoted to this mere handful of canvases. And, God knows, it wasn't sour grapes, she told herself. She wouldn't want them herself for anything in the world. "Immortal," one critic had actually said. "The final proof of his boundless genius," another. "A legacy for which the entire human race is richer" had announced a third. They were all equally ludicrous, each baying together like a pack of dogs, just as they always did, attempting to outdo each other, like the fashion writers after a successful collection. Their words could be about a new style as easily as about paint on canvas.

Yet, all it did, in the end, was to make her own pictures the more valuable. She couldn't really object if they wanted to rediscover Mistral, Nadine thought. Naturally they had all pounced on the *Cavaillon* series, when the old man had singled it out in his will, and naturally they had all insisted on treating Fauve as if she were the star of the whole sideshow. She didn't begrudge Fauve her cheap little moment in the limelight. It would dim quickly.

Nadine was so lost in her thoughts that she was surprised to find the coiffeur had presented her with a mirror so that she could inspect his work. She checked the back of her head carefully. She could see that it was perfectly acceptable but it wouldn't do to let him think that she was too easily pleased. "Perhaps you've made it a bit too tight at the side," she said, smoothing her hand under the shimmering hair that curved under her chin.

As he worked she looked around her. There must be a dozen women here she knew, Nadine realized as she exchanged nods and smiles around the big room. She had had no idea that so many of her friends came to Alexandre, that so many of his clients were the women she was accustomed to dining and lunching with. They all looked, in her opinion, overdone. Why had the Comtesse d'Ornano added that twist of false braids to her lovely black hair? And the Princesse Laure de Beauveau-Craon had chosen, for some strange reason, to wear sprigs of tiny purple orchids in her chignon. Quite odd. As for Baronne Guy, her long blond locks were imprisoned in a sort of gilded net. Madame Patiño, Princess Alexander of Yugoslavia, the young Baronne Olimpia de Rothschild—all of them with highly decorated hair. Didn't they know how fussy it looked, how unsuited to real life? If this was what Alexandre's stylists did to women whose taste was normally good, she had better be on her guard.

"If I might suggest, Madame," the coiffeur said, "perhaps we might try something a bit more formal?"

"Don't touch it," Nadine snapped. "It's fine."

"As you wish. I thought that for the ball tonight . . ."

"I'm in mourning," Nadine said quickly.

"My regrets, Madame." He was plainly relieved that he had not been tactless.

"I couldn't possibly go to a ball."

"Of course not, Madame. It is painful, is it not," he murmured. "Particularly painful to miss this ball, the first time that the Princesse Marie-Blanche has opened her château since her husband died. That's why we're so crowded this afternoon. They say it will be the greatest ball since the last one of the Baron de Rédé's."

"Yes, that was a beautiful evening," Nadine said mechanically.

513

Princesse Marie-Blanche? So her affair with Phillipe had continued even while the Prince lay dying, even after his death, *even now.* Otherwise, why would she not have invited as close a friend as Nadine to her ball? The only possible explanation was that Phillipe was, in some way, going to be the unofficial host. Strange, that she had not heard any gossip about Marie-Blanche and Phillipe, for Marie-Blanche *led* Parisian society. When Marie-Blanche said dance, they danced; when she said drive fifty miles out to the country for a ball, they drove the fifty miles and counted themselves among the blessed. What would Marie-Blanche *want* with Phillipe Dalmas, for God's sake?

As Nadine stared into her own sharply outlined eyes in the mirror she tallied up in her mind the number of unattached middle-aged men in Paris who were charming, good-looking, well-dressed and heterosexual, who danced well, played cards well, played polo well and were adored by every hostess. Besides Phillipe she knew of three—no four, counting Omar Sharif. And how many women were there who were rich—many of them far richer than she—unattached, and desperate for an escort, let alone such a man? *Dozens.* Dozens and dozens. Her heart shriveled, a foul and evil dust filled her mouth, and a pain she would not have believed existed, ignited in her abdomen, a pain that seemed to be a burning rat eating at her insides, a rat on fire running wild with feet of hot lead.

No, she had not heard any gossip about Phillipe and Marie-Blanche. She had not heard any gossip because she had no invitations . . . no invitations worth speaking of, only a few unquestionably third-rate invitations that she hadn't deigned to decline. Faced with the choice between Princesse Marie-Blanche and Nadine Dalmas, people would, of course, choose Princesse Marie-Blanche. She would make that choice herself. There was no contest.

As she tipped Monsieur Christophe, so much that he actually looked surprised, Nadine had only one thought. By chance she had worn a black suit today. She must wear only black from now on. She would find a small hairdresser in her neighborhood, where she wouldn't run into her friends. Acquaintances. She had no friends. She would wear black for her father and she would decide what to do with the rest of her life, a life in which she would, no doubt, often be described as Jean François Albin's ex-employee, as Phillipe Dalmas's ex-wife, for who was Nadine Dalmas? *Who cared?*

She walked down the street looking for a taxi to take her home.

An empty taxi passed as she stood, transfixed, staring at a headline in *France Soir* displayed on the wall of a kiosk. "*Fauve Lunel— Prendera-t-elle le nom de Mistral, son pere?*" Would Fauve take her father's name? Who gave a damn what she did, that tawdry bastard, that interloper, that cunning tramp? Why was she being treated as if she were Julien Mistral's *only* daughter? "I," Nadine wanted to scream out loud at everyone passing by, "*I am Mistral's daughter!*"

When she decided to stay on for a few weeks in Provence, Fauve had taken a room at Le Prieuré, and then, when it closed for the season in November, she had moved into the Hotel Europe in Avignon.

One morning near the end of November, she drove her rented Peugeot toward Félice, determined to make a decision about *La Tourrello* before the day was over. The house had been full of people since the *Cavaillon* series had been revealed. She had had to act as hostess to a great variety of guests; journalists, art historians and museum curators. But now the question of what to do with the *Cavaillon* series had been settled. Yesterday the last canvas had been carefully crated and loaded into the padded trucks that would take them to Amsterdam, where they would begin their slow progress from continent to continent, from major city to major city, to every last one of the museums that had asked for them, carrying their festive message of brotherhood throughout the world. If she had kept them in *La Tourrello* only a relatively few people would have ever seen them except in reproduction. Someday the transcendent canvases would come back to her, but for many years to come, the *Cavaillon* series would belong to mankind.

Now that the studio was empty, now that the storeroom had also been cleared out of all but the family portraits that Fauve intended to keep for herself, she would be able to make a reasonable and leisurely judgment about the house. Except for the future of the *Cavaillon* series she felt as if nothing she had decided on since she left New York in October had been based on firmly collected thought. She'd had to dash into things, she'd been pulled along by events, and by the end of every day she'd been so exhausted that she'd fallen into bed with nothing on her mind but the appointments she had the next morning. She'd hired a young widow, Lucette Albion, from Lacoste, to come in every day and keep the house clean, and make lunch and coffee for all the visitors. Today the last of them had gone home, and *La Tourrello* would be completely empty, since it was Sunday and Lucette had gone to a wedding in Bonnieux, in which her two small children were going to be bridal attendants.

A mistral had been blowing for the past few days and Fauve was bundled up in a warm plaid jacket over loden-green wool pants and a creamy, cable-stitched, Irish fisherman's sweater, but that morning the wind had left the Lubéron as capriciously as it had arrived. The too-bright sky had turned an ordinary soft blue again, and frilly curls of clouds were draped like ribbons here and there, the party decorations of heaven. The only sign of true winter was the bareness of the fields. The windbreak borders of cypresses were green and alert, and in the olive trees, the leaves of the trees were so much like a silver stream that Fauve almost expected to see fish swimming in them. As she drove along she could hear the sound of shotguns in the hills as the farmers went looking for game birds; children's shrill, excited laughter rang out as they played Sunday games, liberated from their perpetual homework, and at the entrance to many a *mas* stood a table on which ripe fruit was displayed for sale. Fauve stopped at one of them, and bought a pear and an apple for her lunch.

She was getting roundish—well, a little anyway, she thought as she drove past Les Baumettes. Everyone she'd met had been so hospitable that, no matter how tired she'd been by the end of the day, she had often found herself eating a large dinner with Jean and Félice Perrin or with Dr. Lucien Daniel and his wife, Céline, or with some of the other new friends she'd made in Avignon, in Apt, in Bonnieux. In Félice she often shared a meal with Pomme and Épinette, both of them as tart and irreverent as ever, in spite of their married dignity. And, of course, she saw Adrien and Beth Avigdor.

Eric hadn't been around much, she reflected, feeling, against all common sense, that he should have been. But he had two important new houses under construction on the other side of the Lubéron mountains, in Les Baux, and it was a curiously long and complicated drive over little country roads from there to Avignon, since the Autoroute bypassed Les Baux entirely. He had designed the large vacation houses for a pair of Swedish industrialists and Eric had to supervise much of the building himself since the master workmen of Provence had not become less unpredictable as the demand for their services escalated. This part of France was a paradise for masons, carpenters and stonecutters. They could pick and choose their jobs. Eric intended to have those houses ready for their owners by spring, if he had to stay in Les Baux and watch them go up inch by inch.

Naturally he was as busy as she was, Fauve explained to herself. It was not by design that they had met so seldom. No, not by design perhaps, but couldn't he have *made* more time for her? Couldn't he have, damn it, been a little more desperate to see her? Nine months ago that man had wanted her to leave everything that made up her world and marry him. Now, his father and mother, for God's sake, treated her with more loving kindness than he did. To hell with Eric Avigdor! Let him spend his life nipping at the heels of hod carriers, she thought scornfully, as she opened the front door of *La Tourrello* with a key picked from that heavy ring that had become as familiar and unremarkable as her lipstick.

Fauve wandered around the salon of *La Tourrello* checking to make sure that Lucette had emptied all the ashtrays and removed all the wineglasses from the table where, yesterday, with Adrien Avigdor and Jean Perrin and varied gentlemen from the Amsterdam museum, she had toasted the departure of the *Cavaillon* series. The salon looked too neat, with all the pillows plumped up, all the surfaces of the tables clear. She hadn't bothered to buy any flowers for the house since she wasn't living in it. It felt like an office on Sunday, a place that wasn't meant to be opened up and lived in, Fauve decided, and retreated to the kitchen, where she discovered the leftovers from yesterday's big celebration lunch neatly put away in the refrigerator. Cold chicken, a half of a liver pâté, cheeses, the last bottle of white wine, still almost full.

As she set the food out on the kitchen table, she decided to start to diet seriously tomorrow. In a week, by the time she got back to New York, she'd have lost the five pounds she must have gained. She'd be home before the Christmas decorations were put up in the stores on Fifth Avenue, home for all the parties, home for the first big snow of the season. No, Fauve corrected herself, the decorations were already in place; they appeared before Thanksgiving. The first snow had come a week ago Maggy had told her the last time they'd talked, so now it must be already covered with grime; black flakes falling on white snow from the solid gray New York skies. Off-duty taxis; puddles of slush at every street corner so wide that you had to wade right through them to crowd into an overheated bus if it didn't rush right past your stop; the constant wail of sirens as if the city were perpetually on fire somewhere or other—but parties, perhaps a welcome-home party, the annual Lunel Christmas party, dancing at Doubles where she had a membership, the Horowitz concert for which Melvin had written he had tickets, the Avedon exhibition, Bobby Short at the Café Carlyle and Baryshnikov and bagels: Where else but in New York?

Fauve looked for the tomatoes Lucette had brought in yesterday. Good, there were enough left for a salad with the chicken. Or perhaps she'd only eat the tomatoes and fruit when it was time for lunch. It wouldn't do to return to the agency an ounce heavier than she'd left it . . . the models would be only too delighted to jump on her for the lack of discipline she preached to them. Somehow it was all right for the personnel of the agency to be as cozily plump as they liked, but Maggy and Fauve Lunel were supposed to be model-thin.

Fauve's mind fell into a reverie in which the treats of Provence were mixed and jumbled; the *tapenade*, that relish made of black olives that was spread on bread like butter; the stars that fell so low to earth through the night sky that a walk after dinner felt like flight; the café in Félice where she could sit watching the whole village pass by, knowing more people by name every day; the color of the light, the color of the sky, the color of the stones—the color of the light, the light. Sighing, she blew her hair out of her eyes and resolutely turned her mind to the problem of *La Tourrello*.

She could rent it as she had first planned, or sell it. Jean Perrin had assured her that either choice would present no problems; there was an enormous demand for properties all over the South of France and the luxuriously appointed home of Julien Mistral would command a huge price. It was as famous as it was unique, with its marvelously restored buildings, its swimming pool, its central heating, its comfortable bathrooms. She would rather sell it outright, Fauve realized suddenly. The apricot trees, the vines, the asparagus fields, the olive groves—all the fertile land of *La Tourrello* was in a shameful condition of neglect. How could she trust a tenant to oversee the work that had to be done? No one who merely rented a house would want to make the effort that was necessary to bring the domain back to its former productivity. On the other hand, anyone who bought the property would do so with the knowledge that the farm would bring in a steady and substantial income when it was again worked as it should be.

Yes, the ideal buyer would be a rich family man from somewhere in the sunless north of Europe, a man who had always wanted wide abundant hectares in Provence—didn't everybody dream of just that?—who would hire a local farmer and his wife to come and live here full-time, a man who would be able to spend his summers in Provence, and to fly down from Munich or Copenhagen or Brussels for the sun in the winter, two weeks at Christmas, a week at Easter; bringing the children of course; perhaps in a private plane that could land at the airport outside of Avignon. They could keep a car at the airport and be at *La Tourrello* within a half-hour after landing.

Fauve thoughtfully provided herself with the pear and the apple she'd bought on the road, as she walked through the rooms of *La Tourrello*, imagining herself the wife of the prospective buyer. She'd keep a few of the gleaming wooden antique chests and tables, she decided, but she'd change the carpets and the draperies and get rid of all the upholstered pieces—the place was *underfurnished*. The house cried out for bigger couches, deeper chairs, less pointedly simple fabrics—it needed color, it needed warmth, it needed, above all, *things*. Strange, she had never minded the artful austerity of the decor before, but then she had always thought of it as Kate's house and it had suited Kate. Well, it didn't suit her—still, who knew—perhaps it would be perfect, just as it stood, for the wife of that rich Belgian? She was almost certain it would be a Belgian. They endured some of the worst winters in Europe.

Her own bedroom in the tower? It would probably become a guest room, unless they had a teenaged daughter who fancied it for herself. Fauve hoped that they would have a daughter, someone who would lie on the bed and dream with her eyes wide open.

What would happen to the studio? Fauve asked, as she found herself in front of its doors. Perhaps they'd use it as a game room, even put in a ping-pong table? Yesterday, she had been too busy making the final arrangements with the people from Amsterdam to lock up the studio herself after the *Cavaillon* series had been carried out, so Jean Perrin had done it and given her the key before he left.

She had never seen the studio empty of paintings, she realized, as she hesitated outside the doors. Did she want to go in? Did she need to go in? Did she dare to go in?

She told herself not to be absurd and unlocked the studio. The room she had always thought of as huge, vast, enormous—was just an ordinary size. A big studio, to be sure, but with Mistral's paintings gone, not that intimidating after all. A human size. Fauve understood that it was because the walls were bare. Her father's work had always opened up into another dimension; no matter what its subject it had led the eye beyond the borders of the canvas. Now there were just the walls and the high ceiling and the glass and the beams. The only reminders that Mistral had worked there were the worktable, the ladder and the easel with the blank canvas on it.

She put her pear and apple, both still uneaten, down on the least paint-stained corner of the worktable and automatically, without a thought, she set about gathering up the many brushes that lay scattered about. It had always been her special task after a day's work, picking up these brushes and cleaning them in the sink in the small room off the side of the studio where Mistral kept his painting supplies. Her father had always cared for his own brushes as meticulously as any good craftsman. In spite of the disorder there always was in his studio he started the day's work with clean brushes, and when he taught Fauve how to paint he had also taught her how to tidy up after herself.

She saw that it wouldn't be an easy or quick task. Both of her hands were filled with the brushes that he had put down on the last night he had ever painted, flung down hastily, she realized as she looked at them in dismay. They were matted, caked, stiffened with dried paint. Probably they should just be thrown out. It would be more work than she had realized to bring any life back to these mistreated tools. Yet Fauve found herself moving toward the sink on which stood the covered jars of turpentine and thinner.

Slowly, lovingly, painstakingly she began the slow job of cleaning Julien Mistral's brushes. Finally she left all but one, which hadn't been used, to soak overnight. She went back out to the worktable with the clean, single brush and stood irresolutely in front of the blank canvas, her mind blank, her hands still. She lingered there, with nothing left to decide, with no thought of what she intended to do next, until she found herself gliding backward in time, as, caught in a slow tumble of memory, she felt Julien Mis-

520

tral's large hand cover her own, she felt it press down, communicating power to her, guiding her fingers as he had done so many times after the first day, that day when she was eight years old. She heard him give her those familiar orders. "*Regard*," she heard his voice say to her. "Do you *see*, Fauve? *Regard*, always *regard*. You must learn to see."

And she did see, in a moment of complete definition, what she was going to do. It was more than just a knowing, it was a sudden admission of a long denied but total need, pure and assertive, without any complications, an absolute order.

Try. She was a painter. She had always been a painter. She had rejected the painter in herself when she had rejected her father but now . . . now . . . all she was sure of was that she must try. Walls had been torn down, doors had been flung open, a vast open meadow lay before her, a meadow she could not cross without risk, a meadow that, once crossed, would lead her into changes unguessed at, into tasks and trials she could only begin to imagine. But she had to try.

Fauve knew that she was at the very beginning of a long voyage of discovery, an adventure that beckoned her on irresistibly. On the other side of the meadow was a mystery, an unknown world that must be explored. She felt full of marvelously imprudent impulses, eager to meet the mystery, ready to dare, ready to try, ready to change.

A pulse that had never stopped beating quickened in Fauve's wrists and fingers. Powers and faculties that she had suppressed and turned away from began pushing themselves forward and upward with the power of young buds opening in the spring sun.

She would have to begin over again. Not at the beginning, but nevertheless, again. She must have lost technique, facility, ease—the machinery of an artist had probably rusted like the Tin Woodsman of Oz, left out in the rain. Paint and she would have to become intimate once more. But she'd known the language before . . . it wasn't all that easy to forget, particularly since she had never lost that nervous habit that made her hand pick up any available pen or pencil and draw lines on paper.

Fauve found herself sitting on the worktable looking at the canvas, a brush in one hand and the apple in the other. Would she eat it or paint it? She laughed out loud and bit into the apple. She'd paint the pear.

35

If she telephoned right now she would find Maggy and Darcy reading the Sunday papers after breakfast up in the country, Fauve calculated, counting the five hours' time difference. She jumped off the table, snatched up her pear and rushed from the studio to the phone in the library of *La Tourrello*.

She dialed the long-distance operator and then, before there was an answer, she put the receiver down hastily, overcome by belated second thoughts. This abrupt decision, this change of direction that she'd made so suddenly—how would it affect Maggy and the life she and Darcy had so carefully constructed for themselves, a life in which they were so well organized, so comfortable and so happy together?

Was this not precisely the sort of selfishness Fauve asked herself, within which her father had lived? He took any action that was best for him, regardless of its consequences. Was she now about to put her work ahead of all other obligations in life? Was her sense of purpose, her physical and spiritual need to paint, the very same feeling that he had known? Was this not the urgency that had driven him? *And blinded him?*

Fauve sat very still and tried to imagine herself putting this morning behind her and going back to the Lunel Agency. She could save her weekends for painting, after all. She would spend her days overseeing the fortunes of the two hundred best models in the world, trying to care again, as she had before, about everything that happened in the competitive hothouse of fashion. She'd been brought up to do that, hadn't she?

Not really. Not at all, now that she stopped and gave it serious consideration. When she graduated from high school, Magali had never indicated to her that she had a secret hope of one day renaming the agency Lunel and Granddaughter. It had been her own notion to plunge into learning her job as if that were the answer to all her problems. If Fauve knew one thing about the modeling business it was that you shouldn't work in it unless it *mattered* to you. When it stopped being a genuinely sickening disappointment to see a Wilhelmina girl instead of a Lunel girl on the cover of *Vogue*, it was time to get out.

As Fauve picked up the phone again she told herself that she knew one thing for certain; Maggy would want her to be honest even if she wouldn't be happy with the truth. To put painting ahead of many things was what every painter had to do. She must remember not to put it ahead of everything. At least not all of the time.

Fauve asked Darcy to get on another extension and she told both of them what had happened to her that morning. She was as direct and clear as she knew how to be. There was no point in trying to tiptoe around the facts or pretend that she hadn't made up her mind.

"Well," said Maggy, after a pause, in a voice that sounded either far away or very muffled, Fauve wasn't sure. "Well, I must say, Fauve . . . I'm not sure exactly how surprised I am."

"Magali, it isn't that I haven't thought what this will mean to you," Fauve said earnestly. "I know what a stickler you are about one of us being at the agency every day and I realize that either you're going to have to work full-time now—or somehow compromise and rely more on Casey and Loulou."

"I was beginning to wonder what was taking you so long, it's not as if it's been absolutely necessary for you to stay on in Félice all winter . . . you could have found people to handle your business there for you. Darcy, how many times have I told you that something strange was going on with Fauve?" Maggy asked, like someone who has won a bet.

"Magali! Don't you realize what I've been saying? I don't want to run a model agency, for God's sake."

"Well, *that's* understandable. Not everyone has the calling," Maggy said with a trace of smugness in her voice.

"You don't care?" Fauve cried incredulously.

"Not that I want to interfere in this career talk," Darcy interrupted, "but, Maggy, I just thought I'd better tell you that I've made up my mind that I'm absolutely opposed to your building that greenhouse onto the dining room."

"Damn it, Darcy, you know perfectly well that I've been planning to grow orchids all winter long after Fauve came back," Maggy said in irritation. "You can't do that without a greenhouse."

"But she's not coming back, the dirt under your fingernails doesn't come out from spring till fall . . . I didn't marry a female Nero Wolfe . . . I married Maggy Lunel. I know you're bored to death with four-day weekends. You've been ten times more fun to live with since Fauve left for France. No greenhouse."

"Darcy! How long have you known . . . about the weekends?" Maggy demanded.

"Let's say that I prefer to remain inscrutable."

"Are you two talking to me or to each other?" Fauve asked. "Is this a private discussion? After all, I'm paying for this call." Jean Perrin had told her that she would eventually inherit at least twenty-five million dollars but none of that sounded real to Fauve. However, long distance was long distance.

"You should have called collect," Maggy said. "We would have accepted it. Now listen, Darcy, does this mean that you *refuse* to let me build the greenhouse?"

"I thought I'd made that plain."

"In that case," said Maggy, "I *refuse* to give up my Fridays at the agency."

"What about Mondays?" Darcy countered quickly.

"On one condition. I'll spend Mondays in the country with you if I can buy that little bit of swamp just on the border of our place."

" 'Bit of swamp'? It's about seven acres! What do you want it for?"

"A water lily garden, like Monet's at Giverny," said Maggy in a visionary tone.

"That'll mean bulldozers," Darcy grumbled.

"But only for a few weeks. And just think, darling, we could have a rowboat and a little summer house and you'd row me out there for martinis in the summer before dinner."

"We're agreeing on three days, right?" he bargained. "Friday night through Monday?"

"It's a deal. On Monday I'll let Casey and Loulou and Ivy take over for me—it's usually a day that starts slowly anyway."

"Ivy?" Fauve asked, astonished.

"Ivy Columbo. Is there more than one Ivy? She decided modeling was too short-term for a career so she's starting as a booker. As a trainee supposedly, but that girl's so bossy that the word hardly applies. She reminds me of—me. It's a shame to retire the best pair of runway knees in the business but on the other hand she's engaged to some gorgeous Italian she met in the Sistine Chapel when she was in Rome with you last March. I like her, she'll do," Maggy said with satisfaction. "But, Fauve, naturally, if you come back, if you change your mind, your job is always open. You know that."

"Thanks," Fauve said absently—in the Sistine Chapel?—as she imagined the tugs-of-war that would take place on Mondays. Loulou had more seniority, Casey had more brains, but Ivy had . . . more of everything.

"Now, where are you going to live?" Maggy said in a practical voice.

"I thought you understood. Out here, in *La Tourrello*, of course."

"Live there alone!" Maggy became every inch a grandmother. "I don't think that's a good idea at all."

"You!" Fauve sputtered. "You who used to dance till dawn every night and were carried around stark naked on a platter and lived in some dive in Montparnasse with God knows whom—and probably smoked opium . . . you're a fine one to talk!"

"I see Adrien Avigdor has been reminiscing. He must be getting senile . . . I never, ever smoked opium. Not that it wasn't offered, mind you. Anyway, all that happened when I was young and foolish. By the time I was your age I was earning an excellent living and very respectably too."

"With an illegitimate child and probably carrying on like crazy with Darcy," Fauve suggested softly.

"I don't think I'd met Darcy yet, had I, darling? When was Lally's treasure hunt exactly . . . was it . . . ?"

"Magali, never mind the exact date," Fauve interrupted. "Anyway, I won't be here all alone. I'll ask Lucette if she wants to come and live here with her kids. She's sharing a house with her in-laws

525

and hates it, so I'm sure she'll jump at the chance. And the place will be full of men working on the land. *La Tourrello* will never be empty again," Fauve said joyously.

"By the way, Fauve, I thought you should know that I saw Ben Litchfield in '21' last Thursday," Darcy said, with the air of one who feels obliged to add every last item to the scales. "By God, Pete Krindler's given him table 9 and he's only thirty. Anyway, he asked when you'd be back as he left."

"Who was he with?" Fauve said automatically.

"An exceptionally pretty girl. She must be a model."

"Who's *she* with?" Fauve asked, sitting up in genuine interest.

"Us," Maggy replied dryly. "It was Arkansas, as Darcy knows perfectly well."

"Arkansas! Now why didn't I think of that? But that's perfect! She learns fast and it keeps Ben in the family. Just be sure to tell Arkansas that he does this really odd thing every Sunday morning, but not to pay any attention, it doesn't last long."

"I'll tell her no such thing," Maggy said, outraged.

"Then she'll just have to find out the hard way. I imagine she has already. Give her a hug for me. Oh, Magali, I've sent you that picture Father gave you, the one Kate gypped you out of . . . you know, lying on the green pillows, remember?"

"Hardly a picture that anyone could forget," Darcy said. "Just where do you think we can hang it?"

"You'll find a place," Fauve said blithely. "I've kept the other six for my great-grandchildren."

"Great-grandchildren? Fauve . . . you're not . . . you aren't . . ." Maggy stammered.

"Really, Magali, how could I possibly be? I'm not married, after all," Fauve reproved her. "But if I were pregnant, it'd be a clear case of genetic predisposition. Darcy, do you remember that panda you gave me once?"

"Vividly."

"Well, would you think I was being silly and childish if I asked you to send it over to me? He's sitting on a rocking chair in the living room of my apartment."

"Certainly not. Everybody needs a panda. Is there anything else you want from your place?"

"Actually . . . this house is bare as a bone. Maybe you could get a moving company just to pack it up and send it over?"

"Pack what up?"

"Everything in the whole apartment. Oh, I know it'll only be a drop in the bucket but it'll give me a start on filling these rooms."

"Why not?"

"Oh, Darcy, you are such an understanding darling. I'm so glad you made Magali marry you."

"She made me marry her, actually."

"I never knew that," Fauve said, fascinated. "How did it happen? Tell me all about it?"

"I think this conversation has gone on quite long enough," Maggy broke in. "Fauve, darling, you're doing the only thing you should do—I'm deeply happy for you, I'm happy for me, and I'm happy for Darcy although I'm not sure he deserves it. A man who breaks promises about a greenhouse . . ."

"There's somebody at the front door. I hear the kitchen bell ringing," Fauve said hastily. "I have to hang up. I'll call again in a few days. I love you both."

Lighthearted and lightheaded, she ran to the front door and discovered Eric Avigdor standing there, leaning on the door jamb, a jacket slung over one shoulder.

"Ah ha. The master builder. Come on in."

"I got home from Les Baux late last night and I went looking for you this morning. When you weren't in the hotel I thought you might be here so I just drove on out and dropped in . . . that all right?"

"Of course, I'm delighted to receive any son of my dear friends the Avigdors."

"You sound awfully . . ."

"How do I sound?" she asked, twirling around, her flaming mantle of hair flaring out combatively, her beauty focused and dazzling, as she well knew.

"I can't quite identify the tone," he said cautiously.

"I'll take that as a compliment. How are your houses?"

"Coming beautifully. The most important part of the construction is over, they'll be ready on time. I'll be back to my normal schedule soon. Listen, Fauve, I really came to tell you that I was sorry I haven't been around much but you've been so busy that it didn't seem as if you'd have any extra time anyway—and now Papa tells me that you're going back to New York next week."

"Duty calls," she said, giving him a wicked darting glance out of the sides of her great, misty-gray eyes. This, she thought, was the way her mother must have treated the men who couldn't help falling in love with her. She felt purely Lunel, for which she couldn't be blamed, could she?

"I guess it does," he said expressionlessly.

"Would you like some lunch?" Fauve asked hospitably.

"I don't want you to bother—look, come on, I'll take you to that little hotel, the Hostellerie in Bonnieux that has such good food."

"I'm too hungry to wait and I've got a kitchen full of leftovers that we might just as well finish. All I've had to eat since breakfast is an apple, and that was a lifetime ago."

She led the way to the kitchen where the table was already laden with the food she'd taken out earlier. The cheeses were properly runny now, the pâté and chicken had lost their refrigerated chill, and while Eric sat drinking a glass of white wine, Fauve set the table and sliced tomatoes for a salad.

"I've never seen you looking so domestic," he said broodingly.

"This is nothing. I'm a demon cook. My specialty is Chicken Paprika with lots of sour cream."

"Sour cream? What's that?"

"*Crème fraîche*, only better," answered Fauve, who had long considered this insoluble gastronomic problem and didn't believe she was committing blasphemy.

"Somehow I've never thought of you as a cook."

"*If* you thought of me at all," she murmured, measuring olive oil.

"That's not fair!" he almost shouted, putting down his wine.

"Oh, all right. I apologize. Cheap shot. Come on, lunch is ready."

They both ate hungrily, almost in silence. Fauve bent her head and her eyebrows pulled together in a straight orange line as she concentrated mightily on not looking at Eric's hands or the way his wrists emerged from the sleeves of his sweater, or at his throat or his face, not at his face, particularly not at his face.

"You know," she said finally, in a thoughtful, reportorial tone of voice, "I never would have taken you for a person who'd forget a sacred promise. Darcy promised Magali a greenhouse and he's taken it back, but that's different, I can understand that. It was a question

528

of checks and balances. You, on the other hand, *seemed* very sincere."

"What the hell are you talking about?"

"You promised to take me to Lunel, remember? I always hoped that I'd find a clue there, an illumination that would tell me something about my identity. How many years ago did you promise me? You still haven't done it and I don't see that you have any intention of taking me there," she said calmly, remorselessly keeping any note of reproach out of her voice.

"Goddamn it, Fauve, that's just too much! You go away without a word, you disappear for years, you reappear in Rome for only two days, you disappear again, you show up out of the blue six months later because of something that has nothing to do with me, you spend all your time surrounded by lawyers and dealers and new friends and newspapermen and photographers, now you're about to disappear again, and you have the incredible, breathtaking nerve to accuse *me* of breaking a promise!"

"You don't deny that you promised?" she repeated calmly, with a sweetly innocent smile that ignored his outburst as if she hadn't heard it.

"Of course I promised. I have the maps in the car to prove it. God, you're *rotten!* Lunel is south of Nîmes and north of Montpellier—it's just a little off route A9. If we got in the car now we could be there in just over an hour—taking the shortcut through St. Rémy and Tarascon . . . it's not far from the ocean, it's on the edge of the Camargue, actually it's just a few miles off the map of Provence, it's in Languedoc, properly speaking."

"You've been there without me!" she cried accusingly.

"Of course not. I'd never do that."

"Then how come you're so sure where it is? Eric, where's my pear?"

"Pear? . . . I just ate it . . . I'm sorry, I should have asked if you wanted half. What's wrong with you?"

"You ate . . . you ate . . ." Fauve squeaked, hardly able to articulate the words, " . . . my first . . . *subject!*"

" 'Subject'? It was only a pear . . . I swear to you, Fauve, I never went near Lunel but I wanted to know exactly where it was . . ."

"Why?" she asked, recovering with difficulty from her fit of laughter.

"Just in case," he said, "you ever came back and remembered that you wanted to go there."

"How long have you had those maps in your car?"

"Ever since you left . . . when you were sixteen. When I got a new car I just took them out of one glove compartment and put them in another."

"Then I think I'll decide to forgive you. At least you meant well, even if you show a lamentable lack of follow-through. Good intentions count for something, I suppose . . ."

"I'd call it a hell of a lot more than good intentions."

"What *would* you call it?" Fauve leaned on her hands and looked directly at him across the kitchen table. "Would you call it sentimental? Would you call it nostalgic? Would you call it a romantic gesture in the direction of a way you used to feel?"

"*You little bitch!*"

"Oh?" She managed to raise her eyebrows in polite inquiry while her heart turned cartwheels of jubilation.

"Don't try that game with me again! You've already had your fun in Rome, remember? Letting me think you still loved me, letting me stay hopelessly in love with you, slipping away at the last minute, teasing, sadistic, heartless—just as you're doing now . . . there aren't words to tell you what I think of you." He rose to his feet.

Fauve, too, stood up and walked rapidly around the table, transfigured, certain, so certain, as certain as she had been in the empty studio, welcoming life.

Eric looked at her and his world was reinvented. The one love of his life, her face blushing and prodigal with love that equaled his own, was holding out her arms to him in a gesture that encompassed all their shining, unequivocal future.

"Are you trying to say, in your original way, that you still love me?" Fauve asked as she put her arms around his neck. "Are you trying to ask me to marry you? Because I warn you, I'm in the mood to take any kind of risk this afternoon, this is the time to pin me down if you want me, I'm feeling astonishingly reckless, I'm flying high."

"There's never been a second when I didn't want you—I thought you didn't want me," he murmured as he looked into the mystery of her eyes and penetrated to its heart. "But," Eric added, drawing back, suddenly troubled, "I don't want to take advantage of your mood . . . you've led me a hell of a dance . . . what if you change your mind tomorrow?"

"Eric, it's not a mood. Nothing has ever been less a mood. I was just teasing, I couldn't help it, I had to make you mad to get through to you. I've wanted to marry you all these years—remember your dream about running off together when I was sixteen? I had that dream too, over and over, but I was afraid to admit it because I knew what it would have to mean, where it would have to take us. I've never had an intermittent heart but I did have a lack of faith— oh, not in you but in the possibility of absolute trust—that's over now. There are two things I hope for in life and neither one of them will be right without the other. I want to be your wife and I want to try to paint . . ."

"Paint? How did that happen? When—no, never mind—tell me later—it's perfect—I've always known you had to go back to it."

"Would you live here, at *La Tourrello*, Eric?"

"This house has been waiting for us, don't you know that?"

"I'm a slow study . . . but yes, I know now."

He traced her lips with his finger, feeling his heart pounding in his chest. "Do you still want to go to Lunel? I don't want to keep breaking that promise," he said gravely.

"Not now, not today," she answered.

"Don't you want to see it for yourself?"

"I'm not in any hurry," Fauve said pensively. "I don't seem to need to anymore. But Eric, I would like to take a drive—not far— just down the road—I *have* to buy another pear."